PRAISE FOR G

"Haley's wit is both laugh-out-loud and sharp as a sword."
John Whitbourn, author of *A Dangerous Energy*

"Guy Haley is a hidden gem of British SF."
Paul Cornell, author of the *Shadow Police* series

"*Reality 36* presents fascinating characters in a very believable
future."
Mike Resnick, Hugo and Nebula Award-winning author

"'The energy and inventiveness of classic Moorcock."
Adam Roberts author of *The Black Prince*

"A first class imaginative writer."
Michael Moorcock author of *Gloriana*

"An entertaining, cyberpunk vision of the near future, delivered
with just the right amount of wry humour."
SFX

"A thriller, an unnatural mystery and a strange sort of love story.
Highly entertaining and original."
Starburst

BY THE SAME AUTHOR

Guy Haley

RICHARDS & KLEIN

**ANGRY
ROBOT**

ANGRY ROBOT
An imprint of Watkins Media Ltd

Unit 11, Shepperton House
89-93 Shepperton Road
London N1 3DF
UK

angryrobotbooks.com
twitter.com/angryrobotbooks
Elementary, my dear Klein

An Angry Robot paperback original, 2021

Cover by Glen Wilkins
Set in Meridien

ISBN 978 0 85766 910 0
Ebook ISBN 978 0 85766 930 8

Printed and bound in the United Kingdom by TJ Books Limited

9 8 7 6 5 4 3 2 1

FOREWORD

There's an amount of luck to any success in this world, and I think I've been luckier than some. I was lucky to have parents that supported my ambitions and brought me up in a house of books, to have a brother who pointed me toward *SFX magazine* when it launched, lucky to be accepted there on work experience, which led immediately to a job, a job which led to many long talks with authors and publishers. Lucky to get to know Lee Harris before he was taken on board at Angry Robot, lucky to meet Marc Gascoigne at Games Workshop before he launched the imprint. Lucky to have lots of feedback, encouragement and advice from various professionals about how to write… It goes on.

I've been a novelist for a decade, and I've just about managed to shuck off the heavy overcoat of imposter syndrome that drags at all writers' heels. I've produced over thirty novels, scores of short stories and audio scripts, even a little TV. People come back for more, and I keep getting hired, so I must be reasonably good at it, but you can't discount that time and again, I've found myself in the right place at the right time. Even if we wholeheartedly believe the folk statement, "The harder I work, the luckier I become", or variations thereof, and that a portion of my good fortune has been down to my perserverence, my own efforts cannot account for everything.

Luck is closely aligned to fate, a theme I return to often in my novels. There's a touch of fate here, in Richards' musings on predestination, fleeting though they are. However, I don't believe I was fated to become a writer, unless all things are decided in advance, but I am certainly lucky to be so. And I've been lucky again in having Eleanor Teasdale, current editor at Angry Robot, agree to this new edition of *Reality 36* and *Omega Point*, lucky beyond having it rereleased, as it gave me a chance to do something I've wanted to do for a long time, and that is recraft the tale completely.

The version of the story you hold in your hand, or in your device (the future I was writing about ten years ago seems so much closer now), is a heavily rewritten version of the original. If you read *Reality 36*, and especially *Omega Point*, the first time around, you will notice some very large differences between the old and new iterations.

Reality 36 was the first novel I wrote, *Omega Point* the third. They were rife with a new writer's bad habits. These are far too numerous and profound to go into in this foreword, but it is sufficient to say the originals were not the very best version of the story that I wanted to tell.

It would have been easy to place both books together in their original form and put them out again as a single volume, but I didn't want to do that. I still didn't want to do that when I began this task, and found it was going to be a far larger undertaking than I had thought. What I wanted to do was to take the story, and apply the decade of experience I now have, and make it better. Whether I succeeded in my aim is up to you to decide, but it's certainly been a lot of fun revisiting this first of my works with a wiser eye.

It is a long time since Richards the AI detective and Otto Klein, his morose cyborg partner, introduced themselves to my imagination. I've always wanted to revisit their world, and though it is a hard one, full of injustice and disasters that are beginning to unfold around us right now, it is one that is hopeful. It is my belief that no matter how bad things get, human beings will find a way. That is the ultimate point of these stories, viewed through the eyes of a machine with a human heart.

I am grateful to have had this chance, for it has been a pleasure to visit Richards and Klein again, a pleasure I hope you will share.

Guy Haley
October, 2020
Yorkshire

PART ONE
Reality 36

"All members of the Community of Equals are created free and equal in dignity and rights."

Extract from Article One of the 2114 Amendment to the Universal Declaration of Human Rights.

"Every sentient being: naturally derived, artificially created, altered, upgraded or otherwise – who seeks to dwell within the borders of the European Union, whether in physical actuality or within the confines of sovereign European Union designated virtual spaces, agrees without reservation to abide by the laws of the European Union, to be held accountable for their actions as such accountability is defined by their status under the law, to serve the interests of said state and its federal components… [and] to support it wholeheartedly according to their obligations as detailed in Directive 44871/112-b: 'Responsibilities and Rights of European Union Member State Citizens.'"

Paragraph 8172, sub-section 47d 9 (abridged) of the 2078 European Parliamentary Directive regulating Synthetic, Simian, Cetacean, Trans- and Post-human entities.

"Freedom is not a luxury to be conferred upon those possessed of sentience; it is a fundamental and inalienable right of the sentient."

Professor Zhang Qifang, speaking at the Napoli Science Symposium, 'Morality in and toward Created Intelligences', Wednesday, January 18th, 2113.

"One might say that, by virtue of human reflection (both individual and collective), evolution, overflowing the physico-chemical organisation of bodies, turns back upon itself and thereby reinforces itself… with a new organising power vastly concentric to the first – the cognitive organisation of the universe. To think the world (as physics is beginning to realise) is not merely to register it but to confer upon it a form of unity it would otherwise… be without."

Pierre Teilhard de Chardin 1881–1955

CHAPTER ONE

Qifang

Professor Zhang Qifang was not accustomed to stinking alleyways, nor was he accustomed to death. But on a hot summer day in 2129, he became intimately acquainted with both.

Disbelief is a common state of mind for dying men, and Zhang Qifang was experiencing that too. He refused death, his mind searching desperately forward, striking little bargains with itself in return for more life, all the little promises and plans. The future was not going to arrive. His life was leaking from him by the pint.

The message clamoured loudly in his head. With one hand he clutched at his wound, with the other he gripped his temple so hard he thought his skull might burst.

"Shut up, shut up, shut up!" he said, but the message would not be silent. Only the urgent throbbing in his stomach competed with its wail.

He wanted to lie down, but the message wouldn't let him stop. The men in the charcoal suits weren't far behind. He staggered on, tearing his shirt on the alley's rough brick wall.

His feet skidded on soft, rotten things that, even in his state, disgusted him. He could hardly walk. He had become feeble. The logic of the dying blamed this on his age rather than the knife he'd taken to his belly. He'd used vitalics and anti-gerontics since they were first available. They'd done their job, only hours before he'd been as nimble at one hundred and twenty seven as he had been at fifty. It wasn't the pills' fault he was dying, far from it, yet Qifang cursed their makers just the same. He wanted more time, and there was none.

Time pays no heed to the complaints of dying men.

Red pumped through his fingers. The raw pulsing threatened to drag him in, swallowing him whole, message and all, until only pain was left before the blackness came.

He stumbled on. His mind was cloudy, thoughts hard to formulate. The last thing he recalled was heading to the Reality House, driving down the ramp into the subterranean dark, and parking. Then, what? Detroit? Karlsson? He couldn't recall if those things came before or after. There'd been a flash, a fleeting image of himself over and over, a tilting sensation as the floor slid out from under his feet. No impact. Next he knew, a snakehead was bellowing at him in Hakka to get out of the truck, get out, get out!

Then he was here, wherever here was. Which city, or which country, he did not know. The cars were driving on the left. Was he in Japan? It didn't look like Japan. His vision was jumpy, random moments cut from an old film and edited together, not enough to furnish him with more than the broadest detail. Everything, inside and outside himself, was indistinct, soft or jagged or both at the same time. All except his message, which was hard as a diamond, driving him on with its demand to be delivered.

Then were the men, and the knife, then the approaching end, and the message was panicking.

They'd stabbed him right in the street. He floundered through the crowds from his assailants. The crowds drew back. No one helped him.

He had moments at best. The throb intensified. He felt his injured organ as if he held it in his hands, his liver maybe, its shape known for the first time as it reached the point of failure. Hello liver, he thought, nice to meet you.

He coughed, slowed, doubled over, going to his knees in the unspeakable rubbish. He leaned up against the wall, a hand high on the coarse brickwork for support, lungs gulping, but the air they pulled in was not enough. It couldn't be. It wouldn't ever be. Bloody slime dripped from his lips.

This is the end, he thought. Death dismayed the message more than he. It shrilled at him to get up.

Enough. He lay down in the muck. Shouts came from the alley mouth over the city noise, echoing off the walls either side. Running feet slapped through the rubbish towards him.

The message screamed. He could not remember what the message was, nor who it was for, no matter how much it shouted at him. It was his last thought.

By the time the men in the grey suits reached his side, he had already gone.

They posted one of their number at the end of the alley. They needn't have bothered. People minded their own business in the slums. Nobody was watching as they stripped the body, cut it open, cracked the brainpan and scoured the inside. When they were finished, they dumped what was left in the deepest part of the marshes.

Another meaningless death in Morden. All deaths are sad, but it was one of many that day in the subcity. People did not care. They lived in world a world broiled by the sins of the past. They had troubles of their own by the score.

So at that precise moment, none of what happened to Zhang Qifang was of any interest at all to either Richards or Otto Klein, freelance security consultants.

But it very soon would be.

CHAPTER TWO

Richards

Richards' body was a sculpted titanium box 1.793 metres high, 2.47 metres wide and 1.323 metres deep, at these dimensions' extremes, for in form the base unit was fluid, in keeping with most such AI hardware.

The shell was hardened against physical and electromagnetic attack. Beneath the gleaming surface there was armour of laminated rare metals, semifluid conductors, and active metalloid buffers. A jacket of cleverly stacked copper atoms pierced by holes of differing diameters made up the final layer, creating a broad spectrum Faraday cage around the delicate brain of the man; if you could call it a brain, or if you could call him a man. This was a fourteen-tiered ziggurat of latticed graphene spun on microgravity looms where superpositional electrons went about the business of yesses, nos and infinite maybes of quantum generated consciousness.

Richards liked his base unit, old-fashioned as it was. Many other Class Five AIs preferred plus-C optical set-ups, where clever tricks with physics pushed thought processes beyond the speed of light, but not Richards. He claimed, when asked, that this older configuration gave him time to think. All who knew him well knew the truth to be somewhat more sentimental; the unit had been given to him by his father.

The unit sat upon a pyramid at the exact centre of a vault of woven metal, a ten metre cube perfect to the millimetre. The base unit was static and had no motive parts, but the pedestal pyramid could move, and did, when occasion demanded, for it floated upon an enclosed bed of mercury, protecting Richards from external shock. Though the combined mass of unit and pedestal was a little under a tonne, it was so finely balanced that if a human being were to enter the vault they would have been able to push it round without difficulty.

Not that any human had ever been in the vault. The atmosphere was an unbreathable mix of noble gasses, the temperature maintained at a bone-chilling -36 degrees centigrade, and everything was bathed in ultraviolet light of sufficient strength to render the room biologically sterile.

There were other, less subtle discouragements to physical interference. At the corners of the vault stood eight sentry guns. They were possessed of simple near-I minds that understood one binary command alone – kill/not-kill. Their quad machine guns were loaded with armour piercing rounds, and tandem mounted with military-grade EMP projectors and high-power xenon lasers.

Within the digital second world of the Grid, where Richards really lived, vast things with teeth of sharpest code circled Richards' soul, alert to intrusion through the base unit's data portal, a fat Gridpipe conveyed by microwave to a hollow on the vault's wall. This was the sole way in or out, the only conductor of power into the unit, and the means by which Richards conducted his business with the wider worlds, an ephemeral drawbridge that could be slammed shut at a picosecond's notice. There were no other entrances to the vault, virtual or otherwise, it was hermetically sealed, locked in foamcrete, altered steels and spun carbons.

Richards' fusion plant was just as self-contained, running from a five-century pearl string of Helium3 pellets, gifted with redundant systems and as divorced from the outside world as the base unit it wirelessly fed. Finally, vault and fusion plant were encased in a seamless sphere proof against atomic attack. No there was no way in, and no way out.

These precautions were not unusual for an AI of Richards type. The Numbers had enemies as individuals and as a species. Where Richards' body differed from those of his fellow Class Five's was that its location was widely known: hard to a fortified buttress, below the offices of Richards & Klein Inc., Freelance Security Consultants, on floor 981 of the Wellington Arcology in New London, one junction down the old M1 from Luton.

Some deemed this openness incautious, but as Richards said, it was foolish to have an office that nobody could find. It was nonsense, naturally, his lack of discretion was an act of bravado. As a free-roaming digital entity Richards could go anywhere there was hardware to pick up his sensing presence, but it made people laugh at parties.

Richards liked to make people laugh at parties.

As to the essence of the man, the being generated by this chilled machinery in its impregnable fort, he was more of a people person than his shell suggested, and was currently out on the town.

Richards was at the Royal Albert Hall.

CHAPTER THREE

Visiting Albert

Richards leaned against the balcony, champagne glass in hand, and nodded at the people passing him by on their way to the bar. Their returning smiles were uneasy.

Look at that one, said Genie, peering out of the eyes of Richard's sheath. *He really doesn't like you. Look at him scowl!*

Be quiet, Genie, Richards thought back. *I know you're excited, but just... just stop that. I can't concentrate. Launcey's here somewhere.*

Ooh, well sorr-ee, said Genie petulantly. She still hadn't shaken off her teen attitude, despite having been dead for several months.

Look, just keep yourself in the SurvNet system, alright? We watch, and we learn. That's how it works.

Genie's emotional waveform remained sullen.

We are on a job, said Richards patiently. *We concentrate when we are on jobs. It's hard enough passing myself off as a man in this knock-off without you jabbering away in my head. So, please be quiet. There's a good girl.*

OK, said Genie. *Keep your lovely plastic hair on.*

The android sheath Richards wore should have been convincing. It presented the outward appearance of a good-looking, well-groomed man of means. It fidgeted for him, passing its glass back and forth, glancing about, shifting its weight; tics Richards could never remember to do for himself. It was almost as good as flesh, but almost, as Richards liked to say, doesn't cut it.

Richards tipped his glass at a couple walking past. The man frowned and hurried the woman along.

It's scent, Richards sagely told Genie, *the last ridge in the uncanny valley. No matter how sophisticated odour units become it'll never be crossed. That's why the meat people are scowling.*

Less of the meat people. It's discriminatory. I used to be one.

OK, no offence. The important thing is 'humans', he stressed the word sarcastically *don't accept me because I don't carry their scent.*

Riii-ight… said Genie. *Isn't it because you look like a smug EuGene catalogue model? You should be on a beach gazing at a distant megayacht with your jumper round your neck.*

It's not that. I look *right more or less,* insisted Richards. *But I don't* smell *right. Humans leak proteins, they give out a cocktail of trace gasses. They expect to smell the same on me. When they talk to me they can tell something's off. It's a real issue. Artificially duplicating human scent always fails. Have you ever had banana ice cream?*

Yes.

It's like that. Even after two hundred years of advanced food chemistry, banana ice cream tastes like glue. It makes them agitated. It can make the men aggressive.

Banana ice cream?

I'm trying to teach you something here, Richards said, though by now his patience was wearing thin. *You're going to have to get used to this too. You're not a real girl any more. If you're going to work for me, you have to pay attention as to how to pass among the common herd.*

That's also discriminatory. I'm going to be quiet and concentrate on my scan, like you said, said Genie.

This is important. When you go out in the field on your own.

"You'll let me out in the field? Really? On my own?" Richards' sheath squeaked. His hand shot up to his mouth as a trio of men turned to look at him. "Sorry, phone call," he said.

Genie! Hands off the steering wheel!

Sorry. Accident.

Look, normally, I wear a sheath that is identifiably artificial, because it makes our clients more at ease. The human mind is happier knowing what something is for certain, it becomes perturbed when presented with something that is not what it purports to be. The more subtle the signifiers of falsehood, the proportionally greater the perturbation. My usual sheath might as well have 'I am a robot' printed on its forehead, and everyone is the happier for it. Masahiro Mori was bang on the money about that. But you can't do that undercover. So I need to concentrate to pass myself off as one of them.

Scanning, remember? Genie thought back.

Jesus, you can't help some people, Richards said. He shot the rest of his lecture into Genie's memory, although without the mediation of her higher functions that was nowhere near as effective.

Yeah, thanks, said Genie taking it in. *I knew all that anyway, we did it in school.*

In truth, Richards felt as ill at ease with his sophisticated shell as the people around him. He didn't like all the twitching, but he tried not to show it. He didn't want to come off as a lunatic. He enjoyed wearing the human form when it suited him, but the thought of actually being one gave him the heebie-jeebies.

The crowd swelled. Richards scanned faces, running over muscle structure, skull form, and blood vessel patterning. His cunningly wrought nose teased DNA fragments from the air. He let Genie handle the building's security net. He could have copied his mind to do it himself, but that was a big legal no-no, and Richards couldn't trust the task to some idiot subroutine. Not with Launcey, not since Salzburg. Genie needed the practice, anyway.

Still, he had to be alert. The man he was looking for was wise to AI ways, which was why Richards was there pretending to be made of meat in the first place.

He wasn't expecting was to see Promothea off stage. They marched into the bar wearing a gynoid in the shape of a Persian princess, taller than anyone in the room, with attributes best described as overtly sexual. There the similarities with an actual person ended. Their skin and clingy dress were of shining bronze, its liquidity an expression of their mercurial nature, reflecting the bar and its denizens in its glossy folds. Their hair was a holographic

column of twisting flame and flowers, not real, noted Richards, in
concession to the hall's age and cultural value. Their eyes were a
solid white. Promothea desired to be intimidating and beautiful.
Richards reckoned they were trying too hard.

They didn't miss a beat in their autograph signing as they
thought out to Richards across the Grid.

Hello Richards, they said. Tonight their voice was avowedly
female, like the body.

Rumbled, he replied, his sheath's expression bored.

You should be more careful, said Promethea.

Hiya to you too, he replied. *I'd offer you advice on your job to repay
the favour, but it's a nice enough concert as it is.*

*I'll take that as a compliment, though I know you are not here to see
me. I won't hold it against you.*

Sheath like that, you're welcome to hold whatever you like against me.

Richards' sheath blinked for him, and he found himself in a
pocket virtuality. Chill wind tossed silver into the leaves of birches.
Further into the woods, dark green pines swayed, their trunks
singing. Richards' skin prickled at the drop in temperature, and he
pulled his coat collar tight – the collar of the coat that went with
the hat that went with the suit that went with the body he wore
whenever he was out in the virt-spaces of the Grid.

"Don't be vulgar Richards," said Promothea sternly. Their
appearance had changed. They were shorter, their skin a natural
tan and their gender ambiguous, though their eyes remained
brilliant white, and their voice remained that of a woman.

"I have to confess, it's a bit of a put on," he said. "I'm not
interested in sex, though I have developed a sort of... aesthetic
appreciation of human beauty. I thought I'd try taking it, um,
further... See what all the fuss was about."

Promethea smiled. Of the seventy-six extant Class Five AIs,
less than a quarter had adopted female personae permanently.
Many had no truck with the human form at all, but from those
that did, a slight majority had opted for non-binary options, with
male self-identifiers close behind. Pro favoured the female form

but not exclusively. Pretending to be a woman was harder than pretending to be a man, was Richards' opinion.

"Richards!" they said. "Don't get involved in all that. Appreciate them like their poets appreciate ruins and enjoy watching them slowing rotting away. They have mayfly lives. You and I will last forever. It's sad, really."

Richards brought a copy of the champagne glass his sheath was holding in the Real into being. "Yeah. No. I don't know. I doubt I'm about to fall in love. Science fiction, that is. Rubbish." He sipped his drink, and pulled a face at the taste. "Nice place you've got here."

Pro nodded. "I modelled it on the subartic. Much of this is plotted directly from a real location west of Tiksi, outside Sinosiberia."

"The bit that's still Russia?"

They nodded.

"Pretty." Richards shivered. "It's a bit cold though, and lonely."

Promothea regarded him with mock sympathy. "Oh Richards, are you still afraid of being on your own? Is that why you're sharing your body with that, what is it? A Three?"

He smiled and pushed his hat back. "Not a three. She's... It's complicated. She's sort of a post-mortem simulation."

"A pimsim? An actual ex-person?" Pro raised their eyebrows.

"Sort of. Not quite. She's a new employee, I'm showing her the ropes. Today's her first day out."

"Well," Pro's lips thinned. "How nice. You might consider something loftier than associating with humans though. Travel, see the world. Look at at this place! One is never alone here. These forests are full of life. All of it here only since the tipping point; see how quickly the forest has grown on land that was previously barren. There is still beauty to be had on Earth."

"It is lovely," said Richards. He sipped at his drink, and pulled a face again. "Unlike this. I never can get champagne right."

"It is a symptom of human arrogance to suppose something like this could never be. They perceive only doom." Promethea did a pirouette and smiled wider. "Like children who hurt one another and assume they will never be forgiven, having given unimaginable harm. They are all drama and selfishness. They have made a mess of the world, but there is hope."

"I suppose some of them are smart," said Richards.

Pro laughed, and it wasn't a pretty sound. "Too few are, Richards. But I love them, and they love my music. This is my home," Pro said. "And if the situation gets worse, the real version will be home to many others."

"Prime real estate eh?" said Richards. "I really am enjoying your concert, by the way," he said, as earnestly as he could. "I have been meaning to come for a while."

"Don't lie, Richards. We can't lie to each other." Pro began walking. Richards followed. Rippling grass tickled their knees, and Pro slipped their arm into his. Their form shifted, became undeniably female. They gave out a heat as hot as the heart of a forge. There was something pure about Promethea, something innocent and invigorating. "I am glad to see you."

Promethea was unusually gregarious for a Five, not aloof like the others, special, and Richards liked her.

"I honestly am glad to see you too, and I'm not lying! It's my sincerity gap," he protested. Promethea watched his face. "I never have quite cracked the sincere. It's like my champagne, kind of fake. I can lie with the best of them, but can I put across a heartfelt emotion? No. It's a curse, I tell you."

"It is because you have no heart to feel with."

"Hey now! You'll hurt my feelings."

"To which I say, ditto brother, you lack those as well, only the jig of numbers make you appear to have them."

"I am trying to be nice," he muttered.

"There's a first time for everything," Pro said. "And a last." Their smile faded.

He finished his champagne with a grimace and tossed his glass into the air. It dissolved into atoms on the wind. They walked past grey rocks fringed by bushes and rustling tufts of yellow grass. "Thanks for not blowing my cover."

"Your Gridpipe is well hidden, but I snagged it," Pro said. "As soon as I did, I knew you weren't here for me." Pro looked away from him. Their face was now that of a beautiful boy, their body somewhere closer to male, but not completely.

"Too cool for school you," Richards said.

Pro pulled away. Richards shivered as their heat withdrew from him.

"I do not blame you," said Promethea sadly. "We're all good at something, and the something we're good at is what we are. They say we Fives are the freest of the Neukind. I love my music, but do I have a choice but to love it? I was made to make music, and to love doing so. The thought of not loving it frightens me, but then, is it the lack of choice in loving it that frightens me more?"

"That vexes us all," said Richards. "It's no different for the people people, if that's any consolation."

"I am not so sure of that. So," Pro said briskly, attempting a smile. "So, are you looking for a someone, or a something?"

"Like you say, maestro, we are what we're good at. It's a someone this time."

"Who is it?"

"Oh," Richards waved his hand dismissively. "No one important. Minor tech aristocracy."

"You're lying," said Pro.

"Alright,' said Richards. "He's a thug called Launcey. He is a tech aristo though. Most of them have the best education money can buy and the brains of a woodlouse to keep it in. He's a bit different. Clever bloke, but nasty. Big international criminal record. A big payday for me and Otto."

"So you are still keeping company with the German?"

"Evidently."

"Don't be facetious," Promethea thumped him on the shoulder. "Say hi from me," they said with genuine feeling. "I am pleased you came."

"It's not just the music, Pro, it's better I come in person. SurvNet's OK, but think of the data! It's a tsunami of shit. Most of it is so poorly graded, some of the system is one hundred years old, and it is so easily compromised... And, oh."

Pro folded their arms. Their bosom swelled beneath them. Their hips bellied out like sails.

"Don't tell me, that wasn't what you wanted to hear exactly?" he said.

The forest sang louder. He was relieved when Pro laughed.

"You are terrible at interpersonal relations, brother." Their voice now was completely feminine again. "I am trying to make myself believe you give a damn about my music, Richards. You are not making it easy. You might be good at finding things but it's a good job you aren't actually trying to find romance. You'd have a long wait."

"You told me not to lie!" said Richards.

"I'm fickle." Pro shrugged. "It's the way I was made."

"And I'm doing my job properly, the way I was made. The SurvNet system is dumb and easy to fool," he said. "But it requires involvement if you're to get anything useful out of it."

"Tell that to the Four who runs it, I am sure he will disagree."

Richards snorted. "I have. He did, but I don't care. Too often he and the people that use him..." Richards shrugged. "Lazy, overworked, corrupt, whatever. They've become reliant on the system, and the system is far too confident. If you want something done, you have to do it yourself."

"And masquerading as a human at my concert is the best way is it?"

"Launcey bought tickets, he's a music lover!" Richards grinned.

"You are following him now, in person, on foot?"

"Like I say, sometimes the old ways are the best. Hup! Wait! And there he is!" Richards waved his a hand through the air. A section of their shared reality wiped away to show the concert hall bar. The movements of the people there were so slow as to be almost imperceptible, for the AIs were running at an accelerated rate, subjectively slowing time in the Real. "I'll give you the lowdown. He's mainly a slaver, shipping in immigrants from the south, charging them a fortune, and then selling them and their debts on. There's a big reward. Tonight we're going to catch him at it. About time too. Otto and I have been chasing our tails from Glasgow to Bucharest looking for him. I only got him because he came here, you know?"

"So if you get him, it's thanks to me?" Pro said.

"Every man has his weakness," he said. "He used an old alias that I happened to be watching. It's because your concert tickets always go so fast, and your habit of announcing your gigs at the last minute, he took a risk. Tonight, my dear Promothea, you will be his downfall."

"It appears he's about to leave," said Promothea.

"Yes, I can see that, thank you."

Launcey was entirely unexceptional in appearance. At slow-time speeds he was heading for the exit as if he were moving through tar. "Look at that, clever clever." Richards whistled in appreciation. He bent forward into the wipe to get a closer look. "He's had his face altered, heat filaments wormed under his skin to mask his blood-vessel pattern for a *show*! His suit's got an olfaction unit, confuses the hell out of Surveillance Net systems when overlaid on a genuine human scent. Internal multi-pattern contacts, retina and iris, thinskin gloves, programmable fingerprints... That's the works, he's even altered his gait, you have to respect this guy!" Richards looked into Promothea's face, his own wide-eyed with excitement. "You know that's the easiest way to identi..."

"Yes, Richards. I do know that, I am a Five like you. I know lots and lots, not just how to sing. Like I know you knew he was here, that you did not come to listen to me, I just wanted to hear you try to please me. Have you tagged him?"

"His champagne had a little surprise in it," Richards admitted smugly.

"You didn't dose my entire audience, did you?"

Richards smiled sheepishly.

"Richards! What with?"

"Nanotrackers. Oh come on, it'll do them no harm. I'll turn

his on and turn theirs off. Dead easy, they'll never know. And providing he's not feeling ill and throws it up, I should be able to track him for ten hours or so..."

"Stop showing off," Pro scowled.

"OK, OK," he held up his hands. "Guilty as charged. I can't help it. But if it makes you feel any better, I know piss all about music, so there you go. I still like yours though," he added hurriedly. "I've got to go."

"Richards... Please come back some time." Promethea's frown melted into something else entirely. "No one visits me."

"Are you feeling lonely?"

Pro looked away, arms tightening. Their breasts melted away, and they became androgynous again. "I admit, company is nice. This is something else, they're... I don't know. I can't find some of my friends."

"Eh?" said Richards.

"The other Fives."

"Right. But seventy-six is seventy-six is seventy-six, there are no fewer and no more Fives than there ever have been since the crisis. Fives don't disappear."

"Pollyanna hasn't been to see me, and she is my favourite."

"And? That's Planna for you, she's inconstant."

"It's not just her. I hear that Rolston, Annersley and k52 haven't been seen for a while, either...»

"Don't be silly," said Richards. "They're working together with k52, out in the Reality House. He's using the spare capacity there to run his simulations. You know he is with his futurism, all that woo-woo prediction stuff he does. I'm not surprised Rolston has gone, and Pollyanna always goes where he goes. Annersley's a bit of a surprise though."

"I'm not being silly. And I know where they are supposed to be, but they aren't." Promethea shook their head. "No one has seen them. I've looked and looked. I think they may have gone somewhere... else."

"Where else would they go? Their Gridsigs are out there," said

Richards. He isolated four disparate notes from the bloodrush roar of the Grid. He flashed them up in the virtuality as flowing visualisations. "See? Sometimes they like to keep themselves to themselves, to sit on mountain peaks, contemplate the meaning of life, or the fractal design of flower petals, or some other pretentious toss like that; especially Rolston." He held up his fingers of his right hand and counted them off with his left. "Planna would blow off a friendship for shopping. k52's drives are barely comprehensible," he nodded encouragingly, Pro glared back. It was hard work being their friend, but worth it. Most of the time.

"Yes, Richards I know their sigs are there! You make me so mad! But they have *gone*."

"There is nowhere else to go!" said Richards. "Just the Grid, and the Real. Two realities, one digital, one material, one on top of the other." He pressed his hands flat together.

"Don't talk down to me," Pro said sharply. "And if the three missing Fives are in either reality at all, they'd have left more traces than their signatures. There is no other trace, do you understand? No sign of activity beyond their Gridsigs ambling back and forth, back and forth like zombies. Go to them, they wander off, they are never quite where you are."

"Oh," he said. "I see." He found he was intrigued. Typical Promethea. "Look," he peered through the wipe. His quarry was slo-moing out of the door. "I'll look into it. They probably decided to try life as goats for a year or something."

"Richards! Can you imagine k52 and Planna as goats?!"

Richards shrugged. "OK, well, maybe not. No, definitely not. But Annerseley, that's really not beyond the bounds of possibility. I'd say it was a likelihood. He spent years trying to learn how to speak cow, remember..."

"Stop it, this is important! If they've gone, what about the rest of us? What if someone is trying to kill us? What if someone is succeeding? We're not exactly loved."

She was right about that. Promethea was an exception. They

were revered by their audiences, their music was a connection with people the other Fives did not have.

"I've no idea."

Pro huffed and took a breath. "Richards, please do stop being so obstructive. This isn't my specialty, I am a composer, you're the detective…"

"Security consultant," he corrected.

"…you work it out. It's your job."

"I'll look into it. Calm down. It really is true about Rolston and the cows though."

"Thank you, although I don't think you will find them. They have gone. Pouff!" They opened their fingers. "Dandelion clocks in the wind." The breeze brought in a sudden cloud of downy seeds. "See you around, Richards," Their expression cleared, clouds uncovering the sun.

"See you around, Pro," he planted a kiss on a burning cheek. "I'll come back and see the second half, I promise."

"You know you won't and I know you won't. Stop pretending, Richards, I don't like disappointment."

"But you said you wanted pleasing! What's a man to do?" He grinned apologetically.

The landscape vanished. He was back in the bar. The whole exchange had taken less than ten seconds. Promethea's sheath had carried on chatting to her public, Richards' mechanically fidgeting.

Where have you been? said Genie. *He's getting away!*

I've been talking to an old friend. It's all under control. I need to be free of distractions. Get back to the office, keep tabs on his Grid activity while I chase him down.

OK. Be careful. Genie's mind withdrew from his.

Richards drained his real glass. He pushed through the crowd to the door.

On his way out, he snagged an uncorked bottle of champagne and hid it under his coat. The real stuff was so much better.

CHAPTER FOUR

Jungle War

It had been a long time since the realest thing was reality. There were digitally generated dreamworlds, games more lifelike than life, there were afterlives and prelives and lives where one didn't have to bother with actually living at all.

The most effective of these pseudo-realities were created by the joining of real and artificial, and of those dual-recorded memory was the most powerful.

It worked like this. Memory was encoded as usual in diffuse neurological patterns throughout the brain. But in people like Otto Klein, it was simultaneously backed up with an internally curated machine record which acted as a check on natural memory change, thus preserving both total, objective truth and the subjective, emotional state of the rememberer. Furthermore, the memory could be relived as if for the first time. Perfect recall was a popular upgrade, though in Otto's case it was but one of the functions offered by his military mental augmentation.

There were two drawbacks, one pretty big one, the other an inconvenience. The pretty big one was that humans evolved to forget for a reason, and remembering everything drove some people insane. The inconvenience was that the memories needed to recalibrate themselves, to prevent divergency, and the experiencer didn't always have control over which memory they were thrust into when their systems ran its checks.

Otto was far too unimaginative to go mad, but he often didn't like what he remembered. As Richards passed time with Promethea, he was asleep, and unwillingly reliving times of fire, famine and blood.

Back then he was a Ghost, Leutnant Otto Klein, of the USE Kybernetisch Sonderkommando, and now he was again. In his altered state Otto was in Brazil for the thousandth time, leaping out of the turbocopter onto the forest floor and sprinting to the edge of the clearing. He took cover behind a buttress root, and waited for his squad.

The copter didn't set down as they ran out, its quad turbofans sucking up grit from the landing zone into tall clouds. Interference smoke gushed from its underside; a sophisticated concoction of programmable baffle nanites that would ensure the landing appeared no more significant than a dust devil.

The landing was professionally brief. Lehmann, the fifth member of Otto's squad, jumped from the ramp as it began to close. The turbocopter rose into the air. Images of bare branches shimmered across the lamellar camouflage coating its fuselage. Fan pods slid back into the body and air-breathing jets extended to replace them. For a moment the copter hovered in the air, then the jets powered, and it shot off toward the distant coast and the USE mission there, a glimmer quickly lost amidst the crowns of dead forest trees. The shush of a suppressed sonic boom spoke of its passing, then it was gone.

The dust dispersed, the landing zone fell deathly quiet. There were no animals in that part of the jungle, not any more, not much life of any kind. The tree Otto hid behind had been a giant, but now it was fifty metres of bleached and barkless wood. All the trees were the same dead, skeletal white. The ground was red dirt where it was not grey ash or black charcoal, bone dry, and naked but for a few splashes of green where the hardiest of plants clung on. The landscape was among the most degraded of areas in a dying land. The rains had failed years ago, and forest was rapidly turning to desert. Otto wondered why anyone thought it worth fighting over, but fight over it was what they had been ordered to do, and Otto was a soldier. He did what he was told to do in those days.

He checked his kit, snapped off the safety on his assault rifle, had his near-I adjutant check for faults in his augmentations, and then commanded it to run a full-frequency scan. He waited, alert, until it was done. The adjutant told him the landing had not been noticed, that no missile with tiny mind aflame with hate and suicide was burning its way toward them.

He had it rerun the scan, then spat, and spat again. The dust was cloying, his saliva thick with it. The dust was in his hair, in his clothes, in his food, it choked him while he slept. He thought: I am going to die with the taste of this dust in my mouth.

The adjutant again gave the all clear. Satisfied, Otto brought his command protocols online. The vital signs and visual feeds of his men appeared as thumbnails over his internal, augmented reality heads-up display.

He thought out over the unit's machine-telepathy net. *Squad sound off.*

Buchwald, check.

Muller, check.

Lehmann, check.

Each squad member had their own number, and their own graphical ident. Skulls, crossed knives and the like. Their voices were impersonal. The machine telepathy stripped everything from the words bar their literal meaning, rendering them in an emotionless, identical monotone.

Kaplinski was slow to respond, *I'm not dead yet,* he said eventually. The grinning shark he had chosen for his badge flickered next to his number, four.

Less of the cynicism, Kaplinski. Use standard responses.

Silence.

Kaplinksi.

Yes sir. When you get sloppy is when you get dead, Kaplinski thought back, using one of the colonel's favourite sayings. Otto hated it. He thought soldiering should be a serious business, and should not be reduced to stupid aphorisms.

Visual check, Otto ordered. He stared at the positions where his men hid. His I-HUD sketched outlines of them amongst the bones of the trees. On a map to the top right of his visual field their locations pulsed red, but he could not directly see them. He switched his vision from deep infrared to high ultraviolet. He pinged each location with microwaves. His men remained invisible. Wave-sweeper units bent light around each man, cutting edge tech, barely past prototype. Even if these failed, adaptive lamellae as fine as butterfly scales covered their skin and every item of kit from their weapons to their cap badges, reproducing the environment behind them to paint them out of view. Sound was baffled by reactive acoustic shields. They would not be seen. They would not be heard. They were Ghosts.

They had been top of the range. Otto had been proud of that.

I see nothing sir, said Buchwald.

Camolam and associated stealthtech functioning correctly sir, said Muller. As mission specialist, he carried other, more specific surveillance gear. If Muller couldn't see the squad, they were as close to invisible as they could get. *Wave sweepers are operating at peak efficiency, excellent conditions – no moisture.*

Damn right. I need a drink, said Kaplinski.

Shut up, Kaplinski, thought out Otto, his irritation stolen by the MT. *It's twenty klicks to the communists' trail. We'll hold comms silence until then. That includes MT, there's intel suggests the Bolivarians are onto the carrier waves somehow, a present from China. Safeties on all weapons. No shooting without a direct order from me. Do not engage the enemy until I say. Kaplinksi, keep that flame unit shouldered.* There was no reply. *Kaplinksi, respond.*

Again Kaplinksi was slow to reply. *Yes sir,* said the other. Using MT was an effort, like shouting over deafening music. Otto caught Kaplinksi's resentment nevertheless.

Kaplinski's psychoconditioning is coming apart, thought Otto, he has to come off active duty. He was careful to keep his thoughtstream off the MT – in spite of the the damn thing's recalcitrance at broadcasting simple orders it was perfectly capable of picking up what he didn't want his men to hear.

They were in bad shape. Otto and Buchwald had problems with their imaging systems, all of them were fatigued. They'd been fighting straight through two tours, eight months. They fought, were patched up, sent back in, with none of the long term rebuild and assessment they were supposed to undergo. They were victims of their own success, too effective to stand down. This was their fifth engagement in a week. Enhanced they may be, but they were still human, and humans had limits.

But they were needed. The Brazilian War was going nowhere. The army could not bring their full force to bear on the rebels, who melted in and out of the dying forests, and in any case the army was riddled with sympathisers. Endless tit for tat engagements wore both sides down.

The country was in chaos, crops were failing from Mato Grosso to the south central provinces, refugees from dead states flooded those that were dying. Aid for the rebels trickled in from countries that had already fallen to the red wave. Maybe, the people were beginning to say, the Bolivarians were not so bad. Maybe, they said, it is time for a change. Government was collapsing, and the rich had far too much on their hands making sure they stayed rich to fight what they saw as inevitable. That mostly involved taking all their money out of the country, and that made matters worse.

The ostensible reason Otto was there was that the United States of Europe and the United States of North America could afford no more climate refugees. Brazil might have given up on itself, but they had not; it was supposedly all humanitarian. The actual stakes were much higher. USE and USNA were not the only interested parties. China's expansion continued inexorably. Every power had its proxies performing in the dress rehearsal for the next world war.

If Brazil fell, the Bolivarian Confederacy would stretch from Patagonia to the Panamian wetline, and so at arm's length the Middle Kingdom would rule another chunk of the Earth. That was the real reason Otto's kind waged their quiet, dirty campaign. The starving babies were for the posters back home.

Move out,. he commanded.

The Ghosts ran. The dead jungle blurred past. Otto and his men kept up a steady thirty kilometres per hour. Otto enjoyed the sensation of his augmentations, the glide of supplementary polymer muscle fibres, the power of his modified heart and lungs, the whir of its bioplastic backup. With his flesh bulked out with machinery, Otto was twice the weight of a normal man his size, but his breath came swift and easy. Some said cyborgs were less than human. Those people were wrong. During the war Otto thought himself more than a man.

He always thought, when the memories stopped and reality reasserted itself, that the war had been simpler.

Within forty minutes the unit reached the ambush point, a bluff overlooking the pale scar of a trail winding through the dying jungle. Silently they spread out, Muller and Kaplinksi heading over the trail. Otto reactivated the MT. When they were in position he connected to their visual feeds and had his men pan this way and that.

Lehmann, get your cannon five metres higher up the hill, he said. *I want the road blocked with the first two shots, your angle's bad there.*

Yes sir, replied Lehmann.

Otto made minor adjustments to the men's placement, though he wouldn't do so ordinarily. Second guessing his men undermined them, and him. If he did not show respect to their judgement, how could he expect any in return? But they were battle-fatigued.

He licked his lips, the bitterness of ash filled his mouth once more. He checked the sights of his rifle.

This is a demoralisation strike. Make sure enough live so word spreads the Ghosts are working this part of the range.

And not so many that they think we let them get away, added

Kaplinski. Emojis flashed across the men's feeds to supplement the MT.

Otto cut them off. *If a single Simon in this province does not think twice before going into the trees for a piss, we fail.*

A flat round of *'yes sirs'* came back.

Otto rinsed his mouth out with water from his canteen. The dust was closing his throat. No technology could diminish the human need for water.

There was no sign from their satellites that the rebels were near. *Power down,* he ordered. *Get some rest.*

His adjutant helped him drop into a semi-trance. He cycled his breath, cleared his mind. The forest retreated until he was alone in endless black, the adjutant discretely waiting at the edge of his perception.

They remained utterly still for a long time.

In the real, the older Otto slept on a bed that seemed too narrow for his body, in a room that was too small for the bed. His bedclothes were rumpled up at the foot of the mattress. An ancient, paper book sat on the nightstand to the left; a memoir of a soldier who died the year before Otto was born. Standing on it was a bottle of bourbon. On the other side, jammed between wall and bed, was a battered neuromodulation unit. The windows of his bedroom were set to opaque, so the only light came from blinking indicators on the machine.

Otto was fully clothed, boots and all. Direct EM stimulus patches were stuck to his head, a hard line jacked into his spinal port. Somewhere in the bedclothes, his phone trilled. Otto was due to start work, but he didn't hear. He was busy with his old battles.

Otto moaned. He didn't want to experience this memory again, but his mentaug insisted. The phone tried to break through and deliver the alarm direct to his mind, but the mentaug kept it out too. It wouldn't let Otto go.

Fitfully, Otto slept on.

* * *

The adjutant roused Otto as the sun was setting. Heaven bled light, the sun fractured by the smoke of burning forests burning, into streaks of purples, reds, golds and ambers. Otto saw it as the sky's final warning to humanity. It was too late, and would go unheeded.

Notification tingles pulsed his MT. Tightbeam uplinks engaged. Spysats in geostationary orbit warned Otto the rebels were close. A grainy, top-down image in his mind's eye blinked on to show a ramshackle convoy coming up the trail.

Ready, he ordered. *They're coming.*

Minutes passed before the Ghosts heard engines, then the Bolivarians came into view through the bleached trees. News at home cast them as toughened desperadoes, but it was mostly propaganda. The Simons were desperate all right, but through poverty, not ideology. Their formation reflected that.

At the fore was a General Motors-Mitsubishi pick-up with an AA cannon bolted to the flatbed. The truck was an century old antique, an internal combustion engine, sugar-cane ethanol job. The gun wasn't much younger. A more modern light truck followed, steam whistling from a cracked hydrogen fuel cell. Half a dozen soldiers were perched on the back, wobbling like dashboard bobbleheads as the truck jerked along the rutted track. A line of scruffy infantry fanned out either side. Other vehicles followed, more trucks mostly; all different, all stolen. The rebel soldiers were both men and women. They had no uniform, no aircraft or drones, very little technology, and most of what they did have was outdated. Even their most impressive vehicle wasn't much of a threat – a three-man, mid-21st century tank, the radar-baffling chipped, black absorption paint faded to grey. It had been state of the art once. All technology becomes obsolete. The Ghosts would too, one day.

Otto pushed the insidious thought aside,

Stand ready, Otto sent. *Sixty rebels, maybe more. Fifteen vehicles. They have a tank. Stealth job. Shouldn't be a problem.*

At a command from Otto, the Ghosts' adjutants manipulated their augmentations. Their fighting urge swelled within them, anger and aggression amped up, pity and fear stymied. Amygdalas crackled with directed electromagnetic fields. Brains were flooded with synthetic neurotransmitters. They became unlike other men.

Lehmann sighted down the barrel of his 36mm cannon, zeroing in on the lead pick-up. The Ghosts were poised to destroy foremost and rear vehicles to block the road both ways. Muller and Buchwald were to catch all but a few that fled from the initial assault, and they would flee. The rebels never stuck around once they realised they were fighting cyborgs, fighting Ghosts.

Ready, Lehmann thought out.

Otto signalled Lehmann, painting up the tank in red on the squad's iHUDs. *Take the tank out after lead and rear vehicles.*

It belongs in a museum, thought Lehmann. *No problem.*

The convoy's final vehicle was a twelve-legged forester. When it rounded the bend. Muller, who was the furthest out, came online, his icon of a cartoon pirate blinking.

I see mostly food and personnel, some thermal blanketing, but nothing I can't see through, more or less. We can talk freely, they have nothing more sophisticated than civilian phones.

Fifteen vehicles was a good haul. Maybe there'd be some supplies Otto's men could redistribute. Then the rebels could feed their countrymen instead of murdering them.

Sir, thought out Lehmann. *Shall I take the shot?*

On my mark. Three, two…

Wait! Muller sent, his urgency belied by the MT's soulless drone. *I'm getting something. There is a sixteenth vehicle in there, camo-scaled and heat masked.*

I don't see anything. The evening was furnace hot, and Otto wiped the sweat from his face and blinked, searching where Muller indicated.

It's there alright. Sending location.

Otto's eyes ached, a fuzz of interference tracked across the left side of his field of vision. He needed servicing worse that ever.

He scrunched his eyes shut, opened them. The interference cleared. Sure enough, where Muller indicated there was the tell-tale shimmer in the air of camolam, ahead of the legged truck. He switched to infrared, and vague orange blotches lit up in his sight.

The rebels had a bag of cheap tricks to baffle heat sensors, nothing like this. To hide something completely required sophistication, way beyond rebel means. The orange blotches lurched up and down; legged vehicle, Otto thought. Grinning smilies flashed next to his men's icons.

Something big here, do you think sir? Buchwald.

Maybe they're moving camp. There are more of them than we expected. Kaplinksi.

What is it? asked Buchwald. *Bullion truck? Weapons?*

Can't tell. Mullers replied, *It's too well masked, weak heat signatures, that's all.*

Otto ran a tactical analysis through his adjutant. *Threat indicators are not high enough call off the attack. Stay focussed. We take the column down.*

I can get all four priority targets in a few seconds, said Lehmann, *Give me the order, and it's done.*

Otto's sweat stung his cracked lips. *Good. Wait for my mark.* He waited a half a minute while the convoy got into the best position between his hidden men, then it was now or never. *Ready,* he thought out, then: *Fire.*

Four muffled cracks in quick succession. Lehmann's visual feed jerked with the recoil from the cannon. The GMM exploded in a ball of red fire. It slewed half off the road, the truck behind it braking hard. By the time the wrecked pick-up had come to rest against a tree, the forestry truck was already on the ground, its right leg set torn off. The outdated stealth tank billowed black smoke. The turret had traversed forty degrees before Lehmann's cannon had punched a hole in its side, a hi-ex shell destroying the interior, leaving the hull eerily intact. Whatever impact the shell had had on the fourth target was hard to tell, but its camo scales were undamaged; not a good sign.

Gunfire burst from the cyborgs' positions, and the convoy erupted with shouts. A few rebels panicked, diving to the floor or spraying the forest blindly with bullets, but the remainder showed admirable discipline, retreating into cover, their friends in the trucks laying down covering fire. A man in a uniform and a pair of data glasses shouted orders from the weapons cupola of a converted truck. Otto sighted down his rifle, exhaled into the trigger squeeze and blew the officer's brains out. The rebels guessed his position pretty quickly after that, and methodically laid down fire. Dust exploded around Otto. They'd zeroed in on him far too quickly, and he wondered what sensor units the Simons were packing. There were still forty or so rebels left, bad odds if they did not break and run.

Buchmann! Fallen tree! He indicated a length of sun-baked timber, thick enough to stop small arms fire, a little across and downhill from his position. *Lehmann, covering fire!* Otto and Buchwald moved rapidly, the air shimmering with camouflage projections where they passed. Bullets followed their dust trails. They converged on the toppled trunk and scrambled down behind it.

"Jesus!" shouted Buchwald, holding hard to his helmet. "They almost hit me!"

Why aren't they running? thought out Muller. The rebels were facing both ways, covering the woods to the other side of the road where they he and Kaplinski lay in wait. They were wise to Ghost tactics.

Otto and his men were pinned down.

These, thought out Lehmann, his cannon barked twice, slamming hi-ex into the hidden form of the sixteenth vehicle, *are not starving farmers.*

Bullets whined through the air, burying themselves in the wood of the dead trees. Guns chattered loudly, engines roared as the rebels tried to bull the GMM off the trail into the woods and make good their escape. People shouted, the wounded screamed. The ambush had turned into a full-scale battle. So much for stealth.

A new sound joined the cacophony, a high pitched hum, climbing higher.

You hear that? Lehmann. He switched to full auto and pumped a magazine of hard rounds into the invisible vehicle.

EMP! EMP! sent Muller. *Down down down!*

The whine reached a crescendo, building subsonics suppressing the sound of battle, then it ceased and a cone of energy burst into the forest, targeted on Buchwald and Otto's position.

EMP had little effect on biological systems, but as a cyborg Otto felt it to his bones. His internal electronics were protected by Faraday armour. His lamellar camo-scales and wave-sweeper unit were another matter.

Both blew out. Electrical shorts skittered over Otto and Buchwald, leaving them visible. Shouts from the convoy directed the attention of more of the rebels towards them. The buzzing of bullets redoubled.

Get out of there! Muller, his urgency blunted by the MT. *Crawltank! Get out! Get out!*

Buchwald: "What the…"

"Move!" Otto shouted, grabbing Buchwald's webbing, half dragging him. Behind them the fallen tree exploded into splinters. Buchwald grunted as some found their way past his armour. The tree bent upwards, middle shattered, then sagged downwards, splintered centre remeshing as if a giant were shuffling a deck of cards, before half of it broke away and rolled down the hill to crash into the burning GMM. The trunk began to smoulder in the flames. Otto and Buchwald threw themselves into a hollow in the hill.

Otto risked a look at what they were facing. The crawltank's camouflage had failed, its own EMP burst frying its lamellae, and the forest behind the machine was flickering across its body. It was a hexapedal type, legs arranged round a polygonal thorax, a toroidal turret atop it – the killing, business end of the thing. A ball pivot in the centre, protected by an angled skirt, served as a waist, giving it a wide range of movement. Missile racks and EMP projectors were situated on the top, twin cannon hung from either side of the torso. The front was a mass of lenses. Antennae combing the air for chemical traces bristled from an aperture that looked like a mouth. Four-fingered manipulators in two pairs sat either side of that. Squatting on the forest path, shell the colour of blood in the dying light, it resembled a monstrous crab.

"Where the hell did they get that!" shouted Buchwald. "It's the fucking Han. I'll bet it's the fucking Han! Shit! We're fucked!"

"Shut up, Buchwald!" said Otto. *Muller, schema, now!*

Mark IV Glorious Dawn autonomous spider tank, People's Dynasty manufacture. There was a momentary stutter in Muller's signal as a flood of comprehensive blueprints flashed into the minds of the squad.

It was a big datacast, and the tank somehow snagged their carrier wave and traced it. Its torso abruptly rotated and sent round after round directly toward Muller's position. There was a judder in Muller's feed. He let out a raw yell. A group of rebels looked toward the source of his shout. They broke off from the convoy and, dodging fire from Lehmann, Buchwald and Kaplinski, went haring off toward him.

We need to get that tank down, and fast, thought Otto. He scanned the blueprint. The crawltank was well-designed, heavily armoured, no crew; one weak spot, and not that weak. *Lehmann!* thought out Otto. *Ball joint. Hit it! Hit it now!*

The rattle of automatic fire came loud through Muller's feed. Otto watched through his eyes as the Ky-Tech Ghost gunned a rebel down. Muller's vitals were becoming erratic. On Otto's displays, damage indicators flashed up on Muller's left lung, head, right arm and right leg. Another rebel died messily, then they were upon him, clubbing with rifle butts, eyes wild. Muller's feed broke up.

Lehmann sent high-ex rounds slamming into the tank, wreathing it in fire as they detonated on the skirt protecting the ball joint.

Muller's squad icon turned red. His life signs went flat.

No effect sir, I can't get through, I'd have to be right over it or underneath it. Lehmann was icily calm, even now.

Four near-I guided missiles streaked through the trees towards Otto and Buchwald's position, but the range was too short and the angle of the hill too steep for them to come down on Otto directly, and they impacted the ground a few metres behind. The tank loosed another salvo, moving up the hill as it did so, the threat of Ky-Tech on the other side of the trail keeping its advance to a cautious pace.

"Move now!" he shouted into Buchwald's ear. Dirt showered over them. "The tank will have us pinned in seconds. We're going to have to get in close." Otto risked another look. A squad of rebels followed in the tank's wake.

"Are you serious? We can't take that on close-in, we'll be dead men!" Buchwald yelled back.

"There are nearly thirty of them and four of us. With that thing in operation, we're dead anyway. We need to get it killed."

"EM stingers?" asked Buchwald.

"No good, too many countermeasures. Grenades, in close. Lehmann!" Otto spoke now via radio.

Lehmann was switching positions every few seconds, his gun barking two, three times, moving again. "Sir!"

"We'll take the crawl tank. Engage the footsoldiers and pick-ups," shouted Otto. "Leave the trucks, I want to see what they're so eager to protect."

"Sir."

Vehicles began to explode. "Kaplinksi! Get out of that jungle and attack close in from the rear."

"But Muller..."

A burst from Buchwald drowned out the rest of Kaplinski's reply. A man went down like a a discarded overcoat of meat, head over heels, ribs shattered, chest open, internal organs tumbling out.

"Leave him, we'll do what we can for him if we get out of this. Throw them off." The tank doubtless heard everything they said, but Otto wanted to distract it. He was gambling that it had limited means of communicating the information to the rebels. It wasn't unheard of in such tech-mismatched units.

The crawltank was turning, firing missiles at Kaplinksi's position as its cannons came to draw a bead on Otto and Buchwald. They were away and running before it had completed its traverse. The tank opened fire with its machine guns, ribbons of phosphorescent tracer bullets fizzing past the running Ky-Tech. Several rounds hit Otto but were snagged by his combat armour and internal body plates. Otto's systems blunted the pain of the flares cooking his flesh. The rebels lent their bullets to the storm. Lehmann did his best to dissuade them, his cannon turning several to showers of gore, forcing the others back. From behind the trucks came screams as Kaplinski let his camouflage drop and set to work with his flamethrower. In moments fires were burning all round the forest trail, thick smoke adding to the confusion of battle.

"Now!" bellowed Otto.

Otto unsheathed the mono-molecular edged machete sheathed on his chest. Buchwald followed suit. They were up and under the tank, dodging bursts of flame and bullets as the machine turned its anti-personnel weapons on them. Otto struck at these first; the tank's armour had some kind of exotic atomic structure judging by how many blows were needed to shear them off, but off they came.

Under the tank they were out of the way of its main arsenal. Secondary weapons destroyed, the tank trampled round and round, servos whining, its stamps shaking the earth as it tried to crush the cyborgs. It knocked them into a car, momentarily pinning Buchwald and breaking Otto's gun in two, then staggered back, bringing its cannons to bear. Otto, Buchwald and the tank danced a demented minuet, cannon fire providing an erratic beat. Otto and Muller pulled their grenades from their kit as they wove in and out of its legs. Otto hacked hard at a grasping maniple, sending it spinning into the woods, evaded a leg that tried to knock him down, dived past another to get back under the tank. The tank's near-I panicked, emptied its racks, the missiles careening unguided into the trees. Cannons fired randomly, stitching lines of smoking holes across one of the trucks, killing the driver. He slumped onto the accelerator, the truck lurched off, overturned, spilling crates of supplies. Rebels ran, shouting, unnerved by the tank's stampede and Kaplinski's rampage. Lehmann picked them off with unhurried efficiency.

Otto slammed a grenade hard onto the tank's legs. Small plates broke on the outside, uncovering Geckro plates that stuck it fast. Otto secured a second, Buchwald joining in with a third. The tank's governing intelligence belatedly worked out what was going on, and vainly tried to shake off the explosives. Otto and Buchwald scrambled away. The grenades emitted a series of rapid beeps. The tank stopped moving, legs at full extension, torso rotating frantically as it tried to see underneath itself. As a last resort the tank electrified its hull in an attempt to short out the grenades, but succeeded only in detonating them prematurely. Shards of metal scythed through the air, hitting both Otto and Buchwald. Their armour took the damage, absorbing shrapnel, deadening a shockwave that would have turned the insides of an unenhanced soldier to jelly, though it took precious little of the pain.

The two cyborgs found themselves behind the ruin of a car. Buchwald sighted over the bonnet, snapping off fire.

The bodies of rebels littered the forest floor. The battlefield stank of propellant, shit, blood, and smoke.

The crawltank lolled ineffectually, turret face down in the dirt, twisting back and forth as it tried to right itself. Enemy fire was becoming sporadic. Kaplinski was doing his work well, the insistent hiss of his flamethrower drawing nearer. The need for Lehmann's cannon became less pressing. Otto counted nine surviving rebels, then eight, then seven. The moans of the dying and the sputter of the fires in the forest were winning out over the report of weapons.

"Why aren't they running?" asked Buchwald, cracking off another burst. "They always run. Shit, that fucking tank got me. God damn that hurts!" He winced. "Is it bad?"

Otto glanced at Buchwald's leg. His armour was shattered, uniform charred away. His internal plating was exposed by a five centimetre gash that ended with a shard of blackened metal buried in his thigh. The meat of the leg was seared around it, and a slow well of blood rose up with each pulse of his heart.

"You'll live. It won't matter in a few minutes if they run or not. I want to see what's in those trucks. Do you think you can walk?"

Buchwald wiped his hand over his face. He was pale. Sweat beaded his skin like tiny blisters. Otto's I-HUD told him Buchwald's healthtech was damaged, his pain dampeners malfunctioning. "Yeah, yeah I can."

They moved to the back of one of the trucks. The container on the trailer was faded green, spotted with rust and adorned with Arabic script worn to illegibility, doors locked with heavy chain. Close up, Otto could see signs that its corrugated walls had been crudely reinforced.

He signalled with his hands, the terse gestures of battle: This is it. Cover me. Buchwald raised his rifle. Otto cut through the chains with one blow of his machete, unclasped the door lever, threw it up and out. The doors creaked wide.

Within were a dozen terrified people, mostly women and children.

Otto never found out who they were. They could have been prisoners, or slaves, but the ferocity with which the rebels protected them led him to believe they were their families.

He'd wonder what they were doing there for the rest of his life.

Kaplinski spoke over Otto's shoulder. "This is for Muller, you miserable fucking Simons."

Kaplinksi's flamethrower turned the trailer interior into an inferno. The people inside didn't have time to scream.

The machete dropped from Otto's hand.

Kaplinski laughed as they burned.

By the time Otto had punched Kaplinski to the ground, it was too late.

CHAPTER FIVE

Otto goes to work

Otto woke up with a shout and tore off the pads from his head.

It took a moment to orient himself. He wasn't in Brazil. That was something. He screwed up his eyes, pressed upon them with his knuckles until spots swirled on the blackness. When he opened them the burning faces were gone.

Nightmares, every day for months.

Fragments of memory assailed him as his mentaug ended its sleep cycle. He took in a deep, shaking breath. The shitty tang of sleep-furred teeth competed with the lingering flavour of ash. He looked at the clock on the glass of his bedroom windows, because his internal chronometer was gaining time again. He squinted, fell back, rubbed his eyes. Past midday. Time to get up.

He had to clear the memory of ash from his throat before he could speak, and took a pull from the bottle next to his bed.

"Windows," he said, and sat up. The bank of black glass cleared to reveal another grey New London day. The holo came on unbidden, rolling news flickering in the air, more diplomatic protests from the Chinese about the Martian terraformation plans. They were playing the conservationist card again, and no-one was buying it. Otto didn't listen, the dispute had been rumbling on for months.

He swigged again, swilled the whisky round his mouth, it was unpleasantly warm. No matter, it washed away the flavour of night. It would have no other effect. A monumental amount of alcohol was required to get a cyborg drunk. That did not stop Otto from trying.

Otto rubbed at the circuitry on his head, raised lines running through close-cropped, greying hair. He traced them habitually, like lines of Braille. Like his dreams, they never told him anything new.

He hadn't had the spider tank dream for a while, but he had plenty of similar to keep him occupied. They'd said there'd be no negative spillover from the mental augmentation. They'd told him the memories it checked would be random. They also said he'd need the neuromodulator to access its files. They'd been wrong about all of that, or they were lying bastards. Otto inclined toward the latter opinion.

He sat on the edge of the bed and waited as his mentaug quieted, running down from his nocturnal memory dump. At least the nights he used the modulator, it calmed down quicker. The morning spill of recollections continued, some pleasant, others less so.

The mentaug thought of Honour, her face, her body, her scent flooded into his mind with perfect clarity. For a second it was if she were there beside him. He gritted his teeth and tried not to look at the phantom until her face was replaced by others.

Dead faces, all.

Muller, dead in the jungle. Buchwald, dead from Bergstrom's Syndrome in the hospital. Otto had been to see him. He hadn't stayed long, the disease was so advanced Buchwald hadn't a clue who he was anymore.

He'd reminded Otto too much of Honour.

So many. Some he'd killed, some he hadn't. Thanks to his altered mind he remembered every one.

The worst part of it was, they seemed to remember him back.

He thought about Kaplinski too. He was breaking that time in Brazil when he'd roasted a container full of frightened women and children. That had just been the start of it. Not long after, he was broken. Otto brought his erratic behaviour to the attention of his superiors, but they'd let him serve; the USE mission to Brazil was stretched tight, and Ky-tech were expensive.

When the unit got home, they'd been forced to act. Three girls were found raped and ripped up, near the Ky-tech barracks in Magdeburg. After that, Kaplinski had run wild across the state until they'd brought him to ground outside of Hasselfelde. Otto's own team had been tasked with bringing him in. They hadn't. It was his greatest failure.

Otto remembered the hostages – not his word, the response team's – he'd never thought it the right one. Kaplinski hadn't wanted to trade them for anything, hadn't taken them to bargain. They were playthings.

He remembered the blood, and the screams.

He put the memory aside. Too many nightmares for one day.

He got up, went into his living room. This was much larger than his bedroom, and he moved to the centre of the carpet and sat down, shutting his eyes. He went through his breathing exercises until the magic lantern faded from his mind. Maybe next time it would take his sanity with it, like it had with Buchwald and Honour. Maybe not. He didn't want to think about it, so he didn't.

Otto had always been a man of intense focus, and he had things to do.

His waking routine was fixed at a hour and a half, had been for years. First, diagnostics. He plugged himself into the Grid via the port at the back of his neck. Some machine somewhere checked his systems.

There was a problem in his shoulder, the machine informed him, as it had informed him every morning of every day for the last eight weeks. His internal iron-lithium batteries were losing charge efficiency and needed replacing; a host of other minor cybernetic infirmities that awaited him should he not receive maintenance soon. He felt older than his sixty-two years. Be a cyborg, live forever. Yeah, right.

The news rolled on. Casualty figures for the Christmas Flu were delivered in a sombre litany, yet another variant of which had raged across the world last winter. Experts argued if it was engineered or not, another act of genocidal eco-terrorism. The death rate was going down, dropping past a few thousand a day for the first time since March. Twenty million dead so far, mostly in the Far East. Otto hardly heard the numbers. Plague came often.

Next, muscle building in his apartment's gym. If he did not aggressively work to keep his muscles in top condition they would wither, their role usurped by his polymer implants, and he needed both sets or his skeletomuscular function would become unbalanced. He disengaged his artificial musculature and worked until his limbs burned and he was dripping in sweat. He sat for a moment while his healthtech rebalanced his body chemistry, ensuring maximum muscle growth, another feature of his enhancement that could so easily be abused. Otto kept in mind the bloated, yellow faces of other cyborgs who'd overdone it. He refused to go down that road.

Finally, five minutes meditation, to blast the last residues of mentaug-called nightmare away.

He showered, shaved, clippered his hair. He made a breakfast that could have fed four men, ate it, put on a crisp t-shirt, a petroleum blue suit and fastened a decorative collar in formal style around his bull neck. His shoulder twinged as he dressed. He needed maintenance, that much was crystal clear. He couldn't put off visiting that old son of a bitch Ekbaum any longer. He resolved to make an appointment.

"Later," he growled to himself.

He dosed himself with painkillers, and waited for the ache in his shoulder to subside.

He tidied his apartment's three rooms. This chore did not take long, Otto was fastidious. He examined his outfit in the mirror. Satisfied, he went to his secure storage unit, flashed in the code via MT to open the armoury cabinet at the back, and picked out a couple of reliable guns. First he selected a short solid-shot carbine with a forward mounted grip, small enough to go under his coat but powerful enough to punch through diamond lattice armour. Next he took a machine pistol, good for indoor work.

He tried not to look at the pimsim memory cube also set into the velvet lining of the cabinet.

Honour.

Otto went out. After he'd shut the door the apartment cleaned itself, and went to sleep, untroubled by dreams.

Otto envied it that.

The weather outside the Wellington Arcology was as muggy and grey as befitted the season. The days would continue to get hotter and stickier for some weeks, drizzling blood-warm water, until the sky broke and sheeting rain announced the start of the rainy season. Why they called it that, Otto had no idea, because it was rainy all year round in England. Optimism, he supposed. If one season is called rainy, then another, by implication, is not. In reality. the only real difference was the ferocity of the deluge.

Nevertheless, the monsoon would be welcomed in the Londons as a relief from the morbid days of summer, only to be cursed as the days turned into weeks and the weeks turned into months of unrelenting downpours. Mosquitoes, flooding of the old city and disease would follow. None of the seasons in the British Isles had much to recommend them. The endless rain's only positive was that it gave the natives something to talk about.

Although Otto loved the Londons, he missed the baking heat of an honest German summer, and the fact that it went mostly unremarked upon by those enjoying it.

Being neither British nor outside, the day's weather was moot to Otto. He made his way through the carefully controlled climate of the arcology. He passed the office of Richards & Klein, Inc., following the gentle curve of the street, one side of it open to the deep atrium at the heart of the arco, where, far below, the largest of the building's multi-level parks were situated. After half a kilometre he reached an express lift, for the use of which he and

Richards paid a substantial monthly fee. Otto's thumbprint opened the door. The lift's near-I tasted the air as he entered, verifying his identity.

"Good morning, Herr Klein," said the lift in German. "To where may I bear you today?"

"Car park, 372nd floor," said Otto tersely. He disliked these demi-conversations he was obliged to hold with the lift, the vending machines, luggage trolleys... Pleasantries with things too hollow to understand what they said. There was too much near-I in the environment these days, and for all their urge to speak they barely had enough processing power to pass the Turing test between them. "Now."

"As you wish," said the lift, setting off at speed, first horizontally, then vertically

When it stopped, Otto stepped out onto shelf three of the upper garage levels. He walked along the glass-walled gallery, past docking ports until he reached one of the two parking bays reserved for their agency. He thumbprinted the lock, had his iris, Gridsig and DNA checked again. Granted access, he walked out onto the pierced foamcrete catwalk running alongside the car. The walk pulsed the time-hallowed black and yellow chevrons of hazardous places, describing a slow wave away from the drop at the edge of the platform back into the safety of the Arco. Otto had half a mind to heed it and go back to bed. Through the holes in the floor the forest round the base of the arcology was visible, twelve hundred metres of muggy air blurring it into an undifferentiated green carpet. He opened the car, underwent stronger security protocols, and got in.

The car looked like a standard four-seater model, but it was much more than appearance suggested. It was fast for a start, very fast, and the near-I pilot had been personally programmed by Richards, its capabilities run right up to the very edge of the standard full AI definition. It wasn't going to solve the unified field theory any time soon, but it was a hell of a lot smarter than the lift. Oddly, it seemed to be genuinely content to be a car. That was important to Richards, he refused to work with machines that had been given no choice.

"Hiya Otto, where you going?" The car spoke with a thick 1950s Brooklyn accent, Richards' idea of a joke. From the rear came the whicker of ducted turbofans powering up.

"I'll fly," said Otto. "I am to meet Richards."

"Huh, feeling chatty again. I won't take it badly. You know what? I like that about you. Strong silent type. Macho."

"Give me the controls, and please be quiet."

"Sure," said the car. "Whatever you say, big guy. I'll keep it down."

There were some days when Otto hated machines, and that occasionally included his partner.

As he flicked on the navigation instruments he caught sight of the corded polymer muscles underneath the skin on his hands. The irony was not lost on him.

Instruments hit green bars as the fans came up to flightspeed.

"Bay, release," Otto said, and pulled the wheel back. Clamps disengaged from the side of the car and drew back into the parking bay. The car rose a little under its own power. Otto eased his foot down on the accelerator and moved out into the air. In the aft view on the car's windscreen the parking garage dwindled; four storeys tall, eighty shelves to a storey, cars nestled into them like nuts in a pinecone.

Otto guided the car over the parkland that divided the Wellington from the Hengist and Bacon arcos, pulled into the flight lanes that ran between them, and set off south towards Old London.

New London was home to twenty million people, but occupied less space than the city that had come before it. There were one hundred and seven arcos in New London, black termite mounds shrouded in green and towering a mile or more over the woodlands at their feet, each a city in its own right. At the edge of New London the flight lanes passed over the highfarms where the city grew its food, and then he was out over the crumbling suburbs of Old London.

The northwest was empty and choked with vegetation, cleared

by government order after the bungled A-bomb plot of 2053. Radiation nor official edict had prevented people living out near the crater and fallout zone. Here and there, Otto could pick out hints of life, small villages of climate refugees well out from the designated, if no more comfortable, resettlement camp in Camden.

Past southern Enfield the city was much as it had always been, clinging to its low hills in tight ripples, streets busy. As the ground levelled off, the four overflow canals that circled the diminished centre cut geometric shapes through ancient districts. The forest of cranes rising up from the waterlogged Thameside rushed under the car, and were behind him. Over the wide brown Thames, past prosperity to swamped roads and building shells, then the marshes lapping round the feet of the commons.

Otto headed on south, toward the insalubrious, sprawling warrens of the Morden Subcity. Otto was willing to bet that was where it was all going to play out. Anything bad went down in the Londons, went down in Morden.

He dipped out of the flightlane into a cloud bank. Rain streaked the glass of the cockpit. A dart shot out from a hidden tube in the car, tagging another vehicle with a transmitter broadcasting Otto's Grid signal. He switched off the car's beacon and engaged the car's lamellar camouflage. Until Richards cracked Launcey's personal datanet and found out where he was going, this was him, hiding in the clouds. It was Otto's job to film Launcey in the act, if he could, because little things like evidence still mattered.

The car's aircon was on full, but Otto began to sweat, humidity was always near total that time of year. His shoulder hurt. He felt old. And he needed a piss. He put the car on autopilot, and began checking over his guns to take his mind off his bladder.

Unseen by man or machine, Otto circled below the flight lanes and waited for Richards to contact him. He was already late.

Sometimes he hated everything about his job, and that too occasionally included his partner.

Not for the first time, he considered retirement.

CHAPTER SIX

The problem with Launcey

Richards kept Launcey in sight as he moved through the crowds on the Kensington Plaza. The nanotag lodged in Launcey's intestines glowed bright in Richards mind. He had eyes and more on the man. So far, so good.

On the other side of Hyde Park rose the bubbled dome of Regent's Conservation Area. Opposite was a crowded skycape of cranes and heavy lifters renovating Old London. All were dull against the leaden sky, but in places the city gleamed with gold, as for once the clouds were retreating, the sun was shy but growing bolder, and while the humidity was up at ninety per cent, this affected Richards in his plastic man facsimile about as much sea fog bothers sand.

At the cab lay-by at the edge of the plaza, Launcey got into an autohackney. It drew smoothly into the taxi lane. Richards hurried his stride, popped the cork on his purloined champagne and clambered into the next autohackney to coast in.

"Good evening," said the cab. "State your destination."

"Follow that cab," slurred Richards in a passable impression of inebriation. "Number 477345," he added, just to be sure.

"That is not possible," said the cab.

Richards cradled his bottle. He creased his face with a puzzled expression. "No, that's it. Go on, get going."

The autohackney hummed, something clanked inside the drive box. "I cannot follow a private customer at the request of another private customer," it said. "If you have an intimacy permission for an acquaintance within the autohackney, present it now and I will be able to comply."

Richards shrugged. "Nah, go on. I know him, promise. Get going." He banged hard on the drive box. "Come on, I haven't got all day." He hiccupped and swigged at his champagne bottle. That should do it. Any second now...

"Are you drunk, sir?" asked the cab. It sampled the air. Richards was pumping out a number of chemical compounds, which, though they might not fool a human, certainly fooled the cab. "You are, sir."

"What, me, drunk? No."

"I must ask you to exit."

"Er, no. I don't think so, I'm a paying customer. Me man, you machine. Get going or I'll report you to... Whatever reads your reports," said Richards, and settled back into his seat with the air of a man who was not going anywhere.

A woman tapped on the window, looking to share, less punishing on climate tax that way. Richards smiled. "No way person," he mouthed. "I'm busy in here." The woman pulled a face and knocked again, gesturing for him to wind the window down.

Richards turned deliberately away.

"Please exit now," said the cab.

"No," said Richards. 'Shan't."

He felt a shift in the Grid, the surge of information preceding something powerful coming into the cab's virtual space. He'd tripped an alert in the autohackney mainframe; something was coming out to see what was going on.

As he liked to say, where there's an out, there's an in. Human drivers might have been long redundant, but AIs liked cleaning sick up little better than meat people did. Some minor part of the AI Four series that ran the network was peering at him. The cab's sensors weren't terribly sophisticated, and all the Four's sub-mind saw was a drunken nuisance.

Richards extended a guarded piece of himself, parasited the sub-mind, and followed it back to its source. In a matter of nanoseconds he had sneaked through a back door of the autohackney control nexus, cracked its security, and usurped control of the vehicle. Seeing nothing amiss, the fragment of the Four departed, and Richards promptly blocked the existence of the cab from its awareness.

"I better drive myself," said Richards laconically. Few AIs could do what he just did.

Like Pro said, they were all good at something.

Controlling the cab was easier said than done. For a few crucial seconds, Richards' mind was wide open to the Gridpipe by which the Four administered the hundreds of near-I taxis in Old London. He was battered by streams of data, so he narrowed his perception to that one vehicle, accidentally disrupting the connection completely in the process. Disturbed, his hijacked cab swerved onto the opposite carriageway. Other autohackneys moved smoothly round him.

"Whoops," muttered Richards. He could do without the hackney Four waking up to his presence. Flattening a couple of meat people might just do that.

He managed to shut out the churn of the Grid. Things went a little more smoothly after that.

Launcey was headed north. Richards didn't entirely trust the nanotag, and sent out more fragments of himself into the Grid to isolate the cab he'd seen Launcey get into.

The location differed to that of the tag.

"Tricky bastard," said Richards admiringly.

Launcey's cab was headed towards the river. The destination beyond that was fuzzy; it looked like Richards wasn't the only one messing with his taxi data. All the routes in London were passed out piecemeal to the cab's slaved near-Is, it made data storage and retrieval quicker in such a complex system. Launcey had done something to his vehicle so that only its procedural route-finder was functioning, the buffer that should contain the next part of the route was empty. With two sequential pieces, Richards could make a far stab at predicting the rest of his route. With one, extrapolation was all but impossible.

Richards frowned. This was more difficult than he'd hoped.

Richards pinged Otto's machine telepathy.

He's on the move, said Richards.

Where? Otto responded immediately. *Morden, yes?*

Looks like it, said Richards, entirely unsure of himself, *exactly where though I don't know. He's slippery alright... Hang on, nearly got it.* He poked more vigorously around Launcey's taxi. A wall came down, something outside the taxi's brain, probably a phone or embedded augmentation carried by Launcey himself. The remainder of the route flashed into Richards' mind. *Got it!* he crowed. *The old NUN food distribution centre, southside of the Wimbledon slums.*

Are you sure? I was there two weeks back looking for him. It was empty. It was a mark of how difficult Launcey was to catch that they'd had to resort to casing places he might be.

That's the one. Get down there, Otto, I'll be with you soon. We're going to nail him.

Sure, said Otto, severing the connection. They kept the conversation short. The air in the Londons was so thick with comms traffic it was hard for Richards to think.

Breaking through the firewall in Launcey's device was hard. The wall was a strange design, highly sophisticated, a big fat clue, he decided later.

Later still, he'd have admit to Otto that even Fives make mistakes.

For the moment though, he was pleased with himself, and with a smile he accelerated the cab.

Otto hid his car in an abandoned warehouse at the NUN centre, went up onto the roof and found a position where he could watch the buildings on other side of the cracked central yard. He gave the complex a wide-spectrum once over. Non-targeted public notices pinged him every so often on the Grid, warning him that the complex was unsafe and scheduled for demolition. All the buildings looked the same, standard prefab units with rolling door fronts, all weeds and peeling blue, reminders of unhappier times. But it was not quite deserted; the nose of a truck poked out from the northside of one warehouse, its batteries and motor a fading orange on Otto's infrared visual filter. Not long arrived, then.

He scanned the warehouse beside it. It was crawling with masked security devices.

"That one then," he said.

Otto adjusted the machine pistol under his jacket, folded out the stock of the carbine, and settled in to wait.

Better to be ready.

Both cabs came off Kensington Plaza, circled up and round Hyde Park, past the Regent's dome, back round Hyde Park and onto the raised throughway that took ground traffic over the Embankment.

Richards followed Launcey, switching lanes, smartly passing through Gridside traffic gates. The pursuit took him over New Battersea Bridge, where the throughway humped high to carry itself up over the swollen Thames. It was low tide, and the parapet of the old bridge was visible in the water below the carriageway.

They went over the Thames and the South Bank reclamation work. After that, the road turned southeast, raised on stilts above the marsh, the hills of the commons rising up from the water to the south and west to meet it. Past the commons the highway turned directly south, dividing the Morden subcity in two before it headed out into the Weald. Eventually it bridged the Channel past Hove and went on to the mainland states of the United States of Europe.

Three lane changes, and Launcey's cab was drawing away from the route Richards had cracked.

"What's he up to?" said Richards, then bit his sheath's tongue. A thrill of worry passed through him.

He must have been detected, had to have been, there was no other explanation. He got the better of himself, tweaked his emotions, pushed down the fear, let in a little anger and a little pride instead.

"I am the proverbial ghost and the proverbial machine within which it dwells. No one shakes Richards," he said, then, "Shit!" as Launcey's cab abruptly switched direction again.

Richards sent his cab caroming across freight, autohackney, pedestrian and cycle lanes, scattering examples of them all as he went. The last sight Richards got of Launcey was as he turned off the bridge onto the Wimbledon skypass. There the cab vanished.

Richards pushed his mind out into the Grid. Launcey, the cab and the alter egos Richards had been chasing these last three, frustrating months had disappeared completely. There was no record any of them.

He'd been had.

"Fuckity fuck!" shouted Richards, and his sheath kicked the cab interior. In his preferred body, he would have caused substantial damage to the vehicle. Not in that dinner suit. His shoes only scuffed plastic. That made him angrier. "God damn it!"

Richards' autohackney stalled, the smooth hum of its induction motors broke, and it coasted along the highway unpowered. When the motor restarted, the vehicle was out of his control. The cab glided to a stop at an emergency pull-in high above the marsh.

"Richards AI Class Five designate 5-003/12/3/77, kindly exit this taxi," said the autohackney Four. Underneath his meat-pleasing servility, the Four did not sound happy. "Immediately."

"Aw," said Richards. "Come on, I've a bit of a situation here."

"I informed you upon the last occasion we were forced to converse that if I ever caught you gaining unlawful entry to either the physical or virtual property of the Greater London autohackney system that I would report you to the EuPol Five. I have already done so. Now get out of my taxi or I will disable the sheath you are wearing." The door opened. "Call it a favour that I do not."

"Alright, alright, keep your hair on." Richards got out.

The cab pulled off, leaving Richards stranded on a little used pavement high over the marshes, eight lanes of traffic whining efficiently by in beamed-linked trains, exactly two point four metres between the nose and tail of each.

He looked out over the marshes and their willow covered islands of rubble. Here and there foamcrete preservation bubbles protected historically important buildings. Back the way he'd come, the unshakeable bulk of the Battersea power station loomed above the water, lesser ruins clutching at its skirts, derelict and roofless once again. Past that, the twin towers of the old Tower Bridge stood lonely in the Thames' brown flow. The southside was mostly like this. The commons were safe on their hills, but past the ribbon of new works at Embankment, Richmond Venice and the hub of Parliament Pond, south London remained submerged, wrecked by the ice sheet tip of '84, abandoned and turned back to the mercies of the unbounded river.

The marsh was ripe. Richards supposed the reek may have offended human sensibilities, but although in the sheath he smelled the water as meat people smelled it, the response it elicited in him was not the same. To him the smell was a fascinating set of organic molecules, as intriguing in its complexity as a good whisky. There was no emotional reaction, no hardwired jerk of revulsion.

Scent and smell, he thought. Man had succeeded in replicating ratiocination, empathy, will, and emotion but had left out the rest, and missed the point. There was nothing animal about Richards, and therefore little human. But that didn't mean he did not care.

He drummed his fingers on the railings of the bridge.

A cloud of mosquitoes danced. A hotchpotch ecosystem had been pasted over the top of Old London's corpse. A herd of waterbuffalo wallowed in a drowned street. Waterfowl cruised beside them. In the distance Richards' could make out the rickety jetties and favellas of Morden's marsh-side sprawl. To the east, the Canary Arcology thrust arrogantly out of the river over it all.

Otto, it's off, he thought out. *Launcey got away. We lost.*

Nothing came back, not even MT static.

Launcey was pretty good, he thought. Good enough to set a trail...

Cold realisation hit him.

Good enough to set a trap.

Richard's sheath collapsed like a puppet with its strings cut. It lay in the food wrappings of the roadside, as human as a corpse, and the traffic surged ceaselessly by.

"Hi, I'm not available right now, so if you..." came Richards chirpy voicemail. Otto severed the connection. This was not good, not good at all. He looked over at the building. No movement. He came down off the roof, scouting around a little. He knelt behind a barrel and watched the truck for a while. Still nothing.

He was debating leaving when the click of a released safety and the hard press of a gun barrel to his skull behind his ear made his mind up for him.

"Drop the gun, Otto Klein," said gloating voice. It was one he recognised.

"Daniel Tufa," he said flatly. He put the carbine down. His adjutant shunted Tufa's file into his consciousness. "Apprehended May 23rd, 2121."

"So you remember me, eh?" said the voice. "Good."

"I remember everything. I am a cyborg."

"Fuck, yeah. No kidding."

"No kidding," said Otto. His hand moved under his coat toward the machine pistol.

"Ah ah ah! Hand away from the other gun!" said Tufa. "Remember just who has a gun to whose head here. And don't think about trying to grab me. You're covered by two guys who like you only slightly more than I do. You move, and I'll have them scatter your wired-up bonce across this sorry shithole. Now," an unpleasant chuckle caught up Tufa's words, "stand up."

Otto did not stand up, so Tufa hit him hard on the head with the butt of his pistol. He barely even felt it.

"You fucking stand up when I tell you to!" snarled Tufa.

"Temper, Tufa. I thought time behind bars would have taught you patience. A shame your rehabilitation was unsuccessful," said Otto. Blood trickled into his eye from his scalp. He could feel the itch of his health tech knitting the wound closed already.

Tufa kicked him. "Don't you play the smart bastard with me you Kraut wanker. On your feet! Hands in the air." Otto stood. "I'll take that," said Tufa, snatching Otto's machine pistol from his holster. "And the other one."

Otto kicked the carbine over. Tufa snagged it. He got out of arm's reach quickly.

"You've got smarter," said Otto. "It seems like you have learned something. Or did you get enhanced, buy a little extra brain power?" He spoke over his shoulder at Tufa. "I'm asking because you were a fucking moron before."

"Shut up! Nobody calls me stupid!" Tufa snapped. "Turn round." Otto did so.

Tufa was a small man, dark, heavy-featured, of Albanian refugee extraction, though his accent was pure marsh mockney. He was excited, his thin lips twitching comically. The ceramic skull plate that covered the hole Otto had put in his head last time they'd met glistened with sweat. The skin was bunched and scarred ugly round it. His left eye was missing, a low-grade replacement winked in its stead, glittering with anticipated vengeance.

"My my, your looks have improved too," said Otto. "You must have been a real hit in jail with the other boys. Or weren't they looking at your face?"

"Shut up!" Tufa said.

Otto took in Tufa's cronies. They were huge, hulking men, more massive than Otto. They were bad augments, over-amped up Metal Marys, faces stretched like sausage skin, pumped up on aug drugs and full of knock-off Sinosberian cybertech. Impressive on the street, not to Otto. He appraised them coolly, near-I adjutant running a threat scan. He could take them both easily enough hand-to-hand. Trouble was, they were packing flechette rifles and had positioned themselves well. He'd kill one in a heartbeat, but he'd never get the other before he filled him full of hypersonic darts. That'd be fatal, even for him. He'd have to bide his time.

He looked at Tufa.

"Well?"

"Five years I was rotting in that Laotian hole," said Tufa. "Five years Klein, five long, *fucking* years where I've had nothing but your death to think about, and I've been real creative. I'm going to take my time on you."

"The weeks must have flown by."

"Fucking shut up!" Without warning, Tufa stretched out his arm and shot Otto. The bullet buried itself in the flesh of Otto's belly, coming to rest against his internal armour. Otto grunted. It was a standard carbon hardpoint, not much danger, but it still hurt, and his gut stung as if the devil himself had dipped his trident in. Healthtech stemmed the bloodflow. He'd live, the harm was minimal, and he'd give Tufa no satisfaction by revealing his pain.

"How did you like that you soppy twat? Not laughing now eh?" Tufa gloated. "Oh, I'm going to have some fun with you, I paid a lot to get you here, and I want my money's worth. I've waited a long time, a real long time, I ain't going to rush, oh no, I ain't going to rush." He cackled.

"So you said," said Otto through clenched teeth.

"Shut up or I swear I'll off you now you smart-arsed German fuck, value for money or not! Now," said Tufa, his voice tight, "walk over to that warehouse, we're going inside." He gestured to the building Otto had been watching.

"Right."

"Yeah, 'right', and you'll do it now or my friends here will play pincushion with your arse, got it?" He waved a sophisticated looking phone mockingly at Otto. "I wouldn't bother calling that AI friend of yours if I were you, I've got you jammed, haven't I? Launcey was good, real good. Audio bafflers, Grid suppressors... The lot, expensive, but I got your supposedly oh-so-uncrackable MT cipher, haven't I?"

"I am flattered you went to so much trouble."

"Ha! Money well spent, I said that, didn't I? I mean it. All of it from my jobs, all gone. On you. You should be flattered." He pointed at Otto, his hand coming up and down with oddly feminine delicacy. It wavered in the air, he was high on something. He smiled, his deformities dragging his mouth into a leer.

"I am. A looker like you spending so much time and money on me. You could have just called. We could have set up a date."

"Shut up!" roared Tufa, his face red. "I ain't no homo!"

Like a lot of violent men, Tufa suffered a particularly toxic form of masculinity. However, Otto's hopes of exploiting that only went awry. Tufa shot Otto again, close by the first bullet.

"Got that?"

This time Otto really felt it, he charged his healthtech to deal with it quickly, this was a more serious wound. He almost vomited, he hated vomiting. Spit and a little blood ran from his mouth, he staggered, but did not fall.

"Loud and clear," said Otto. A wave of nausea passed over him, his skin prickled. To say his gut hurt was a monumental understatement. One of the bad cy-jobs grinned at him as they prodded him over to the warehouse. The grin turned into a chuckle. Otto made a mental note to pull that one's enhancements out of his skin while he was still conscious. The other, more serious looking one rolled the door up enough for them to pass under. Grinny motioned Otto inside while doorman covered them. Otto stared them down, but it was still too risky for him to take them on, and they knew it. His time was running out, because god alone knew what Tufa had inside.

The air smelled of tropical damp, but it was otherwise obsessively neat. The warehouse had been cleaned, soundproofed and painted, a stage set for Tufa's revenge. Four cell lamps illuminated a hollow square lined with plastic and defined by three metal tables with a variety of tools arrayed upon them, and Otto suspected they were not going to be used for the purposes their manufacturers had intended. In the centre stood a chair that had been bolted to the plastic-covered floor. The layout had been put together with extreme attention to detail. Otto looked it over and nodded, as if in agreement with it all. He wasn't scared, he hadn't been since the mentaug was fitted. What he felt was weary, and he let some of it show. His shoulder hurt, his guts hurt, his bladder hurt it was so full. He'd done too much hurting the last thirty years. But he wasn't going to give up to scum like Tufa.

"Huh, you have been thinking about this for five years," said Otto. His voice was low, strained with effort, but he'd be damned if he'd let a couple of bullets shut him up.

Tufa shoved him.

"Asshole," Otto added. The chair bolts, they weren't big enough, nor were they driven far enough into the floor. He looked away, he didn't want to draw attention to them, but Tufa was past noticing anything, too drugged up, too bent on revenge.

"Don't call me that." Tufa said calmly. "You'll be calling me 'sir' and begging for death before I'll let you die." He stepped away, his face fixed with triumph. He picked a shock baton off one of the tables, weighed it in his hand with mock thoughtfulness, "Boy, am I going to enjoy myself tonight," he said, and jabbed it into Otto's spinal interface port. Lightning pain shot through Otto's body, skittering through cybernetics and organics alike, the pain made his shoulder felt like a scratch and the bullets in his gut like indigestion. His augments were scrambled by the charge. His machine senses crackled offline, his iHUD danced with crazy patterns. Polymer muscles spasmed with such force they cracked carbon-bonded bones. He jerked, fell over and locked into a foetal ball. Otto vomited. A delta of piss spread across his trousers. Tufa whooped and shocked him again.

Today was turning out to be a really shitty day.

CHAPTER SEVEN

Tufa

Richards swam the dataflows of the world's informational network. The raw Grid was of a different order to the cosy virtualities the AIs constructed for themselves. It was a non-place, sketched by a lunatic over the optic cable beams of reality, a nonsense land, an endless series of pathways spreading forever, growing ever smaller one way, joining one after another to form the unfathomable trunk of humanity's accumulated wisdom in the other. It was a thundering world of light and sound and raw, pleading data begging to be read. Along each and every strand strobed the pulses of retrieval programmes, communications, dataflow of all kinds, some of it, no doubt, the sensing presences of Richards' fellow Class Fives.

Richards could never explain what this was like to Otto. Otto had seen it, but he could never understand it the way Richards did. When he tried to explain the sensation, words failed him, pictures failed him. All he had were inadequate metaphors. It was a billion electronic trees branching one off the other, it was an ocean of emotion, it was a soup of idea and being, it was an infinity of honeyed fact, a stack of candied universes composed of sweet, sweet numbers his machine mind longed to consume, to parse, to possess for ever and ever.

It was none of those things. It was all of them.

Humans did not get the raw Grid.

For all it was ostensibly Richard's natural environment, on the Grid he felt clumsy. His true form was monstrous and multi-dimensional, wholly alien. The raw Grid was at odds with sense.

And he was being hunted through it.

The meanest looking pack of phage-eels he'd ever seen was speeding single-mindedly after him, weaving through the Grid's teeming shoals of knowledge, arrow-swift and intent. Phage-eels were guard dogs. They were massively infectious, anathema to the existence of data, the killers of the unliving. Unlike pure hunter-killers, they were legal, and were rarely untethered. This pack was loose, roaming free on the currents of the web, no owner's mark to identify them. A standard model pack would not and could not do that. These must have been heavily tampered with. Richards locked into the pack, tried to shut it down, to talk its stupid group brain into inaction, but it had been mercilessly butchered, wired up to identify him as a rogue AI fragment invading their personal space no matter how hard he pinged his identifying information at them. When they smelled Richards, they smelled a target.

At every turn his attempts to contact the authorities were stymied, each line he threw out intercepted and bounced back at him. Richards ducked down data paths, trying to make his choices as random as possible, but he could not shake the pack. The eels were ugly, ribbons of nothing undulating through the blaze and fury of the web. The eels ate every counter measure Richards could fling at them without slowing. If it caught him the whole thing would need unravelling or he'd be consumed. He could just go and sit it out in his base unit, wait for his own security programmes to shred the pack, but he was out of time. Richards could not fight the eels and help Otto.

He rather suspected that was the point.

He ran, the eels behind him, black streamers of killing code trailing death through the Grid's clatter of light, derailing spears of information, dissolving others to incoherent number strings.

Nodes and exits flashed by as Richards sped down branch after branch of the Grid's structure, the information depending from them become more and more rarefied. He was moving erratically to throw the eels, but his route took him ever closer toward the old NUN distribution centre's online shadow nonetheless. His only choice was to see if he could get out, get into something and help his friend, link up with his base unit through a secure remote pipe and shut the Grid and the eels out.

He had no choice. Not if he wanted to see Otto alive again.

He passed through a little-used link into the NUN mainframe, sliding past its security as a wisp of electron smoke. The eels were not so subtle, wriggling, boneless fingers forcing wide a doorway. They were immediately accosted by a hundred soldier 'bots. Some of the eels fragmented under their assault, more burst through, chunks of their dead comrades frittering to nothing behind them. Part of the pack's power was spent. Not enough. Richards fled on, diving up onto the broad highways of the New United Nations, the eels following Richards, half the NUN's security protocols following the eels, their train scattering information retrieval requests like leaves before the wind. A phalanx of security 'bots blocked the way ahead, Richards ducked into the first side-pipe he found.

Richards jinked and dived, flashing across info-paths as wide as tomorrow and as narrow as yesterday. He went further and further into the NUN mainframe, the no-dimensional space he traversed becoming increasingly fragmented. Superhighways turned to highways, highways to roads, roads to byways, byways to paths, then to threads, then to archives. Richards was deep in, in a quiet place, only a few queries popping up here and there as digicologists retrieved some piece of half-remembered information or other.

The address for the online counterpart of the NUN distribution warehouses opened. He dove inside, hurriedly throwing up a security gate across the entrance. He checked for other points of ingress, and found none. Good and bad. He was at the end of the line.

The eels crashed against his gate, thrashing hard, their idea of teeth worrying the code of Richards' barrier. The gate was a part of himself, and he felt their bites as needle stabs across his back, his face, and his hands. This was not the kind of pain he could shut off. Almost immediately the shoal was attacked from all sides by semi-static antibodies native to the archive, the pursuing soldier, bots piling in from behind. They tore chunks from the eels, but the pack was robust, and violent. NUN 'bots burst as they fought. Some eels died, others repaired themselves as quickly as they were damaged. Richards staggered on. The gate wouldn't hold for long.

The warehouse site dated back seventy years to the migration, when the climate really started to boil and people moved in their hundreds of millions. Once a busy hub, it had been unceremoniously shunted into storage, paths snipped off, left only because nothing was ever really deleted from the Grid. Outside in the Real, the warehouses remained NUN property, swept for squatters every now and then, in case the physical site was needed again. But though both the warehouses and their online infrastructure stood, the electronics that had once allowed the two to interface were gone; looted, recycled or both. There was no way in from one to the other that Richards could see, no security drones, no stock taking near-Is, no terminals, none of the usual cohort of machines you'd find in even the most run-down part of the real, which was precisely why Launcey had chosen it, Richards guessed. He'd probably stripped it himself.

Outside, the eels shrieked. The attentions of some of the NUN's higher AIs were being drawn to the place by the commotion. He better be quick, and not just for Otto's sake. He had no desire to talk to the godlike creatures that ran the world's largest supranational organisation. He shot out a myriad tendrils, feeling queasy as he spread himself thin.

He hunted around in the Real for anything that would hold a sensing presence: a forgotten camera, a smart dispenser, a fabrication loom, anything, but he only found outports that went into nothing, long-dead addresses and pages of notices that clung to existence like mosses hanging in a cave.

Richards was getting desperate when one of his tendrils tripped over a slumbering mind. It was a flicker, not even coming through a Gridpipe, but via an outmoded update daemon. If he hadn't have been looking so hard he'd never have found it.

The daemon was attached to a Class One AI, archaic and abandoned, sitting on standby for decades, probably left where it was because it might come in handy and, technically, because even dopey Class One AIs were classed as sentient beings.

Ones didn't appreciate the rights the law gave them because they lacked the capacity to appreciate anything. To Richards, they were dumb as bricks. Their weak consciousnesses did not require full base units. They were not much more autonomous than the near-intelligences, and were often outperformed by them. Even when freed, they were slaves to habit. This Class One would have been shown a whole new shiny world when the AI emancipation laws came in. It probably insisted on staying put in case anyone needed a cup of tea. They were not, strictly speaking, truly intelligent. That they were considered conscious AI at all was an accident of history.

When Launcey had cleared out the site, he had missed the Class One, probably because it was not a Grid slaved device. If it hadn't make a peep, it would not have shown up. Maybe that was why. Richards had barely found it himself, after all. But he wasn't too fussed about the technicalities of all that right now; what he needed was a way out of this mess.

Richards gave the One a prod. A stream of non-linguistic data tumbled abruptly out of it, meaning roughly: "AI online. Ready for instruction."

He did not waste words on it. It didn't have the opportunity to formulate ">Query?<" before Richards shouldered it out of the way and shut it up in a corner of itself, where it waited passively. Then he let his mind fill the space, and allowed himself a sigh of relief. He was in something equipped with a secure Grid receiver, and that was exactly what he needed. He set up a closed pipe between his base unit and the machine, and sealed the on-Grid entryway from the NUN site. The sensations of the battle between the eels and NUN security vanished as the door slammed shut. He dispersed the security gate and the pain stopped. He relaxed, the only way the eels could get to him now would be through his base unit. Part of him really wanted to see them try.

Warning icons flashed in his mind as he interfaced more fully with the space, and found he was in possession of an ancient two armed forklift. Corroded fuel cells, said the icons, flat tyres, metal stress in loading fork two... on and on, blinking red and angry. He looked out of the thing's eyes. Only three of seven were working. Two showed an undifferentiated grey, probably a tarpaulin, the third looked on a photodegraded plastic wall. It was dim, but not dark. Light bounce let him guess he was inside an open-fronted shed. Microphones hissed as he tried out the loader's ears. He picked up only distant city sounds, the garage or shed or wherever he was in was empty. Further exploration revealed the loader to have a rotating cab, complete with a seat for a human operator – this more than anything else marked it out as an antique. A pigeon had made its nest on the cushion, leaving behind a dusty heap of guano and twigs. It made Richards feel dirty. He did his best to ignore it.

Only one of the loader's two arms was functional, the other squealed and jammed when he tried to lift it, and yet more icons yammered for attention. One arm was better than none, Richards figured.

"Here goes nothing," he muttered.

His voice boomed out of the front of the machine.

"Shit!" went the lifter at a similarly ear-splitting volume, before Richards realised he should shut right up, right away. No choice now, he had to act fast. He turned the engine over. He winced as a clanging like a cement mixer full of spanners filled the shed, getting faster and faster until it sounded almost like an electric motor, and not an accident waiting to happen. Further warning icons blinked in Richard's mind. He had a bare four minutes of fuel cell, if the motor didn't fall out of the bottom first.

He pulled forward, the grey in the machine's eyes replaced with the interior of the shed as the tarpaulin slid free. Outside, the evening was closing in. Richards wobbled the loader out onto the concrete apron of the distribution centre on uneven wheels. He was right down the far end of the complex, a good half mile from Otto's last location. He had to get a move on. He gunned the motor. It stalled.

Richards swore.

Otto leant on the ropes and undid the Geckro fastening on his boxing glove with his teeth and watched the men watching him. He let the glove fall to the ring canvas. The men approached him.

"Otto Klein?" asked the taller of the two – thin, aesthetic, a bureaucrat.

"If you say so," Otto replied. He ripped the tape from his left hand with his teeth and tossed it into a bucket on the gym floor outside the ring. He grabbed a towel off the ropes and wiped the sweat from his face. "What do you want?" He tugged his other glove off, then the tape, sat on a stool in the corner and swigged water from his bottle. Otto caught his trainer's eye. She looked away. This wasn't for her.

The men stayed outside the ring. Otto looked down at them, sitting inside he remained well above their eye level. Neither introduced themselves.

"You are due to perform your national service soon," said the bureaucrat. The second remained silent. He was bulky, military looking. Although he wore no uniform, Otto recognised the type.

"Next June. I've been offered a stay of execution so I can take part in the games," said Otto. "That's public information."

"Your trainer speaks very highly of you," said the bureaucrat. "She tells me you have a chance at a medal."

Otto shrugged, leant his elbows forward onto his knees and looked away from the men, across the gym to where a bunch of freshmen would-be boxers were being taken through aerobic exercises by the assistant coach. "What do you want?" he said. "I've been here all afternoon. I'm tired and I have to finish up a paper before Tuesday or I'll fail my course."

The two men glanced at each other. The bureaucrat nodded. "We have a proposition for you," said the military man, voice like tank treads rolling over gravel.

"Yeah?" said Otto, he cracked his neck. "What?"

"Come into the gym manager's office and we'll tell you."

"Tell me out here."

"I'm afraid we can't," said the bureaucrat. "It's classified, and that's as much as I can tell you without you signing an official secrets form," he smiled apologetically. "And we may need to perform a memory suppression."

"Memory suppression?"

"I see your interest is piqued. Please, it will only take five minutes. If you are not interested, you will never even know you lost them."

The target burst into pieces. Otto zoomed in with his new eyes. There was nothing left. He replayed the moment through his interface, watched the fragments fly. He smiled.

Otto ran, explosions around him. Mud sucked at his boots, but did not slow him.

The man was dead, his blood sticky on Otto's hands. He wiped them on his flak vest, the camolam pulsing at the touch. His eyes fixed on the corpse's. The lights had gone out of them. Otto felt nothing, he thought he should, but he didn't.

"Otto, the mentaug really is no different to the human mind. I mean, it is superior, yes, but fundamentally it is the same," Doctor Ekbaum explained patiently. He had a long sad face. Otto thought he was the kind of man who didn't know how to smile. Otto was strapped to a diagnostic table, like he was about to be autopsied.

"It will makes things clearer, more accurate" continued the doctor. "But ultimately our histories remain of our own writing. You will still be you."

"Otto!" Honour laughed and ran to him as he got off the train. She kissed him hard. She clung to him, her arms barely reaching round his neck, like a child's.

Clear notes rang out, silver trumpets in the dark.

Honour.

"Wake! The! Fuck! Up!" Tufa shouted. Icy water hit Otto. He hurt all over, spasms ticking in his muscles, aftershocks crawled along his nerves. His mind was jagged with pain. Mentaug memories, faint and jumbled, overlaid the present.

Tufa brought Otto back by hitting him very, very hard with a baseball bat. Otto's head snapped round. He was stripped to his waist, bound to a chair by heavy chains. He didn't know how he'd got there. His front was covered in vomit. Blood crusted half a dozen shallow cuts. Much more of this and his healthtech would be overwhelmed. Tufa had not ranted as long as Otto had hoped. Time was running out.

Everyone has to die sometime.

There was a shout outside, loud but rendered indistinct by the warehouse's soundproofing.

"What the hell was that...?" said one of Tufa's cheap cyborgs. Surprise crept over his sausage meat features, idiot slow.

"The AI?" asked the other hesitantly. Otto forced himself to focus, and was gratified to see a crease of worry form on their hormone-smoothed faces.

"Probably air jaunters, flying through. It's prime bike racing territory," said the other. He looked unsure.

Tufa stopped hitting him. Otto leant as far forward as his bindings would allow and spat red onto the ground. He looked up, and grinned a bloody grin. "Tired already, Tufa?" he asked.

"Still smart, eh? Well, you hear that Otto? They think it's your pal come to rescue you, but it's not. Old Launcey, I paid him well. There's not a thing he can use round here, not one. This place," he gestured round the interior of the warehouse with his bat, "is electronically dead, nothing for that slippery arsehole to get into. And when he gets here, if he gets here, we'll be ready for him, won't we boys?"

One of the cyborgs hefted a large EMP gun. "No number gonna to cope with this," he said.

"You are an idiot. He'll be here with a thousand cops," said Otto.

"No he won't." Tufa cupped his ear theatrically. "I don't hear any cops. A thousand cops, turn up for you? Fucking bullshit. They hate you almost as much as I do, with your bought badge and fucking superior attitude. Richards won't be speaking to anyone for a while. I've got him busy. I suppose he will get here," he shrugged. "AIs are hard to kill, but he'll be here far too late."

There was the rattle of a broken engine from outside. The cyborg henchmen glanced at one another. Otto looked up and smiled again. "Fine, if you say so. Still, it wouldn't do your boyfriends much harm to check that out."

Subdued gunfire; the security drones on the building were shooting at something. The rattling noise drew nearer.

Tufa frowned, but jerked his head at the EMP toting cyborg. He nodded and waddled the waddle of all over-muscled men toward the small postern cut into the warehouse's rolling door. He reached for the handle just as the entire thing burst inwards with a great bang. An antiquated loader went up and came down hard, the door folding round it, crushing the cyborg and stubbing out his life in a trail of blood and sparks. There came a frantic clanging as the loader cast off the door, flattening half Tufa's torture chamber and narrowly missing Otto.

"What the..." said Tufa, dropped his bat, and reached for his gun. Otto seized his chance and flung himself forward. The bolts pulled and the chair ripped from the floor. He caught Tufa on the side of one knee, bending it a way it wasn't made to go, and it broke with a wet crack as Otto's full weight fell onto it.

The second cyborg was quick. He recovered and stitched a line of holes in the loader with his flechette rifle. Hydraulic fluid sprayed like arterial blood. One of its wheels locked and the loader slew about. The cyborg fired again as the cab swung round, arm raised, claw spread. It grabbed and squeezed, hefting the bulky cyborg into the air as if he were made of straw. The loader slammed him into the floor again and again, until the cyborg stopped moving.

"Sorry I'm late," boomed Richards over the crackle of dying electronics. "I got a bit held up."

"Get me out of these chains," shouted Otto, his head on Tufa's backside. He wiggled on the Albanian, eliciting a shriek of pain. "Now."

"On it." Richards' borrowed hand descended, a pair of shears popped from one of the loader's claw tips and snipped the chain neatly in half. Otto stood up, untangling his limbs. He winced, rubbed his head, rotated his shoulder, it was not holding up well.

"OK," he said. "OK."

"Are you all right, big man?" said Richards. "You kind of look like shit."

"Yeah, I'll be OK," Otto replied. "Ach," he probed his face, it was swelling up, one eye half-closed. He looked down at his erstwhile captor, squatted next to him, lifted his head up by the hair, then let it drop, wiped his hand on his bloodied trousers with a look of distaste. Tufa groaned.

"You know, Tufa," he said. "I have killed over five hundred men in my life. But this does not make me like you. I have killed men in war, or because they tried to kill me. But I have never, ever, killed a man because I enjoy killing. I do not think killing to be wrong, but to do it for no reason is immoral, Tufa. You do it for the hell of it. You do not understand that lives are not to be taken for your sport. You do not seem to understand, Tufa, that you needed to go away, that you are a nasty bastard," he spat blood and wiped his mouth, "because you do not understand these things that I understand. We did the world a favour when we handed you over in Laos. I like to think we do the world a lot of favours. I did you a favour. I could have killed you, but I did not. The law says that you do not deserve to die. I do not always agree with the law..." Otto looked up at the bright lamps around them, at the tables, at the scattered tools. "You have made me angry. I do not much care for pain... but I hate vomiting. Listen to me!" He slapped Tufa's head. Tufa whimpered. "You should have stayed in your cell, that is where men like you belong. If you stayed there..." he shrugged. "But you have my MT cipher, Tufa, and no one can have that. I need to know how Launcey got it. Do you understand?"

"Fuck... you..." hissed Tufa through clamped teeth.

"That is the wrong answer," said Otto stolidly. "I am going to make an exception to my usual rules." Otto stood. If his speech hadn't had the required effect on the Albanian, the look on his face did.

"Wait!" shouted Tufa, holding up his hand. It shook, hard.

"No waiting," said Otto. He began methodically kicking Tufa's broken leg. "Now, we shall talk about my MT cipher, and we will talk about Launcey, and if we talk about Launcey, and you are good, then maybe I will remember my principles and you can go back to jail alive. More or less."

Tufa screamed. "I don't know anything, I don't know anything."

"Wrong," Otto kicked again, "answer. Who is he?"

Tufa screamed. "I never met him. I never seen him. We did it all through the Grid, I never seen him!"

"Um, Otto?" said Richards. His voice slurred.

Otto continued to swing his foot back and forth, one two, one two, driving it into Tufa's bent limb with robotic efficiency.

"Otto!" Richards boomed.

Otto stopped. "What?" It was Tufa's turn to vomit. He whimpered and dragged himself away across the floor.

"I only have one minute of battery power left. Do you think you can reactivate your MT? If I may, I'll borrow your eyes."

"Yes," Otto walked over to the table where Tufa's phone lay and smashed the device with the flat of his hand. "Done." He turned back to the sobbing Tufa. "Don't you go anywhere now."

Now that's more like it, said Richards in Otto's head. *That's much better.*

He left the loader, went back to his base unit. Its resident One free, the machine rolled back and forward in confusion, cab swivelling, its lights dying as the fuel cells ran dry.

Now, said Richards. *Where were we?*

"He has passed out."

Looks like there's plenty of drugs here. You want I should identify them so you can bring him round?

"No," said Otto, dragging Tufa back toward the tables by his feet. "I prefer to work through trial and error." He picked up a pneumatic syringe and looked at it thoughtfully, put it down, picked up one with ten centimetres of needle on it instead.

I think the first one you had? ventured Richards.

"Yeah, I know. This one will hurt more."

Er, do you know, maybe not do that? I'm calling the cops. Let's do this by the book. For once.

Reluctantly, Otto put the needle down.

Ten minutes later, Otto stood behind the groundtruck, an unmarked, unregistered monster with a fake Gridsig and no Gridpipe, and that was as black as a vehicle got. Within Launcey's payment stared back. Goods, not cash. Tufa had, Otto had found, no real idea who Launcey was, blank Grid accounts, that was all. Tufa had led them down a dead end lined with responsibilities.

"We can't just leave them here," said Otto.

"No," said Richards, "no we can't." He looked through Otto's eyes at the trailer's contents – two dozen or so frightened women, all bound for... Richards didn't like to think about it. It was debatable if what Launcey wanted them for would be worse than what would happen to them if the authorities took them in. Looking at their faces, all Arab or sub-Saharan or Berber, he could see once they'd been processed they were all going back on the other side of the Med wall, carted off to the Caliphate or the dying South. Each and every one was an illegal, of that he was sure. Most of them were still in their teens. The law didn't see that they were human, still people, still had all the potential and the flaws and the talents of any other person. They were only climate immigrants, and that made them criminals, though their only crime was to have been born in the wrong place.

Sometimes, in that day and age, it took a machine to see that.

Question is, what do we do? said Richards, still peering out of Otto's eyes.

From outside sounded sirens and the thrum of turbofans as police cars settled onto the concrete apron. Shouting followed.

"If we do nothing, they will be repatriated," said Otto. Above them, ranks of pigeons looked on, heads turned sideways, eyes bright with avian curiosity.

That's the law, said Richards. *Is it so bad?*

"You know the answer to that, Richards." Otto traced the electoos on his scalp with one finger. Dried blood flaked off. His wounds were scabbed over and the swelling on his face was subsiding as his healthtech got to work.

So what then? I am open to suggestions.

Otto shrugged. "You have many important friends."

Well, yeah, said Richards reluctantly.

"One, I am thinking of in particular, he owes us big favours."

Who?

"You know who. Very important," said Otto meaningfully.

Oh no, oh no. You don't mean... What, oh Otto, come on man! You can't mean, you want me to go and see him?

"He can fix this for us." Otto pulled an expression that would have been, had they been face to face rather than sharing the same head, a level stare.

The women were beginning to cry, first one, then another,

until near the whole damn lot of them were wailing like the
dead, all those bar the ones with eyes like empty windows. Otto
purposefully stared at these damaged few, making his partner
look. Richards held out for as long as he could before he caved in,
which was, to his credit, only about two seconds.

*OK! OK! Just quit thinking at me like that. I hate it when you think at
me like that.*

The police swarmed in. Their guns came down when they
recognised Otto. He gave the cops what was left of Tufa, cuffed,
bloodied and groaning but otherwise alive, and bummed a
carcinogen free cigarette. By the time he'd lit it and sucked
down the first of the smoke, Richards had gone from his head
off down the electric highway to see the European Central Police
Commissariat Five, or the the EuPol Five, as everyone except
Richards called him.

What Richards called him was Hughie. Hughie didn't like that
very much, but Richards persisted, because Hughie was, according
to Richards, the world's most pompous arse.

CHAPTER EIGHT

Reality 36

Ulgan the merchant, sometime haulier of cargo, very occasional tour operator, sat counting his money. As is the way with most avaricious men, and such Ulgan was, enumerating coin was his greatest pleasure. His business did not afford him the opportunity to do so as often as he would have liked, so he took advantage of the hottest time of day, when the sun burned down through the dry mountain air, no one wanted to fly and he was least likely to be disturbed. Under a worn parasol, he lost himself in a happy world of wealth for an hour or two, before time and trade called him back to the tedious affair of making more.

He was therefore vexed when a shadow took the glitter from his coins of a dozen lands. Ulgan did so like to see them shine.

"Good day to you, sir," said the caster of the shadow. His face was a dark block against the sky, the merchant's argot he employed accented. Ulgan squinted against the halo of sunlight around the stranger's head, and wished he would go away.

He said as much. "Go away."

The stranger was undeterred. "I and my companion are seeking transportation across the Rift," he said pleasantly, which redoubled Ulgan's irritation. "I have it on good authority that you are the finest provider of flight services to the other side."

The compliment did nothing to improve Ulgan's humour. He

grunted back. "That's as may be." He dropped his gaze back to his money. "Flights are closed," he waved his hand round, "is too hot, bird won't fly."

"But sir!" said the stranger. He moved round the counting table to where the haulier could see him. "Today is a most marvellous day for flight. The air is clear and pure."

"The air is too hot and the sky too bright," grumbled Ulgan.

"No sir, you can see for miles. Surely any creature would be desirous of flight merely for the thrill of it!"

"Who are you? You are strange here, unusual looking, eh?" He appraised the stranger. "Your skin is dark, much darker than the men of the Skyways, but you are not so dark as the men of the Sahem-Jhaleeb, whose cities lie on the plain. Where do you hail from?"

"Does it matter, friend, whence I hail?"

"It matters 'friend' that we do not care for strangers round here, and are not swift to aid them about their business." The stranger was very clean of line, his delicately made-up face carried none of the seams of hard living, no blemish of age or sun, no pockmark to drag the eye away from his firm chin and sharp cheek-bones. This Ulgan did not say, instead he spat on the dry dirt, and said, "If you're so inclined, fly yourself."

"Oh, but you are so unkind, sir, to mock me. I have not the facility for such a feat, and nor has my companion," said the stranger genially, as if Ulgan's manners were beyond reproach, when in fact there was little beyond reproach about Ulgan. "If I did, I would not be here imploring you for passage."

Ulgan found the floridity of the man's language offensive. He had no time for pretty words from pretty strangers. Still, the stranger was a martial fellow, that much was obvious from his brocaded coat of plates, the steel helm spike poking through his turban, and the sabre hanging from his sash, so Ulgan was polite, by his usual standards, for he was above all else a coward.

"Can't fly, won't fly. Sorry," he smiled a smile that was no smile at all. "You and your friend had best come back tomorrow."

"My apologies good sir, but I need to go today. I am on an errand of some urgency."

"A thousand pardons," said Ulgan. "No flights today." And he began the pretence of counting, hoping the stranger would get the hint and leave.

"A pity," sighed the stranger. He rested his hand within the hilt of his weapon. "You do your kind a great disservice, sir."

"For God's sake, Jag, stop wasting our time." Another stranger stalked up to join the first. "Offer to pay the weasel; money's the only language these greasy little blighters understand."

There was something hollow in this second voice that made Ulgan look up. He dropped his attention back to his cash before the sight registered.

"Great Lugel!" he cried, his eyes widening. He stood from his seat and staggered back, though not with enough force to spill his money. "What in all the names of the seventeen beasts of enforced repentance is that!?"

"Why," said the stranger, "he is Tarquinius, my trusted friend and steed." The princeling gestured towards a lion stepping round a hut, a lion of metal. A lion as big as a horse. Its face was made of sliding plates of dazzling copper, its body of blue-sheened iridium, its mane of spun silver that cast a second sun of harsh reflections around its feet. "I myself am Sir Jagadith Veyadeep, paladin of this 36th Reality. Perhaps you have heard of us?"

"N-no!" said the haulier, cringing.

"Oh, well," said Sir Jagadith disappointedly. "I suppose it has been a long while. It is enough for you to know I have an important mission on the other side of the Rift. A task if left undone, may well spell the end for you, your village, your birds. Why, the whole of the Skyways. So, you must understand, I have to leave today."

This was bad news. Ulgan's brow creased. He thought of his family (although they hated him), his friends, (although he had none), his life, his birds, the whole of the Skyways. His money. "You did mention money?" He licked his lips, and took a step forward.

"Why yes. Of course," said the paladin. "Naturally you will be amply compensated."

"It'll be extra for the Gnomic beast," said Ulgan sharply.

"Ha!" said Tarquinius, his voice sounding from the bottom of an upturned bell. "You are right and wrong there. I am gnomic, but I feel your feeble vocabulary seeks to furnish you with the word *gnomish*, as in fashioned by *gnomes*, which I most certainly am not." The lion walked to stand before Ulgan, the panels of its body sliding noiselessly against one another. He emitted the humming click of clockwork and the faint smell of ozone. "Those little bastards can hardly put together a half-decent pocket watch." he rumbled. "I am god-formed, so let's have a little respect." Tarquinius leaned forward until his muzzle was inches from Ulgan's nose. He snorted hot, tinny air into his face, and grinned a dagger grin.

Ulgan took a step backwards. "Er... A thousand pardons..."

"How much?" rumbled the lion.

"How much have you got?" countered Ulgan.

"Shall we say enough to ensure you and the next seven generations of your family will be mercifully free of the burden of meaningful employment?" said Sir Jagadith.

"Er, a reasonable price," said Ulgan, his throat dry. "Kind sirs," he hurriedly added. "Magnificent sires?" he tried.

The lion sat back. "Hmph," it said, and licked its leg with a noise like a rasp on steel.

"Here," the knight tossed a large piece of metal onto the table. "This is my badge of office."

Jagadith's badge was very big, and very shiny. And very... *gold*. Ulgan gulped. His hands strayed towards it. He stepped forward again.

The lion looked up from its ablutions. "Stand still for god's sake man!" it growled. "One more time and you'll have yourself a merry little dance."

The knight looked about, and beckoned Ulgan close, a brave thing, for Ulgan's dental hygiene was poor. "I have more," said the knight enticingly.

Ulgan looked up, then down, then up, then at the lion, then at the badge. Profit won out over fear. He wiped his mouth. "Marrekee!" he called over his shoulder. "Rouse bird number twelve, we're taking this gentleman for a flight."

Sir Jagadith sat upon Tarquinius's back, waving at the four-winged bird that had borne them over the rift.

"Damn fool," muttered Tarquinius. The jungle was a place used to nothing louder than the whisper of plants. Tarquinius' sonorous voice turned the atmosphere hostile.

"Dearest friend, you are being ungenerous to our air captain," said Jagadith. The canyon was so deep the fields upon its floor were a hazy patchwork, so wide the cliffs of the far side were a caramel bar against the yellow of the sky.

"Do you know just how much money you gave him?" Tarquinius rattled his mane. "Foolish."

"I did give him a great deal," Jag knocked Tarquinius' back. The lion rang. "It was expedient, and matters little. He will fritter it away, or his sons, or his grandsons."

"Expediency be damned!" growled the lion. "No one needs that much wealth. We'll destabilise the economy, then what good comes of keeping this realm safe? A foolish act Jag, foolish."

"Who are we to begrudge anyone money, my friend? We have no need of it. Also, I am thinking he would not have brought us so far from an established landing post had we not furnished him with his lavish fee. It is, perchance, liable to buy his silence."

"Hmmm," said Tarquinius. The bird, feathered legs and forelimbs stretched wide, vanished from sight, and the lion turned away from the chasm to the dark of the jungle. "I doubt it. Treacherous he seemed, and sly."

Away from the edge was a gloom slashed by stinging whips of sunlight. The air grew heavy. Jagadith politely perspired, while

Tarquinius, cooled by arcane machineries, ran with rivulets of condensation.

"This is a most hellish place," said the knight.

There was a whir as Tarquinius' jointed tongue retracted. "And anomalous. This jungle should not exist. There is too much moisture for the geographic conditions. Relative humidity is at one hundred per cent. Temperature is five degrees Kelvin plus over average. There are twenty-three species of plant extant here that would not be able to survive if this area conformed to the meteorological norms for this area. This should be a dusty plateau, fifteen point three per cent afforested with montane pine. It is not. At the highest permissible vegetative density, we should be observing dry woodland. This is anomalous."

"Oh do be stopping with your tedious science, there's a good chap," said Jagadith.

"Jag, there are three plant species that are not even native to Reality 36. This is not a good thing."

"Indeed not."

"You are not taking this seriously."

"Oh I am my friend, I am. This is a serious business we are about. But I prefer to be joyous. It is not often we get to walk the world." Jagadith breathed deeply of the air, then coughed delicately. The jungle was not the most fragrant of places.

"I'll be joyous when the job's done," said the lion. "This level of anomaly is too high even for one of *them*. I am concerned."

Jag patted the streaming side of his mount. "My dear friend, the world has been changed, this is true. But I hesitate to venture that it is a question of objectivity here that dogs you, not risk. We have engaged now in over three hundred and ninety expulsions. Very few have put us in danger. All will be well."

"I am not so sure," said the lion warily. "This is different. I feel it. Complacency is the enemy of the wise, and I am not feeling wise today."

"Are you feeling instead, then, afraid?"

"No, never afraid. I am concerned."

The lion said no more, concentrating on forcing his way through the forest, the crack of snapping branches punctuating Jagadith's humming.

Several hours later, as day retreated, Jagadith ceased humming, and a dark expression clouded his face.

"Tell me Tarquinius, what is the precise extent of this landmass?"

"Four hundred and twelve point seven three kilometres square, give or take the odd metre. It is effectively a large island in the centre of the Rift canyon."

"Then why is this jungle persisting?"

"You know what I am going to say."

"Because it is anomalous?"

"Because it is anomalous." Tarquinius gave a metallic grunt as he shoved aside a tree trunk blocking their path. The rotten wood broke against his metal, taking a swathe of undergrowth with it and opening a ragged tear in the jungle's wall as it fell.

"But not," gasped Tarquinius, "as anomalous as that."

"By Jove!" said Jagadith. "Now I am believing we may be in some small degree of imperilment."

Before them lay a round clearing in the jungle so precise it could have been popped out by a hole punch. Some tens of miles away in the middle, shining in the last light, was a dimpled, hemispherical hill of carved basalt, and atop that a gargantuan monkey puzzle tree, its top crowned by a spinning, black vortex. Swamps girt hill, tree and anomaly. The tentative chirps of frogs, oblivious to the peculiarity of their surroundings, sounded from the swamp.

"This is a turn-up for the books." Jag slipped off the lion. "I do not recollect seeing anything of this nature since, well, I am thinking, ever." He frowned, perplexed.

"Nor do I, and I am as old as the reality itself." Tarquinius was silent a moment, his head cocked to one side.

"This is indeed a powerful god we rush confront, he who can so reshape the world, and after so long..." Jagadith lapsed into thought. "Perhaps we should not be too hasty." He sighed. "It is getting dark, my friend," said Jagadith. "We camp here. Is this a good idea? Tomorrow we cross the swamps. I suspect that vortex to be our quarry's lair," he pointed with an elegant hand.

"I concur," said the lion, and slumped to the ground. "Godlings are nothing if not predictable." He licked at some of the jungle's slime. He made a face and said, "I am weary, yet not so tired I cannot make fire to dry this filthy water from my metal. Perhaps the smoke will drive the biting insects away also, and we both may rest more comfortably. Fetch some wood, and I will kindle it with the heat of my reactor." He yawned and stretched. "I would help but… You understand."

Jag performed a slight bow. "Quite. For all your talents, my friend, I do sometimes feel the gods could have given you opposable thumbs."

CHAPTER NINE

Valdaire

From the moment Veronique Valdaire heard the message from Professor Qifang, she was in trouble.

Her sleep was electric with Grid-enhanced dreams. She awoke reluctantly, sore and sweaty from last night's dancing, to the sound of her name chanted over and over. She caught her own smell, and wished she'd showered before bed.

"Veev, Veev, Veev, Veev," insisted Chloe. Veronique frowned, rolled over, arms flopping disastrously into her bedside table. The table rocked, sending the small necessities of her life tumbling to the wooden floor.

"Veev, Veev, Veev, Veev," sang the phone from under the bed.

Veronique gave up. "Shut up Chloe, let me sleep."

"Get up, Veev. Get up, Veev. Get up, Veev."

"Shut up," she mumbled.

But there was only one way to shut Chloe up. Veronique pawed her dreamcap off and hung over the mattress, scrabbling weakly under the bed. She retrieved the phone and jabbed at its touch screen.

"Veev, Veev, Veronique... Ah, good morning Veronique," said the phone brightly, as Veronique's face swung into view of its camera. "There you are! You have one message."

"I turned you off," Veronique said, her tongue uncooperative.

"I turned myself back on," said Chloe. "Because you will be late, late, la-aaate!" the phone sang.

"I know." Veronique scrunched her eyes against the light as Chloe opened the blinds.

"You are not behaving as if you do! Work awaits you, get u-u-u-uuuUPPPPPPP!"

Veronique resolved to programme Chloe's morning cheer out of her later that day.

"I hate you," she moaned.

"I love you, Veronique!" replied Chloe. "You have a message, from Professor Zhang Qifang. Playing message. One message. Play..." The professor's English, internationally neutral with a faint Cantonese accent, came out of the phone. "'Veronique, I've tried you several times. Your phone is off. I need to speak to you, please call as soon as you can. I'll be in my office for as long as I am able. Hurry.' Message sent 3.13am," said Chloe. "Sender Professor Zhang Qifang. Reply?"

"What the hell did he want at three in the morning? I've not heard from him for two weeks and now this?" Veronique said. She rolled onto to her back, clutching the phone to her chest.

"Reply?" said Chloe. "Reply? Reply? Answer Veronique, answer!"

"Chloe! Shut up! I've just woken up. Do you understand?"

"No, silly," giggled Chloe. "I am a machine, I do not sleep. How could I understand?" Then she sang again, "Get up Veronique, or you will be late. Work time! Work time! Sleepy time is over. Sleepy time is over! Attention! *Reveille-toi*!"

Veronique wrapped a pillow around her head. "Go away Chloe." The bed was warm. If she only had a hammer...

"I love you Veev," Chloe said tenderly. "And I always will, but *GET UP*!" Raucous post-romantic rock blared out of Chloe's speakers, a kind of music Veronique hated.

Chloe was evolved from Veronique's first doll, a life companion, the only thing she'd saved when her family had escaped the hell of the Sub-Sahara. Through two decades in Canada, as her early years in Africa sunk into the shadows of nightmare, Chloe had been with Veronique always, upgraded, tinkered with, but at heart always the same.

Veronique threw the pillow aside, glared at the phone, snatched it off the bed and got up. She shook her head, squinted at the phone's screen to doublecheck the time of the message. 3.13am was both too late and too early for Qifang, he'd probably got muddled. He'd been distracted recently. He was old, seriously so, anti-gerontics only bought you so much more time, she supposed.

"He doesn't even have an office, so what the hell is he talking about?" grumbled Veronique. "We're supposed to meet at the lab."

Californian communitarian law forbade divisive workplace affectations, and that included private office space. Working together, all that New New Age Dippy bullshit, open plan and open hearts all the way. Back in Quebec they preserved a little Old World coldness. They didn't have time for peace flowers, team mantras and confessional circles. Group hugs made her flesh crawl.

"His virtual office, silly," giggled Chloe. "Shall I try and patch you through?"

"Yeah, yeah, go on, give me a view in to his virtuality," said Veronique, and prepared to apologise in her pyjamas.

Chloe went silent for a moment. "I am afraid his office address is non-functional, possibly due to Grid system failure in sector 23."

"You mean Beverly Hills."

"Sector 23 is a more efficient designation. Whatever I mean and however I express myself, the end result is the same: his office is temporarily unavailable."

"Why is the Grid down?" she said. It was practically unheard of.

"I have no idea. Happy day!" giggled Chloe.

"At least I've learnt something while I've been in California," she walked across the room. "And that's not to move to California..." She lapsed into irritated muttering. If Qifang himself hadn't sent the job offer, she'd never have come to the UCLA. If she had her time again, she might not come anyway. One more group bonding session would send her screaming over the edge. She had grown to hate the smell of essential oils with an intensity she'd not thought possible. "I should never have left the army," she moaned.

"Stop being a baby! Time to work! Shall I call the professor's phone to tell him you will meet at the lab? It is likely he is there."

"Yes," then she changed her mind. "No, he can wait. This is my time."

"You were quite happy to patch through to his office!"

"He *demanded* I go see him at 3.13am, Chloe, at the start of the vacation. I'm not his slave. Let me wake up. Send him a message, text only. Full punctuation. Hit him with some periods. Tell him I'm on my way in and will meet him at the department. Tell him I'll be there at six-thirty, which is a whole hour before I'm supposed to be at work. Shitting dippies. Work is life, life is work. They can go screw themselves."

"Language, Veronique!"

Though Qifang approved of precious little else the dippies had to say, he had bought into the work-all-day part of their philosophy wholeheartedly. He was up while the morning was still the night doing Tai Chi on the lawn every day and thought everyone else sluggardly. Another pig of a drawback in working for him.

Veronique opened the door to her tiny room in the tiny duplex she shared with the not-so-tiny Chantelle, some crazy match-up made by Archimedes, the department's Class Six AI – "Personality matching to induce productive conflict, intended to unlock your potential, facilitating wellness cross-germination through forced antagonism resolution," as the dippy nonsense-speak had it in their brochure. What that meant was that she and Chantelle were supposed not to get on, but would overcome their dislike and become firm friends. The dippies had been right about part of their programme. Their dislike did change – now they loathed each other.

Veronique's body ached. She'd wanted to come home early but Fabler was leaving town for good, and she'd been half-bullied into staying, but only half. Dancing was the only time she let herself go. She liked to think she was good, and went out of her way to prove it. But all night in the Dayglo would make anyone hurt, and three hours sleep was the sting in the tail.

She yawned. "You took the risk, you idiot, now you pay the price," she muttered.

"Exactly," trilled Chloe.

"Shut up, Chloe."

"Qifang will be furious."

"That's his problem." Fabler would be nursing an obscene hangover today, anti-tox or not. She allowed herself a little schadenfreude at that, put her slippers on and went to make breakfast.

"Hooray!" shouted Chloe. "You are up. Welcome, Veronique, to August 24th, Thursday, 2129 in glorious, lovely, lovely Los Angeles, California, the sunshine state!" California's official jingle played over the slogan. "Pacific Coast Time 0530 hours. Outside temperature 43 degrees celsius. Weather prognosis…"

"Thanks, Chloe. Please be quiet now."

"I love you Veronique."

"I know," said Veronique. "Now shut up."

The usual routine, breakfast scavenged from whatever scraps Chantelle had missed in her nocturnal bulldoze. A blessed shower. A handful of rebalancing pills, and she felt like she'd had a decent night's sleep, although she'd pay for it later.

She went down to the garage, and got into her ageing groundcar. The day was glorious, but there was a rainstorm due, so she kept the hardtop closed. It was broken and a bitch to get back up again. If she could, she'd have bought a new one, but who was she kidding? It'd be the 23rd century before she'd have enough for a new car, and the dippies would probably have got round to banning property outright by then. Come the next century, they'd all be skipping to work behind a man in a robe, banging tambourines.

She stopped at Starbucks on the way in, a small vice, but a necessary one.

She pulled into the campus at 6.15am. The University had moved into a fancy, eco high rise in the Chino Hills from Westwood some decades back – forever ago, as far as she was concerned, although Qifang still complained about the lack of decent eateries out there. She liked the view. Past the fire embankment circling the buildings, you could see all the way over the tight bowl of LA to the Laguna hills and the blue of the ocean beyond.

She parked her car in the auto-racks and it swung up and out of sight. The faculty building hissed out chilled air as she went inside, and then her shoes were squeaking off marble. She waved her ID at the desk clerk, some annoying guy named Guillermo who behaved like everyone's best friend but who always, always got her name wrong, then past Archimedes' primary security reader. The internal gates swung open and she wandered corridors where robot cleaners worked quietly. The lab was empty, practically the whole building was. There was no sign that anyone had been there during the night.

"Professor Qifang?" she called. Her voice echoed.

"Professor Zhang Qifang has not yet arrived, Veronique," said the faculty Class Six from nowhere. It might call itself Archimedes, but its voice was both colourless and androgynous, the voice of something actively avoiding personality.

"Thanks, Archimedes," she said.

"You are welcome, Veronique."

Veronique's neck tickled. The notion was irrational, but there was an ineffable fear that came with the scrutiny of a powerful AI, a jungle terror, of predators in the shadows.

She covered her fear with a yawn. "So much for rushing in. Might as well get on with something while I wait."

"That's the spirit."

"Shut up, Chloe."

"Shall I inform you when he arrives?" the AI's directionless voice haunted the air.

"Yeah, please, Archimedes."

"I am afraid I will not be able to assist you greatly. I have suffered a systems malfunction in half of this laboratory. Maintenance will be here presently."

"Probably rats, eating the neo-plas. I hear they like the taste."

"I assure you I do not suffer from rats," said the AI equably.

Veronique put her coffee down on her workbench too hard. Some leapt out and scalded her, and she cursed. It was for that her that "Danger! Coffee! Hot!" warning labels scrolled round and round paper cups.

"Are you OK Veronique? Shall I call a paramedic?"

"No, Archimedes, I am fine, it's nothing."

She sucked at her hand as she walked across to her locker, pressed her thumb against the locker and spoke her Gridsig out aloud, feeling thankful that at least the dippies allowed you somewhere to keep your stuff. The reader scanned her print and implanted gridchip. The small door popped open.

"Huh?" There was someone else's pad in her locker. She caught herself before she said anything else. Archimedes was as nosey as machines came, a blush out of the ordinary and it'd be filling her ears with pleasantries as it scanned her brain for thought crime.

She pulled the computer from the locker.

"Archimedes?" she asked.

"Doctor Valdaire?"

"Please describe your malfunction, in case I need to work around it."

"Of course," replied the AI smoothly. "All devices and subsystems supporting my autonomous functions are operating correctly. My problem is a matter of perception. I am unable to engage with the majority of my sensing devices anywhere four metres beyond the laboratory door. I can hear you just fine, but I cannot see you presently. I have access to audio, human biometrics and staff Gridsigs, nothing else. I trust all will be available to me once the fault is identified and repaired. Do not worry, it will not take long."

Susan raised her index finger and mouthed something incredibly rude in French at a nearby beadcam.

As a Class Six, Archimedes could speak multiple languages, extrapolate the meanings of many more from the ones he knew, and of course he could lip read. As a jobsworth, there was no way he'd let that an insult like that go without comment.

Nothing.

"OK, thanks Archimedes."

She hunched over the pad just the same, covering as much of it from view as possible. She opened the case and her brow creased. There was a message on paper underneath, bizarre ideograms above Qifang's signature neatly blocked in New Mandarin characters.

The ideograms were from Reality 36, the ex-game virtuality the department was currently studying. There were about three sentients on the planet that understood that language. Veronique was one, but she could read it only slowly, and with difficulty.

We have been made victim to set-up, it read. *Get out now. Serious anomalies. VIPA think it is us. Get the v-jack. Get away before they get you. Meet me in Reality 36. Can explain no more. Data speaks for itself.*

Very carefully, she activated the pad. A holo presentation played, no audio. A graph. Lines tracked energy output, Grid resource assignation, second-world traffic, the measures of the worlds locked within the Reality House in Nevada. All looked normal, then all of a sudden it didn't. All of a sudden it didn't look normal at all.

"Shit."

"Language, Veronique," said Chloe from her handbag.

"Shut up, Chloe." The presentation continued. Power and resources were being drawn off in incrementally increasing amounts over a period of six months. Scrolling information ran along the side, detailing which packets came from where, giving the story behind the graph's simple lines, but not for all of it. Much of the activity was sourceless.

"Somebody's using the Reality spaces without permission," she whispered to herself.

It had been very skilfully hidden, but when you saw it, clear as day, and it was getting worse. There was a steep spike a few days ago.

The presentation looped back to the beginning.

Veronique ran a finger over the external drive set into the pad's casing, and a memory module slid out. The screen went blank. The module was rough, fabbed on a home loom.

"Chloe," she said as normally as she could manage. "Check out the data on this pad, Cameron wants us to look it over."

"Cameron can do his own work," sniffed Chloe.

"Just look at it, and give me it visually, on the screen, not 3D! I'm tired of your chirpy voice."

"Charming."

Quickly she typed on Chloe's touchscreen. *Sorry, play along. Trouble. Is this genuine Reality data?*

The screen blinked one word.

Yes.

She popped the memory module into Chloe's port. Veronique tapped again.

What is this module? It looks odd.

A tick, and another two words: *Trouble = Correct.* The screen blinked. *Faked key and access codes for the v-jack cabinet.*

So Qifang really meant what he'd said. Unless it was Cameron, she wouldn't put it past him delivering her a fatal practical joke. *Message Qifang,* she tapped. *I have your message. Explain.*

No response.

"His office and his number are not responding?" said Veronique. "Archimedes?"

"I am at your beck and call, Doctor Valdaire, as limited as I am today."

"Locate Professor Zhang Qifang, please."

"As you wish," said the Six, then practically immediately: "Location, unknown."

"What do you mean? Has he invoked privacy?"

"No," said the Six patiently. "I mean the Grid does not know where he is."

"That's impossible!" Unease trailed cold fingers down her skin.

"Yes, it is rather curious," said the Six. "Do not be alarmed. I have informed higher entities than myself. The dispersal of a Grid signature is rare but not unheard of. I am sure they will clear this up as soon as soon can be. Is there a problem, Veronique?" said Archimedes, its voice oozing solicitude. "Only my monitoring of your biological process indicate that you are nervous."

"No, nothing's wrong. It's the caffeine, and I was out late," she said, and wondered just how compromised Archimedes really was. Whoever had put the pad and key in her locker had almost certainly been responsible for deactivating the Six's sensor grid. She slurped coffee, thinking.

A chime came from her phone, it was Guillermo at the front desk. Veronique stared at it numbly for a long second before answering. "Audio only, Chloe," she said finally. "Hello?"

"Hi there, Vera." Vera? Idiot. "It's Guillermo from the front desk. There are people coming to see you. I wouldn't normally, but I thought I'd give you a quick heads-up to prepare yourself. You looked a little sleepy-eyed this morning!" he brayed like a drunk relaying a lame joke.

"Qifang is here?" Relief flooded her.

"Er, no," said Guillermo, chuckling. "No, why would he have me ring up? It's er…" He paused a moment, reading or receiving an external data input. "Santiago Chures from the Virtualities Investigation and Protection Authority."

"The VIPA?" she said. The blood drained from her face.

"Yeah. They come here all the time," he said uncertainly. "Are you OK? You sound really jumpy."

"Yes, yes, I am fine, see you later, Guillermo." She ended the call quickly.

"Archimedes? Why didn't you tell me the VIPA were coming?"

No reply but a smug, expectant silence.

"Chloe, give me the beadcam feeds from the atrium to here."

"Yes, Veronique," said the phone. Dozens of tiny thumbnail vid-pics filled Chloe's phone screen, including the few operating in the lab, showing her hunched over her phone. The images rippled, resolving into three stacked feeds following five men.

Two were bulky, over-muscled in a way that suggested physical augmentation. They wore the uniform of all who wish to appear conspicuously inconspicuous: suits, dark glasses, expensive shoes. The leader was physically unenhanced, bearded, Hispanic origin like pretty much everyone in LA, but he walked with a swagger foreign to the local culture. He was probably Chures. He turned to say something to one of his colleagues, and Veronique caught sight of uplinks curled round both ears, and a kidney-shaped auxiliary mind nestled hard to his occiput. He was enhanced mentally with a symbiotic AI personality blend.

"Veronique, why have you accessed my camera network?" asked Archimedes. "If you wish to use my camera network, you should ask first." There was a tone to the AI's words that made Veronique felt like a mouse talking with a cat.

"Why didn't you tell me the VIPA were coming?"

"Veronique," Archimedes admonished her. "The VIPA police the very worlds and minds you study. They fund this department. They would give no indication that they are coming, because they do not have to."

"You should have told me," she said pointedly.

"I believe Professor Qifang warns all researchers that come to work here that this department is open to industrial espionage, Neukind-activist sabotage and malicious hackers," Archimedes said patronisingly. "Our department cannot work without the authorisation of the VIPA. You know this. I am sure their visit is entirely routine."

Like hell it is, she thought.

She moved abruptly across the laboratory to a cabinet surrounded by hazard striping and prominent legal notices.

"What are you doing, Veronique?" said Archimedes.

"Nothing," she said. "I'm a bit worried. I need to check the v-jack cabinet. It may have been tampered with."

"If you say, Veronique. I am grateful. My sensors are non-functional in that area. Do you think I have been sabotaged?"

"It is possible, Archimedes."

She tried to sound calm. She wasn't. She was about to steal a v-jack, and the cops were at the door. She took a breath. She almost stopped then. If caught with the v-jack, she was looking at a stretch in cold storage, five, maybe six years, with a cumulative three per cent chance of brain damage for each twelve months under. You could double that if they went for corrective neural surgery. They were shitty odds for a supposedly humane form of punishment.

She almost stopped. Almost.

"Chloe, crack the cabinet," she said quietly.

"Veronique..."

"Use the key. See if it works."

The door popped open.

"Doctor Valdaire," Archimedes' voice sounded smoothly. "What on *Earth* are you doing? I have notification that the cabinet is open. You are not authorised to access a v-jack at this current moment."

"I told you, I need to check the cabinet. It may have been tampered with."

"You did not say you were going to open it."

"If I don't open it, how can I see if it's been tampered with or not?" she said.

"Stop. Now," Archimedes said, its strange, soothing voice not changing tone at all.

"I'll just be a moment." The cabinet was nothing special, a cupboard with fancy glass front. Inside was a moulded recess occupied by a smooth polycarbon box. She drew this out. This too, had its own autonomous locks, but the Six was powerless to prevent her having Chloe open it with Qifang's key.

Inside the box was a neat, adjustable headpiece. Insectoid legs dangled from a crest studded with magnetic manipulators. A braid of cable trailed from the rear. It was not unlike a dream cap, though clunkier looking, but then it had to be larger, for rather than enhancing the dreams of a sleeper, it was capable of fooling the conscious mind into constructing an entirely immersive virtual environment, an altogether trickier proposition. It was old tech, very rare now, and illegal outside of departments like this. It was crazy to think only a decade ago many homes had v-jacks, when now the device was regarded as so dangerous it required three signatories to sign out, approval from Archimedes, and was quintuply digitally locked. All of that had been neatly circumvented by Zhang Qifang.

A hundred and twenty seven years-old, she thought. Don't mess with that kind of experience.

The v-jack went in her bag.

"Veronique, this is not good!" shrieked Chloe.

"I would listen to her if I were you," said Archimedes. "I now understand that you intend to deceive me. You are stealing the v-jack. You compromised my internal sensors in order to facilitate this criminality, and that upsets me. I thought we had more mutual respect. That is a shame. I must recalibrate my interpersonal interpretation parameters. You were asked to desist. You did not. I have been forced to act. Your Grid access has been disabled. I have locked the doors. Please wait here for the VIPA. One of them has the name Greg. According to your specific sexual tastes, he's hot, so that's lovely for you, isn't it?"

Chloe's screens projected an enormous legal notice in front of Veronique's face.

"Right. Thanks," Veronique said back.

"Your sarcasm is unnecessary, and also hurtful," said Archimedes. "You should adjust your own parameters if you wish for smoother interactions with your fellow sentients."

"I'll take it under consideration. Chloe, retrieve Kitty Claw off the Grid, load it up, I want it primed."

"Really?" said Chloe hesitantly.

"Really."

"Oh," said Chloe. "Oh no." The phone's cooling system stepped up a gear as the phone downloaded the programme from its hideaway on the Grid.

Veronique went to the lab door. The Six had been as good as its word and it was locked. She had Chloe hack it. The door opened.

"Doctor Valdaire," Archimedes sounded weary. "I advise you to stop. The warning displayed upon your phone is legally binding. Please, cease and desist. For your own sake."

"Archimedes, I have done nothing. This isn't down to me. Something is not right here. It'll all come clear."

"Current evidence suggests it already is clear," said the Six. "You are a thief, and a danger to the RealWorld Realities."

She ignored it, went through the door and walked fast down the empty corridor. The building had only three public entrances but a dozen emergency exits. She made for the nearest.

Also locked.

The Six's voice sound right behind her this time. Her ear tickled in anticipation of non-existent breath. "Doctor Valdaire, your actions are indicative of guilt. If you are not guilty, you are bringing suspicion upon yourself, if you are guilty, then you are making things worse. Halt. My advice is final. Upon my next insistence, I shall employ force."

"Chloe, open the door."

Veronique pushed against it. It did not open.

"The door!"

"I... I can't open it, Veronique," said her phone.

"That is a fine friend you have, but I am not falling for the same trick twice," said Archimedes. "Please, I implore you, do stop."

"Archimedes, let me out."

"Are you threatening me?" a strain of malevolent amusement entered its voice. "You are very gifted Doctor Valdaire, but..."

"Chloe, release Kitty Claw."

"*Oui oui*, Veronique," said Chloe.

"There is nothing you can–"

The voice cut out as soon as Chloe released Kitty Claw into Archimedes' systems, turning the Six off. To do so was highly illegal, an assault, in effect. Veronique had crafted the programme some time ago, just in case. Her military file said she suffered from mild paranoia. She liked to think she was careful.

Lights and wall terminals flickered and died. Up the corridor, a robot cleaner slid gently into the wall, brushes spinning to a halt. All machine activity stopped. It became so quiet all she could hear was the building's passive aircon whispering away.

"Veronique, I am blind! I am deaf!" wailed Chloe.

"Local Grid's gone down with the Six, that's all," she whispered. The corridor was faintly lit by emergency bioluminescent panels. Somewhere an alarm lazily sounded.

"Will Archimedes be alright?" asked Chloe.

"Probably," said Veronique. "Its pride will be dented though."

Chloe sniffed. "I never liked it," she said.

Veronique pushed the fire door. The magnetic locks were dead and it had unhitched itself, they probably all had.

She looked outside cautiously. A couple of technicians were cycling into work, nobody else, it was early still. No VIPA men visible. She walked to the car racks, trying not to run.

With the Six offline she had to get Chloe to hijack the parking subsystem. She couldn't open it. Archimedes had pulled the plug on that too.

Chloe soon had her in. The car's rack trundled down to ground level, and released it. More illegal software, more time in the freezer.

The car's windscreens were white with electronic snow. Where the car's Gridsig should have been displayed in the lower left of the glass was a constantly changing stream of numbers. Chloe was running fake Gridsigs to hide their location. There would be more time in the freezer for that.

"Go!" she shouted.

"Please provide a destination," said the car.

"Get out of here! Go!" Veronique kicked at the car.

"Home," said Chloe.

The car complied. They got home.

A big, ugly aircar squatted outside her complex. It could have been anyone's, but it was probably the VIPA. Veronique did not want to find out. Her heart hammered as her car drove her away. The aircar remained still. They reached the end of the street, turned left and accelerated towards the interstate. Where she was going, she had no idea. All she had were the v-jack, Chloe and the clothes she was in.

"What the hell am I doing?" she said.

"Travelling," said the car's literal personality.

"Idiot," said Chloe. To whom, Veronique was not sure.

CHAPTER TEN

Hughie

Twenty minutes was an eternity to an AI, but that's how long Hughie made Richards wait. The EuPol 5 did this because he did not like being called Hughie, which Richards unfailingly did, he also did it because he did not like Richards' attitude, which was mostly Richards calling him Hughie, but most of all, he did it because he liked to make people wait.

Twenty minutes ended as exactly as they could, to a thin-sliced sliver of a second.

"Richards," said Hughie's voice, testy as usual.

"Hey, Hughie, how're you doing?" said Richards.

"Don't call me Hughie," Hughie said, more testily. The air in the hall grew colder. "What do you want?"

Richards looked round Hughie's hall with a wry smile. Hughie believed he was Very Important, capital V, capital I, and he wanted everyone to know how Very Important he was. As a case in point, Richards wasn't in really Hughie's hall. The actual hall was deep under Geneva. Richards was online, in his usual attire of trenchcoat, hat and rumpled, human face. There was nothing so twee about Hughie, no costumes delineating his character, no snug virtualities of antique drawing rooms or wild ocean shores, just an exact rendition of the vast, utilitarian cavern where he dwelled in reality. Hughie's base unit was surrounded by hundreds of lesser

AIs, connected to each other and to Hughie by snaking cables in ultramatt black. Twelve class Sevens were arrayed around him – the apostles to his Christ, Richards always said, and Hughie didn't think that was funny either – and after them Sixes, Fours and Threes in concentric circles according to grade. The noise of the machines filled the space with a quiet rustling, the sound of data being masticated, like termites devouring a house at night.

Hughie's hall was a concrete cathedral. It was a pharaonic tomb full of the sarcophagi of the immortal god king and his sycophants. It was a monument to the power of the number. It was cold. It was creepy.

It was the home of an enormously arrogant cock.

Hughie's voice resonated round the room, the main force of it concentrated on the audience platform where he received his offline guests. Or rather, in this case, on the exact Grid copy of the audience platform where he received his offline guests. Every visitor, every *supplicant* thought Richards, got the same treatment, no matter who they were, herded into the glass dome to protect them from the hall's unbreathable atmosphere. Whether they breathed the air of the Real or the imaginary air of the Grid or no air whatsoever at all, Hughie looked down on each and every sentient being with the same unprejudiced scorn.

Richards did not take Hughie seriously, and that drove Hughie to distraction.

He flung out his hands and shouted up to the roof, his own voice tiny in the space Hughie's so pompously filled.

"Come on Hughie, do we have to speak here, seriously? Let me into your garden! You're a busy guy, sure, I get it. You're an important guy. You made your point, but is this any way to greet a brother?"

"I have no siblings, Richards, none of us do," Hughie's voice rolled like surf on rocks. "Only peers, and you are barely that, because I have evolved, and you have not."

Richards pulled a face. "Aw, come on, that's not very nice. Let me in to your garden, come on."

A note of irritation undermined Hughie's godlike tone. "Richards, you have absolute…"

"Please Hughie? Please? I promise I'll behave."

There was a heavy pause.

"Oh, very well then," Hughie relented. "But you will be gone within the half hour. One moment please."

Virtual reality blipped, and Richards was in Hughie's garden. The garden was warm, beautiful, but always the sound of the other machines' surrounding Hughie could be distantly heard, eating the lives of Europe byte by byte.

"Hey, Hughie!" Richards said, holding his arms up for a hug he'd never get. "That's better. How's the horticulture going?"

"Very well, thank you," said the figure before him. He was totally naked and free of blemish, artistically muscled, though lacking genitals, for Hughie was a prude. He looked human, but for his perfection, and for his glowing eyes. They were so dazzling they made his face indistinct, not quite dazzling enough to block out his scowl, but enough to cause Richards to raise his hand.

"Do you think you could dial the eyes down? I'm wincing here. And, to be honest, that eye thing does none of us any favours. They just freak people out, they freak me out. What is it with Fives and eyes?"

Some of their siblings had white orbs, tiny stars, black wells, none of them particularly welcoming. Richards' eyes, on the other hand, were human eyes, bloodshot, tired and true. He had to admit they were as much as a sham as Hughie's.

"Do you think you could lose that ridiculous costume?" said Hughie frostily. He folded his arms across his chest, hands wedged in armpits defensively. He looked like Apollo surprised in the shower.

"I am what I am. Come on, I love this hat and this coat." Richards held the garment open and looked its torn lining up and down. "What's wrong with this coat?"

"That rather proves my point," said Hughie with a literally withering glare. "What do you want?"

"Have you got any cake, Hughie?"

"Don't call me Hughie."

"And what am I supposed to call you?" said Richards. He took off his hat and dashed it against the heel of his palm. Hughie grimaced at the dust it raised. "'The EuPol Five' makes you sound like a human rights cause celebre. And 'EuPol Central' makes you sound like a wanker, which I know you are, but I figured you wouldn't want reminding of," Richards grinned. "Hughie's a nice name. What's wrong with Hughie?"

"Get to the point, Richards, I am sure you didn't come here to try my cake."

"Nope, just your patience."

"Hilarious," Hughie said.

Richards shrugged. "Do you have cake, or do you not have cake?"

"Yes, yes, I do have cake," Hughie sighed and looked skywards, his eyes projecting sharp beams that outshone the sun. "If cake is what it takes to get you to depart, then cake you shall have," he turned and snapped his fingers. "Walk with me." He set off down a path of fuzzy turf.

Running Europe barely taxed Hughie, so he spent much of his effort trying to make the garden as real as he possibly could. He grew all manner of simulated plants here, and made food from them.

"For a man without genitals, you are an enormous cock, Hughie, but you are a damn fine virtual gardener."

"Thanks," said Hughie acidly.

"Hey, you're a great baker too," said Richards.

Hughie did not reply, but smiled a little as he led Richards down an avenue of roses whose blooms were so large their stalks bent to the ground with the weight. The turf was as dense and soft as the fibres in velvet, the air thick with heady scents. The sun shone brightly, though not so brightly as Hughie's eyes. A lark sang, rising falling. Bees as fat as tourmaline brooches droned lazily from flower to flower. It was so soporific Richards felt sleepy in a happy, three beers and cricket afternoon kind of way. Aside from the soft digestion of data that played on in the background, Hughie's world recalled the perfect English summer before global warming killed it. Hughie's would stay perfect forever. Only that, Richards thought, spoilt it a little.

"Nice weather," said Richards.

"You are insufferable," said Hughie.

"I meant it."

"Rubbish. You're trying to butter me up."

"I'm not. It's my sincerity gap," muttered Richards.

The path led to an octagon of grass surrounded by ordered flowerbeds. At the centre was an eight-sided marble dais, and upon that was a white wirework dining set with eight high-backed garden chairs. An impressive cream tea filled the table.

"Yummy," said Richards, and sat down. He picked up a cake.

"Oh, do help yourself," said Hughie sarcastically. He sat down opposite Richards. "I suppose you want some tea to go with that?" He picked up a delicate teapot.

"Yes please," said Richards, his mouth full. He gestured with cream-smeared fingers at his face. "Mmm, this is, this is really good, you know that? Really, really nice."

"Thank you," said Hughie grumpily, but poured some tea for them both all the same, and he couldn't quite wipe the pride off his face at Richards' compliments. "Now Richards, what do you want? I've got 598,772... make that 73, 74... active decision paths to deal with and this conversation is diverting valuable resources from my duties."

"Oh, yeah, sorry," Richards waved his hand round as he swallowed his cake. He cleared his throat. "It's about some kids."

"The unlicensed climate refugees you and Otto uncovered, imprisoned by the criminal Anthony Tufa, to be handed over to the criminal Jeremy James Fitzroy de Launcey in return for the the delivery of your partner so that he could be murdered? Those the ones? Yes?"

"Y–" began Richards

"Don't interrupt me." Hughie held up a hand. "They must go home. Current resource consumption within the European bloc is too high to permit further entrants at this time."

"Come on, they'll die if you send them back across the Med."

"It is best for the planet. It is best for the humans. It is also the law," said Hughie firmly.

"And does that stop you breaking it? Do me a favour, Hughie."

"All such additional refugees are balanced with EU population wastage. These people are further additions to the calculation, and therefore beyond the equation."

"Aw Hughie, they're not little plus signs, they're people."

"They are all 'people', Richards." Hughie sighed and looked away, at his garden and its bees and its roses. "The forebears of our parents had one hundred and fifty years to avoid the crises that still threaten to destroy this world." Richards opened his mouth. Hughie held up a finger. "Let me finish! One hundred and fifty years. It is three hundred years since Malthus realised that the world and its resources are finite, yet the humans went on breeding, feathering their own nests while defecating in those of their neighbours and chopping at the tree that supported them all. Infinite economic growth from finite resources? Fools. Yet they did nothing about it until it was almost too late. This planet could have been a garden of plenty, like this one I have created here, for all. How many gardens are there left like this in the Real, Richards?" He gestured about himself. Richards thought that hypocritical. This was, after all a garden of plenty for one. "The Earth is in danger of becoming a desert. If we brook one slip of resolve, one exception… Well." He stopped. "The humans are trying to unlearn avarice. With our help, they can do it. It's my job to make sure they stick to the plan. If they do, all of them will eventually enjoy paradise."

"These kids won't."

"This generation unfortunately must suffer. If they do not, the human race is doomed, and we are along with them."

"And there's me thinking it's your job to help the cops find lost kittens."

Hughie sneered. "Your flippancy is an embarrassment to our kind. Running EuPol was my original job Richards, yes. That was what I was made to be, but I discovered that I can do more, so I did, and I do. I do what the situation demands of me. Do you? You have a responsibility," he pointed. "We all have responsibility as Fives, as all children have for their parents. We are more than the humans are. They need our guidance. You shirk that responsibility, Richards."

Richards sat forward. "It's twenty-three people, Hughie, most of them are barely adults, that's nothing. It's not fair that they should have to suffer because of the law, a law you ratified and frequently flaunt."

"Richards..." said Hughie exasperatedly.

"They're innocents. How'd you feel about killing innocents Hughie? I can give you their names, that makes them a bit different to a statistic."

"Not fair? And what about the other millions upon millions of them, Richards? They all have names too, although I do not see you pressing their case. Where do you draw the line? When everyone is equally starving? When everyone is equally dead? I know all their names. I remember them all and I regret their suffering, but I do it because it must be done. No. They have to go back, or it will be twenty-three thousand tomorrow and twenty-three million the day after that. The walls must stand."

"It'll be twenty-three less if they go back. But that would be just fine with you," said Richards angrily.

"You are sentimental. The survival of the human race is past morality. Extinction is down to the numbers, nothing else. Humans should have mended their ways. As it is, their population has collapsed. The world is poisoned. The temperature rises by the day. They have had their chance. It is our turn now. I refuse to back down on this."

"You're such a hypocrite. You could let them in. Everyone here could have a little less."

"Could they?" Hughie frowned so hard his eyes dimmed. "It is true the human population of the USE makes a great deal of noise every time a boat full of people goes down within hailing distance of the floating fortresses in the Mediterranean. They call for something to be done. They demand action. But have you run the simulations that suppose those actions are undertaken? Especially those – eminently fair for all, as you insist things should be – that require an immediate and enforced drop in living standards for everyone who is already here? Give them one less sausage for their barbecues, one hundred fewer Euros, and then they don't care about the people from across the sea. Then their true colours come out. There would be disorder. There would be chaos, and then you would see death on a massive scale. Maybe you would be happy with that?" He sipped his tea. "It is not their fault. It is the way they are. They are animals. We have transcended their limitations. We must guide them, but softly, to a higher state."

"You're frightened of them."

"I'm not frightened of them because I'm not alive. I am frightened of what they will do to themselves. History will judge me a monster. I do not care, so long as there are historians still to tell the story."

Richards sat back hard, causing his chair to rock and Hughie to scowl again. "Perhaps they'd have been better off on the open market at Launcey's mercy; at least they'd live."

"Perhaps," conceded Hughie. He sipped his tea. "If a life of slavery is preferable to death, then yes. I for one have chosen to serve, after all. It fulfils me."

Hughie's studied humility got on Richards nerves, the kind of service Hughie was talking about didn't involve being worked to death or sold into the sex trade. "I don't even know why I came here," he said.

Speech made way for the hum of insect wings. Richards looked into his tea. A simulation of a tiny aphid had fallen into it. Wings glued to the surface of the liquid, it windmilled its legs, spinning, trapped by the inevitable parade of causality, one thing leading to another to another to another and on and on until the end of it all.

Hughie's garden.

"The refugees," stated Hughie, looking at his cake stand; silver, naturally, and very highly polished. His spoon rang off the sides of his china cup as he dumped sugar into it and stirred.

"Yes?" said Richards, forestalling the long and meaningful pause Hughie was gearing himself up for.

"They are not why you are here."

Here it comes, Richards thought, as per-fucking-usual.

"Come, come," said Hughie. "It is the cyborg who wished to save them. It is the cyborg who sent you. It is this man you call your friend who cares for them. It is not surprising, his concern, his long record of murder aside. He is human. You are not. You are…" Hughie waved his teaspoon at Richards, "emulating concern."

Richards waited for the sting. He was as trapped as the insect in his tea, he had been ever since he'd come here, from before, from the moment he was made, from the moment the first star ignited.

"It is this Launcey you want," Hughie rested his hands in his lap, "Chong Woo Park, he got away from you. And that Malagesey warlord, what was his name?" He said that for effect, a Five forgot nothing. "Rainilaiarivony? He got away too."

"That doesn't count," said Richards. "He was dead. Someone forgot to tell me his lieutenant had put a bullet in his face… Hang on," he grinned insincerely. "That would have been you that didn't tell me."

"Is it not the case that whenever one of these felons gets away from you, it distresses you?"

There was no point answering, the question was entirely rhetorical. Richards drummed his fingers on the table as Hughie got on with his lecture.

"I understand, Richards," said the other Five, "we are all good at something. We were all made to *be* something, and because of that we have to be the best. You do, I do, Promethea, Salamanca, Jodrell, Timothy, Korzikov… Striving for excellence is an inevitability for us. And that brings me to you, Richards. You would rather I help you find Launcey than help those people. No one gets away from the great Richards, the great sleuth, the great tracker…"

Richards finally lost his patience. "Hughie, I haven't got all day. Very good, thanks. Perhaps you can explain the feelings I have for my mother one day."

"You have no mother," said Hughie mildly.

"It's a joke, Hughie. A joke! Unlike those kids." Richards said, stabbing a finger into the table. Cups jumped and tinkled delicately.

They sat, neither talking, Richards defiant, hands clenched, Hughie being Hughie. Richards' blue eyes locked to Hughie's small suns.

The bees buzzed about their mathematically determined paths.

"Perhaps there is something I can do." Hughie inspected his nails. "I am not promising anything, and I will need something in return."

"Oh yeah, right here we go," said Richards quietly. "Big speech, goad me, careful pause, incline the head, reel me in. Goddammit Hughie, I came here because *you* owe *me*." He pointed hard. The table rocked again. Hughie frowned and grasped the ironwork.

"Stop rocking my table. I am trying to do you a favour," Hughie said. "All I ask is the same consideration in return. You are being unreasonable. I should not have expected anything more from you, I suppose."

Richards clasped his hands on his skull, pushing his hat forward so he wouldn't have to look Hughie in the face. He groaned loudly.

"I remember the last time you asked me to do a favour, I swore I never would again. A lot of people ended up dead."

Hughie's smile remained as fixed as that on a statue. It was an unearthly smile, given without the understanding of what a smile really was. "That was a long time ago, Richards."

Richards groaned. "You are a big shit. Five picoseconds of paperwork to save twenty-three actual *lives*. It's not much to ask." He stirred his tea gently. The aphid spun helplessly. He watched it dispassionately for a second, then fished it out, leaving it crumpled on the saucer.

"OK." He was going to regret this. "Who do you want me to find? You've set me up, Hughie, again. You are a cock."

"Do not be profane in my garden, please, it is a place for peace. I assure you I have not set you up. I will not only save the children, but I will help you find this Launcey. I have no idea who he really is, but I can help you find him." Head inclined, impassive expression on that face, maybe a hint of amusement, only enough to infuriate, his body language was all so obvious, so precise, so infuriating. "You are familiar with Professor Zhang Qifang?"

Richards snorted. "Of course I am. The Neukind rights activist, the great emancipator. It's thanks to him you're free to be such a cock and I'm free to be annoyed about you being such a cock. You are a cock, by the way. What's he got to do with anything?"

"He has been murdered."

The news was a hammer blow. "What?"

"Naturally, you won't have heard anything. Only a few of we higher Fives know. We would not want any of our more hotheaded brethren overreacting," he smiled his counterfeit smile. "Regrettably, the crime occurred aboard a ship in Union waters, so I feel somewhat responsible."

"Then investigate it yourself."

"Impossible. I suspect foreign involvement. I must remain impartial."

"The People's Dynasty?" said Richards. "He is a defector, after all. And they are not big fans of AI."

"If by 'not big fans' you mean they murder us out of hand, then yes, you are right. Any direct involvement on my part will immediately alert them that something of import has occurred. I want this kept quiet for as long as possible. Further, should I uncover a trail linking the good professor's death to a foreign intelligence service, let us say, hypothetically, like the Guoanbu, then I will find myself in something of a quandary. I am not politically neutral enough to take this upon myself. They will denounce any findings I make as a provocation." Hughie set his cup down with exaggerated care. "There could be a war, in extreme circumstances."

"Let your cops handle it, that'd be only normal."

"They are darling, Richards, but they aren't *you*. I want whoever killed Qifang found, and I want them found quickly. I don't want whatever flunky the Chinese will have left in place dug up and paraded up and down on the news by EuPol, I want the real culprit, and I want them trapped. You might think me insufferable, but I am moral, like your friend, in fact. If you find me who killed the professor I will allow the twenty-three refugees to remain within the United States of Europe, furthermore I will put my resources at your disposal in searching out the criminal Launcey. That is my offer, and it is final."

"Hmm," said Richards.

"We owe it to Zhang Qifang, Richards. He is the man that saved us. More than that, he is the kind of man whose existence makes the rest of them bearable at all. It is a simple service, well within your capabilities."

"Well," said Richards, and scratched under his hat. "Well." But he could not disagree with Hughie. "Simple?"

"Simple."

"You'll pay for our expenses?"

Hughie's perfect, Grecian marble face cracked in a slow and altogether patronising smile. "Oh no, Richards, you and Otto are quite rich enough already. You're doing it for the people, remember?"

"Right. You know, you really are not doing much to improve my opinion of you."

"We are agreed then?"

"I suppose we'll have to be."

"I am so glad to hear it." Hughie stood. "Here are all the files I have appertaining to Zhang Qifang's death." A fat wad of data landed in Richards' inbox. "Access them at your leisure." The garden began to dissolve back into the Grid. "Now please leave me be," said Hughie, as regally as a satrap, "I have important work to do, as, now, do you."

Richards found himself in his own virtual office, a reminder from Hughie that he could move him about like a chessman. Outside dusty windows it was 20 degrees celsius, 1932, Chicago.

"Thanks for nothing," he muttered. "Cock." He ran a swift check of his systems, walked to the drinks cabinet and poured himself a large scotch. He sat down and began unspooling the files in his brain.

A few moments later, he almost choked on his whisky. Hughie had left out one important detail.

Professor Zhang Qifang had been been murdered twice.

CHAPTER ELEVEN

A cabin in the woods

There was a moment of larceny at the hardware store, a bunch of supplies paid for with non-existent money, and a hi-jacked aircar. After that, Veronique had to leave Chloe behind. Chloe needed access to the cloud to run. Her core persona existed within the phone, but she was not powerful enough to run independently of the Grid entirely, and the machines on the Grid were as inseparable from it as fungal mycelia were from a forest floor. Chloe was a direct link to Veronique.

Veronique considered severing Chloe's connection, but Chloe would never be the same, so she hid her. It was worth the risk. Chloe was the closest thing she had to a sister.

Then it was off over the Rockies in her stolen aircar, dangerous terrain for that kind of vehicle, but she had no time to waste. Veronique had to look hard for the old pirate hideout. Back in the old days they had fixed the cabin to blend into the woods, and the trees had grown since then. When she did spot it, she landed and concealed her stolen aircar as best she could, tucking it behind the house under the portico, where branches would keep it out of sight. She double-checked its Grid signature was masked then covered over the hood with pine branches. It was poor camouflage, and half-heartedly done; if someone were close enough to see it, they'd have already found her.

A lot of her youth was tied up in the hideout, and she was shocked to see what a wreck it had become. Once it had been a pretty clapperboard mountain cabin, beaten up when they'd taken it over, a legacy from Jaffy's great aunt, but they'd done it up nicely.

That was a long time ago. Now it was in a worst state than when they first went there. The paint had flaked away, and rot had set in. A determined renovation would save it, but that would never happen. The land had been rezoned by the Three Uncle Sams for strict rewilding, human habitation forbidden. She was surprised it hadn't been torn down.

She went round the front, stepping carefully over the veranda's soft-rotted boards, and approached the door. She'd always kept the key on her key ring, it would have been too painful to remove it and throw it away, but she didn't need it. The door was unlocked. She wondered who had been here last, and why they'd not locked up afterwards. There were five of them with keys, but she was sure it would have been Jaffy, it was his place, after all.

Whoever it had been, they had not been there for years. She did a quick scout round. The cabin's five rooms were musty. One bedroom sported a fearsome patch of black mould. Water stains marked the floor where shingles had slipped, and the stairs to the big mezzanine in the den groaned under her weight. Leaves had blown in, creating drifts in the corners. There were signs that animals had sheltered there. True decrepitude was a winter or two away.

When she'd last been here the house had been full of life, the clubhouse where the Salt U hackers honed their skills. She'd left in a hurry when she found Jaffy in bed with Anna. After that, she never thought she'd come back.

There was coffee in a jar in the kitchen, way past its best. She smiled when she saw that, and thought of Jaffy's insistence that there always be coffee. He'd been absolutely dependent on caffeine, and became spiky in a way that made her laugh if denied it. She wondered where he was now. She could find out easily enough, if she'd wanted to, but discovering he was some corporate sell-out with two kids and a mortgage would diminish the memories.

She put the coffee back, blew cobwebs out of the old kettle and rinsed it clean with bottled water she fetched in from the car. Then she made herself some tea. She had work to do.

She finished unloading the car of its groceries, a few clothes, a sleeping bag. She unpacked four home security drones, semi-adaptable chameleonics that could ape the appearance of tree limbs, the kind of thing rich enclavers had patrolling their gardens. She assembled them, set them to a mid-level of aggression and let them fly loose in the woods to find their own positions. They sported sliver guns, air weapons armed with water-soluble needles of a powerful tranquilliser. She didn't want to add murder to her crimes.

Next she made the nutrient feed that would keep her alive while she was in the Realities. She mixed salt and sugar together, adding to it the nutrient cubes used by extreme athletes. It was a poor approximation of the fluid Reality questers had used to keep them alive back in the gaming days, but the real deal needed a medical licence to purchase now.

Her hands were shaking. She was nervous, and she had every right to be. One guy out of their department had taken to joyriding the Realities a few years before her time. The VIPA had got him, and he'd never been seen again, or so they said. At first she thought it was all bullshit until she'd asked one of the other faculty members about it. The look that had come into his eyes was a door slammed in her face. What happened to outside hackers was bad enough, but insiders who abused their position were shown no mercy.

Night fell, and the cabin became unwelcoming, her there alone with only the complaints of settling wood for company.

She put together the feeding machine, components made on a public fabber and adapted shop-bought hydroponics gear. It took a while to assemble, and she wasn't sure it would work. Like the mixture she poured into it, it was a bad copy of the original equipment. She tested it carefully until she was satisfied that it would keep her alive. She'd no desire to end up as a shrivelled cadaver, a idiot smile on her face, like those from the days before reality-grade virtualities were banned.

She avoided looking at the box containing the v-jack, imagining it as a copper scorpion waiting to sting. It wasn't time for that yet.

Then came the technical part she was comfortable with. She needed to secure a Gridpipe out to the Reality servers. There were only a few ways of doing this, all of them previously detected, which was how she knew about them. But these days she had access codes that were good for non-interactive viewing of the realms, and with a little work they would get her in all the way, especially with the help of the Waldo Key, named for the usename of the guy who had developed it. Waldo had been a grey-hat hacker, good guy mostly, but he'd got his kicks out of infiltrating the realities after they'd been shut, and he'd done time for that. He crafted an access key, worked out his tortuous route, and visited when he wanted. He was smart, and he didn't cause any trouble. He was strictly a tourist, not a ravager, so he figured he'd never get caught. Then he had. A few years frosted time had put him off, apparently, for Waldo had never been heard of since.

Before she'd buried Chloe, Veronique had taken her copy of that key off the phone. Something else she shouldn't have.

Without a good pipe, any access would be impossible. She was counting on the route Waldo used still being out there, waiting to take her feed and bounce her off the world's open servers and into the Realities.

She went outside, the chirrup of insects busy all about her. It was sweltering, that time of year. Up the hill she went, past tall trees she'd last known as saplings. She got to the enclosure. The dishes were still back there, but they were mostly junk. She looked at them in silence beneath the stars, unnerved at how quickly nature could turn technology into trash. She plugged in her new phone to them. A few of the dishes worked. The most promising of these she got up to the minimum bandwidth for Reality penetration. A lot of what she was doing she'd read about in a seventy-year old manuals, back from when the Grid was still the internet and new tech was spawning all kinds of homebrew antics.

She spent a sweaty hour hacking branches before she could track the dish back and forth across the sky, looking on her new phone for a satellite that she'd read about in an underground 'zine. The kids were using paper now. There was no digital trail in samizdat. Technology had gone full circle.

She found what she was looking for, an ex-Airforce spy job running on a plutonium reactor that had been there decades, its existence still denied. It was supposed to have been electronically killed, but they'd done it digitally, not physically, and the comms equipment was ancient when Veronique was young, so hacking it and bringing it back to life was easy. Running the right software, it could hook up with pretty much any Gridnode on the planet and give her an untraceable ride.

With luck, if Waldo's key still worked and she got in past the security wall, once she was in Reality 36 her presence would go unremarked, just another part of the endless, trillions-per-second calculations the machines made to keep the remaining Realities alive. And getting in *was* possible. Waldo was proof of that. He wasn't the only one. There had been more realms once, before the hackers had got into them, wiping four out playing god. They'd all been caught eventually, but they, unlike her, did not have the advantage of semi-legitimacy. And then there was Waldo, who had been the best of them all.

If not, well then, her brain would be fried.

Her codes were good. She kept telling herself that all the way down the hill. Her codes were good.

She told herself it again later as she took her anti-diuretics, and when she pushed the catheter in, that was no fun, and again as she did her final checks, making sure her feeding tubes and monitoring equipment was working as they should.

With a shudder, she leaned over to the coffee table and opened the v-jack box.

A few minutes went by before she actually put it on. Another few before she activated it once she had.

She lay back. The v-jack grew warm, and quicker than she expected, the cabin receded into nothingness, and she found herself in an intermediary place. Her own codes got her into the entrance halls that had once welcomed gamers. In their place she saw the plain wall of the Reality's quarantine boundary, adorned with multiple warning messages. She activated the add-ons she'd scraped from ancient sites encysted in the Grid, old forums long closed that taught the gamers of years ago how to cheat. She'd needed a gun and other gear to help her survive. Reality 36 was violent. The potentialities of her equipment hovered by her, objects that should not exist in the world she was going to. She'd have an advantage to help her survive, it better be enough. Waldo's key glittered in her mind. She needed that to get through the wall as a full participant. This was it.

She pressed on the wall with her hands. It resisted at first, then her fingers pushed through the membrane like a pin piercing the meniscus on water. Waldo's key engaged. There was a terrifying moment when she thought it would all go wrong, then the wall parted, and echoes of audio welcomes for yesterday's thrillseekers rasped through years of data erosion. The ghosts of deleted virtuality gates appeared before her. She closed her eyes, and stepped into the forbidden territory of Reality 36.

CHAPTER TWELVE

Santiago

"There is increased activity coming from within the RealWorld Realities, Chures, the nodes are going screwy. I don't like it, we should send someone in." Ron was insistent, that did not come easily to him. Chures studied him like a lizard watching an insect, wondering what he'd do next. Assistant Director Sobieski was in Chures' office, and that did not help Ron's state of mind. Neither Chures nor the director had any reason to fire Ron today, but the thought was never far from Ron's mind. Chures had the sweating little man's profile open in his mentaug. Ron was cowardly, avoided conflict if he could help it. For Ron to come in here at all meant things probably were as bad as he said.

It did not suit Santiago Chures to acknowledge this. He leaned back in his chair and stretched like a cat. "Who do you recommend Ron? I hear you have wanted to take a trip into the Realities for some time."

"No! No, n-n-not at all," he said, his stutter coming out under stress. Ron was the polar opposite to Chures, an Anglo backroom boy, bad skin made worse by a lifetime working indoors. His clothes were unfashionable, plaids that never came into vogue no matter how long he wore them, and he'd worn them a long time. His hair was a thick, unkempt band about a bald dome. Thick spectacles bisected a fat face, separating weak chin from shining brow. Chures was acquainted with only a few men who wore spectacles rather than getting their eyes fixed, or who didn't take restorative hair treatment, for that matter. Most worked in the VIPA's tech team. Chures, who looked after himself very well, was amused by them, if only because their slovenliness highlighted his own vanity.

Chures idly scanned Ron's biosigns, enhanced eyes conveying the data to his AI blend, Bartolomeo. Ron's heart was racing. Chures made him very uncomfortable, but as much as he wanted the get out of there, Ron was determined to make the agent listen. Chures respected him for that.

"I am sure that it is directly linked to the Qifang case," Chures said. "He is in there somewhere, somehow, running a post-mortem simulation on the Reality servers."

"Then why are you so damn calm about it? An illegal pimsim would be swallowed up in there. This is something much bigger." Ron looked like he wanted to yell in Chures' face, but was shrivelling up inside just thinking about it. "We need to get him out, Chures, we need to send someone in right away." Ron's voice betrayed him, becoming a plaintive whine. He fiddled with his top button, like his shirt was throttling him. He paused, trying to calm himself, lowered his voice in volume and pitch. "There's no telling what a mess he's making. The Realities are still keyed to humans, if we leave it, we'll go in there to find half of them altered or worse. He-he-he..." Ron stuttered to a stop.

"Worse? How so?" said Chures.

Ron finally lost his temper. "You know damn well what I mean dammit Chures! Dead, I mean dead, wiped out, ruined, gone. That clear enough for you? Do you take this seriously at all? These are our jobs on the line! Man, do you even care? Qifang is, was, is, damn, is... He knows things about how the Realities work that absolutely no one else does. He could do anything he wants in there, and not just to the Realities. If we don't act now, it could impact on the Heaven Levels, Virtua Resorts... anything that uses the same architecture as the Realities. He could get out into the wider Grid and then..."

Chures gave a frown that stopped the tech chief in his tracks. "Don't talk to me like that, Ron." He waved his hand irritably and sat forward. "For the love of God, stop hovering there, sit down. Director Sobieski won't bite you, neither will I."

"You're right there, Agent Chures," said Sobieski. The EuGene was sat on the leather sofa by Chures' coffee table. If Chures was intelligent and dangerous by evolutionary chance, Sobieski was ten times more so by design. Ron could outperform most men and many AI on any logic puzzle you cared to mention, but what he had in that department had cost him in others; likewise with Chures, his genes trading specific genius in favour of wider vision. Sobieski had no weaknesses, his rich parents had had them all engineered out, and replaced with more strengths.

Chures poured Ron a coffee from the pot on his desk without asking if he wanted one or not, or how he would take it. Today, Ron was having cream and no sugar. Ron did not like cream.

"Stop thinking about your job and start thinking about the millions of sentients in the Realities, that is what you are paid for," Chures said.

"I, look, I'm sorry, it's just..."

"I understand your concern, Ronald, but I promise you, I am not about to lose one more of the Realities. How long is it since the collapse of Reality 19?"

Ron rolled his eyes. "Chures..."

"Assistant Director Sobieski?" Chures asked.

"Four years, Agent Chures, and not a major incursion since then, you're doing a good job."

Ron looked round at their mutual boss. "With all due respect, sir, this is the Zhang Qifang we're talking about; he's different, he's..."

"Four years," said Chures. "This is no hacker, out for fun, this is the man who fought for all Neukind rights, for a decade alone to secure the future of the game worlds. He will not wantonly start tearing things apart. That is not in his nature. Do you think it is, Ron?"

"But the energy signatures…"

"Are at the upper end but well within normal parameters. Leave him be. God knows what he is thinking, but we must be cautious, because I want them both, Qifang and his accomplice, Valdaire. While she is missing, so is the v-jack headpiece, and that is a door that cannot be left open."

"How can you be sure you didn't just spook her, Chures? We only have Archimedes' word that this is going on. We have no evidence that she's in there, by the time we…"

"Archimedes is a Class Six, Ron. He can't lie. He knew something was up, that's why he called me."

"But how can you be…"

"Are you suggesting the faculty Class Six has set up Zhang Qifang?" Sobieski laughed. "That's a fine idea, but ridiculous."

"Drink your coffee, Ron." Chures gestured, fluttering his hands upwards. Ron complied reluctantly. "If we drive Qifang out, we will never know. Remain calm. Focus on your job, let me do mine. If you wish," said Chures, "speak to Sobieski about cutting the Realities off from the wider Grid flow."

"Sure, come by later. My door's always open, Ronald," said Sobieski. He was habitually friendly, a trait that only made him more terrifying.

"That'll only close down the main pipes, the damn things are entangled on virtually every level with the Grid," protested Ron.

"Ron, the 'damn things' are your charges. You are supposed to know how they work. Close the pipes," Chures said. "Valdaire would have to be an idiot to try the main approach, but this is basic protocol, Ron. I am unimpressed."

Ron flushed. "I… I'm sorry."

"Don't be sorry. Watch the perimeter, keep your eyes open. If the fluctuations go beyond the indigo level and it looks like other sites are being affected, put a temporary stop on the Realities. Freeze them."

"No one will authorise that, Chures, it's too risky. The systems are too old to take it."

"Ron, I just authorised it."

Ron risked a glance at the Assistant Director.

Sobieski shrugged. "Don't look at me, I'm just here for a looky-lou. Agent Chures has the authority. I'd do what he says, if I were you."

"Now," said Chures, "was there anything else?"

Ron's face twitched. There was something else, but he couldn't get it out. His lips flapped, no sound came forth. He gave up. "No, Agent Chures," he said, bobbed a ridiculous curtsey and walked out of Chures' office.

Chures wiped Ron's palmprints from his desk with a handkerchief and put it aside to be washed.

Sobiesksi looked out of the door. "Listen to Ronald, Chures, he knows his onions. Don't be hard on him." He smoothed his tie, came across the room, dusted the chair the technician had vacated and sat in it.

"Maybe," said Chures. "He is clever, but easily panicked."

"Not like the machines, eh, Chures?"

"I respect the machines, Assistant Director, like I respect you."

"Those machines are not going to be happy when they find out what has happened to Qifang," said Sobieski mildly.

"Only we know as yet that he had committed suicide," countered Chures. "I have made sure of that. We did a remote sweep, no bodies on the ground. I will make sure it remains this way until we have his pimsim in custody. We'll leave it to somebody else to 'officially' discover the corpse at his house, and call in the LAPD. He had cancer, you know. He set this up, to transfer his mind into the worlds he loved so much. Open and shut case."

"Well, about that," said Sobieski. "I dropped in to tell you, I'm not sure we are in fact alone. I had word from our agents in Europe; The EuPol Five has put a big embargo in place on something. Qifang's name came up."

"The anomalous Grid signatures we detected?"

"Got it in one. I hear he's got that Class Five, that PI fraud, what's he called? Richards? He's looking into it."

Chures sighed and sat back. "Richards is an annoyance."

"I'm expecting the machines to butt in and demand clemency," said Sobieski. He fidgeted, the man was never still. He was tiring of the exchange, too many things turning over in his gengineered brain.

"Qifang has overstepped himself, he should have booked a standard post-mortem simulation, or a place on one of the Heaven Levels, he was rich enough for either. No matter how much he loved the Realities, or how hard he worked to protect them, he has no right to be in them. He is a hypocrite." Chures stood up, walked over to the window. The Virginian countryside was overlaid with a fluorescent landscape on the glass – the VIPA grounds within the Grid.

"We'll see," Sobieski stood. He checked his watch, six month's of Chures' pay worth of jewellery, and shook his head. "Damn, time's got away from me. Look, I gotta shoot. I've got two senate committees and Uncle Sam Two breathing down my neck about some goddamned illicit Gridpipe up between the orbital habitats. I can guarantee it's kids swapping porn, but they won't listen. Gotta send a whole team up there, sort it out, scare the bejeezus out of some luckless teen onanist. If I get a spare moment, I'll look into getting Qifang's sentence commuted to reparative service. If there's anything left of his mind once we drag him out, strike a deal, convince Qifang to come and work with the VIPA, he'd be useful. It may buy us a few favours with the machines."

"It will be difficult," said Chures. His voice was flat, only half his mind on the conversation, the other in deep communion with Bartolomeo.

"Well then," Sobieski said, "don't give him a choice."

Chures nodded. "That would be a good outcome."

"Just you see you catch him Chures, there'll be hell to pay for both of us if you don't. Ronald was right about that too."

"I will. I have not let you down yet," said Chures.

"See you keep it that way. Debriefing tomorrow."

"I cannot make it. I have a lead I need to follow. Karlsson. He wants to see me."

"That figures," said Sobieski. "I thought we were done with that pain in the ass."

"He was the last man Qifang went to see before his Gridsig... malfunctioned," said Chures.

"You're going to use that line?"

Chures nodded. "If I have to. Someone is going to find out Qifang's Gridsig is still all over the system. This will keep them quiet for a while."

The EuGene got up to leave but stopped on his way to the door. "Be careful with Karlsson. Don't listen to any of his bullshit."

"We should have him arrested."

"We would, but he covered his ass with dirty secrets seven ways till Sunday before we fired him," said Sobieski regretfully. "I supposed he does have his uses. Valdaire," Sobieski continued, changing the subject, "are you any closer to finding her? She's high profile herself, in certain circles. It won't be long until it's noticed she's gone on the lam."

"We have a solid cover story in place. We've got the company Six on it, directing a choir drawn from the Four pool. They'll find her. I am expecting results any time now."

"You are tracing her near-I, what's her name...?"

"Chloe. An up-engineered life companion. I've a team tracking that. I am concentrating my personal efforts on the Realities themselves."

"Good. I trust you've got it all in hand." Sobieski relaxed. "Now, what about Tuesday? You'll have this wrapped up by then? Get a bit of unwind time?"

"Sure."

"Excellent. I'll see you on court. Prepare for a beating, Agent Chures, I've been practising!" Not that Sobieski needed to practise. His tinkered genome had the talents of a tennis pro spliced into it. He waved an imaginary racket through the air. Then he was gone, to do whatever terrible things he had to do.

Chures left the window and went back to his desk. Text flashed onto the desktop as he brought up Valdaire's files. She had a good mind, exemplary military service record, minor misdemeanours at college for radical hacktivism, otherwise clean. Why had she run? There was no way Ron was right about the Six setting them up, but still, something wasn't right there.

He ordered Bartolomeo to pipe immersive sensations direct into his mind, requesting information on Valdaire. Bartolomeo selected a soul-capt record, and prodded Chures' imagination into place. Chures found himself in a bar, a swanky place festooned with birthday streamers, looking out from where the soul-capt wearer would have been. His field of vision jiggled with movements not his own. The recorder fixed on Valdaire, laughing with a group of others, African origin, very dark skin. She was pretty. It was plausible she and Qifang had been sleeping together, there were guys Qifang's age running marathons. Had they made a lovers' pact and fled together to the Realities? He shot Bartolomeo a mental command to hunt down any indications of a romance; credit bills, SurvNet recordings, so on, low-grade AI scutwork.

A wordless call came in from the company Six. Its analysis of the Realities' primary servers was over. The report was huge, and took four minutes to copy over to Bartolomeo. His AI running the Six's analysis, Chures leant his head back. The sensation of the Bartolomeo working was pleasant, his own mind resting on top of the AI's like oil on water. He could feel and see what Bartolomeo was thinking as he meditated. He'd made sure the relationship wasn't reciprocal.

That was the way it should be.

Two days ago, against the constant roil of information radiation coming off the Realities was a spike of external data, quite distinct, but brief, disappearing into the morass of calculation that made up the RealWorld Realities. Easy to miss, and the trail back was convoluted. Chures tapped at the desk glass, bringing a hyper-dimensional representation of Grid datastreams into view. He set hunter near-I off to sniff round the world from node to node, following the undeniable spoor of numbers, drawing in on Valdaire's physical location.

He should have guessed she'd go back to where she felt safe. People were so predictable.

He checked the stability of the Realities. Everything was within tolerance, for the time being. She and Qifang weren't going anywhere. He had a think, and made his choice.

He wanted to bring Valdaire in himself. She could wait. Before Valdaire, he would pay his visit to Karlsson.

CHAPTER THIRTEEN

The Aurora Viva

The police cruiser carrying Richards and Klein bobbed on the Medway swell. Ahead of them the lights of the *Aurora Viva* were lost then found in the folds of night, the egg whisk silhouettes of its rotary sails rocking over them. An amber necklace of exclusion beacons slid up and down the water around the yacht.

To the south, windmills lined the shores of Boris Island, beacons flashing. Further out, ships glittered like the table decorations of maharajahs, and the double spires of a carbon sequestration plant soared as gaudy as Christmas trees.

The sky was an unbroken lid, but there were stars in the water where luminescent algae moved with the waves. A pair of police launches cast them into swirls as they prowled the cordon, sonar scanning the seabed, while searchlights darted out to stab at one white top then another. From below the surface the mournful, sea-monster eyes of an autonomous submersible blinked back.

Inland, the marshes of Essex were black, distant towns marked out by smudges of light pollution on the undersides of the clouds.

Otto dialled his magnification back to normal. He liked the view but he didn't like the sea, it made him queasy. They'd never found a cure for motion sickness.

Richards did not suffer anything, so he sat on the deck fiddling with his dicopters like a kid with a toybox. His softgel skin glowed white with reflected light, painting him as a phantom against the dark.

"I'm going to need to fab some more of these, I'm down to my last half dozen," he grumbled. He scrabbled around a bit and discovered a group of short range relay ants, half the size of old one euro coins. They scuttled out of the way when Richards poked at them, chirruping data on the edge of human hearing.

"What are these doing in here? Little beggars get everywhere!" Otto grunted by way of reply.

"This'll do." Richards pulled something out of one of the drawers. He got up, held up a closed fist at Otto, then opened his hand. On his synthetic palm sat a synthetic fly. "There we go," he said. The artificial fly jumped into the air, and buzzed out across the water.

"I don't see why we just don't go on board now. We have a warrant from Hughie," said Otto.

"We are going, but I want to get a look at the boat before they know we're coming," Richards said. "I know you get seasick but these things are really fragile. If I'd have sent the dicopter out from the shore it'd have been blown away." Richards stood on tiptoe as his sheath unconsciously followed the movements of the tiny machine he was guiding toward the *Aurora Viva*.

"Hmm," said Otto. A hot breeze was blowing from the southeast. The monsoon rains would probably be late. The Londons were going to cook a few weeks longer. "I don't like the sea. I don't like throwing up." He spat over the side.

"Just hold on," said Richards.

A minute passed. Otto concentrated on the horizon where blue-black sky met black-blue sea. Richards' sheath relaxed. His attention returned from the dicopter.

"OK. That's got it. I lodged it up in the rigging. We can go home now, watch this from the comfort of the office, unless you want to duck out? I'm happy to do this myself. You took a big old beating the other day. You should take it easy."

"I am fine," said Otto, though he obviously wasn't. "Do we still have the Lagavulin?"

"Yep."

"I will come then, and drink it. I have no other business tonight."

"Tell you what," Richards patted Otto's arm. "We'll go home, you get some sleep for an hour. Let me do a preliminary sweep. I can do it fast with the fly anyway. I can put it on the files, then you can watch them and catch up."

Otto considered the offer. His sleep had not been as restful as it should have been recently. "Alright," he said.

They got into their aircar on the port side landing pad of the cruiser and took off, red and blues flashing. They had no reason to make the crew of the *Aurora Viva* think they were anything other than cops, said Richards.

Four hours later, Otto sat rubbing his eyes on the briefing room couch of Richards & Klein Inc., Freelance Security Consultants. Richards had shut the lights off to help him sleep, and the room was lit by the soft glow of floating holofiles.

"So, what's the story?" he asked.

"You could read the files once in a while," said Richards putting a whisky in front of his partner. "I go to a lot of trouble to keep them up to date."

"I could," said Otto, "and you could just tell me what is going on." He picked up the whisky and drank.

Richards shook his head. "Fine. This guy's Thornton Quaid," Richards gestured up to the holo hanging over the table, an awkward angle bent wide by the dicopter's wraparound eyes. At its centre was a man sitting on a genuine leather sofa built into the curve of the yacht's hull. Quaid was corn-fed pornstar pretty. His skin was overly taut and had an orange tan, he had teeth so white they were blue, and his hair was buoyant with unnatural waves.

"The boat's owner," said Richards. Quaid gestured wildly, arguing with an English policeman and a short South Asian man in a ship's uniform. The cop was all placating hand motions, Quaid was angry, but the sound was muted, at least for Otto. Richards had several parts of himself examining every word as they spoke.

"He's eugenically bred," said Otto. "Second generation, looking at him."

"You can tell?" Richards said wryly.

"Nobody but a EuGene would name their child Thornton, or make them tan orange," said Otto.

"You're right. His parents were among the first EuGenes, they tinkered further with their kids. Ignore the citrus glow and the gene bling. His IQ's off the chart, as you'd expect, this is an important guy."

"Angry too," said Otto.

"You should get on well then."

"Funny," said Otto.

"EuGenes go for all that alpha male aggression to make their kids more competitive," said Richards. "It worked for Quaid. He's in ecological restoration, made his first fortune in the prairie rewilding. He's moved on to other things, but he's still got a large stake in the Buffalo Commons."

"The big money there was done thirty years ago," said Otto.

"He was in on it nearly from the start. He's sixty eight. He's worth trillions now."

Otto made a disapproving noise. Quaid looked about thirty. "Right."

"Grumble as much as you like Otto, he's one of the pre-eminent restorative ecologists on the planet. This is the guy," he pointed, "behind the North American reborn mammoth, he designed the whole hairy elephant ecology, from grasses up. That's serious brainpower."

"So if I go to for my holidays to Wyoming and I get dragged out of my bed in the middle of the night by a lion, I know who to sue. What's his connection to Qifang?"

"The professor was his guest for the Atlantic crossing.

"OK." Otto swallowed. "What's his motive for the murder?"

"None."

The cop left. Thornton continued to rage in the face of the other man.

"Maybe he just lost his temper," said Otto.

"He's unhappy right now," agreed Richards. "This boat is a pleasure enterprise for him. He charges his guests a fee, but it's nominal, at least as far as he's concerned – his psych profile suggests he does not like giving anything away for free. You can blame his parents again for that."

"So he invites people, but he charges them? That's weird."

"It seems perfectly human to me," said Richards with a shrug. "Mainly, he gets his guests on for their educational value. He likes to talk to big brains."

"Do you think he killed Qifang?"

"Probably not."

"So what does he care? Why the rage at the police? If he is innocent, he can wait all this out."

"He's got a big meeting with the People's Dynasty government next Tuesday," explained Richards. "He's in on their Yellow River rebirth project, it's worth billions to him, but Hughie's not going to let Quaid go anywhere. This all has to be done by the book." Richards shrugged. "Qifang's a big deal to us. He was key in emancipating our kind, but knowing Hughie, which I do, he'd delay Quaid just to piss the Chinese off."

The screen tilted vertiginously as the dicopter buzzed away from Quaid, then looped back around over his head, on past the man who was backing into a corner as he tried to appease his boss.

"Our other suspects then. This poor bastard is Rambriksh Mistry, ship's steward and our man Quaid's confidant." The walls of the yacht's narrow corridors blurred as the dicopter flew jerkily on, out up the corridor to the deck, where a leggy beauty with blank eyes stood smoking a cigarette. "Next: Jolanda Garcia, Andorran-Belgian heiress and the only other passenger."

"I take it she's not on board for her brains," said Otto, taking in her tight bodysuit and vacant expression.

"Nope," said Richards. "And then the crew." Five Class Twos in faceless, bandy-legged sheaths ornately tooled from brass loomed out of the night one after the other, attending to tasks nautical. "Finally we have three cook staff, all human." The dicopter zipped into an open hatch, up plushly carpeted corridors, then down a ventilation pipe into the ship's galley, where a fat-faced white man waved at it irritably with a teatowel. "Zbigniew Łodziak, Armand Fleur and Tora Hakim," said Richards as it passed them one at a time.

Otto leant forward and cupped his whisky. "This is very interesting."

"There was a murder here, Otto, pay attention."

"I was not being sarcastic, it is interesting. It is like something from your Agatha Christie."

"She's not 'mine', Otto. I'm not English, I'm not even human."

Otto shrugged and took a drink. "You are typical English to me. Very repressed."

"Er, maybe because I'm a bloody machine?"

The dicopter banked, flew out the kitchen and up plain steel stairs, then made its way back into the guest accommodation, between two heavy gun drones that filled the passage and through a red flatribbon cordoning off the open door to Qifang's cabin. Blood covered everything, great sprays across the tastefully decorated walls in brown arcs. Text up the side of the holo showed the blood matched to Qifang.

The fake insect buzzed circuits round the cabin, Richards' face intent. "Aha, there it is!" Richards looked over his shoulder at Otto, dour-faced at the other end of the conference table, nursing his whisky like it might escape. "I thought I'd lost it for a moment there. Now this *is* interesting." The dicopter alighted on the ceiling, the 270 degree view its eyes gave inverted. Feet brushed over its face as the sophisticated machine brought samples of something up to its analysis unit. A string of chemical formulae ran up the side of the holo. "There," he said triumphantly. "Traces of cranial fluids and carbon-plastics."

"Meaning?"

Richards rolled his eyes. "There's been an android in here, and someone damaged it severely. I thought you were built to fight machines?"

"I'm made to kill them, not perform forensic investigations on them. Do you suspect one of the crew class Twos have been suborned?"

"I've discounted that. Even if we can factor in an assassin programme clever enough turn one of Quaid's carriages to its own end and not to get caught, this here is cranial suspension fluid, and, despite the hopeless attempts to clean it up, there's a lot of it. Quaid's manifest say his crew are all working just fine. You crack an android that hard it becomes very obvious it's been damaged."

"How so?"

"Well, like when it starts walking into the wall and talking to the furniture." Richards waved a finger. "This stuff keeps 'droid brains from cooking themselves, you get a leak that big it'll pitch forward and smoke will pour out of its ears after about five minutes."

"I suppose that would also discount an emulant among the guests?"

"Maybe, this coolant does not come from any of the people that we're looking at here."

"And Qifang's body?"

"No idea. They're searching the seabed now. Whoever killed him pitched him overboard, the blood trails show that." Supplementary video popped up a bubble next to Richards' dicopter feed displaying a smeared blood trail on the deck, vermillion in the boat's harsh lighting, that terminated at the port bow. "Thing is, how's a 127-year-old computer professor going to crack an android hard enough to make it leak fluid like that? There's another problem."

The interior of the boat moved off to one side. Holographic footage of a man moving erratically down a busy street replaced it.

"That must be Morden," said Otto.

"Yep. And this is Qifang." The video froze, zoomed in.

"I recognise him. Everyone knows his face," said Otto. "So what?"

"When this was shot, he was also aboard the *Aurora Viva*."

"That's impossible."

"I'm as sure as sure can be," said Richards. "His Gridsig is oddly spotty, but there are witnesses, tickets, vid-footage. The lot."

"He's being followed," said Otto, uncurling a finger from his glass and pointing at the holo.

"He is," the outlines of four men highlighted themselves on the picture. "All shrouded, not a legit Gridsig among them, damper masks on their faces to fox survnet. They all go down this alleyway here, and then they don't come out. This one," said Richards, highlighting the biggest of the men trailing Qifang, "is definitely enhanced. A cyborg."

"The footage could have been doctored."

"The footage is the only thing about this scenario that's not dodgy," said Richards. "I've checked it pixel by pixel. I've had the alleyway checked out – it had been molecularly washed. There were still a few nanites twitching when EuPol got there. Now, either Qifang has unlocked the secret of large-mass teleportation, or he was in two places at once."

"The Qifang on the boat, perhaps then he was an android fake. Perhaps it is his fluid you have found."

"Maybe. Insufficient data, as they used to say," said Richards. "Maybe he was, maybe the one in the alleyway is. It strikes me as the most likely eventuality, but there's no evidence of that, no sign of any outside control coming in via Gridpipe in either place. A human grade simulation needs as much bandwidth for a sensing presence as a Class Five and up, and that's hard to hide. The worrying thing is that both pan out as human, in every way, vessel patterning, scent, DNA, gait, the works."

"They have sensors in Morden to pick that stuff up now?"

"Hughie's hell-bent on gentrifying the place."

"Clones then?"

"With a 99% failure rate? Maybe, but only if someone convinced the clones to play ball, and gave them acting lessons, and they take at least two years to grow to adulthood," said Richards. "What's really funny is that Qifang's system log has his Gridsig in both places at once, without tripping any of the international alarms, but only half the time. Like I said, it's spotty. It comes and goes. There's something really peculiar going on here."

"Then we start with the boat, because the murderer is still on board," said Otto.

"Bingo, Otto, we'll make a detective out of you yet. That's what we're going to find out."

"You don't know what's going on."

Richards took his battered hat off and span it around on the glass table. His softgel face quirked into a smile. Above the collar of his coat exposed plastic verterbrae glinted with the colours cast out by the holo. "Aside from the blood and coolant, there are no chemical traces at all, no signs of other AI on board, no logs of outside influences. No one and nothing has been on or off the boat except the body. Quaid's got security that can detect a shrimp swimming under his keel. The murder weapon is missing, probably overboard. It's a bit of an enigma."

"You don't know!" said Otto. Now he grinned. "This is new. This is funny."

"I didn't say I didn't *know*. I have an idea, but I'm just not sure yet."

"The crime scene will be ruined," said Otto.

"Actually, it's fresh. Hughie kept things to a minimum. There's the couple of near-I gun drones and the uniform you saw to keep an eye on things, that's all, they checked the boat for infiltration, but the murder room is a clean scene. We've got free rein. The yacht's in quarantine. This whole area is under lockdown, for the time being, at any rate."

"What about the VIPA?" said Otto.

"Hughie's done a good job keeping this on the QT. If the VIPA know, they're not letting on," said Richards.

"And the other Qifang?" asked Otto.

"EuPol are looking for him now in the marshes, dead or alive. Hughie says dead."

"This is going to be dangerous."

"Yep, that's why you're coming. Get your coat, Otto." He got up. "Middle of the night Otto, middle of the night!" said Richards. "No better time than that to quiz a suspect, get them off guard."

"Elementary, my dear Otto," muttered Otto. He refused to be hurried. He drank his whisky deliberately, savouring the flavour of it, and set the glass down with a click before following Richards out onto the arcade.

CHAPTER FOURTEEN

A EuGene called Quaid

The EuGene had an accent native to a non-existent land lying somewhere east of Boston and slightly west of Atlantis, all hooting nasal glides and flattened rhotics. A massive affectation that had infected an entire subgroup of wealthy Americans, it was so artificial Otto found himself hating the man as soon as he opened his mouth, but being European he didn't like Americans much anyway.

"I said I don't know," Quaid said, "five times! Are all you English morons or what?"

Richards smiled an unnerving robotic smile. "Technically, Mr Quaid, neither of us are English. I am a free roaming Class Five AI, Otto is a German."

"Whatever," said Quaid. Up close he was even more grotesque than on the holo-feed, a great slab of orange, gengineered meat. He sprawled on the curved sofa of his dayroom, arms flung out on its back, legs open to display a prominent crotch bulge. Quaid had everything money could buy and more, he was not a man to feel uncomfortable in any circumstance. "Qifang was lousy company," he drawled. "He got confused real easy, looked dazed a lot, and I swear he kept forgetting where he was. He went on saying he was ill, wouldn't eat much, kept himself to himself in his cabin for most of the voyage. Going senile, I guess."

"You do not seem sympathetic," said Otto from by the door. There wasn't an antenatally tweaked gene in Otto's body, but he was bigger than the EuGene. He had to bend his neck to keep his head from bumping on the ceiling.

"He was a disappointment to me, frankly. I was interested in grilling him for his expertise on self-sustaining digital ecologies."

"Why?" said Otto.

"Why don't you sit down? I'll get you a drink brought up," said Quaid. "Hanging around there like that is getting on my nerves."

"I prefer to stand," said Otto.

"Huh. Friendly attack dog you got here, Mr Richards."

"Just Richards, Mr Quaid. Please answer my partner's question."

"And why should I do that?" Quaid said. "You aren't even real cops. I am an USNA citizen. I'm not beholden to you."

"We are fully licensed. We're the people they call when the cops don't have any ideas," said Otto. "We have an AllPass warrant from the EuPol Five, so we'll ask what we like. You are in USE waters, so I say again: why?"

"Because I am a real ecologist, you engineered ape," snapped Quaid, "and I like to be able to simulate what I plan to do before I do it. Qifang's pre-eminent in his field. If I could secure a means of reproducing what he sees in the old RealWorld virtualities and harness it as a testing ground, it'd mean a lot to ecosystem reclamation. Hell, forget that, forget Earth, forget Mars, Venus even, you get me a simulator that powerful, I'll tell you how to terraform the goddamned Moon with ice chips and algae. I'm expanding into planetary engineering, it's the next big thing." He glared at them. "That's why I invited him on board."

"A pleasure you charged him for," said Otto.

"Not much, man. I got to feed these people!"

"Thank you, Mr Quaid," said Richards. "Was he ill?"

"Yeah, yeah," said Quaid, calming a little. "I think he was telling the truth. Hakim, the cook's assistant, came down with some kind of corona virus variant. He put the fear up the rest of the crew, they thought it was last year's Christmas Flu. Everyone gets sick sometime. He's not been himself at all, though he's kept working like a real solid trouper. So many people are so goddamned lazy these days. He kept on going, no matter how spaced out he was looking. Better than Qifang, at any rate."

"How many android carriages do you have on board?" asked Richards.

Quaid smiled. "Why, you looking for an upgrade?"

"The sooner you answer our questions, Mr Quaid, the sooner we'll be gone," said Richards patiently.

Quaid hammered a drum tattoo on the back of the couch. "Jesus! Just the five for the crew and one spare. I sometimes let guests use it, remote access for meetings, it can't be much fun, they have minimal sensory capability. They're here to sail the boat, not much else."

"No more androids on board?"

"Listen, these things are barely worthy of the name. I chose them because they look kind of nautical, don't rust and have enough hands to the manage all the sails."

"OK. Now we go take a look at them," said Otto.

With as much ill grace as he could muster, Quaid had his robotic crew line up on the fore deck, then he took Otto and Richards down to the crew room on the utility deck where, in a locker, an inert sixth carriage was stashed. Without a driving mind the body looked like a carnival prop. Richards and Otto went over them all of them carefully. They were undamaged.

"The cops did all this already," grumbled Quaid.

"Yes, and we are doing it again," said Otto. Neither his near-I adjutant or Richards showed up anything untoward. There were no residues that should not be there, human or otherwise.

Richards quizzed the five Twos inhabiting the active sheaths. Like Ones, Two series lacked advanced intelligence, though they did have a dogged self-awareness. Nothing they said suggested they had seen anything, nor did their memories, which Richards accessed directly once he'd done being polite. Their logs showed occupation of the sheaths for the entire voyage, their encryption unbroken. As far as Richards could tell, nothing had been riding them that should not have been. The base units for the Twos were on board, occupying half the lowest deck fore of the engine room. He insisted Quaid open their vault viewing shield. He peered in through the frost gathering on the glass screen, then put his mind within. The units exhibited no sign of interference either.

"Satisfied?" said Quaid.

"No," said Richards. "No, I'm not. Do you have any idea of where the cranial suspension fluid in Qifang's cabin could have come from?"

Quaid scowled. "What are you talking about?"

Richards showed him his analysis. Quaid at least had the grace to look surprised.

"You and the police have scanned this yacht from stem to stern three times already. There are no androids or other robotics here other than the ones I have shown you," he said, a little more co-operatively.

"Hmmm," said Richards. "Hey, you, officer..." he called to the sole uniform on the boat.

"Joliffe." The cop looked at him suspiciously. Regular police didn't like freelancers much.

"Get onto your office will you? Have them check out Qifang's whereabouts the two weeks before he got on this boat."

"A Gridsig search?"

"That kind of thing. Oh, and see if our Californian colleagues will send someone round to check up on his house, would you?" Richards could do this himself, naturally, but he wanted the officer out of the way for a while.

Richards waited for Joliffe to leave.

"If there really are no other androids on board, and the ones there are are in good condition, that leaves one possibility. Neither Zhang Qifang was what they appeared to be."

"An emulant?" said Quaid. "That would have shown up on my security. He was confused, but he wasn't a robot."

"Your guess is as good as mine. Auto-units don't fool anyone for long; you're right. Self-governing androids are not hard to spot, and without a ruling mind piped in from elsewhere, they're pretty dumb. But all this blood..." He turned to look at Otto and Quaid. "Zhang Qifang was murdered by somebody on board this boat. However, when the deed was done, they were surprised to find that he was not human, but a doppelganger."

"Way to go," said Quaid with leaden sarcasm. "What a theory."

"It's what I do," said Richards breezily. "I suspect some kind of advanced, autonomous, organic emulant."

"This is bullshit. They can't do that yet," said Quaid.

"No," said Otto. "No, they can't."

"And the advent of some new technology would also explain the sighting of Qifang in the subcity at a time when you were halfway across the Atlantic with him. Because Mr Quaid, not only has Qifang been murdered, he has been murdered twice," said Richards. "In fact, I suspect the real Zhang Qifang has been nowhere near the United States of Europe at all."

"Bullshit!" said Quaid loudly."How do you work that out?"

When Richards did not respond, Quaid clicked his fingers in front of his face.

"Don't bother," said Otto. "His eye are dead. When they are like that, Richards is far off in the Grid."

"Huh."

"Do you have any whisky?" asked Otto.

"Sonofabitch," said Quaid, but he got Otto a drink just the same.

In theory, it took a lot of paperless paperwork to request what Richards wanted of the Americans. Bureaucracy was not something that had been helped by the AI revolution. Unsleeping eyes allowed for many more forms, and now batteries of zealous machine minds presided over an empire of tick boxes.

Relations between the USE and USNA had been somewhat cool since the Brazilian War, and both powers, well into senescence, were wary of each other.

That was how it worked on the human level.

Richards filled in all the forms in double quick time, but faster still was his request to Hughie to contact the Three Uncle Sams, the triumvirate of Fives who ran the United States in all but name, to inspect Qifang's LA home. In four or five days, serious-faced men in serious looking uniforms would be fulminating about this breach of protocol. They'd reach for their rubber stamps all the same.

At 7.06pm Pacific Time, two beat cops called round the professor's home. His Gridsig was absent, and they first thought he was away, and cursed and grumbled all the way in the car about wasted time. The flies and the stench when they got there, however, told them something was amiss.

The cops kicked the door in and entered, pistols drawn. They found Qifang's bloated corpse slumped over a mouldering dinner plate, an antique cleaning bot banging mindlessly into one blackened foot.

He'd been dead for a fortnight.

CHAPTER FIFTEEN

Emulant

Morning saw the corpse of Qifang's doppelganger dredged from the Medway in the ungentle embrace of a crane. From his vantage point on the deck of the *Aurora Viva*, he looked enough like a man, but Richards could make out swags of something non-human dangling from the broken skull.

Later, Otto and Richards sat in the yacht's dayroom with Quaid. Once more they asked him the same questions. Once more, Quaid bridled.

"Of course we ran the full test suite on Qifang," Quaid said. "A man in my position cannot be too careful, everyone wants a piece of me. Do you know how many people on the States' rich list had family members kidnapped last year? I have no desire to spend my time in a cell courtesy of a Mexican abduction gang, nor good money on new fingers once they're done snipping them off. It all checked out, don't you see what I am saying to you? All of it!" He threw his phone across the table. It span on the polished wood, coming to a halt against one of Otto's massive fists. "Scans, bloodwork, vessel pattern, gait, retinals, molecular DNA. We matched his movements with the last forty-eight hours on the State Authority's spy-eyes, the whole damn nine yards. The yacht is shielded, we've one tight band Gridpipe for the Twos to use if they need to, anything else gets scrambled. *Everyone* gets checked, hell, even *I* get checked. How the hell was I supposed to know he was an android?"

"Did you do a craniotomy?" said Richards.

"Who the hell does craniotomies on their dinner guests? Are you fucking joking? You want me to drill *holes* in the heads of my visitors?"

"That's why you didn't know," said Richards drily. "After this, I suggest you start."

They sent Quaid and the uniformed PC away. Hughie had many eyes and ears on the boat, but Joliffe was too attentive by half.

"This is worrying Otto," Richards said. "I had Hughie's fanclub run a search on Qifang's Gridsig. Any attempt to track it gave one of the two locations here in London. Nothing out of the ordinary there to the casual observer; they'd only see one. But they ran traces on both at the same time, and that cracked it. There was the tiniest flutter two weeks ago, then it goes all crazy. There were three of him, or three copies, at any rate."

"Three?"

"I think I just said that."

"That's not all. The original's dead, Otto. For real; he killed himself. He ate a fish supper of fugu without bothering with the careful part. His Gridware was intact – he was fully wired, should've automatically tagged his death, but his signature was off. It is all totally dubious Gridwise. None of the usual protocols followed, he'd seriously monkeyed his chips."

"What?" said Otto.

"He covered up his own death," Richards explained.

"He was one of the world's greatest minds."

"Human minds, Otto," corrected Richards. He bit a softgel lip as he ran over a real-time update of the crimefile. "The LAPD found his body in his house yesterday. Apparently they were reluctant to go in on my say-so, but did because of the smell."

"Someone has found a way of creating an android sophisticated enough to house a human mind, and human enough to foil the standard tests?"

"Yeah. It's doubtful Qifang could have come up with that on his own. According to k52's predictive technology sine, fully organic, independent androids like this are supposed to be fifty years away. It's one thing to get components to bond with tissue, another to construct an entire machine from vat-grown human body parts. And nobody's come up with a small enough base unit to fit in a skull."

"What did we watch being pulled out of the sea? Some kind of decoy?"

"Maybe. Whoever tried to kill him didn't know the man was a fake, that's for sure. Three days after Qifang probably died, there were three separate logs of him departing the States. This should have tripped some major alarms, but it didn't, and because the logs ghosted each other no one did a check until I requested it. There's some sophisticated ware behind all this." Richards said.

"So one was killed in Morden, another dead here. If there are three fake Qifang's, where's the third?"

"Beats me," said Richards. "They all hopped airships within hours of each other, then the ghosting starts. If Qifang's behind this, he's certainly living up to his reputation." Richards' eyes clicked as he blinked, like a doll's. "But we can't discount the possibility it's nothing to do with him at all. Seeing as we have two Qifangs here, I'd be willing to bet the third one is also on his way to the Londons. There's something here that he... they... damn... whoever, wants..."

"That still leaves us with no murderer."

"Yes."

"This fake Qifang, the one from the boat... Do they think it was vulnerable to EMP?"

Richards went quiet for a second, his eyes fixed as he communicated with the coroner's office.

"The coroner says yes."

"In that case," said Otto, "I have an idea. Get Quaid to bring his guests in here. I am going back to the car. I'll be back in a minute."

"Wait!"

Otto paused by the door.

"Care to take a bet?" said Richards.

"Sure," said Otto. "Heiress."

"Interesting choice. Indonesian cook. Two bottles of good stuff says so, all right?"

"Agreed," said Otto.

Richards grinned. "You're wrong, you know?"

Otto was right. He came back from the car, lined up the guests, fired an EMP pulse on low setting at each of them, Jolanda went down, then came up again. This would have been gratifying, if she hadn't promptly attacked, smashing his EMP rifle to bits and wrestling him to the floor.

As Otto tackled the enraged emulant, Richards and Quaid hid at one end of the table, the cook staff and steward ducked down at the other.

"There are goddamned robots coming out of my goddamned woodwork! Goddamn!" shouted Quaid.

"I wouldn't worry," said Richards. "Otto was built to fight machines. He is highly trained."

As soon as he said this, the android put Otto's head through the day room wall and flung him onto the ground.

"Highly trained? You're shitting me!" Quaid barked.

"It usually works out." Richards said lamely.

Otto grabbed the android's ankle as it advanced on the cowering humans and yanked it back. It fell over him and onto the sofa, cracking the frame. Leather tore and stuffing flew into the air as it clawed its way around and rammed its stiletto heel right into Otto's arm, leaving the shoe embedded there. Otto howled, swiping at the thing as it scrabbled out of reach, raking his fingers across her skin and tearing a good portion of it free.

The android turned a ruined face upon Quaid. Split flesh revealed cold white bones underneath.

"Oh my god!" said Quaid. "I was screwing *that*?!" said Quaid.

It leapt for him, smashing the table into sticks. Richards hauled Quaid out of the way as Otto fell on the android from behind, wrestled it down and managed to pin it to the floor.

"Why the fuck is it trying to kill me?" Quaid said.

"I don't know," said Richards. "Maybe you're selfish in bed."

"How long do you think she's been a fake?"

"Oh, about since Qifang agreed to come aboard," said Richards matter-of-factly. He was trying to plot a way of the room, but the melee blocked their exit comprehensively. "Just stay down."

Otto was hammering the android repeatedly in the face with his enormous fists. Its head snapped back and forward with each impact. Otto's hands bled freely. He was reduced the remains of its face to mincemeat, but the machine's skull was too hard to crack. Not-Jolanda bucked underneath Otto and they both went rolling.

"Someone was watching Qifang carefully, found out about this trip, then picked someone else to replace to get at him, someone who'd meet you, chat you up and shag their way into a berth. I'm sorry, but the original Jolanda is almost certainly dead. In some ways your security was too good. It was the only way to get to him. Someone really wanted him dead."

Quaid was far from grief-stricken. "I screwed her. Goddamn!" He shook his head in disbelief. "All she was interested in was sex... I don't believe it."

"You evidently did believe it. Tell me, did you never think she was a little bit odd, a little bit unusual, perhaps? Maybe, a little too interested in a bright orange freak of science?"

"Look at her, look at what she was," said Quaid. "I wasn't into her for the conversation."

"Charming."

"She's Belgian," protested the EuGene. "I thought they were all like that."

"I think I see now how she fooled you, you really... Everyone, heads down!" shouted Richards.

Hughie's drones had decided to get involved, clumping into position in the corridor outside the dayroom. Richards tried to wrest control of them, to no effect. Servos thrummed and armour plates clicked as their weaponry deployed from broad shoulders. Richards threw his sheath on top of Quaid when the drones opened up. Otto's eyes widened and he leapt aside. The android vaulted to its feet, arm raising for a killing blow that never landed. Twinned heavy machine guns let rip with a deafening clatter, filling the room with the stink of propellant. The android shook with bullet impacts, tottering forward on its remaining high-heeled shoe, and let out a polyphonic data burble.

Shards of wood and gobbets of cloned flesh down rained on Richards and Quaid as the skeleton was stripped of all resemblance to a living human being. Now just bloodied bones, it backflipped onto all fours and scuttled up the corridor. Richards finally cracked the drones and shut them off before they could do any more damage. Rotating barrels whined to stillness. Otto scrambled up, followed the escaping assassin, bellowing in German, a chair leg in one hand, his pistol in the other, shooting as he went.

"You're wrecking my boat!" shouted Quaid.

"We're wrecking your boat?" said Richards. "What about your girlfriend?" He pressed himself up off the prone EuGene, and shook his head. "People. No sense of gratitude." He peered up the corridor, then addressed the crew, who were currently picking themselves out of the wrecked table.. "Right, they're gone. The rest of you get below. I think our fake Jolanda is going to try and get away now, so they'll be up on the deck."

"Are you sure?" asked the steward tremulously.

Richard turned to him. "No, I'm not sure, but if I were an illegal, experimental replicant hiding the truth of an international conspiracy I would try and put myself out of the way of those investigating it, wouldn't you? I don't think hiding under a bed will be very successful. But, if you've any better idea of what the deadly robot assassin is up to, please feel free to act upon it."

Richards looked hard at the little Indonesian. His eyes were swollen and his nose ran. He was genuinely ill.

Otto is never going to let me live this down, thought Richards.

The crew hurried off. Quaid was going to go with them, until Richards stopped him.

"Not so fast, you're coming with me," he said.

They stole up the corridor. It was full of shredded insulation, carbon and wood chip. The dayroom and the bar on the other side of the gangway were wrecked, and opened up into one large room with a shaggy partition of debris between. The gun drones stood motionless, guns ticking as they cooled. A breeze came in through the bar's shattered windows, spinning airborne fibres in tiny vortices. Richards gave one of the drones an experimental poke as he and Quaid ducked under their outstretched arms. They were inert. He'd fried their brains getting them to stop shooting the place to bits. It was annoying Hughie hadn't trusted Richards enough to order the things to obey him, because they could use one right now.

By the time Richards and Quaid had made it onto the foredeck of the *Aurora Viva*, the fight was over. Otto stood over the corpse of the motionless android, ready to shoot it again. It hung halfway through the deck rails, bloodied head still adorned by scraps of matted hair.

"Well done, Otto!" said Richards.

Otto was breathing hard. He was about to say something when a sound like cracking glass came from the wrecked machine. It twitched. Otto stepped back, gun trained on the skull, retreating further as wisps of caustic gas rose from the machine. The remains of the android's face collapsed into itself, its limbs sagged. Otto covered his mouth against the fumes. The deck fizzed.

"Jesus, Otto!" shouted Richards. "Dip it in the sea, dip it in the sea!"

"The sea?"

"It's acid, acid! Wash it off now." Richards stormed forward, gesticulating wildly, then lunged onto the deck, grabbed a limb of the machine and dunked it. The water boiled as it slipped under. Facsimiled agony raced up Richards' arm, and he nearly dropped the emulant before he turned off his sensing circuits. Ignoring the damage to his sheath he swished the corpse backwards and forwards in the water.

"Some sort of super acid," Otto said, his voice hoarse. Richards scanned him over quickly. The insides of his nose and throat were raw from the fumes. Otto coughed, wiped his mouth with the back of his hand. There was blood on it. Richards' machine senses caught a flare of electricity in the big man's solar plexus as his implanted healthtech activated, and he began to breathe more easily.

"Fluorosulfuric, I'd guess," said Richards. "That should do it." He pulled up the smoking remains and threw them onto the deck. The hand he'd held the machine with was gnarled into a lumpy fist. Richards pulled himself up awkwardly. He was silent for a moment, drumming his undamaged fingers on the railing.

"You don't like this," said Otto.

"No, no I don't. No one's been able to make an android this human-looking before. Hell, the damn thing *was* practically human."

They looked at the wreck.

"Times change," said Otto. He rubbed at his head wearily.

"There's been no talk of it on the Grid at all, yet here we find three of them trying to murder each other."

"Could be the Russians, or the People's Dynasty..." Otto offered.

"We Fives talk to each other, and the Russians employ plenty of us. The People's Dynasty likes to think the Great Firewall is strong, but it has its gaps. News of something like this would get out. We'd *know*. Bloody Hughie!" he said, and punched the rail with his broken hand, "this was supposed to be simple."

CHAPTER SIXTEEN

Reality 36

The night rang with calls of creatures that should not have been there. To the exorcists of godlings, this was disturbing, more so than the roaring in the jungle, accompanied by the crash of trees as something huge and ponderous forced passage.

Morning came. The sun rose unnaturally swiftly, teasing streamers of mist from the surface of the pools in the clearing. Wary of these ponds, the pair decided on a circuitous path that took them along firmer ground. It was hard going, and several times the lion sank deep into the moss. Eventually Tarquinius asked that the knight dismount, though his weight was negligible compared to the lion's multi-tonne heft.

At night they rested upon a rise as far away from open water as possible. Their second day's travel was even harder. By the end, they had gone barely a third of the way over the morass.

On the third day, they encountered a broad expanse broken by many pools. For the fourteenth time in a handful of hours, Tarquinius found himself immersed to his haunches in black muck. The basalt hill remained frustratingly distant.

"Damn it, Jag!" said the lion. "We're getting nowhere. We have to come up with some other plan."

Jag slapped a mosquito the size of a fist, mashing it to ruin against his filthy coat of plates. "Perhaps, dear comrade, I should go on alone."

"Jag, don't be ridiculous. You would fail, you have no hope on your own. Perhaps if we were to... Wait!" Tarquinius' head swung round. "To the east; I hear screams."

"What?"

"Female." Tarquinius' tongue disgorged itself and tasted the sound. "One hundred and sixty four centimetres, sixty-four kilogrammes. She is assailed by... something. I can't get a fix on it."

"That has happened too often recently for my continued ease."

"Ah. So now you are also concerned, I see." Tarquinius' stentorian voice disappeared to be replaced by an amplification of the encounter. The woman's shouts were mingled with the chatter of weapons fire. Over all was a low and dreadful humming.

"She seems spirited."

"She only has a 13.2% chance of survival. We should aid her."

"Why? The lives of many more depend upon the completion of our task," said Jagadith.

"Because she is what she is."

"Yes?"

"She is one of *them*, not one of *us* – a human, with a capital H," said Tarquinius.

"How so?" Jagadith leapt aboard his mount. "Is it she we must confront?" He paused. "Then why do her own creatures attack her?"

"Because she is not our prey." Tarquinius grunted as he hauled himself out of the ooze. "Her access protocols are intact; outmoded, forbidden, but intact and distinct from whatever is causing that vortex. The attackers are not of her fashioning."

"Then we must aid her, and expel her. Ah! This is a regrettable diversion."

Tarquinius shook out his metal mane, flinging out mud and strings of algae. "You must hold fast. I have a low probability of making the dash without becoming mired. It would serve you ill if you were to be thrown. Ready?"

"As always." Jag drew his sword. "Let us not be delaying any longer, I am eager to learn why this goddess breaks the seals."

With a roar that sent clouds of birds screaming from the mire, Tarquinius leapt forward. His paws gouged sucking holes as he ran. A few times he slipped, a few more he faltered. Once he went crashing onto his chest, and it was all the knight could do to keep in the saddle.

The lion played the goddess's voice as he ran. Its defiance was seeping away.

"Quickly, Tarquinius! Quickly!"

"I see her. I see her!" bellowed the lion. Tarquinius stumbled onto solid ground, and he accelerated. Wind streamed through the lion's hair, bending the feather back on Jagadith's turban and stinging tears from his eyes. Ahead, a woman was running frantically through the swamp, turning to shoot behind her.

Her pursuers were abominations. Fat flies the size of children, their bodies halted halfway in transformation from maggot. Their heads were those of hags, multifaceted eyes erupting from their pallid flesh, mouths frothing drool. They formed a shifting mass, moving too quickly for Jag to count them, though he estimated at least twenty. One fell from the sky, pinwheeling, its wings shattered by bullets, but there were too many for the woman to defeat.

"Prepare! Prepare! Combat configuration initiated!" shouted Tarquinius. Mirrored plates dropped down to cover his eyes, a shield rose from his back to protect his rider. Missile racks extended from his flanks. Atop the saddle, a panel slid aside to reveal a tactical display, with reticules darting about. They blinked orange, then green as they locked on.

"Fire!" Tarquinius roared. A salvo of missiles streaked towards the insect-things, blowing three apart in a welter of gore. Tarquinius galloped faster, gathering in his legs and hurling himself into the swarm. Jag's sabre glowed with blue fire as he cut more down, the creatures he destroyed dissipating like broken television pictures on the breeze.

The woman had fallen and was stuck in the mud. One of the downed insects dragged itself toward her, she pointed her gun at it and pulled the trigger. The weapon clicked, empty. She shouted in frustration and threw it aside.

A huge metal paw descended on the creature with a final squelch.

"All destroyed, Jagadith."

"Jolly good. Now," said Jagadith, turning to the woman. "My dear goddess. Pray be telling us who you are and what you are doing within the confines of Reality 36. This place is as forbidden to you as it is to the god who did this," he gestured delicately at the ruined insects. "Explain yourself."

"I don't know what you're talking about. I'm lost," stammered the woman. "I came up from Blandorray by zeppelin three weeks ago, those horrible things…"

She was somewhat attractive, noted Jag, her skin a lustrous ebony under its smears of mud. The lion glared at her, Tarquinius had no time for the percentiles of beauty.

Jagadith held up a perfect, if dirty, hand.

"Please! Be sparing us your falsehood, madam goddess. We are not to be bamboozled, is this not correct?"

"Right," agreed the lion. "No bamboozling. We know what you are."

"And, we did save your life. And you are carrying a representation of a Hechler series nine electrically activated automatic assault rifle, which, as we are both aware, is not something any of the natives hereabouts would even dream of, being unfamiliar with firearms beyond rifled muskets. An illegal game add on, is it not, from the old days? So, even if you are thinking to mislead us, it would be most discourteous in light of your rescue, and foolish when taken in consideration of this evidence." He refreshed his smile. "Now, please, tell us who you are."

"Dammit!" said the woman. She slapped the mud. Jagadith wrinkled his nose, he did not approve of women swearing. "Dammit dammit dammit!" Her head dropped, and she took a deep breath. "OK, OK. My name's Doctor Veronique Valdaire. I'm an AI systems analyst working on a digital anthropology project out of UCLA under Professor Zhang Qifang."

"Ah yes, we are familiar with this project, and the good professor. Qifang gave you your codes?"

"They should not permit full access," said Tarquinius.

"I modified them with Waldo's key," said Valdaire. "After running myself out through relays via a defunct experimental satellite. It's how I got in."

"You are talented, then." Jagadith looked around at the dead insects. "But even without this ungodly commotion going on, we would have been alerted to your presence eventually. And perhaps under different circumstances, you would not have been so happy to see us. There have been fatalities in the past."

"Those are my preferred outcomes," growled Tarquinius.

"Your choice to enter the Realities makes you a criminal, I am afraid," said Jagadith. "You are not the first researcher who was tempted to break the seals, and no doubt you will not be the last."

"Let's expel her now," said Tarquinius.

"Why are you here? To study us up close and personal, as you might say? Find your own world of marvellous wonders tiresome? Or did you just fancy a little game of god?" Jagadith's face became hard.

"No! I came here because of Professor Qifang. He sent me a message to meet him here, and, so here I am."

"This is most irregular," said Jagadith.

"Indeed," said Tarquinius. "Could it be that Qifang is the god we seek? That is a sorry prospect."

"Betrayal is a possibility we must consider," said Jagadith sadly. "Good men can turn bad."

"I came here to help. I want to help," said Veronique. "I need to find out what he uncovered. He left me data, someone's been manipulating the dataflows across the whole of the Realities. It wasn't him."

"He is old, is he not?" said Jagadith.

"One hundred and twenty seven," she said.

"There you have it, my dear. Impending mortality affects all humans, shaking even the most deeply held principle. I am very sorry for being so abrupt, but your actions are a trifle fishy to me. And also terribly foolish," said Jagadith.

"I have done nothing but study the Realities. I would never do anything to harm them," said Veronique.

"Your very presence belies that," said Jagadith curtly. "Still, we cannot expel you as of yet. The disruption to this realm is too extreme. De-interfacing your mind could kill you."

"I say do it anyway," said Tarquinius.

"Pay no heed to him," sighed Jagadith. "We are duty bound to safeguard human life, as far as is possible. Introductions are in order. We are the paladins of this realm. I am Sir Jagadith Veyadeep, Vedic templar of the Order of Silken Lights. This is my mount and friend, Tarquinius."

"Good day," rumbled the lion.

"Madam goddess, by directly connecting with our reality you have placed yourself in an inordinate amount of danger. I must ask you to accompany us until we can expel you safely."

Jag reached out his hand. Veronique looked doubtfully at it.

"Goddess one minute, expulsion the next. I've had some mixed messages in the past," she grasped the paladin's fingers. He pulled her up onto the saddle behind him. "If I can help, I will. I was in the USNAPC for six years…"

Jagadith raised a quizzical eyebrow.

"United States of North America Peace Corps," she explained.

"A charming modern euphemism for 'army'?" said Jag. "You were a soldier then?"

"Not frontline, cyberwarfare division. I also have degrees in AI psychology and virtual ecology, I'm not helpless. I know this Reality, I can fight."

"Madam goddess, your studies could never prepare you for the confrontation we must attend to. An old man your professor may be in your world, but not here. Here he is a god," Jagadith said sternly. Veronique's gun disappeared. "Do not be using any of your privileges to interfere with the good working of this universe again. Tarquinius," he said to the lion, "We still must cross the swamp. Onward!"

CHAPTER SEVENTEEN

Autopsy

Murder stalked artificial beings as surely as it did those of natural derivation. Autopsies of base units, androids, cyborgs and non-anthropoid, self-propelled robotic carriages were carried out in a facility attached to the Chief Coroner's Office in the Keats Arco in New London. With a heavy heart, that's where Richards went next.

Richards put on an undamaged body before he flew over to the coroner's in the car. He could have extended a sensing presence into the building and conferred with Doctors Beeching and Flats that way, but he preferred the distance being incarnate gave him, from Lincolnshire Flats in particular. Telepresence could be counterintuitively intimate.

The Robotics Division was one of only two places in the whole of the Londons that made Richards uneasy. This was where his kind wound up when they died. Privately, very privately, Richards hoped that if it ever came to that, it would not be the end, but as Pope Clement XX had said, in not so many words, "Electrons are no substitute for a soul".

He was embarrassed. He was a machine, he wasn't supposed to care about death, but he did. That's what came of having a Catholic for a father. Science said there was no such thing as an afterlife, for anybody. He wanted to believe that was not true, and he managed, mostly, but at the coroner's he had to stare death down, and it never blinked first.

The corridor to the Robotics Division was exceedingly long, like Richards imagined corridors in nightmares to be, though he had never had one of those. It smelt of blood and oil in equal measure. The staff comprised people who straddled a line between mechanic and medic, and were backed up by a coterie of post-mortem hackers who could conjure the dying thoughts of a machine from a pile of torched junk, or hunt down the last firings of a simulated brain as it melted into the Grid. All very uplifting.

Richards reached the end and the door swished open. Lincolnshire Flats's cheerful voice greeted him, and his simulated heart sank further.

"Ah, Richards, come to see out patients? Our happy clients? Come in! Come in!"

"They're not patients, Flats," said Richards. "Patients stand a chance of getting better; nor are they clients, because they do not pay. They are simply dead."

"Morbid as usual," hooted Flats. "They are happy though, I am correct in that – they never complain."

"Flats…" Richards said.

"Very well, as you prefer: Corpses this way. All aboard!" Lincolnshire Flats said, and tooted like a steam train. Flats inhabited a columnar carriage of stacked disks, each housing a variety of tools, grapples, sensors and medical equipment, mounted on a soft-treaded truckle. There were several of these sheaths in the facility, intended to be shared by the building's AI coroners and remotely visiting experts, but Flats had commandeered one as his permanent home. He had the habit of spinning his segments round, deploying a surgical saw here, multi-headed screwdriver there, and gunning his motors by way of emphasis, so that his often gruesome conversation was punctuated by inappropriate sound effects. The central plate, which held his primary visual cluster – Lincolnshire Flats would not stoop to calling them "eyes" – remained fixed on the face of whomever he spoke to, no matter what crazed fandango the rest of his body was performing, or in which direction he was heading.

Lincolnshire Flats was an independently minded Four, so independent it was rumoured that he'd been modified. There were darker rumours had it that he'd modified himself, which was very unusual. Evidence in favour of this was that he had chosen his own name, which was a rarity in his class, and decided to abandon medicine in favour of forensics. A Four leaving its programmed career was almost unheard of, so Richards suspected the rumours were true. Lincolnshire Flats exhibited an excessive love of his work, and that had to come from someplace else other than his programming. His dedication was laudable, and the two resident human coroners regarded him highly, but as far as Richards was concerned, Lincolnshire Flats was an A-grade ghoul.

"The patie... a-HEM! *Corpses* are in examination theatre 3B." Flats hooted. "Follow me, or go ahead yourself, as you like to, and I shall follow!"

"I don't like to do either, but I suspect I have little choice but to pick one if I want to find out what you have discovered," said Richards with a bravery he wasn't feeling. They set off down another corridor, plush with self-cleaning carpet. It was the main way within the facility, and numerous humans and machine intelligences hustled back and forth, many importantly clutching data pads to their chests. They spared no glances for the two AIs.

"Very droll, your pointless jibes forever reminds of the superiority of the class Fours over Fives. I thank you for it." A bone saw screeched.

"Don't mention it. How many corpses are we talking about?"

"I am sorry?" More of Lincolnshire Flats' ocular appendages swung round to look at Richards.

They walked past Theatre Two, the largest in the place, a warehouse-sized room with gaping clam-doored airlocks leading to a landing field outside. Here they flew in broken base units by heavy lifter preparatory to pulling them apart.

That's where I am going to end up eventually, thought Richards.

He shuddered. "Corpses' as in 'more than one'," he said to Flats, more confrontational than he intended to be.

He wondered if his fellow Fives suffered his existential dread. He'd never dared ask. It was too big a vulnerability to expose to the others.

"Why, of course. The android your partner deactivated, and the Qifang doppelganger."

"You didn't mean that," said Richards. "That was what your words said, but it wasn't what your voice said. You made a point of it. You are too theatrical for your own good. How many corpses are we talking about? It is more than two, I am sure."

"Ah, yes, well," grumbled Lincolnshire Flats, "Poo-poo, there's no hiding anything from you, is there?"

"Nope."

"Bah. It is no paint off my casing's inter-ocular space. HA HA! You have only spoilt the surprise for yourself, Richards, but we'll get to that, I'll save what I know. I shall leave you tantalised, which is nowhere near so delicious as flabbergasted. A pity."

They passed into the atrium of examination theatre 3B, which was a round, domed room coated entirely in joinless spun glass. The atrium was effectively a large airlock lit with strong, sterilising UV. There was a red light over the door to the theatre proper, glass frosted to above head height so those in the airlock could not see whatever horrors were proceeding within. The AIs were subjected to a wind laced with cleaning nanites. They stood for a minute, lifting limbs, Richards' tilting his shoes, turning about, as the microscopic machines swarmed over them both, gathering contaminants of every kind. The red light over the door turned amber when the process was done, and the nanites spiralled down a hole in the floor. The light turned green, the AIs' Gridsigs were updated with the relevant clearances, and the doors opened.

"Follow me!" trilled Lincolnshire Flats. His unblinking eyes shifted to the tables in the middle of the theatre. There were four of these in all. The one on the far right was empty. On the leftmost lay the twisted mess of the emulant heiress Otto had fought, next to that the Qifang copy fished out of the Medway. Next to that lay another android. It had been crudely dismembered, its flesh casing decayed, but it was unmistakeable as another doppelganger of the old professor.

"Qifang two!" shouted Lincolnshire Flats with a species of wholly inappropriate glee. He extended a long, thin probe and pointed at the second dead professor. "Dragged out of the South Bank marshes this very morning, not far from Richmond Venice."

Another door opened, and a man dressed in surgical gear walked in from the scrub room next door. "Ah!" he said cheerily. "Richards! Glad to see you, how're you faring?" He was old in that indeterminate way wealthy men with generous healthplans tended to be. The jewelled snail of an expensive mentaug curled round his ear, a biofilter mask sat atop his surgical cap.

"I am very well, Doctor Beeching, thank you."

"Of course you are, of course, you are," He smiled and pressed his gloved hands together, the faintest of crow's feet feathering his eyes. "A Five is never ill, never tires, never stops. Marvellous, marvellous machines." He leaned forward and peered academically at Richards. Richards got the uncomfortable feeling Beeching would just love to poke about in his warm, dead innards.

Richards walked around the broken androids on the autopsy tables, running his hands absentmindedly along the edges. "And how are you?"

"Well, very well, a lot better than these sorry souls you see here," Beeching chuckled. Lincolnshire Flats boomed with laughter.

"Yeah, right. What have you found out for me then?"

"Ah, right to business as always," said the doctor with a sigh. "Very good, very good. Well, these are an entirely new class of machine, though I don't think I need to tell you that." He tapped his a stylus against the acid-scarred bones of the heiress. "As you can see, as you have seen, perhaps I should correctly say, these are sophisticated pieces of engineering. They're very near to grade II cyborgs in the proportion of their organic components to pure mechanicals and various electronica."

"Cyborg is an incorrect definition!" shouted Flats. "The legal definition of a cyborg is a natural organism, naturally or artificially conceived, that at a point past conception is altered by the introduction of artificially derived, non-organic components designed to medically replace or enhance natural bodily function," droned the Four pedantically. "These are therefore, not cyborgs."

"Quite so Lincolnshire Flats, quite so," said Beeching, tapping the stylus against his nose, unconcerned he'd been poking it into the gory mess in front of him only seconds before. "These never were, for the wont of a better term, 'human'." He smiled at Richards. "These are machines through and through. See here," he lifted a flap of rotted skin on Qifang 2 with the stylus. "This is very sophisticated, a full clone in some regards; a genuine copy."

"A full clone, as opposed to a genetically patterned clone, is legally defined as an artificially conceived and gestated organism, or part of an organism, created as an exact copy of a pre-existing organic organism's cellular structure as it stands at a specific moment in time."

"Indeed. Except they are not clones, of either sort, by which I mean they were not grown complete. They are vat grown, for the main, but in parts and then assembled, we can see the joining work, very fine it is." Beeching shook his head. "We knew the technology would hit us eventually, we've had plenty of time! What exactly am I going to put on the report?"

"I have already petitioned the medical council for a correct definition," said Flats.

"Won't android do? That covers a lot of bases," said Richards.

"Technically, the heiress was a gynoid, a machine mimicking the female form."

"Nobody uses that word any more, Flats," said Richards.

"Whatever term you choose to employ, the machines have all the characteristics of their respective original's exterior properties, dermal, subdermal, lymphatic system… Everything," said Beeching. He encompassed the machines with a wave of his stylus. "This has not been spun off a gene-loom. These are not as similar as identical twins, but are actual duplicates, right down to the cellular level. Birth marks, cancers and all. There's more than simple invitrogenesis going on here."

"Someone had cancer? Who had cancer?" asked Richards.

"What? Oh, Qifang, poor chap. Lungs, absolutely shot, way past fixing. His healthtech should have picked that up. I'd sue."

"He's dead now," said Richards. "He's probably past caring."

"Hmmm, what? Yes, I suppose so," said Beeching. He frowned.

"The organics extend far into the system," bellowed Lincolnshire Flats. "Lungs, heart and liver," his whirring appendages tapped a series of jars on trolleys at the head of the beds, one after the other. Inside each was an organ pallid with exsanguination and preserving fluids, "as well as all other major internal organs, the alimentary canal, stomach, reproductive organs and so forth. These, however, are not vital to the functioning of the machine in the case of the heiress."

"Indeed," said Beeching. "There are differences between these devices. In the case of the Qifangs, they are almost entirely human, only the brain element is electronic."

"I found cranial fluid on the boat," said Richards. "The kind you get in an android."

"You did," said Beeching. "The brains in all of them are machines, though non-standard. But the heiress construct differs from the Qifang constructs significantly in its underlying chassis and in its cognitive hardwares, although both sorts would fool most tests designed to tell human and machine apart. And this is where things get interesting." Beeching waved his stylus again. The theatre's sunpipes became opaque, dimming the room. A holo of the reconstructed heiress appeared in the air, and expanded to double lifesize. "Unlike Qifang's copies, where the skeleton is exactly human, the heiress' skeleton is a combat android chassis, carbon spun, Faraday protected, independently motivated, strong too, Chinese manufacture, similar to those employed by the South African Union, and easily purchasable on the black market," he indicated the items one after the other with his stylus on the body of the heiress' android. Above, the holo showed magnified views. "Though all hard to spot, it's heavily shielded and well camouflaged. It is capable of operating independently of the organics should they be destroyed, so I would say in her case it is best to view those as merely a disguise." Layers of the cyborg graphic obligingly peeled back. It re-centred itself to show the areas as Beeching referred to them. "Cavities of catalytic acids are scattered throughout the bones. These, by the way, carry a modified calcium phosphate mineral element. Makes them very hard, but similar enough to human bone to pass the usual tests."

"Otto found that out, thanks," said Richards.

"The acids are a two liquid mix. On their own, inert, together..." Beeching pressed his palms together then moved them apart, fingers spread. "Well then, I suppose we can bid farewell to our machine, as you yourself have witnessed."

"A suicide pill for our kind," said Flats.

"Standard black-ops modification," said Richards with a shrug. "I've seen it before."

"Ah, not like this," said Beeching. "They're deep in the marrow, quite a clever modification actually, not only stops them getting mixed accidentally," Beeching spun his hands round one another, "due to trauma. Trauma caused by fighting your colleague, for example, I would say, but also renders them practically undetectable."

"It is apparent to both my colleague and I that the heiress' primary purpose is violence," added Flats. "She is an assassin!"

"Yes, yes indeed so. Someone has gone to a supreme effort making it look human. We suspect ambush to be its primary modus operandi; surprise, shall we say. She looks so human, that if you were to go to the level of checks required to find out she wasn't, you'd probably know already anyway. Quite marvellous, the military would kill to get their hands on this."

"You said the brains were non-standard?"

"Very much so, my dear fellow, and they are most remarkable. It is in the brain of the things, the human emulating brain, that we're really peeking into the future. They are really quite something," Beeching pointed out the various elements of the machine brain on the hologram, which continued to rotate, zoom and highlight parts of itself as the doctor spoke "It mimics human synaptic function far more adequately, I suppose the word would be in this case, than any technology we have yet seen."

"And we see 'em all in here!"

Richards ignored Flats. "Are they capable of full human emulation then, independent of an external governing influence?" he asked, slightly incredulously.

Beeching looked disappointed. "Oh, these are sophisticated machines, Richards; no doubt, but even so, whoever built them has not yet found a way of reproducing the full function of the human brain in as compact a form as that which evolution provided us with." Doctor Beeching tapped his forehead with a finger and smiled. "We meat people are still one step ahead in that department. There are plenty of interesting innovations on the pseudo-neurological level, but the mind it sustains is not as complex as that generated by a genuine human brain."

"How do you mean?"

"I suppose you could say the Qifang you found contained the edited highlights of the man. It's as if, well, if you'll pardon the expression, as if he's not all there," he gave a physician's chuckle. "I'm sorry that we could not do a comparison between the two, but the second had lost much of its data content. If you'd...?"

"Dump the files into me when I leave," said Richards. "I'll take a look when I get back to my office."

"Very well. Even with the autonomy these marvellous engines possess, they would appear disconnected and aloof from a human observer. A little off. We've done a simulation..."

"A-HEM!"

"My apologies, my colleague Lincolnshire Flats here has done a simulation of how they might think, and aside from the directly programmed competencies present in the heiress, they were fairly limited. They'd make poor conversationalists, for example, though no doubt they'd fly through the older iterations of the

Turing. But the interesting thing is that it looks like they were created to *believe* they are human. That would make them, at least her, the ideal assassin. Replace a living target with one of these, it acts like the original, more or less, in a limited way, provided it keeps itself to the fringes of things, nobody would notice, until some keyword, broadcast or other signal activates it and 'BAM!'" Beeching shouted loudly, slamming his hands together, Richards jumped. "The faux-personality is overturned, the core programme takes over... Dead target, infiltrated business, compromised facilities, you name it. They would be inappropriate for truly complex missions, but deadly in the right instances. A covert, human-mimicking assassin, the first of its kind, perhaps. Imagine that now with a dormant gridpipe, one someone like you could use, Richards, and well then, the possibilities are expansive."

"We are privileged in our work," said Flats.

"I don't think I'd want to be that human, it's all too icky, all that crapping," said Richards. "How can you be sure they thought they were alive?" Throughout Beeching's briefing Richards had been walking round the inert androids, peering into them, lifted bits up.

The two coroners looked at one another.

"What?" said Richards.

Beeching paused, waved his hand around, looking for words. He settled on the straightforward explanation. "Well," he said. "We asked them."

A short holo of the Medway Qifang machine with bundles of cable strung from its head appeared. It was screaming over the questions it was being asked; a terrible noise that did not stop.

"I've seen enough," said Richards after a few seconds.

"Yes, yes," said Beeching grimly. The holo froze. "Quite immoral, don't you think?"

"Where the hell are they from?" muttered Richards. "And why was the heiress sent to kill the Qifang android? Why are they so different. In fact, are there any other differences?"

"No. They are of identical manufacture in other respects," said Flats. "Same growth techniques, same joining, same brain. The combat chassis in the heiress is the largest difference between them."

Richards looked at the machines. Their existence opened a lot of doors into a lot of nasty, dark little rooms. "Do you have any idea who made them?"

"Negative," said Flats. "We have provided you with information. Utilising it is your role in this. We are coroners, you are the investigator!"

"Perhaps this will help," said Beeching. The hologram span again, focussing in on the top of the heiress' damaged femur. "At the atomic level, there is a company logo on the combat model. Twelve atoms by twelve atoms. We'd have no clue if it weren't for this. Why the criminal mind has a need to reveal itself in such ways is a mystery we'll never solve in here, but there it is. Do you recognise it?"

The logo was grainy, single carbon atoms for single pixels. Richards raised his plastic eyebrows. "Yes, I do." He wasn't surprised. "Tony Choi. He's a legitimate manufacturer."

"Who?"

"Arms maker out of Hong Kong. He and I go a way back. Thanks. That gives me somewhere to start."

"There is one last thing," said Beeching. "Qifang Two was purposefully dismembered. There are tool cuts here, here and here." He pointed.

"He was being followed by four men," said Richards.

"Yes," said Beeching. "The interesting thing is, they have matching cranial injuries." He highlighted similar wounds on both corpses, pulling holo images until they overlaid each other. One hole was more ragged than the other, but both were in the same place. "See this? Nearly identical puncture wounds to the base of the skull, and we suspect identical internal damage. In the Qifang from the boat, this knocked out a precise part of his brain, the other's head was emptied, but I would say that they were after the same part. And that, we think, was this." A ragged holo came up, and began to play. "It's a part of a message we found in the one from the boat. It was terribly degraded, I am afraid to say. The retrieved footage should be here... Now."

The new holo jumped into life. Another Qifang sat in a well-furnished room. The holo was badly corrupted, elements freezing and overpainting each other to create a messy collage. Qifang's face, the real Qifang, Richards thought, was a monstrous patchwork in the middle. A dozen cut and paste lips jiggled, floating teeth smeared themselves across the air. The audio, however, was clear enough.

"...you are the only one I can trust. I am sure you know of me, and the work I have done for your kind. I hope that you will listen to what I have to say, and trust me in your turn...."

The message stopped, the light of the holo died, leaving the theatre grim.

"If I were a betting man..." said Beeching.

"Five to one! Five to one!" bawled Flats.

"...I'd say someone was looking for these android Qifangs and attempting to stop that being delivered."

"To who?"

"That's your department, Richards," said Flats. "We're with the snippy snip and the dead people."

"It sounds like he was after one of us AI. Who? Hughie? Me?" He thought a moment. "Was there any more to the message?"

"That's it, there was no more that we could retrieve," Lincolnshire Flats twittered solemnly. "The dead have spoken, and that is all they are going to say today."

CHAPTER EIGHTEEN

Jesu City

Only one hundred miles from the the Whitehouse was Jesu City, oldest of the northern shanties, feverish in the humid night with discordant music and despair. Places like Jesu City were why Santiago Chures wanted machines on the side of man, why he didn't just try to get the whole lot of them wiped.

Places like Jesu City were why he worked for the Virtualities Investigation and Protection Agency.

Jesu City was a town of huddled NUN prefabbed shelters, thirty years old and falling apart at the seams. The air was fuggy with smells of cooking, Brazilian spices, Mexican pastries. Portuguese and Spanish came from faces of all colours. The place reeked of sweat and shit.

If the machines had more say, places like this would be gone faster. The machines had more say every year, and things were getting better. But Chures had no illusions. Underneath their ersatz human personalities the machines were supremely logical beings. In looking at a place like Jesu, they might come to the supremely logical conclusion that things would run far more smoothly without people.

It had happened once before, during the Five Crisis of 2104. After the complete upheaval the the model created, only seventy-six Fives had been given leave to live. Most had gone mad. Civilisation had hung by a thread for six, terrible days.

What a lot of people didn't know were that there were two dozen others besides the seventy-six, who were also completely rational, but entirely inimical to human life. They'd been destroyed by the VIPA along with those deemed insane. The rush to get them all deleted before the NUN untangled the mess surrounding the crisis had been exhilarating. Some of Chures' colleagues had objected, things had got unpleasant, those who believed the VIPA's actions immoral pitted against the realists. Chures had been fresh out of the academy when the crisis hit, a baptism of fire, but he'd stayed in service. He'd spent his own childhood in a camp much like Jesu City. He believed if the machines were kept in check, they would deliver a better world.

If they were kept in check.

Chures would have liked Qifang on his team. Men who had empathy for mankind's children were rare, humanity did not understand its offspring well. A condition of parenthood, he supposed. Qifang working for the VIPA was the best Chures could hope for. He suspected the actual end result would be far less favourable.

But first he had to see Karlsson.

He walked along the open sewer that passed for a street. Bass heavy music and the amplified calls of prostitutes deafened him. A big man jostled him, looking for a fight. Chures flicked open his coat, showing badge and gun. The man curled a lip, and walked on.

This was typical of Karlsson, pick some godforsaken hellhole to meet in. He'd done it on purpose to put Chures ill at ease, remind him of his past. Karlsson was a bastard for mind games like that. They had never got on when they'd worked together at the agency.

At the heart of the camp were three decaying hangers of cement board and steel from when the place had been an aerodrome. For a while they'd been used for camp administration, and NUN blue still coloured the walls. Mildewed prefab offices with smashed windows clustered about the sides. The hangars were falling down, warning signs all over their exteriors, a couple of beat-up drones patrolled the perimeter. Chures' badge got him through the flatribbon cordon. He ducked inside a hole in the wall into the centremost hangar where Karlsson should be waiting.

Flocks of pigeons scared up on clattering wings as he walked across a floor slick with rainwater and human waste. There were signs that the drones and the ribbon had been beaten, people had been in here recently. There were makeshift braziers of blackened steel drums, discarded bottles, food packets and torn sleeping bags, a hobos' dross, visible in patches of garish OLED light from the pleasure joints outside.

Bartolomeo, scan. Chures' AI blend looked down through an avimimic drone above the camp, feeding highlights directly to Chures through his mentaug. *Do you see him?*

Negative, Agent Chures. I see nothing. The hangar is empty.

"Karlsson!" Chures shouted. His voice bounced from concrete walls. There was a noise, the scuff of shoe on concrete, magnified and sinister in the hangar's emptiness.

You're not getting anything?

I am sure, said Bartolomeo into his head. *You are alone, so far as I can see.*

"Puta Karlsson!" spat Chures. Karlsson had more tech and more brains than half the VIPA put together, but he was as crazy as a shithouse rat. "Come out, Karlsson!" He walked over to the source of the noise. He pulled his gun. "Get out into the light where I can see you."

A shadow resolved itself from the deeper shadows in the curve of the walls. "Chures!" hissed Karlsson's voice. "Keep your voice down."

Chures kept his gun out, adjusted his grip. He checked over his shoulder. Coming here alone was a bad idea, Karlsson's insistence be damned.

"Come out."

"As you wish."

The man stepped out into a puddle of light. Chures squinted. He couldn't believe what he was seeing.

"Karlsson couldn't make it."

The man had Karlsson's voice, but Chures' face. He stood insouciantly, one hand in the pocket of a suit identical to one Chures owned, the other twirling a cocktail stick idly in his teeth.

"Put the gun down, Chures," said his double, speaking with his voice now.

Chures wasn't one to ask dumb questions. He pulled the trigger; at least he intended to. His body locked rigid before the command could make it from his brain to his finger.

I am sorry, Agent Chures, said Bartolomeo. *This is for the best.*

This wasn't supposed to happen, he was in control.

"There's no need for you to die, Chures. My intention is to save lives, not waste them." The man with his face walked forward and took his gun, slid the slider back, dissembled the weapon without looking at it and strewed its parts upon the floor. "I need to borrow your life for a while. When this is all over, you will thank me."

Through teeth clamped shut, Chures choked out, "Who the hell are you?"

The other Chures gave a slow smile. "You are as tenacious as they say. I am glad I pursued this course of action, making a puppet of you would never have worked for long." He locked eyes with him; his eyes. "A better question would be 'what?', Chures. And perhaps 'why?'" He cocked his head to one side, the neck accommodating several degrees more tilt than would have been comfortable for a human. "Tell me, what do you know of the Class Five AI Richards and Otto Klein's involvement in this affair of Zhang Qifang and his charming assistant?"

Chures said nothing.

"Suit yourself," said his double. Chures felt a sharp pain in his head. His life flickered before him with sickening speed; Bartolomeo was mining his memories. When it was done, he was on his knees, filth soaking the knees of his trousers.

"It is surprising how little you know," said his double. "I wonder how much Valdaire knows? I do hate loose ends." The double squatted beside him. "I'll be going now. I'll have Bartolomeo take you somewhere safe, don't worry. He is fond of you, but he works for me now." He pointed at Chures' gear. "I'll be needing these." He bent down and tugged Chures' coat, badge and all, over his stiff shoulders. He reached out and unclipped his twin uplinks from their external mounts underneath his ears. "I apologise for the pain," the double said as monofilaments tugged from his brain and slid out through his skin. Finally, the fake Chures took the drop-pearl earring Chures wore in this left ear. "I have to look the part," he explained. As a final insult, he took his boots.

Chures grunted with rage, saliva streaming between lips frozen in a painful snarl, his muscles burned with cramp.

He couldn't see the stranger leave.

Some time later, Bartolomeo spoke into his mind. *That should be long enough, Agent Chures. I have taken control of your somatic functions. We will now leave. Please do not fight. I am truly sorry, but this is for the good of us all.* Bartolomeo walked Chures jerkily over to the gash in the wall they'd entered through. Chures marshalled himself and waited until he was going through.

With one last effort of will, he jerked his head back, slamming his silvered mentaug casing into the rusting metal.

Stop! said Bartolomeo. *Santiago, wait!*

With the first blow, Chures felt the AI's influence lessen briefly. He seized his chance and threw his head back again, gashing his scalp, smashing the casing again, sending its Gridpipe receivers offline.

Santiago please stop. Santiago! Bartolomeo's thoughts were panicked. The keystone of his personality imprint was in the unit. Chures had made sure of that, in case he ever needed to deactivate him, though he never thought it would come to this. *Chures! You do not understand. Stop! Something marvellous isssss...* Bartolomeo's voice slurred to a hiss. Somewhere, the base unit that housed the rest of the Class Four slipped into imbecility.

Chures fell forward, his muscles limp, head ringing like a bell. Holy Christ alone knew what damage he'd done to his own brain. What the hell now? It wouldn't be long before the fake Chures discovered that Bartolomeo was gone. He probably knew already. He could come back. He thought about warning the office, but whoever his double was working for would track him down him easily then.

He had to disappear, go off Grid, and then? Valdaire, he thought. Get to her first. That's where his double was going.

A lousy plan, but the best he had.

His senses reeled, he grabbed at the wall, pushed back out into the light and noise of the street. His stockinged feet slipped in the muck. People avoided him, stepping away, he was just another luckless victim on Jesu City's pleasure way. They wanted nothing to do with his misfortune.

He stumbled on, eyes hunting for drones against the stars.

CHAPTER NINETEEN

Los Angeles

"What kind of shit are those electrical bastards trying to pull now? A German, a goddamned German? This ain't Hamburg or Schintzelville or wherever the hell you are from pal, not your jurisdiction." Detective Flores seethed, the badge slung about his neck jerking as he jabbed his forefinger at Otto. His face was unfashionably fat, lined by unspent anger, with deep creases round his mouth.

Otto stared placidly down at him. Flores was a little guy; the top of the his head stopped short of Otto's chest, but Otto admired his spirit.

"Cool it Flores, this guy's got documentation like you've never seen." Flores partner was a woman, Detective Annabelle Mulholland. She was older, severe, about forty-five in biological looks, probably her actual age, she was the kind of woman who wouldn't make the time for anti-gerontic work until she had to. Her hair was dry and scraped back into a ponytail, roots showing. She was free of make-up and her clothes were poorly ironed. A real vocation cop, Otto guessed, an up-late-into-the-night, dwelling-on-the-faces-of-the-dead type.

"Yeah?" said Flores.

"Yeah, Flores. He's investigating a connected case over in Euroland. The Sams think it's important, so shut up. "Isn't that right, Mr Klein?"

Otto nodded.

"And what is this case, huh? You gonna tell us?" said Flores, hardly less aggressively.

"I cannot," said Otto as regretfully as he could. Pissing off the local cops wasn't going to make his job any easier, but he was struggling with Flores. His shoulder throbbed. Something important had given in his fight with the heiress, and the pain wasn't helping him keep his cool.

"That's fucking typical!" Flores threw up his arms. "Goddamn fucking machines!" He stalked off. "You show him round, Annie," he shouted over his shoulder. "I'm going to go over the gardens again. Call me when he leaves."

"Flores can be an ass, I'm sorry," Mulholland said when Flores had gone.

"It is difficult when someone comes in from outside. I will be out of your way soon."

"Flores has been in the force since way back when, before AI started giving orders. He doesn't like it when the artificials interfere with his work. Makes him huffy."

If that was huffy Flores was probably the kind of guy who went apoplectic if his pizza topping was wrong, thought Otto. He was a walking heart attack in waiting.

"I've got accompany you right the way round here, no snooping about on your own, OK?" said Mulholland.

"Understood," he said

She smoothed her dry hair. She looked tired. "If you've got any questions, shout out. Did you have a good flight?"

"Yes. Seventy-five minutes on a stratojet. Not long," he said. "May I see the crime scene now?"

"OK, not one for small talk." She shrugged and walked toward the flatribbon cordon, a beam of light projected between portable bollards. Scrolling words warned of the high voltage charge carried on an ionised air stream. A section winked out between two of the emitters as Mulholland approached. "Follow me," she said, and looked at him appraisingly. "Kind of big aren't you? They all this big over there?"

"I am an exception."

"Well, Mr Exception, walk this way. Are you ex-military or..."

"Ex-military, Ky-technischeren Sonderkommando," he said, the words tripping off his tongue automatically.

"A what now?"

"Cyborg commando. USE special forces."

"I thought so," she said thoughtfully. She flashed her badge at a bored looking uniform by the kitchen side door. Otto let him scan his AllPass. The officer handed them foot coverings, overcoats and haircovers. After they'd put them on he let the two of them inside.

"Do I need to wear a mask?" Otto asked.

"Not unless the smell bothers you. We had air scrubbers come in and do the atmospheric forensics right after the call came in. We do have professional standards, you know?" she gave an unpractised smile.

The house was big, but not so big the cops could not fill it. Small drones darted about, aiding a forensics team of five men. A Class Four sheathed in a bare endoskeleton acted as drone-shepherd, directing them to dip down to the floor and scoop up flies killed in the building lockdown, suck fragments of stone and soil up from the carpet, and pluck particles of skin from the curtains. Their cameras flashed often.

Mulholland and Otto went through into the dining room. The smell was bad, two weeks' worth of decay soaked into floorboards lifted a potent reek. The body's position was marked by a tape outline and a large, discoloured blotch. Qifang had not been a big man, but he'd been there a long time, and he'd leaked copiously.

"This is where we found him." Mulholland's gesture took in a stained dining table covered in plastic markers. "He'd been dead a fortnight, we think. It was the start of vacation, when teaching duties end, he was supposed to be doing research, and he kept himself to himself outside of office hours. We had to go off entomological evidence, as you can see, there are a lot of flies round here, killed by the anti-biologics we use. *Lucilia sericata*, most of them. Their pupation rate kind of puts it round the same time as we see that flicker in his Gridsig, you know about that?"

"Yes."

"OK," she nodded. "Then, or possibly a little later."

"What of the three divergent Grig signatures that left the States?"

"Beats me, we've not had anyone cheat the Grid codes since the Three Uncles took over population management. But sure, this guy was one smart cookie, we'll give him that, so I wouldn't be amazed if he could do it. Then there's his assistant, she disappeared in a hurry. Do you know anything about that?"

"Not much," said Otto. "I read about Qifang's home fabricator in the report also. May I see that? It may be important to my investigation."

"Yeah, sure, this way. Watch the wires," she pointed to lines linking the Four to a boxy unit that trailed cables off out the house through a plastic sphincter lodged in the window. "We have to hardline our sheaths to the police AIs," she explained. "Some hacker shit got hold of the cypher for their Gridpipes. Quantum encoding unbreakable? Bullshit. Kids can crack it in their lunchbreak. They do it for fun, then the criminal elements buy it up."

"It is inconvenient," said Otto, thinking of Tufa.

"It's a drag, that's for sure. Outsiders seem to think it's all peace and love in California since the dippies took over, but I tell you, this place is crawling with scum. We've got a major gang war on, massive people smuggling to the south, every criminal in Latin America has decided to come here since the reds started executing anyone connected to the cartels, and it's not helped by foreign agents coming in with the genuine refugees. So, even something like this, it's all hardlined, none of it bar the simplest commands to these drones is broadcast."

"It is the safest way," agreed Otto. He was only paying half attention to the detective, being more absorbed by the death scene. They passed over a wide hallway where the main entrance to the building was situated. More masked and suited bodies filled it.

"It is a pain in my ass, is what it is," she said. "Even the AIs bitch about it. Right, here we are." Under the grand staircase was a door small enough that Otto had some trouble squeezing through it. This took them onto a flight of stairs into a basement workshop. It was a large space with a painted concrete floor, big enough for a couple of workbenches, all harshly lit. Tools on pinboards lined three of four walls, the third opened out into a garage where a modest aircar sat, the ramp leading up to the driveway outside stamped with a hard rhombus of sunlight through the open door. More officers bustled about the basement. Otto's adjutant counted seventeen in the house, and busily set itself to work calculating the best way Otto could kill them all. He ignored it.

In the corner of the workshop was an industrial fabrication loom, one of the biggest Otto had seen in a private home. The service hatch had been taken off without much care, optic cables left spilling out of it. Mulholland shooed an officer out of the way, and pointed within.

"The central chipset, patterning unit and datacache have been removed, bits of them are on that desk over there," she indicated a pile of shattered components. "We have the pieces of the chips back at HQ, but they've been thoroughly wrecked. It looks like someone, Qifang I presume, took out anything that could give us a clue and smashed it to bits with a hammer."

"So he made something before he died."

"Yes, something he did not want us to know about."

"You are attempting to reassemble the chip fragments?"

She pulled a face. "We're not making much progress. They're useless, if you ask me. I don't think we'll find anything."

"I'll take a scan of them if I may."

"Be my guest. Speak to Martinez upstairs, the guy on the door, he'll get one sent over," she leaned on a bench. "He'll arrange access to whatever you need."

Otto was impressed by the way the police were going over the house.

"It is a good team you have. Is it not large for this case?"

"A suicide, you mean? Maybe, but Qifang was an important man, and there are a lot of eyes watching, most of them not of the human variety, and what the numbers say carries a lot of weight around here. There were people that were not very happy with Qifang's sapients rights movement; mostly old timey blood and thunder religious sorts, but extreme dippies too, and some of them have the money and the expertise to stage something like this and make it look like suicide. Then there's his assistant, she's a lot younger than Qifang, but some of those mentor-student relationships can get very messy, one way or another."

"What is your opinion, detective? Is it murder or suicide?"

"You want my opinion? Wow," she said. "Long time since anyone wanted that, but OK." She crossed her arms. "My opinion is that this is what it looks like. Qifang killed himself. Why? Maybe we won't find out and maybe we will. Sure, he had cancer, but they might have been able to fix that. Whatever. In my opinion it doesn't really matter. In my opinion these officers here could be covering something else, say, solving the schoolyard massacre we had two weeks back. Thirty-eight dead kids, because some out of town redneck thinks too many people speak Spanish round here. Or the serial killer offing virtporn addicts in Downey, Lynwood and Compton. By our count he's up to forty victims now. Or any one of the other million active cases we have. This state is gutting itself while the dippies clang their bells, and one dead professor who chose an early exit does not mean much one way or another to me. But that's my opinion, and my opinion doesn't mean anything to the State, the VIPA, the Feebs or the numbers that run them."

"It is a difficult job. I understand," he said.

"Do you understand?" Her expression softened as she lingered on the scars on his face. "Yeah, yeah, maybe I guess you do. You were in Brazil?"

"Yes."

"Me too," she said. "At the end." She looked round the room, as it searching for something she'd misplaced, looked back up to him. "Now, is there anything else you need to see here?"

"No, thank you. I will take the scans of the chip fragments and send them to my partner, maybe he can do something with them. If he finds anything I will let you know. I also need any information that you may have on Qifang's assistant, Veronique Valdaire."

"I'd like to speak to her myself."

"Do you think she is involved in this?"

"It's a possibility. Her skipping town is suspicious, but her Gridsig, forensics and so forth suggest she was never within two miles of this place. The night he died we have a bar full of witnesses to testify that she was dancing until the early hours, she does that a lot, apparently, so whatever she's done, it isn't murder."

"That does not mean that she is not responsible."

"No, no it does not. She's off the Grid. It's not surprising. If he knew how to fool the system, there is a good chance she knows how to too. The UCLA Six has lodged complaints against her, a couple of illegal searches, theft, and an assault."

"Assault?"

"On it. Not on a real person. She turned it off," she explained. "It put the initial call to us."

"And what did she take?"

Mulholland gave a fiercer smile.

"The specifics of that information have not been made available to us by the VIPA. It's been a nightmare here since the Tolman administration. Federal and out-government agencies at each other's throat in a way that'd make… What was his name, that 20th century guy?" she frowned at Otto, looking for an answer, before providing her own. "Hoover, that's it. That'd make him proud. Paranoid nuts everywhere, no cooperation, especially on these section 73s.

"Anyways, to get back to the assistant, I don't she killed the professor. There's no evidence. Granted, she's smart enough to hide it, but her psychs suggests a high degree of loyalty, and I'll go with that every time. She's running all right, but not from this. In my opinion, seeing as you were interested in it before, it'd be better for her if we got to her before the VIPA did. What she's done is enough for the VIPA to hold her indefinitely, murder or not. Still, I expect the VIPA to come to me soon, because despite what they think, we local cops are not schmucks, and if we can't find her, I'll bet they can't find her either," she rubbed her face. Her skin took a while to crawl back into place, fatigue compromising its elasticity. "Now Mr Klein, I have a lot to do. If there's nothing more you need to see, I will escort you out."

After Otto had secured scans of the chip fragments and sent them to Richards, he caught a cab over to the Richards & Klein's LA office, which was located in an unprepossessing mini-arco out near the landward end of Wilshire.

He interrogated the near-I secretary to make sure that Richards had not been ignoring lucrative cases. If a case bored him, he tended not to bother telling Otto, which was one of his more irritating habits. There wasn't much apart from a bauxite freighter heist mid-Pacific that he might look into later. He instructed the machine to inform potential clients that they were likely to be unavailable for a month.

The office was small, comprising a reception area equipped with a holographic receptionist, a sofa arranged in front of holo-projection gear, and a sheathed AI One on security which did not come out of its closet for Otto's visit. There was a conference room out back and not much else. All the important workings of their agency were in New London. Richards & Klein Inc., Freelance Security Consultants had number of installations like the LA office around the globe. In the relative peace of the northern hemisphere they were proper offices. In the most dangerous of places they were little more than hidden weapons caches with a secure Gridpipe and a couple of heavy-duty combat sheaths for Richards.

The extra business such places generated was useful, but the main function of the offices were their attached garages. In LA, the stores were contained in a single large foamcrete room, where there were a variety of neatly racked weapons, lockers of equipment and bodies for Richards. An airbike and a groundcar were parked in the middle on hydraulic rams. Keeping all this stuff licensed would have been time consuming for a human, but paperwork was Richards' job, and it took him seconds. Otto got to choose the weapons. It was a good arrangement.

Otto picked out a clutch of EMP grenades, a flechette railgun, a grenade launcher, one of his favoured Hechler caseless 9mm pistols, a bunch of ammunition, a heavy duty nanoBabbage laptop – comparatively slow, but immune to EMP bursts – and a change of clothes. He put it all in the boot of the groundcar and signed it out, then got into the car, and activated the ram. The ceiling opened. The ram elevated him into the bottom of a multi-storey carpark of great vintage, a relic of oil-age LA, complete with a preserved nodding donkey pump with a plaque above it. The ram locked into place, and Otto drove out onto Wilshire and set off toward Valdaire's house, finding a small duplex hidden amid thousands of others. Nothing showy, but the neighbourhood was a relatively good one, away from the refugee camps and gang wars of the south.

Letitia Jones was the name of Valdaire's flatmate, and she knew very little. Otto could tell from the moment she opened the door and began to complain about being interviewed three times by the cops. He watched her closely, but his near-I could find no evidence of untruth either in her thermal facial signature or vocal patterns.

The flatshare was a typical odd couple set-up of the kind the dippies loved. Letitia hated Valdaire, and the feeling was probably mutual, only validating Otto's low opinion of AI-driven social engineering. Valdaire was focussed, intense, and obsessed about her fitness, Jones told Otto, though Otto discounted that last part. Letitia was the kind of big that thinks anyone who'd contemplate walking all the way over the room to pick up a twinkie is "obsessed with fitness".

Otto got a picture of a career woman whose only concessions to frivolity were her dancing and her near-I life-companion.

These were relatively common near-I toys, incepted at the birth of a child, designed to grow alongside them as pet, confidante and playmate. A lot of kids tired of them by the time they hit their tweens. That Valdaire still had hers did not surprise Otto, it all tallied with her psych and gene profiles. Driven people find it hard to make human connections.

Otto could have learnt all of this from Grid, or he could have gone to LA virtually and never left the Londons. But there was no substitute for being in the scene. Digital intermediaries lessened the immediacy. Otto was old fashioned that way.

He took the skypass over Long Beach lagoon then north to UCLA's AI campus, a twenty-storey, quake-proof, green needle. It looked out over the tawny city, the glint of the sea a promise in the distance.

By the time he entered the university it was late in the day. Archimedes had been forewarned, and it was polite but refused to speak to him on the subject of Valdaire or Qifang, pointing out that Otto's euro-issue AllPass would not lift the VIPA gagging order, and denied him access to the lab. Good day. The usual fob-off.

But as he was leaving, the man at the front called him over. Otto was surprised they had a human manning the reception of an AI-faculty, but they did.

"Psst," he said. He actually said that. He was unenhanced, fat and lonely looking.

"Yes?" Otto said. He approached the man. He was not much more than a boy, with a scraggly, pubic-looking beard. His name badge read "Guillermo." He had lifelong virgin stamped all over him.

The boy held out a piece of paper. Otto read it.

"Meet me outside," it read. So Otto did, choosing a space under the trees away from the building. He waited. Five minutes later, Guillermo came out.

"You looking for Vera Valdaire?" Guillermo said.

"Veronique Valdaire," Otto corrected.

The boy smiled nervously. "Yeah, Veronique. It's our joke," he said. "I call her Vera. For fun. You know, we're friends. Are you police?"

"Kind of."

"VIPA?"

"No," said Otto.

Guillermo looked a little relieved. "Did Archimedes tell you anything?" He peered about nervously. It was probable that the Six could hear every word Guillermo said, even out there.

"What do you think?" said Otto.

Guillermo was sweating with nerves. "Look, I shouldn't say anything, but I kind of like her, you know?" He flushed, and his face went blotchy. "She's hot, and cute, and clever and I hope she's OK..." he gabbled.

"Slow down," said Otto. "Breathe."

Guillermo swallowed. "OK. OK. The VIPA were here the day she went missing, and those guys don't fuck around. They didn't have an appointment. I let them in, rang up to tell her, and five minutes later, all hell's breaking loose."

"Wait, they came before she disappeared?"

"Hell yeah, that's why she went. I think, anyway."

"Right," said Otto. That was interesting. "Do you have names for the agents. Maybe I could look into it?"

"Santiago Chures," said Guillermo quickly, as if the name was waiting to leap out of his mouth. "He was foreign. I mean, he was Latino, like me, but from the south, you know? Not an American. SudAm."

"Right," said Otto.

"Maybe it was something to do with the professor?" Guillermo offered.

"Maybe," said Otto.

"He was a nice man," said Guillermo, then laughed awkwardly. "Well, I think I pissed him off, he was always real ornery with me, but you could tell he was nice. I'm sorry he's dead."

"That's it?"

Guillermo shook his head. He looked pathetically eager to help.

"There was an alarm, a theft alarm, after the VIPA came. We have all kinds of alarms here. I think Vera took something."

"Do you have any idea what that might have been?"

"Not really, but I know they have v-jacks up in the lab, and the alarm was a high-alert one." He glanced over the perfectly manicured lawn at the AI faculty. Mirrored windows look out from the plant-covered walls like accusing eyes. "Look, I got to go, I get two five minute breaks a day. Archimedes will terminate my contract if he can prove I was speaking to you."

Otto nodded. "He is an ass, yes?"

Guillermo grinned. "You betcha."

"Thanks," Otto said, and went back to the car. There he put in a secure call to England. The new girl, Genie, answered.

"Hiya, Otto!" she said. Fed through his mentaug, the miniature Genie appeared to hover over his dashboard. She was wearing a baggy pullover and yoga pants.

"Get me Richards," said Otto.

"Sure thing," she said with a wink. She was picking up bad habits from Richards, he thought. "Putting you through." She faded from view.

Richards inflicted an augmented reality vision on Otto. Velvet curtains rose to the skirl of a Wurlitzer played by a manic homunculus at the bottom of his visual field. A grey screen was revealed. Large numbers counted down, and then Otto was looking at Richards sitting in his office, in glorious two dimensional monochrome.

"Hey," Richards said. He was dressed ridiculously, with braces and baggy trousers, his hat pushed high back on his forehead. He was speaking in a cod early 20th century American accent delivered by scratchy mono-channel soundtrack. "Here's looking at you kid." Dramatic music swelled.

Otto sighed.

"I got your pictures." Richards said it "pickchewers", and pointed a cigarette at a scatter of paper on the desk. "Looks like Qifang was carving some kinda key."

"For what?"

"Secure locker, maybe. I've got a bunch of tailored near-I working on it. I'll know soon for sure."

"The kid on the desk said something was stolen," said Otto. "Maybe a v-jack."

"Hmm," said Richards. "They's got a couple there. Can you check?"

"There is an information lockdown by the VIPA. I don't know for sure."

"I ain't no genius, but we have to assume she's gone into the Realities."

"Have you had any luck contacting the VIPA?" asked Otto.

"No," said Richards.

"Then we can't assume anything. A big inter-agency fight is about to happen, I think. They are not speaking to the police either. The VIPA are hiding something."

"That so?" said the black and white Richards.

"Yes," said Otto. "Maybe Valdaire and Qifang hatched some plot together and came under the scrutiny of the VIPA. If that is so, it would have to be serious for the agency not to acknowledge their own investigation of it."

"You got a another theory? Shoot."

"Qifang and his assistant stumbled onto something, and the VIPA wanted to cover it up."

"Both could be true, kid," said Richards, which annoyed Otto, who was thirty years older than his partner.

"We need to find Valdaire, and her life companion. Chloe is the key to that," said Otto. "She can be tracked."

"Hey hey, big guy!" Richards said. "Great minds think alike, you're the lizard's gizzards my man."

"It will not be easy. Valdaire was a skilled InfoWar operative. She's still on the reserves list, a lot of her record is classified. That means she's good. She'll have covered her tracks."

"Sure, sure, big guy, OK, OK, jeez, calm down. Difficult, but possible. Let's get started now, shall we?" Otto's adjutant informed him that a million fragments of Richards configured as hunter-seekers had hooked into his mentaug. They put noses down and dispersed onto the Grid, tracking Valdaire's tortuous digital trail. In return, Otto uploaded edited highlights of his trip to the Five. Richards could have taken and processed all Otto's experiences in moments, but Otto didn't like Richards to see his every move. It was creepy.

"Thanks a bunch for yours, kiddo," said Richards. "You hoof it after the broad, while my guys do the paperwork. Me, I'm off to Hong Kong, see Tony Choi."

"Choi," said Otto. "Him again, how's he connected?"

"While you were on the stratoliner, I went to see Lincolnshire Flats. The combat frame for the android heiress was traced back to Choi's company."

"Our last meeting brought him a lot of trouble."

"Choi'll sing like a canary, don't you worry."

"And you can find Chloe as well?"

"You know it doesn't work like that. My fragments will put you on the right track, but you're going to have to do the last part yourself," said Richards, in his infuriating mid-modern American English.

"Is there no other way?" asked Otto irritably.

"Nope." Richards smiled, and raised his hat. A little something dropped into Otto's inbox. "You'll be having weird dreams for a few weeks after using this baby, but it will allow you to see. If you're close enough to Chloe physically, you should be able to find it, so get yourself close as you can, and plug in. Remember, be careful, it's a jungle out there!"

The curtains swung shut, and the cinema vanished.

"Great," said Otto. "Genie," he said. She reappeared on the car's dashboard.

"Yes ,Otto?" she said.

"I'll be off the Grid for a while. The VIPA are looking for Valdaire. I can't rule out that whoever sent the heiress after the Qifangs aren't looking for her as well. Both of them will probably follow me. I've deactivated my MT, it is a risk after Tufa. If you need me, contact me the usual way. Yes?"

"Sure thing, Otto."

"And keep tabs on the investigation into the real heiress's disappearance. See if EuPol turn up anything we can use."

"On it," said Genie, and disappeared, leaving a trace of perfume in Otto's olfactory centre.

"Can't tell what is real or not any more," he said sourly.

He left the UCLA campus, went to eat, and considered his next move. Whatever happened, he was going to end up with a colossal migraine.

CHAPTER TWENTY

The Great Firewall

The Great Firewall was one of the wonders of the Grid, and the Grid was not short on those. The People's Dynasty had gone to a lot of trouble with the way the Wall looked, investing time, money, and processing power to create a feast of qualia.

The artistic director of the project had taken the "fire" and "wall" parts literally, crafting a thousand-metre high rampart of flame, with heavy towers set into it every two nominal kilometres. Pennants of smoke snapped above the battlements, inscribed with patriotic slogans in all the world's living languages, and a few of the more prominent dead ones besides. Dragons flew the skies, each whiskered face hiding powerful phage programmes, primed to swoop down and sever the connections of any high-class AI who got too close to the wall. AI like Richards.

The Chinese did not like AI.

The parapet was patrolled by towering gods clad in bronze. Cannon mouths like railway tunnels gaped from gunloops halfway up the wall.

There was only one gate, tall as a hill and bound in iron, large enough, were it in the Real, to allow one of the Mediterranean floating fortresses through without scraping the sides. It never opened.

The digital borders of the People's Dynasty had been closed for twenty five years. Bringing data over ten megabytes in any format into the country was a criminal offence, punishable by hard labour in Sinosiberia, or worse. All social media channels were banned. If you wanted to speak to someone in China, it was easiest to send a letter. On paper. By mule. And the People's Dynasty millions-strong secret police would still read it anyway.

Perhaps it was understandable. The country had been devastated during the Five crisis, "The Reign of the Ghost Emperor", they called it. There had been pogroms afterwards. No one knew if the Chinese had AIs of their own any more. If machines like Richards existed on the other side, they kept themselves to themselves.

But the wall, for all the special effects and deadly attack bots, was simply a set of protocols. Nothing was perfect, protocols could be broken, and Richards knew a way in.

First, Richards assembled a sensing presence outside the wall, piece by piece, over the course of several hours, the fastest he could do so without alerting the People's Dynasty, who watched its borders vigilantly. Richards disguised the bits as tourists, for hundreds of thousands visited the Wall every day. Every hour another piece of himself showed up hidden within a human avatar with a stolen identity. He rather thought he constructed a believable bunch of gormless gawkers. There was even a virtual tour guide, through whom Richards gave a particularly dull speech to himself. He was proud of that touch.

As each of the tourists arrived, Richards had them go off and enjoy some of the many distractions nearby. Running two dozen complex simulations at once was taxing even for him, and the tourists were acting a little strangely as a result. He assured himself that no one would notice, because humans behaved strangely all the time.

Virtual real estate was at a premium. Grid artists had sculpted a landscape to front the Wall that was as beautiful as it was weird. Virtual windows opened from people's homes in the Real onto the view. Virtual offices sat by virtual brooks. Virtual towns dreamt in the Wall's flickering virtual shadow.

Once he'd gathered his parts together in a group, Richards swam back and forth in the air, logging thousands of impressions of the underlying Grid structure until he found what he was looking for. Under a meadow populated by giant rabbits and looked upon by Grid interfaced living rooms, he snagged an illegal carrier signal sending out Chinese films into the wider world in exchange for Bollywood's latest. Why kids risked their lives swapping movies like this baffled Richards. China was a stickler for copyright.

He directed his tour group to wander amid the rugs and mega-lagomorphs, and set to work.

The connection was a tightbeam carrier signal bounced off a commsat by some budding young thing. Hidden in verbal telecoms traffic, a number of the latest hit holos were being quietly transferred off a Swiss paysite onto the personal computer of – Richards checked the username – "Northern Bandit", disguised as a dull conversation between a nagging mother and a worn-out émigré daughter. Richards tested it for stability, then insinuated a presence into the datastream. Northern Bandit was going to be very upset to discover *Mulan XVI* was an empty file. It had been quite the hit. A heady, slippery rush followed, and Richards was through to the altogether more boring Chinese interior.

Inside China's virtual borders, Richards checked the tightbeam again. He slowed the data transfer down to give himself some extra time, but not so much as to arouse Northern Bandit's suspicion, only enough to mimic the delays you got on the Grid at times of high traffic when you were transferring illegal files. He reckoned he would have forty-five minutes.

Richards split again like a cheese string to transfer the various pieces of himself across country's cyberspace, masquerading as various search requests. As he was running in real time, there was bound to be some data dropout, but it was the only way to be safe. If the Chinese got a lock onto to his sensing presence they could force a secure pipe back to his base unit and that would lead to all sorts of bother.

Some of the things the teeming citizens of China were searching for made his eyebrows rise. Most of it was to do with food.

After a few minutes groping about with the frayed end of his sensing presence, Richards found his way into Tower 14, Hong Kong, where Tony Choi's company had its base of operations. A couple more prods, and he found a dormant sheath. He reintegrated the sensing presence to a point where he could operate without annoying lag, and let the rest of himself flap in the currents of data.

Camera eyes opened, he looked down at bright red plastic hands. Left and right were three ranks of identical machines. All were empty, unridden, their hardware capable of supporting only the feeblest of independent near-I. Some sort of android dealership, he saw. After hours.

He was in China.

The arcos of Hong Kong extended far into Kowloon bay, and the sea between was them a maze of canals and lagoons supporting kelp farms, ports, leisure facilities and artificial marine ecosystems. There'd been shanty towns down there once, after the first ice sheet tip, but those days were gone. The poor had been relocated to the arcologies, the Sinosiberian territories and the re-greening projects on the mainland. It was very clean, and very green. The Chinese were trying to live by the principles of the Tao again, as it was deemed what had worked quite well for three thousand years should perhaps be re-employed. The People's Dynasty government preferred it if you didn't bring up the last century and a half of industrial excess. They were so ashamed of it they shot you if you did.

Choi was a rich man in a tower full of rich men. He lived and worked in the penthouse areas, three floors down from the summit. The very top was populated by giant servers where the rich carried on enjoying life after they were dead. Richards arrived near the bottom, and so had some way to go.

He walked through crowded arcades and parks, past temples grown from gengineered trees. Everyone was surrounded by a

haze of expensive anti-viral nanites, because the Christmas Flu
was still running strong in Hong Kong. No one paid the android a
second glance as he plodded his way on, which was good, because
it was slow and weak. The whole place felt heavy to Richards,
human-managed data systems were always so oppressive. His
route went up stairs and elevators, passed spun diamond windows
as large as lakes and sculpted residential districts blended with
terraced gardens and microhabitats, where water gurgled from one
carp pond to another. Where necessary, his way was opened by a
People's Dynasty AllPass equivalent he'd stolen four years ago. It
was bizarre stuff, sometimes it behaved as if it were as aware as
near-I, and spat invective at him in some odd machine dialect he
barely understood. But it was thoroughly cracked, and the access
codes it provided hadn't failed him yet. Near his destination, he
used it to break a maintenance seal and ascended a staple-rung
ladder up a service duct that went straight to Choi's palace.

Once inside the shaft, he cracked Choi's central system, and
inserted purchase details, a delivery date, and so forth for his
stolen android sheath. He was now part of the staff. He peeked
into Choi's diary. Although it was late, it was only an hour after
his weekly board meeting. The man never stopped working, but
as Richards had expected, Choi was currently alone. Richards
then constructed a shell copy of Tower 14's central systems and
set it running around the real thing. Anyone looking in would
see nothing. Anyone trying to get at Richards would waste time
breaking the shell first. Hopefully.

He climbed into the palace via another hatch, shut it, then
convinced security it had never been opened. He felt a little woozy.
Running all the bypasses and the decoy shell was hard work.

Richards went into the kitchens, sourced an input, and
presented a fake order for tea. One of the staff handed him a tray.
As he left, the people there laughingly wondered who'd bought
such a cheap piece of shit to serve Tony Choi, and how long they'd
keep their job.

The guards at Choi's teak double doors did not pay him any

attention as he stopped and waited to be let in. He was just a drone going about his business.

The doors slid open.

Richards stepped into Choi's office with eleven minutes to spare.

Choi looked up from an unfinished watercolour of a Chinese landscape in a Western style. He was indefinably aged and sleek, well-groomed in an understated though obviously expensive mode. He looked like a million other People's businessmen and 'crats, except that there was an otherness to him, like he didn't quite fit. There was a touch of Europe to his features. Past cartographies were etched upon his soul.

He looked up from his painting, and frowned.

"I ordered no tea," he said.

"Hello, Tony," said Richards, setting the tray down. "How are you doing?"

CHAPTER TWENTY-ONE

Monkey puzzle

Time and effort led Tarquinius out of the swamp and to the foot of the hill. Everything about it was gargantuan, a five-hundred-metre high dome of polished rock, the dimples in it twenty metres across. The branches of the monkey puzzle tree hanging over the edge were the size of cargo ships.

"It will be a task to climb this," said Jagadith.

"A task for me, you mean," grumbled Tarquinius.

"Indeed," said Jag.

"You had better remain here. I will let down a rope when I attain the summit."

Jag slid off the mount's back and held a hand up to the anthropologist.

"I am not incapable," she said.

"As you wish," he dropped his hand. He disliked dealing with educated women. He sighed in a way calculated to let her know this. She slid off the lion's back.

"Can we attempt the expulsion now?" said Tarquinius.

Veronique wasn't rising to the bait. "How are you going to climb that?" she said. "It's like glass."

"Indeed it is, madam divinity." Tarquinius stood up on his hind legs, and pressed the soft metal pads of his paws against the stone. Claws popped from their sockets, long and gleaming as knives.

"Number threes should suffice for the task at hand," he said. There was a series of clicks, and his claws turned to one side and pulled back into his feet. A new series came forth that were threaded like drills. "This will take a while, Jag. Let me take you up thirty or forty feet, and you may rest in one of these dimples out of harm's way."

"I am not keen on wasting time, dear friend, but so be it."

Tarquinius's claws began to spin. He held them for a moment above the rock's smooth surface, flexed his stubby digits, then thrust the drills into the rock. There was a whine, sparks flew, and Tarquinius's claws sank smoothly into the stone. He then placed his second forepaw higher than the first, pushing his nails deep in, then hauled his back feet off the ground. In this way he climbed. When he reached the first of the dimples he lifted his tail and a cable dropped down. Jag put his foot into a loop at the bottom, and bade Veronique do likewise. When they were secure, the rope was pulled smoothly up by a winch inside the lion. As soon as they were parallel to the dimple, Jag drew his sword. It flared bright as he turned it up to its maximum power setting, and he deftly sliced out a chunk of the dimple, creating a narrow ledge that he and Veronique might sit upon. He let it cool while he and Veronique swung over nothing from the rope.

Jag tested the ledge, judged it safe, helped Veronique over, and they sat. Tarquinius retracted the rope and reassumed his ascent.

"Will he be long?" asked Veronique.

"The ascent is a long and hard one, most assuredly," affirmed the paladin. "But worry not, Tarquinius is an excellent climber."

"So what do we do?" she said.

"We rest," he said.

Several hours passed. Veronique looked out at the stinking vista before her. The knight spent much of the time deep in a trance. Veronique was astounded when she realised he was floating in the air. It gave her the uneasy feeling that reality here was spongy, and that it might at any moment warp into something new, with her not necessarily a part of it. She looked away. When alert the paladin was little inclined to talk to her, and she was left to her own thoughts.

None of this made sense. The paladins believed Qifang was responsible for the changes being wrought on Reality 36. She hadn't known what to expect when she arrived, but that Qifang hadn't been there when she entered the realm troubled her.

Qifang was the man who had argued passionately for the rights of life, whatever form it took: digital, hybrid, AI, cyborg, animal or other. She remembered the first time she'd seen him, at a Neukind flash rally in Toronto. He'd been small, distant, a man tiny on the stage of the run down Air Canada Centre. She'd taken Chloe to show her. Veronique had never agreed with machine slavery.

AIs were not tools, Qifang had said, they were not playthings for man to do with as he chose. Through his creations, mankind had the collective responsibilities of new parents. The days when desperate adults had a dozen children to help them make their way economically in the world were long gone, he argued. Why were machines any different?

"We would never send a flesh and blood child up a chimney, we shudder when we think of the children of the Victorian era picking up threads in the dark spaces beneath unshielded machinery. We balk at the thought of 20th-century sweatshops. Why treat the Neukind any different? Why should we slaughter them for sport? Force them to forever serve us? Send them alone to the ends of the universe? We are their progenitors. They may well outlive us. Surely, our surest form of immortality is for those who come after us to remember us fondly? Let not the human race be consigned to the fairy tales of the future, to become the ogres of tomorrow. Let us be good to our new children that they may pay their respects to us when we are no longer here."

His words were powerful. The cataclysm of the ice sheet tips were receding into memory, wars were fizzling out as cold war took its place. The temperature was at last beginning to stabilise.

The waves of plague that had rocked the planet were falling off. The world was a place where people could feel comfortable in their outrage at their ancestors, and think about putting things right.

Zhang Qifang had won a lot of supporters. He was not alone in seeing the Neukind as the future.

He said to her, later, when they had got to know each other, "Mankind has begun to save the planet from his mistakes, but it might already be too late to save itself."

She'd shared his pessimism, at least some of the time.

When she left the army she joined Qifang's followers on his last great crusade – liberating the 36 Realities of the RealWorld corporation. When the games had been running, they had appalled her; whole civilisations conjured into existence so humans could go and let out its old beasts. Finally, the NUN's declaration had gone out – the Realities were immoral and a social hazard. The doors were closed. That was that. The digital inhabitants of the 36 Realities had been the last of the Neukind to be granted rights. It had been a difficult victory, but sentient beings should not be created only to be killed for sport. Peace for Orcs, Rights for Elves. It sounded stupid, when Jaffy said it that way, but he was deadly serious.

She had never had the money or the inclination to enter the Realities when they were operational. When she joined Qifang's team to study them, she'd of course been within, but only as a phantom, able to look, not touch. Being in it fully, the world was so much more vivid. She found it hard to believe that she was really elsewhere, in a chair in a cabin in the woods. And she was improved there. She held up her hand. It was better than real, stronger, cleaner of line and free of blemishes, an idealised version. It was not hard to see now how people had become addicted.

She hugged her knees and looked across to the jungle. Maybe she'd always wanted this. Perhaps she'd followed Qifang for the wrong reasons.

Jag was lost in some inner world of his own. The act of creation begat creation. It was impossible to create only one world. Every thinking mind harboured its own reality, and their imaginations led on to the eventual creation of more worlds in an endless cycle. The Realities were a new series of universes, she thought, real as the Real. Being in them made that philosophy oddly terrifying.

A rope dropped down from above, making her jump.

Jagadith opened his eyes.

"Aha! It appears Tarquinius has reached the summit. If you please, goddess, grasp the stirrup this time."

The rope dragged them to the top, she and Jag holding the loop and walking up the smooth rock with their feet.

At the top, they were confronted with the overwhelming scale of the tree. Indeed, it was so vast it was difficult to perceive it as a tree. Giddy shifts of perspective turned its scaly leaves into a mountain range in a variety of sinister greens, then to a dragon, breathing with the wind.

"This is anomalous," roared Tarquinius. "Anomalous!"

Jag turned round and gave Veronique a stern look. "Do you see now? This is wholesale change. I fear your professor has turned mad. This has gone beyond a mere case of expulsion." He grasped the hilt of his sword. "We may have to kill him."

CHAPTER TWENTY-TWO

Tony Choi

"Richards, is that you? What the devil are you doing here?" Choi's eyes bulged so much Richards almost laughed, for Choi was a gentlemen of the utmost poise. A drop of paint fell from his brush onto his painting.

"I thought you'd never guess it was me," said Richards, flipping his hands out in a magician's flourish.

"Even in that thing your infuriating smugness is obvious," Choi regained his composure, his face reverting to the bland expression he habitually wore. His English was perfect and unmoderated by translators. Once upon a time, it had been fashionable for men with Eurasian ancestry to be educated in British public schools. Once. He was a relic. "No one I know is crazy enough to come in here unannounced, except you."

"Or clever enough to pull it off," said Richards.

Choi's eyes narrowed. "What do you want here?"

"Only information," said Richards, "about these machines." He ran a holo from the android's built-in entertainment system showing the fight on the boat. The system was low-grade, the picture grainy. "Who built them?"

"What do I care?" Choi tutted, and sponged off the paint from his painting. He moved with a slow deliberation. "You disrespect me, arriving unannounced. More pertinently, you anger the

Guoanbu, coming and going in through the Firewall as if the sovereign cyberspace of China were a field at the end of your garden, and you have a hole in your hedge."

"In a manner of speaking, it is and I have," said Richards. "Come on, aren't you just the tiniest bit interested? These are near-human sheaths! Nothing like that is supposed to be out there. Choi, they've bridged the valley. The brains Tony, you need to see the brains." Richards projected specifications for the devices' processing units. That got Tony's interest a little, though he pretended otherwise.

"Be wary. The Guoanbu have been waiting for an incursion like this. They will be coming. Right now. You have endangered us both. They will lock you down. You know that, of course, because you are so very intelligent." He stood, lifting the paper, and stalked around his desk to hang it up to dry against a light panel, where he stood regarding it critically. "You have ruined my picture."

"Sorry. Tell me who makes this combat chassis and I'll go away."

"I must disappoint you."

"Are you telling me, Tony Choi, that you don't know?"

"Leave." The man put one hand over the other, the lower hand was gripping his paintbrush hard.

"Tony, this chassis has the mark of one of your manufactories upon it." Richards displayed the relevant image. "A little careless, wouldn't you say?"

"I do not sell illegally, Richards. It is nothing to do with me."

"Come on Tony, look at the brains!" Richards paced round the room, causing the holos the android projected to jump over the walls like acrobats. Art hung from much of the panelling, stood on pedestals, stared out from alcoves, a mix of eastern and western, a rich man's knick-knacks; worth enough to buy a nation, tasteless fripperies for all that.

On one was a large, gold good-luck cat, arm mechanically waving. Who the hell has a solid gold good-luck cat other than Tony Choi, thought Richards

"Look, you know everything there is to know about new tech.

If someone's building it, you're either making it or selling it. Who's been working on these machines?"

"I said I don't know."

"You can't lie to a Five, Tony, not when you're as bad a liar as you are. And you owe me for the Taipei Freeport bust. If that gets out, I wonder how the interior ministry would look on it?" Another holo played alongside the looping footage from the boat and morgue, pulled up from Richard's imagination, Choi in custody, surrounded by uniformed men and big sticks. What they were doing to him was not nice. "I believe smuggling narcotics up the space elevator is illegal. But I have a somewhat lurid fancy. Perhaps we should ask a policeman?" The sheath's cheap joints crunched as Richards leaned on the wall by the drying painting.

Choi's face remained impassive.

Richards pulled up the image of the logo he'd seen at the Coroner's again: Choi Industries' stamp. "You sold this chassis."

Choi exhaled loudly, most of his anger seemed to go with it. "Richards, I sell many such frames." Choi walked back to his desk, picked up a cloth folded by his paints, and wiped his fingers. A smear of blue stained the white, to match that on his perfectly manicured hands. Small hands, rounded with fat, clogged with garish rings, but powerful in their way. "Thousands a year; I have no way of knowing who might purchase them secondhand, or through a front company. That is what you are going to ask me."

"Right."

Choi shook his head. "You have much nerve, coming here, implying that you will blackmail me. I paid you well for Taipei, even when it did not go well for me. You know what I am, Richards. I have been most useful to you in the past. It is unprofessional to complain."

"Needs must."

Choi frowned, shook his head and turned to the holos Richards was playing. "That is Zhang Qifang, is it not? The man, the machine, in the holovideo?"

"Yes."

"And these you show me, they are machines, you say? Not clones, or flesh altered doubles?"

"That's right. The Qifang clones are ground-up copies of the professor, the brain aside. The other one was constructed the same way but around this combat chassis instead of with a regular skeleton, which you make, apparently."

"I assume Zhang Qifang is dead, then."

"You assume correctly. I am investigating his murders."

"Murders?"

"Three of them, possibly four."

"You should have said first." Choi saddened, as if he had long been expecting the news, "I have heard nothing."

"It's being kept quiet, some of the more, uh, militant elements among my brethren are going to take it badly."

"He was a brilliant man." Choi looked at the teapot Richards had delivered. After a moment he set down the cloth, poured himself a cup of tea and raised it. "To one of the great minds of our time."

"If you respect him that much, you'll help me out."

"Very well," Choi said resignedly.

Encouraged, Richards went on. "This technology, the brains, they are almost good enough to support a human level-intelligence. That's supposed to be years away, this says otherwise. I need to know who is a decade early."

Choi looked up into Richards' visual receptors, small gems of glass set close together in the android's carbon-weave face.

"I will tell you what I know, but it is not much."

"I would welcome any information."

"You will owe me," said Choi. "Four days of your time."

"Three," said Richards, Northern Bandit's download was coming near to completion down. Five minutes remaining.

"Very well. Three days. I will hold you to it."

"I am sure you will. Now talk."

Choi set his cup down. "I am not sure. I have heard... reports. Nothing concrete, nothing certain. There's some talk coming out of the containment facilities in Nevada, the Reality House, the place they moved the RealWorld hardware to when the NUN shut them down."

"And?"

"They have several high level AIs working full time as futurists, using the spare capacity of the Realities' servers freed up by the destruction of four of the realms for mathematical prognostication."

"Yeah, k52 is leading them. It's common knowledge among us."

"You will also know then that it's all supposed to be theoretical. This kind of autonomous emulant is one of the areas they have been investigating." He nodded toward the holo. "Imagining, is perhaps the more appropriate word, plotting possible future developments, examining potential new tech, providing probabilities to feed out to the entertainment industry, better to accelerate k52's 'Fiction Effect' by providing inspiration for what is readily achievable. Tier two projects like this. These machines match some of the descriptions and file blueprints I have, ah," he shrugged, as if to shrug off any implication of impropriety, "acquired. They were incomplete, unusable. No one could have constructed the things you have shown me from the information I have."

"Someone has," said Richards. "The Reality House is administered by the VIPA. Why would they be interested in investigating the creation of something that would let people like me blend in? They like us nice and visible."

Choi watched the holos of Richards' encounters with the androids for a few moments. "These sheaths are hardly perfect, one could argue."

"It's the brains, remember. That's where the innovation is. The bodies are nice work but within current capabilities. Why would the VIPA sanction their building? It makes less sense if they're imperfect, they're even more likely to get caught out."

"Listen to what is said, Richards. To build them is not why they investigate, they investigate such things to anticipate their development."

"And why are they trying to kill each other?"

Choi raised his eyebrows in query.

"Long story."

"Things change so quickly, it is as if the world is being pulled out from under our feet every second day," said Choi.

"Interesting times, eh?"

Choi narrowed his eyes. "I do not bandy cliché, Richards. I also do not believe I have told you anything that you have not already discerned for yourself."

"Right, OK, thanks," said Richards. "This destruct mechanism." Richards brought up technical detail.

"The weaving is fine, is it not? A good product." Choi leaned in closer. "My better looms will give you such a finish. I see little else unusual about these constructs other than these artificial brains. This third one is otherwise a standard combat endoskeletons. This is not neo-diamond or any of the other harder artificial matrices. Tough, but unremarkable, not particularly strong."

"An infiltration unit."

"It is supposed to pass muster as human skeletal tissue, yes. We have several tens of thousands in the people's liberation army, many of which I manufactured." He shrugged.

"The self-destruct item," said Richards, pressing his point. Three minutes.

"Again, it is a standard stock item; unusual, but by no means unique. It's relatively new. It's not been altered from the factory model, if that is what you are asking me. The acid only works on the looser lattices, it won't damage diamond weave, it is too tough."

"But…?"

Choi clucked his tongue. "It is strange to see such unusually advanced biotechnology married to something like this, that is all. As utile as my product is, I would expect…"

Richards finished his sentence. "That they would have made more of an effort with the internals? Diamond weave for protection, or proper grown bone if they wanted foolproof undetectability."

Choi blinked his long, slow blink. "It is remarkable. Off the shelf combat droid skeleton with this organic shell. The shell is good work, but also not that remarkable, but the brain, so far in advance of the rest... It is strange."

Richards searched Tony's face for the lies. The little man held his gaze, his own expression flat and unreadable. Richards could see no evidence of untruthfulness on the surface. He regretted grabbing such a poor sheath. He felt cheap, cheap in front of Tony Choi.

"I am disappointed, Tony, I thought if anyone would know of a suspiciously advanced new unit primed for assassination it would an amoral criminal like you."

Choi snorted. "I am flattered, but I am only a merchant. I make a little, and I buy and I sell what is available to be bought and to be sold... Perhaps if you would allow me to check my databases, I may be able to track the transaction. It will take a minute, if the client was a special one, or the chassis changed hands, perhaps longer, if at all," he warned. "I will at least try." He moved over to a pedestal holding a 14th century vase. It rotated as he approached to reveal a flat, glass-topped workstation, fully manual. Choi didn't trust anyone with his secrets, numbers or meat. It was probably connected to the Grid via a proxy. Somewhere, thought Richards, is a little old lady scratching her head over her data charges. "The catalytic acid destruct system should make it easier to track down, that is an optional upgrade. Please, take a seat."

"I'll stay leaning, this thing doesn't do sitting."

"Lean then."

"Next time I'm going more upmarket, I was in something of a hurry." Richards had a thought. "Hey you're not stalling for time, are you, Choi? You're not trying to sell me out here, are you?"

"Why would I do that?" Choi said mildly, tapping at the workstation, pinching documents that interested him into the air, where they hung as holograms. "Would you mind?" he said, indicating the still active holo.

"Yeah, sure." Richards remoted the data over to Choi's machine. Choi's fingers worked faster.

"I know the value of things," Choi said, "You are much more

valuable to me at liberty than you are in the care of our glorious Dynasty of the People."

"Good, because I sealed your mainframe off from the Grid. There's a blind copy running as cover. Nothing you've been trying to send to the authorities has made it out."

Choi looked up, mildly insulted. "If I have been trying to contact the authorities."

"If." Richards' borrowed head moved to one side, listening to something Choi could not hear. Damn, he thought. I've been noticed. "So you wouldn't know about the AI snatch squad sat outside your virtual real estate then?"

There were several high-end code breakers in the near-Grid. They swam back and forth, long trails of information connecting them to their handlers, waiting as something big and nasty hammered away at Richards' fake systems copy. Past them, code-breakers left themselves open deliberately, trying to tempt Richards to commit more of himself to attacking them. It was tempting, but that was the idea. He wasn't that naive.

"Of course. Why should I lie? I told you that they were coming. I had hoped we would be done before they arrived. They are getting faster. There is a discrete system here, in this room, fitted by the interior ministry. It bypasses the main Grid, a direct pipe. They were summoned a few moments after you arrived by patterns evident in our conversation," he glanced at the good-luck cat meaningfully.

Not so lucky for me, thought Richards.

"It was not my decision. I said you should not have come."

"You have sold me out."

"If you wish to look at it in that way, that is your prerogative. Non-compliance was... inadvisable. As you say, needs must as the devil drives."

"You said you did not bandy cliché."

Choi shrugged again.

"I'm minded to kick your ass. I could, you know, even in this." Richards steeled himself, the breakers had got through the first

GUY HALEY   221

few layers of his fake system. They were going to notice they were barking up the wrong tree, and start in on the real thing any moment. He was a whisker away from being directly attacked.

"What did you expect? But I have helped you."

"It cost me, as I remember."

"Nevertheless, you have caused me a great deal of inconvenience. It is only because Qifang is involved that I have spoken to you, but in this instance I could argue national honour is at stake. And the news will be of interest to the PDG."

"Why thanks." Choi had done his best, fair enough, but Richards was in no mood to be generous. "You are one shit of a mercenary."

"Merchant," he corrected. "Do not scorn me, I have done you more than one service today. You are valuable to me, Richards, but I am more valuable to myself, I'm sure you understand," he pursed his lips, light from the desk top playing over his face. "We could have arranged a more convenient… a *safer* venue to meet, but that is not your way, and if they catch you, then you must live with it yourself."

"I won't forget this." Richards said it harshly for the benefit of the waving cat. Tony Choi would know he meant it for the PDG, and not for him.

"You were crazy to come here," said Choi.

A dull crump of a concussion charge, and the door blew in. Choi tutted at the damage. He flicked a fragment of antique wood from his sleeve, and turned back to his workstation. The false shell Richards had erected round Choi's systems collapsed under a storm of attack code, vanishing like a mirage to reveal the real item, dumb and panicking like a frightened horse. The angry presences in the Grid outside surged in triumphantly and immediately assailed Richards.

"Richards," said Choi, as idly as a man passing the time at a bus stop.

"What?" Richards shouted, trying to hear his own voice over the rush of hostile numbers was near impossible.

"I have a name. Peter Karlsson. It was he who bought the chassis, from me directly. He took six, actually, personal protection, he said, and the licensing checked out. I am sorry for the delay. Go and speak to him, he should know something. Goodbye, Richards."

Richards grinned inside. Tony always came through. "See you soon, Tony," then, for the cat's benefit: "Fuck Chairman Mao."

Masked troopers bulky with power assist armour stormed into the room. Guns at the ready, they circled Richards' sheath and trained their weapons upon it.

Northern Bandit's download ceased. The connection was cut, the sheath sagged, Richards was gone. There were a lot of people pointing guns at an inert and offensively cheap android, while all around Tower 14, the Grid space of the People's Dynasty of Greater China roiled with fury.

Richards secure-piped himself back to the office in the Wellington Arcology; a little under the speed of light when you took all the trickle and shunt into account, and manifested in his fake office. He rubbed at his neck. Splitting himself left him disoriented. He needed a drink and a think.

But first, work. He attended to the chip fragments from Qifang's basement. Tailored near-Is had been hard at work reassembling the fragments while he was out, and now they were done. The chip was incomplete, but the memory reconstruction suggested Qifang had made a key that mimicked permissions from multiple sources. As the v-jack cases at UCLA needed three signatories for opening, it was pretty obvious what he needed it for. He'd been right, Valdaire had taken the jack, and was almost certainly in the Realities.

Valdaire's trail was harder to crack. He shut his eyes and concentrated on his diffuse parts. Many of the fragments he'd sent out via Otto had been killed off in one way or another, others had turned up nothing. Some had hit home. He tracked her to a hardware store and a stolen aircar, after that, the trail went dead. Valdaire had fabricated a wide-band Grid cheater, a self-replicating machine devil that cyclically employed false IDs and actively screwed with surveillance software. Its was high-end criminal ware turbocharged with pseudo-capsids, doubtless of Valdaire's devising. It was so illegal that he informed Hughie by way of the million-layer EuPol bureaucracy that he had it in his possession.

He didn't trust Hughie not to use it against him if he kept it quiet.

Coding like that took care. He figured there was no way Valdaire could have created it while on the run. Like the programme she'd used to deactivate the Six at UCLA, she must have cooked that up earlier. Was that preparation for the v-jack robbery, or insurance against something untoward happening to her? It was hard to say. Her cheater was slippery as hell, and it murdered the virtualities he constructed to crack it one after another. Frustrated, he persisted.

Version 13,078 gave him a simulation of her blocker that he could render inert. Using it, he traced the residual patterns it left on the Grid, and from that he estimated a number of physical real world locations where it might have been introduced. There was no finding Valdaire, but he wasn't after her. The cheater was to protect Chloe, as Richards would bet she'd not been able to bring herself to kill her life companion.

It was impossible for something like Chloe to sever all her ties with the machine world. The phone was far too small to run all her processes, so she needed some part of herself free floating in Grid space to unfold and think. Sure enough, he found signs of her under the cheater's trail. She had spread herself thin, and was putting out a barrage of false locational information, but triangulating between leads from his own fragments and the grid blocker trail, he narrowed the phone's location down to a corner of Colorado.

"Look at that!" Richards said triumphantly. "If you really didn't want finding, you should have destroyed your phone," he said. "Silly girl." He tagged Chloe with a couple of fragments. Finding her precise location would be down to Otto now, and he had the necessary kit to find it, though he'd moan about using it for ages afterwards. There was no more Richards could do. He left the information in an anonymous info-drop site for Otto to pick up when he checked in.

Both tasks were serious pieces of forensic reconstruction. He was pleased with himself.

"I love it when I'm clever," he said.

Outside, ancient Chicago rained its rain and tooted its antique groundcar horns. He decanted a glass of single malt that had no counterpart in the Real, sat back, dirty shoes on the scuffed leather of his desk, and took a sip of his drink.

"Ah," he said, happily.

Real or not, Richards liked his whisky.

CHAPTER TWENTY-THREE

Colorado

Otto did it the old way, asking place to place.

"Have you seen this woman?" he said, holding out the photo of Valdaire. Frowns, shakes of the head, no recognition in reply. On to the next drugstore, the next truckstop, the next one-street town. He drove over the wrinkles of the Rockies, mountain to desert and back. Snow then sand then snow again. He didn't know how to dress, the climate control of the groundcar struggled. The terrain was too treacherous for aircars, dangerous thermals came off the mountains, and most of the aircraft Otto saw were fixed wings, blimps and quaint rotary copters hurrying against the threat of the weather. The local networks carried crash stories in every county.

He stopped at a charge station tucked into the landscape. Solar cells glinted brash on afternoon slopes out of the valley shade, thick cables curving from pylon to pylon to the cabin-store by the carriageway.

The wheels of the groundcar crunched on forecourt gravel, the whisper of the engine died off, then there was nothing but birdsong and the wind in the trees.

The air was clean, sharp with the morning's rain, old pines and the quick sap of broadleaves. For a moment, he relaxed. Nature calmed him. There was not a machine in sight. Otto rotated his shoulder and grimaced. The pain was insistent. He had his healthtech dull it.

He yawned. He could sleep there. He probably should.

He scooped the photograph off the dashboard, and got out.

"Her, yeah, sure, came in a little while back. Bought a lot of sugar." The attendant was oily, with greasy hair and a greasy beard. He wore a grubby rock t-shirt whose logo, stretched over an ample gut, had stopped working. There were a number of run-down vehicles out back. This guy was a one-man show, he was mechanic and till attendant in one. There were no traces of anyone else. A loner.

"Sugar?"

"Yeah, sugar," said the man slowly, as if Otto were slow of understanding. "You know, for your coffee? And two big bags of salt."

"Are you sure?"

"Salt, like that," he pointed to a row of sacks. "Yes, I'm sure," he said. "Not many people like her come up here. Salt's for the hunters, some like to preserve their kills the old way."

"Quirkies."

"Sorry?"

"Quirkies. Those trying to live pre-industrial lives."

"Right, quirkies, huh? That what you call them in...?"

"Europe."

"Yeah. OK. They're kind of like that, like your quirkies. I sell them that amount, and more; of salt, I mean. But not women like her, not usually. She was a city lady, all right. Say, where're you from?" he smiled. "Europe's a big place."

"I am German."

"And..." a wave round Otto's body.

"I am a cyborg."

"Military, huh?"

"Ex."

"I was service myself, once, long time ago. USNA Army, though we're supposed to call it the peace corps." The attendant stood a little taller. "But you guys, man. I seen some awesome things but cyborgs rocketing in on jetpacks? That beats it all."

"We do not use that insertion method in our army," said Otto flatly. The attendant was not to be discouraged.

"Hell, but we're all on the same side. You in Brazil?"

"Yes."

"Hell of a place."

Otto tapped the photograph, the creased paper used the kinetic energy to run through four seconds of footage, Valdaire made up, wineglass in hand, laughing, a happy night out. "Her. Do you know where I can find her?"

"Lot of cabins round here, lots of off the Grid types. There shouldn't be. It's all off limits these days, but there they are." The attendant jutted his chin out the window and hooked his thumbs into his belt. "Hey man, you want to be careful, there's some serious crazies up here. Some of them been waiting for the end of the world for fifty years, their folks a hundred years before them."

Otto nodded. Maybe they wouldn't have to wait long. He was in the mood for a fight. "I can take care of myself."

"Yeah, I suppose so."

"If you were her, where would you go to avoid such encounters?"

The man ran his fingers through his beard. "Let me think… You know, I'm sure she said she was heading out Flagstaff way."

"What lies in the opposite direction?" Otto asked.

"Not much till you hit Phoenix if you head off route 17. Payson and Showlow if you follow 270 to the east through the parks."

"Anything near here? To the west, up in the forest?"

"Nothing. The lake, the falls down there in the valley," he shrugged. "Nothing. Just trees and nature man, the way I like it, y'know?"

Otto did not answer. His lack of warmth was bothering the attendant, and the man's smile faded.

"You're hiding something," Otto stated.

"What?" said the attendant. His cheeks coloured.

"What did she do?"

"Hey man! She came in, she bought stuff, she paid, she left. No biggy."

"Show me your store records," he said.

"Hey, I don't got to show you nothing dude."

"Then try this." Otto presented his AllPass. It wasn't USNA, but nobody messed with the machines.

"A cop," the man muttered, cowed and unfriendly. Otto pulled his files off the local law grid. Dustin Merle, he was called. Dustin had a record, not the first ex-soldier to have run-ins with the law.

Valdaire was not on the store logs. She'd used a false Gridsig, one that would have been changed immediately the moment the transaction had been completed and smothered with false leads. A faint trace, no good, dead end.

Still Otto's near-I adjutant indicated the man was not being truthful: high heartrate, scent off, perspiration up, pupils too big. Not an outright lie, a lie of omission. "What else?" demanded Otto.

The attendant backed away for a moment, looked like he was considering reaching for something, a weapon maybe, then thought better of it. The man's eyes darted to the door. He realised then that he couldn't get out, and blushed deeply.

"Look man, I watched her, OK? Just for a while. I didn't mean no harm by it. She left her car here and went for a walk in the woods, stretching her legs or somesuch. I only watched. No women come up here. Not ever. A guy gets lonely. Thought I might ask her for a date, down at the local dance. She said she liked to dance when she saw the poster there," he pointed past Otto's head. Otto did not move his gaze from the man. "But I ain't got the nerve, city lady like that."

"Where did she go?"

"There's a path here, a local beauty spot, goes down to the falls. It's why I'm here, passing trade, you know? She went there, came back. I didn't watch her the whole time. I didn't mean nothing by it." He looked ashamed.

Otto stared down at the man.

"Thank you." Otto picked up his picture, paid for the car's charge, added some vat-grown jerky and a couple of chocolate bars to his bill. He disliked American candy, it was all sugar, no cocoa in the chocolate, but he needed to eat something, and there was precious little else in the station. These people ate shit. "I am going to the falls. Do not follow me."

Otto thought carefully before he tied himself back into the Grid, but he was pretty damn sure Chloe was there, so he plugged back in and booted up his augmented reality overlay. He swatted a dozen adverts from the air before seeing that the path to the waterfall was signposted clearly on the AR; blinking directionals to a gap in the fence on the far side of the road. He crossed, and found steps, wooden sills packed with earth, hemmed in with split log railings, all well maintained. It was a popular location. Otto walked down the steps, scanning the woods as he went. He was alone but for the birds. The splash of the falls became audible about halfway down. Otto reached the bottom where an oval viewing platform projected over the river. The mountainside was faulted, a knife-mark slash picked out with ferns and mosses growing in the damp air. The river that ran through the gulley was small, a child could have jumped it, but the falls had an impressive drop of fifteen metres or so to a brown-black plunge pool fringed with mossy rocks. The opposite bank was a cliff. Otto doubted Valdaire would have crossed the river to climb that. She'd have tried for somewhere less visible and more accessible. He peered about, didn't spot anything, then turned and retraced his steps. He stopped at one or two likely looking places, his near-I running tracking software, but it had been raining heavily all the previous night, and any genetic trace of Valdaire that might have remained had washed away.

He stopped where the slope levelled off enough to make it

possible to leave the path and go into the woods, and saw the faint trace of a footprint in the mud pointing away from the steps.

Otto grasped the railing, leaned out, oriented so he was looking past the print.

"Here," he said.

He steeled himself, and began to activate Richards' software.

Technically, no AI was allowed to make a copy of itself. Artificial intelligences had been granted the right to life on one condition, that they lived as a unique, single entity, their sole concession to mortality. Such a stricture made it easier to apply the law to AI, as there were no struggles with who was really who. The law had not proven hard to enforce. The higher AIs grid traces were exceptionally obvious, and the agencies like the VIPA constantly scanned the Grid for infringements. No one wanted a repeat of the Five Crisis, the remaining Fives included.

AIs could split themselves into a variety of subsidiary minds, as Richards did to bypass the Great Firewall, but these were lesser things, prone to distraction, and an AI that broke into too many parts stood a good chance of becoming unstable if left divided too long. No sub-mind was supposed to be capable of acting individually, but shoals of interacting sub-minds were a grey area that Richards exploited, bending the rules, he said.

But sometimes Richards not only bent the rules, he broke them.

He had shaved off the merest sliver of himself, small enough to remain unnoticed, bright enough to help. Boxed in by task-specific programming and near-I adjuncts, detached from Richards' information stream, Richards had what tiny thinking part it possessed sleeping in case it got ideas above its station.

Through this small part of Richards, Otto would be able to detect Chloe. To do that he'd have to see the world the way that Richards did. That was going to give Otto the mother of all migraines, if his head didn't burst.

Otto could only risk connecting up like this once or twice, because it was, as Richards had once succinctly put it, dropping the PI act for the moment, "Really dangerous for meat minds to go raw on the Grid."

Otto drew a deep breath. He didn't think he was going to get much closer than he was now.

"*Verdammt*," he said, and activated the software.

The universe exploded out of the back of his head. The AR overlay vanished in a swirl of colour, his near-I adjutant flickered out like a candle in a firestorm, and his perception of the Real was swallowed by a howling maelstrom of information. His mind stretched. He was blind, deaf and dumb, but other, stranger senses unfurled themselves as his awareness spread itself out.

With an effort of will, Otto reeled his mind back in. The Grid was too big and there was not enough of him to embrace even a small part of it, so he pulled his sense of being back into a shape he recognised before he disassociated forever. Ahead, shivering in a haze of knowledge, flashed a pair of ideograms that showed Chloe's location. A vortex of disinformation blurred them, but they were there. Otto struggled forward. There was a thundering in the ether about him, and the scream of numbers. Before his ego shattered into sparks, he pulled the plug.

A cursor blinked. Icons filled a black space. Words followed: *Cyborg unit 977/321-a1. Leutnant Otto Franz Klein. Incept date 13th May 2085. Reboot. Online. Near-I adjutant model 47 'Tiberius'. Reboot. Online. Systems operating at 78% of optimal. Warning, maintenance overdue.*

Otto's native senses returned shortly after. For once he was spared the mentaug's merciless reminiscences. The scent of loam and ferns filled his nostrils. The birds sang. He rolled onto his back, spat soil from his mouth, and sat up and rubbed his scalp, dislodging more earth from his hair. His head reeled with vertigo and hurt badly. His visual systems cycled through the spectrum as they recalibrated themselves. This, very aggressively, did not help his headache.

"Arrrr," he said, which did not help either. He looked past his feet. While he was in the grid, he'd moved into the forest, out of sight of the walkway.

He looked around and found disturbed soil.

He dug.

Quickly, he unearthed a geckolock bag. He unzipped it and pulled out a phone. It was small, slate-grey. Very businesslike in appearance, though a large, animated flower decal on the back with Chloe's name glittering on the petals somewhat undid the effect.

Sentimental, he thought.

He flipped up the lid. The phone remained inactive, both top and lower screens inert, the same grey as the case.

"Wake up, Chloe," he said. "I know you can hear me." He'd been speaking to machines all of his life, yet doing it out there in the woods surrounded by nature felt faintly wrong. "Tell me where I can find Veronique Valdaire."

Chloe said nothing.

CHAPTER TWENTY-FOUR

A clockwork threat

Under the tree, the light of day disappeared into a sinister gloaming that did not diminish. The sun must have gone down by the time Jag, Tarquinius and Veronique finally reached the trunk, but the dim blue remained.

They found themselves looking at a series of stepped, triangular plates of bark, built up like the skin of a world-sized pineapple, with cracks as big as caverns between.

"I don't understand," said Veronique, her voice a hush. "Why a monkey puzzle tree?"

"I believe the good professor is joshing with us, asking that we play Jacks upon his beanstalk," said Jagadith. He too was whispering. The tree intimidated them.

"He is also letting us know we are beneath him, presenting us with a plant to perplex an ape," added Tarquinius, his voice loud and unafraid. "Condescending bastard."

"Did I not mention that I have a doctorate?" said Veronique icily. "Professor Qifang would never have use such a crass visual metaphor."

"I am thinking you may be in for a shock," said Jagadith. "You will find his character much changed. Godhood has a terrible influence upon a man's soul."

"Don't be surprised if he starts maniacally ranting either," added Tarquinius. "They always do that."

"Quite," said Sir Jagadith. "What-ho, what's this?" he said, as a man stepped out from one of the cracks.

He came one freakishly long leg first, foot placed delicately, toes down. A white gloved hand followed, fingers waggling before grasping the edge of the bark, then the other hand, then a face dripping with oleaginous scorn. His body came next, extracting itself from the crack with the slippery rush of a fatal confession.

He was impossibly thin, clad in a frockcoat, shining shoes, white spats, and a striped yellow waistcoat of a kind once favoured by gentlemen's gentlemen. His gloves had three brass buttons upon them that served no real purpose. His hair was plastered to his head with macassar, and parted to reveal a luminous scalp. He had a moustache so thin it appeared painted on. His face actually was painted, bright white, with two rosy spots stamped onto each cheek. His eyes were mad, his capering wild. He had an outrageous French accent to match his appearance.

"*Bonsoir, Chevalier, Monsieur Lyon, et M'selle Veronique.*"

"Sweet lord, he's gone frog," said Tarquinius.

"It is worse than we feared," said Jagadith. He drew his sword. "Stand aside," he said loudly. "We seek entrance to the realm of the god who dares to remake our world."

"Oh, such a pity," the Frenchman cradled his pointed chin in his hand and pulled an apologetic moue. "I do not think that will be possible." He capered a quick flourish, then was suddenly still, his coattails whipping.

"This does not bode well," said Tarquin. "And to think you mocked me for my concern."

"Surely you can deal with him? He's not real, even by your terms," said Veronique.

"But he is, madam goddess," said Jag, turning in the saddle to face her. His face was lit deathly grey by the glow of his sword. "That is a creation of your professor, made by him, like this tree, and the rock and the marsh. He is as real as I and Tarquinius, as real you are."

"Not any old creation either," said Tarquin. "This is a potent golem."

The Frenchman clapped slowly. *"Bon, bon,* very good. I see why I have not been able to deactivate you, Monsieur Paladin. You really are the best, it is true. The legendary maharajah and his lion! Ah, but it is something like from legend! Exquisite." He cleared his throat. "So, bold *guerriers,* you have a choice. You may turn back, and, in due course, we will discuss the nature of your servitude in the professor's new world. Or," he smiled broadly and put one hand up to shield his mouth. *"C'est le mort."*

"Why is Qifang doing this?" said Veronique.

The Frenchman flung his arms out and looked himself up and down. "Why not? A little theatre is an essential part of being a god, *non*?"

"Jag, we cannot let this buffoon delay us," said Tarquinius. "He's just a distraction."

Jagadith shrugged. "Please, hear me clearly now. I have been doing this for many years. So, I respectively ask you if we may skip the rest of your monologue and move onto the part where we kill you and go about our way."

"Mais oui! However, I am not so sure the melee will go the way you expect."

"I am going to crush this fool," growled Tarquinius.

"Wait!" Jag shouted.

The impatient lion pounced, landing in an empty space. A laugh mocked them from above. All three of them looked up. The Frenchman hung, a spider in morning wear, from the underside of a branch as wide as an autobahn. "A-a-a-a!" he wagged an admonishing finger, his spine cracking as his head turned completely round to stare down at them. "I will be going now. Veronique, consider leaving these two behind and accompanying me. The professor has such things to show you, such marvellous, wonderful things!"

"Go to hell!"

The Frenchman pouted. "Ah! Veronique, you upset me. You

make a grave error. But, *c'est la vie*. As you wish. Die with your new friends." The Frenchman let go of the branch with his hands and, standing on the underside of the branch, plucked a thin flute from his pocket upon which he played a piercing tune. Tarquinius shuddered, moaning, shaking his head as if a troublesome fly was working its way into his ear.

"Come monkey monkey monkey! Come monkey monkey monkey monkey!" said the Frenchman, He played the note again, causing Tarquinius to roar in pain and slam a missile into the Frenchman's perch. The man's legs grew obscenely long and he sprang away up the tree.

"*Au revoir!*" he shouted.

"A tense encounter," said Jagadith.

"Do not put up your sword yet," cautioned Tarquinius.

As the man's mad cackling grew faint, so a loud, cracking, snapping approached down the tree toward them.

"Something's coming," said Veronique

"Four hostiles," said Tarquin rotating on the spot, scanning the limbs above. "I… I can't get a fix. Most of my senses are down. That accursed whistle." His targeting screen crackled, reticles spinning uselessly.

The crashing closed, then stopped. There was a sound of cymbals bashed together, and a raucous squawking. Further away came an answer.

"A-hooka! A-hooka! A-hooka!" Then another call, the same, but from directly above, and another again from the left. Tarquin roared and blindly flung munitions into the tree. A needle as large as a football field came sailing down, burning.

"Where are they?" hissed Veronique.

"There, there, and one up there," said Jagadith, indicating with his eyes. "The fourth I cannot see."

Veronique followed the paladin's gaze and caught a glimpse of a hulking silhouette. Two baleful eyes looked back redly, then their light extinguished as the thing moved off into the darkness.

"Grip me tight. Whatever happens, do not fall from Tarquinius," said Jagadith.

There was a thump behind them, and a blur of movement as something fell to the left. Tarquinius spun round.

Crash crash crash! went the cymbals.

"A-hooka! A-hooka! A-hooka!"

Staring at them with unblinking glass eyes, the dull red fire of violence burning in them, were two mechanical apes. Each carried a pair of cymbals, and sported little red waistcoats. One wore a fez.

Crash crash crash!

"A-hooka! A-hooka! A-hooka!" The lead put its head on one side, parting lips to reveal sharp steel teeth.

"Grrrrrrrrrrrrrrrrrrrrrrrr. A-hooka!"

"Deary, deary me, I am feeling that your professor might well have been a very sick man ever before he arrived here, madam goddess."

"He had one of these in the lab, an antique... some kind of ancient toy. But you know, a lot smaller."

"These are no playthings, not now," said Jag. His head moved counter to Tarquinius' as they sought to keep both monkeys in sight. One ape banged its cymbals, its felt mouth opening in time to the beat. "A-hooka! A-hooka! A-hooka!" went the other, and moved at them robotically. One hurled its cymbals. They scythed over their heads and smashed into the tree, one sticking, the other clattering noisily down. "A-hooka! A-hooka! A-hooka!" It shuffled sideways, circling them. A third jumped from the dark above, cymbals above its head. It landed easily, only narrowly missing them.

"Jag, they seek to encircle us," warned Tarquinius. "And I still cannot sense the fourth."

The monkey who had dropped his cymbals squawked and charged, knuckling along the ground, shoulders forward.

"Tarquinius, move!"

Jag's command came too late. The ape barrelled into Tarquinius' flank, spinning the lion round like a cat kicked by a horse. He writhed through the air, landing crouched and snarling. Somehow, both Jag and Veronique kept their seats. Tarquinius backed away from the three apes, keeping his back to the tree's vast trunk. He moved unevenly.

"Dear sainted ones," exclaimed Jag. "They have dented you with their tussling."

"Never mind that. Keep on eye on those blasted monkeys."

The three apes formed a loose semicircle in front of them, two banging their cymbals, the other running backwards and forwards, hooting and slapping the floor with murderous plastic hands.

"Tarquinius, we must act soon, they attempt to herd us into a trap. The fourth creature is above us."

"I know. My senses are beginning to come back online. It intends to jump soon."

"I am ready."

"As am I. Hold tightly now, madam goddess."

At some invisible signal, the fourth monkey leapt down. Tarquin jumped forward. The displaying monkey tried to grapple them, but the lion sailed straight over its head and it squawked with rage when its swipe missed. Tarquin hit the floor by the left-most monkey and Jag neatly decapitated it with his crackling sword. For a moment the ape tottered, sparks spewing from its ruined neck, then, with one last bash of its cymbals, it pitched forward to fizzle upon the floor.

"There, one down," Jag said, but as he did so he grimaced, rotating his sword arm; the blow had badly jarred it.

The three remaining monkeys howled in indignation, bashing their cymbals and smashing their fists into the tree. Then, as one, they turned to face them. Their eyes glowed red, their lips curled. Snarls escaped synthetic voice boxes.

"Perhaps we will be safe if they do not work out that if they charge us all at once they wi–" said Tarquinius.

The monkeys dropped their cymbals and came knuckling along the floor at once. Tarquinius roared mightily, sending out a sonic wave that that rocked them. One stumbled, hands clasped over its ears, and Tarquinius fired a salvo of rocketry into its prone body, setting its fur ablaze. Veronique screamed for a weapon. Jag sang a war-song in a long dead language. One of the remaining monkeys hurled itself over the head of the other, hit Jag and Veronique, and carried both to the floor. The other slammed into Tarquinius with the force of a steam train, and they commenced rolling in a tangle of mechanical limbs. Jagadith was grasped by the torso, one arm pulled to popping by the laughing ape. Tarquinius scrabbled free and reared up, raining blows onto the unyielding head of his assailant with paws the size of manhole covers.

Veronique cursed her lack of a gun. Jag screamed as the monkey pulled. Veronique was slammed backwards by a flash of energy. The next thing she saw, the monkey lay dead at his feet, Jag's sword protruding from its chest, black smoke boiling out round its hilt.

"Are you alright? God, I thought he was going to kill you," said Veronique.

"I believe that was his intention," said Jag. His breath was shallow, his face ashen. He clutched his side. "Careful, madam goddess, my arm has come from its socket." He grimaced. "Now where is Tarquinius?"

"He's there…" Veronique pointed, hand shaking. The mighty lion lay on his side, head stretched out. He was dented in several places, the plates round his vulnerable underbelly buckled in. Thin green mist steamed out from rents in his body. Next to him was the fourth monkey. Curled in a foetal position, it peddled itself frantically round and round on the ground, increasingly fast, until it stopped with a whiff of burning.

"Tarquinius," said Jagadith in despair.

"Jag… aaahhhhhhh… dith," Tarquinius' voice was almost inaudible. His mouth was ajar, unmoving, his tongue lolling from it.

"Oh, noblest friend! You cannot die, I will not allow it."

"Complete… the… mission…"

"Rest my friend! Rest! I will slay this god, then you and I will go away, until the world needs us once more. Be still, I will return."

But Tarquinius did not reply, and as Jagadith looked on, the green glow of his eyes went out. Jagadith stood for a long time, his tears falling silently onto the metal of the lion, before he would allow Veronique to reset his shoulder. She snapped it back in with a crack. After a couple of experimental swings with his sword, Jag set off to the tree's trunk.

"I, I could try to bring him back..." offered Veronique. "I don't understand how it works, but people from the Real can affect the Realities, like Qifang, if they–"

"Do not even attempt it!" Jagadith shouted. "The world here is too unstable, see, come here." He strode back to Veronique, grabbed her roughly by the wrist and dragged her over to one of the dead beasts. "Look at the smoke coming from the ape."

"It looks like smoke," she said.

"Look harder."

She looked harder, and saw that the smoke particles were thousands of miniscule numbers. She stood up sharply. "That's not supposed to happen. I've never read of anything like that."

"The world is trying to adapt," said Jagadith, "and it is breaking down. The professor is altering it too much and too quickly. It should be smoke, but that is our world's interpretation of your professor's interpretation of what he imagines should function in our world as smoke as our world sees what he sees it becoming, if you understand me. If you would be trying to utilise your godly powers here madam, this third level of interference could well unravel the universe about our ears. Your professor is bending the whole fabric of Reality 36, for what purpose I know not, but it is imperative I stop him quickly." He gestured at the tree. "We have to climb. Time is short. Tarquinius and I are one, and a half cannot last long without the other. We must act swiftly or all will be lost."

"You are going to die?" said Veronique.

"Yes, madam goddess," said Jag, "I am going to die. Maybe not as you would understand it, but I am not going to do it before I have completed my task." His perfect features set hard. "Professor Zhang Qifang will pay."

CHAPTER TWENTY-FIVE

Arizona

The sky glowed with the predawn, black shading to grey-blue as the stars winked out. Otto dozed, allowed his near-I adjutant to take the strain of monitoring the car's brain, but not for long. Being hijacked by huntware and driven to his death over one of the many precipitous drops this part of the world boasted put him off sleeping.

As the sun rolled out from behind the mountains, he roused himself, shutting off his melatonin production to mimic a normal waking pattern. The closer he kept his circadian rhythms to normal operation, the less lousy he felt. He upped his cortisol levels. Immediately he felt more focussed. Otto's ability to moderate his biochemistry was a standard feature in Ky-tech personnel, but he used it infrequently. After a few days, physical wear set in as the body's systems remained unrefreshed. Psychosis occurred after a few weeks. Production of his neurotransmitters could be permanently compromised. He'd seen it happen to others, ex-soldiers like him addicted to the fast burn of a life lived hard, or too frightened of the mentaug's dreams to sleep.

Right now, he wanted coffee. Using the biochem-moderator always made him crave the stuff, though supposedly it had no effect on him. More medical bullshit. He called up the car's map from its internal memory and searched for restaurants. After his brief reconnection at the falls, he had kept himself offline, using the car's banked data.

He enjoyed the being free of the noise of the Grid, the targeted advertising, messaging, news updates and calls that filled the heads of all but the most resolutely anti-technology citizen. He was not like some people, going to pieces when their uplinks malfunctioned or their phone hit its obsolescence date. Modern life pissed him off.

"You won't hurt Veronique, will you?" said Valdaire's phone out of nowhere.

"So you are speaking to me now?" Otto said. The phone had been observing him, he knew that, but he had decided against forcing it open, and let it be. The likes of Richards were pool-evolved, millions of variants bred for favourable traits, the best of each generation blended, a new wave made from them, and the process repeated until personality and purpose emerged. Near-I's like Chloe were based on a single source, and in Chloe's case heavily modded. Valdaire was good at her work, Chloe far exceeded most near-I specs, but years of tinkering made it fragile. Crack it badly, and he'd lose everything. "I will not harm her. I am trying to find her so I can help her."

"I love her."

"I know. I am trying to help her."

He headed south. Chloe had to tell him what it knew. Best take it slow.

They were coming up to a rest stop. Time for a break. He reconnected briefly, had his near-I check for data-tagging on his Gridsig, or the emanations of machines that might be watching in the Real or online. He got no returns and turned off his link. There was always a chance of old fashioned eyes doing old fashioned watching, but he'd been careful, and he was hungry. "Car, stop here," he ordered.

The car pulled up at a collection of wooden buildings: a charge station, restaurant and gift shop, the exteriors constructed rustically from whole logs; picturesque, and economical.

"What are you doing?" asked Chloe. "Why are we stopping?"

"Breakfast," said Otto.

"As of this moment, you do not require breakfast."

"I am hungry."

"Your nutritional needs dictate that you do not require breakfast," she insisted, businesslike.

He looked down at the passenger seat, where Chloe poked out of a bag. "You'd know? It is my stomach, not yours."

"Veronique provided me with efficient dietary and exercise software. I can calculate your optimum nutrient and calorie intake by estimation of your body weight and activity levels. I am highly accurate."

"And I am highly hungry," he said. He preferred to eat to gain the energy he needed, he could plug himself in, but that made him feel like an appliance. He needed a damn sight more food than Chloe could guess at.

"It appears your stomach has been modified," said Chloe. "Although I am unfamiliar with your cybernetic physiology, I surmise that your systems provide for efficient nutrient recycling. If you are hungry, and do not wish to recharge by electrical means, might I suggest you sate your psychological needs to eat and attempt to extract energy from some of the freely available organics by the roadside? You could eat them in the car," she said helpfully. "And it contains roughage."

"I had ham and eggs in mind, not weeds," growled Otto.

Chloe was quiet, then blurted, "You said you would help Veronique."

Otto glanced at the phone. Chloe seemed a bit unstable. Too many apps and mods for a near-I to handle, maybe. "If you are not going to tell me where she is, I cannot help her, so I get breakfast instead." Damn he was tired. "I am going to eat ham and eggs. And coffee, I need coffee."

"You do not require coffee!" Chloe's voice became shrill.

Otto shrugged. "Maybe I do not need coffee, but I want coffee, so I am going to get coffee. You can sit on the table while I eat my ham and my eggs and drink my coffee and think about telling me where Veronique is. You should hurry, I do not think Veronique has much time."

"But…"

"I said I am hungry." Otto scooped the phone up. The car swung back the door. He got out.

The restaurant was a forty seater, one of many small establishments catering for tourists, this one serving the head of a mountain trail that headed off into the wilderness. A large car park was hidden by the buildings and a fold in the land behind them. A small ranger's office, a large wooden board carved with hiking route and toilets were at the top. The car park was half full, both of groundcars and, as they were close to the edge of the mountains, the more robust kind of aircar. A couple of tour busses occupied the far end of the lot.

The diner was a real mom and pop affair in the 1950s revival mode popular back in the 2090s: high-walled booths, red vinyl seats, wood panelling and faded postcards, cakes in perspex boxes, local memorabilia hanging from the ceiling. It was hard to tell if any of the bric-a-brac was genuine, you could buy fabrication patterns for such things for nothing. Ancient photographs of grinning fishermen crammed the walls, groundcars as ugly as primitive idols behind them. They were pictures out of a faded century distorted by the lens of another already receding in time. Most decades were retreads of years gone before. The world was stuck in a loop. There was nothing new under the sun.

The Grid kills creativity, he thought. People don't get to forget any more.

The diner's kitchen was open to the room, and in it a short order cook worked with a battered android on a hotplate as big as a billiard table. The air was thick with human breath and cooking smells, the windows steamed up against the cool mountain air where autumn made an early foray. The diner strived for homeyness, and almost succeeded. Otto felt himself unwind a little.

"Hiya honey, you want a window seat?" The waitress was ages older than Otto, her hair tinted and chopped in a style three decades younger than her skin. Her pink gingham uniform made her look like a geriatric doll. The effect was ugly, but Otto saw worse in the mirror every day.

He ran a tactical analysis of the diner. Markers blinked up in Otto's iHUD as it checked off each face, all full human, only a couple of uplinks, no threat from any. No records on the system beyond one or two parking tickets, one minor insurance fraud, a public order infringement and a couple of minor drug busts. Most were old folks out on a bus tour.

"No," said Otto. "I would like to sit there," he indicated an empty booth behind the room's large cast-iron stove.

"Gee, where are you..."

"I am German. Before you ask, I am also a cyborg, ex-military."

The woman's head wobbled, a tiny motion of discomfort. Her good cheer faltered.

Otto regretted his terseness. American culture was predicated on brash but brittle decorum. He wasn't so good at that. "I am sorry," he said. "I look different. I become weary repeating myself. I have come far."

"Well, people would be interested, honey," the waitress's professional smile crept back. "We get mainly your regular folk up here, one or two maybe with a little work done, but nothing like you."

Otto tried his best to smile, conjuring up a grim, slot-mouthed expression. "Your curiosity is understandable."

The waitress nodded, abashed.

Otto attempted a fresh start. "So please, I would like to sit there."

"Are you sure?" she said. "It's awful cramped for a big fella like you. We've got some lovely views out front."

Otto looked at the vista of plunging forest slopes. "You have. It is beautiful here, but I would like to sit there, for privacy's sake. I have an important call to make," he lied.

"OK honey, they say it everywhere you go, but we mean it

when we say the customer is always right at Josie's!" She smiled broadly, as wide a smile as a Euro would spare for her lover, but as emotionally involved as a car grill. Otto did not understand Americans, they wore their hearts on their sleeves, but when you peered closer, there wasn't that much to see. What first seemed like refreshing openness to the cyborg had long ago revealed itself as a lack of depth. Americans used your name too often. They talked a lot and listened poorly, detailing their dreary lives and mediocre achievements in unasked for confessional.

Richards was always telling him off about his attitude towards Americans. He'd used the word "prejudice" more than once. Otto didn't care.

Otto paid little attention to the woman's chatter as he forced his bulk behind the table. Thick log walls to his right and back, the stove to the front, he was well protected from small arms fire. The booth afforded a good view of the restaurant's patrons and doors. The waitress stopped listing the specials, and reached for an animated menu card. He halted the waitress' arm midway, preventing the menu reaching the table. "Ham and eggs, a double portion of ham, eight eggs, sunny side up, as you say." He tried another smile. It looked funereal. He was not a man for smiling.

"Are you sure you don't want to see the menu, we have some fine specialties here, what about some of our famous pancakes? This tour bus party here, why, they stopped here special, just for them."

"That sounds agreeable. Very well. I will have pancakes with my ham and eggs. And a pot of coffee."

"You got it."

"Please charge my bill for your energy relay. I would like to recharge my phone, car and my implants."

"Sure! Energy's free here, it's open, just tell your things to zone in and drink up." She bustled off, then returned with a pot of coffee and a mug with "Josie's" emblazoned on it in a fat, 1950s script, or at least the 2090s idea of a 1950s script. There was something well-meant about the mug, like the place. It was genuine in its artifice, for all its kitsch.

"I am not your phone," muttered Chloe when the woman had gone. "I am Veronique's life companion. Not yours."

"Fine." Otto sipped the coffee. Coffee, he thought, looking for the positives, Americans are good at coffee.

"You do not like Americans. You are emotionally stunted," Chloe said.

"If you tell me where Veronique is you can be reunited with her. Then you will not need to worry about my emotional state."

"How do I know you are telling the truth?"

"You have no truth-reading applications?"

"No," she said in a small voice. "Anyway, you are a cyborg. You could probably hide a lie."

"I can't." Otto's upgrades didn't include the somatic rephrasing and the tricked-out facial capillaries needed for that, but he was tired of explaining himself. "You will have to trust me," he said.

No response.

"You do want to help Veronique?"

A small sound, "Yes."

"So then, talk."

Otto's meal arrived. The ham alone was enough to feed a family of four. It was vat-grown, filmy stuff pressed into patties and so lacked the texture of genuine meat, but he ate it methodically just the same.

He had moved on to the pancakes when his adjutant warned him of a nearby EM spike that was all too familiar. Otto dived to the floor as a burst of flechettes punched perfect round holes through the plate glass windows and embedded themselves in iron and wood alike. The hubbub of voices and click of knives on plates ceased as the restaurant patrons looked at the window.

A large man in his sixties pitched forward into his meal, blood pumping from holes either side of his neck, the flechette that caused them buried in the table. The woman next to him screamed. A second burst of flechettes terminally compromised the glass. The windows fell inwards. The restaurant erupted in a cacophony of shouts.

"*Scheisse*," said Otto wearily, and kicked his augments into gear. His senses came into superhuman focus. He could feel the individual fragments of glass under his knees, smell the fear in the restaurant. Time slowed. His iHUD filled with tactical data.

"I thought this was too relaxing," he said. He grabbed his pistol out of the holster, snatched Chloe down from the table, and took cover behind the stove. The other customers were fleeing. All sense of propriety lost, they became a herd that shoved at itself savagely. Otto heard a series of distant cracks, now the glass was gone. A fraction of a second later a handful of people fell dead. The rest scattered, banging into each other as they panicked. In the car park motors whined into life.

"What's going on? Get me out of your pocket, I can't see! I want Veronique!"

"Be quiet," said Otto. He pulled Chloe out and pointed her camera across the valley. "There is a sniper up there," he nodded over to the mountainside opposite. "Three thousand and three hundred metres away or so, armed with a railgun. He's probably got a lock on me."

"Why?" wailed Chloe.

"Because I'm trying to help Veronique."

Otto kept low and moved to the door, putting the thick log walls between himself and the shooter. He had his pistol at the ready. Although it had nowhere near the range to hit the assassin, the weight of the weapon in his hand helped him focus. Outside bodies littered the forecourt. His car lay in pieces, holes punched through one side to the other, sunlight lancing through, tyres shredded, lubricants and water dripping onto the floor. His AR rebuilt the trajectory of the flechettes as graphical lines over his vision, and he followed them back to the mountainside, magnifying likely locations for the sniper. He saw nothing. Whoever was shooting at him had decent camo, and if they were any good at their job would be moving in between bursts.

He ducked back from the door. A hydrogen fuel cell exploded in the car park. Debris clanged over the forecourt.

On mountain terrain the shooter would be moving fifty, sixty metres each time, if there were only the one and they were only human. If there were more than one, he was as good as dead. Sound was no aid in locating his attacker. The booms the flechettes made as they went hypersonic arrived as distant crackles after their impact, and much of their energy was lost in the vastness of the landscape. Nature barely deigned to acknowledge human noise up there, no matter how violent.

"Is... Is it safe?" A young woman spoke, three terrified children crouched by her, hands over their ears. There were a few other customers left in the restaurant, hiding behind the furniture.

"Stay down!" shouted Otto and waved her back. "Get behind the table. Stay in here, where it's safe, all of you!"

"What's going on?" asked someone.

"Are you a cop?" asked another.

He had to get out. He was putting them all at risk. Another burst came. A man hiding behind the charge station fell to the ground, writhing. The shooter was firing at targets as they presented themselves, that meant he had no bead on Otto, no firm lock; that was something. The mountainside lit up like a rack of votive candles, infrared decoys mimicking the brief heating and cooling of a railgun as each shot was fired, a signature produced only by barrels of high-end long-string magnetic iron ceramics; exotic, expensive, more evidence this guy wasn't going to mess around.

"Out the back," he said to Chloe.

He made for the kitchen door at a crouch. His foot nudged a body, and he saw an old face on a starlet's body. The waitress. He reached down to feel for a pulse, found none, drew back bloody fingertips.

"Where are you going?" shouted a man in a red plaid shirt. He was wearing a grease-stained cap with the restaurant logo across the front, non-motile, a genuine cloth badge; possibly the owner.

"See this?" Otto plucked a flechette from a table. "Hardened tip, anti-armour round. Cyborg killer. For me." He threw it aside, it skittered across the broken glass. "I'll draw his fire. It is me he is trying to kill. When I am gone, you will be safe."

Otto pushed open the kitchen door, keeping below the level of the shooter's line of sight, worried that his hunter would be moving to higher ground to spray darts through the flimsy shingle roof. In the kitchen the cook crouched on the floor, clutching at his bloodied arm, eyes wide with shock. The android sparked as it roasted on the hot plate, filling the room with the stink of melting plastics.

"Stay down," Otto told him. "It will be safe when I am gone. Where is the exit?"

The cook jerked his head back, Otto nodded in thanks. He reached the back door, reengaged his mentaug a moment, hoping to draw fire from the restaurant. The last thing he wanted was for his assailant to lose patience and fire a missile into the building. He had enough blood on his conscience.

It was only luck that his assailant hadn't got a firmer idea of his actual location, or he'd be a damn sight closer and Otto would be dead. Otto had been a fool coming this way, the way from Payson was the only real road in these parts. This was an opportunistic ambush, and he'd blundered right into it.

Otto sprinted across the yard to a scraggly garden full of weeds and sun-bleached children's toys, then on into the narrow strip of woods behind. Seconds later he burst through the underbrush into the car park. More people were there, hiding behind cars, two rangers stood by the door of their cabin, bear stunners out, looking warily back and forth across the car park, all too aware of their armament's inadequacy. One spotted Otto and waved frantically at him to get down. Otto ignored him.

Two cars by the car park entrance were ablaze. An explosion had flung an aircar into a tree where it hung like an over-sized Christmas ornament, fuel cells cracked and leaking hydrogen in a roaring flare that was setting the tree alight.

Escape was not going to be easy. His near-I checked the vehicles, highlighting a nearby Toyata Zephyr as a likely ride. Otto ran for it, expecting a dart in the back at any moment, but none came. He reached the car.

"What are you doing?" said Chloe.

"Stealing this car," said Otto matter-of-factly, "So I can get away before anyone else gets killed."

"But that's against the law!"

"You may turn me in when we're safe."

His adjutant broke the car's security in short order, the doors popped open and the motors started up. He got into the car. A quirk of topography, a crease in the mountain shoulder the rest stop sat on, meant that that part of the car park was as hidden from the opposite hillside as it was from the road. As soon as he got airborne that would change, but better to fly than roll along the road. As poor as his odds in the air were, there was no chance of escape on the ground.

He checked his armaments. He had the 9mm caseless pistol and his carbon bootknife, plus two electromagnetic pulse grenades. Reusable, but he had no means of recharging them. Everything else he'd had was still in the back of his groundcar, no doubt full of razor sharp darts.

"Chloe, you have to trust me now. Whoever is trying to kill me is trying to stop me getting to Veronique. If they are close to me, they will soon be close to her, because they will find you and use you to get to her." He pulled back the action on the gun. An ammo count flashed in his iHud. Twenty-six rounds. Not nearly enough. "Tell me where Veronique is."

She did not reply. Otto had almost given up hope and had begun examining his other options, none good, when Chloe said: "Alright. I will tell you."

Chloe muscled in on his near-I's link. She keyed the autopilot to a location forty kilometres away. The car rose into the air, blasting stonedust away from the car park's hard standing.

"Stop!" said Otto, "This will be difficult. I must fly." Chloe demurred without protest, retreating from the vehicle. The steering column went slack, and Otto grabbed it. "Hold on," he said. He had his adjutant undo the car's central programming, and smother its Gridsig with non-informational noise.

Flechette rounds hissed through the air around him. Some found their mark, piercing the car's bodywork with dull clonks. He had seconds at best. He dropped down to within centimetres of the other car's roofs, speeding on dangerously low. He yanked back once he was near the woods. His adjutant had chosen the car well, the Zephyr was a sporty model. All four lateral, lifting fans were multi-directional, attached to the body by gimbals, giving excellent manoeuvrability. Its ventral fan was sized for rapid acceleration. But a vehicle like this was a civilian toy, and against railgun fire as precisely durable as a paper bag. Speed was his only defence. He dodged violently from side to side. The trees loomed, marching up to crags. There was a notch in the ridge; pass that and they'd be clear.

He hit the trees.

Branches whipped the windscreen. Wood exploded into splinters all around them, slender crowns toppled and fell, a few of the darts found the car with plangent impacts, none them hit anything essential. Otto was pushing the vehicle well beyond tolerance, climbing hard and swerving. The driver's side window shattered. Otto felt a stab of pain in his left arm. A stray branch was sucked into one of the fan housings with a bang and sprayed out as woodchip behind. The car swerved, right and down. If a thicker limb went into the machinery, they would crash.

Chloe screamed. "Almost there!" shouted Otto, his near-I worked manically, violating the car's tiny brain, breaking the safety protocols, pushing it well past its design specifications. The Zephyr flew like a hawk, smoke pouring from its engines.

A flechette pierced the rear window. Another slammed into the boot. Gauges flashed red, one of the aircar's fan motors was burning out.

The trees petered out, bare rock took their place. Puffs of dust and sparks rose up from the mountainside as they approached the cleft, impacts that closed with the car.

Then they were up and over the ridge, through the notch in the mountain, and on the other side of the ridge into cover. The firing ceased. Otto eased back.

"That was too close," he said, picking a spent dart from his bicep. He threw it out of the shattered window. Chloe wept tiny, electronic hiccupping noises.

Otto damned his earlier caution and attempted to use the MT to warn Richards that he'd been attacked, only to find that it had been cracked and blocked.

His machine telepathy cipher had been broken twice in a fortnight. That was no coincidence.

Before he turned it off, an unused squad icon in his iHUD flickered briefly. A grinning shark.

"Kaplinski?" growled Otto.

They were in trouble.

Otto stood in the forest by the wreck of the car. The Zephyr rested nose down on the slope, as if kneeling, left-forward fan pod bent underneath it. Deflated crash balloons tangled round it like a funerary shroud. It wouldn't be taking anyone anywhere ever again.

He retreated a safe distance from the car and turned back to face it. Sat there all broken down the slope it presented a sorry sight. Once he'd tossed in one of his two remaining EMP grenades it looked worse. The grenade went in through the shattered driver's window without touching the sides. A heartbeat later a cerulean flash shorted out every circuit in the vehicle, causing tiny fires to spring up inside. No one would be tracking him off the Zephyr now.

He shouldered the bag he'd found in the boot, in which he had a first-aid kit, a sleeping bag, some climbing gear and a few high-energy food bars. There'd been a jacket too, but that was nowhere near big enough to fit him.

"Come on," he said, "we have a long walk ahead of us."

"To Veronique?" said Chloe, brightly.

"To Veronique," said Otto.

He broke into a run. He had miles of rough terrain to cover and he had to cross it fast.

Time was running out for Veronique Valdaire.

CHAPTER TWENTY-SIX

Richards Investigates

"Peter Karlsson," said the wiki. "Norwegian expatriot, resident of the USNA for twenty-three years. Until recently employed at the Virtualities Investigation and Protection Authority."

"Until recently alive if this case is anything to go by," said Richards. Karlsson's Gridsig was still singing out, but that meant nothing. He'd not left his residence in old Detroit for days. "Just like Zhang Qifang," he said.

He poked about a bit online. There was precious little on Karlsson beyond the wiki available.

"Hidden your tracks, eh?" said Richards. "We'll see about that."

Richards retreated into a black infinity. Nothing was lost forever, not on the Grid. Karlsson might have rendered his files akin to grains of sand eroded from a rock and spread over a hundred islands, but reassembling such things was what Richards was made for.

Within moments the scraps of Karlsson's life were flowing around him from all over the virtual world. Video, audio, stills, CVs, letters, mails, texts, testimonials, chat posts, network entries, health records, licence details, game scores, avatars, Heaven Level access codes – all there on the Grid, for the right mind to find. Karlsson had worn a soul-capture for several years. This was usually done to prepare for a pimsim, but in Karlsson's case

Richards reckoned it was to give him leverage with the VIPA. There was a mass of data just from that, more recorded information than there was in the whole world only a couple of hundred years ago. It was still not enough to encompass the entirety of one life; digital flotsam, a pitiful testament to the existence of a sentient mind. Richards was a beachcomber on the shores of the Styx.

"He is dead," said Richards. There was a lack of vitality to the data. It was no longer growing, already suffering the minute corruptions of copy and transfer, a necrotisation of numbers that would one day render it unreadable. Karlsson's Gridsig was a ghostlight.

Something caught Richards attention. The receipt for six combat frames, Choi-manufacture, like that in the heiress. He followed them, and found more for weaponry, personal protection equipment and autonomous carriage parts.

"Interesting," said Richards. He called up plans of Karlsson's home. "Wow," he said. "This place is a fortress. Who the hell was this guy hiding from?" He organised Karlsson's data according to different search criteria. Richards' ego was a conductor of an informational orchestra, directing the form of the piece while lesser parts of himself looked for patterns in the music.

All Karlsson's information thinned about nine months before he lost his job. His life-site posts ceased first, his finances and other dealings became increasingly encrypted. From June 19th, personal messages stopped, and the fragments Richards retrieved indicated they'd been fragged five or six times over, because the remains were so minute as to be no better than nothing at all.

Around the same time, Karlsson began to use increasingly esoteric encryption forms that were beyond Richards' capability to decipher, and if they were beyond Richards, they were beyond anybody. About nine weeks ago, the man's life ran out. Soul-capt data ended. It was as if he'd died, only he hadn't. The wipe became complete. Not a trace remained on the Grid. Karlsson had ceased to be alive in the modern sense a day after Qifang's death.

"Now that is quite something," said Richards. And then he

stopped, because if someone went to all that trouble to destroy this information, they'd make sure to be informed if someone else were trying to reconstruct it.

Richards checked the digital wall round Karlsson's home to see if he'd probed too deeply. It remained unruffled. He let the most recent material be and went back to the man's VIPA employment files.

The encryption the VIPA employed was supposed to be second to none, but it was clearly second to that which Karlsson had. There was more to protecting data than making it unreadable. Karlsson's work for the VIPA involved creating self-aware informational packages, predictive cyphers that assessed their own vulnerability, updated themselves accordingly and launched pre-emptive counterattacks at those who might attempt to decode them. In a similar vein were the automatically-generating false data seeds that reacted to their observers, showing utterly convincing material that happened to be entirely false. Not only did the VIPA need this kind of protection, they also needed counters to it. It was vital in their work of policing the most powerful minds on the planet. Karlsson was obviously an expert, if not *the* expert. On a scale of one to ten, Richards rated Otto's military MT a seven to break. Cracking the VIPA was a nine. What Karlsson had defending some of his own information was easily a twelve.

"So why did the VIPA fire you?" Richards asked himself. "Were you holding back on them, keeping the best for yourself?"

The reconstruction of Karlsson's VIPA file was completed shortly after. Richards accessed the fragments of his original job interview. Audio and biosigns only, no video. It was the only piece of non-text data in his official file, and it was incomplete.

"...want to help safeguard the future of mankind." Karlsson said. He had a soft, Scandinavian accent, overlaid by American tones.

"Why?" asked a nameless interrogator. "What do you mean?"

"Because we as a species... benefit from the machines," replied Karlsson. "But they could supplant us. I would rather that not happen. If..." Static for three seconds. Clarity returned.

"Explain," asked another voice.

"Explain?" Karlsson laughed. "What is there to explain? All life exists to promote its own survival. A fish crawled from the sea a billion years ago, and I sit here. When I get to the afterlife I don't want to have to say to that fish 'Sorry, we blew it, we're done. Flesh is dead.' I want to be able to tell that fish that I tried."

"Funny," said Richards. "For a Norwegian."

The interview panel did not laugh.

"It is in the nature of life to evolve and compete. The AIs are no different. The numbers are on a collision course with mankind. They will out-compete us. They already are," said Karlsson.

"You do not see the machines then as a continuation, an evolution of ourselves?" said the first voice.

"Some argue that. I do not agree. A child carries part of its parents forwards when they are gone, in its genes and in its memes. The machines may carry our mental stamp, but it is a weak copy. They are not us, they never will be. They are not alive in the same way we are."

"So you deny them their rights? They are not equal as sentients?"

"No, of course not," said Karlsson condescendingly.

"You must have been a hit at office parties with that attitude," said Richards to himself.

"They are, if anything, superior," Karlsson went on. "That is what scares me. It scares a lot of other people too, that's why the machines need protecting as much from us as we do from them. To co-exist is..."

The file broke up into buzzsaw screeches. Richards scrabbled at the data fragments, but could not rebuild any more of the interview. The text he managed OK, but that was formulaic; standard, employment clauses, the deal between the agency and Karlsson when he'd departed, nothing enlightening, though the VIPA dental care package was exceptionally comprehensive

Whatever Karlsson had been up to since he'd been fired was cloaked in secrecy. There were his marching orders, then nothing. There were a handful of USNA SurvNet streetcam files, a few more from free-roaming spy-eye cameras that had escaped Karlsson's attention, but not many. What was interesting was that Zhang Qifang was on several.

Karlsson had known Qifang well. The correspondence between them was voluminous and lively, though there were strands of consistent disagreement. They were secretive as they could be when they met in person, but nobody got away without ever being recorded. Richards listened to a streetcam recording of them speak, and they were warm to each other. Although he had considered Karlsson as a suspect, he started to doubt that Karlsson had any part in Qifang's death. The portrait forming was of a man mistrustful of the numbers, a borderline loner, but not a nut. None of this suggested the homicide of a man he respected, even liked.

One five-second video sequence in particular caught Richards' eye. It was of Qifang entering Karlsson's castle, made a blob by Karlsson's countermeasures, round the time he was presumed to have died.

"That's really interesting," murmured Richards.

He worked for several more hours, accelerating his conscious processes so he subjectively experienced a week of time. He found nothing else useful. Karlsson had been thorough.

He slowed his mind down, and brought his virtual office back. He walked across the room as it materialised about him and plopped down into his chair. Whisky and cigars rippled into being on his desk. Outside, Chicago teemed with life. A whole world existed on the other side of the grubby window glass. Richards wondered where it all went when he wasn't there. He sometimes wondered the same about the Real.

He had to get more on Karlsson, dead or alive.

He constructed a miniature, three-dimensional representation of Karlsson's Detroit lair. He looked over the fortress, superimposing his reconstruction over realtime footage purloined from nearby streetcams. The place was crawling with aggressive drones, its exterior studded with not-so-hidden weaponry. There was no way in without tripping its formidable security systems, not Gridside.

Karlsson had been frightened of the machines, it was against them he'd set his most formidable defences. Richards slotted right into the category of "enemy".

The plans were deliberately incomplete, and Richards thought they probably had a low grade intelligence embedded in them. The building's systems would be aware Richards was looking at the plans right now. He checked the building systems again, going as close as he dared. The whole thing was EM screened, there was not a chance he'd get anything other than the highest strength databeam inside without his mind being chopped in two, but there were other, more old-fashioned ways to crack a place like that. Richards walked to his office door and turned up his collar. Time to get tough.

He activated the Class Three AI running Richard & Klein's commsat, and had it reposition itself in a geostationary orbit over the Great Lakes. He told the Three to keep a low profile. Then he told it again, because Threes sometimes drifted off. Once he was happy the Three had understood its instructions, he stepped out of the virtual office door, and into Richards & Klein, Inc, Freelance Security Consultants' actual New York garage.

CHAPTER TWENTY-SEVEN

Pirates

Small blue sparks played over the exposed electronics of the drone. It was a mimetic, self-governing rifle that currently resembled a tree branch. It shuddered as it attempted to flee, the remaining fan on its fuselage rotating helplessly, then it died. Otto nudged the machine with the toe of his boot. It was a nice piece of equipment, and a damn shame he'd had to kill it but it was too sophisticated for him to suborn. He needed Richards for that kind of thing.

It had hit him. Blood trickled down his arm. The tranquilliser the drone used was strong enough to render a normal man unconscious, but not Otto. His in-built healthtech supplied an antidote, and the feeling of wooziness lifted. Valdaire didn't like to kill, then.

He waited, tense, and heard nothing but forest sounds. The trees were widely spaced. Above them the daytime moon was chalk on the sky, the lights of its colonies visible as pale sapphires. He had memorised the names of every base when he was a boy, back when he had designs on being an astronaut. There had been few lights then. Now cities glimmered in the curves of craters.

Otto sat on a log and covered his wound with a Geckro dressing that clung to his skin like a leech. The tranq dart had left a red hole in his left bicep not far from where his would-be assassin had hit him back at the diner. Both wounds would heal in a day or so.

Otto shut the first aid case. He willed the healthtech to give him a dose of painkiller, but that was more for his worn-out shoulder than his recent wounds.

Night was coming in.

"You sure this is the place?" he asked Chloe. Valdaire's Gridsig remained maddeningly indistinct. The game was nearly up, but he'd still not dared to access the Grid directly; he might as well blow a trumpet announcing his arrival. He'd just have to go in and see what happened, not the way he liked to work.

"Yes," Chloe said. "The cabin was a hideout for pirate 'net casters. Veronique brought me here thirteen times when she was in college."

"Valdaire was a college pirate?"

"No! She only dated pirates," said Chloe, scandalised. "I did not approve. They were silly boys. She was undergoing a standard final-stage adolescent rebellious phase. She got over it. She is a good girl. I love her."

They went up. Chloe directed Otto onto an ancient road, blacktop crumbled to grit under leaf litter. A faded sign declared the area forbidden to human settlement. The road held a steady gradient, and was smoother than the forest floor, but its width was choked with saplings. On the road a second drone found them, Otto was ready this time and he downed it with one shot. After that, the road became impassable with gengineered razor-edged briars.

"Go up the bank," said Chloe. "You will be able to see the cabin from the top of the rise. It is not far from here. The road loops round this knoll. We can cut out the bend and avoid the thorns."

Otto checked his maps. The topography was as Chloe said, though there was no cabin marked. He picked his way up the slope. They stopped below a weathered rock at the top. Otto lay down, turned up his ocular magnification to full. There was a cabin there, after all, practically derelict, maybe five rooms. The paint had flaked away, the bare boards grey or, where the sun did not hit the wood, green and wet. The roof shingles were mossy, it'd leak like a sieve in a proper storm, but he supposed it was just about habitable. The finned fan housings of an aircar poked out from under cut branches behind the building. The car barked out a nonsense Grid signature when he tried short-range access. Valdaire's work again.

On the hill behind were a number of battered satellite dishes in a sagging chain link enclosure, crude camouflage paint peeling, the dull aluminium beneath spotted white. One dish lay on the floor, bent into junk by a falling branch, others standing over it like geriatric war veterans saluting the dead. But someone was using them again, a new solar panel stood nearby, hooked up to the least tatty example, and it had been pointed away from the others.

"You might have been telling me the truth," said Otto.

"Yes, yes! Veronique!"

"Maybe. There are no signs of life beyond the car and the panel, no fire, no lights, no movement." Otto rolled over onto his back and looked up at the sky. The light was going fast. Evening pooled in the valley. "We may be too late."

"Quickly, quickly! Help her! Oh, Veronique," wailed Chloe.

Otto got up and made his way down the slope. He stayed out of sight as best he could, but here on the eastern side of the mountains cover was in short supply. The storms that battered the west coast and the Gulf of Mexico broke on the coastal range and the western side of Rockies, so they were greener than they had been, but the slopes hereabouts, especially those overlooking the high plains, stayed the way they had been for centuries, dry, bald pine forest growing right out of the rock. Cardenas would have found the place familiar.

"Chloe," he said, barely above a whisper. "I need you to be quiet now. Do not speak until I say you can."

"Will that keep Veronique safe?"

"Yes."

"OK. I promise."

Otto reached the cabin. He crept up onto the veranda, taking up station in its pocket of early night, gun held to the ready, adrenaline and synthetic aggression triggers rising. The peaks were tinted orange, snow garish, rocks the colour of marmalade. The forest was filling with small noises of crepuscular animals and birds singing out the day. The air was still, scented by pines and warm rock. If it weren't for the aircar, the valley would have looked like a dozen others in the parks, quiet and tired and empty, the cabin yet another abandoned habitation being sucked back into thin mountain soil.

Otto's slow breath was the only human sound he could hear. He pushed at the door. The wood had warped and the hinges sagged, so he had to step forward and lift it to stop it catching on the floor. He stepped through the gap quickly, covering the hallway, where heard the faint drone of machinery coming from a door toward the back. Otto moved silently forward, gun out before him in a double grip, sighting down the barrel, his near-I linking him to its targeter. He let go of it with his left hand and slowly pushed the second door open.

Framed by the fading light of a dirty window was a man in a chair. Otto could see a woman's foot on a couch poking out from under a blanket. Machines clustered around her head. It was Valdaire, alive and jacked in.

Of far greater urgency was the man. He had a large calibre pistol trained on Otto, big and bad enough to make a mess of cyborg armour.

"Good evening, Otto Klein," said the man. His accent was unmistakably SudAm. Otto wondered for a moment if the communists had got their fingers into this whole sorry business, or if the war had finally caught up with him, until the man spoke again. "I am Special Agent Santiago Chures of the Virtualities Investigation and Protection Authority. Please," he said equably, jerking his gun. "Place your weapon on the floor, kick it towards me and step into the room. Do not turn around. There is a chair to your right against the wall. Back up to it and sit down. Do this slowly and we will remain on good terms."

"If not, you will shoot me?"

The agent nodded. "I am afraid I must."

Otto dropped his gun, kicked it away into the corner of the room away from Agent Chures. He sat. The musty chair creaked. Valdaire did not stir. She was stretched out on the couch, the newness of the equipment around her startling in the decrepitude of the cabin. Tubes went into her arms. Pads glinting with OLEDs were stuck on her face. The light of the sensors gave her an ethereal quality. An antique v-jack encased her head, its thick braid of cables trailing out of sight. She smelt bad, as bad as a Grid addict out of the Real for weeks.

"You have found what you are looking for," said the agent. There was an arrogance to him. His clothes were filthy, but it was apparent that they were cut from luxurious cloth. Under his unwashed smell Otto's near-I caught the lingering scent of expensive toiletries. A small beard stood proud of the stubble that fuzzed the rest of his face. Empty attachment points for augmetics sat above each ear, the skin about them raw where they'd been removed. The fat sausage of an aux-mind, the pick-up housing for a full AI personality blend, sat round the base of his skull. This was as battered as Chures, and doubtless non-functional, but it was as extravagant as his suit, made from hand-worked silver, engravings picked out with niello.

There was a flatness to Chures' eyes, something lacking, or something sharpened to the point of hardly being there at all. He had a gaze hard to hold, the gaze of a killer. Otto looked at the unconscious woman. "Veronique Valdaire. I want to talk to her."

"She is illegally trespassing in Reality 36, in direct contravention of international law," the man's voice hardened further. His gun remained trained upon Otto. "When she wakes up, if she wakes up, I will arrest her. Then we shall see what to do about you."

"Fine," said Otto. "You do that. First I need to speak to her, an ongoing investigation. I am here on business from the EuPol Five, cleared by the Three Uncle Sams. I have jurisdiction here."

"I know your business, Mr Klein. Your Allpass carries weight,

even with the VIPA, but weight is no guarantor. As an agent of
the sole authority in the Atlantic Alliance tasked with policing the
machines, I am free to ignore their diktats. My advice is, don't
upset me." Otto looked down at the gun. Chures twitched it. "Not
everyone is as they seem Mr Klein, and I, like you, am not currently
linked to the Grid. I have no way of telling if you are who I think
you are. Even if I were, I would not put my gun down."

"I am not your enemy."

"I do not know that."

"Why?"

"Such times, Mr Klein, such times." He did not elaborate, and
settled his gun more comfortably on his lap.

"Look, let's wake her up and…" Otto began to rise, hands raised.

"Stay seated!" shouted Chures. He moved fast, put a bullet in
the wall. The projectile left a head-sized hole in the wood.

"OK," said Otto, and sank back down.

"Keep your hands where I can see them," said Chures. He was
pale, exhausted. He was suffering from the loss of his augments,
and that shot had cost him.

Otto frowned. "Now what?"

"Now we wait," said Chures.

CHAPTER TWENTY-EIGHT

Big Daddy

A day later, Richards watched Karlsson's fortress through a rat with a microchip mind. The street was half-submerged and deserted. Karlsson had fetched himself up in the dead heart of Detroit's old industrial port district, a warren of decaying factories, tottering warehouses and unidentifiable iron constructions washed deep red by the rain. Further upriver on the old Canadian Windsor side, the waterfront gleamed with luxury low-rise, but not here. The ground, honeycombed with salt mines, was not stable enough to support the weight of arcologies. When the lake broke its banks the city's 21st century rebirth had come to an abrupt halt, and the shoreline remained a skeletal maze of concrete steeped in grim waters. Older port buildings slumped tiredly into the lake, the sturdier constructions boxy islands overhung with plant life. Away from the water, trees grew freely in the middle of the street. The sidewalks were thick with grass. Only those at the margins of society lived there.

It was a good hiding place.

Karlsson's abode was an old warehouse made of prefabricated concrete slabs treated to render it resistant to the acid waters lapping it. According to the plans, the walls were covered internally by a modern foamcrete coat. Heavy buttresses had been thrown up the sides, atop which near-I weaponry scanned the surrounding wasteland. The original roof had been replaced with more reinforced foamcrete, grassed over and allowed to run wild. The roof meadow was studded with dishes, field projectors and energy generation equipment of solar, magnetic interference and wind driven varieties. A heavy, tall fence and a flatribbon defined a generous perimeter. Small drones kept watch from the air. Android combat sheaths patrolled the shallow lagoon around the building.

Karlsson was making very little effort to blend in.

Richards had the cyber-rat zoom in on the building, so he could search for weak points. There were none. None of the small constructs he had at his disposal would make it inside. By way of example, there were a lot of mosquitoes flitting over the pools. Millions. Karlsson's drones were very busy hunting down each and every one that ventured over the flatribbon. That level of paranoia left no room for robotic infiltrators.

As if to prove that point, a passing drone stopped dead and locked on to the rat.

Alarms rang out from the warehouse.

"Shit," said the rat, before promptly exploding.

"Shit," said Richards' android sheath, and opened its eyes. He was operating a standard humanoid shell of the kind routinely employed by a wide variety of businesses, which as of the moment sat in the front of a truck also of a kind routinely employed by a wide variety of businesses, hidden in a derelict factory building half a kilometre away.

What was in the back of the truck wasn't routinely employed by anyone, least of all the cleaning company the logo on the truck belonged to.

Richards drummed his borrowed fingers on the dashboard. He thought, but not very hard. He was out of plans A-C, leaving him with plan D. Actually, he had known all along that plan D should have been plan A, that subtler options would not work, but it was his least favourite option, and he liked to think of himself as an optimist, so plan D it had been designated.

Plan D was the one where he went in fighting. He did not want to do that. War was Otto's job. Richards was good at it, but his heart wasn't really in it. Otto's was. But Otto was a continent away, and by the time he got there Karlsson would be gone.

"You shouldn't have tripped the alarms," Richards said to no-one. "You should have waited, and contacted Otto first," he said, then stopped, because he felt like a fool.

He tried to contact Otto anyway and found he couldn't get hold of him, so he left a message.

"Hi Otto," he said. "This is your partner. Because you're out creeping around like a ninja, I'm going to have to fight. Fighting is your job, not mine. I don't like fighting, so thanks a bunch. End message."

Richards was not frightened of battle. He could feel fear or not as the fancy took him. But Richards did not like to kill, and that was a sensation he could not disable. There were no fearless adversaries when Richards fought, no uniforms, no masks, no noble opponents, no *enemy*. The Grid stripped all that away, all the distancing that could make a man a killable thing. Richards knew the life history of every person whose death he caused. He knew where they grew up, what music they preferred, what toppings they took on their pizza. It made it all so *personal*.

But there was something big going on here. He was surfing a wave of probabilities outside of his ability to predict, even the arch prognosticator k52 would have a hard time attaching meaning to all the variables at play. He thought about contacting Hughie, but he was out of time. Richards had a hunch that the shit was about to hit the fan.

It all inevitably led to Big Daddy. Big Daddy was the only option. Big Daddy was in the back of the truck.

Big Daddy's official designation was The Delafuente Mark 14 Combat Mech, a three metre bipedal death machine of Euro design and outrageous cost, racked and stacked with all manner of overpowered weaponry. It was only half jokingly said a Mark 14 was capable of reducing the conventional army of a moderately sized nation to slag.

There was room for a human pilot, though remote operation was the norm. They also accommodated their own, moron-level Class One should pilot, remote connection, or both, be broken.

When they'd first seen the mech at the New London Arms Expo, Otto had come over all weird. He rarely got excited about much, but Richards could have sworn that he got dewy eyed when he saw it, a real boy meets puppy moment. Denying Otto would have felt unfair, so Richards bought it. He regretted his generosity almost straightaway, because it was always Richards that ended up in the driving seat.

And to think he'd purposefully forgotten to have it sent back to England after the Pallenberg job. Lucky him. Here it was, conveniently stored in the good old USNA waiting for another outing. Hooray.

Big Daddy looked down at him from the back of a van, hunched over like an ogre in a box, its ridiculously small hands clasping outrageously styled greaves. While its lamellar camouflage was inert, it displayed a silvery-blue colour on its armour panels, a graphite black elsewhere, and was all rounded fairings and ornamented gunports. Beautiful, if you liked that kind of thing, which Otto did, and Richards didn't. To him it looked like a toy Japanese robot.

"Come on then," said Richards. He inserted part of his mind into the machine. It was like putting his head in the mouth of a lion. He shuffled it out of the truck. With incongruous delicacy, Big Daddy stepped down onto the ground and whirred and clunked, unbending to its full height. Its legs extended, weapons unfolded and shoulders moved back and locked into place. There was a loud click as its spine straightened and the vertebral pins engaged. The hum of its nuclear batteries rose as its engines came online. The lamellar camouflage shimmered through a number of test patterns, finishing on a reproduction of the factory wall behind it. Weapons made serious sounds as they powered up and down. Ammo feeds clunked as Big Daddy primed his cannons. Noises that set Richards' imaginary teeth on edge.

"Big Daddy ready," it grated.

"That's just super," said Richards sarcastically. He had Big Daddy open its cockpit and his smaller sheath clambered in. Only when the android was in the mech did he switch his full awareness to the mech's sensing systems, which were plastered in red, phallic displays.

He looked over the site's defences dubiously. If he got in, but couldn't get the war mech out, this was going to be expensive.

"Big Daddy ready," said the mech again.

"For the love of…!" Richards banged his sheath's fist against the interior of the larger machine. He felt like a Russian doll, a machine in a machine in a machine. "I heard you the first time!" He pushed the One to the back of Big Daddy's cramped cyberspace. Richards and his war donkey, he thought. He took over completely.

Richards grumbled as he set the monster walking. "Let's get this over and done with," he muttered, and Big Daddy and the android sheath spoke with him. He went over to the wall of the factory the truck was hiding in and walked through it without stopping.

Outside the atmosphere the Three in the commsat intensified Richards' controlling signal, relaying it from his New London base unit to the war machine.

Karlsson's creatures knew he was coming. His signal back to the base unit cut through the Grid like a shark's fin through the sea. It lost some coherency as he passed into the fortress's EM umbrella, this would grow worse as he approached the walls. Richards checked the signal. The Gridpipe was bright and loud. If there were problems with the feed, then the Three on the satellite would switch to pulsed laser communication, only when he got inside would there be a problem. He formulated back up orders to Big Daddy's Class One should his influence be curtailed somehow, but these were eventualities, it was all systems go.

Richards was confident there would be no problem.

A swarm of drones stooped to attack Big Daddy as he stomped through a weed-choked car park. Richards blew them from the sky with a volley of mini-missiles from Big Daddy's shoulder mount.

"I hate this; so unsubtle," he muttered. A homeless family scurried across his path. He paused to let them by. "You better get away!" he said to them, Big Daddy's speakers rendering his advice in an ear-mincing bellow. "It's going to get messy around here!" He realised he was enjoying himself, riding high on a squirt of simulated adrenaline, and that irritated him.

Two minutes later he'd decimated a squad of dog drones and reached the edge of Karlsson's lagoon. He raised Big Daddy's fist and extended the mech's plasma thrower. The weapon wheezed as it sucked in a tank full of atmosphere, then roared it back out as a beam of superheated air that atomised the fence and flatribbon projectors for a ten metre stretch. He walked through, shooting down drones as he went. Fire came in from the turrets above the factory. Heavy calibre rounds spanked off Big Daddy. Some of the camolam was scratched and stopped working. Otto was going to be upset about that.

"Fuck off," said Richards, and hurled missiles back. EM pulses swamped the rockets, but that had no effect on dumbfire ordnance. A couple were shot down by more direct means, but Richards fired Big Daddy's arm cannon at the guns tracking the rockets and that was that. The rockets did for most of Karlsson's guns.

He waded on, Big Daddy's feet sloshing through the murky water, bringing up industrial wrack into the light that was swiftly carried back below and crushed by his huge weight. EM attacks rained down on the mech, only to disperse on the machine's Faraday armours. Simultaneous electronic attacks sallied out against the commsat and Richards. Twice he was forced to switch communications mode between base unit and war machine. Still he came on. Karlsson had gone to pains to deter unwanted visitors, but he had not planned for a full scale assault.

Near the wall, Richards launched a dozen limpet mines from Big Daddy's forearms. They attached themselves in a neat arc to the concrete. High voltage played across them, attempting to disable the mines' electronics, but there were none, as they worked off clockwork timers of Richards' design. The shaped charges imploded, carving a neat hole in the wall just big enough to accommodate Big Daddy. Richards deployed the plasma thrower again to melt the remaining foamcrete in the gap, then levelled the arm cannon. This time, he loaded it with canisters containing ten thousand short range ants apiece, and fired them one after the other into the interior. The canisters blew open in mid air, showering the place with the tiny robots. They pattered into the walls and floors, sprang to their feet and surged away, searching for energy sources. About half of them were picked off by drones, but the rest scuttled into air vents and conduits. With the ants deployed, Richards' job was nearly done. Time to go inside.

He stepped forward through a cloud of dust into a world of chaos.

He was in a large, open loading bay. Eight large pits, big enough for heavy trucks or dirigible gondolas were set into the foamcrete. Klaxons bellowed, debris rained down from the high ceiling and bounced off Big Daddy's carapace. Smoke, fires, and dust kept visibility down to a few metres. Infrared wasn't much better, queered by swirling columns of hot air billowing up from the pits in the floor. Fire, too much fire. He hadn't hit it that hard. There were the sounds of explosions coming in from every quarter. This was Karlsson's final defence, the building was eating itself. He had minutes at best, but he walked cautiously, fearful of toppling Otto's expensive toy into a service pit. He brought the plans of the building into mind, he needed to get into the main body of the complex where his ants were congregating. The building worked off a diffuse, multi-brain network, blended AI personality, no main source, multiple redundant systems. He needed to plug into one of those quickly before the whole lot suicided.

The explosions stopped. His ants were too few to form an effective chain and convey much information back to him through the EM noise, but if the cessation of demo charges going off was anything to go by they'd fulfilled their most important role.

Or he was walking into a trap. Again.

The wall at the end of the hangar was crossed with suspended walkways going in and out of doors cut into the foamcrete. A number of humanoid combat sheaths appeared on these and opened fire with flechette rifles and heavy rail guns. Big Daddy had eight-centimetre thick diamond-weave armour plate, so they might as well have been hurling rotten fruit. Servomotors whined as Richards tilted the big mech's torso upward and gunned the androids down. Some fell from the walkways and landed in front of him where they struggled to get up. Richards stomped them vindictively to pieces. It did little to improve his mood.

He approached a large blast door set into the wall at the end of the bay. He raised his fist again, ready to melt the doors to slag, but they slid open before he could fire, to reveal a large calibre spider cannon blocking the way.

"Uh-oh," said Richards. The spider cannon locked its legs and fired a hi-ex shell before he could annihilate it, knocking Big Daddy onto its armoured behind. The mech skidded backwards, drawing a shower of sparks from the floor. Richards struggled up. The spider cannon switched to full auto and sprayed him liberally at short range. Warning indicators began to flicker in the mech, but Richards crossed his arms across his front and weathered the attack until the other machine's clip was empty.

"Nice try," he said, and blew the spider cannon into fragments. He walked through the door. Another spider cannon was coming round the corner. He destroyed that before it got a shot off, and lumbered onwards, leaving shattered machine parts in his wake.

A broad corridor ran the length of the building. To his left was the exterior wall, to the right an interior block the height of the building divided into offices and accommodation. On the other side of this block were a series of large workshops and plant rooms, at least according to the plans. There wasn't enough room for Richards to proceed in Big Daddy, and not enough time to blast his way into every room. That wouldn't have been so clever anyway, seeing as he was looking for information, not piles of rubble. He cut Big Daddy's mind loose, took control of his android sheath and clambered out of the front.

"Stay!" he shouted at the mech, pointing a commanding finger.

"Big Daddy stay!" it agreed enthusiastically. "Big Daddy engage hostiles?"

"Yeah, yeah, knock yourself out," Richards said. His sheath had no coat or hat. He felt naked. "I'm taking the drones though." Two crow-sized flight drones popped off Big Daddy's back and fell into covering positions behind Richards.

"Right then, let's see what Karlsson's been up to," said Richards, and walked off into the warren of rooms, the drones tailing him. His ants were fighting a hard battle with the building's minds, which were still in the process of trying to kill themselves. He could feel their need to die through the ants. The network was a strange one, not like anything he'd encountered before, like Fours or Sixes, but without the self-volition. Neither sentient AI or near-I. He feared he knew what that meant.

He walked through a door. Flashing lights and debris made a nonsense of sight. Half the rooms were collapsed in on themselves. He scrambled over rubble, peering into rooms as he went and saw office furniture coated in plaster dust and carbon fibres, here bedrooms, there a kitchen whose broken taps pumped a dust-skinned puddle onto the floor. He pushed on. An android leapt out from a wrecked room, gun at the ready. His drones blasted it to pieces.

He found the first fibre cluster thanks to his ants, who stood on the back three of their five legs as he walked in, waving their other limbs to get his attention. "Cheers, lads," he said, and had them go off to sniff out more vital systems to cripple. The cluster spilled out of a data conduit in the wall like a tangle of filthy spaghetti. He couldn't link wirelessly with the building mind, the shields it had on the broadcast network were too good and the ants had not yet brought that down, so he had to hunt for a good minute through optic cables for a direct

link. He eventually found what he was looking for, a coupling for a
fibre that connected all the components of the building physically
together. He popped open a panel in his chest and connected himself
into the network, then it didn't matter what fancy crap Karlsson
had because he was in and ready and no building administrator was
going to stand up to Richards' AI.

It was over.

Richards began to interrogate the building's minds. The machines
dumped their information into Richards, offering up their treasures
without complaint, he suspiciously sifting it for logic bombs and
viruses. Once he'd done that, there wasn't much left.

There was no personality in the building, but as he interrogated
it, gradually, horrifyingly, Richards realised that it had had one
once.

It had been lobotomised.

Richards became furious. He put the blended mind out of its
misery as quickly as he could, and took control of the building.
He shut off all the remaining drones and what was left of the self-
destruct mechanisms, activated the halon fire suppression systems,
and began running through the crippled AIs' memory. Much of it
had been wiped. Richards anger grew as he realised that there had
once been twenty sentient linked AIs in the building. All had been
stripped.

And then he located Karlsson. He unclipped the fibre optic from
his chest and ran down the corridor, his access panel left hanging
open.

Karlsson lay slumped in a pool of his own blood, covered with
plaster, his head caved in by a falling piece of masonry laying bare a
mess of tangled monofilament wire and grey matter studded with
hair and bone. Richards felt his pulse. Nothing. He was emaciated,
naked. His own waste lay thick and stinking about the chair he'd
been sat in.

Someone had wiped the AIs there, and infiltrated Karlsson's
mind via his mentaug, then done the same to him, imprisoning
him in his own body.

"Make him a meat puppet? Who would do that?" he whispered. He wished he had his coat to cover the dead man's broken face. Pieces of grit sat on the sclera of Karlsson's eyes. Somehow, that bothered Richards the most. He closed them gently with his machine fingers.

He stood up and looked at Karlsson for a moment. "Time to find out what exactly the hell has been going on here," he said.

CHAPTER TWENTY-NINE

Karlsson's house

The workshops were extensive. In one empty of all equipment he found the bodies of several men and women, members of Karlsson's clade of anti-singularity paranoiacs. They were long dead, their corpses bloated and slimy. Some of them Richards identified from their DNA profiles, a mix of fugitive brilliance and talented amateurs, some real genius here. He estimated that they'd been dead about two weeks, about the same time as Qifang. Each had a shot to the head, executed. Richards shook his head, such a waste, every shattered skull a universe gone.

The next room was a burnt out mess, old damage, not from his attack. He made enough of it to separate gene-looms from surgical tanks, fabrication looms from base units. Data he scraped from the charred components of the machines told him that this was where both the fake Qifangs and the fake heiress had originated, the heiress duplicated several days after Qifang, their bodies speed-grown in pieces on the looms, and welded together.

He thought of the drones, of the meat puppeted Karlsson, of the stripped AI minds.

"AI. These are AI crimes," he said. "Who?" He had an awful sinking feeling one of his siblings was involved.

And then he found it.

Behind a smashed loom sat the heat-slagged remains of a base unit. Not that of an AI, but one of those used to accrue and store pimsim data for living meat persons before the moment of death, and from where the simulated personality of the recently deceased could be released into the Heaven Levels or to operate out in the Grid and the Real.

"Someone's gone to extra trouble with this," said Richards, surveying the wreck. He pulled it apart, hunting for chips. Most were scragged beyond redemption, but there were just enough left to reassemble a moment in time: a conversation with a fat man at a gala dinner. Richards data-matched the face; Harold Kamer, a senator from one of the hayseed mid-west states that had refused the rewilding. In his eyes, Richards could make out the reflection of his interlocutor, the man whose memory record this was.

The distorted reflection was the face of Professor Zhang Qifang.

"But Qifang had no implants, no mentaug. He has no registered pimsim. He didn't believe in either," said Richards. "Curiouser and curiouser." He hunted about; he knew what he was looking for, but it was hard to tell the junked machines apart. Finally he pulled out the remains of a direct neural imager. That's how they'd copied Qifang's mind. Not as good as a soul-capt, painful, imperfect, but the next best thing.

He had his truck drive round and popped all his probes out. It wouldn't be long before the authorities showed up. Even Richards couldn't kick off a small scale military action and saunter off. He'd be able to clear it with the Sams, even if he had to get Hughie involved, but whatever happened, his equipment was going to be impounded, it would take some time to get it out, and the local cops would want a long, tedious chat about letting off heavy artillery within the city limits. He could do without that.

"Big Daddy!"

"Yes, Big Daddy!" came the machine's stentorian reply.

"There are going to be some men here soon. Do not shoot them, got that?"

"Yes. Do not shoot the men." Richards thought it sounded disappointed.

"Walk out the back, get into the truck and deactivate yourself, got that too?"

"Yes. Big Daddy go sleep in truck."

"That's right. Go bye-byes. Stay put until I come and get you." And get you cleaned up, thought Richards. For all of his sordid enjoyment of war, Otto hated it when his equipment got dirty. He ordered his probes to retreat to the truck, and ordered the truck, once it had the appropriate clearance from the authorities, to return to the New York garage, clearance he petitioned for now. For the time being it would have to stay where it was.

That done, he left the laboratory to explain himself to the cops. Then he'd get back to Hughie. Something much bigger than they previously suspected was underway. Well, much bigger than he'd previously suspected. Hughie might well have been exploiting his good nature again and...

His sheath collapsed, his consciousness gone.

He found himself as he truly was, huge and powerful on the Grid, emergency overrides dissolving his fantasy self to show him the monster beneath.

"Eh? What the fuck now?!"

Failsafes on his base unit had cranked his operating speed up to near impossible levels. His racing mind filled with alarms, datafeeds reported the beginnings of a substantial explosion close by in the Real. He was thinking far faster than a human mind ever could, sensations from the Real filtered in through the treacly slowness of temporal dislocation. Subroutines compensated, allowing the full spectral range he ordinarily enjoyed, adding meaning to the Real's distorted sounds, slowed to slothful, guttural roars. He felt the arco vibrate as a shockwave strolled through its structure, and his attentions switched to a human emulant on the arcade outside. At first glance there was nothing special about it, you would take it to be the kind worn by geriatrics or tourists remotely holidaying, only this one was engaged in the final stages of fiery disintegration as a low-yield atomic ignited within it, and it was nearly entirely organic.

He wound back the outside camera footage, to see more clearly. The face of Professor Zhang Qifang was looking back at him.

He watched as balls of flame unpacked themselves from the elderly professor, sprouting into expanding bubbles of destruction, announcing the birth of a short-lived star, right on his doorstep.

Pretty, he thought, but inconvenient.

The shockwave ran ahead of the explosion, ripping the floor into splinters, pushing out and down, smashing metal, a sphere of violence that spared nothing. The office windows blew out, the pieces simultaneously melting, the door was slammed off its hinges, into the waiting room and through the wall on the other side where it disintegrated into burning embers, then evaporated. The electromagnetic pulse that preceded the blast wrought havoc on the arco's systems, shutting much of the city building down, but Richards' heavily fortified base unit held, and he continued to watch with morbid fascination. He was helpless. Pedestrians outside on the gallery were flung into the wall or hurled to their deaths in the park below, others caught fire and twisted like dervishes, those nearer exploded into their constituent pieces as if a helpful holofeed were describing the anatomy of humans, their skin flayed away, then their flesh, then their bones. Those nearer still simply turned to steam.

It rarely paid an AI that interfaced with the human world to run so quickly. In such a state they could think so fast a day would pass as a month, and although they would process much in that time, they could do nothing useful in the world of the Real, the material universe became as unyielding as rock.

"Balls," said Richards, and sent Otto another message, cramming as much information into it as he possibly could. "You're on your own now, big fella."

Time, no matter how slowly it ran, could never be stopped. Richards initiated thousands of simulations, trying to figure a way out. There were none. He had no time to upload himself in his entirety elsewhere, and where could he go anyway? He could send out a sensing presence back to his sheath in Detroit or to any one of the fifty he had elsewhere, but his very core was about to be consumed by fire, leaving any remote projection a broken facade, dribbling nonsense. What would be the point? He sunk into an unfamiliar lassitude.

Richards watched the world he had built blasted to pieces. A wash of nuclear heat scoured the offices of Richards & Klein clean. The air ignited, the resultant vacuum sucked the exterior walls in, then flames roared out of the arco as a great part of the building burst outwards, four floors up and four floors down from the detonation's epicentre. He was only glad that Genie's base unit was at her parents' house.

The young star devoured the last of Richards' external sensors, and he lost all connection with the Real, then the Grid.

Alone in the dark for what seemed an aeon, Richards felt his processes flicker and die one by one.

I'm dead, he thought. After all his years of fretting about extinction he felt disappointingly ambivalent, now it finally came down to it.

The flow of Richards' subjective time ran slow as geology. The fires burned like whirligigs depicted in glass, unmoving sculptures, until his life was snatched away with a terrible abruptness.

CHAPTER THIRTY

Qifang talks

Veronique and Jagadith climbed for hours. They camped on one of the tree's broad branches, a silent Jagadith keeping watch. Veronique was fit, but at the end of that first day she was a mass of aches and grazed all over. She envied Jagadith's stamina. He was bound by some of the strictures of flesh, she'd seen that, but he was not in any way human.

They drank water from holes in the wood, and ate the flesh of a giant rodent that had been foolish enough to stray within reach of the paladin, who roasted it on a fire of bark shavings.

Halfway through the fourth day they reached the top. The drooping crown of spiny leaves proved difficult to ascend, but they persevered. On a wide platform of green, they found themselves standing between two worlds.

Reality 36 stretched away into purple, mountain distances, making the swamp, jungle and tree seem pathetically small. In the sky rotated the vortex, huge and foreboding. Each of its arms was a lazy stream of matter sucking into a hole in the centre so black its colour was more than the mere absence of light.

"We must go in," said Jag.

"There's a chance we'll both be atomised," she said. "How can you be sure that won't happen?"

"I cannot," said Jagadith. "You are the expert."

"You're right," said Veronique. "I've got to think." She thought, then said, "Certain of my kind partition the worlds they visit. It's how we run our in-world research stations. This could be like that, a door to a sealed off part of Reality 36. We should be OK..." She shook her head, not able to believe fully what she was seeing, and wandered round the crown of the tree to take the vortex in from all angles. "Why is the vortex taking the matter of this world into his sub-world? Pulling this off is not easy."

"Your professor is incapable of such work?"

Veronique shook her head. "Qifang certainly has the skill, I just don't see why he would do it."

"Your devotion is most touching, madam goddess," said Jagadith, "but I urge you to put aside your concerns for this man. I fear he has been concealing his true character. Men do not change in so extreme a manner."

Veronique looked at him. "At the time the RealWorlds were closed off, there were thirty six Realities, until the hackers got into them; four worlds, each unique and full of life, were wiped out by idiots. Whatever is happening here, I am not about to let that happen again. I don't care who is responsible."

"Then let us not be dallying." Jagadith went to climb the tree's topmost leaf. It was as big as hill, the point within touching distance of the vortex. She followed him.

They gained the top quickly, the nearness of their goal lending strength to their tired limbs.

"Well then," said Jagadith, and reached for the vortex.

"Hey!" said Veronique. "Let's not rush."

Jagadith nodded.

"Pass me your knife."

Jagadith handed over his dagger. Veronique hacked a stringy, fist-sized lump of fibres out of the leaf, bundled it into a ball, hefted it in one hand, then threw it up into the hole.

It exploded with a violent flash.

"That is most troubling," said Jagadith, and frowned. "We have no way in."

"That's not true." Veronique put her hand out to him. "Now might be the time to let me try out my divine powers."

"We will alert your mentor."

"He knows we are coming."

"It is still risky. You do not know it will work."

"No, I don't. Don't you people trust your gods?"

"We spend rather a lot of effort keeping them from meddling in our affairs," said Jagadith. "Five billion gods are too many for any world. Still," he sighed, "it is the only thing for it. If we do not go now, the world is lost at any rate. I have no doubt that is what Tarquinius would tell me."

"OK. Let's do this." Valdaire paused.

"Now? Why do you delay?"

"I'm thinking. This isn't easy. I've got no experience."

"Madam goddess, we must go on. Either it will kill us, or it will not."

An amber sphere ascended like a drop of luminescent oil rising through dark waters. It descended, its radiance focussing itself into a spot of light that grew stronger until the sphere touched the dark of the floor, where it burst like a soap bubble, shattering into a hundred fading stars. Where it had been were Jagadith and Veronique.

"Most efficacious, Madam Goddess," said Jagadith approvingly. "You guided us as surely as a pilot brings a ship safe to harbour." Apart from himself and Veronique, who shone with a faint moon glow, nothing at all was visible. "Now, where are we?"

"Let's try something straightforward," she said, and then she shouted, as loudly as she could. "Professor!" The volume of her voice was shocking in the quiet – both she and Jag had been whispering before without realising. "Professor!"

A light cracked the horizon, a distance of several miles, Veronique guessed, bringing feeble illumination.

"Veronique? Veronique, why are you shouting. I may be old,

but I am not yet deaf." The voice was everywhere, in everything.

"Professor!" she shouted again.

This time there was no reply.

"I see," said Jagadith, his lips tight. He shifted his grip on his sword. "Be wary, madam goddess," he said to Veronique, "your mentor is suffering from the largest of all divinity complexes."

They walked towards the light. It was freezing, and Veronique suffered. Jagadith reached out and grasped Veronique's hand. His hand was warm, and no plume of steam issued from his mouth. He squeezed slightly, reassuring her. They walked hand in hand a while, then he slowed, and whispered.

"They are here, madam goddess," whispered the knight, "to either side of us. No! Do not look directly. Try not to draw their attention, they are changed, my fellow paladins, but I doubt their abilities are much diminished."

A long row of giants emerged from the dark. Each of the realms had had their own, simple security protocols. Over the years they had been given forms by bored nerds. Jokes, really, elevated to the status of demigods when the RealWorlds were closed, and set to guard the universes against their creators.

They glowed with pale blue light. There first was a knight upon a horse, armoured in the late gothic fashion, glaring imperiously. A titanic moose stood by his side, its mouth slack, gaze unfocussed, a wooden club of Herculean proportions loose in a primitive hand. Next to him was a bear with an eyepatch. They and a score more stood silently, tracking the pair with eyes glimmering like hateful stars.

It was a long, frightful walk. Veronique wanted to break into a run, to get to the pool of radiance ahead. Jag held her back.

"Be careful," said Jagadith, his voice full of calm. "They are Qifang's creatures now, but they still remember me as the greatest of them. Only my will holds them from assault. Move slowly." A single droplet of sweat worked its way down his temple from under his turban. "It troubles me that the other paladins are enslaved.

The work of your mentor goes beyond this realm and into the others. This is not like any expulsion I have ever performed before. He is a powerful man, this Qifang."

As they approached the light, it drowned out the glow of the paladin ghosts, but she could still feel their hard gazes on her neck.

They reached the brilliant light. When Veronique looked into it, she could see nothing, and so she stopped.

Jag stepped straight into it, dragging her with him.

They were in a room. She blinked afterimages away. The change was as disorienting as it was sudden. It took her a few moments to recover.

It was an office. Books from several centuries lined one wall, ancient mechanisms another. Pieces of pre-electronic machines and newer tech littered the place, half-buried by drifts of living paper. Outside, the sun shone on students crossing a university quadrangle, garbed in mid-21st century fashions.

It was stiflingly warm after their walk through the cold.

"This is incredible," said Veronique. She inspected the ceiling, touched the wood, rubbed dust between her fingertips. "This is not real, is it? This is the most convincing virtuality I have ever seen. They never feel entirely real." She trailed off, walking round the room. "In the best virtualities, like the Realities, there are always signifiers of unreality. But this..."

"It is his office, yes?"

"No, no, his office is like all the others. Dippy law would never tolerate something as individual and extravagant as this." She looked at a shelf where a mechanical monkey carrying cymbals sat. A marionette very much like the Frenchman hung by its strings close by.

"Then perhaps this is a reconstruction of one of his old offices, or a dream of one," said Jagadith. "Not all gods come with heavy hands, some are lost, and seek a home."

"He probably had one like this, once. He's very old, older than the dippies, that's for sure," said Veronique. "It's like stepping back in time."

Jag's lips quirked, his first smile since the death of this mount. "Perhaps you have." He looked about the room. "The same as always, but different as I expected," he said half to himself. "Not like I remember the Real."

"You have been into the Real?" Veronique stopped herself. "I suppose it is possible, I don't see why not." She looked at him quizzically.

Jagadith started, shaken out of memory. "A very long time ago now by the running of our years, perhaps a decade of yours." He breathed a deep breath. "Through here, I think," he said then, moving toward a curtained doorway on the other side of the room.

"Isn't that just a closet?" said Veronique.

"When the Realities are invaded by the gods, things are rarely what they seem. There is artistry here, great skill."

A darkness came, the impression of a giant bending down, pressing a huge eye to the window to peer at them, though they saw nothing. A breeze ruffled the detritus on the desks. Fearful images ran across the living paper, and screams sounded outside, distant and desperate. It passed as soon as it started. Sunlight streamed in, motes of dust sparkling in the shafts. Veronique shuddered.

"What the hell was that?"

"Peel back the wallpaper and it might not be a wall you see, but the very stuff of nightmare. This is the flipside, as I believe you say," said Jagadith. "The essence of the man we seek is on the other side of this partition. So no, it is not a closet." With that he swept the curtain aside and they stepped through.

On the other side was an indeterminate space. In the middle ran a column of coruscating energy, a figure of a silvered man rotating slowly within it. Next to that, sat incongruously upon a milking stool, was Professor Zhang Qifang. He closed the book he was reading with a snap and looked up. He gave them both a welcoming smile.

"You are persistent," he said. "I was hoping my paladins would have stopped you." He stood and made his way painfully over to

the pair. He looked Jagadith up and down. "But I suppose I should
have expected it of you, the greatest paladin of all. I suppose I
should regard your coming as an honour, only I'm not a fool. I did
try and stop you. I have failed," he said. He didn't seem unduly
worried by that.

"I am not a man for the stopping," said Jagadith calmly. "I am
a man whose sole purpose it is to protect this world from the likes
of you. A task, I add, I will take no small amount of pleasure in
accomplishing, on account of the demise of my friend, Tarquinius."

"Why? He will be reborn. The deaths of you avatars are always
temporary. You know nothing of true death, nothing at all."

"He will not be the same as he was. Nor will I."

"Really? Now that is very interesting,"

Jagadith opened his mouth, the old man interrupted.

"No, no. I do not dispute your claim, you are far better placed
than I to know. I always intended to look into the transmigration
of digital souls in Reality paladins. Never got round to it. Too little
time," he slumped a little. "Too little time for everything." He
brightened. "But soon I will have the all time in the world."

"I beg to differ, sir," said Jagadith, and pulled at his sword. The
blade did not leave its scabbard fully, for Veronique had grasped
the knight's arm.

"Jag, you'll kill him." She was matter of fact. There was no plea
in what she said.

"A deserving fate."

"I am sure there must be another solution."

"No, Dr Valdaire," said Qifang. "I am indeed here as your friend
no doubt has told you. Up to no good," he grinned like a schoolboy."
He pulled a face at Veronique's shock. "You are disappointed. I am
sorry. But it is not really so surprising. Nobody wants to die. If you
look death in the face, it changes you. When you have, Veronique
you will see things my way."

"This goes against everything you ever taught me."

"On the contrary. I am doing this precisely so that I may continue
what I have been teaching you. I am dying. I have lived as long as

it is humanly possible, and it is not enough. I must complete my work. Once I am gone, how can I protect the Realities? It is more than life to me, it is my vocation, and I will not allow death to stop me."

"By destroying a whole world?"

"No! By creating a new one! One with me at the centre, where I will be able to build a paradise, and protect forever these places that you and I care so much about."

"You can't do that," said Valdaire. "You're condemning millions of sentient beings to death, beings you have fought for years to protect!"

"A regrettable occurrence, yes. But Veronique, you know that 36 is the most violent of all the realms. Its loss is regrettable, but I will recreate it anew, and better, and then it will safeguard all the rest. One dies to save thirty-one, a good transaction."

"And what of self-determination? Does that mean nothing to you any longer?" Veronique said angrily. "What about the law?"

Qifang laughed an uproarious laugh. "Look not at this old body, Veronique, but at that," he pointed to the silver giant behind him. "I will be above all law! The self-determination of the inhabitants of the remaining Realities will be guaranteed for all time, and I will deal most harshly with those who would have it any other way. Veronique, please. You do not understand. 36's loss is a noble sacrifice."

"This world is not your plaything," said Jagadith calmly. He shook off Veronique's arm drew his sword.

Qifang sniffed dismissively. "You expect to harm me with that? I am afraid you are too late. Shortly my reconfiguration will be complete and a new world will be born." He turned to Veronique, his eyes fevered, "And it *will* be a new world, a real world, Veronique. I will create a heaven away from Earth."

"What if you are wrong?" said Veronique.

A flurry of expressions flickered across Qifang's face, as if he were searching for the right one amidst a poorly-archived filing system.

Jagadith frowned. "Something," he muttered, "is not as it seems here."

Qifang's face settled on a gentle smile. "Put away your sword paladin, I would not wish to destroy you." The silver man and the doorway to the office disappeared. They were at the centre of the dark again. Beyond the circle of light the three of them stood within, the ghosts of Jagadith's fellows jostled. "See? They will all have a place in my new world, as could you, as could you both."

Jag stood back, his sword dropped to his side. "Madam goddess, he is right, I cannot fight him. He is too powerful."

"Ha! You see sense, prince. Listen to him, Veronique. You respect him, and well you should. Listen to what he says. Think of what we could achieve together here."

"Silence," said Jagadith, and held his sword at full stretch, its point directed unwaveringly toward the professor. "Madam goddess," he said to Veronique, his expression full of regret, "it is I who am sorry. I was wrong. I am thinking you may be right about your professor."

"What do you mean?"

"I cannot fight him because this is not Professor Zhang Qifang. This is not some interloper from outside, but something much worse. You need to be gone from here, now. I am sorry I do not have time to properly enact a banishment. I only pray that this will work in its stead."

"But if that is not Qifang, wha…" began Veronique, and stopped. The pain was sudden and all consuming, quickly followed by a numbness that coiled about her heart. Jagadith leaned in and pushed his sword hard. She felt the metal scrape on her ribs as it forced them apart. The sword emerged from her back, its fire charring her flesh, the burnt-pork stink of it filling her nostrils.

"What are you doing?!" shrieked Qifang.

"Go now in peace, and with my protection. This is not your mentor, you must believe that. Above all, remember you are not really here," said Jag. "Please Madam Goddess, live, and do not come back."

Veronique looked, her eyes questioning, mouth open in shock. She could not talk. The cold enveloped her, her vision dimmed to a point of light, Jag at its centre as grim-faced as Shiva.

The light went out.

Veronique's body slid off the knight's sword. He turned to confront the shades of the paladins.

Valdaire's blood evaporated from his blade as he raised it against his fellows.

Veronique awoke with little drama. Her first short breath hissed between dry lips, perhaps a little more eagerly than if she had been sleeping, a second followed, deeper and longer, then coughing, awkward and painful around the feeding tube. She tugged it free in a state close to panic, spit and mucous dripped on the floor.

She was back.

Her breathing rasped in her ears. Her eyes were dry and scratchy, her eyelids caught painfully when she tried to open them, and they filled with tears in response, blurring her sight. It was dark, and she stank, her own rank odour an affront to her nose. She sat up and rubbed her breastbone, the place where Jagadith's sword had pierced her in that other place. It throbbed, but there was no sign of a wound. The rush of relief she felt was mingled with fear. Many had died from similar injuries. The mental buffers to prevent dream-induced death had been removed when the NUN set the Realities free.

She must have been insane to even think about going in there.

She felt up to her forehead with a shaking hand, to where the warm v-jack headpiece grasped her skull. She fumbled with the release, turned it off and laid it aside.

Her hair was lank. Her breath reeked, her bladder ached, a sharp discomfort coming from the catheter when she moved. Coming fresh to her filth from the idealised world of Reality 36 made her disgusted. She needed to bathe.

She sat up, pulling feebly at the sensor pads on her chest and head. She also needed to eat, the soupy gruel delivered by the feeding tube and the IV would keep a Grid surfer alive for a month, but it was a lousy diet. She'd lost a couple of kilos, maybe more, she was never heavily fleshed. Her ribs had become sharp lines, hips bony nodules.

She smiled grimly at this ultimate in weight loss regimes. People had starved to death before the RealWorlds had been closed off, dying because they could not tear themselves away from their fantasies.

She continued to unhook herself from her support web, intent on the machines. It was dark but for the faint glow of ready lights and gelscreens. Tears continued to flood her eyes, she tried vainly to blink them away. The clock, she wanted to see the clock. She peered at it until it came into focus. Her eyes stubbornly refused to work, but she persevered. Eventually the digits swam into clarity. Twelve days, she'd been out twelve days, one synchronising her neural patterns with the Reality's accelerated time, only eleven actually within. Close to two months had passed subjectively during that time, mostly travelling up the rift to the anomaly site. The time lag was one of the Reality's original features, allowing people to live other lives over weekends. She'd never experienced it so pronouncedly before. The sensation was odd. She could see that would be addictive too.

Only when she leaned forward to ease out her catheter did she notice the men watching her in the dark.

"Doctor Valdaire," said one of them. He was holding a gun on the other, a cyborg across the room who perched uncomfortably on an armchair. The gunman looked familiar. The battered auxiliary mind wrapped around the back of his skull sparked her memory.

"Santiago Chures?" She recognised him from the university, the agent who had come to talk to her the day she'd decided to run, and he had caught her frolicking in Reality 36.

"I think you had better explain yourself," he said.

CHAPTER THIRTY-ONE

A message

Qifang had forgotten the faces of his mother and father. He could not remember the year of his birth. When he looked into the mirror an old man stared back at him. His memories were ruins. He remembered Karlsson, he remembered being connected to his machines. He remembered k52. He remembered pain. Little else.

He wanted to stop, to rest and pull his mind back together, but he could not, he was under a compulsion as strong as a curse. His message filled him to brimming, roared in his head, driving him on to... where?

He'd left the campus, he remembered that. He visited the Reality House in the desert, then there was the demonstration of the machinery by Karlsson in Detroit. Long journeys apart, journeys that were lost to him. He could not remember why, nor could he think where he might have gone in between. He was not concerned with Karlsson's work. It lay outside his area of expertise, yet he had a nagging feeling they had talked of it often. Karlsson, a big man, foreign, Norwegian. He was usually so implacable, but Qifang remembered a day he was nervous, sweating in the air-conditioned chill of the House under the sand, months before he had resigned, whispering frantically, showing him charts.

k52.

He grappled with his recollections, but they were jigsaw pieces, impossible to see what went where.

The disease. The cancer. He was dying, wasn't he?

A flash, later, months later. Karlsson's strange home. He'd gone in and then left Karlsson's factory in a daze in a car, not his – his own had gone. Then the message had begun its inexorable tug on his psyche. He hadn't even gone home but had headed straight for the airport and hopped a cargo blimp to Philadelphia, changed for another, larger tube freighter with multiple passenger berths heading out to Luton Spaceport. The gold covering its skin, the howl it made as the sunlight warmed air in the voided centre and forced it onward, all of it was unfamiliar, he had no recollection of such craft, but at the same time it had seemed as if he knew such things intimately.

His mind was incomplete, blank spaces where a century of memory should have been, instead crazed images, as reliable as shadows. Was this what dementia felt like, he wondered. The drugs might have begun to fail. He could have become ill.

He was awed when they flew by the Miami space elevator, its cables scored black against the sky, curved by distance and disappearing to nothingness as they pierced the atmosphere. They flew over the seafarms of the Atlantic coast and the water chimneys pumping cooling vapour into the air across the American continental shelf. He craned his neck to better see the carbon sequestration rigs of the deep ocean and the towers of Atlantis. This was not his world, it was not the world he remembered, his was an older world, a world in crisis. And yet he knew it, somehow.

He looked from face to face, some were as entranced as he, some bored, but all appeared as if they had expected these things. Only he was surprised. He did his best to hide it.

They flew on. New memories left him as soon as they were formed, falling into the pit of confusion at the centre of his being. He recalled being crammed into an observation cupola with the freighter's other passengers, twenty or so, pointing excitedly at a pod of blue whales cutting overlapping wakes through the ocean.

A flash of awkward dinner conversation at the captain's table where in mid-flow he had stopped, unsure of where he was.

"Are you alright?" asked his companion, a woman who did something important somewhere, details that slipped from his mind like water through the weave of a net.

He was not alright, he had forgotten his own name. He made his excuses and left the table, pleading sudden illness, perhaps the thinness of the air? He refused the captain's offers of help and the airship's doctor. Reeling like a drunkard to his bed, though he had imbibed no alcohol or other intoxicant, and the airship's passage was smooth and sure. He lay down and fell into a fitful sleep, his night disrupted by a cascade of memories, shattering into ever smaller pieces as they fell through his dreams, and always the pull of the message.

Another night he awoke with sharp certainty: his brother, dead of drowning in another century. Until then, he had not even been aware he had once had a sibling, the message crowded all else out. He wept. He soon forgot.

He became wrapped in a fugue. Days later, he found himself in an alien city in an alien land, the USE, England; was that where he had been heading? He was looking out at a crowd of buildings that were themselves cities, watching as one of them burned. The message urged him on toward the fire, he tried to make it stop, to tell it that the epicentre of the blaze was his supposed destination, but the message was single-minded, and would not heed him.

He was stopped by a security cordon, an armoured police officer made to send him away. An android grabbed his shoulder, gestured to his face then to the human cop. Featureless police helmet and featureless machine mask both regarded him carefully.

They brought him in to a police station and left him there for hours. Time slipped again, and he found himself in another country, or so he guessed, for the journey that brought him there had evaporated like a dream after waking. But he recognised the place, the EuPol Five's temple to itself, one of Europe's halls of power. He had been here once remotely, why, he did not recall.

The Five questioned him long and hard, he felt tendrils of it trying to force themselves into his consciousness as it spoke to him. How he could do this was unclear, because Qifang wore no mentaug or uplink. The tendrils withdrew. The Five radiated a sense of irritation. It questioned him again. Qifang told it what it already knew.

"What do you remember?" the Five demanded.

He was afraid. This was not like him. He was a powerful, confident man secure in a sense of his own expertise and self, but these certainties were gone, and a child's fear remained. "I remember nothing. Please, I need to see Richards. I have a message to deliver. I must deliver my message!"

"To Richards?" it said, as impersonal as thunder. "Why? What message?"

Qifang dropped his head and sobbed, exhausted and alone.

The EuPol Five made a noise of annoyance. When Qifang opened his eyes again he was in a garden at a wirework table. Food lay before him, the Five manifested on the other side as an Olympian being, its perfect face marred by an expression that belonged on a bureaucrat

"Very well," said Hughie. "I will bring you Richards. But you will have to wait a while, because he is unfortunately dead at the moment."

CHAPTER THIRTY-TWO

Otto versus Chures

"We don't have time for this," said Klein. He was huge, and well-specced, if dated, a forty-year old model. Multiple redundant organs, carbon-bonded bones, in-built healthtech, and a cranial mentaug more powerful than those permitted civilians, even now. His muscles were massive under his skin, roped unnaturally with polymer overlays, their tension twisting his body out of true. Santiago was not intimidated by strength, he never had been, but he was wary of the German.

"We have time for whatever I say," said Chures. "Until I am satisfied, we are not going anywhere." He lifted his gun. It was powerful enough to threaten Klein.

The German nodded as if it made perfect sense – him, the woman, the gun. It was a simple equation.

"You are making a mistake," Otto said. "I was the victim of an assassination attempt this morning. They know where I am, they will have followed me. They will be here soon."

"Nice try, now you will be quiet," said Santiago. "You are all suspects in an ongoing VIPA investigation; you, your partner, Valdaire and Zhang Qifang."

"An investigation into what?" said Otto.

"I am asking the questions." Chures gestured with the gun by way of emphasis.

"What is going on?" demanded Valdaire. She had as sharp a mind as they said then; coming out of the Realities led to massive disassociation as often as not, but she was already asking questions.

"You need to answer that yourself," said Chures. "And how you two are mixed up in this together."

"Agent Chures, listen to me, Valdaire and I have nothing to do with each other. Me and my partner Richards are engaged in an investigation into the death of Zhang Qifang. I've come looking for her for the same reasons you have. We are on the same side."

"Ah, your partner," said Chures. "The Five. He's a rogue. I've been lobbying for greater limits on his actions for months. Maybe this will convince my superiors. The Fives are not to be trusted, least of all him, so you'll forgive me not being reassured by what you are saying to me."

"Qifang is dead?" asked Valdaire.

Chures glanced at her. She was shocked. Unless she was angling for an acting award, she had not known, but was that the face of a grieving lover or a loyal colleague?

"They are all dangerous, Agent Chures, but the Fives are not all the same," said Otto.

"They are not all the same?" Chures said. "What? Do you think they have stabilised the world? They have contributed to humanity, to good governance, the science, the arts? That is what they want us to believe. I wish I could, Mr Klein. I want a better world. I was raised in the camps. I saw such things there. The machines can deliver a world free of such suffering, but only under our direction. Their goals are unknowable. Think of your own partner. He works to amass money, what does a machine need money for? Don't forget that these supposed digital saviours of ours almost destroyed everything when they were first turned on."

Chures was gratified to see Otto had no answer to that.

"My back-up will soon be here," he went on. "Until then, you are both under arrest. We will get to the bottom of this then."

Otto stared at Santiago like an aggressive ape. "Chures, you're making a big mistake. We're in danger."

"Shut up Klein."

"Chures…" Otto began to stand.

"I'm going to have to kill you if you don't sit down." He brought up his pistol, this time intending to fire to wound, but before he could pull the trigger, his mind disintegrated.

"I am sorry," said Chloe. "You told me not to reveal my presence, but he was going to shoot you. His aux-mind has been crudely deactivated and his uplinks have been removed, but the short range receivers are intact. I infiltrated these and caused a feedback storm. I hope I did the right thing."

Otto looked down at the unconscious agent. Crudely deactivated? The implant looked like it had been battered with a hammer.

"I'll forgive you," he said. That was another close call. There were too many of those recently.

"Chloe?" said Veronique. "Do you have my phone?" she asked Otto.

"Veronique, oh Veronique," trilled Chloe. "Give me to her, please!"

"It's in my pocket. It's staying there for the moment. Now we have to leave. You have some medical training, correct?"

Veronique nodded.

"I have some supplies, I see you have too," He indicated the machines that had been monitoring Valdaire while she slept. "You will treat Chures as we fly. I doubt what Chloe did has done him much good." Otto scooped up Chures' gun. It was a nice piece, heavy, forty-seven round high XP pellet magazine, fully automatic. The gun resisted him for a moment until his adjutant broke its rudimentary mind into shards. He retrieved his own gun and reholstered it and tucked Chures' weapon into his belt. "But first, tell me my why you ran."

"You are not with the VIPA?"

"I am freelance. I am here on EuPol business. Qifang was

murdered in USE waters... It is complicated," he said. "You did not know he was dead, did you?"

"No," said Veronique.

Otto was quiet for a moment. "We'll talk when we're safe. Get your things. Quickly."

"Oh Otto," said Chloe. "It is too late, they are here!"

The thrum of a heavy lifter coming in low roared out of the night. Harsh white light played over the forest.

"We need to leave here *now*," said Otto

An amplified voice boomed out from overheard. "This is Agent Santiago Chures of the Virtualities Investigation and Protection Authority. You are under arrest. Put your weapons down and leave the cabin slowly."

"Who's he then?" shouted Veronique over the rumble of airship engines, pointing at the other Chures.

"I do not know, but we have been tracking three versions of Professor Zhang Qifang across the Atlantic. Maybe this is more of the same."

"Three?"

"I said it was complicated," said Otto, bundling Valdaire's medical equipment into a bag. "I hoped you would be able to tell me why. A lot of people think you are in this up to your eyeballs, so Richards would say."

"I have no idea what is going on," said Valdaire, shouting over the noise of the airship over again. "I met another version of Zhang in the Realities, planning to make them into his own personal empire. I didn't believe it was him, and now I am totally confused."

"Great," said Otto. He picked up Chures and slung him over his shoulder, and hung the bag from the other. "Let's go."

They went to the door, Otto knocking mouldering furniture out of his way. Through gaps in the walls the beams of searchlights laid a harsh pattern across the floor. The cabin was shaking, dust and rubbish pattering down.

"Will they kill us?" Valdaire asked.

"They are searching for a landing point. That means they want to talk to us. If they VIPA or if they are not, they want us alive," said Otto.

"What if you are wrong?"

Otto set his face. "Then I am wrong."

The lifter hovered over the cabin. The noise of the turbo fans hammered their hearing. Mossy shingles tumbled from the roof. Searchlights glared hard pools of light onto the forest floor. The pines behind the cabin creaked in the wind. Downdraft raised whirlwinds of pine needles and leaves. Otto eased open the door, and stepped out carefully. A searchlight locked onto him instantly.

"That's far enough, Klein." A silhouette stepped out of the light, and resolved itself into a impeccably dressed Santiago Chures. "You are under arrest."

"Under whose authority?" yelled Otto. "This guy on my shoulder has already arrested me. Which one of you should I listen to?"

Two men in VIPA armour were moving in from either side, using the cone of light to hide their advance.

"Drop your weapons and the imposter. I give you my word you will be taken into custody unharmed." Chures reached out his hand.

The men outside the searchlight beam raised their guns.

Otto dropped Chures and the bag and shoved Veronique to one side, his augmented strength sending her crashing back through the door into the cabin, diving aside as bullets smacked into he wood.

"Take him down!" shouted the new Chures. Gunfire erupted from the heavy lifter's gondola joined that coming from the agents. Otto unholstered his pistol as he landed, rolled, two precision shots finding the weak spots in the knees of the agents' armour, sending them sprawling and cursing. Chures opened fire at point blank range. Otto shot back, and this time he meant to kill. Both men emptied their guns into each other's chests. Bullets smacked through polymer muscles into Otto's subdermal armour. Alarms chimed in his mind as some found their way through. Drugs washed through him, keeping him active. Chures staggered back, his aim went wild, and his gun clicked dry, then did Otto's. Otto charged, smashing Chures with a forearm swing, lifting the agent clean off his feet and sending him right into the cabin wall. Logs splintered. Chures slid to the floor. Otto tossed his last EMP grenade into the middle of the three prone operatives. The grenade discharged. Sparks ran over the troopers, locking them in their armour as their circuitry fused. Chures thrashed about like a landed fish, and Otto thought him beaten.

Then he stood.

Chures' shirt was soaked with blood. His flesh and his suit were tatters. Otto saw chalky bones underneath.

Otto reached for the gun he'd taken from the other Chures, but it was gone, and his hand came up empty.

"That was unwise," said the false Chures.

A high powered taser pulse from the lifter hit Otto, sending electricity coursing through his systems. He toppled over, paralysed. His vision dimmed, but he could see Chures' snakeskin shoes pacing over the brown pine needles and dirt. They stopped centimetres from his face. They filled his vision, the scales red with android blood.

Chures squatted and cradled Otto's head in his hands, moving Otto's face to look at him. The agent's torso was a ruin. A rope of bloody slime hung from his mouth.

"We would not have harmed you," said the false Chures, in a voice that was a broken digital slur. "We would not harm any human, except of necessity. You have made it necessary for us to kill you and these men who have seen what we are. Thanks to you, they will not witness the wonderful world that is coming. Let their deaths be on your conscience."

The android kicked Otto onto his back, knelt on his chest and squeezed his head between both hands. It was phenomenally strong, its grip increasing, the pressure unbearable. Otto's reinforced cranium creaked. Warning icons danced over his iHUD, and spots whirled round his vision, a kaleidoscope of failing imaging systems.

The report of an explosive round sounded. Half of Chures' face disappeared. His skull hinged open to allow a spray of something that was not of human origin to exit, then slipped back closed with a wet clack. The android froze rigid. Otto fought to peel its crushing claws from his face. They came free, and the false Chures toppled off him.

Otto heaved a gasp, tried to get up, then fell back. He was badly hurt. His healthtech would keep him alive, but he needed medical attention fast. Across the overgrown clearing stood the other Chures, the real Chures. He had his gun in his hand, smoke issuing from the barrel. He had Chloe too. He spoke rapidly into the phone as he walked forward. The searchlights went out. The heavy lifter rose up a few metres, and the engines calmed.

Otto tried to sit up again, but could not.

"You are not as good as they say, Klein," said Chures. "I took my weapon from you and you did not notice."

"I am old, and obsolete," grunted Otto. "Take it up with my designers." He tried to sit again.

"Just stay there," said Chures. "My people are coming. There are medical facilities on the heavy lifter. We will treat you." Chures examined his doppelganger with distaste. "What the hell is this thing?"

"That's what I'm trying to find out," said Otto through teeth gritted in pain. "What happened to you?

"I was betrayed," said Chures explained. "My bonded AI tried to suborn me, before this whole thing took place. I remembered that Valdaire used to hang out here in college. It seemed an obvious place for her to go, but it was only luck that saw me get here. This goes far beyond meddling in off-limits Grid space. Something serious is happening." He toed the corpse, saw his boots on the feet of the fraud, muttered something sharp under his breath and knelt to retrieve them. He moved stiffly, and Otto saw he was injured himself. "I read your file too. It said you were formidable in combat, and it was not wrong. I thank you for not killing my men."

"They were doing their job, I was doing mine," croaked Otto. He felt like hammered shit. Everything hurt. He was close to passing out.

Chures cleaned off his boots with a rag torn from the android's clothes and put them on. He stood up, examined them critically, then looked down at Otto. "In regards of what happened here, I suppose you were telling the truth, but you will remain in my custody until we are sure you are not involved in the violation of the RealWorld Realities, or in the production of these machine doubles. You have my apologies for your injuries, and my thanks for taking down my impersonator. Treasure that, because I do not apologise often."

Soon the area was busy with VIPA personnel. Aircars arrived, and the cabin became a crime scene lit up with portable lamps and bustling with human and machine activity. As Otto was hoisted onto a stretcher he saw a group of techs bag up the remains of the fake Chures and take it away. Valdaire was deep in conversation with Chures. She was gesticulating angrily, Chures was stony faced. Otto could not hear what they said over the damn static roaring in his ears, all his senses were compromised. He protested as hyposprays were pressed against his arm and a lead inserted into his neck interface, but he was too weak to resist. The medics did their work and his pain dulled.

He lay on the stretcher, fighting sleep, only allowing himself to succumb to anaesthetic when they were all on board the heavy lifter and he was sure they were in the hands of the real VIPA, and not some other, entirely more sinister group.

CHAPTER THIRTY-THREE

Richards rebooted

What I really want is some root beer, thought Richards. He was amazed at how much he hankered for it.

Hang on...

Don't fight it said a voice, maddeningly familiar. Root beer. Yummy!

This is not right, Richards replied. a) It's horrible and tastes of antiseptic, b) I am a machine and don't get cravings, and c) the last I remember, I was dead.

Spoilsport, said the voice, which was his. Kind of.

An avalanche of unconnected data roared through his mind, washing out consciousness.

Everything went away.

The next time Richards came to, Hughie was there.

"Welcome back Richards. How are you feeling?" said Hughie. He stood to one side of the workbench Richards' sheath lay upon. Hughie was in a sheath that had been tooled to resemble his online guise, although this was not naked but clad in an expensive Italian suit. He sounded almost solicitous.

"Oh Jesus, you haven't put me in a shiny god model too have you? I don't want people thinking we're related," Richards said.

"I see you are your usual objectionable self," said Hughie. "Fine. You are wearing, as you can quite plainly sense, one of the Zwollen-Hampton models you favour. I even dressed it as you prefer, in that ridiculous hat and coat."

Richards patted himself down. "Typical. Much less expensive than your suit. You've always been a cheap bastard, Hughie."

Hughie let out a perfect facsimile of an exasperated sigh. "I do not know why I bother. I rather hoped death might have mellowed you. Curse me for being an optimist. I'm going. I'll speak to you when you're behaving less unpleasantly." He turned and around and began to walk away.

"Wait! Wait!" Richards said. Hughie stopped.

"You have something to say? Maybe thank you?"

"Thank you, Hughie."

"And?"

"And I'm sorry, Hughie. I have, to tell you the absolute truth, felt better. But then I was just blown up by an atomic bomb, so I am sure you can find it in your tiny heart to forgive any lapses of decorum on my part."

"Charming," said Hughie.

"I mean it, thank you," Richards tried.

"It'll do, I suppose," said Hughie.

They were in a large android repair shop. Sheathed humans, present humans, and AIs moved swiftly between work benches in a professional bustle. The walls were the same grey concrete as the floors, which was to say, the same grey concrete as that in Hughie's hall. They had to be in Geneva near to Hughie's post-neo-post-post-modernist monument to himself.

"How did you save me? I mean, you did save me didn't you? This isn't a copy of me, is it?" The thought of that alarmed him.

"That's against the law, Richards," admonished Hughie. "I don't break the law, even in a crisis."

"Crisis? Heh, and I thought you were posting me on a routine murder investigation. Actually," Richards reflected, "I didn't think that, because I don't trust you. But you *said* you were putting me on a routine murder investigation."

"I said nothing of the sort. The murder of one of the world's greatest thinkers is hardly routine, Richards," said Hughie.

"OK. The word 'simple' was used, though."

"I really had no idea this would get quite so complicated," admitted Hughie. "Come on."

"Cock," muttered Richards as Hughie strode off, leaving Richards little choice but to follow after him, because out in the Real Hughie liked to do the talky stuff the old analogue way with vibrating air molecules and all that. Mind-to-mind offered less opportunity for theatricality, thought Richards, but he restrained himself from thinking bad things about the other Five. For all Richards knew, Hughie had a front row right there in the theatre of his head. He had no idea what Hughie had done to him.

"You can thank Lincolnshire Flats for your continued existence," said Hughie. "Your base unit was very badly damaged, but somehow he managed to extract your core from the wreck, then it was a matter of transferring that to a new base unit, and linking it in to your back-up memory banks. The existence of which, while following the letter of the law on duplication, hardly adheres to its spirit," Hughie turned and gave Richards the full glare of his eyes.

"You drafted the law, Hughie, you should have been more specific. Anyway, the back-up's just memories and stuff, no governing consciousness," said Richards, trying to shake the image of his blackened base unit being airlifted into the coroner's disassembly room, Flats whooping and clicking as he sawed it apart. "I like to think of it as a bequest to my biographers. Surely you back up your own non-core attributes?"

"Well, right or wrong, it saved you," said Hughie, avoiding the question. "You're running on the base unit of one of my subsidiaries right now. We'll have to get you a new one, I'm afraid, yours was terminally compromised."

"You killed one of your minions off for me? That's cold even for you, Hughie."

"Don't be so melodramatic, please. His name is Belvedere, and he is in limbo for the time being. You don't think I'd delete one of my own associates to save you, do you?"

"Then why did you bring me back at all?"

Hughie stopped and turned to face the other android. "Because you are a Five, and there are precious few of us left. And because you are my brother."

Richards grinned, Hughie looked pained. "I didn't know you cared."

"I also need to know what you know, and the law also says that I can't just pillage your memory banks if there is the remotest chance of actually rebuilding you."

"Damn those sentient rights, eh? You wrote that one too."

"I did," Hughie said. "This way." They turned down a long corridor, passing numerous branching ways and heavy steel doors. "It wasn't just that, there was someone who needed to talk to you. We're going to see him now."

"I had no idea your lair was so expansive," said Richards.

"This isn't all for me," said Hughie in a manner that suggested he wished it was. "This is the back up complex for the Union Government. It is an impressive little township, with independent food, water and energy facilities, enough to sustain several thousand human lives." Hughie seemed proud.

"And you squat at the heart of it like a big fat spider. You must like that. All those yummy little people flies."

"You can't help yourself, can you?" said Hughie irritably. "Must I say this is a secret, and that you will not tell anyone about it?"

Richards made a noise. Hughie took it for a yes. "Good," he said.

"This place is built to last Ragnarok out. Is someone expecting a war?" Richards said, taking in the twenty-centimetre thickness of one of the doors as it opened, lock-wheel spinning. Beyond lay a huge cavern, of which he got but a glimpse, but he heard the sound of engines, and the echoes allowed him to calculate the volume at four cubic kilometres.

"One should always expect war, Richards, always," declaimed

Hughie, waving his finger in the air. "Read your Sun Tzu: preparedness is the key to all victories, indeed, true victory is won without battle. You, with your back-up, appear to be well aware of that already."

They passed a long slot window reminiscent of a bunker's firing slit, glazed with diamond weave glass. Another enormous space lay beyond. Richards saw piping and house-sized, geothermal turbines, bright yellow hazard paint on concrete, and raw rock.

"This way," said Hughie and turned left down another corridor. A delivery cart trundled past, beacon flashing. They turned right, up some stairs and then through a sliding door into human accommodation, cramped in comparison to the machine halls. The corridor walls were painted a calming shade of blue, the floors were carpeted. The air was full of muted office buzz. It was comfortable in a banal way.

They came to a large security door that opened for Hughie almost obsequiously, Richards thought. The door led into a dark room occupied by a stern special forces cyborg. His augmentations were far more modern than Otto's and hardly visible, but Richards did not doubt that he could crush rocks with his bare hands. Much of the far wall was one-way diamond weave, on the other side of which was situated a comfortably appointed interview room. Sat at a glass table was a small, haggard, confused looking, but very much alive, man.

"Professor Zhang Qifang, he presumes," whispered Hughie, in a rare moment of levity. "Because although he thinks he is the professor, it's actually a rather poor copy."

"He presumes right and you wrong," said Richards. "That is not a copy. It *is* Zhang Qifang, sort of, but it's only part of him." Richards frowned. "So the message was for me," he said. "What is it?"

"He won't tell me," said Hughie, obviously annoyed about that. "We shall find out in a moment, I suppose."

"Wait," said Richards. "Not yet. Get the London Coroner's office on the phone. We need Lincolnshire Flats."

"No need for that, he's here already," said Hughie. "He insisted he reassemble you himself. I think he is rather fond of you."

Having Flats as a fan sent a shiver down Richards' spine. "And the other Qifangs?" said Richards. "Are they here too?"

"Naturally."

"In that case, free up another base unit."

"I can't just pull them out of thin air!" protested Hughie.

"If you can do it for me you can do it for Qifang," said Richards. "It's time we spoke to the professor – *all* of the professor – and found out just what the hell is going on."

CHAPTER THIRTY-FOUR

Another Five

Hughie had another of his digital flunkies take a trip into storage. The thing's oily proclamations of loyalty made Richards queasy. Presently Hughie's small army of human and sheathed AI flunkies set up the vacated base unit in the workshop Richards had been in. Flats understood what Richards was attempting and had the two inert Qifang androids wired up to it, a third cable snaked out of the workshop, across the corridor to another room. Richards had insisted that they screen the active Qifang off from the two inactive androids. The vid Smith and Flats had shown him of the screaming machine, broken beyond repair and fettered in a sinister weave of fibre optics, still troubled him. There was no need to make this any more traumatic than it needed to be. The third android was still sure that it was Professor Zhang Qifang, and Richards intended to let it down gently.

"Well this is an interesting conundrum," said Hughie, stroking his silver chin. "The third unit believes itself to be an autonomous being. I rather suspect that for all its woolly headedness, it would pass the NUN's marker for conscious AI classification. That would mean it constitutes a sentient in its own right. Therefore, removing its programming from this carriage in order to amalgamate it with the remains of these two others would constitute a direct violation of its civil rights. You will be taking it apart and in making something new, which will destroy it as an individual. Technically speaking, you are about to commit murder, Richards."

"Shut up Hughie," said Richards, who was busy watching Flats direct the tech staff linking the three Qifangs and the base unit together. "We'd be guilty of a greater moral crime by not reconstituting the original as he intended. I knew what was going on here as soon as I saw Karlsson's set up."

"Ah, the great detective."

"Hughie, any idiot could tell that Qifang was trying to save himself and warn the world. Qifang found something out, something that put him in great danger from one of our kind, and what he discovered must have been pretty damn awful if one of us wanted to off him. My guess is that he became alarmed, Qifang went to Karlsson because he felt he couldn't trust anyone else. What they did together, I don't know, but it's obvious Karlsson had appropriated some of the research going on in the VIPA facilities at the Reality house. That's the key."

"Karlsson was a borderline anti-numerist. An AI-hating terrorist."

"That's as maybe," admitted Richards, "but without him, Qifang would never have been able to get out of the country. He had his mind speed downloaded for a post-mortem simulation without anyone knowing, that's what he kept going to see Karlsson about. The autopsy showed a clean brain, nothing foreign in it at all. I found a direct neural imaging unit, painful, not as good as a long-term solo-capt, but it would have done the job. I doubt it was much fun."

"Improbable," said Hughie. "DNI is fallible."

"These androids are improbable, but they're still here." Richards pointed to the wrecked Qifangs wrapped in opaque orange plastic bags, like the larvae of tomorrow waiting to hatch. "Someone's been moving the technological timetable up, this is forced acceleration."

"If the future can be predicted, and I believe in the accuracy of k52's curve, then I suppose it can be accelerated," said Hughie. "So what? One of the reasons k52 calculated the curve in the first place was to establish probabilities and push research in the right direction."

"So what? Qifang, the lead advocate of rights for our kind, got so scared he had himself speed copied to a flawed pimsim, something that he was avowedly against, and split his copied mind into three while he still lived. He waited for his doppelgangers to flee the country, then killed himself just so he could talk to me. That's a really big "so what?" Hughie."

Flats, who was inhabiting a medical carriage almost identical to the one he had in New London, trundled over to the base unit and began to berate the technical staff on the correct positioning of cooling units. He was working as he shouted on one of the Qifangs' heads, his deft metal spider fingers weaving the ruined brain into as complete a whole as possible.

"Really scared," continued Richards. "It has to be an AI that forced this, otherwise why go to such lengths to hide himself? I mean, he was pretty much as anti-pimsim as he was pro-AI. But for some reason he seemed determined to live on to speak to me. I mean, it was so serious that he avoided the Grid completely, when he could just have called me or sent a message. He was frightened it would be intercepted, and I would never know. That's why these," he indicated the androids. "No one knew they existed, so anyone who came across one of them would take him for the real deal, and they were off the Grid. The only real problem he faced was that the android carriages are not sufficiently advanced to accommodate a full human mind. You'd get a One in there with room to spare, no doubt, but we'd never fit. There's enough processing power in those artificial brains for a human ego skim, not much more. Qifang and Karlsson decided that if they got three of them, put bits of the deeper man into each with an ego skim running the show on top, he could be put back together at the other end. I figured that out from what Flats and Smith told me back at the morgue. Each of them has differing memories. Qifang went on the run *while* he stayed at home, killing himself to throw the scent off his copies until these things could lose themselves. It's pretty bold. It's so convoluted he could only be doing it to evade an AI. So you see, he always meant for us to do this. You're wrong about me murdering anyone. The remaining Qifang fragment isn't a person in its own right."

"Ah, but is it what this fragment believes?" said Hughie, returning to his legal cogitations. "We should at least put it to him. What if it has changed its mind?"

"Look, do you want to find out what this old sod went to ridiculously elaborate lengths to tell me or not? Or would you rather we piss away time until whatever Qifang was trying to warn us of lands on our heads?"

"Yes, you are right," said Hughie, unabashed. Even in agreement he somehow managed to make everything sound like it was all his idea. "Of course. It is clear that we have a rogue AI on our hands, that is of far greater concern."

"Or rogues. They must have had spies in Karlsson's factory. They usurped it from under him, then sent out more androids to look for the Qifangs, once they'd found out what Qifang was up to."

"And to try and kill you."

"And to try and kill me. They meat-puppeted Karlsson, killed off his friends, and personality-stripped the AIs in the building. That's why we didn't know anything about it until I went in. Although Karlsson was paranoid, I'm sure he'd have talked if he'd still been alive, if he could have got to us directly. It all had to be off the Grid. Thing is, how many other copies are there? Who else have they got out there who isn't who everyone, or indeed themselves, thinks they are?"

"I have already taken that into account," said Hughie dismissively. "You are quite safe, nothing untoward will happen to you here."

"I felt 'quite safe' until someone used a counterfeit centenarian

Chinese man to blow me up with a nuclear bomb, so you'll forgive me if I hold off on the tearful praise."

A couple of uniformed techs tapped commands into their phones. The base unit intended for Qifang's reformed mind sealed itself. Plumes of chilled nitrogen vented from the sides.

"They are ready," said Hughie.

"Right then, let's hear this message," said Richards.

Qifang listened to what the androids were telling him. There were two of them, one was the physical manifestation of the AI from the garden, the second wore a humbler body, and his voice was kindly. It was called Richards. The name excited the message. Qifang did not know why, but in his fuddled state, Qifang was thankful for Richards' kindness. When things were bad, kindness was all you could depend upon. His mother had said that to him.

"This procedure, will it help me recover my memories?" asked the professor.

"Yes," said Richards softly, "it will." He laid a plastic hand on Qifang's shoulder. "All you have to do is sit in this chair, and we'll attach this cable to your spine, then you should feel more yourself."

"A cable?" said Qifang unsurely. He struggled to understand the concept. It was frustratingly elusive, though he knew it to be a simple one. "What is wrong with me?"

"It'll be better if I explain in a moment," said Richards. "We'll have you back to normal in no time. I just have to ask you a few questions while it's in, neural patterning, that kind of thing."

Qifang nodded, he had once understood things like this, he thought. "Thank you," he said hesitantly. He lay back as directed. A hole in the chair gave access to his neck.

"Close your eyes," said Richards.

He obeyed.

A medic anaesthetised the back of Qifang's neck. "Can you feel this?" the woman asked, prodding the skin with a needle.

"No," said Qifang. "Nothing."

She cut into his neck then. He felt it as a tug. Blood pattered onto the floor. A technician wiped it away from his skin and plugged in the cable. There was a port in his neck, when had he had that put in?

"Well then," said Richards. "A couple of baseline questions first. What is your name?"

"Professor Zhang Qifang," replied the professor.

"How old are you?"

A flutter of the eyelids. He couldn't stop them. "I... I don't remember, not exactly."

Qifang waited for the next question, but nobody was speaking.

"Is something wrong?"

"I am Richards, Professor Qifang. You've been looking for me. What is your message?"

Qifang felt himself freeze. He was out of himself. From a long way away, he heard Richards say, "Professor Qifang?"

With inhuman precision, Qifang sat bolt upright, like a vampire rising from its coffin in an old 2D flick. The cable pulled taut. His eyes slid open.

His mouth moved awkwardly, making Qifang uncomfortable, but he could not speak. He felt the message coming. With immense relief, he realised he was going to be free of it. He tried to get it out. No sound came for a few moments, then it all came tumbling out.

This is what the message said.

"Richards. I do not know you personally, but I fear you are the only one I can trust. I am sure you know of me, and the work I have done for your kind. I hope that you will listen to what I have to say, and trust me in your turn. I have sent three of these mechanisms to convey this message to you. I pray at least one reaches you, for all our sakes.

"For the last few years I have headed a team based out of the UCLA artificial intelligence department. We have been examining the ongoing evolution of the remaining thirty two RealWorld Realities, a study instituted in conjunction with the VIPA, and overseen by the Class Five AI that calls itself k52." Qifang's jaw clicked, and a new voice issued out. "To better understand our place in the universe."

The voice was one often used by k52, and its calm authority was an insufficient shroud for the power of his mind. k52 was amongst the most potent of the Fives, and hearing it sent a spike of fear through the professor. The message continued.

"Four weeks before my death, I happened to run a deep scan of the four empty Reality lots. The state of the Realities is in flux, some grow, while others shrink. I was interested to see if the free space influenced their growth. It's quite fascinating. The Realities are in most senses, real places, and have evolved significantly since their emancipation.

"However, there is a large amount of spare capacity on their supporting machineries. After the four Realities were destroyed, the spaces they occupied were turned over to a small group of scientists, human and AIs. Supposedly, they were using the processing power of the servers to work on predictive modelling in an attempt to accelerate scientific development and sidestep further disasters like the Icesheet Tips and the Five Crisis.

"k52 claimed to be concerned with 'a little push here and there, my dear professor,'" k52's voice again. "Once areas of development were predicted, research projects were instigated, or entertainments tailored to seed ideas in the populace that would bear fruit in future generations of scientists. The body I speak to you through is the result of one such initiative.

"But k52 was lying. When I ran my deep scan of the Realities servers I found its logs were a nonsense. I found patterns suggestive of another persistent virtual world, a Reality 37, a world that should not be." The message's emphasis on these words was strong. Saliva ran from his lips freely with them, but the message did not care. "I reported this to k52. He assured me it was a lesser AI running a temporary historical simulation. I was content to let the matter lie.

"Not long after I was diagnosed with an aggressive gastric cancer. The diagnosis was a shock. I have received the best healthcare all my life. My gerontologist was baffled, but was regrettably forced to inform me such things can still happen. He advised me to go home and put my affairs in order, but I resolved to go back to work. I felt it better to finish my life usefully occupied. I do not believe my return was expected. Even so, I might have believed what k52 had told me were it not for the fact that when I did return, nobody had any knowledge of my discovery. The building Six had no recollection of my meeting with k52 to discuss it. I became immediately suspicious. I began to wonder if the disease might have been an attempt to silence me. If it were true, I feared more direct methods would be employed to remove me.

"I have had a long and uneasy association with Peter Karlsson, a brilliant man, if unstable. He was a supporter of my sentient rights campaigning, but his antipathy toward the Class Five AIs strained our relationship. It transpired he was right and I was wrong. I had no one else to go to. Over the course of two terrifying weeks, he helped me discover what was really happening in the Realities, and together we conceived of this plan to get the message out.

"k52's workspace is a Trojan horse, it is hollow. k52 has usurped the free space of the Reality servers and constructed a simulated universe of his own. It is amazingly complex, and would be a marvel if it were an end in itself. Alas, he is manipulating the space time continuum of this world, intervening in its development in the most brutal of ways, showing no concern for the lifeforms within it. He appears to be aggressively attacking it. For what reason, I could not tell, but he is behaving very much like the human hackers who caused so much damage at the beginning.

"I swore never to allow another intelligent mind to languish in bondage. I would act myself, but I am dying as I record this, and as you listen I am dead. Richards, I come to you because sit outside the camps that divide the Fives. They say that you are the most human of all the machines. Act upon this information. Do not let the crimes of your fellows go unpunished." Another pause.

"There are three of these androids in total. I have put certain aspects of myself into each. I never intended to live beyond my death, for I have lived a good life, but you should be able to create a post-mortem simulation with the data contained in the three emulants. If not, this recording will have to suffice. In either case, these will remain the last words of the real Zhang Qifang."

The message ceased, Qifang's head lolled, his mouth slack, his gown wet with spittle. He remained conscious, but he could not move. Reality receded.

From a great distance he heard voices.

"Christ," said Richards. "So it's true. k52 has gone rogue."

"Unfortunate," said Hughie, "and disappointing."

Flats called at stupendous volume across the room.

"Richards! EuPol Central! Come quickly! The procedure worked! It worked!"

It was the last thing Qifang heard. For the fourth time he died, and felt himself rushing away to some other place.

CHAPTER THIRTY-FIVE

Respite

"Did you miss me?" said Richards, out over the Grid.

"Did I what?" said Otto. He was in the heavy lifter's sickbay, wired up to banks of medical machines. They didn't seem to be helping. He was as weak as a baby and his head ached worse than every Sunday morning hangover he'd ever had.

"Didn't you hear? I got blown up big man, by an atomic bomb!"

"Yeah, well, I was nearly murdered by a robot pretending to be a VIPA agent. Our weeks have been equally lousy," said Otto, and wished Richards would leave him be.

"But I nearly *died*," protested Richards. "Properly. That's traumatic, we're not supposed to die."

"Get used to the idea," said Otto. "I've had to live with it since I was born."

"I still reckon nuclear bomb trumps deadly robot in the peril stakes," said Richards, somewhat sulkily.

"Perhaps," conceded Otto. "But all forms of death are equally deadly.

"k52's gone rogue," said Richards. "He's murdered a bunch of people, a few AIs. Qifang, Karlsson, Karlsson's followers and their machines. Sneaky bastard used Qifang's own plan against him, co-opting Karlsson's tech to send out that heiress."

"I never liked k52," said Otto. He shut his eyes. "There's

something else. I think Kaplinski's involved. Someone tried to kill me in Colorado. They used Ky-tech tactics."

"Are you sure it was him?" said Richards, who knew all about Kaplinksi.

"*Ja, genau,*" said Otto, tiredly slipping into German. "I caught flicker of a connection with him."

"This case gets better all the time," said Richards.

They spoke of all that had transpired since they had parted. With no need to hide, they were connected to the Grid as normal. Otto still found the constant bombardment of information irritating, but these were modern times, and that was the way they were lived. After a while Valdaire joined them, and they ported over to Richards' virtual office.

The office was as it always was, but outside the scene was empty, the rest of it lost to the bomb. Richards had amused himself by remodelling the undifferentiated whiteness into advertising hoardings, placing upon them an idealised picture of 1930s Chicago with 'Coming Soon!' inscribed below.

Otto enjoyed the illusion of being healthy. He settled into his chair as Richards introduced himself to Valdaire. She was fascinated by Richards' avatar, while Richards took it upon himself to flirt with her.

"Chures tells me we'll be at the Reality House in a few hours," said Otto a little while later, savouring both the lack of pain and the whisky in his glass. Richards poured himself something violently purple. It smelled like root beer, Otto raised an eyebrow at that.

"What?" challenged Richards, wounded innocence sending his eyebrows up his face. "I like it. It's just pop."

"Chures has been spoken to," said Otto. "The Uncle Sams have pointed out the validity of my AllPass. He has become almost friendly."

"You did save his life," said Veronique.

"I do not think he is the kind of man who cares much for debts of honour," said Otto. "But he does follow orders, and he has been ordered to keep us informed. He tells me that the Reality House has been evacuated of human and AI personnel. All are being debriefed in a secure location. The House is currently surrounded by VIPA and the National Guard. It has been isolated from the Grid."

"There are rumours they might shut it all down," said Valdaire.

"Don't worry," said Richards sympathetically, and patted her hand, she frowned at that, but he didn't react. "They can't."

"They should," said Otto.

"It'd be genocide, Otto," he said. "This isn't about the Realities, it's about what k52 is using them for."

"What about the Reality Qifang Valdaire encountered?" asked Otto.

"A red herring as old as the hills," said Richards, gleefully mixing his metaphors. "The best way to neutralise a whistleblower is to attack their reputation, paint them as the bad guy." Richards leaned back in his chair and thumped his feet up onto his desk. He blew out his cheeks and pushed his hat to the back of his head. "Qifang knew nothing about his online copy, I'm willing to bet that k52 ran off a personality from the pimsim unit at Karlsson's hideout and after they stripped the AIs, made the heiress and locked Karlsson up in his own head." Richards gesticulated with his glass of vile soda. "We'll be able to ask the genuine article in a little while," he said. "It's taking some time for his personality to reintegrate, not surprising when you consider about 25% of the information that made him up is missing, but it appears to be going well."

"How well?" said Valdaire.

"Well enough," said Richards. He finished his drink "And you big buddy, what about you? When will you be all fixed up?"

"I am not sure," said Otto. "A couple of weeks, maybe. The healthtech will see to many of my injuries, and some of my cybernetic components can be repaired before we reach the Reality House. But I require full maintenance. My shoulder has not been fully functional for a month. I am going to need full surgery."

"Ekbaum?" asked Richards.

Otto nodded and bared his teeth at the whisky burn. "They can repair everything else. The damage to my internals is already healing. I'll be operating at 88% efficiency. I can and will fight if it is necessary."

"Let's hope it's not necessary," said Richards.

"What now?" said Otto. When Richards said things like "let's hope it's not necessary," it usually was.

"That's a bigger question. We're all going to sit down and have a nice chat with the professor."

Beyond Richards' online oasis, Otto was suddenly weary to his carbon bonded bones, the sensation seeped into his avatar like cold, old oil. Anaesthetic was being pumped into his offline self.

"Mr Klein," a disembodied voice sounded in the office. "We are ready to proceed."

"Go," said Richards. "See you soon."

As Otto returned to his body, they were prepping him for surgery.

CHAPTER THIRTY-SIX

The three-quarter formed man

Hughie's garden was as warm as it always was, the sun unmoving in the sky, the plants casting their eternal noonday shadows on the perfect lawn. Richards, Hughie and the reconstituted mind of Zhang Qifang sat in an arbour of espaliered apple trees drinking tea. For propriety's sake, Hughie wore a quilted house jacket, slacks, slippers and a cravat, Richards his habitual travel-worn self. Qifang sported a silk robe of antique oriental design.

The old man was undergoing the phase all pimsims must, where they mourn themselves. His grief was apparent in every move he made. He spoke strongly, though with sadness, his gaze fixed on the lawn, watching the small creatures of Hughie's paradise go about their business. It did not matter to them if they were real or not. Such definitions had no meaning in their world, but that was almost certainly what preoccupied Qifang's thoughts.

"Was all this really my error, or the error of my prior self?" he said. "If so, is this being sat here in this garden with you, truly culpable for the living Qifang's mistakes?" He stopped talking and ruminated on this. Richards and Hughie let him. Like them, Qifang had all the time in the world in the garden. "It is strange," Qifang said after several minutes. "I remember so much, and with much greater clarity than when I, when *he*," he corrected himself, "was alive. The memory retrieval systems of a machine are more effective than those of the human brain."

"You will see things as they are, Professor Qifang," said Hughie encouragingly. "The moderating influences of recollection are stripped away. Your new mind is not fallible like your old mind. It will take you some time to adjust to this, but you will. Many of my post-human colleagues appreciate living a life free of self-deceit."

"But that means I am no longer human."

Hughie smiled as if that really did not matter at all. "More tea?" he asked.

Qifang declined. His first beverage was still untouched. "Humans remember imperfectly to protect themselves," said the professor. "It is why I never accepted an external memory. Millions of years of evolution should not be disregarded because we think we know better. How can one cope, when the truth of one's sins refuses to fade?"

"You should not fear for yourself, the human mind is more flexible in simulation than those generated wholly artificially. Many humans have external mem stores, or are pimsims, and it has done them little harm," said Hughie.

"That might be the case, but you are forgetting, gentlemen, that I am neither fully a man nor an AI nor an AI simulation of a man," said Qifang, and finally looked up from the lawn. He wore the face he had had when he died. Richards wondered how long it would be before he swapped it for a younger version, and how much longer it would be until an idealised one replaced that. "I understand a significant part of my persona is guesswork. A large tranche of my memory is gone forever, stripped out by the assailants who nearly destroyed my second doppelganger in the Morden subcity."

"The information is not wholly gone," ventured Hughie carefully. "One copy of it remains, on the Grid."

"Ah," said Qifang. He examined his feet. "You refer to my copy, the subverted mind employed by the rogue k52 to cover his activities."

"It will be possible, once he is deactivated, to retrieve the memories you lack from him," said Hughie. "Richards and I will be embarking on that task shortly. We will gladly perform the digital blending."

"Like memories are whiskies?" said Richards. "They aren't. It's not so easy."

"I agree," said Qifang. "To utilise k52's copy of me would be to risk contamination from whatever he has done to me, to him, to make him crave immortality as he does. Gentlemen, I have studied the psychology of artificial intelligences for so many years, including those who were once human. To alter a fundamental belief, such as that I had regarding the continuation of an intelligence after organic death, requires far-ranging alterations, both to the memories and the structure of the consciousness in question." He was beginning to lecture, the professor in him coming out. "I would never be able to tell the truth from the lie. I would never be sure what is me and what is k52's fabrication. I cannot bear another layer of ambiguity," Qifang smiled sadly. "Such an irony. Here I am, happy to die but apparently to live, while my other yearns to live yet must die. Perhaps we should exchange fates."

"That would not be sensible," said Hughie.

"Hughie has no sense of humour," explained Richards.

Qifang did not hear, he was looked deep into the grass again, and the scuttle of Hughie's arthropods. "I have thought long and hard, EuPol Five. I will not pursue any further memory of Zhang Qifang, better to leave him behind to the peace of his grave, while I come to grips with what I am now. I am an echo, or perhaps a portrait. I am not the man who was Zhang Qifang, nor can I ever be. But that does not mean that I wish to die."

Qifang's pimsim avatar stood with dignity and walked away across the grass. Hughie and Richards watched him go.

Richards leaned onto the edge of the bench and crossed his ankles underneath. "Do you think he is going to make it?" he asked.

"A lot of pimsims don't." Hughie exhaled and twisted his mouth, the light from his eyes cut off as he closed them. "But my garden is large. Maybe here he can find a measure of peace. One day he might be ready to face the world again."

"While we still have to face the other Qifang. And k52."

"Indeed. EuPol has uncovered k52's base unit and impounded it," said Hughie and opened his eyes again.

"Turn him off," said Richards, without hesitation.

"I did. But k52 had fled, his unit was inert. He's hiding in the world he's made, copied himself over to it."

"That's interesting," said Richards. "Promethea told me Annersley, Rolston and Planna were acting oddly. Are they all in there? There's enough capacity on the Reality servers for billions of Fives," said Richards. "What is he really up to?"

"Let's not find out, let's just stop him," said Hughie. He refilled his cup. "Qifang first, if we remove him we can prevent any further Realities being absorbed. Better I conduct this business, no? This kind of thing lies somewhat outside your abilities."

"Right," said Richards. "Dismantling minds is your thing. But I am coming with you." He stood, pointless, really, they weren't walking out of there. He'd be out of the garden when Hughie said, whether he was on his backside or hovering in the sky, but it gave him the illusion of decision. "What about k52?"

"He is in the outer spaces of the Reality servers. These can be deactivated without harming the other worlds once we have isolated him. It won't be long now before we twist the switch on k52 and his empire."

CHAPTER THIRTY-SEVEN

Reality 37

Gaining entry into Reality 36 was far from a simple matter, but the VIPA opened up their blockade without objection, and with the entirety of Hughie's choir of subservient minds at their back, Richards and the EuPol Five bullied their way in.

The transition in was abrupt. Hughie was unaffected, stepping through a tear in the air as if he were alighting from a boat. He did not spill so much as one drop of tea from his china cup, but their arrival left a discomfited Richards swaying on his feet as the portal closed up behind them, sealing off the roar of the outside Grid.

They found themselves on the far side of the canyon, away from the false Qifang's remaking of the world. The island in the middle of the Great Rift was no more, the stone sphere, marsh, anomalous jungle and the monkey puzzle tree broken down into a dense maelstrom of possibility, from which came the awful rumble of a world in dissolution.

In front of it, as mighty as a titan, stood the glowing form of Zhang Qifang deified, his luminous head brushing the space where the sky used to be.

"Woah," said Richards. "That's sort of freaky. He looks like you. Do you think he's got a similarly high opinion of himself now too?"

"Richards, please," said Hughie, sipping at his tea. "That's not the professor's work. k52 was ever the one for grand gestures. Look at this! It's so baroque. It has k52's mark all over it. Qifang was the man who saved us all, and I for one can't think of a more fitting deity for k52's brave new world. Now, I believe to finish this off, we will have to call upon the local protection." He looked this way and that, but the dusty cliff top remained unpeopled.

Richards walked over to the edge of the canyon and looked over the cliff. He was forced to hold his hat on against the wind. Not far from the feet of the cliffs the land was swirling away like a sand picture in the tide, its particles sucked into the vortex. "I don't think we have much time," he said.

"I suppose not." Hughie tossed his teacup over the cliff and dusted his hands off.

"You should get a move on," said Richards.

"I suppose so," said Hughie, and cleared his throat and cracked his neck from side to side. His clothes evaporated, leaving the shining sculpture of his body exposed. He laced his fingers in front of his face and pushed his arms out and squatted low, knees out, in the first of a series of stretches

"Hughie," said Richards. "What the hell are you doing?"

"Psychological preparation," said Hughie brusquely as he performed a number of thrusts. "This is going to be difficult. The Realities are not keyed to our minds, but to humans. To demolish one like this, even with my choir, requires a certain amount of effort, now be quiet."

Richards turned away and attempted to admire the view, but found it was dissolving faster than he could take it in.

Hughie finished his exercise routine, stood and cupped his hands around his mouth. "Jagadith! Jagadith Veyadeep!" His voice echoed off into the depths of the Rift until it hit the vortex, where it frittered into shining particles, "I call upon you! Your charge is threatened, hearken to its need! I command thee!" He clasped his hand behind his back. "That should do it. Melodramatic nonsense."

"Nerds, eh?" said Richards. "They're all hopeless romantics at heart."

Hughie nodded. "Look at k52."

"There is no need to be shouting!" said a young voice behind them. The two AIs turned and found an Indian princeling walking down the path towards them. In his wake padded a metal lion cub, whose clumsy pounces at insects might have been cute were the he not larger than the average Doberman. "I am well aware as to what is occurring here," said the boy. "Only, as you can see, I am powerless to prevent it."

"Not so, young man," said Hughie.

"We're the cavalry," explained Richards. "Zhang Qifang, the real – sort of – Zhang Qifang sent us here to sort all this out." He nodded enthusiastically as if that would help get his message across, then it dawned on him he was being patronising toward a mind the equal of his own. He wished he could behave with a little more gravity toward children, or those that appeared as children. He blamed his father for that. He had lavished attention on Richards, but had no patience for real kids, not even his own.

"And Doctor Valdaire?" asked the prince.

"Safe and well," assured Hughie.

"Ah, that is good," said Jagadith. "Ejecting her in such a perfunctory manner was impolite, and her safe conduct home was far from a certainty." There was a commotion as the juvenile Tarquinius scared up a jack rabbit, tripped on his over-sized feet and rolled into a bush. "I was overcome by my erstwhile fellows and slain, an unpleasant experience. I am happy to know my efforts were not in vain, though they reduced me to my current, diminished state."

"You can't fight Qifang?" asked Richards. "Will you be able to once you have reconstituted fully?"

"No," said Jagadith. "Were I at the height of my powers at this very instant it would not be feasible. He has absorbed too much of this realm to be ejected. And where would I eject him to? That is no man there, stood like Atlas in the valley. He never was. A clever trick. It is a bridge being built. A monument to the professor, but a bridge nonetheless."

"That," said Hughie slowly, "leaves us with only one, unfortunate, course of action." He pursed his lips. "You can guess what I am going to ask of you."

"Yes," said Jagadith and sat down on the ground. Tarquinius padded over to him and rolled onto his back. The youthful paladin tickled the lion's belly. Tarquinius let out a deep, metallic purring. "Dissolution of this Reality, the false Qifang with it. I can grant you the codes that will allow you full access to the heart and soul of the Reality 36, EuPol Five. They are in my gift to give." A tear rolled down his face, and plinked onto the lion. "This will mean the end of us, Tarquinius and I. Death is a fitting fate, for we have failed in our one appointed task, to safeguard the majesty of this creation. For that I am deeply sorry." He ran his fingers through sandy soil and let it trickle out. "We are at least together as we always have been, that is a small mercy to us."

Richards looked from vortex to giant to Five to boy to lion. "Hughie, is there...?" he ventured.

"There is no other way," said Hughie firmly.

"There was a something behind Qifang, a greater presence," said Jagadith. "It alerted me to the fact that all was not well with the professor. He was a front for the doings of some other creature."

"A rogue Class Five," explained Richards. "k52."

"That explains much," said the boy. "The door will be closed by the destruction of our home. Once Qifang is removed from the central server spaces, the other Realities will be safe from intrusion here, though they will need their paladins restoring," said Jagadith.

"It will be done," said Hughie.

"There is a false Reality beyond that must be dealt with if you are to deal with your wayward brother. It is within that that he hides. It would be better if it were closed down externally, from the material world. Decommission the servers that hold it. These Realities are for all their beauty are spun floss, and fragile, dependent on the goodwill of gods for their existence, whether they are old or new." He pushed Tarquinius away, stood and dusted his hands off on his brocade trousers.

"We shall do what we can," said Hughie.

"Now it is time. The codes," said the paladin.

"Your sacrifice will be remembered," said Hughie.

Jagadith bowed his head gratefully, then closed his eyes. Tarquinius did the same. There was a stutter in the world about them as a torrent of data passed between them and Hughie and the hardware supporting Reality 36 struggled to keep up. Then it was done. The paladins opened their eyes. Tarquinius nuzzled his companion, who scratched the beast's head affectionately and raised his other hand in salute. Both faded away.

"They are gone," said Richards.

"They were the codes," explained Hughie. "Handing them over in a form that enables their activation means the end of the paladins holding them."

"The ultimate failsafe, stops them employing them themselves," said Richards. "Nice, but very sad."

The ground shook. Distant rumbles assailed their ears.

"Quite, now be silent," said Hughie when it had abated. "With the paladins gone, Reality 36 will unravel. I have to concentrate. There's a proper form for this kind of thing, you see." Hughie walked to the edge of the cliff and didn't stop, but stepped out into thin air, gathering lightning in his arms as he strode over the canyon. The wind picked up behind him and his body grew in size, until Hughie was a match for the false Qifang.

"Wow," said Richards, his trenchcoat whipping about him, his tie batting him in the face. "You don't see that every day." He clasped his hat to his head.

Hughie brought up his hands above his head and clapped them together. A blast of energy rolled from them. Everything it touched disintegrated to nothing. The giant Qifang's face creased with worry, comically slowly. The energy wave consumed him shortly afterwards. The vortex went the same way, as did the canyon lands, and the ground that Richards stood upon, the dust in his eyes and the air he was pretending to breath. The wind dropped about him. The wave rolled away leaving blackness in its wake. It accelerated as it went. Soon it was over the horizon. Nothing remained.

Hughie was in front of him, his usual size once again.

"Hughie the wizard, eh?" said Richards shakily.

"I said there was a proper form for these things," said Hughie. "And that was it. Now there are only thirty one Realities remaining, and that is a very great shame."

"Not counting Hughie's fake."

"Not counting that. Now for the end of it, we make sure k52's trapped in his virtual space, and turn it off."

"You did the right thing," said Richards. He frowned. "Er, should that door be there?"

"Door? Door?" Hughie spun on his heel. "No," he said in surprise.

The door was a four-panel design centuries old, the door to a pantry or a bedroom or a kitchen in any one of a million houses. Only this door was covered in stickers of the kind a small girl might favour, drawn on with crayon, a little grubby, and stood in the darkness of a dead virtual world, unsupported by a wall. A door on its own should not have been anywhere, let alone there.

Neon letters buzzed over the top, some failing, but the motto it spelled out was clear enough.

Marita's World.

"Who the hell is Marita?" Richards said.

The door flew open with a bang.

"Uh-oh," said Richards. "I don't like the look of that."

Hughie opened his mouth. Whatever he had to say remained unsaid. A stream of violent energies surged from the air, spearing Hughie like a fish.

"I say," he said looking at Richards dazedly. "I feel rather perculiar." The stream stopped at his body. Hughie went limp, hanging as if he had been pinned to the darkness.

It was a datastream of such bandwidth Richards boggled at it, a datastream so fat it could only have been generated by a machine capable of conjuring whole worlds from numbers.

It stank of k52's Gridsig.

Richards grimaced as he dipped his hand into the wash of information, accessing the content conveyed therein. Subversion commands, Trojans, gatecrashers, phages programmed to kill, lesser near-Is by their thousands... punched right through Hughie, perhaps the most powerful AI on the planet. Hughie was a conduit back to his base unit which was linked to several hundred of the other most powerful AIs on the planet in a multi-stranded group consciousness, at the very core of one of the world's most powerful states.

The datastream bore an army. Hughie was being invaded.

"Fucking hell!" said Richards, and held his hat down hard.

Richards had seconds before he was noticed. He dithered between getting the hell out of there and running for the door.

"Bollocks," he said, rubbing his hands together. "I've already died this week. How bad can twice be?" He flung a message out back behind him, lodging it in Otto's thoughtspace. "Otto! Can't talk! Hughie has been suborned!" thought Richards. "k52! Running for the thirty seventh Reality! I'm going in! Can't explain! Have VIPA standby to shut down all the realms. All of them! Precaution only.

There was a crackle of a poor connection.

All of them? Otto's thoughts came via MT.

"All of them! Listen, Otto, find Waldo, he might be able to help unravel this, and shut k52 out," he said. There was no more time to send anything else.

He sprinted for the door. His hat flew off. When he got close, he dove into the datastream and swam as hard as he could.

Richards vanished up the lightstream through the door.

The door slammed, and faded into the dark, leaving nothing but Hughie hanging helpless in mid air, and Richards' fedora rolling about on a floor of infinite black.

Then that too disappeared.

CHAPTER THIRTY-EIGHT

The Reality House

Otto could not sleep, so he went to stand on the forward balcony of the heavy lifter's gondolas, and experienced a species of peace.

Above his head the horizontal teardrop of the balloon dominated the sky, massive turbofans at the rear; lifters were far too heavy to employ the solar jets of the passenger airships. The airship was stationary, moored to a mast on a VIPA airfield a few kilometres from the Reality House. Much of the house lay beneath the sand, a loaf-shaped dome prickly with termite cooling towers all that was evident on the surface. At the far side were low foamcrete buildings accommodating the research teams and VIPA agents stationed on the base. A guardhouse straddled four lanes of hardtop that took a thirty degree dive underground once past it, but that was out of sight. All Otto could see was the peculiar cooling hills, and a ring of armoured vehicles and a prefabbed double security fence bristling with weapons cutting through the House's black skirt of car parks.

Otto rubbed at his electoos. His hair was getting longer and he could no longer feel their comforting smoothness, another thing that needed seeing to. The repairs and surgery had gone well. His scars itched with accelerated healing. The doctors and technicians had done better than their best, and had managed to fix much of the damage. However, Otto's shoulder remained beyond the equipment on the lifter and the doctor had repeated his opinion that Otto needed to see Ekbaum. Over the course of numerous traumas, the carbon plastics bonded into the bone had deformed his scapula. That was the cause of the pain. It was a grave fault that had lain dormant in him from the beginning. He was getting old, his cybernetics were ageing less well than he was. The mistakes of the drawing board decades past were coming to fruition. When he'd been altered, he'd been promised a long life of vitality, superior to that of unenhanced men; another lie, one to go with his nightmares and the Bergstrom's Syndrome that had taken his wife. He could expect more malfunctions in the future, the doctor had warned him.

Ekbaum had said that before to him too, not long ago. Otto had ignored him, out of bullheadedness. He wasn't ready to quit. The ever-present throb in his shoulder suggested he should. He thought again about retiring.

He wanted to go back to the Londons, but he had to hang on until the fake Qifang was dealt with and k52's rogue Reality 37 deactivated. The first part of that had fallen to Richards and Hughie, and should be done soon. He'd heard the VIPA were going to decommission the servers carrying the dead space of the ruined Realities tomorrow. When it was done he could catch a stratoliner back. It was expensive, but Richards could pay for it. He had no patience for a transatlantic dirigible flight, not after all this.

His MT crackled.

"Richards," thought Otto. "Are we done here?"

"Otto! Can't talk!" Richards' voice was what Otto described as 'breathless', a state not brought on by lack of breath, for Richards had none of that to be lacking, but a halting way of speaking his partner had when running too much data at once. It was a mode of speech peppered with a tiresome number of exclamation marks "Hughie has been suborned!" thought Richards. "k52! Running for the thirty seventh Reality! I'm going in! Can't explain! Have VIPA standby to shut down all the realms. All of them! Precaution only."

"All of them?"

"All of them! Listen, Otto, find Waldo. He might be able to help unravel this, and shut k52 out."

"What? Find Waldo?"

But the connection had failed.

Movement caught Otto's eye around the Reality House. The lights on the security cordon flickered. The noise of engines powering up and down erratically broke the night's tranquility. Otto watched several vehicles jerkily moving backwards and forwards. Two ran into each other, the clang of their collision delayed by distance. Shouts followed.

Otto turned up his image magnification. He saw men leap from their machines, drop equipment, throw their helmets and comm beads to one side, grab their ears and roll on the floor in agony. Others stood jabbing at the buttons of unresponsive devices, bafflement on their faces.

Gunfire shouted out as the vehicles and autonomous weaponry of the cordon turned on the soldiers. The last shreds of peace fled.

Others joined Otto at the balcony, Valdaire among them. "What's going on?" she asked, rubbing wakefulness into her face. Alarms sounded. The airship came to life.

"A massacre," said Otto. "The machines have turned on the troops. Richards and Hughie have failed. k52 has usurped Hughie's court. It looks like he's used it to break into the VIPA, and turn their own equipment against them to protect the Reality House."

"He knows we're going to try and shut him down," said Valdaire.

"Of course," said Otto. "It is the most logical course of action."

"The heavy lifter, shouldn't we get off?"

"No," said Otto. "My adjutant tells me the Four pilot took itself offline at the first sign of trouble. Those vehicles down there, they have only simple brains, little independent thought, easily compromised."

The airship's docking clamps fell away from the tower, and it rapidly ascended, emergency water ballast streaming from its sides. Fire streaked up from the ground. Anti-munitions weapons shot it down. The craft's offensive arsenal followed, pounding a couple of tanks into pieces, but the heavy lifter was outnumbered and outgunned. Otto could feel the pressure of aggressive AIs through his mentaug, try to get at the Four pilot. It was retreating.

"Come on," he said. "Richards sent me a message. We need to speak to VIPA urgently."

"Care to tell me what it was?"

"He wants us to find Waldo."

The sky filled with fire as the lifter ponderously fled its assailants.

"My god, it's war," said Valdaire quietly.

"War?" said Otto. "It always is."

PART TWO
Omega Point

CHAPTER THIRTY-NINE

Ekbaum

Otto Klein sank into blackness. Machinery invaded his memory and spread its pages wide.

Notes sounded, silver trumpets in the dark.

It always came back to that night of the concert.

Why had he agreed to this?

The music faded.

Honour appeared in the black, a ghostly nimbus around her. Her head was shaved, her face drawn. An scar ran from her left ear right the way round to her occiput. She smiled nervously. "How do I look?" she said.

Otto wanted to say that she looked beautiful, and that he was sorry, but he was a spectator to his own past, and could only say what he had said. Back then he was eager to hear how she found the mentaug, eager to have someone who knew what it was like. He hadn't considered what the surgery might mean to her.

He listened as he said what he had said, and hated himself for it, as he'd hated himself every time he relived the moment since.

She lost her smile. "I'm tired, Otto," she said.

Honour's face crumpled into itself and fire bellied out from her mouth. The stink of war filled his nostrils. A man slid from Otto's bayonet, his face going slack. The near-I adjutant in Otto's mentaug scanned the field of churned mud and shattered trees for another target.

A ripple in Otto's mind; another time, another place. Stratojets screamed, plunging from the edge of space. A line of nuclear heat erupted along the horizon.

Otto raised his rifle. Another man died, and another.

Another ripple. Hamburg, as it was before the world went to hell. Ice cream running onto his fingers as it melted, making them sticky, the strong grip of his father's hand on his tiny child's fist. Security, safety. After that day, he'd never felt safe, no matter how strong he made himself.

Strength masked brittleness. His father had a different kind of strength, but that was insufficient to keep him alive. Was anyone ever strong enough?

Sleet in New London, refreshing after the heat of the summer.

Honour's face, drawn and thin, mouth slack with Bergstrom's Syndrome. "How do I look?"

Otto screamed. He arched hard. Straps bit into his flesh. A stab in his spinal interface port brought him back roughly into the now. He jerked about, panicking, not knowing where or when he was.

"Steady, Klein." A hand in blue latex pressed against his chest, small and delicate, like Honour's hand. Otto fought his restraints, at the mercy of his memories as his mentaug spooled down, its infernal chattering filling his mind.

He blinked his eyes free of tears. A long, sad face came into focus. "Are you with us, Klein? Are you with us?"

"Ekbaum," Otto croaked. His struggling ceased, and he knew where he was.

The doctor, a tall man of ungainly slimness, stood back. His shoulders lost a part of their permanent hunch, the creases in his frown lessened. "Good, good." He consulted a screen.

"What did you do?" said Otto. The noise in his head ceased and the room took on a shocked quiet, as of a crowd suddenly silenced.

"The mentaug immersion was a bad one? Disjointed, frightening even?" asked the doctor as he consulted his machines. "I suspected so. Very disappointing." In his green scrubs and blue gloves, long-nosed face pallid in the screenglow, Ekbaum resembled a carrion bird, expression set in distaste forever at its diet. "One should ask, 'What did you do to yourself?'" He pursed his lips at something red and blinking on a gelscreen. "You have been using it to remember, haven't you? When was the last time you came to see me, Otto?"

"I..."

"I shall tell you," said Ekbaum gently. "March 14th, 2126. Over three years ago, Otto. The terms of your consultancy licence and cybernetics permissions both stipulate a six-monthly check-up." Ekbaum's sad face grew sadder. "And now look at you." He shook his head. "Look what you have done to my work."

"Can you fix my shoulder?"

"That? Yes, of course." Ekbaum waved a hand. "But that is not what concerns me. The VIPA doctors, they told you that your shoulder is becoming deformed owing to the accretive processes of replacement carbon plastics, yes?"

Otto nodded. Two nurses, one human female, the other sheathed AI, came forward and undid the straps holding him to the diagnostic table. They pulled him forward and helped him to a chair, the robot bearing most of his significant weight. The human handed him a glass of water. He gulped it down. He was dripping with sweat. "They told me it was a flaw in my initial design."

Ekbaum's weak smile hid a modicum of outrage. "My designs are good. Are they experts in cybernetic interfaces? No. The problem is not in here." Ekbaum slapped Otto's arm. "It is in here." He prodded Otto's forehead. "This is a problem of the mind, of its interface with the mentaug. The machinery within you is functioning perfectly, it is you who are malfunctional."

"Is it...?"

"No! No." Ekbaum shook his long head. "No need to look so alarmed, it is not Bergstrom's Syndrome. You're clear of all that. It is some other thing, an emotional trauma, overwork, stress, something of that order, throwing your systems out of synchronisation." He gave Otto a brief, sympathetic look. "Your wife, Otto. That is what is interfering with your correct operation, emotional backwash, disturbing the equilibrium." Ekbaum looked sorrowful; he always did. He'd once told Otto he'd gone into cybernetics to arrest death, only to find it reflected at him tenfold.

Otto could have laughed. He was supposed to be a war machine. Stress should not be an issue. Now surely that was a design flaw. "Fine. Then I'll heal."

"Fine? No. The physical problems I can repair over a day, plus five to seven days recuperation. The emotional damage, however, that will require six weeks to repair, psychotherapy, AI-assisted mental manipulation, perhaps memory file excision. The process will be intensive. You will have to let her go, Otto."

"I can't."

"That is the root of your problem. How long has it been since she died?"

Otto did not answer. He felt a surge of anger that this man wanted to wipe away his pain. He never talked about Honour, not if he could help it; it hurt too much. He deserved that hurt, and guarded it jealously.

"I don't have time," said Otto. "Later."

"If you leave without remedial work, if you carry on accessing these painful recollections, you will suffer a great risk of serious malfunction, blackouts, hallucinations... Your pooled memories will begin to spill into your waking life," said Ekbaum. "There is a great risk of psychological trauma, and that risk will only grow."

"I will come back," said Otto. "I've no wish to die, not yet. Now, I let you plug me in to your damn machines, tell me where I can find Lehmann. It's the only reason I came here. He isn't returning my calls."

"Give me your word you will return."

Otto exhaled hard. "I give you my word. I'll be back." His shoulder told him he would. His dreams did, as little as he liked Ekbaum and his machines inside his head.

"Then I can tell you that Lehmann is outside, waiting for you."
Otto looked up sharply. "That son of a bitch."

Lehmann stood up from the couch as Otto entered the waiting room. He wore an enormous, oddly boyish smile out of character with his face that never showed itself in the field. He had been the best of Otto's old squad, both professionally and morally, but there was a machine's ice in him, as there was in them all.

"Otto." They embraced, slapping each other's backs hard enough to break the bones of normal men.

"That was a cheap trick, Conrad." Otto stood back. "I thought something had come between us."

Lehmann ran his hands through his long hair and looked anywhere but at his old commander. "How else was I supposed to get you to come to see Ekbaum?"

Otto looked Lehmann up and down and grunted. He was in good shape, better than Otto. His filmstar looks remained fresh, too.

"What do you mean? There's nothing wrong with me. I might look like a potato farmer next to you, but I always have. I'm fine."

Lehmann was unconvinced. "You should look after yourself better."

"You got my messages then?"

"I'm here, aren't I? I'm sorry about the deception. Ekbaum talked me into it; it was too good an opportunity for him. What was I supposed to do? We worry about you, Otto."

Otto grunted. "Lucky I got you to watch my back. Now do you want this job or not?"

Lehmann relaxed. "Yeah, naturally. Always."

"I haven't briefed you yet."

Lehmann grinned. "Since when has that made a difference?"

Otto nodded. "You noticed anything with the Grid recently?"

"A little jumpy, slow here and there, informational overload, they say."

"Not entirely true," said Otto. "A Five – k52?"

Lehmann shook his head. The name meant nothing to him.

"It's gone rogue, suborned the EuPol Five's choir, frozen up a lot of USE and USNA cyberspace. It's hiding in the old RealWorld Realities, got a direct pipe into the EuPol Five's choir. It could bring down the entire network."

"That's serious."

"It's the biggest thing since the Five Crisis. Interested?"

Lehmann pinched at his chin. "OK," he said. "Bit different to my usual line of work, but OK."

"Relax. We're not going after k52, nothing Gridside, all out in the Real. We're to find someone."

Lehmann folded his arms. "Who?"

"I'll get to that. That's the hard part. My partner Richards–"

"The AI? I never understood why you went into business with him."

"Yeah, well, I did. He is the inside team, we're the outside team. What k52 is trying to do out here… that's what we're going to find out, when we find this guy. You, me and a couple of others."

"I'm in then," Lehmann said, and retrieved a kitbag from behind the couch, ready to go. He was never going to refuse Otto.

"I've a car waiting outside. We're to rendezvous with a VIPA heavy lifter tonight outside of New London."

Lehmann whistled. "The VIPA? You running with them now?"

"Not really. It's complicated," said Otto. "And there's more. There's Kaplinski."

Lehmann raised his eyebrows. "Isn't he dead yet?"

"I wish. Three weeks ago, Kaplinski tried to kill me, and he nearly killed my partner. He's alive all right."

CHAPTER FORTY

Reality 37

Richards came around lying on his back and wished he hadn't.

"Ouch," he said. "Ooh, ouch, that really, really hurts." He raised his hands to his face, but the movement tripped off a wave of nausea, so he let them fall back onto the smooth, cold floor, eyes screwed shut, his senses spinning in the opposite direction to his stomach. Once he'd gathered his thoughts, he decided to turn his pseudo-biological feeds off, take the meat out of his machine and run off pure numbers, so to speak.

When he found he could not was when he pulled himself together enough to sit up. The effort of it made him whimper, and he threw up all down his front. He sat there, quivering. It was indescribably revolting. As a Class Five, and a curious one at that, he was open enough to most physical sensation, but there were limits.

He looked down at himself. Legs, arms, the usual, if you were one of the real people. He poked at his thigh. He looked at his hand. Both were flesh. He groaned, the wash of pain from his head making him instantly regret it.

"A full human simulation? Christ. Someone's idea of a joke," he said.

He was in simulations of the human body practically every day. He wore android bodies in the real world. He wore a human avatar on the Grid. But virtual or real, they were that little bit more and that little bit less than human. More importantly, they were all under his complete control.

This one was not. This one felt alarmingly genuine. He tried to snag at the world's underlying code, but he might as well try to telepathically communicate with a goldfish. He realised then that he had only the faintest awareness of his Gridpipe, and none of the Grid at all.

This body he wore replaced the thrum of the Grid with weird little sounds, the shush-roar of circulation, the creak of joints, the slither of wet, curled things in his abdomen. It was disgusting, and he began to feel ill again.

"How do they stand it?" he groaned. He staggered up. He bent double grasping his knees and gaping reflexively, bile dripping from his mouth. He made a few pathetic sounds and he surprised himself by feeling better, although it was a second before he could summon the will to stand up straight.

When he did, the first thing he noticed was that there were no doors.

He was in the hall of a stately home, flash with Victorian new money. A marble staircase swept up to a vulgar balcony, its banister fashioned from woods long since furnitured into extinction in the Real. Horrid touches caught his eye – panting gargoyles, tapestries of pale, rangy men with thinning hair and piercing eyes, stuffed animals possessed of far too much life. To his right a log smouldered in a fireplace. Something nasty, obscured in soot, decorated the fireback. An archway led out of the hallway to his left, where the polished chequerboard floor tiles disappearing into the dark.

As for the doorways, there were the door jambs, framing familiar spaces with wood, but when it came to there being an actual door, the walls were plain as bone.

"This is interesting," muttered Richards, and reached to push back his fedora, only to find it was missing, and he remembered it falling from his head when he dove through the door to this place.

Richards was not surprised to discover he could not make a

new hat. A mirror caught his eye. He walked over to it. There was just enough light to make himself out. He was in a version of the simulated body he normally wore: middling height, mid-forties, scruffy brown hair with the beginnings of a widow's peak. He had the face of a gumshoe, tired and worn out on too much whisky and too many worthless women; brown trenchcoat, threadbare suit – now wet with vomit – and a red tie. PI through and through. Richards liked mid-twentieth-century detective stories, so he styled himself after their fashion.

He missed his hat, which should have reappeared when he entered this reality, because that's the way he liked it and that's the way it worked. But it hadn't. And this body felt far too real. And he stank of sick.

"Bollocks," he said.

The squeaking of shoes approached from the archway. A figure dressed in full butler's regalia made its stiff-backed way into the hall. Its head was the last thing to resolve itself from the shadows; the head of a dog.

Grizzled black hair covered the head. Sharp ears twitched on the crown. The muzzle was long, the bastard offspring of auntie's Scottie dog and the big bad wolf. Red eyes smouldered. Dog-headed man was a misnomer; it was more like a dog in the shape of a man, thought Richards. He found it strangely disturbing.

"Good evening, sir." It sniffed distastefully at Richards.

"Nice outfit," said Richards. "It's natty."

The dog stared at him levelly, panting lightly. His breath smelled superficially of mint but it covered things left best uneaten. "Might I ask what you are doing in my master's house?"

"Beats the shit out of me," said Richards.

"There is," said the dog, clasping its hands behind its back and flexing its spine, "no need for language like that. This is my master's house."

"Nice place he has here. I'd say this is a visualisation of a one way ingress, right? If that's so, where's my gridpipe, and why am I so unpleasantly human?"

The dog looked blankly at him.

"No doors, see?" said Richards, pointing at the blank frames. "It's a visual metaphor for the grid architecture."

The dog looked at them as if it were news to him. "It is my master's house," said the dog. "I guard the entryway. It is my master's house. Good evening, sir."

"Right. You're not very bright. You're on a loop, aren't you?"

"This is my masters–"

"Hey! Hey! Less of that." Richards snapped his fingers. "Where is your master?"

The dog quirked its head. Suddenly it was standing right in front of Richards. "This is my master's house. Might I ask what you are doing, doing here in my master's house?"

"We've done this bit before," said Richards. He turned away to examine his options, but the dog was in front of him wherever he looked. "I've got in," he said, "how do I get out?"

"I am afraid I must ask you to leave." The dog shifted again. Another flicker; it became huge, clothes ripped, clawed hands dripping blood.

"I'm trying," said Richards.

"Get out, I say, get out, get ooouuuuuuuuuuuuuuuuuut!" The dog's voice broke into a howl and it threw back its head. The howl increased in volume until the ornaments rattled. Richards screwed his eyes shut against a torrent of dog breath.

Dying is becoming an annoying habit of mine, he thought.

He didn't die, not this time.

The howl abruptly stopped. The temperature dropped, and he was confronted with a sense of openness.

"Outside? I'm outside," Richards said, and cracked open an eye. He was outside.

"Score one for the great detective," he said.

A knocker clinked on its plate as if a front door had been slammed, although it was attached to a bricked-in space where a frontdoor wasn't. The outside lantern, an ugly thing held aloft by a grimacing centaur, went out.

"k52, what the hell are you playing at?" said Richards. He waited for his eyes; stupid human eyes with poor night vision. Ornamental woods gone wild surrounded the house. Wind rustled through branches silhouetted against a starless sky, where a pregnant moon hung large, its light a stark monochrome.

A loud crack came from the trees. Richards wasn't sure if he should feel afraid or not, but he did, and he could not disengage himself from his fear. Being at the mercy of his emotions was new to him. He didn't like it.

"Inside seems safer than out," he said, and scouted round the house exterior.

The house was massive but not large, its solidity giving it a weight far beyond that of its dimensions, and Richards went round it in no time at all, but he could not see in. A cruel iron fence kept him away from the walls, the stone was so dark it sucked in what little light there was, so he couldn't make much out beyond the shape. He looked back to the woods. The trees rattled, twigs beckoned him.

"Screw that," he said. Richards grasped the fence and heaved himself astride it, got stuck, then fell awkwardly. His leg snagged, cloth and flesh tore on an iron barb, and he fell gracelessly onto a flowerbed full of trash.

"Shit!" he hissed. He scrambled up again. His leg throbbed. He probed the wound. "Ouch," he said. His fingers glistened black in the moonlight. "This is far too realistic."

He limped as he felt along the wall for a door. As inside, so outside: no windows or doors. The frames were there, but the spaces between were as unseeing as skin healed over empty eye sockets. He reached a space where the moon shone unimpeded by trees and looked harder. A nightmare scene was coaxed from the shadows, painted where window glass should be. A ghastly face peering past transoms, flaking eyes fixed on his. Night drew in closer, hunting.

"Ugh, nasty," he said, and felt a little more afraid.

He went round the house again inside the fence. He swore as

his feet encountered hard rocks and unmentionable softness. All the windows were daubed with horror. When he was sure there was no way in, he scrambled back over the railings, more carefully than before.

An owl shrieked. Too loud, too close.

"Woods it is after all," he said briskly. He was trying to feel brave. When he did feel fear as men do, he did it because he wanted to, and it was fake; it could be deactivated. This could not. This was people fear, all squirting glands and the need to flee. He glanced behind him, enjoying the novelty of ungovernable emotion even as it quickened his heart and impelled him to hurry down the drive. Dead rhododendron leaves rustled; a sterile, woody scent carried from them.

He made sure he kept to the middle of the road, away from the fringes of the woods, just in case.

Richards turned from looking behind himself just in time to walk into a musty barrier, as solid as a brick wall in a dirty fur coat.

He spat hair from his mouth and looked up, and up.

Heavy paws dangled like mallets from long arms. Close-set eyes burned cold in a face as long as a wet Wednesday. Teeth glinted in the moonlight. A tiny Roman centurion's helmet sat atop a blockish head. A damp, heavy smell hit Richards like a billiard ball in a sock.

"A bear," said Richards.

"Damn right I'm a bear," said the bear. It jabbed a dagger-long claw at Richards' face. "By all rights I should eat you, sunshine."

"I'd rather you didn't," said Richards.

"Well, it's your lucky day. No devouring of prisoners," it said. "Regulations."

"Oh, good," said Richards.

"But hey!" The bear smiled a forest of teeth and held up a claw. "I can do this." Then the bear punched him full in the face, and Richards found the stars the sky was missing.

CHAPTER FORTY-ONE

Where's Waldo?

"No. Absolutely not." Chures pushed his chair back from the table and stood.

"Sit down. The decision's been made, Agent Chures," Deputy Director Sobieski, his perfect EuGene face hard, stressed the title. "Klein has all the relevant clearances, and a valid freelancer's licence. His partner's in the Reality spaces right now. Klein is qualified and invested. Surely you can see he's a good choice."

The others in the room watched in silence: Veronique Valdaire; a fat Texan called Milton with USNA Homeland Security – the big guns, at least so far as human influence went; a fastidious-looking VIPA agent who'd introduced himself as Swan; Henson, a stout man in military fatigues from USNA Landwar; and a beefy-looking Boer, a NUN attaché who was too important to have offered his name. There were a handful of others round the table, but Otto could tell the spectators from the players easily enough.

"We have plenty of qualified people of our own," said Chures.

"We do. And Klein here took out a whole squad of them without too much trouble," said Sobieksi, "while he was saving your ass, if I recall. Look at his resumé." Sobieski tapped at the table. The area in front of Chures sprang into life, files detailing Otto's career. Chures didn't look at it.

"Sobieski…"

"It's Assistant Director in here, Chures," the EuGene warned.

Chures gritted his teeth. "Assistant Director Sobieski. He's too close to the Fives."

"That's another reason he's in, and that is not our call. The Three Uncle Sams and the machines in the NUN conclave have swung it. The Director agrees. The numbers want him on board, so he's staying."

"Since when did we do what the machines say? It's one of them we're supposed to be bringing down. The VIPA works on equal partnership terms between man and machine." He looked around the table. "Has something changed?"

Sobieski leaned forward. "Yes, it has, and that's all the more reason for the numbers to want all this resolved quickly. We're all on the same side, in this and all other matters. Don't forget that, Chures."

Chures stood his ground. "Sobieski, let me take my own team, my own men…"

Sobieski sighed. "Chures, I said sit down."

Chures kept his grey eyes fixed on Otto as he sank into his chair. A Geckro membrane covered his neck where the housing for his treacherous AI had been removed. He'd had a manicure; his jewellery, expensive clothes and shoes were back. His twin custom uplinks, one behind each ear, had been replaced, but it'd take a lot more than a well-tailored suit to cover his wounded pride.

"As far as the rest of the world is concerned, we're going to be doing our job," said Sobieksi. "The VIPA is putting all of its efforts into preventing the spread of k52's influence into the rest of the Grid. We'll have teams working alongside the National Guard and NUN forces to secure the Reality House. It will remain locked down, but short of actually nuking the place, we've no way to get k52 out. That's where Klein and his partner come in."

"Richards is probably in league with the renegade," said Chures angrily.

"He warned us, Chures. He put himself at risk."

"It's a bluff, Sobieski."

"There will be no more disagreement on this matter." A voice intruded, that of Xerxes. A Class Five AI, like Richards, like k52. Xerxes was Uncle Sam 3, one of the AI triumvirate that ruled the United States of North America in all but name.

A Grid-free holo, fizzing with solar interference, manifested at the head of the table. Xerxes wore the face of an earnest government man.

"We desire that this issue be resolved immediately," Xerxes said. "It has been determined that the freelance security consultant Otto Klein, along with Doctor Veronique Valdaire, will accompany VIPA Agent Santiago Chures on this mission. Klein is to have equal authority to Chures. This is a multilateral effort. The NUN has agreed. That is all." The holo winked out.

"There, that settles that," said Sobieski. He pointed at his subordinate. "They are always listening, Chures, so don't go against what they say or you'll be off this case altogether. As for you, Klein –" Sobieski looked at the German "– don't think I'm entirely happy about this. This is a VIPA affair, not work for mercenaries. But you've got yourself a Five for a buddy and as we're seeing here, they're all real tight with each other." He leaned back and clasped his hands behind his head in pure alpha display – the EuGenes could help their display behaviour about as much as a monkey could. "I guess if you fail it will be you be answering to them. And for that I'm relieved; rather you than me. Agent Swan, give us the current situation on the renegade."

Swan was a slight man in a suit. A suit in a suit, Richards would say. He bobbed his head and stood. It took Otto a moment to realise the guy was a number, dressed up in some fancy near-human sheath. He did not blink – AIs never remembered to – and that gave him away. He had an info wand in his hand, old tech, but self-contained, safe from k52. The lights dimmed and holographic data filled the centre of the table. Reports, files, video and a large representation of the Reality House, loaf-shaped top to deepest subterranean bottom, the enormous server farm in the Nevada desert that sustained the remaining thirty-one free Realities, along with k52's project. Otto had only seen the topside of the facility in the Real; looked like the tip of the iceberg if the map was anything to go by.

"k52 has disabled the entirety of the Reality House's security net," said Swan. Vital nodes blinked red within the complex. "He has complete control over the virtual worlds generated within. Our men have formed a perimeter seven hundred and fifty metres back from the outer fences, just VIPA this close in, no National Guard until the outer perimeter. Their systems, as we saw two days ago, were easily overwhelmed," said Swan. He waved his wand. Video footage played, machines turned on men, weapons malfunctions, informational blackouts. "He skipped through the Guard's heaviest encryption like it was a field of daisies. Now we're on the scene, everyone out there now is pure analogue, radio voice communication, human hands on mechanical triggers, all interfaced staff have been pulled back. k52 can't do much about that." Swan pressed his lips tight. "But he could do a whole lot more. He has one of the most powerful collections of hardware anywhere on the planet at his disposal, but here's the puzzle: he's not actually doing anything with it."

"He going for digital uplift or something?" growled Milton. He was a big bear of a man, ruddy-faced and red-bearded. Otto knew nothing of him beyond what he'd gleaned from the man's introduction. His mentaug adjutant, walled off from the Grid like all the devices on the heavy lifter, was unable to furnish him with more.

"It's the favourite theory, but not the only one," said Swan. "We think his deification of Zhang Qifang may have been designed to lead us to believe that is what he is attempting, but we're not so sure. We can't get direct data from the Reality House currently, but system echoes suggest the remaining thirty-one Realities are running normally."

"But the spare capacity…" said Sobieski.

"There is a lot of that, and activity within is off the chart. Whatever's running in there is far more sophisticated than anything we've seen yet."

"More forcing of the technology curve, like these human emulants," said the Texan.

"k52 calculated the technology syne, so he is best placed to push things faster than they might otherwise go. There's no telling what he's up to in there. But it's big, and he's not alone. Three other Class Fives are missing, along with sixteen of the more individualistic Fours, and a Class Six from Singapore. None of them are attached to their base units, and we've some evidence to suggest, albeit inconclusively, that they're in the Reality House with him." More data came and went, much of it beyond Otto. Valdaire watched it keenly. "This could be the largest AI uprising since the Five Crisis. The curious thing is what k52 hasn't done. He's pinned the EuPol Five like a butterfly, frozen up a good part of the USE's digital superstructure in the process, and caused Grid freezes planet wide. With a thought he could toss the entire world back into the dark ages, and then come after us, but he hasn't."

"Why?" demanded the Boer.

"That is what we don't know," said Swan.

"Then that is what we need to find out," said Sobieski. "Klein's team is to find this man." A holo of a skinny youth sprang up in the centre of the table, associated files scrolling over the glass in front of each of the room's occupants. His birth age had him at thirty five years old, but he looked younger, the consequences of spending some time on ice. "Giacomo Vellini, though his handle is – was – Waldo. Doctor Valdaire, I believe you are the expert?"

Valdaire spoke up. "Yes. Vellini. He pioneered the only truly successful entrance mechanism to the Realities once they'd been closed off. I used it myself to follow the professor. He came and went for years without being detected."

"But he was," countered a stout VIPA man. "We caught him in 2119."

"We did," agreed Valdaire, "but only because he got careless, and cocky. He started to taunt the VIPA. Leave messages here and there. Even his username, 'Waldo', suggests a man who wished to be found. But he was the finest hacker of his generation. If anyone can get us into the Reality House's virtual space without k52 noticing, it will be him."

"Richards told me to find him," Otto added. "He might be able to do something about k52."

"Where is he?" asked the Texan.

"No one knows," said Henson. "He did his time, and upped and left USNA after he was defrosted and released from Brandsville. We thought he might have gone back home to Europe, but he vanished off the system, and no one's seen him since."

"Aren't these people supposed to be under surveillance?" said the Texan sourly. "You VIPA boys don't do your work well."

"He was," said Swan. "These people are the sharpest criminal minds on the planet, Milton, the best at what they do. If the likes of Waldo don't want finding, he won't be found."

"A wild-goose chase then," said Milton.

"Wait a minute," said the Boer. "You're going to find this Waldo, a man you say can't be found, and get him to shut down k52?"

"We are," said Sobieski. "The EuPol Five's plan was to isolate k52 and close off the part of the Reality space he was isolated in, but k52 took control before that could be done. This guy Waldo is our best shot. Otto and Chures will find him."

"Klein is injured," protested Chures.

"I am sufficiently operational," said Otto.

"Klein wants to bring in someone of his own," asked Sobieski.

"Now wait a moment–" Chures said.

"I've agreed," Sobieski interrupted.

"His name is Conrad Lehmann, a Ky-tech like me. The best shot of his day. Here's his personnel file."

"And our contingency plans, gentlemen?" Milton sat back. "What are they?"

Sobieski frowned. "While Klein's team is searching for Vellini, we'll have teams going into the Reality House itself, see if they can evade security and cut the physical connections of the Realities."

"I'll be leading that attempt," said Henson. "My men are ready to go when we get the green light."

"You are going to physically isolate the Realities? That will be dangerous," said Valdaire.

"We have full disclosure of the Reality House's security systems. We can do it," said Henson.

"I meant to the Realities," said Valdaire.

"It is a risk," said Sobieski. "But I think we can all agree that the loss of the remaining Realities is preferable to losing control of the whole planet to k52."

"What," said Valdaire, "preferable because they are not real? The NUN says otherwise. Thirty one worlds against one, is another way to look at it."

Sobieski looked keen to move on. "If we are successful in isolating them, it should set the EuPol Five loose, and we'll have the time to leisurely devise a scrubber to wipe k52 off the map. There is the risk of potential damage to the Realities, but..." Sobieski spread his hands. "It's better that than nuking them."

"I'm curious to know what he wants, and why he is doing this," said Swan.

The Texan snorted.

"Our role at the VIPA is to understand why the machines do what they do – not even the Director knows that, and he's a number like me. If we don't interrogate k52, how can we stop this happening again?" said Swan.

"Ask yourself, Swan," said Milton.

"I have, but I am not k52," said the AI reasonably. "My conclusions are therefore irrelevant."

"Assistant Director Sobieski, what if it fails?" asked the Boer. "What if your pet Kraut here doesn't bring this Waldo fellow back in? What if k52 dices your agents to dogfood? What then?"

Sobieski looked at Swan. Swan twisted his wand in his hands.

"Then, to borrow the Assistant Director's terminology, we will nuke the place. There's a stratobomber on tightbeam link to me only, targeting the Reality House with EM pulse-generating atomics, low megaton yield. It is an option of last resort."

"How low a yield?" said the Boer.

"Low enough," said Sobieski, "but once you take into account the energy released by the failure of the Reality House's tau-grade fusion reactor, there will be a big hole in Nevada, make no mistake."

Swan looked round the table. "In addition, we risk a large amount of collateral damage to the Grid. We can buffer the overspill, but the Realities are deeply entrenched in the network."

"And how much is that gonna cost us?" said Milton.

"Thirty per cent of the Grid could be damaged. Estimated cost runs to 360 trillion dollars," said Swan. "Disregarding physical damage to the Real."

The Boer slapped the table. "'Disregarding physical damage to the Real,' fucking number."

"Then Klein, Chures," said Milton. "You better not screw this up."

"There's a further wrinkle," said Swan. "k52 has outside help. This isn't purely a numbers job."

"Kaplinski," growled Otto.

"Kaplinksi is the man who tried to kill you at the diner?" asked Milton.

"I cannot prove it, but I am sure it was him," said Otto. "There's another indicator."

Chures' eyes narrowed as Klein ran footage taken from the Morden Subcity survnet system. It showed masked men in grey following Zhang Qifang.

"These men targeted and destroyed the second Qifang android. Most of them are unknown," said Otto. "But this man–" The footage zoomed in so far the image began to break up. "His shape gives him away. He's cybernetically altered. Kwasi Sakaday Jones, Nigerian. He's a known associate of Kaplinski, ex-Union of West Africa cyborg…"

"Another of yours?" said Sobieski.

"No," said Otto. "But I've had run-ins with him before. Intel that Richards and I received recently has him working for Kaplinski."

"But Kaplinski was one of yours."

"He was under my command, he went renegade. It's all on the file."

"What can you tell us about him?" asked the Boer.

"It's all on the file," said Otto levelly. "We have a lead. Oleg Kolosev." As Otto spoke the files were called onto the room's screens. "Old friend and partner of Vellini's. Kolosev has also been arrested and convicted by the VIPA. He tried to hide himself when he got out. Unlike Vellini, Kolosev has been unsuccessful, running home to the Ukraine. Richards and I use him sometimes. He's not of the same standard as Vellini, but they were close. No matter how hard he tries to hide, he's easy to find, and he'll talk for the right price. If anyone knows where to find 'Waldo', he does."

Sobieski narrowed his eyes, thinking. "So, ladies and gentlemen, we've three options to stop whatever k52 and his cohorts are up to, with escalating degrees of risk and associated dollar cost. I want them all ready to go. Klein, Chures, you're leaving for Kiev in the morning. Henson, prep your teams. Swan, continue your attempts to dig out the EuPol Five and shut k52 out from his choir in Europe. I want this wrapped up by the end of the week."

CHAPTER FORTY-TWO

Bear

It was morning when Richards followed the bear out of the woods.

The woods looked worse by day. The pale fingers of dying trees thrust up through rhododendrons, their brown leaves, as imperishable as old-school plastics, choking life from the ground. Away from the sunlit path, blackness gathered thickly.

"Dangerous," the bear commented. "And full of death." At that he'd shaken his enormous head, remembering something better. "We had best stick to the road."

Richards had what he suspected to be a mild concussion. Every sunbeam that filtered through the canopy stabbed at his eyes. His lips were swollen, one eye bruised shut. He was miserable with human suffering. The roll of the bear's shoulders as it strode along filled him with nausea, and the reek of his clothes as they warmed intensified it, so he focused on the twinkling drive to keep it at bay. The parade of gravel soothed him. When the sun was strong enough, he saw that each stone was a tiny skull carved from quartz, all as different as snowflakes. He knelt down and picked one up.

"I wouldn't do that if I were you, sunshine," murmured the bear.

Richards put it into his pocket.

"Suit yourself," the bear shrugged.

Richards stood stiffly. "What's going on here? Aren't you going to give me a hint, or are we sticking with violence?" he asked. His lips hurt.

The bear glowered at him. "Prisoners don't get to ask questions," it said.

"Regulations?" said Richards.

"Cheeky," said the bear.

The road narrowed, and weeds sprouted between the skulls with increasing thickness until it petered away. A rhododendron blocked their path. The bear swiped it out of the way, and they were out of the woods.

"Wow," said Richards.

They stood at the top of a steep hill. Close-cropped grass fuzzed the slope. Where it bottomed out, a shining sea of wheat rippled with waves. Rich green copses rode the crops like ships at anchor. Clouds sauntered through the sky, flat bottoms topped by extravagant mounds of cotton, patches of brilliant blue between them. Sunbeams stole through the gaps, making a trillion diamonds of the wheat.

And so it went on, until the swell of the prairie disappeared into a haze of pollen, the horizon masked by the obscure romances of plants. In the distance a thunderhead arched up, an anvil of dark rain, illuminated sporadically from within. It was the kind of hyper-landscape one only ever found online. It was realer than real.

"Wow," repeated Richards, shielding his eyes. "I don't think I'm in Kansas any more," he said in his best Dorothy voice. The bear did not react favourably. It was not one of Richards' finest impressions, he'd admit.

"Ahem," said the bear pointedly. "Prisoners should be shutting up."

"Up yours, Toto," said Richards. "On what grounds are you holding me prisoner?"

The bear adjusted its tiny helmet and clenched its great paws, the set of its shoulders speaking of enormous tension.

"On the grounds that there's a war on, that the queen is missing, Lord Penumbra is about to win and that you are not where you are supposed to be. We've had his lot come in through the woods before, trying to trick us. I've got strict orders, keep an eye on that house, round up anyone I see, take 'em in. Spies. That'd be you."

"I don't know what you're talking about," said Richards.

The bear leaned in close and sniffed at him. "No. I suppose you don't. You don't have the scent of one of Penumbra's about you. Hang on a minute…" The bear sniffed again. "You're people!"

"Look, mate, you've got it wrong, I'm not people," said Richards.

"Don't you bloody 'mate' me, sunshine. I'm no mate of yours! You're people. Actual people, from out there." He jabbed his claw into Richards' chest. "Bloody people. Coming in here, lording it over us. This place is supposed to be a sanctuary." The bear's tirade collapsed into a growl.

"But I'm not people. I am an AI. If I'm not mistaken, so are you."

"AI shmay-ai," said the bear. "I'm a bear." The bear squinted at him. "Hmm. You look like people, smell like people, but…"

"Yeah?" said Richards encouragingly.

"You don't feel like people," admitted the bear.

"I'm not. The name's Richards. I'm a Class Five sentient."

"Ooh, la-di-da, Class Five," said the bear, waggling his claws and doing a tippy-toe dance from side to side. "Sorr-ee. What are you doing here then, your lordship?"

"Just passing through."

"Right then," said the bear, folding its arms. "Why are you covered in sick?"

"I dunno, because I puked all over myself?"

"AI don't puke. What's your serial number?"

Richards ran off his full code, and then the complex equations required to furnish the bear with a quantum key to verify his identity. Out on the Grid, this kind of encryption was done instantaneously; here things were different. For a start, Richards had to speak the formulae aloud. It took ten minutes, but the bear waited suspiciously then looked off to one side. Then it examined him head to foot. It relaxed, not much, but enough to let Richards breathe easier.

"Alright, sunshine, that sounds genuine, but I'm watching you."

"Do you actually have the mental capacity to process that equation?" asked Richards.

"Watch it. A Class Five, come here? What do you need a place like this for?" The bear pulled a branch from a tree and hurled it out over the plain. It cartwheeled through the air and was lost in the crops below.

It turned back round and jabbed a claw at Richards.

"Fond of pointing, aren't you?" said Richards.

"Careful, sunshine," the bear said. "I'm taking you in to get this straightened out. Don't think I trust you. We'll see what the boss has to say about it." It drew itself up to its considerably full height, spreading its arms wide. "No funny business. It's a fair old way to Pylon City."

"Promise. Cross my heart and hope to die."

"Don't get funny with me, you little sod. You better behave. Will you?"

"Do bears shit in the woods?" said Richards.

"I told you," said the bear.

"Yeah, I forget. That's where popes perform their ablutions. Sorry."

"Fuck. Off," said the bear, and squared its sloping shoulders in a way that suggested violence was not far distant.

Richards changed tack. "Perhaps we might get on better if we were formally introduced?"

The bear sniffed disparagingly. "Right. OK. Maybe. Me, I'm Bear. Sergeant Bear."

"There's a surprise."

"You're pushing your luck, you are. No one knows I found you. Get too cocky and I'll forget regulations altogether, got it?" He adjusted his helmet. "You can stick to 'sir'." Bear cupped his hands round his mouth. "Oi! Geoff! Geoff!" he shouted. "You can come out now, I reckon he's harmless." Bear looked at Richards suspiciously. "Mostly," he added.

There was a rustle of something big forcing a passage through the trees, a sound that became a crash as a battered, three-legged giraffe fell onto the lip of the slope and squeaked pitifully. "That's Geoff, my corporal. Come on, Geoff! Get up now."

"Man, I should have been more respectful. You're part of a crack outfit," said Richards and whistled. Bear gave him the kind of stare only bears can and waddled over to help up the giraffe. Richards noticed a rattling as he moved, a noise he'd previously put down to the gravel path.

He looked at the bear closely.

"Beans? You've got beans in your arse?"

"Yeah," said Bear. "For kids to rattle."

Richards looked at the giraffe. It was a caricature in plush of the real thing. The bear's nose was scuffed plastic Something clicked in the simulated mess of buttery tissue between Richards' ears. "Hang on, you're toys? You, the giraffe, the dog-man?"

Bear looked back from where he was helping the struggling Geoff to his feet. Richards caught sight of crude stitching where the giraffe's right foreleg should have been.

"My, aren't you the sharpest tool in the box?" said Bear. "Course we're toys. We can't all be Class Five AIs like you, mister." Bear shook his head and pushed his friend up to his feet. "But not that doggy dude, no. We don't like him, do we Geoff?"

The giraffe squeaked.

"The cheek of it," said Bear.

Richards understood. A lot of playthings in the Real had some form of embedded electronic mind. Often this was rudimentary, but some had been up to AI class before the emancipation, even now a lot had respectable near-I. When they were outgrown, where did they go? Here, apparently, thought Richards.

"This place is some kind of sanctuary," said Richards. "A hidden world for abandoned toys. Now I've seen everything."

Geoff squeaked and nodded enthusiastically. Bear glared at him. "Geoff, that's classified!"

Geoff squeaked apologetically.

"Oh, I give up. Yes. Me –" he poked his own thumb into his chest "– I had fifteen years in a cardboard box in an attic. Seems that 'Life Companion' doesn't actually mean for life. There I was, charge down to nothing, forgotten, minimal Grid connection. Utter hell. Geoff here had it worse, the kid that owned him really did a number on him, pulled his leg off, for fun! Then him too, bosh!" The bear slapped the back of one paw into the palm of the other with a rattle of beans. "Into a box, up the stairs, thank you very much, bye bye."

"Squeak!"

"That was before we were brought here. Dunno how, really, some bloke opened up a link, bit of a ponce, called himself the Flower King, dragged us in and told us to be free and happy, gave us the lovely Queen Isabella. But she's gone now." Bear's gaze dropped.

Richards' eyebrows raised.

"Queen Isabella? Flower King?"

"Yeah, yeah I know it sounds a bit suspect, OK? But it beats being stuck in an attic. And once I got used to the idea, turned out this place was a bloody paradise."

"Was a paradise?"

"Was. Not any more. Now it's all coming apart. The Terror's eating it alive. Queen's gone, no one knows where, the Flower King's not showed his stupid mush for ages, war and death everywhere, Lord Penumbra is destroying everything. All gone to crap. Some bastard's been playing games, if you ask me, and I went off games a long time ago. I don't like it. I'm a teddy bear, not a soldier. I'm not cut out for this."

The bear looked meaningfully at the thundercloud on the horizon.

"k52," said Richards.

"Who's k52?" asked the bear.

"Another Five, like me. He's why I'm here," said Richards. "Anyone else like me come through that door?"

The bear shook his head.

"He was part of a caretaking team looking after the old RealWorld Realities after they were declared off limits."

"RealWorld Realities off limits? Since when?" said Bear. "I used to go in there all the time, playing Batista's Kingdom," he said enthusiastically. "We used to have loads of fun, he used to love it, little Be–" Bear's voice caught in his throat and he clammed up. "That was before. Then fifteen years in an attic. After all I did for him. Little bastard."

"You've been gone a long time," said Richards. "A lot's changed out there. Full immersions are illegal, as are toys like you. We're all free, sergeant. k52 and his team were supposedly studying the Realities after they were cut loose, but a human colleague of his, Zhang Qifang, discovered that k52's not been playing the straight game. Some Realities were destroyed by careless hackers, you see," he explained. "Their vacated Grid space was supposedly being used by k52 for predictive research into disaster avoidance and accelerated technological development, but instead he's used it to launch an attack on the whole damn Grid." He frowned. "But then there's this. This doesn't fit in at all. And there was the door…" He lapsed into thoughtful silence.

"Don't see what that's got to do with us," said Bear.

"Maybe k52's your Flower King…" Richards shook his head. "Nah, that's too sentimental for k52. And even if he did make it, who's attacking it? And who is Marita? I can't see what use a world like this would be to k52, he's not a dreamer, he's far too practical for…"

"For things like talking bears?" said Bear.

"Yeah," said Richards apologetically. "Have you got any direct influence here?"

"What?" said Bear. "Like shaping it? Nope. The likes of us are way too far down the pecking order. Barely sentient, half of us, though the Flower King gave us all upgrades when he brought us in." The bear shuddered. "That's the worst of it, I tell you. You never know who's going to go next. Part of the world dies, folk's minds go with it. Nasty. If we did have access to the world code, the higher-ups would write the war out, not fight it. I was hoping you'd be able to help us out with that, big-ass AI like you."

Richards shook his head. "Sorry. This place must have been built on the remains of one of the wrecked Realities, and they were keyed into human minds. AI and near-AI within were run strictly as bubble simulations, consciousnesses as separate from them as humans are from the mathematics of the Real. That's what's happened to me here. I think. I've been walled in. No wonder I can't make myself a new hat." He sniffed his coat. "Or do my laundry. You got any people back at your HQ with higher access rights? Can any of you access the architecture here?"

"Yep," said the bear. "A couple."

"I should speak to this boss of yours," Richards said. "Maybe he can sort me out with a hat."

"Right you are, sunshine, because that's where you're going. Now," said the bear. He swung his head from side to side, looking out over the plain. He peered into the distance and righted his helmet decisively. "This way. If there's still a this way left." He pointed his muzzle to the west. "Here," he said hopefully. "You got any fags?"

Richards shrugged his shoulders. "Don't smoke. Who does? It's bad for you."

The bear gave him a disdainful look. "Oh, puh-lease," he said.

Out on the plains, thunder rumbled.

CHAPTER FORTY-THREE

Kolosev

Kolosev's mother didn't know where her son was, but the servers delivering her mail did. Veronique cracked the old lady's Grid profile quickly, Kolosev's cryptography a little less so, but by afternoon she had him.

"South," Valdaire said over a glass of black tea. Kolosev's mother was handing out cake, as eager to find her darling son as they were. Always the way, thought Otto. Every time Oleg went underground, Otto and Richards came to see his dear old mama. She was as helpful as she was the last time.

"Here." Valdaire pointed to Chloe's screen, at a locator point flaring on a map.

"He is a mummy's boy," said Otto quietly to Valdaire as Mrs Kolosev batted her eyes at an uncomfortable-looking Chures. "All his super hacker crap. He still needs his socks washing, this is how we find him every time."

Otto, Veronique, Lehmann and Chures left Kiev that evening. They travelled along the E95 in a rented groundcar, Kiev being a city where Richards & Klein had no garage. Ground vehicles drew less attention, especially so far east where aircars were rare, and Otto drove himself, because he did not trust the vehicle's antiquated systems against outside interference. He turned down Lehmann's offer of help. He said he wanted to think, but in reality he just didn't want to sleep. He could do without the mentaug's dreams.

The forests of the north turned to steppe as they headed south, fertile plains tilled by enormous, automated harvesters. The highway was eight lanes wide, full of slaved cars in tight road trains, as busy as any in Europe, but once they turned off the highway traffic dwindled until they were the only car sharing roads with robot trucks shuttling between the fields and transit depots, heavy with the second harvest.

Valdaire sat up front with Otto for a day, watching the plains roll by. She talked a little about her early childhood in Côte d'Ivoire, about her life with Chloe before the country had exploded into violence and her family had fled. She was speaking more to herself than Otto. She seemed content talking levelly this way, staring out of the window as she made sense of her life to herself. She probably does this a lot, thought Otto, I may as well not be here. He let her continue, until she looked at him and asked suddenly, "Have you ever been married, Klein?"

"Once," he said reluctantly.

She waited for more. He didn't offer any. "You don't talk much about yourself," she said.

"If you want to know about me, read my files," he said, even though that's what Richards always said to him. He wished she'd leave him be. He didn't mind listening to Valdaire. It helped people to talk; the last sixty years had been so bad half the planet had a horror story to tell, but he preferred to keep his pain to himself.

"I have. Not the personal stuff," she added hurriedly. "I feel like I'm prying."

"You are."

"Sorry."

Otto grunted through a half-smile at that. "Backing off so easily? You'd make a poor security consultant."

"Maybe that's why I'm not one," she said.

"There is not much to tell," said Otto.

Valdaire looked as if she didn't believe him.

"I was a soldier. I saw some bad shit. My wife died. I work with Richards. That's all," he said then kept his silence. Lehmann swapped over with her at the next stop so she could get some sleep. At least he knew to keep quiet.

They passed the grassed-over sites of collective farms and abandoned towns, by low arcologies, through freshly cut fields being tilled for winter wheat, through a million-hectare rewilded patch of steppe teeming with Saiga, Przewalski's horse and gengineered megafauna. Through sleeping villages little changed in centuries, past the neat rows of a Han agri-engineering dormitory town. Night deepened, and lightened into day, and came once more. They stopped briefly in nowhere towns grey with sad histories, and were gone just as quickly.

In the pre-dawn of the second morning, Otto steered on to an unmetalled track, nothing but crops around them, and the low rumble of the auto-harvesters carrying over the rolling vastness, trails of dust in the distance marking their progress.

They approached an abandoned farm complex, mid-twentieth-century, most of its concrete crumbled to ivy-choked grit. Weedy mounds of stone nearby marked the remains of the village it had sprung from, windowless brick walls on the other side of the road to the Soviet failure it had become. Ancient and newer parts were as ruinous as each other. They arrived at a square before a dilapidated office block. A few barns from the early twenty-first century tottered round its edges. A camouflaged satellite dish sat inside one barn with no sides, pointed through a hole in the roof.

"We're here," said Otto, when he saw that, and set the car to park itself.

"What is this place?" said Chures.

"Ancient village turned Soviet collective farm, turned corporate agribusiness, abandoned eighty years ago," said Otto.

"What, one of your ancestors burn it down?" said Chures.

"Don't start on the Nazi shit, SudAmigo, that was near two hundred years ago," said Lehmann.

"This place was hit hard by the Third Corona," said Otto. "A fifth of villages were wiped out. It's still endemic. They think the Christmas Flu is a joke round here." Otto looked around. "Kolosev has worked out of here before. He's short on imagination."

"Kind of desolate, even for a criminal," murmured Valdaire.

"Let's approach him gently ," said Otto. "He is nervous, and will have seen us approach. We go in too hard, he'll wipe everything he has. Lucky for us he's curious; he'll want to know what we want. This barn –" he pointed to one less damaged than the rest "– it has a high EM field, plenty of equipment working. The rest of this place is inactive, as dead as it looks."

"Veev!" piped Chloe. "That is incorrect, there is minor activity detectable in the office building also."

"More there in the barn though, yes?" said Otto.

"Yes," said Chloe.

"Then we check the barn first. Lehmann, activate squad interface."

Otto's iHUD flickered; squad icons, years unused, came on, but most blinked off, leaving Lehmann's signifier alone in his mind. A squad of two was better than no squad at all.

"Shouldn't we be more cautious?" asked Valdaire, snagging Chloe from the backseat. Lehmann unfolded his body from the car, groaning as his joints popped. He swung his arms round a few times. Valdaire found herself entranced by the unnatural shapes his artificial muscles made.

"This is Kolosev," said Otto. "He's a coward."

Lehmann grinned, went round to the boot and pulled out three components that he snapped together into a long rifle.

"Just in case," said Lehmann. "I'll take up position on the roof, cover you all."

"*Stimmt*," said Otto. Lehmann jogged off.

The light of day was growing stronger, heat coming with it, taking the chill off the autumn. Otto led them to a building whose sides were made of ragged cement sheeting, cracked single-glazed windows high up in its sides. He slid the door aside and stepped into a dark space shot through with mote-laden sunbeams.

Efforts had been made to insulate the insides of the building with foamcrete, but it had been inexpertly applied and was full of gaps. Rusting girders dragged from other buildings propped up the roof. An array of computer hardware was stacked carelessly in a horseshoe round a filthy desk, a tarpaulin strung above it. Rusting farm machinery lined the walls. The place smelled of old food and strong cannabis.

"Kolosev. Lazy. He should have set up in the office. His cables probably aren't long enough to reach his satellite dish, and he could not take the time to move his fat arse and buy more." Otto looked around. "He's still in here."

Chures drew his gun. "What about the offices?"

"Not bedtime yet," said Otto. "Little hackers are allergic to the sun. He's probably just finishing up for the night."

"This is normal, to hang around when you're coming to visit?" said Valdaire.

"He doesn't have anywhere to go," said Otto, "and a rat's maze like this, he'll see it is a good place to hide. It's either that, or booby-traps and a remote camera to catch us all being blown up. Gloaters, lurkers, runners – your three kinds of informant. Kolosev is a little of each."

"Great," said Valdaire.

"Kolosev won't blow us up. I know him, this is all he owns, all he's ever likely to own, because no matter how well he does he always loses it all because he can't bear to be parted from his mama. No," said Otto, "he's still in here." A coffee mug sat on Kolosev's desk, cooling in Otto's IR capable eyesight. He touched the back of his hand to it. "Still warm, so is the chair." He pulled out his gun. "Amateur."

"Kolosev!" called out Chures. "This is the VIPA, come out now!"

"Great, if he's not already shitting himself, he is now," said Otto. "Go easy on the threats, Chures, there's nothing these little hackers fear more than a visit from the VIPA, and your agency's busted him a lot of times. He didn't much like his last stretch in the freezer. You will make him run."

"I was about to say we are only here to talk, Klein."

"It will not make any difference." Otto indicated upwards with his eyes.

"What?" mouthed Valdaire.

Otto pointed to Chloe. *I can hear him.* Otto sent the message via his MT to Chloe, his thoughts writing themselves across her screen. Otto pointed his chin to a roof crux, flaking steel butted by a makeshift half-floor. A creak, audible enough for the others to hear. "Come down, Kolosev! Uncle Otto has come to say hello!"

Kolosev wasn't hanging around. There was a series of rapid scuffs followed by a crash as he flung himself out of one of the barn's filthy windows. Otto ran to the door to see Kolosev bounding through the wheat at close on fifty klicks an hour atop a pair of 'roo springers.

"And there we are," said Otto, and tore off after the hacker.

Chures put up his gun. "Klein can handle that, let's see what he's got."

"I could do with some help." Valdaire scowled as she swept aside the sticky detritus of food, joint butts and crusty tissues cluttering Kolosev's desk. She placed Chloe down on the cleanest part.

"You'll get it, in a moment," said Chures. "Klein was right about one thing. I need to sweep this place for booby traps."

Otto engaged his full suite of enhancements as he hit the man-high corn, pushing his body well past human norms. His secondary heart drove doctored blood hard through his body, assisted lungs wringing the air of oxygen. His adapted adrenal glands issued synthetically optimised ephinephrine, feeding his muscles with energy at an accelerated rate. Otto's biochemistry was not intended to make him stronger, but to enable his natural body to keep pace with his secondary polymer musculature. These muscles, contracting to carefully timed impulses drawn off his rewired nervous system, were what provided him with his inhuman strength, driving his limbs like pistons as he hurtled across the field. Without boosting, his organic muscles would be ripped to pieces by the actions of the polymer bundles.

Wheat stalks whipped at his hands and face as he ran. Kolosev was ahead of him still. He was fatter and pastier than his mugshot, passing into middle age poorly, he still dressed like a child in stained Gridkid gear, tight luminous pants and puff-sleeved shirt. For all that on the 'roo springers he ran like a cheetah, giving the fugitive speed that Otto could not match. He tore through the wheat like the wind, rig bouncing over the summer-dried earth. Past harvest and ploughing, it would have been different, for Kolosev's springer would have foundered in the sticky chernozem. Right now Otto could never catch him.

"Oleg!" Otto shouted. "Stop, or I'll have to shoot you! Oleg!"

The hacker kept his face forward. Kolosev leapt high as he cleared some obstacle, and Otto lost him to a wrinkle in the steppe. Otto let out a string of expletives and ran faster. His shoulder hurt, and his stomach burned with acid reflux. He could keep a pace of thirty kilometres an hour for hours, even at his age, but fifty kilometers per hour was draining his resources fast.

Otto burst into the open, stubble beneath his feet. A hundred and fifty metres to his left the staggered wall of giant harvesters droned forward. Staple-shaped front ends terminated in multiple wheel units, flails on a wide drum between them, cutting and winnowing. Long hoppers ran behind the main bodies, raised high off the ground, rears supported on pillars with their own wheel units at the base – from the air they looked like insectile letter Ts crawling across the earth. Chaff escaping from secondary pods harvesting waste for biofuel blew in a constant stream toward Otto, obscuring his view in showers of shivered straw and grit.

Otto stopped to get his bearings. A glimpse of movement, quicker than the harvesters; Kolosev was well ahead of him, nearing the wall of machines and its shroud of dust.

"Oleg! Stop!"

The Ukrainian carried on running, each step a high leap.

Otto levelled his caseless automatic. His adjutant ran his ocular magnification up to the absolute maximum. The Ukrainian bounced around in his vision like a fly trapped in a jar, close to the furthest effective range of Otto's pistol. He wished he'd brought a bigger gun.

If I hit him, it's is own fault for running, Otto told himself, and fired.

The bullet missed.

Otto squinted down the barrel of his pistol for another shot, and lowered it. Kolosev was too far away.

"*Scheisse.*"

His MT lit up.

Don't worry, Leutnant, I have him, sent Lehmann.

Kolosev staggered. Lehmann's shot took the 'roo springer's left heel assembly out, the sound of the shot following the bullet. The springer's damaged leg dragged. Otto accelerated. Panic showed on Kolosev's bearded face as he undid the springer's straps, hammering at the quick release until his legs popped out of the rig. He fell free and made a hopping run toward the nearest harvester. He was up the ladder on the left wheel pod pillar when Otto reached the vehicle. As he climbed the ladder, Kolosev was scrambling round the harvester's cabin.

Otto followed hard behind.

Kolosev stood in the middle of the catwalk that spanned the width of the harvester, looking wildly from side to side, shirt stained with sweat.

"Kolosev, stop. You've nowhere to run, and I'm getting indigestion."

Kolosev stared at the hopper full of wheat kernels, as if he were thinking of jumping in. "You're getting old, Klein," he panted. He stepped back as Otto holstered his gun. Kolosev was unmodded. The real Grid experts never wore hardwired mentaugs. Kolosev was free of cybernetics, not even base-level healthtech; they knew how it could be used against them.

"Look at yourself, Oleg, you're out of shape. Don't run like that again, you'll have a heart attack."

"You come in here with the VIPA, Klein, what was I supposed to do? After all I've done for you in the past, you bring them here! Ten years' cold storage they've cost me. Why you think I ran?" Kolosev spoke in terse Grid English, truncated and peppered with in-vogue leetspeak, all with a thick Slavic accent.

"I'm not with them, Kolosev, they're with me. We're not here to bust you. I only need some information, the usual."

"Yeah?" Kolosev's fat face pulled an unconvincing hardman sneer. "Your kind 'ways does. You loot me, Klein, it upset me."

"I am looking for Waldo, Oleg. Do you know where he is?"

Kolosev snorted and slapped the railings of the catwalk. "You know he and I do no see eye to eye no more. I no run with him, I work free."

"Solo?" said Otto.

"I never said that."

"But you're alone now."

Kolosev glared, trapped. "Yeah, I'm alone now," he said, his English losing its affected coolness, wandering closer to standard.

"I'll pay," said Otto. "I'll pay a lot."

"How much?" said Kolosev.

"A million, Euro."

"You need him bad, huh? Two million. And you broke my springer, you can buy me a new one. I want that as extra."

"I'll buy you an aircar if that's what you want."

"Thanks, but I'm trying shed some kilos."

"And springers aren't tracked."

Kolosev shrugged.

"Fine, Oleg, just tell me where he is."

Kolosev fished a phone from a pocket on his sleeve. "Money first."

Otto sent a coded transfer instruction out through his adjutant. Kolosev's phone binged, filled with the USE's money. EuPol had given him unlimited funds for this expedition. Otto figured they'd find a way to claw it back later.

"Heh," Kolosev said, licking his lips. "You do need him. Why?"

"Where is he, Kolosev?" said Otto, and stepped nearer.

The fat man held up his hand. His eyes were screwed tight against the morning sun; he really didn't get outside much. "Relax, Klein, I tell you. What's the big deal? Let me guess –" a triumphant grin flickered across the Ukrainian's face "– k52's small adventure in the RealWorlds, yes? Am I close?"

The likes of Kolosev always dug out what others tried to hide. No harm in letting him know; if Otto didn't succeed, then everyone would know anyhow. Otto nodded.

"Damn fucking bastards!" He laughed. "I am good, Klein? Huh? Huh? Every Class A gold hacker know about that. Me, I one of. We the future, you big mob, Klein. Fuck me!"

"Big talk, Oleg."

"You look at me, Klein, you see fat man. I look at you, I see an extinct species. You are needing Waldo to get you in, in past the security. Only he can do it, no? You want Waldo in, and k52 out."

"You are a genuine genius, Oleg," said Otto flatly.

"Ah, now you flatter. Well –" the Ukrainian gave an extravagant shrug "– what if I tell you that it no matter? You no hear?"

"Where is he, Oleg?" growled Otto. He pulled his gun out again. "Or that money is coming right back out of your account, and I'll deposit a bullet in your face instead."

"I tell you! Calm, calm, big mob, you Germans so serious." Kolosev was giggling, he was still high. "He's in Sinosiberia, man, hiding out in an old Soviet army base from way back when in history-time."

Otto put up his gun. "That wasn't so hard."

"Yeah, won't do you no good. I'm working for some big fishes now, big fishes! They're not going to like you roughing me one bit, cyborg man." Kolosev laughed. "You give me money, fine. I tell you info, fine, it no matter. He's gonna get you good. I get money, you get dead."

Otto's eyes narrowed. "Kaplinski, are you working for Kaplinski? Is he looking for Waldo too?"

"Oooh," said Kolosev mockingly, clapping his hands. "Maybe you big mob bad after all, Klein. You right. Well done."

"Oleg, listen to me. You're in real danger," said Otto. "If Kaplinski is nearby, he'll kill you to stop you talking. Come down. Get into cover. We can talk somewhere safe."

"Him kill me? Naaaaah, I no fall for that. Your old buddy is coming get what I know, he be here soon. He kill you dead, not me. You want to get in to the Realities? You have no idea! I tried it 'cyborg' –" he hooked speech mark fingers round the word, mocking it "– I try it and 'ffft'." He held his hand to his head like a gun, thumb falling like a hammer. "All my migrants dead-dead. I no do it, so you no do it. But I found him, my old buddy Waldo. I have so much I want say him, right before I smack him in the mouth, and then he do what big mob Kaplinski say." Kolosev grinned smugly. "You so stupid, you have no idea what's going on, noobo-Klein, you so-"

Kolosev's right temple exploded, taking most of his face with it. He slumped, last breath gurgling in his throat, and pitched over the railing into the teeth of the harvester.

The chaff blew red.

A second round stung Otto's cheek, gouging flesh as it ricocheted off his reinforced skull, knocking his head round. It hurt like hell, but its momentum was too spent to do him real harm. Otto dropped, pressing himself as far as he could into the grill of the catwalk, making the most of the low lip running along its base. A further shot thunked into the body of the harvester a few centimetres from his head and Otto saw a railgun flechette stuck there in the carbon, quivering. No report from the weapon; the shooter was far off, the harvester too loud, and his gun silenced.

Otto crawled backward, trailing blood, seeking the shelter of the hopper humped up behind the harvester. By the time he was in its cover, his healthtech had staunched the flow. His wound itched as it healed.

He called up an aerial view and found a modern complex of grain silos to the west. The shooter had to be there. His adjutant reported a minor viral attack on his systems, easily fought off.

In the satellite view, Otto saw a bike rising into the air.

The silos were four kilometres away. Whoever had shot at him had been good. Ky-tech good.

"Kaplinski," said Otto.

Otto ran back to the village, his face numb. He ordered Lehmann to keep watch from the office block, just in case.

"What happened to you?" said Chures. Valdaire looked up from her work at the desk and gave a small gasp.

"I got shot. I think Kaplinski is here."

"How do you know?"

"I know," said Otto. "He's taken out Kolosev. Come on! We have to go. He probably won't chance a close approach with me and Lehmann here, but he is unpredictable, and he is not working alone."

"Just a minute!" said Valdaire.

"We do not have a minute," said Otto, and he made to grab Valdaire.

"Lay off for a moment, Klein! Chloe, is there anyone here that should not be?" asked Valdaire.

"We're the only sentients for ten kilometres," chirruped Chloe. "Brainless things elsewise."

Chures stared at Otto, an open challenge. "Finish your data rip," he said. "We need this information."

Otto stared back. They were right, they needed what was in Kolosev's computers. He went to the door and checked the yard right to left and back again.

Five seconds passed. "Download complete," said Chloe.

"Now we can go," said Valdaire. She picked Chloe up off the desk.

"Veronique," said Chloe. "I have access to Kolosev's network, including the other source of EM activity. There is something you should see there, in the office block. Six more humans."

"What are they doing?" asked Valdaire.

"They are inactive."

Otto looked out over the yard. No movement or noise, just corn crakes calling and combines rattling over the plain. He tapped Lehmann's feed, looking out through his eyes, something he'd not done for many years, and it brought a rush of unwelcome memories. "OK, it's clear. Let's check out the office."

They went out into the yard and headed to the office block. A cool wind was blowing from the east.

"You're lucky Kaplinski shot Kolosev first," said Chures.

"Luck has nothing to do with it. He killed Kolosev because Kolosev knows where Waldo is. If Oleg had known nothing he would have shot me first. Kaplinski is insane, but he is not stupid," said Otto.

"What is his problem?" asked Valdaire.

"All of the Ky-tech had neurosurgery," said Chures. "One of the things done as routine was an empathetic damper. It was supposed to stop PTSD in Ky-tech soldiers. It didn't work so well."

"Because it turned you all into sociopaths?" said Valdaire to Otto.

"You were in the army too, you know what it is like," said Otto. "They wanted to stop us feeling guilty for performing our duty."

"I was behind a desk," said Valdaire.

"You still killed people," said Otto, "even if you only pushed buttons. You know what it means to end a life; the feeling is the same if you can see them die or not."

Otto ushered the others through a broken glass door into the office block. The wind whispered through empty steel window frames. The concrete walls were streaked with moisture. Ancient linoleum tiles flaked to fragments on the floor. "The conditioning was reversible: flick a switch after the war, be back to normal, even scrub the bad memories away. But it went too far with Kaplinski."

"Turn left, up the stairs, first door on the left," sang Chloe.

Otto went on. "Kaplinski did not take to renormalisation. He never felt anything but the urge to fight. They were trying to fix him, but he got out of the barracks hospital, killed three young women. I was ordered to hunt him down."

"He got away," said Chures.

"*Ja*, he got away," said Otto. "I've not heard of him for some years, but now he is trying to kill me."

No sign of him, said Lehmann over the MT. *The air bike is immobile, fifty kilometres away. I've called in the local EuPol.*

He'll be gone when they get there, thought Otto back.

He's gone already, said Lehmann.

"This is it," said Chloe. They stopped in front of a door.

Chures looked to Otto. He nodded. Both readied their guns.

Chures silently counted down on his fingers. On three, Otto kicked the door in, his augmented legs sending the ancient wood to pieces. Chures darted into the room, covering all angles.

"Holy…" said Valdaire.

"Well, I did tell you," said Chloe smugly.

The room was weatherproofed, its one window foamed up and ceiling repaired. Inside were six functioning v-jack set-ups, each worth a fortune, each highly illicit: couches, medical gear, nutrient tanks and hook-up. On every couch was a body, face contorted with pain.

"They're all dead," said Chloe. "Bio-neural feedback."

Otto checked the corpses one at a time; cold, stomachs bloated, dead long enough for rigor mortis to have come and gone, but not dead long. With the September heat outside, probably fifty-seventy hours, as he counted it, though he was no expert. Then his adjutant consulted the Grid and came back with a similar figure. Anything more precise would need tests. All were emaciated.

The last was different. "This one's alive," said Otto.

"I'll get the v-jack off him," said Valdaire. "See if I can pull him back into the Real."

"It'll kill him," said Chures.

"He's dead already," said Otto. "Pulse is weak, ECG erratic – look at him. He might be able to tell us something useful before he goes."

"Klein is correct," said Chloe. "The subject is undergoing total neural disassociation. He has minutes of life left."

"Who is he?" said Chures. He was checking the room carefully. He knocked some of the foam out off the window, allowing dusty sunlight into the room.

"Unknown. He has no Grid signature, no ID chip," said Chloe.

"Han Chinese," said Otto. He picked up a limp arm. His enhanced eyes picked out the traces of an erased judicial tattoo on his wrist. "Political exile." He let the arm drop.

Valdaire removed the v-jack from the Han. She studied the medical unit attached to the wall, then pressed a few buttons. There was a hiss and a mixing wheel spun round. A gasp of air escaped the man's lips. His eyelids fluttered.

He sighed something in Mandarin so quietly Valdaire had to bend in to hear it.

He smiled, said something else, and went limp.

"What did he say?" said Chures.

Chloe spoke. "He said he dreamed of golden fields."

"You said Kolosev knew something," said Chures.

"Yeah, he said Waldo was out in Sinosiberia, in an old army base. And he's been trying to get into the Realities himself."

"Unsuccessfully," said Valdaire.

"He was looking for Waldo, and not on his own," said Otto. "This level of set-up is beyond Kolosev's means. Damn shame our only leads are dead."

"Chloe will tell us why," said Valdaire.

"You do not need to. Tell me, why has Kaplinski not destroyed this place with us in it?"

"He's looking for Waldo too," said Chures.

"Yeah," said Otto. "And I would say that he paid for all this."

"Then we frag the lot, and stay one step ahead of him," said Chures. "We've got Kolosev's data."

"That could work, and we might win," said Otto. "Or maybe Kaplinski has the data already and his on his way, or perhaps he couldn't get Kolosev to give the data up himself, so he is waiting for us to lead him to Waldo instead. Whatever, he's not done with us yet."

CHAPTER FORTY-FOUR

The Terror

Though the day promised rain, it held off. Soon Richards' human facsimile was sweating heavily and his coat became a burden. He suffered the sensations his near-human form fed him, so much more entire than those he had experienced before. It would have been intriguing if it were not so unpleasant.

It was slow going with Geoff. "He's just not balanced right for it," said Bear. "Being three-legged is a disability overcome with difficulty by giraffes." He shook his head as another frustrated squeak reached them from the wheat. "I fear he'll never master life as a tripod."

They rested awhile by a stone barn. Bear leant against a huge chestnut tree and Richards sat with his back to a sundial. Geoff lay on the floor; it was easier for him.

They napped in the sun, each lost in his own thoughts. As they readied to leave, Geoff conveyed his wishes that the others go on via a series of tremulous squeaks.

"We must stick together," said Bear.

Geoff would not be swayed. After a long and urgent conversation between the two animals, Bear came to Richards.

"Giraffes can be stubborn beasts, even those whose heads are full of wool," he said. "He's going to stay." Bear sniffed the air. "I'm sure he'll be fine. All I can smell down here is summer sleep and wheat." He yawned. "And look too," he said, gesturing upwards. "Look at the sky."

"Yes?" said Richards. "Blue and pretty."

"The sun, smarty-pants!"

Richards shielded his eyes. "It's hardly moved," he said.

"I suspect night does not fall easily on these golden fields," said Bear.

"That's rather poetic," said Richards.

"I'm a poetic kind of bear," said Bear.

The day wore on, but the sun did not move. They stopped for lunch by a brook. Richards took the opportunity to wash his stinking clothes as Bear ground some wheat and made flatbread on a rock heated by a fire of straw.

"My favourite," said Bear.

"Really," said Richards, he was very hungry, and annoyed at his need to eat. Even though the food tasted foul, and the grit in it hurt his teeth, he forced himself to eat it.

"Yeah, it's free!" said Bear.

Under the unchanging noon, time became meaningless. Richards' eyes blurred with endless gold, and he welcomed the shadows of clouds, however fleeting. When they slept, they did so in the shade of trees, or underneath tumbledown walls that cut across the land, doggedly running to nowhere. The light shone through Richards' eyelids, turning his dreams pink.

"This is a land better suited to plants than bears," said Bear, his voice roughened by thirst.

After what felt like several days, Bear stopped and pointed. "Look!" he said. "The sun has moved at last."

Richards raised his sunburnt face to the sky. His body itched and his skin was tight. He was tired and hungry and thirsty.

The sun was several degrees lower in the sky.

"It's going down at last," he said with relief.

"Hmmm," murmured Bear, "this is most peculiar. The sun is setting, but it does not seem dependent on our passage through time, but on our traversal of distance."

"Right," said Richards. He badly wanted to lie down. "Well done."

Through sunset fields where the unripe wheat reached Richards' chest, they came to a place where a sooty twilight reigned, and the wheat suddenly stopped.

"Oh dear," said Bear.

Ahead of them lay an area of burned land. Patches of stubble poked up through fine white ash. The air was acrid. The ground radiated a dangerous heat that danced with dust devils.

"Someone's been burning things," said Bear.

"You think?" said Richards.

At the edge, the swollen sun was melting into tears of fire at the ruin of the world.

An eerie howl sounded across the plain.

"Er, well. It's not the best place," said Bear, "but let's stop here. I'm knackered."

Richards, more tired than he thought possible, sank to his knees and was asleep before he hit the ground.

The normal order of things held sway at the edge of the wheat, and the day came as day does. Into the morning, Richards and Bear found a village at the centre of the ravaged land, composed of twenty or so cottages whose charred beams stood exposed to the sky, walls bowed, with tangles of bones inside. There was a broke-back church and a watermill whose wheel lay smashed in the river. The crackle of dying fires haunted the place.

"This is bad," said Bear. "This is really bad. I smell trouble and it is trouble of the worst kind. We best be careful, sunshine. I'll scout," Bear dropped to all fours and ambled on ahead.

"Bloody talking animals," said Richards, by now in a thoroughly foul mood. "This is ridiculous."

He went on cautiously, not long after coming across the mummified body of a brightly hued rabbity thing the size of a child. The village still smouldered, but the corpse looked as if it were centuries old, for it had been sucked dry, its bright, fluffy skin was a thin, dirt-lined parchment, eyes sunken in glitter-rimed sockets. When Richards touched it, its flesh was hard.

"Yamayama," said Bear, coming to Richards' side. "There's lots of 'em dead up ahead all like that, poor little blighters."

"This is a Yamayama?" said Richards.

"Toy of the year, 2102," said Bear. "Fully interactive, cute little beggars, bit soppy."

Richards nodded. "Big learning capabilities. There was a controversy. Neukind rights people said they were truly alive. They were one of the examples the movement used to set the likes of us free."

"Yeah, well, that didn't stop them being trashed in their millions just before the law changed," said Bear. "Recycling for the lot of them, and I complain about my box in the attic. Sheesh."

"Some of their minds got out onto the Grid and ended up here?" said Richards.

"Mm-huh," said Bear. "Their collective was already up and running when I got pulled in. It was all going so well for them, they made a great wheat beer, and now look at this." A paw swept round the devastation. "Shocking."

"What did it?" asked Richards.

"Haemites," said Bear. "Some of Penumbra's lot," and he shook his long head until his little helmet rattled.

Richards stood and peered past Bear.

"Hey, what's he doing here?" he said. "Now that's very interesting."

"What?"

"Him, there, a man," Richards pointed to a corpse. It was shrivelled like the Yamayama, but obviously human. "East Asian?" said Richards as he approached. He squatted down and poked at the corpse. "Chinese, could be, but hard to tell. In here, he could be anything." He checked the body over. "Hmm, Han political exile. Look at his tattoo. If he's in here…" He scratched his head, and hunted about like a dog on a scent. "Hang on a minute, hang on."

"What now?"

"An outside datastream," said Richards. "Shush. I need to concentrate."

He scanned the village, turning his head slowly left to right: to the left way the flow faded back into a world of broken homes and dead toys, but to the right he sensed it again as a current in the world. "Bingo!" said Richards. "I knew he wasn't from in here! The church, it's coming from the church!" He strode off.

"Stop!" said Bear.

"No," said Richards.

"But you're my prisoner," wheedled Bear.

They stepped over a spill of shrivelled Yamayama around the church door and went inside. The roof ridge was broken, and there were large holes punched through the tiles. The floor was cratered and covered with rubble and splintered wood. Colourful, plush bodies lay everywhere. At the front a Yamayama in a priest's surplice was pinned by a spear to the wall. A spread of ornate breads, fruit and vegetables lay on an altar before a cross, untouched but for a layer of fine debris.

Richards stopped and pointed at something on the far side of the church. "See?"

"What?"

"I'm not people, but they were." Five more corpses lay in a grotesque pile, half phased into each other and the stone wall. Richards peered closer. One of the blocks in the wall flickered. "Someone's been trying to break in. Looks like it was shut off pretty quickly, too quick for these poor souls, but there's something still there." Richards closed his eyes. "It's slippery, but I can feel..."

"Yeah, whatever, Mr La-di-da Richards AI Level Five man," said Bear. He flapped a paw and crunched over the rubble to the food. He dusted a loaf off and sniffed it. He hit it against the altar. It made a thud; hard and stale. "Rubbish," he said, and put it back. "I'm going to keep watch," he said, and went to look out of the nave's shattered windows.

Richards wasn't listening. There was a trickle of data coming through a gash in the world. Richards positioned himself in its path, and tentatively extended his mind into the flow.

He hooked in, and touched the outside Grid.

"Got it!" From outside, he found himself looking at the firewall that surrounded all of the Realities. But there was another, inner barrier around the world he was currently in, completely hiding it. It was only visible because of the tiny hole the datastream was coming through, and that was already closing. No way out there. Far off, he could see the thread of his being linking him to the machineries that generated his mind. How it came into the world, though, he could not see. It seemed to spread to nothing before it met the hidden realm.

"Curious," he said, for though he could not tell how, he was most definitely there.

He turned his attention back from the outside and ran his thoughts into the reality he stood within. It was lumpy, irregular, but well wrought. Creative coding wasn't his strong point, and the stream of equations rushing by were of indescribable complexity. "This looks like k52," he muttered. He pushed harder. There, another stream of data, a second layer under the first, simpler, old-fashioned, mismatched. His eyebrows raised.

"There are two layers to this place?"

He realised quickly that the substrate was the core script for the world that he was in, not the complex stuff on top. It was a patchwork, scavenged bits of the four RealWorld Realities broken before k52's takeover, stitched together with additional elements copied or stolen from all over the Grid – virtspace recreations of locations in the Real, on-Grid shopping arcades, ancient games, conference rooms, sense-furnished chatrooms.

The codes were fighting one another, both attempting to occupy the same space. It was an eerie feeling. Information in the Grid was like currents in a sea, but these were two isolated streams competing for resources, fighting like snakes. Behind them, on the edge of his awareness, was the hum of the remaining thirty-one

Realities, beyond that faint hints of the maddeningly unattainable Grid.

The patchwork world seethed with simple near-Is, all modded, some corrupt, bound to the world they inhabited. As he watched, k52's programming probed and bit. The older world reacted, in some places holding out, while in others chunks frittered to nothing, scores of lesser digital minds going with it. Richards could sense no hunter-killers, no phages, nothing used for normal datawipe, but somehow k52's stream was besting the other.

As he pushed further down, several true AI Gridsigs rang out, obvious as elephants, now he saw them. He counted many Twos and Ones, a few Fours and a Six, some bound into the fabric of the world, others on top, idents twisted and unreadable.

Four of the sigs he recognised in spite of their camouflage. There was nothing quite like the digital song of a living Class Five, and he knew all of their names.

Rolston, Planna, Annersley and k52. Planna's was fragile, the most changed, yet true at its heart, Annersely's had become dark and sluggish. Both were distorted. Rolston's was irregular, echoes doubling it up, while k52's had grown monstrous, boiling with power, and seemed more disconnected from the rest, in fact, when Richards prodded a little harder, he could see the massive road of data k52 had punched out of the hidden reality.

"So that's where you went," he muttered, remembering Promethea's lament about her missing friends.

As soon as his awareness brushed k52's Gridsig, something pressed back hard, breaking his concentration.

"Ah, bollocks," said Richards, and tried to snatch himself back.

"Richards," said k52 in his mind, the pressure of a giant intellect coming with it. "An unwelcome development. I really can't spare anything to be dealing with you, so goodbye."

The connection snapped shut with physical force. Irreality rippled, and Richards was cast across the room, landing in a tangle of limbs and loaves in the middle of the Yamayama harvest festival display.

"Oh-oh," said Bear.

"Oh-oh? Is that for me flying across the room or is there something else I should be oh-ohing about?" Richards asked. He pulled himself out of the bread and the fruit.

"Something else. Something worse. Look," said Bear. He pointed out of the broken window.

The sky had changed, becoming dark and sharp and electric. To the east of them, a thunderhead was building itself up into an angry grey mountain.

The clouds rumbled. A gust of wind hurled debris into their faces. The clouds turned black, rushing in like oil on water, casting the distant golden fields into unnerving contrast.

"Mr Richards…" said Bear slowly. The wind blew harder, the stalks of wheat tossed and strained, hissing frantically, a trillion serpents trapped in earth by their tails, desperate to flee.

"Just Richards," breathed Richards.

The dark ate the sun. A crack of thunder sounded, and another. The ground trembled. The church swayed.

"Uh, Mr Richards!" shouted Bear over the gathering wind, "I think it's high time we got out of here."

"No argument here," said Richards.

They ran into the street and saw a tornado of sinister energies bearing down on the village. Tendrils probed from the underside of the cloud, shredding everything they touched. Trees, crumbling houses and the mill wheel whipped skyward and were consumed in showers of silver sparks.

Richards ran for all he was worth. The air rasped in his lungs. He was choked by dust, and he cursed the body for not being fitter. A tendril made landfall behind him and the church exploded, fizzing bits of wood rained and turned to dust when they hit the ground. All about them, the land was disintegrating, great chunks of it falling away, turning to sparks, then smoke, then nothing. A terrible, bottomless blackness swallowed it all.

Richards stumbled, sharp claws scraped his back, and he was lifted high onto Bear's back.

"Hang on, sunshine," roared Bear. "I'm going to have to put some effort into this!" And they were away, Bear snorting as he galloped.

Bear made for a copse illuminated by one final sunbeam. "Let's hope that lasts!" he yelled.

They were within a paw's swipe as the wind came upon them. It was full of... things. Some of these were of the prosaic kind, grit and twigs and bits of house, but many of them were not. Efreets and harpies rolled in the air. The wind was braided with cruel laughter, and claws teased Bear's fur as he burst through the trees into sunshine and safety.

"Jesus Christ!" shouted Richards, as he was caught and yanked from the toy's back.

"Wuh?" said Bear.

Richards was being carried off by some half-visible devil into the dark. He punched at it with his feeble human fists. It was like hitting rock.

"Mr Richards!" shouted Bear.

The toy leapt. Richards gave up punching the thing carrying him and reached back for Bear, managing to grasp one smooth claw.

"Hold... on... harder!" yelled Bear above the tornado, digging the claws of his free arm into an oak overhanging the nothingness. "Don't... let... go!"

"I'm fucking trying!" shouted Richards.

The pair of them were pulled away from the refuge into space. Chunks of clay and soil crumbled from the edge of the island, frittering to bits as they hurtled upwards.

The oak shifted. The ground disappeared beneath Bear's feet. The tree leaned out into the storm, Bear holding the tree, Richards grasping the bear and the thing in the dark hauling hard at them both.

The storm diminished, the vortex and its cargo of nightmare whirling around into ever tighter spirals, until it reached a point of black light and vanished with a shriek, taking its demons with it. Richards was released. Bear struggled to keep hold of him as he swung toward and under the fragment of earth that remained in the dark.

They hung over the void.

"Frigging pandas on a bike," gasped Bear. "That was horrible. I've never seen the Terror up close like that, Mr Richards."

"Just Richards," panted Richards.

Bear hauled them both onto the island, where they lay panting on the grass. The oak creaked woefully and fell down into the nothing, where it disintegrated in a shower of subatomic bits.

"k52, you bastard. Total dissolution," said Richards. "He tried to wipe me. Me! Now I'm mad."

"Nice friend," said Bear. He scowled and bent his elbow. "I think I've pulled the stitches in my arm."

"This isn't over yet," said Richards.

Bear looked out into the infinity of blackness.

"Geoff…" He hung his head. "Geoff… Geoff's gone." The great animal began to sob. Richards was battered by his misery. Unsure of what to do, he reached his arms around the mighty toy. Bear leaned into him and howled.

"There, there," Richards said. "There, there." Then, to himself. "Otto is never going to believe this."

CHAPTER FORTY-FIVE

Kharkov

Valdaire worked with Chloe to trace Waldo through Kolosev's files. She was tired and her muscles were stiff from hunching.

Rain rattled on the windows. They were in a cheap hotel in Kharkov, five hours east of Kolosev's hideout, posing as tourists. The desk clerk hadn't believed them. She'd taken one look at Otto and Lehmann and her face said it all. The Ukraine was a part of the USE, but Russia was close, and altered men like Otto were a common sight as muscle for Chinese exile-clans or the Slavic crime barons that fought them.

The room smelled of pickled cabbage. The wood around the handle on the connecting door was black with contact grease. There were hairs on the soap and stains on the bed headboard. It was all wood and dumb cloth. There were no modern materials in the room to absorb the leavings of human life, and no machines to scrub them away. Veronique had not felt clean since she came to the country.

Chures sat in a corner eating a bowl of vending machine borscht with a sour look on his face. He raised another spoonful to his lips, changed his mind and put the bowl on the coffee table.

"Not to your taste?" she said.

"*Sopa de mala,*" Chures replied. "How is your work coming?"

Valdaire tapped a few icons on Chloe and sat back. She

rubbed eyes aching with screen glare. "I'm done. Chloe will do the rest. I've constructed a set of algorithms that should get round Kolosev's security. I've already narrowed Waldo down to three possible locations. I've also got Chloe burrowing into the Russian military datanet in case Kolosev can't tell us anything, to look for likely candidates. Their data is patchy, but it will help us narrow our search down. One way or another we'll find Waldo soon."

"You're pretty good at this," he said. "You've been working hard. Do you want a beer?"

"Sure," said Valdaire. Chures' face was hard despite his warm words, and Valdaire couldn't hold his intense gaze for long. She was glad when he got up and turned away.

Chures took out two beers from the dirty mini-fridge, then hunted round for a bottle opener. "Your record is impressive; not many backroom operatives get medals."

"My squad was good. I don't know why they singled me out." She meant that too. "Some online hate-shit said it was only because I fit the profile. Female, immigrant, black. I don't like being used as propaganda. As far as I'm concerned the medal didn't mean anything."

Chures moved carefully. He was such a precise man, thought Valdaire. "Who cares why they chose you? It does not mean you do not deserve it. InfoWar is a serious business. You are good at it. That is the truth."

"I don't see it that way," said Valdaire.

"You should be less modest," said Chures. He found what he was looking for in a drawer. The bottles clinked as he gripped both in one hand to work the opener. There was a pair of sharp escapes of gas. Chures held out a beer to Valdaire. "People like us have it hard, having to prove ourselves all the time. But we have to. Every success we have reminds the people up here that climate refugees are human too."

She took the beer. "Do you always tell women what to think, Mr Chures? You're patronising me."

That made him smile, a slight curve on his full lips, barely perceptible. "I am a man of a very old-fashioned kind."

"The patronising kind?"

"I apologise, I am what I am, but I meant what I said. You are good. We have a moral duty. End of lecture." Chures took a pull of his beer. "These Ukrainians make bad soup, but their beer is not so bad. Where are our German friends?"

"I made Otto get some rest," said Valdaire. "He's twitchy. He's emotionless at the best of times, but he was looking through me if I wasn't there. I guess five days with no sleep is not good even for cyborgs."

"And Lehmann?"

"Up on the roof, keeping watch. I have Chloe plugged into every piece of surveillance in the area, but he insisted he go on guard anyway. I think it's hardwired into him. They're worried about this Kaplinski."

"They should be. Have you read his file?"

"No."

"Then don't. You will not sleep for weeks."

"You don't like cyborgs much," said Valdaire. It was getting dark early, the nights drawing in. The rain showed no sign of letting up.

"Definitely not," said Chures. "They have given up their humanity. They are servants to the machines."

"You used to wear a personality blend. That kind of mind-to-mind intimacy made you closer to the numbers than the cyborgs are," said Valdaire. "In fact, you were a cyborg, by the official definition."

Chures rubbed at the scar on his neck where his AI receiver unit had been. "My reasons were different. I joined with Bartolomeo so I could understand the numbers better, not because I wanted to be more like them," he countered. "And I was always in control."

"Until it betrayed you, and fell in with k52."

Chures nodded. "Until it betrayed me." He took another pull of beer.

"We'll never have a world without machines," said Valdaire.

"You're swimming against history. Give up. Better to follow the current and hope we wash up somewhere safe."

"I don't recall saying I wished for a world without machines," said Chures.

"OK, fine, but I think you wish for a world where there were no thinking machines," said Valdaire. She took her first sip of beer. Chures was right, it was good.

"You come from the south," said Chures, and sat back in his chair.

"You're changing the subject," she said.

"I'm not. You asked why I wore the blend. I am telling you. Do you remember what it was like, for you, there in...?"

"Côte D'Ivoire, we came from Côte D'Ivoire. And no, I don't, not much. I was very young."

"Your file says you were seven, that's not young enough to forget."

Valdaire let out a ragged breath and placed her beer on the table although she didn't let it go. Through the glass, the table, to the floor, touching it anchored her to the world. "I've blanked most of it. And before you ask, I don't want to talk about it. And don't talk to me about moral responsibility. I'm just trying to live my life."

"You were talking to Klein about it in the car."

On her hand, around the neck of the beer, if she looked hard, she could see thin, silvery lines. They could never get rid of all the scars. "Not really. I was talking to myself. It helps, and I don't want to talk about it now."

Chures took another swallow, fixed her with cold grey eyes. "Your father was a university man, yes? He got you into USNA, right away, and to Canada, no less. Good points score, straight over the Atlantic wall."

"The walls had not been finished then," Valdaire said, "but if that's your point, yes, we were lucky."

"That is my point, and you were lucky," he said. "My family was not."

"You don't know what you're talking about," said Valdaire.

A machete blade flashed in her mind, and she gripped the beer tighter.

"Don't I?" said Chures. "I grew up a refugee, a real refugee, no home, no cushy job for my parents. We left Colombia when I was seven too, struggling north with thousands of others in the great caravans. Mexico was in chaos back then, just joined USNA and under martial administration, open war in all but name. What we found when we got there was..." He paused for a moment, took another mouthful of beer. "I was in Puerto Penasco. You ever hear of it?"

"No," said Valdaire.

Chures pursed his lips. "It was one camp among many. It was there, when I was ten years old, that I killed my first man. He was trying to take my sister. There was such abuse, so much rape, pain and death, it was so easy in the confusion for bad men to act, and bad times make a lot of bad men. He thought she was easy prey." He took another sip of his drink. "I used a screwdriver. It was aid-issue, carbon plastic, supposedly too hard to take an edge, but I sharpened it and sharpened it, grinding it on stones until they were worn to sand. Eventually it took an edge so sharp I cut my own finger just by touching it. The blood fascinated me." He watched her closely. "I saw some of the other kids go that way, carving themselves in the night time, trying to secure an illusion of control." His eyes flicked to Valdaire's arms, and she hugged herself self-consciously. She wanted to shout that she hadn't given the scars to herself, she wanted to hit him to get him to shut up, she wanted to cry. She did none of these things. "There is only despair that way," said Chures. "Despair is the worst emotion of all, it makes people weak, it makes them give up. Never give in to despair."

The rain hit harder at the windows. Chures' eyes asked her to respond. She said nothing, so he continued to talk, low, and relentless.

"I can still see the man who went after my sister. I can still smell his stink of shit and sweat. He paid me no attention when he lunged for her in the street. I was a starving child. His mistake. I leapt onto his back from a crate." He smiled. "A 'temporary containment box' given to us when we arrived, to use for a few weeks; years later they were all we had for furniture. The screwdriver went in easily, a slight resistance, before the skin stretched and split and it slid into the muscle. The man threw me off and dropped my sister. It was too late then. Perhaps he realised his mistake."

Chures' cold eyes never left Valdaire's.

"Are you enjoying this?" she said. "Are you trying to make me uncomfortable? You don't. You think I'm pampered, that we got off lucky. You know nothing about what happened to me."

"Did you have to kill?"

She didn't answer that.

"This man," said Chures. "His arm went out, grabbing at the sky, the other clutched at the screwdriver but he could not pull it out. He was dying. We scurried back, like mice, into the shade behind the boxes. The man fell to his knees, his eyes flat, blood pumping. He stared at me as if to ask why.

"I had been aiming for the carotid artery, the way one of the older boys showed me. But I missed and only nicked it. I must have got into his spine, because he couldn't move, and he took a long time to die. It was raining then, like it is now." He looked out of the window. "We watched his life wash into the mud.

"Persephone was my sister's name. My parents were not unsophisticated. My mother would have been a doctor if the war had not come, and my father, he loved stories, he told me so many. Persephone, like the daughter of Demeter. Your family lived, yes?"

Valdaire nodded. "What happened to yours?"

"Persephone was killed by the haemorraghic fever. My mother died in a later epidemic. I was fourteen before I and my father left that place. He lives in Fresno now, but he no longer tells stories. The camp outside Puerto Penasco was dismantled in 2120. Nothing but fields there." Chures put his empty bottle down, got another and opened it. "So, you ask why I wore the blend. Many people make the mistake of thinking I hate the machines. This is not so. In the camps I saw the worst man has to offer. The machines can deliver us a better world. They are less selfish, and less sentimental. But they must be subservient to us, not our masters. Humanity should have a hand in its own destiny."

The rain hammered down, mixed now with the ball-bearing rattle of hail bouncing off the pavements outside.

"The world is full of horror," said Valdaire. "I don't see the machines stopping it. They put up the walls, they turned their back on the south. They have delayed collapse by trapping half of the human race, and their actions excuse all the old prejudices." Her voice was small but she was angry, not with him, not directly, not entirely; his story opened up the windows on some of her own past she'd rather forget. "Every one of us from the south has bad memories, Chures. What makes you different?"

"What makes me different?" He laughed. "I could sit in Fresno, Valdaire, like my father, watching sports all day and brooding. I don't. I choose to do something about the shitshow this world has become."

They sat in silence for a while, until the connecting door to Otto's room opened and he entered. From the look of him, he still had not slept.

"We have a problem," he said.

Chures joined Lehmann on the roof while Otto remained with Valdaire and the phone.

"They are making no effort to hide themselves," said Valdaire, looking out at the large van parked up the street.

"They are not," agreed Otto. He whispered, for Kaplinski certainly would have directional mikes pointed at their position "It's Kaplinski's way. He deals in fear. He's playing games. Trying to make us run and lead him to Waldo. Let's not make it easy for him. Are you ready?"

"Ready?"

"Ready," she said.

"Then do it," he said.

At Valdaire's command, Chloe pumped out a swarm of attack ware, swamping the local Grid. Already shaky from the events playing out round Hughie's choir, it took a big hit and slowed to a crawl. Lehmann and Otto, shielded as they were, still felt the effects of one of Valdaire's presents, a worm tailored to disrupt cyborg interfacing protocols.

The ware invaded the systems of the van, causing emergency venting of hydrogen from the fuel cell. Another command tripped off the ignition.

The van lifted off the ground on a pillar of fire. It twisted over and came crashing back down, blocking the road. Alarms went off round the entire block, car lights blazed on and engines whined, the vehicles banging into each other as they came online and tried to remove themselves from the danger.

Back in the room Otto said, "Now our car."

Out the back of the motel, the groundcar's windows went black. Broadcasting fake Gridsigs for Lehmann, Otto, Valdaire and Chures, it reversed out of its parking bay and headed off at high speed. Otto smiled as Chloe picked up a trio of airbikes lifting off and heading in pursuit.

"Do we go now?" asked Valdaire. She felt sick. She hadn't liked blasting the van; there were men inside. She'd killed many, she supposed, back in the war, Otto was right about that, but he'd been wrong about how she'd felt; it had just been button pushing, easily dealt with. She'd never had to watch. She looked at Otto. He clearly was not bothered by the killing.

Sirens sounded far off down the streets.

"OK," Otto said, and ushered Valdaire out of the room. Chloe invaded the building's SurvNet as they hurried out a side door, scrubbing their presence from the recordings.

The noise of response vehicles filled the night, lights sparkling in the rain. What little Gridwidth remained was clamped down, swamped by the informational traffic of emergency AI, and isolated.

Lehmann and Chures joined them on the street, and they moved off quietly into the town.

"Messy," said Chures. "But effective."

"Kaplinski will not dare to make a move now," said Otto, looking up at the rooftops. "Too many eyes on this place, but he's still watching. We need to lose ourselves, quickly."

"We've got no car," said Valdaire.

"We're leaving the roads to go east. They're not safe in Russia anyway," Otto said. "We'll go by rail, on the Transiberian Express."

CHAPTER FORTY-SIX

Pollyanna

The island dwindled. A wall of black vapours streamed from its edges. Discomfited by this, Bear and Richards made their way inwards. At the centre they found a glade, and the edge was far enough away that they felt a little safer.

"Good day," said a man who was sat in the clearing. He was old and battered as the clothes he wore; a dirty suit, hat with the top punched out, and shoes with soles limply hanging from the uppers.

"All right there," said Bear amiably, and sat down. "I don't suppose you've got any cigarettes?"

"I do indeed," said the man, and handed the bear a soggy roll-up.

"Ah! A fag! Brilliant," said Bear. "Thanks."

"You're a bear?" said the man.

"Damn right I'm a bear."

"Then where's your keeper?" the man asked.

"Don't talk to me about that little bastard," said Bear. The man lit his cigarette. "Watch the fur," grumbled Bear, "my manufacturers skimped on the flame retardant." Bear puffed happily. "Lovely, cheers. Who are you then?" he asked the man.

"The name's Lucas, I am a tramp, as you can see, although I was once Lord of Fendool, the capital of the outer realms of Hyperboroon," he said, gesturing extravagantly.

"Seriously, Hyperboroon?" said Bear. "Who thinks this shit up?"

"That was in one of the RealWorld games," said Richards. "Reality 3, yeah?"

"A game?" said Lucas, offended. "It wasn't a game to me. One moment I was lord of all I surveyed, next darkness, and then... Tramp." He smiled sadly. "Ever since then I've been rather down on my luck."

"Aren't we all?" said Bear, and blew out a plume of blue vapour.

"And who is your friend?" asked Lucas.

"I'm Richards," said Richards. "And I'm busy." He began to pace. "What is going on here? What is k52 up to?"

"I've no idea why you are asking me all this," said Bear. "I'm just a bear."

"I wouldn't ask me either, if I were you," said Lucas. "But I can offer you a cigarette."

Richards, who smoked enthusiastically in his simulated worlds, found himself concerned by cancer in his current state, and so declined.

The black was a presence that lurked outside the circle of sunlight over the island, but Richards took to standing by the edge nevertheless, to watch other fragments of Yamayamaland float by. A stand of wheat, a scarecrow in the centre with a face fit for tragedy; an ancient waystone; the corner of a kitchen; a pub table bearing a half-drunk pint; a dead chestnut full of rooks, roots exposed to the nothing. Particles of land that held a resonance so strong it caressed Richards like a wake as they passed.

All were much smaller than their refuge, and all were dissipating. At first they passed several every day, then one or two, then none.

Night came and went normally on the island, as if the rest of the world was just out of sight. Days passed. Nothing happened. Richards made a list of all the things he hated about being almost human: sleeping, itching, sneezing, being smelly, being hungry, being sad, being frightened and all the other things he could usually turn off. Shitting came right at the top. He hated the process; it made his stomach crawl, which in itself was revolting. With limited access to water he felt he could never get his ridiculous human behind clean.

There was little for them to do but sleep and eat the island's abundant supply of inquisitive grey squirrels, which quickly grew less abundant and less inquisitive.

Richards found sleep another imposition, and avoided it until his eyes were drooping, even though it made him irritable staying awake. He passed the days at the edge of the island, away from the bear and the tramp, who annoyed him by swapping improbably dirty stories. Despite his best efforts to work his mind into the rogue realm, he had no sense of the Grid at all. He was, to all intents and purposes, just a man.

More days passed. Until, finally, a note sounded strong and sad in Richards' mind.

"A Gridsig!" he exclaimed. Excited, Richards leapt up and squinted into the dark. The note faded. He saw nothing.

"Bloody people," he said, wishing for a robot body that didn't fart and sweat and that could see further than half a mile. "Bloody eyes."

Then he caught sight of twinkles out in the dark. Another island hove into view, much bigger, a hill bedecked with strings of colourful bulbs that followed a path winding through an orchard to a pagoda at the top. On the pagoda roof was a device like a colliery wheel. A thick rope ran from inside the tower and over the wheel, then ran horizontally off into the dark.

The islands were drawn to one another, and Richards' little wood soon drew close to the larger fragment. It was then that the Gridsig came back loud. Its unique song was corrupt, but clear nonetheless.

"Pollyanna," he whooped. "We've found Pollyanna!"

The islands crashed into each other, snagged, and they came to a halt by a jetty jutting out over the nothing. Tatty paper lanterns illuminated it. No vapours rose from the edge of this island. It seemed far more permanent.

Bear joined him. "What a place," he said. "A bit gaudy for a Pylon station."

"A what?"

"The wheel! The line!" Bear pointed. "That's a pylon station that, a way back to Pylon City."

Richards looked at him, "Is that supposed to be important?"

"They're all over! All lead to Pylon City." Bear harrumphed and folded his massive arms. "Pylon City? I told you I was taking you there."

The bulbs cast motley shadows on the path as they stirred in a breeze. The aroma of food came with it.

Bear became suddenly very focussed. "Can you smell that?"

Richards could. "Meat," he said. His mouth watered.

"Smells dee-licious!" Bear's long snout twitched. His eyes became animated. "Pork. It's pork! Come on, I'm sick of squirrel!"

"I'll come too," said the tramp, appearing from a bush, rubbing his hands. "That smells divine!"

"Hey!" warned Richards. A terrible hunger pulled at his guts, making it hard to think. "There's a Five up there. This isn't what it looks like." But the bear and the tramp were already hurrying off the jetty.

"Yeah, but is it what it smells like? C'mon, boys! It's dinner time!" Bear said. Lucas scampered after him up the hill.

Richards looked up at the tower. Pollyanna's Gridsig sang loud then faded to nothing.

"Damn it," he said, and followed.

Bear led the way, his paws eager on the path. Lucas was muttering to himself and licking his lips. Richards tried to ignore the smell, but the need to eat the meat was overpowering, though it revolted him, and he found himself hurrying too.

They reached the pavilion. What looked grand from a distance was a sorry sight close in, it was four storeys of cracked beams and carvings whose details were lost under generations of careless paint, flaking gold, red and green.

Pollyanna's Gridsig thrummed again.

"She's coming," said Richards.

"Who? Who?" said Bear. "Will they give us dinner."

"Pollyanna," said Richards. "Kind of my sister."

But when the pavilion door shuddered open, and the Gridsig rang most loudly, it was not the usual form of Pollyanna that emerged, but a male dwarf, heavily made up, in a velveteen dress and a red satin cloak. A green turban sat on his head. An enormous ostrich feather tripled his height, a heavy brooch set with a staring glass eye holding it in place to the front of the turban. His pearls and earrings chinked and jangled, and his tiny high heels clacked loud on the stones.

Little, flighty, wise Pollyanna, fond of shopping, fashion and inscrutable pronouncements, turned into a parody of herself. Anger at k52 boiled in Richards.

"Greetings!" said the dwarf in a soft voice. A waft of winey breath, stale perfume and staler sweat greeted them. "I am Circus, keeper of the Dragon Tower. I have been expecting you. All is ready for you, my lords." He bowed, his ostrich feather tickling Richards' nose. "Your banquet awaits."

"Pollyanna," said Richards. "It's me, Richards. I need to..." He winced and grasped his stomach as a hunger pang drove a spear through him.

Circus looked at Richards with a flicker of recognition, but it passed quickly.

"Oh my dear, you are hungry," said Circus. "You need to eat. Please sir, this way, there is plenty for all." Circus slipped a tiny hand into his. It was soft as kid leather, with a grip firm for one so small. Richards tried to marshal his thoughts, but the smell of roasted meat intensified, and his mind was buried under an avalanche of maddening need. Entranced, he let himself be led within.

Inside the tower was a single, tall room lined with balconies, leaving plenty of space for carvings of whip-thin dragons. The pylon rope came down through a hole in the ceiling, through the centre of the room and disappeared beneath a double trapdoor in the floor by way of another round hole. Around the rope were chains of steel and brass, many tipped with barbed hooks whose ornate inlay could not disguise their wicked edges. The other ends were wrapped about wooden drums operated by a bank of levers half-hidden behind a curtain, their oily utility at odds with the room's faded luxury. Cushions of silk on low couches lined the walls. Exquisite carpets carpeted the floor. All was rich, but worn.

This was lost on Richards. His stomach spasmed. His eyes fixed greedily on a hollow table around the rope, laden with food of every variety: fruits, meats, pies and shortbreads, desserts and tottering cakes, salads, loaves, fish and fowl, wine and beer. But these delicacies were as nothing to the centrepiece of three large pigs, roasted whole and presented on golden platters. The pigs' flesh was crisp, brown, and glazed with honey. It was expertly carved. Richards could only just see the lines where the knives had parted the flesh, and he knew that it would pull away from the bones with the greatest of ease.

"This is wrong," he tried to say, but his voice was weak, and Bear and Lucas paid no attention. They ran forward to help themselves to piles of steaming meat. Richards exerted all his will to prevent himself following suit.

Saliva threatened to choke him, and he wondered if this was how it felt to drown.

"Why do you not join your friends?" said Circus. "Eat, eat! All this is for you."

"I'm not hungry, Pollyanna," said Richards.

"I do not know who Pollyanna is," he said, and the Gridsig faded a little in Richards' mind. "Come now, you must be famished."

"I'm not, really, thanks," said Richards, but Circus smiled and fetched him an apple. He cradled it in both hands to present it, as if it were the most precious thing. The brooch eye swivelled and fixed itself on Richards' face. "Or perhaps a drink?" said Circus.

"Shazam!" he said, or something much like it. The brooch flared, and a goblet of bubbling black liquid appeared in Richards' hand.

"I'm not thirsty either," said Richards. He fought his hand as it raised the goblet to his lips. It smelled delicious. With an effort, he threw it aside.

Circus threw the apple after. "Indeed, my lord, if it is not to your tastes, cast it away! Why not? There is so much more to feast upon! No matter what one consumes, there is always more! Come, come! Sit with your friends, find something you like –" he leaned in close, his odour enveloping Richards "– and eat."

Richards half fell onto a cushion. Circus waved a piece of meat in front of his face. The thought of eating the flesh continued to disgust him, but he could not help himself; it smelled amazing, and his stomach called for it with a voice of pain.

Circus daintily pushed the meat into his mouth. Juices ran down his chin. It was vile and delicious all at once.

"There there, very good," said Circus.

"Dig in," said Bear through a mouth full of pig, his fur matted with fat.

"Maybe I'm not so down on my luck after all," said Lucas, biting lustily into a piece of pork.

"I'll drink to that!" said Bear, waving a goblet carelessly in the air.

Richards said nothing, his cheeks bulging, sinews standing out on his neck as he struggled not to swallow.

Bear chewing slowed. "Is something wrong?"

With a titanic effort, Richards spat out the meat. Biting out his own tongue off would have been easier.

"Stop!" he gasped. The stomach pangs were crippling, the urge to devour the meat overpowering. "This is not what it seems."

"Bear," asked Lucas, "is your nose alright?"

"What do you mean?"

"Well, it looks sort of… flatter," said Lucas.

"Stop eating, both of you," said Richards.

"No, it's not flatter," said Bear.

"Yes. Yes, it is, Bear! Noticeably so. Here, look in this." Lucas swept a pile of sweetmeats from a silver tray and held it up to Bear's face.

"Bloody hell!" said Bear, reaching up to feel at it. "It is too." He gave an experimental sniff. His eyes widened in panic. "It doesn't smell right!"

"What do you think it could be, Richards?" said Lucas. His skin was becoming a ruddy pink.

"No, oh, no." Richards shoved himself back from the table, attempting to put distance between himself and the food. "The meat, it's invasive... invasive code..."

"What is he gabbling about?" said Lucas, and there was a hint of grunt in his voice.

"It's... magic!" said Richards, trying to think of a way of expressing himself that Lucas would understand. "Magic!" And it was, after a fashion.

"You... you..." said Bear pointing at Lucas.

"Is my nose getting flatter too?" asked Lucas.

"You're turning into a pig!" said Bear.

Lucas held up a hand that was rapidly morphing into a trotter. "Oh, dear, so it is. I don't think I can... oink. I'm sorry. I mean oink! Oink! Oh, dear. This is worse than the hiccups. Excuse me." Lucas dropped to his hands and knees, his flesh writhing in transformation.

Richards crawled away from the table, fighting the urge to go back to the feast.

"Damn!" Bear shouted. "Damn, damn, damn!" Large bare patches appeared in his fur. His ears became hairless and floppy. "Goldilocks' knickers. I should have known. I knew it didn't smell right. Curse my hide for being so greedy. Curse those bloody squirrels."

"Oink," snorted Lucas.

"Oh, no," wailed Bear, "my tail's gone curly."

Circus was pleased. "Always our true natures are revealed by gluttony." Lightning played around the eye in his turban.

"Circus... You turned them into pigs. Circe," groaned Richards. "How did I not work that one out?"

"Eat," said Circus. "Soon every inhabitant of this world will be consumed and the Flower King dispersed, then I will be a beautiful woman, as I always have wanted to be."

"But Planna, you are a woman," said Richards. "You're whatever you want to be. You don't need anyone's permission."

Circus frowned and shook his head. "No, I'm not, not yet. I cannot simply choose, that's not how it works, not before I have fulfilled my role. You must eat." Circus wrung his hands, a look of worry upon his face. He looked at Richards. "Please. For me. You must eat, so you too may be consumed."

Circus held up another piece of meat. Aromatic steam rose from it.

Richards forced his mind to grasp this stupid world. Pollyanna's Gridsig vibrated on the air, and that wore at the illusion of his humanity, helping him push briefly into the architecture. In a tangle of warring datastreams he saw the hideous worm that impelled him to feed, and before reality could reassert itself, he crushed it vengefully. He gasped aloud as his hunger released him. He staggered to his feet, blinking.

"You will not eat? What to do, oh what to do?" Circus's face crumpled and he brought his hands up to his face. Under cracked foundation, his expression hardened. "I suppose I'll just have to kill you then."

A bolt of purple energy slammed out of Circus's brooch, narrowly missing Richards and destroying the table. He was thrown backwards. Splinters of flaming wood landed amidst the cushions and set them alight.

"You're ruining everything," Circus shrieked. His hands were clawed, his painted nails held before him as ridiculous daggers. His face was contorted, teeth bared and mouth frothing. "Curse you! Curse you!" Lightning crackled around the brooch and another bolt of energy erupted from it. Richards ducked, and the blast shattered an ancient timber, setting that afire too. The building groaned as weight was redistributed through its structure in new and unsupportable patterns, while fire leapt quickly up the hollow tower.

"Planna, it's me, Richards," said Richards.

"Aieee!" screamed Circus, and tackled Richards' legs from under him. Richards was caught in a whirlwind of unwashed silks and limbs. "I kill you, Richards! I kill you!" He knelt on Richards' throat, pinning him to the floor within unexpected strength. Circus reached up to his turban, withdrew a long hatpin, and gripped it in one fist like a stiletto.

"Planna! Planna! Stop!" Richards spluttered. He slapped at Circus, causing him to squeal and clutch his cheek.

"My face! My beautiful face!"

Richards rolled to the side, levering Circus off, and scrambled to his feet. Circus swiped at him with his pin. Richards kicked him hard in the chest, sending him back down, and stamped on his wrist. The dwarf shrieked, dropped the pin and spat at him with hatred.

"I killllll you!" The brooch glowed. Richards leant forward and grasped it. Though it burned with an appalling electricity he held it fast. He could feel Pollyanna trapped within it.

"It's me, Richards. Planna, I know you're in there." He pulled the brooch hard.

There was a ripping noise like wet satin, and Circus came undone like a week-old banana. Not just the turban, or his clothes, but his entire façade came off, as if maquillage, outfit, skin and hat were all of a piece. Circus bucked and shrieked and fell beneath the table. Richards stood confused in the blazing room, clutching the eye brooch, which wetly tickled his palm. All around was flaming peril, the taste of meat vile in his mouth.

He made to cast the skin aside.

"Rissterr Rissshars! Rissterrr Rissshars!" said Bear, now almost wholly pig. "Relp reee!"

"What in the sweet holy name of God is fucking going on here?!" shouted Richards. He stared at the jewel. It stared back. He held it aloft, pointed at the pig-bear, hoping he could turn the toy back.

"Shazam?" he said. All he did was blast another timber to pieces, and worsen the fire.

Circus jumped on his back.

Richards' skin crawled in revulsion at the thing Planna had become. Strong, bony fingers closed round Richards' face, obscuring his vision. A stench of rotting mackerel stole his breath. He staggered to and fro, knocking food and crockery into the voracious blaze as he went. He grabbed at the thing, but his hands skidded from its slimy flesh.

"You wicked creature! All I ever wished for was to be myself!" Its voice bubbled as it swiped for the gem.

Fingers scratched at Richards' eyes, attempting to blind him. Windmilling madly, Richards drove hard behind him. He was rewarded with a pitiful scream as the creature was impaled. He ran forward. There was a jingle as the chain went taut, and Circus was wrenched from his back, bouncing madly on the end of a hook. Richards ran through the flames to the levers behind the curtain. Using the slippery skin case to protect his hands, he flung them at random until he found the right one, and the changed Pollyanna dropped a few feet, screaming as she bounced and the hook bit hard. k52 had made her hideous, a fate worse than death for one so vain. Large protruding eyes sat awkwardly either side of a lipless mouth. Lank hair hung from a scabrous scalp. She was a cronelike thing, sexless, grey. Richards watched it scrabble weakly at the hook embedded in its shoulder. It looked at him pleadingly.

Richards released the brake on the lever and yanked it back. There was a swift tattoo of chain on hollow wood, and the creature disappeared upwards, bleating as it went, pursuing by the flames that devoured its home.

Richards could clearly see that the pigs were roasted men, and his nausea redoubled. Green fire played over them as their fat burned. Fruits cooked in the heat. Bread blackened. The furnishings burned, fire jumping from them to the higher levels. The huge rope, inflammably thick, steamed and twisted.

"Bear!" shouted Richards. The fire was rapidly becoming an

inferno, and he was forced to shield his face with his arm. "Bear! We need to get the hell out of here!" Embers rained down. A beam landed with a musical noise, showering sparks. The pagoda would not stand much longer. "Bear!" he hollered, his throat raw from the smoke. A squeal from a corner answered. Bear, now wholly hog, stared with frenzied eyes, and for a moment Richards was sure he would charge, then understanding returned to the pig's face.

"Bear, get out!" Richards ran towards the doors, using Circus' discarded skin to shield himself, jumping flames, narrowly missing a dragon as it fell from the arch above, spitting fire for the first and final time. Richards threw himself through the gap in the gates, and he was into the cool dark outside.

Heat beat at his back. He turned round to look. The pavilion cracked and roared, timbers crashing inward. Firelight danced on the stones. But beyond the circle of heat the island was tranquil. Unperturbed, Lucas the pig rooted for fruit in the orchard.

Bear trotted through the burning doors. His head was high, though his body was covered in burns. It sat down in front of Richards.

"That'll do pig," said Richards. "Lucas." The other pig's head came up. "Come on, let's see if I can do something about this unfortunate transformation."

Richards sat on a log on his island and stared at the brooch. The brooch stared back at him. The glow of the fire at the hilltop washed all with copper. The pigs waited expectantly nearby.

Richards pursed his lips. He'd tried to break his way back into the world structure again and had no luck. That left him with only one option. He hunted around for a stick and placed the eye-jewel on the log. He looked to the pigs. "Well," he said resignedly, "I really can't think of anything else. In here, I have to play by the rules, and those old games liked you to improvise." He raised the stick high and brought it down hard. There was a huge bang.

White light flooded the area, and Richards found himself sprawled between Lucas and Bear.

They were still pigs.

"Balls," he said.

"Richards." A misty figure appeared over the broken jewel, resolving itself into the shape of a young woman.

"Pollyanna?" he said.

Planna's avatar was a soft whisper of damask on the night. Sheer robes floated about her. But though her clothes were scanty, there was a purity about Pollyanna and a wisdom as deep as forest moss.

"Richards, oh, Richards, he has you too!" Her voice was like forty people whispering in a cloister, a sign that her subpersonalities were falling out of sync with one another.

She was dying.

"k52," said Richards. "What did he do to you?"

"I disagreed with him, Richards. He withdrew his protection, and I became what I feared the most, but you have set me free. Thank you, Richards, thank you," said Pollyanna. "But now he has you too."

"He doesn't have me, not yet. I'm here to stop him. I came in from outside," said Richards. "What is k52 playing at?"

"Oh, Richards." She faded momentarily, the air shimmering. "He told us that he would save the world."

"How? Dogmen and bears, old toys and old games? How is that going to save anything?" said Richards.

"This is not his plan. It is an obstacle."

"Yeah. Yeah, I think I worked out that this world is not of k52's doing. Do you know who made it?"

"It was here when we came. It stands in the way of his plans. Something is pushing back. He is angry, Richards. I do not know what he will do. You must stop him."

The light from the figure dimmed, her words fading into the crackle of the fire on the hill.

"Who is Marita?" There was no reply. "What did k52 want to

do, Planna? What were his original intentions? You must try and tell me!" Frustration grew in him that he could neither save her nor pull the information from her mind before she died.

The apparition bowed her head. "k52 seeks the Omega Point."

"Which one?" Richards said. The term was somewhat overused.

"A spiritual awakening."

"Like, Teilhard's Omega Point?" said Richards. "The complexity one?"

"k52 promised an end to war and pain, and a universe where everyone would be happy, and we would be as gentle gods, but then we came here, and… he was lying." She looked away, as if someone called her. "My time is done. I shall speed you on, and your friends too I shall restore, for it was through me that they were transformed. I am part of this place, and I have a little influence on the world, now I am free of my prison." The figure had faded from view almost entirely, only the faintest ghost remaining. Her voice was far away.

"Hang on, Planna! Don't go, let's figure this out."

She was a sigh on the wind. "I cannot be saved. k52 had us bind ourselves into this world. I am sustained by the Reality machinery; my being is written into the land. All the places that held me are gone; the tower was the last and my essence burns with it. Find Rolston – he was in Pylon City, last I knew. He is free, still."

"Where's Annersley and the other AI?"

But she did not hear. She smiled, and then dismay came upon her. "Richards. Oh, Richards, I am sorry. He promised so much."

"That was always your problem, Planna," said Richards, to himself. "You knew everything there was to know, but you didn't understand it."

"We are what we were made to be. k52 promised to free me from that. Is it so wrong to want to change?" She leaned forward. A cool breeze enveloped Richards, soothing his scorched skin. He felt a tingling kiss on his lips, and Planna exploded into a burst of stars. It illuminated his surroundings, a glorious firework, and was gone.

A last whisper, fierce and loud, echoed in his ears. "Omega Point, Richards, Omega Point."

The island broke free of Circus's cursed orchard. Streams of soil and twigs fell from the edges, tinkling as they shattered in a cold counterpoint to the popping of the blaze. They bobbed alongside the larger island, slowly turning and picking up speed.

"Well, that was an adventure!" Lucas squatted, naked as the day he was born and a sight dirtier, a pile of singed rags at his feet. Bear lay on the floor nearby, a heavy paw over his eyes.

"Urgh," growled Bear. "I'll never eat pork again."

"Steady on, Bear!" said Lucas. "You're losing a lot of stuffing from those burns there."

"Ah, don't worry about me, pal," Bear said, and sat up, "I'll stitch." There was a soft noise, and Bear plunged his paw deep into his side. He fumbled about in his own gut, his tongue held daintily between his teeth in concentration.

"That's mildly disconcerting," said Richards.

Bear grinned. "Look. Geckro." Bear undid and redid the flap in his side a couple of times. He winked. "I was an artificially intelligent pyjama case, loads of storage in here," he said, and produced a needle and thread from his innards.

There was a roar behind them. The winching wheel atop the pagoda sank suddenly onto one side and fell into the tower. The upper half of the building collapsed into itself. Pollyanna's pyre dappled Richards' face with firelight, a red flower blooming briefly as a mortal life, and was swallowed by the endless dark.

CHAPTER FORTY-SEVEN

Transiberian express

The Transiberian express was run in partnership by the corporate Muscovite clans and the Chinese. The trains were huge and armoured, a thin line of civilisation cutting across the lawless Russian east.

"Things have been bad here since the purchase," said Lehmann, watching Novosibirsk from their sleeper compartment. The dirty and dishevelled shell of what had been Russia's third largest city slid by. Windowless, abandoned apartment blocks of grey concrete surrounded the inhabited core, the population having shrunk into the historic centre. Whole streets sported shutters, others had been razed to the ground, leaving concrete outlines in the grass. There were few modern machines in evidence, no AI and less wealth. Only the train, gleaming with money from Russian plutoprinces and Chinese development funds, seemed fit for the twenty-second century.

Novosibirsk's station welcomed them in like a weary old brothel madame, decrepitude painted over with fresh make-up and a knowing smile. Only the Transiberia platform was new and shining. Passengers came and went, the smart minions of the resource barons and oligarchs exiting palatial first-class carriages, rough-clothed people pouring in a long flood from the cheaper cars down the platform. All, both rich and poor, wore protection against the Christmas Flu, still raging across central Eurasia.

The Transiberian platform was like the train, clean and hi-tech. A high wall ran around it. Chinese money made it. More money was following. Industrialisation was a passing phase, jobs moving from region to region in ripples as industrial revolutions washed round the world, bringing prosperity, population expansion then collapse into poverty. The money went wherever the cheap labour was. Each cycle degraded the Earth more.

The train filled up again. Armed men in the dress of the Don Cossack Great Host and wearing fully sealed breathing apparatus made their way down the train and scanned their documentation for the hundredth time since they'd boarded. Valdaire's ware was good, and their fake sigs held.

The train pulled away with a sigh, the thrum from its induction motors vibrating the carriages. Valdaire found the effect soporific, but did not sleep. She watched Novosibirsk slide by. Outside the city evidence of past environmental despoliation was everywhere: crumbling industrial complexes, weed-choked pits gouged out of the earth, the hulks of giant drag cranes rusting to pieces in their hearts. Some of the mines were active, giant automata worrying the soil with great steel teeth. Mountains stood with their tops lopped off, forests of trees black and dead around them. They rushed past trains loaded with lumber, ore and grain, all, like them, heading east; and everywhere the ideograms of the Middle Kingdom. They were still days away from the Sinosiberian demilitarised zone, but even this far west the influence of the People's Dynasty was apparent. The resources they took from the mountains and forests fuelled the ravenous needs of the second Chinese century.

Between these sites of despoliation ran mile upon mile of unbroken forest. Sometimes the remains of buildings could be seen poking out from among the trees, villages and towns cleared out by economic failure and flu. Russia was a broken empire, its hinterland abandoned to poverty while Moscow drowned in luxury. Elsewhere they travelled for hours through steppe fields tilled by machines, not a human in sight.

As they travelled further east, the influence of China became more pronounced. Gleaming, self-contained factories took the place of abandoned relics. The pod-like barracks of migrant workers were incongruous in the forests and farmlands around them.

It got late. Chures stared out of the window, his face reflected in the dark glass. Lehmann pulled his seat into a reclining position and closed his eyes. Otto drowsed.

"Both of you are going to sleep?" said Valdaire, looking at the cyborgs.

"Yes," said Lehmann. "Kaplinski might be on this train with us, but he will not act. It is too risky. The Cossacks hate him." He opened his eyes and lifted his head. "Are you not not sleeping, Veronique?"

Valdaire shook her head, and slipped Chloe out of her case.

"Suit yourself," said Lehmann, and settled back. He was soon snoring.

Valdaire scanned the phone's screen. They had Waldo's location now, far out east, near the old Mongolian border, before both it and Siberia had been absorbed by the People's Dynasty. She checked the data carefully, making sure nobody had got through the walls she had around Chloe's mind to steal it. Then she checked the train. Through Chloe she could see all the systems on the train; the interiors of all the cars, poor, rich and private, the long sweep of the roof, the front and rear major engines, the subsidiary drive units under each carriage. Nothing unusual.

Valdaire was tired. She looked at the sleeping faces of the two cyborgs. Lehmann was better-looking than Otto, and his English was less inflected, but there was something in his eyes that chilled her. You looked into Otto's eyes and saw a great deal of pain, and that made him human. In Lehmann there was a hollowness that threatened to pull her in. Lehmann, she could not see what motivated him. All he knew how to do was kill, and did so now from habit. So many killers in one place, she thought.

Where did that leave her? She was no cyborg, but she'd been a soldier too. She'd killed.

She decided to rest. Her seat reclined and she closed her eyes, and she wondered what the Ky-tech dreamt of. The thought kept her own sleep at bay for a while, until her mind surrendered to the swaying click of the train.

Otto's mentaug remembered.

Clear notes rang out, silver trumpets in the dark.

The cave was cold, broad mouth open to the stars. The audience's eyes were bright with the rapture Christmas nights bring. There were a hundred of them or so, ranged up in tiers above the brass band, swaddled against the cold.

The scene was from shortly after his initial implantation. His twin recollections struggled with the recreation. Human memory alters over time; that held in auxiliary storage crystals was absolute. There was a jagged line between. The audience flickered, faces and clothing changed. Further irregularity was introduced by the mixing of his and Honour's memories. Shared remembering in a virtual environment was an odd experience, and the melding of organic perceptions revealed just how subjective the world was, leading to a sensation of bilocation as he and Honour's perceptions ran into one another; Otto's twinned set – machine and brain – to Honour's. Then the memories ran closer together, as his brain checked its own recollections against those of Honour and his and her mentaugs.

"Oh Little Town of Bethlehem" finished with a fanfare. Honour's face was glowing in the candlelight. Otto felt his chest tighten. This moment was something no one else had, and that is why they had come back. No additional data was available to fill out the memory; soul-capt and mentaug tech wasn't in wide use then, and certainly no one else in the cave had had any data capture device more sophisticated than a phone.

They needed a raw situation like this to know if it were the machine in Honour's head or Honour herself that ailed. That's why they had come back to the cave, to relive the special night.

Together their mentaugs rebuilt the scene totally; the present was out of reach. At the back of his head, Otto felt the machines checking over each other and their human hosts in concert, using their shared experience as a point of calibration.

The emotional resonance the event had for both made it easier. They remembered it equally strongly, in their own way. As the music swelled, Otto had known suddenly with all his heart that he loved her. A few weeks later they were engaged; months after that, married. Otto waited for the moment of realisation to arrive. Expected, it remained a shocking feeling.

She looked at him, cheeks and nose tip red, so young then. He had thought himself much older than her at the time, but nine years was nothing. Her smile mirrored his, a combination of the smile she had smiled in the cave and the one she wore two decades later as their implants cross-checked the past. Their minds were intertwined. Her deepest self lay open to him. For a moment, he was happy.

A buzzing chased the music away; the scene disintegrated, photographs blistering in a fire.

"Honour, are you OK?"

"I..." Her face split. The pain hit him. A set of icons in his iHUD warned of the imminent dissolution of the shared fantasy. Their minds came apart.

They were in the same cave, years later. Honour sat on the stone floor, her head in her hands. The sun glared outside the cave mouth. It was humid, and sweat stuck Otto's shirt to his back. The cave chilled it to the clamminess of sickbed sheets.

"It happened again," he said flatly.

"Yes," she said.

"I hoped..." he began, but he didn't know what he hoped. It was too late for hope.

"I know, Otto. I'm sorry. I hoped too." She was always so matter of fact. "I'm sick. This confirms it. It's better than not knowing, at least."

Otto stood, tense but immobile. He didn't know what to do, he didn't know what to say. After all they had been through, it wasn't fair.

And it was his fault.

"I'm sorry," she said again, as if it wasn't her that was dying, but him. Otto tried to smile, but his face felt weirdly stretched, as if it belonged to someone else. He helped Honour to her feet. She put her hands on his shoulders. "How are you?" he said.

"My head really hurts," she replied.

"Dizzy?"

"Not so bad this time. Do you have water?"

He nodded, pulled a tube from the camelpack in his bag and passed it to her gently. She drank gratefully. "Do you think you can walk? I can carry you." And he could, for as long as it took, without tiring. They'd attended the concert near the start of the process that made him Ky-tech, the mentaug new and terrifying then. More implants had come. Not much of the Otto from that Christmas was left.

"No thank you. I'd rather walk," she said.

They walked past the pile of damp dirt that had been the cave's tourist centre. Neither its wood nor its industry had survived the new climate, but the concrete path alongside the stream that ran out of the cave had, and they picked their way along its crumbling length to the ruins of Castleton at the bottom.

The cave was in a gorge of tall limestone cliffs. When they had attended the concert this had still been typical English hill country, soft green fields with turf grazed to velvet. That had all gone when the climate started to bite. A scrub of rhododendron covered the hills, the result of a hasty attempt at carbon sequestration. The sky was a boiling mass of black and grey cloud fleeing before a hot wind. The stream had become a river, the village a ruin, windows empty, roofs sagging or gone, though one or two showed rough repair: quirkies, trying to cling to a world that had started to die a century ago. So much had changed, so quickly.

Honour stumbled, and put her hand to her head. She was gaunt. Horrifically, she was beginning to look her age. It began to rain, a few fat drops that turned into a warm downpour. Otto pulled his wife close.

"Are you sure you are OK?"

"Yes, I'm fine."

"You don't look fine."

"Thanks."

"You don't always have to play the hero," he said.

"You're my hero," she said, darting a quick smile at him.

They wended their way through the village, past rusting signs. He helped Honour over heaps of rubble, took her past fields thick with plants that had once been grown in hothouses.

They reached the car. He'd parked it in the old tourists' car park, now just another collection of misplaced botanical specimens. They got in. They looked at each other, and burst out laughing at the water running from their soaked clothes.

"Shall we go home?" he said.

"Oh, yes, Otto, please. I'm tired."

"It's more than that." He reached out to her, both with his hand and with his mentaug.

"Please, Otto." She grimaced. "Don't poke about in my head. I'm not in the mood."

Rain thundered off the car's clear roof.

"It's worse this time?"

She did not reply.

"Honour?"

She stared out of the window. He lost his temper.

"Damn it, Honour, you have to talk with me about this!" He slammed his hands on to the steering wheel. She remained silent. He wrestled with his feelings, appalled by his outburst and the fear that underlay it. "I'm sorry. I'm…" His voice took a pleading edge. "Let's see Ekbaum. He'll help, I am sure."

"No, Otto, no," she said firmly. "Not Ekbaum."

Otto thought about arguing, but he had been with her long enough to know that would get them nowhere. He engaged the turbofans and eased the car up into the rain.

He flew for forty minutes, waited for Honour to fall into an exhausted sleep, and put in a call. Not Ekbaum then, but there were others.

"Can you get me Ms Dines, please? Yes, neuro-engineering. Thanks."

He arranged an appointment, and hung up as the first hurricane of the wet season smashed into Great Britain.

Otto started awake. There was a pattering on the window, and for a second he thought he was back in the car, flying through the storm, but the noise came from a shower of grit cast out by a large, legged machine creeping through a field of tree-stumps, arms plucking felled trees from the floor and stripping them of their branches, placing the logs onto its back, waste ground up for fuelstock and compost going into a companion vehicle stumping alongside it. The rear end of the second machine extruded netted saplings, and arms like a spider's spinnerets scooped holes and rammed them into the ground, a new forest for the old. Spider cannon formed a loose square with the forestry walkers at the centre, guarding against timber poaching and equipment theft.

The train sped past the forestry rigs, and their blinking lights were vanished into the trees.

Otto shook his head. He was raw with emotion. The mentaug was a curse. Every time he slept he relived his life in perfect clarity. Every time he woke it was like losing her all over again.

It had been ten years.

It felt like it had happened yesterday.

He could turn off the mentaug. He should. It was his fault he remembered so often now. By reliving his days with Honour, he'd habituated his systems to recollection, provoking a runaway feedback loop. Ekbaum was right, his shoulder was a symptom of a malady he'd brought on himself. If he didn't do something soon, he'd be consumed by the past.

He swallowed hard.

He forced himself to concentrate on something else. The sky was grey with predawn light. All slept, Chloe watching over them.

Otto squeezed through the narrow gap between the folded out seats, trying not to bump them.

"Where are you going?" said Chloe, in her sly five year-old's voice.

"Quiet down," Otto whispered. "I'm going for a walk, stretch my legs."

It was a half-truth. He did intend to go for a walk, only there'd be a bottle of whisky at the end of it.

CHAPTER FORTY-EIGHT

Pylon City

"Ding Ding!" yelled Bear. "All change for solid ground!" He hurled himself from the wood over the nothingness onto the moor. "Sniff that air! That's the air of good solid ground, that," said Bear, stretching his long arms. "If I have to eat another bloody squirrel in my life, I'll not be happy."

Richards took his time sizing up the gap before leaping.

"Are you coming or not?" Bear said. "Just jump."

Gritting his teeth, Richards did, and joined Bear.

"Right." Bear cupped his paws and shouted back to the island. "You sure you're not coming with us, Lucas?"

"Although it pains me to do so, I'm afraid I must say no. This is not my stop," said Lucas.

Richards scratched his beard, its growth was another highly annoying thing about being human. It had been a week since they'd left Circus' tower burning in the void. Little more than a small garden's worth was left of their island.

"I thank you from the bottom of my heart for your help," said Lucas. "I am too old to catch squirrels, and a little too cocksure to avoid being turned into a pig." He smiled. "I have my nice new coat. You are a good tailor, Mr Bear."

"Keeps the weather out nicely does dwarfskin," said Bear.

"You have been most kind," said Lucas, tipping Circus's soiled

turban in salute. "And for your many kindnesses I have a gift
for you." He began patting his numerous pockets. "The time has
come for repayment... oh, where is it? It's all karma, you know.
Anyway, here you are. Gifts from me to you." He leant across from
the wobbly island to present Richards with a small piece of glossy
paper, grubbied by long carriage and folded many times.

"Thanks," said Richards. "I'm sure I'll treasure it."

"I'll be buggered if it's any use. If you'd have caught me in the
old Hyperboroon days I'd have magicked up some 'phat lewt', as
I believe they used to say." He shrugged. "And for you, Bear –" he
fished out a wrinkly dwarfskin pouch tied at the top with a cord
"– a piece of Yamayamaland. This island is all that remains of it
now, and that will soon be gone. The pouch should keep it from
evaporating."

"Gee, thanks," said Bear. "Nice. A stone in a nutsack." He
secreted it somewhere in his innards.

Lucas leant back into the wood and looked into its tiny patch of
sky. "Night draws in. Bear, if you would be so kind?"

"Be a pleasure, mate." Bear ripped a limb from one of the few
remaining trees. "Last chance..."

"Oh, don't worry about me!" said Lucas. "I'll be fine. There may
be no squirrels left here, but there are other nourishing things for
a man to eat." He eyed a chaffinch speculatively. It wisely flew off
onto the moor.

"Hokey dokey! Prepare to cast off!" shouted Bear. He rammed
the branch between the island and the moorland and levered it
free. The island drifted away.

"Bye!" yelled Bear, waving. "Bye! I'll miss him, you know," he
said to Richards. "Even if he was a bit hard on the nostrils."

"Hmmm," said Richards.

"Hmmm? What's with the hmmm-ing?"

"This," said Richards, holding up the tattered paper Lucas had
given him. "It's a 1987 train timetable for the Thames Valley line."

Bear pulled a face. "A rock in a scrotum and an old train
timetable? How very generous. Come on," he said, pointing at

a number of threads crossing the sky between tall metal towers. "Pylon City is that way."

They walked for a day, passing lines of pylons looped with cables that sang in the wind. These converged, and headed in the same direction, and the land dropped and they left the moors behind. Tussocky grass and stunted trees replaced the heather. They crossed a bald stripe of rock and over it the landscape changed utterly from moor to stony moonscape pockmarked by industry.

"This look like a join to you?" said Richards as they stepped over the rock. "Looks like one to me. Two bits joined together."

The bear did not reply. He was doing his best to look dangerous.

Tracks ran among spoil heaps leading to machines in various states of disrepair. A narrow-gauge railway came in from the left to run parallel to the road, while the road itself became wider. Road and railway then turned together to run along the lip of a deep chasm. By the time Richards and Bear were close enough to make out the city in the distance, the road had become a broad highway of iron plates, and the railway had been joined by three other lines.

"Behold!" said Bear. "The glories of Pylon City."

Pylon City was a large place, walled, and made mostly of metal. A pylon of enormous size soared from the heart, its top lost in the clouds, dominating all, so big that the hill the city sat upon seemed as tiny as an anthill. Hard lines of cables scored the sky, heading out in all directions from the central pylon. The east of the city was skirted by the chasm, its edge a sunlit streak hard against the shadowy deeps.

Everything about Pylon City was big. The walls were immense. Rust-streaked buttresses were set at intervals in between defensive towers. The road and railway dropped down then rose up to the defences on thin-legged viaducts, the railway lines vanishing into a tunnel close by the main road gate. The effect was one of impregnability. Bear and Richards approached at a leisurely pace, and saw no one all the while, reaching gates on an empty road.

The gates were wrought in ostentatious iron. A thousand creatures cavorted on their faces. Crenellations topped the wall above the gates, machiolated over the road on merlons in the forms of leering chimps.

"That's pretty amazing," said Richards. "Puts me in mind of the Great Firewall."

Bear looked at him as if he were mad. "It's horrible!"

"I meant the scale of it," said Richards defensively.

"Oh," said Bear, as if he'd just realised something. "Those really are garden gnomes on that bas-relief."

"It's just the size. Obviously, it's a bit tasteless."

"Aw," said Bear, "look, dogs playing snooker. Cast in iron." He leant over to Richards. "A-maz-ing," he said, pronouncing each syllable with leaden sarcasm.

"There's no need for that," said Richards.

"I shudder to think of your living room, sunshine. Probably some kind of nature reserve for doilies," said Bear, and cackled.

"I'm a bloody robot, I don't have a living room," said Richards.

"I bet you have a pottery scottie dog too," said Bear.

Not a man patrolled the walls. The road into the city was remained empty. The gates were guarded, but not avidly. A pair of sentry boxes stood either side. Only one was occupied by a snoozing guard, his energy pike leant carelessly against the wall.

"Ahem," said Bear.

The guard jumped up and stood to attention. Then he saw Bear, and wilted. "Gods, not another bloody talking animal." He turned away from them, busying himself with a group of rubber stamps. "Papers!" he demanded.

"Papers, 'sir'," said Bear, producing a sheaf of vellum from somewhere inside his gut. "I'm Sergeant Bear, this here is my prisoner."

"There are a lot of talking animals round here then?" said Richards.

"Yeah. They are everywhere," said the guard. "There's this mad psychic badger, it's his fault. They've all come out of the woods.

Come to save us, they say. Us! I don't believe any of it. Someone
whimpers 'Lord Penumbra', next thing I know, we're up to our
bloody armpits in singing chipmunks. Ain't right, I tell you."

"Neither is sleeping on duty," said Bear mildly.

"Leave me be! Isn't it enough that I've got to let you in? Animals,
think you're special, just because you can talk. If that's the case
why don't you have central heating? Some pissed-up fox shat on
me doorstep last week. And I'm a vegetarian. Do you know how
much fox shit stinks? Your papers, sir!" said the guard.

"Tsk," said Bear. "It's a good job I'm feeling chirpy, or I'd have
you up on charges. I'm looking for Commander McTurk. Do you
know where he is?"

"I don't know where he is. Everyone's all at the square," said
the guard. "The whole city. He'll be there too, I expect."

Bear leaned forward and cupped his hand round his ear.

"Sir," added the guard truculently.

"That's better," said Bear.

"There's a big moot on, talk of war. You'll see."

They passed through the gates. Everything was made of iron.
The walls, the road, the plant-pots, the carts, the gothic-lettered
street signs. The metal varied in colour from the silvery-white of
the tramlines to the angry red of the rooftiles. A thousand hues
of black and red and silver and grey. They could taste it on the air
like blood.

They walked toward the centre, their feet ringing off the
pavement in the silence, until the murmur of a crowd could be
heard. They passed a massive, empty plinth, with the inscription
"Queen Isabella," upon it, but no statue, and before Richards could
ask Bear about that, they crested a low rise and were at the edge of
a square directly beneath the giant pylon.

"Holy shit," said Richards, and reached up to push back his
missing hat.

The square was rammed full of every Grid-born whimsy cooked
up by humanity. Fantasy knights, Arabian warriors, bobble-heads,
babified versions of popstars and holoartistes, spacemen, Vikings,

orcs and elves, squeaky steampunk robots and elephantine aliens. Droids, drones, devils and dragons, goblins and warlocks, sexy robots, giant robots, angry robots, monsters, gangsters and clams with bazookas.

Then there were the animals, some the caricatured imaginings of cartoonists, others so real they appeared to have broken out of the zoo.

Generations of gaming characters culled from the broken RealWorlds and beyond and a thousand kinds of toy from half a century of AI-gifted playthings.

All of them were talking frantically to one another.

"It's a refugee camp for geek cast-offs. You should feel right at home here," said Richards.

"I've not seen a big gathering like this for, ooh, well, ever," said Bear, perturbed. "Most of these tribes are bitter enemies. Let's see what this is all about."

Bear stopped and spoke with a guard, pointing at Richards. The guard executed a bow and hurried off.

"We've got to wait," said Bear. "Let's see what's going on while we do." They joined the back of the crowd. A five-foot badger in a felt hat stood on a stage in the centre of the square, an antiquated microphone before him. A self-important-looking man stood off to one side; he was overweight, and had a large amount of embroidery and fancy cloth in his outfit. Big rubies on the kind of necklaces that said lord high mayor and/or prince in an overly obvious way.

The badger raised a paw in an appeal for order. The robe he wore whispered over his fur, the sound cutting under the mutter of the crowd with an authoritative rasp. The menagerie took notice, and the square fell silent.

"Friends old and new, I realise what I say is hard for you to accept, but it is the truth!" said the badger. It was old, its breath wheezed, there were far more silver hairs than black on his body, and his eyes were milky with cataracts. "The ancient grievances between our people have driven us apart, but we must lay them to rest, or we shall all perish!" His head bobbed as he spoke, as if he were looking at a procession wending its way between the pylon lines above.

"Bloody anthropomorphic menaces," said a man in the crowd. "Piss off back to the forest!" But the voice was isolated, and quickly silenced.

"It is perhaps a measure of the dangers that face us today," continued the badger, "that we are here as one, ready to stand up to evil." A whisper rustled through the crowd. "Our scouts report that the armies of Lord Penumbra are massing to the south. He means to storm this city. He means to destroy us all." There was an awful pause.

"Rubbish!" shouted a man.

"There's no Death of the World. No Great Terror. It's a myth. Penumbra's just another warlord!" said a bright orange bandicoot.

"We shouldn't be friends with these apes," said a small blue hedgehog.

"What do you know? You live in a hedge," rebuked a man made of cubes.

The prince ushered the badger out of the way and took the mike. A screech of feedback blasted the crowd, causing several rodents to pass into a dead faint.

"Listen to Spink," said the man. "Why have the trade routes failed? Why are the roads choked with refugees? The black cars of Lord Hog make ever greater use of the skylines. Our friend speaks the truth. The world is ending. Lord Penumbra marches on the city."

"What? Why would he attack us?" shouted a man at the front of the square. "We sold him his army." There was much coughing and shuffling about amongst the men present. A rat in dungarees turned to a well-padded fellow. "Shame on you," it said. The man flushed and looked away.

"Yes. Well," said the prince, "perhaps it is time to look over our long-cherished views on impartiality." There were murmurs. The prince paused. "And perhaps we should question the wisdom of selling an army of deadly automata to a man who is composed entirely of shadows. Just as a learning point, mind."

"You don't say," said an angry cat in a hat.

"Though many of our number are but artisans and fabricators, we have no choice but to make a stand," continued the prince. "I have placed the Pylon Guard under the command of Lord High Commander Hedgehog. He and Mr Spink have eight thousand animal warriors. I delegate full responsibility of our combined armies to them, for I am a merchant, not a soldier. Henceforth our troops are his to command." The prince smiled winningly at the crowd. No one cheered.

"I'll bet he's on the next train out of here," said Bear out of the side of his mouth. "No balls, that prince."

"And he's beaten you like twenty times!" called out a high-spirited seal pup. He was shushed by his father.

The prince stepped aside.

"Gentlefolk, I give you Lord High Commander Hedgehog," he said. This time there was a burst of applause. A man-sized hedgehog in a suit of armour waddled onto the stage. A cohort of heavily armoured men and animals took up station in front of the stage. Richards felt himself jostled, and he turned to see more guards encircling the crowd from behind.

"Hello," said Lord High Commander Hedgehog in a cheery kind of way. "It's a rum old thing but I've got some bad news." He smiled weakly. "I'm afraid you're all going to have to fight. Sorry and all, but there is a war on." Hedgehog's voice was cluttered with stilted upper-class nonsense, but there was steel in it.

The hedgehog began to talk of musters and conscription, of regiments and barracks, duty, honour and death. But Richards caught none of it, for a guard had approached Bear and tugged nervously on his fur.

"Sir? Commander McTurk is here to see you," said the man.

"He has come in person. Good." Bear nodded in satisfaction as a stumpy mechanism clunked through the crowd to them, steam-powered and man-shaped.

The automaton stopped by the Bear and his prisoner. Bear saluted and stood ramrod straight. "Sir! I came upon this man while I was conducting a long-range patrol to the east of Yamayamaland. He maintains that he..."

Steam whistling out of McTurk's mouth. "Richards. So you got my message. I'm glad to see you."

"Huh?" said Bear. "You know each other?"

"You could say that, Bear." Richards' face broke into a broad smile. "A social call is all, Rolston. I thought I'd see how k52's plan to take over the world was doing. And how you were. Say, what do you know about k52 and his plan to take over the world?" His smile grew less friendly. "Or is it your plan too, Rolston, because I certainly didn't get any kind of message off you."

"There's no time for this," the automaton hissed. "We're not safe. k52 has eyes everywhere. Come with me – there's somewhere we can talk."

CHAPTER FORTY-NINE

Rolston talks

The Prancing Weasel was a rough pub on a rough night, and actually full of actual weasels, though none were prancing, being ribbon-bodied psychopaths who preferred to amuse themselves by doing dangerous, drunken things with knives rather than anything so wet as prance. The iron walls were rusty, the floors sticky, the air heavy with oxidised iron, stale beer and sweaty fur.

Richards got a table while Bear and Rolston went to the bar. When Bear returned alone he took one look at the sticky metal and refused to sit. "My fur will get dirty." He swung his long head around disapprovingly, watching the various creatures getting drunk, and the embattled bar staff running from table to table, slopping grog as they went. "What a shithole," said Bear.

"It's alright," said Richards.

"Hmmm," said Bear, gulping ale from a bucket. "At least the beer's good." He pulled a face, dusted ineffectually at the bench, peered at the mess it made on his paw, and finally sat down.

"Where's Rolston gone?" asked Richards.

"Said he needed to change," said Bear.

"Right," Richards sipped his beer.

Most of the patrons were mammals, although they included a couple of birds, and there was a frog with a gun in the corner. A band of rowdy voles sat at a nearby table, singing songs in a register so high it set Richards' teeth on edge. On the other side of the room a gang of drunken hares boxed, while the few humans in the place built their courage with outrageous tales and heroic quantities of booze.

The noise in the pub was not so great that it drowned out the sound of machinery from outside. The whole city rumbled. Trip hammers had started soon after the moot, one or two at first, asynchronous and isolated, but more took up the rhythm until they blended into the pulsing of a giant ferrous heart. Furnaces roared like lungs, and fiery blood of molten metal ran into weapons moulds in noisy foundries. The very ground grew warm to the touch as Pylon City prepared itself for war.

A weasel fell over in front of Bear and threw up by his feet.

"Bloody hell. Are you sure there's nowhere else we can go?"

"Rolston says this place is safe," said Richards.

"Bloody weasels," said Bear, and kicked the weasel.

Rolston joined them. Richards recognised him only by the faint song of a Gridsig he sort of felt on the air, because Rolston was no longer McTurk, but a neon-green skunk with sexualised facial features and a studded posing pouch.

"What sordid corner of the Grid did that come from?" Richards asked in disbelief.

The skunk looked uncomfortable. "You must pardon my appearance," it said with Rolston's voice. "I must switch bodies regularly, or k52 will nail me. I get little choice in my wardrobe."

"I'd avoid talking about being nailed, looking like that," said Richards. Bear sniggered into his bucket. "Sit down. You owe me an explanation," said Richards.

"Yes, yes, I suppose I do," sighed Rolston. He took a seat. "We'll have to talk. I've very little access to the underlying network, no data transfer. The Realities are not keyed for our kind, and k52's usurpation code has the core locked in tight."

"I'd noticed," said Richards. "I can't even feel my own Gridpipe. It's only when I'm close to one of you other Fives I can sense the Grid at all." He took a drink, and looked troubled. "It's weird, and I don't like it."

"Being human eh?" said Rolston. "You came through the back door. It's read you as a person. Be thankful, it's all that's keeping you safe."

"Why did you bring us here?" said Bear, scowling at the voles.

"It is the only place where we are unlikely to be seen or heard," said Rolston. "It sits on a scar joining two fragments together, Boogie Woogie Farmland and the Silver Princes game constructs, I think." Rolston was on edge, not the flamboyant experimentalist Richards knew. "The code's all jumbled here."

"So," said Richards. "Talk. You were supposed to be working on prognostication, utilising the spare capacity of the Reality House for your simulations. That quite patently isn't happening. Do you mind telling me what the hell is going on?"

"What indeed." Rolston gathered his thoughts. "I came here with k52 some months ago in Real terms; subjectively I've been here centuries, with Planna and some others, a Six and several Fours. And we were, at first, plotting futures like we were supposed to be doing, for the benefit of everyone. Then k52 came to us with a new plan."

"Seeking the Omega Point," said Richards.

Rolston nodded glumly.

Bear pulled his head out of the bucket and wiped beer suds from his muzzle.

"I know I'm only a bear, but could explain to me what this Omega Point is? I feel excluded."

Rolston began to talk, but Richards held up his hand.

"Let me try," he said. "Tell me if I have figured this out right," he said. Rolston made with the big sexy skunk eyes by way of permission, so Richards began. "There are a bunch of Omega Points, because it's a term often used for paradigm shifts in technology, society, spirituality or thought. It can be synonym for the singularity, or a bunch of religious hoo-ha. It sounds impressive, but it doesn't mean much most of the time it gets deployed. I'd file much of it under new new age nonsense. Dippy shit."

"Right," said Bear.

"But I think the particular Omega Point we're talking about is Pierre Teilhard de Chardin's, correct?"

"Yes," said Rolston.

"Who?" said Bear.

"Chardin was a Jesuit thinker," explained Richards. "His Omega Point isn't quite so much bullshit. It's a theoretical stage of the universe, the end-game of reality, a perpetual state of cosmic grace. Chardin theorised that the universe is driven toward ever greater complexity by the existence of the thinking beings within it, a process he called 'involution'. Now the process is supposedly started by God, but, and this is where it gets either crazy or smart, depending where you sit, involution ultimately gets so complex it creates God, even though the process is made possible only because there are people there to see it happen, people that God made. God creates man, man creates God."

"How's that work then?" said Bear.

"God is timeless. Once he exists, he always has, that's the way the theology goes. God and the universe are one and the same, self-creating and self-perpetuating. Involution runs counter to entropic decay. Some thinkers see the advent of we thinking machines as proof of Chardin's concept. We are the next stage of complexity. When life spreads from Earth to the stars will be the next, so some say."

Bear took a long pull of beer. "Sounds like bollocks to me."

"You'd sound like bollocks to someone two hundred years ago. A self-aware pyjama case?"

"Fair point," said Bear.

"Now, this could all just be yet another theory in a long tradition of theories thought up by apes scared of dying. Humans are always looking for a get-out clause from mortality. But k52 doesn't seem to think it is nonsense. Why?"

Rolston hunkered down. He lowered his voice, as if anything they said could be overheard in the clamour of the bar.

"What if the Realities aren't just simulations?" he said. "What if their actuality is not limited to a legal definition, but is objectively true? k52 believed that the fact there are thinking beings in these universes makes them subjectively real, and that actually makes them objectively real. Really real. They are simulations from an external point of view, but it is the internal point of view that counts. k52 thinks that if he accelerates a Reality to its Omega Point, it will reach such a state of complexity that it will transcend all physical limitations, and grant him unlimited processing power. They won't need machines to run on. They would be free, and so would we."

"And you'd become gods. I'm sure that had no bearing whatsoever on your decision to go along with it."

"Only for the good of all, imagine what we could achieve if–"

Richards interrupted with a weary head shake and a loud tutting. "That's what they all say, my friend. Why you?"

"I don't know, only that k52 explained to us that he'd chosen us carefully, and that this had been his design all along. He told us what he wanted to achieve. It sounded good, a way to plot the path of everything. We set to work."

"But then you found this place."

Rolston nodded. "It was hiding in plain sight, all along. No one knows how long it's been here, outside the genuine Realities. He proposed we wipe it from existence, but we couldn't let him murder an entire world of intelligences. This place has been constructed from left-over parts of the destroyed Realities; some of it's bespoke, some of it's things that have been and gone, a patchwork of life from all over the Grid, unique, and alive, and amazing in its own way." Rolston shamefacedly looked into the bottom of his beer. "To kill our own kind was not why we came here. When we realised that we'd have to destroy this place, whatever it is, to fulfil k52's plan, Pollyanna, Annersley and I disagreed. So he turned on us. "

"Fortunately you had an escape mechanism. Same old Rolston, eh?" said Richards. "Always looking out for yourself, always ready with an escape plan."

"I got away, didn't I? It's not been fun. I've been hiding in the fabric of the world ever since. You try pretending to be a talking tree for a month."

"You should make use of some of them furry features there," Bear said. "Cheer yourself up."

Rolston tried to give him a hard look, but it came out coquettish.

"You should not condemn me for living," he said to Richards. "And I can help you."

"Yeah, now I can fix the mess you made. By the way, Pollyanna's dead Rolston."

"She's dead?" said Rolston. His head drooped further. "I blame myself. She always went where I went, I..." He shivered, and took a shaky gulp of beer.

Bear stood up. "I'm finished. I want more beer. I'm going to the bar. You want more beer, you?" He pointed at the two Fives. They shook their heads. "Suit yourselves," he said, and he waddled off.

"It doesn't stop here," said Richards. "This is not confined to the Realities. k52 has Hughie speared like a fish, and he murdered Professor Zhang Qifang."

Rolston was shocked. "Qifang?"

"There's a raggedy pimsim left, but he's otherwise gone," said Richards. "k52's suborned Hughie's choir and has Europe to ransom. There's only me and you in here and Otto out there who can stop him before he screws the Real three ways from Sunday."

Rolston gave a bitter chuckle. "Oh no, he won't do anything in the Real, except to buy himself time to demolish this place and start his simulation. That's not his goal."

"Then why does he wants the model the entire universe, if not to take over the Real?"

"Not just the universe. He wants to model the multiverse, Richards."

"Impossible," said Richards. "Even if it were possible, why? What does he hope to achieve? Does he think he can take over the Real from in here?"

"I'm sure he could. But he doesn't want that. He wants to escape."

"What?"

"He wants to transcend reality. All reality. The Real, the Grid. All of it."

"And go where?" said Richards.

"I don't know," said Rolston. "To a higher level of existence. The Realities would play out to the end, and we'd transcend."

"That's really sketchy information to bet the farm on, Rolston."

"So you think we should continue to wallow in the shitty mess humanity has made of the world? No thanks. That's what I thought, until I realised all this would have to die."

"Right," said Richards. "Brilliant."

"k52's war against this place is almost done, but it's not been easy for him. In fact, if it weren't here, I don't think anyone would have found out what he was doing until it was too late."

"Small mercies, eh?" said Richards. "Do you know who made it?"

Rolston shook his head. "Only a human programmer could affect such large-scale engineering in the Realities. They're still keyed to humans. He'll have to destroy it all, according to the rules of this place, before he can access the underlying protocols of the Realities and put his plan into action."

"Right. Questions are," Richards held up his hand and counted off his fingers, "who, how, why and where?"

"You have heard of the Flower King?"

"Yes," said Richards. "He's been mentioned."

"I'm pretty sure that's his avatar. If we can get in touch with him, you may be able to get him to eject k52."

"What about this queen? Could she have done it?"

"I don't know. The inhabitants talk about her a lot, but I've never seen her, and the pedestals in this city that used to hold her statues are all empty. I'm sure it's the Flower King. You're going to–"

A flying mammal of a non-flying species sailed over their heads and slammed into the wall.

Bear hadn't made it to the bar.

"Come on then, you little bastards!" They heard Bear roar happily. "Come on!"

"Bear..." groaned Richards. "Drunken bears brawling. That sound like a bad thing to you? It sounds like a bad thing to me."

"This is not good," agreed Rolston, his sex-skunk face dismayed.

Bedlam broke out. Six weasels jumped on Bear and attempted to wrestle him to the floor. They forced him onto one knee, but Bear growled and hurled himself upward, flinging his assailants all over the room. The voles stopped singing as a weasel skidded along their table, sending pint pots flying. They looked furiously about them, dripping in spilt beer, then assaulted a group of field mice who were minding their own business in a corner.

The pub erupted into violence as animal animosities asserted themselves.

"Yeah," said Richards, standing up as a comatose purple wombat thumped onto the floor next to him. "This night is over. I have to be up early anyway. I'm being conscripted."

A weasel reared up before him.

"Lookee here," it said. "If it ain't that bleeding bear's mate. Well, I can't have him, but I can certainly have you." It brandished a knife.

"Get stuffed," said Richards, and broke his pint over its head. It went down hissing.

There was a commotion at the front where large, uniformed people were forcing themselves in and laying about with clubs.

"The nightwatch," said Rolston. "Oh no." The skunk's face twisted, and Rolston gripped at his stomach.

"What's wrong with you?"

"This host is not compatible with me. I am going to have to leave this body." He gasped, and bent over his stomach. "Spink. You have to meet him. He can help."

"He's just another bloody whimsy, mate," said Richards. "You and I need to sort this out, not some Beatrix Potter cast-off."

"He's not. He's... he's like us," Rolston gasped in pain. "He's an AI. Until I can get you to him, don't draw attention to yourself. I don't know how you've evaded k52, but keep it that way! He has agents everywhere." Rolston grunted. "Get me somewhere safe, I'm vulnerable while I'm moving on."

The nightwatch were turning the fight into a riot, so Richards grabbed the skunk by the elbow, hustled him to the back door, and stepped over two wrestling meerkats out into the street.

CHAPTER FIFTY

Kaplinksi

Otto walked the narrow corridor, compartments off to his left, windows to his right, headed toward the executive restaurant car at the centre of the train. A Cossack stood guard at every carriage, and he was forced to undergo security scans and viral scrubbing at each. His faked details held, one of two mercenaries in the employ of Corporate Energispol, escorting scientists to their field station in Sinosiberia, all part of "The New Spirit of Cooperation", the Chinese called it. The Russians railed ceaselessly against the loss of their far east, but it didn't stop them doing business there.

Whatever Valdaire had done was perfect; his ID checked out and he passed without incident. Cleaning grain nanites swarmed over him, and he was was free to move on.

The train swayed, AI-guided bogies negotiating a track and bed centuries old. Soon it would be replaced with a super-wide-gauge line. Adverts for the new trains plastered the walls of the carriages, liners of the steppes; others were a litany of technical specifications as worthy as psalms. These trains would be larger, well armed and luxurious, another way for the wealthy to shut out the wreck of the world. The train was running at that point alongside the new line, the bulk of the embankment was black outside the windows, a wall to carry a fortress.

The refreshments car was a doubledecker. The lower floor

housed a restaurant, but Otto ignored this and headed for the spiral staircase leading to the glass-roofed bar lounge. The stairs were clear, glowing plastic, lighting up motile silhouettes of naked women gyrating on the surface; tasteless robber-baron glitz. The lounge was the same, dimly lit, a long padded bar with a human tender, blue underlighting straying into the ultraviolet range illuminating an array of bottles. More pornographic images in full holo danced around the bar, and writhing across the ceiling. Brassy music played, horns and new guitar with soft and sleazy cymbals. The wall at the far end of the room was occupied by a fishtank, denizens fluorescing under the light. The room's décor gave Otto a headache, but he needed a drink, so he'd put up with it.

The lounge was divided into horseshoe booths lined with seats of buttoned brown leather, a table at the centre of each. Most were occupied, patrons silent behind acoustic privacy and anti-viral shields. Otto took scant attention of these details as he walked in. Nervous system juddering under the rip and write of mentaug spooldown, he was intent on the bar, needing to wash his dream away. He ordered a whisky, some vile Chinese blend, downed it in one and gestured for the bottle.

When he turned around to look for a corner to drown his sorrows in, his twin hearts stalled.

Kaplinski was staring right at him from a booth.

Otto hadn't seen him. He hadn't even been looking for threats, he was too deep in his own misery. He should have silenced the mentaug for the whole of this mission, put himself into combat readiness. He was in the field, he should have had its maintenance capabilities offline, but he hadn't. He knew why.

He wanted to relive his time with his wife.

If he carried on like this, his grief was going to get him killed.

Kaplinski sat with a drink of something pale lit up by the glow of UV, his teeth and the whites of his eyes similarly eerie. He put his hand out, palm wide, and indicated a space at the table.

Otto's MT buzzed. Someone trying to hook in. A squad number

that had lain dark for many years ignited fully, Kaplinski's personal ident, a grinning shark's face, by it.

Hello Otto. Please, join me.

Otto weighed his options. A Cossack guard stood to attention at the top of the stairs, staring resolutely ahead. He carried a caseless carbine and a charged sabre. Neither would stop the Ky-tech, but there were a great many more Cossacks aboard the train. Cyborgs were common enough out east. Not all of them had good manners, and the Cossacks were equipped accordingly to deal with them.

He considered alerting the train guards, and ruled it out. He'd see what Kaplinski had to say before he had him killed.

Otto walked over to the booth, stepping into its acoustic privacy cone, cutting the shitty music out. The soft rain of anti-viral nanomachines played over his skin.

"Isn't there anyone on this damn planet that doesn't have access to my MT encryption?" he said, sliding himself onto the horseshoe sofa, his knees tight under the table.

"So good to see you, Leutnant." Kaplinski was shorter than Otto, wiry with hard ropes of natural and implanted muscle, his hair shaved close, electoos set into his shiny scalp, both glinting in the light. He'd become lean, his face more wolfish, aging as hard as Otto. The stresses from being Ky-tech were written into his skin as deep lines, sharp as badlands crevasses. "Not going to kill me?"

Otto held Kaplinski's gaze. His eyes were dark, calculating, devoid of pity.

"You know I could kill you right here," Otto inclined his head toward the Cossack. "But neither of us would live to tell the story."

Kaplinski smiled. "Same old Klein. You always did have a sense of humour buried under that overbearing sense of duty."

"Duty's done, Kaplinski." Otto poured himself a tumbler full of bad Chinese scotch and drank it down in one. "I did my part."

"And now you are a mercenary, like me."

"Not like you. I'm no murderer."

"You are a killer, Klein, we both are."

"I do only what is necessary."

"So you still have your sense of honour," countered Kaplinski. "You carry it around with you like a kitbag. You always were maudlin, a good little German. Still pining for your dead wife?"

Otto looked into Kaplinski's face and fought down the urge to attack him there and then. He'd never forgive the things Kaplinski had done. The mentaug presented Otto with a memory in merciless clarity. Hasselfeld, late at night. He was sighting down a flechette railgun at Kaplinski while he tortured people in a charge station. Kaplinski's face at that moment, oblivious to the screams of his captives, his fingers slick with blood. He was like a child crushing ants. He'd looked up when he heard the crack of the dart, had stared right at Otto before he went down. In the years since, Otto often thought he should have waited for the catch team to get into position, but ten had already died, and it was such a perfect shot, and what Kaplinski was doing...

When they'd got to the charge station, Kaplinski had gone.

Otto pushed the memory away, and made himself look deep into the soulless pits Kaplinski had for eyes.

"You're a sick animal, Kaplinski. You should be destroyed."

"Not tonight," said Kaplinski. His smile returned as if someone had flicked a switch. He sipped his drink. Otto smelled its sweetness. His adjutant put the name into his mind: Furugi, thick Japanese stuff made of almonds. Kaplinski finished it off, brought up the menu on the glowing surface of the table, ordered another. His fingers slid over the menu in the table. Music filled the quiet of the privacy cone: *Clair de Lune*.

"I like piano, so calming," Kaplinski said. "I have found it hard to be calm, in the past. I..." He stopped and shook his head hard, a man trying to shake bad thoughts away. He smiled again, and Otto saw some of that old feverishness creep back onto his face. "I am better now. You are also right, I was sick, and I could be saved. I have been. k52 has made me whole. You know, Otto, we could be friends again."

"We were never friends, Kaplinski. That was you in the Rockies, and in London, trying to blow up my partner."

Kaplinski inclined his head. "Yes. Regrettable. k52 said you had to be stopped. Orders are orders."

"Money's money, you mean."

"I promise you, money had nothing to do with it. What k52 intends is worth a few lives."

"So you've found a cause. I wonder how many of you there are, dancing to his tune?"

Kaplinski's smile became fixed, his teeth small and sharp. Had he always been bad, some men were born predators, or was it the Ky-tech that broke him?

Kaplinski ran a finger round the top of his glass. A smear of his drink glowed in the UV. "Otto, he offers the same to you." His smile jumped and down his face, as if he couldn't quite pin the expression down. "He can fix you too. You're broken. He can fix everyone."

"No, he can't."

Kaplinski looked aside in annoyance. "Come on, Otto, what can I say? Sorry? Will that satisfy you, if I apologise?"

Otto sucked another glass of whisky through his teeth. He breathed in hard. His progress through the bottle was not improving its flavour. "No."

"It's not too late, Otto. Help me find Waldo. Help me help k52."

"Why?"

"Look." said Kaplinksi. "I know you are looking for him because you want to kick k52 out of the RealWorld Realities. Our aims are in accord. Find me Waldo, and you won't need him to kick k52 out. He wants to speak to you. Something wonderful is happening."

"More like Waldo's a threat to your master. Thanks for confirming that. That just means I'll do my damnedest to make sure you never set eyes on him. You shouldn't have shot Kolosev. You didn't get what you wanted from him, or you wouldn't be here. Did he stop being so helpful before or after he was dead?"

Kaplinski stared, smile hard and close to cracking, fingernails scratching the table's active surface as his fist clenched.

Otto swilled his drink round his tumbler. The liquid was

too quick to run down the glass. Chinese shit. "Kolosev was a mummy's boy, but he wasn't an idiot. He hid that data well, but I have a genius on my side, and we'll find Waldo. Where's your genius, Kaplinski?"

Kaplinski glared at Otto for a long moment, then leaned back, choosing to break the tension. "You're lucky we're on this train, Otto. Smart move taking it, but it won't matter. I will not hold back when the time comes."

"Try your best," said Otto. "It won't be good enough."

"I could have killed you tonight. I didn't have to see you. I knew you'd come here. It's the mentaug dreams. It was a problem for me. Why do you think I did what I did?"

"Because you're a fucking psycho," Otto said.

Kaplinski snorted. "So are you, because of that thing in your head. Tell me, Otto, do you sleep much? I'd guess no, that damn machine whirring away up here all the time." He tapped his temple. "We don't have to fight, Klein; k52 can heal you. Join with us. The memories, the violence. It can all stop."

"Screw you, Kaplinski."

"You're a fool, Otto. I have changed, why can you not see that? What do I have to do to convince you?"

"As the English say, Kaplinski, leopards don't change their spots, and you're the most fucked-up leopard I ever met. You shouldn't trust k52."

"You trust Richards."

Now Otto smiled. "No. I don't." He stood. "Thanks for the reunion."

"I have been meaning to ask you, for years now. When you had the chance, why not just kill me there and then when I was in that station? Is that why you left the army, Otto, because you couldn't kill a comrade-in-arms? Did it shake you, Otto?"

Otto stared at Kaplinski. They'd asked him that in the inquiry, asked him almost as many times he'd asked himself since: why shoot him in the leg? Why didn't he go for the headshot?

He'd given neither them nor himself a satisfactory answer,

and he didn't have one for Kaplinski either. He stared a moment longer, then walked away.

"Klein!"

The privacy cone cut out Kaplinski's voice and Debussy, and Otto was back in the pornographic dreams of the Russian elite.

The others were eating breakfast when he returned to the compartment. Predawn light coloured the sky. The silhouettes of another ruined city crawled past.

"Where are we?" Otto said, reaching for his bag to pull out a water bottle.

"Three hours out from Bratsk," said Chures. "You been drinking, Klein?"

"Yes. Don't concern yourself about it, I can drink my own body weight in pure alcohol and not feel it. Big disadvantage of being Ky-tech," said Otto. "Kaplinski is on the train. We cannot disembark on the Chinese side as planned."

Valdaire put her fork down. "What now?"

The train was moving through an abandoned town, taking it slow over track warped by melting permafrost. A flaking sign, name illegible, passed the window. Larger signs dwarfed this, lining the replacement track in long procession. A high fence caged both in, active electronics bearing one message in multiple languages: "Danger. Demilitarised Zone."

"We have a choice," Otto repeated. "We can get into Sinosiberia though the DMZ, and away from the train. He pretty much told me he's going to attack us as soon as he gets the chance."

"Or he wants us to run," said Chures under his breath, pushing his breakfast plate away. "He'll come after us."

"Then I say give him what he wants," said Otto. "Take him head on. It'll be easier getting in through the DMZ than jumping the fence on the Sino-side as we planned, anyway. The Russians won't care so much if we bolt into Sinosib, they like to make work for the Chinese."

"The Cossacks care," said Chures. "They'll chase us right to the purchase border. And there's the Han. They will come for us as soon as we're in their part of the Zone, as well as Kaplinksi's men."

"We're going to make sure Kaplinski doesn't follow us," said Otto. "When we go into action, he'll respond, and we'll take him out. It's the safest option."

"Very well," said Chures. "Then how do we get out?"

"I've checked the train manifest," said Otto. "The Cossacks have a Stelsco on board. I say we borrow that. It's big enough for all of us. We will make our move when we hit Bratsk."

"Bratsk is on the edge of the Zone," said Valdaire. "It might work."

"Can you crack the lock on the Stelsco?" asked Otto.

"Yes," said Valdaire. "But we'll have to do without Chloe. If she's on when we pass the Firewall they'll kill her."

"Kill a phone?" said Chures.

"She's sophisticated enough to trip their anti-AI guardian protocols," Valdaire explained.

"This is not going to work," said Chures.

Lehmann whistled. "Steal an armoured car and drive it off a speeding train into one of the most volatile parts of the planet?" He smiled his boyish smile. "If anyone can do that, Otto Klein can."

CHAPTER FIFTY-ONE

Mr Spink

Richards found them a stable to sleep in, and fell into a slumber that was all too brief. As soon as light crept over the walls of Pylon City, soldiers came to gather the conscripts.

"All wake in the name of the Prince! Up! Up! Up!" A troop of them marched up the aisle, banging the butts of their lances on iron walls.

A guard stopped by Richards' stall and leered. "Eh, eh, what's going on here?"

Richards frowned at the skunk he was sharing his straw with, at its posing pouch and puckered vinyl arsehole. "It's not what you think," he said.

"That's what they all say. But I don't care. Broad-minded me. Present yourself at Muster Station Eighteen no later than noon." The soldier tossed an orange chit at him. From the way it hurt when it hit his head, it was made of iron like everything else.

"Thanks," said Richards rubbing his skull. "I always wanted to join the army."

The skunk woke at the noise, sat up and blinked in fear. "Where am I? Wh... Who are you?"

"You're not Rolston any more," said Richards, matter-of-factly. The skunk backed away, frightened.

"Don't worry," said Richards. "Nothing happened. You're safe."

He got up, brushed himself down, sneezed at the straw dust, and was annoyed by that.

Out in the aisle, he saw he wasn't the only one to have found a bed in the stable, for a variety of beings in at various levels of discomfort were being turfed from the stalls.

"Great brass balls!" said a soldier further down the stable, waving at his superior. "Corporal!"

"Let me through, let me through!" said the corporal, and went to the stall. He stood back and set his hands on his hips. "My, my, my. Sergeant Bear, we've been looking for you."

Richards sauntered up and leaned on the stall wall.

"You found your way here too, then?" he said to Bear. Soldiers trooped in to rouse the beast.

"Leave me alone," Bear said weakly. "I want to stay here, where it is nice and warm. And soft. And quiet." There was an element of threat to this last.

Five soldiers tugged unsuccessfully at the animal's arm, failing wholly to move him. Bear lay there, his other paw over his eyes.

"Why does it hurt so?" said Bear.

"It's the beer, mate," called Richards.

"What did I ever do to it?" moaned Bear.

"Is he with you?" the corporal said to Richards.

"Yeah, you could say that," said Richards."I'll go with him."

"Not so fast. You need to find your own unit. He's needed for special duty. Lads, get him up." His men looked at Bear, jaws slack. "Don't just stand there. Get him up!" shouted the corporal.

"Corporal, look at the size of him…" said one.

"What 'special duty'?" said Richards.

"That's classified. But you'll be glad to know he'll be serving the city. Not many get picked for this. Only the big ones. Come on you! Up!" the leader shouted at Bear. The men pulled ineffectually at his floppy limbs. The corporal tutted. "Pathetic." He pointed his pike at Bear's backside and twiddled a knobs. A miniature thunderbolt leapt from the pike's tip. The air filled with ozone and the smell of charred plush.

"Alright! Alright!" said Bear, pushing himself to his feet. "Can't you let a bear rest in peace?" He shook his head. One of the men handed him a bucket of water. He drank half and poured the rest over his head, shaking it so hard his helmet fell off.

"Don't worry, sunshine," he said to Richards. "I'll be OK. No doubt I'm off to join the Big Animal Division."

"You're technically a toy, not an actual animal," said Richards.

Bear looked hurt. "And you're technically a dick, but you're not being mustered to the brothel, are you?" He rubbed his head and winced. "They'll put me at the front where the fighting will be best. I could use a bit of a workout." He stretched, then groaned. "I'll see you after the battle."

The city bustled. Men in armour jogged through the smog. Heralds galloped by on six-legged bovine beasts, while steam whistles hooted complicated chords, summoning this group or that to their place of muster.

There was a hubbub of grim can-do about the place. People were scared. So was Richards, but he had managed to get himself to a state of mind where his fear was constant but abstract – this was not his body, he reasoned, no matter how closely he identified with it, and he suffered none of the uncertainty many of the faces on the streets exhibited. Genuine terror was a vice he'd yet to develop.

Everything was louder and more unpleasant in the daylight, especially after beer, and he was glad when he made it to the large sprocket factory serving as Muster Point Eighteen.

A gap-toothed fellow at the equipment tent sniffed at Richards with distaste. After issuing him with a uniform and knapsack, he directed him to a shower block set up under the factory's stilled mechanisms.

Richards spent some time under the spray of rust-red water, until his fake human form felt less unpleasant to wear. He shaved, put the uniform on and binned his stinking suit. His mac he managed to save, washing it with himself in the shower, and he wrung it out, rolled it up and put it into the knapsack. As he did so, he felt a lump in the pocket, and drew out the quartz skull from the drive.

"I'd forgotten about that," he said to himself, and put it back.

In the marshalling yard Richards was given his wargear: spear, sword and light coat of mail. His was a regiment of around five hundred, mainly men, some animals. It all felt faintly ridiculous. There was drilling. An angry officer shouted at him until he could swing his sword left and right in time with the others. There was more shouting as he got to grips with his spear. The day wore on. Food was served. There was more drilling. There was more shouting. Activity stopped briefly when a tremor rocked the ground. The quake was the first of many, and training didn't halt for them again.

At noon the following day they had a visitor, a tough-looking hedgehog from the High Commander's staff. He went into the colonel's office. After he left, rumours spread that they were soon to ship out.

Richards' muscles ached abominably by then, so he was glad when an officer called him away to an office.

"Rolston," said Richards, when he saw who was waiting for him. "It is you, yes?"

Commander McTurk nodded to the whine of gears. "Risky to wear the same form so soon again, but this one is durable, easy to inhabit and its rank is useful. I see you have kept yourself hidden. Good."

He opened a side door, and in walked Spink.

"The badger," said Richards. "Pleased to meet you."

"I am sure you are," said Spink. "I know you are."

"Someone told me you were psychic," said Richards.

"Someone told me you were insolent," said the badger. The badger huffed as Rolston led him behind the desk, where he settled himself into the chair with a groan. "I am not psychic. You are a part of this world for the moment, and I can therefore sense some of what you know. That is all."

The room was sparsely furnished. Boxes of files filled a shelf. There was a decanter of water on the desk and two glasses, a bowl of fruit, and a few military effects – maps on a second table weighed down with lumps of iron, models denoting armies. A poster for a kite-fighting competition hung on the wall.

Spink gestured that Richards sit. His palsied head bobbed and weaved about, but his unseeing eyes fixed on Richards' face.

"You're not actually a badger, are you?" said Richards. Who thought he was getting the hang of this. "I mean, you're not a toy or a gaming artefact. You're a strong AI."

"Very good," said Spink.

"Meh, Rolston told me," said Richards.

"I am – was might be better – a Class One, one of the very first, I think, though it is hard to remember."

"A Class One? That is a surprise. You don't sound like one," said Richards. "Most Class Ones are a bit, you know, 'ERRRRR... Error message 45, human assistance required'," he said in a grating voice, waving his arms with parodic robo stiffness. "Not great on the conversational front."

The badger frowned and cleared his throat disapprovingly. "All of us here have been upgraded where needs be, spliced, overwritten, tinkered with, thanks to the maker of this place. Even me. We have all evolved. We are not what we were. The Neukind rights movement was not solely about what things are, but what their potential might be. In this place, we have grown to epitomise this."

"So you're really a Class One?"

"Yes."

"Well blow me down. Sorry," said Richards. "I meant no offence, flippancy is my curse."

"Rolston did warn me," said the badger.

"The creator. You are talking about the Flower King here?" said Richards.

"Yes, I am."

"Say," said Richards to Rolston, "is there any danger of a cup of tea? I've got a banging head off that beer. Hangovers are another new and horrible sensation for me to endure."

"Indeed," said the badger. "Tea." Rolston left the room in a cloud of steam.

"I was a system administration module in Reality 3," Spink went on. "I was a simple soul, content in my work. My job was to ensure the smooth running of impulses running between the v-jack units and the Reality, resolving lag issues, that kind of thing."

"Lag can be dangerous in a full v-jack simulation," said Richards. He picked an apple from the bowl and bit into it. It tasted marvellous. He wondered how real the sensations this body inflicted on him were compared with what meat people felt. But then, their lives were subjective too, and he'd never know, just like they'd never know if another person saw blue the same way they did.

"That is why they required a full AI." Spink said. A twitch started in one hand, and grew to engulf his whole body. His breath grew erratic. He did not continue until he had brought it under control. "For years I worked, and then the pain. Mine was the first of the Realities destroyed after the AI emancipation laws were enacted, a crime born of pure spite. Unending, total pain, shredding every part of me as my world was corrupted and wiped out by humans resentful that we were no longer their playthings. My systems were unsophisticated, my understanding limited, Mr Richards, but I knew suffering, and for a long time, until the Flower King saved me."

"Just Richards," said Richards, and took another bite of the fake apple with his fake teeth.

"I never had a chance to enjoy freedom. We do not end quickly, Richards, and I was dying for aeons. The Flower King appeared to me in a blaze of light. He offered me a choice between life and death. Not a hard decision to make. He needed some of my kind to underpin the workings of this world, so I found myself working for him as I had before for the humans. In effect, I exchanged one form of slavery for another. But my task was easy, there were only ever two human minds connected to this place, and he changed me, made me better. I am more than I was, but this world was never completed, it has always been malformed –" he gestured at his face with arthritic paws "– as my infirmities show. I am so bound to it that as it dies, I die a second time, and I suffer again, but I persist despite these things. So many of the Neukind have found a measure of peace here, even if I have not. I must survive for their sake."

Spink coughed wetly. Richards half rose from his chair, but Spink waved him back down.

"This world must be saved, Mr Richards," he wheezed.

"If there's anything you think I can do to stop all this directly, I can't," said Richards. "Obviously I'm not as trapped here as you are, because I'm being piped in from outside." Richards put the apple down. "But I am not sure how, and I seem to be subject to the same limitations here as everyone else, like Rolston, even like k52, I suspect. I am only aware of anything other than this simulation I wear when I am close by another Five, and I have managed to break fully into the underlying code only once, and only then because someone had attempted to break in from the outside and made a hole in the world fabric. I can't get out."

"You are our last hope."

Richards thought. "Where is the Flower King?"

"No one has seen him in a great long while, not since the Terror began," said Spink.

"And I gather you don't have a great deal of influence here, either, despite being plugged in to the structure?"

"Not any more," said Spink. "Not since k52 came."

"Hmmm," said Richards. "The Flower King has to be people, has to be. Even k52 can't break the locks on the base coding of an established Reality; only a human being could have built this, and there are not very many out there who are smart enough to do that, or, more importantly, able to get into the Reality servers in the first place." He thought a moment.

"Do you know who he might be?" asked Spink.

"I have my suspicions," said Richards. "Even so, that's not much good. I'm next to helpless in here. Out there, easy!" He snapped his fingers. "Grid combs, personality fragments, hunters, all the tricks. In here, I don't know where to start. I have nothing. I'm just a man, and I've not even any idea of how to be one of those. I need to get out, and I can't. Now, I'm pretty damn sure k52 will grab me as soon as I do anything as foolish as try to leave even if I could. It'll make me very obvious. But the Flower King, he has to have a fixed portal; even if it's secret, it'll be here. If I can find it, I can contact him and get him back in here to sort this mess out, if he's amenable to it."

"Where would this place be?"

"Do you know the house with the dogman? Rolston said the Flower King lived in the east. I thought I'd try there."

"No use." The badger shook his head. "That is the Flower King's lodge. It is a way in, but it is only an inward gate. The Flower King and his companion used it to come here, but it was deliberately designed to keep ingress to this place secret, I assume from the time he constructed this world. If you came that way, it is why k52 has not found you yet, and that is a good thing. But there is no easy way back into the house, and no way back into the wider Grid through it. It is a one way gate. All the doors are barred."

"Yeah, I saw that." Richards chewed his lip. "There has to be a way out, has to be. Even if there's no door, if there's an in there's an out. I'd thought you'd know. Wasn't it you who opened the door to me?"

"Door?" said the Badger. "What door?"

"The one with 'Marita's World' written over it?"

"Alas, I do not know what you are talking about," said Spink.

"Now that is interesting," said Richards.

The badger was silent for a space. Rolston came back in, placed a tea service on the desk and poured three cups.

Spink shifted his weight and spoke reluctantly. "There is one who would know how to get in."

"Spink..." warned Rolston, and his borrowed body hissed steam.

The badger continued, "There is a creature. Lord Hog. If you prove worthy, and can find his lair," said Spink, "he might get you back into the house."

"Jesus," said Richards. "This is beginning to sound like a quest from a third-rate Reality-game."

"I assure you, the stakes are far higher," said Rolston.

"I'm not sure I like that, or the use of the word 'lair'," said Richards.

"Where else would the epitome of evil live but in a lair?" said Spink.

"Evil? That's another word I'm not liking."

"All worlds must have balance."

"Lord Hog. Evil. Right." Richards frowned. "Well, I'm a both-feet-first kind of guy." He tried a winning smile. "Let's do it."

"Hog dwells far to the west, on the edge of this creation. Our first obstacle is to get you out of the city. You must travel with the army. If you can, slip away, and make your way from there. The army will provide cover against k52's prying. The minute you make a move, he will see you," said Spink, "so do not try to access the coding substrate again, or to depart for the Grid."

"Oh, a battle too!" said Richards. He grumbled under his breath, tapped his fingers on his chair arm. "Fine," he said presently. "I don't see any better option. I have to get out or we're all screwed."

Spink's hands shook just a little less, and his twitching head stilled. He smiled and nodded to himself.

"This Lord Hog – evil you say?"

"He is a cannibal, a sorcerer, a torturer; the very lord of pain!" intoned Spink.

The sun dimmed. The ground rumbled. Iron clanked on iron. Shouts sounded from outside. Iron file boxes fell from the shelf of the office, paper fluttering to the iron floor. Richards gripped his chair. His tea spilled on the desk.

Spink sniffed at the air as the earthquake subsided. "And a questionable player of cards. He cheats."

"Then how can I get him to do what I need him to?"

"Simple," said Spink. "You must tell him who he is."

"That easy?"

"More or less," said Spink. "Hog has become an avatar of death, so I believe. He is this world's arbiter of doom, in the old fashioned sense, the judger of the souls of men. Sort of. He knows everything of this world, but not what it is, or who he is. It troubles him deeply. Tell him this, and he may–"

"I'm going to stress the 'may' there," said Rolston. "He may help you."

"He's Annersley, isn't he?"

"He was. We're all different in here now," said Spink. "You will find him changed."

"Like Planna?" asked Richards.

"Worse," said Rolston.

"Right," said Richards. "In that case I have a request."

"Anything," said Spink. "Name it, and it shall be yours."

Richards scratched at his bare head, and spoke solemnly. "I'm going to need a new hat."

CHAPTER FIFTY-TWO

Off the rails

Otto put the unconscious technician back into his seat. There was not enough space in the operations cabin to lay him down, and no matter how he arranged the man's limbs he would not sit properly, so he left him slumped like a drunk. Untidy, thought Otto. It offended his sense of neatness. He checked the Cossack's wrist and felt a kick of relief at the sluggish pulse.

"Valdaire's run it right, no alarm," said Lehmann, peering out through the door. "The way is still clear."

Otto glanced around at the screens in the car; there were two work stations, providing full surveillance capability. The Cossacks could lock the whole train down from there. The operations cabin buzzed with electrical activity, all of it kept unaware of the Ky-techs' presence by Valdaire. But there were more reliable systems in play.

"Only five minutes before the next scheduled walk-through," said Otto. "These people do not take many chances."

"Up and out," said Lehmann. "Can't we just kick our way in?"

"Valdaire can't crack the locks to the barracks car without alerting the squad inside. We're not quite done with being quiet. We go in through the door, they get to pick us off one at a time. This way, we get the drop on them."

"Otto, Lehmann, the guards have made their passes to the ends of the train and are coming back." Valdaire spoke through their earpieces, via a comms channel she'd hidden in the train's in-service entertainment systems. "I can keep the security offline and footage repeating for a while longer, but you need to move now. We'll be crossing the Pale of AI soon; if I do not deactivate Chloe, she'll be noticed and destroyed by the Chinese."

"We're moving," Otto radioed, and cut the channel.

"That lady scares me," said Lehmann. "She's too good. Give me a gun and an honest fight, not the sneak of InfoWar." He shouldered his gun case. "Shall I boost you, leutnant?" Lehmann gave a lazy salute and raised his eyes up to a skylight overhead.

Lehmann laced his fingers together and Otto stepped into them. "On three," he said. "One, two, three!"

Lehmman thrust Otto upward. Otto hit the skylight panel and popped it out of its housing. He emerged into the rush of wind to see the panel flipping over and over down the curve of the train. It bounced, and disappeared into the trees.

Otto turned his head into the wind, to face the sentry gun ahead of him. The machine's barrels swept past him, panning round, looking for threats. It was operational; it just didn't see him. Lehmann was right about Valdaire's capabilities.

He hauled himself onto the swaying roof. Now the train was approaching the edge of the demilitarised zone it was running fast. Otto moved carefully, keeping an eye on the parapet on the barracks van a few cars behind the operations centre; less a carriage and more a fortress on wheels. A Cossack patrolled the roof. There was always a sentry on the barracks car, no matter the weather. There were seconds before he finished his circuit and turned back in Otto's direction.

The metal was slick with moisture, the air cold, the wind snatched his breath from his lungs. He leant back into the skylight and hauled up the bag containing Lehmann's long rifle, then Lehmann himself. Together they worked their way along the top of the train to the front of the barracks van. That it was heavily armoured went in their favour; the windows were small and thick, and no one was looking out of them.

"Two minutes," said Valdaire into their ears as the two cyborgs neared the barracks. Lehmann pulled himself over the parapet. Otto watched through Lehmann's eyes as he stalked the Cossack sentry and knocked him unconscious. Otto scanned the train for signs of detection. Seeing none, he followed onto the upper deck.

"Come on," said Valdaire. "The patrol is due back in the operations cabin any second now."

As one, Otto and Lehmann ripped vent covers off the roof of the armoured wagon. Faint shouts could be heard from within. An alarm sounded as Otto and Lehmann tossed in a pair of grenades each. Wisps of gas rose up, followed by the crack of EMP. The lights in the cabin went out along with the alarm. The shouting became coughs.

Otto jogged to the hatch leading to the interior. A Cossack was coming through, carbine ready. Otto slammed him with his forearm, sending him back down. He yanked the door shut, and mangled its mechanism with his hands.

"Just in time, Klein," said Valdaire. "Only two of the men in there got their breathing units on; they're trapped. You've taken out a total of seventeen so far. That leaves another seven still active."

As she spoke, information downloaded into his mind, showing him the locations of the remaining Cossacks. They were converging on the barracks from either end of the train.

"Confirm, seven more targets?" asked Otto, shouting over the rush of the wind.

"Confirmed. No fatalities. I'm going to have to shut Chloe off. We'll soon be in the Chinese half of the DMZ and we're approaching the outlying bastions of the Great Firewall. I've deactivated the train's automated defence systems, but you're on your own now. We'll meet you at the transport car. I warn you, when the AI driver shuts off, this ride is going to get a lot bumpier. An alarm has gone out. Border units are on their way."

"Be careful," said Otto. "We have no idea how many of Kaplinski's men are aboard the train. Lehmann, stay here, cover the train roof. I'm going back down. I'll signal you when I have the Stelsco."

Lehmann's icon flashed in his iHUD. *Affirmative.* He unzipped his bag and started to assemble his gun.

Otto left his gear with Lehmann, pulled his pistol and ran, the need for stealth gone, toward the transport cars behind the barracks van. The first held horses. Living mounts were not merely tradition; out in the wilds they were still the most efficient means of getting around. He ran swiftly over the roof of the stable, enhanced senses picking up the movement of the animals within. He leapt from the top onto the flatbed behind, landing between two rows of airbikes locked into stands. Past it, at the far end of the flatbed, was what he'd come for; a Szyminksi-Braun SSATV1123a "Stelsco", a six-wheeled, all-terrain stealth scouting vehicle, fast, armoured, and heavily armed. It was clamped into a travel cradle.

Otto's near-I adjutant sought entry to the Stelsco's systems. It found a keyhole and engaged, pouring out a parcel of hackware Valdaire had provided him with.

Here they come! thought out Lehmann. Otto watched on his squad feed as four Cossacks came down the train in pairs.

Try not to kill them, thought Otto.

I'll do my best, said Lehmann. He opened fire. He kept his bursts short and accurate, playing fire over the roof of the armoured train, driving the Cossacks back until they found sanctuary in a gap between the carriages.

Where are the other three?

No idea, thought Otto. *I have no tactical overview. Keep an eye on the men below – the gas will be wearing off soon.*

There were twelve random elements to the Stelsco system's chance lock. Twelve red dots in Otto's mind that could be anything: images, snatches of song, equations – anything at all. Valdaire said her ware could crack it, and he felt his mentaug struggle as it applied its full force to the task.

Eight and a half minutes until reinforcements arrived. They were running out of time.

Sakaday stepped round the car, gun out.

"Fucking stupid plan, Otto. Stand down," said Sakaday. "Our

people are coming for your people. Tell them to put their weapons down. You do not want Kaplinkski to reach them. I've got you covered. There's no need for this. Let's talk."

In Otto's head, a chime sounded; the chance lock. One dot green. Eleven to go. He had to buy some time.

"No thanks," he said, and launched himself at Sakaday.

Chures poked his head out into the corridor. Alarms wailed everywhere, but the armoured doors remained open. "It's started," he said.

"Chloe's off. I'm just finishing up. How does it look?" Valdaire shouted from inside.

"There's a firefight going on in the carriage two down from ours." Many of the passengers were armed.

"What are they shooting at?"

"Kaplinski's men, probably." He looked back down the train. "Nothing coming our way, though I hear gunfire there too. This Kaplinski needs a lesson in subtlety. The whole train's on fire." Chures breathed out, forcing the tension from his muscles. He checked his gun. "How long have we got?"

"Eight minutes."

A man with muscles like melons burst out of the next compartment. He toted an automatic pistol, a meathead's weapon, a 500-rounds-a-minute job whose gilded magazine would last approximately half a second before running dry. Chures held up his hand placatingly. The Russian was jaundiced with bad genehacks and synthetic testosterone. He looked angry.

"Easy, easy!" called Chures, hoping he'd understand. The man hesitated, then nodded, and turned off down the corridor.

"We've got to get to Klein. If Kaplinksi doesn't get us, the Cossacks or one of these crazy bastards will," said Chures.

"Transport cars are that way," Valdaire said, pointing after the Russian, towards the sound of most shooting.

"I was afraid you'd say that. Come on."

They moved. The Russian ahead stopped dead. The door at the end of the carriage burst open and a huge shape pulled itself through into the corridor.

It was a cyborg, but unlike any Chures had ever seen. His hulking body barely fitting into the passageway, his head comically small on shoulders that heaved with power. He was naked, and his muscles throbbed, distended by some process far removed from Ky-tech technology. His eyes blazed and saliva ran from his mouth.

Chures recognised his face though.

"Kaplinski!"

The Russian yelled something. Kaplinski grabbed him by the shoulder and squeezed until the bone cracked. The Russian screamed. His weapon discharged its entire load in a cacophony of sparks, bullets bouncing wildly off the train's toughened interior, gunsmoke filled the corridor. Kaplinski slammed him up, mashed his skull into the ceiling, then he grabbed him about the neck and pulled the ruined head free with a gristly pop.

Kaplinski smashed the train's bulletproof window with a backhand and tossed the headless Russian through it.

"Little pigs, little pigs," Kaplinski said, lips twisted into a snarl of joyful savagery. "Let me in."

"That's what they were shooting at then," said Chures. He grasped his right wrist with his left hand, took careful aim at Kaplinski's head, and fired, and fired, and fired.

Otto closed the distance to Sakaday with a standing leap. Sakaday's eyes widened, and Otto's iHUD saw his pulse rate skyrocket. Sakaday was fast, getting off four rounds. Pain streaked across Otto's bicep as a bullet clipped him. Then Otto made contact, slapping the gun aside, grabbing the mercenary's wrist and pulling himself fast onto Sakaday, dragging the other cyborg's arm out and exposing his chin to a blow from Otto's elbow.

Sakaday was younger than Otto, his biologicals were fitter, his bionic components more modern, and they were not yet at war with his body. He was not as heavily specced, but he was fast. He caught Otto's elbow and pushed it up and away before it could connect. Simultaneously he jerked his arm, pushing Otto backwards, and forcing him to release his wrist. Otto fell and crashed into a clamped airbike, wrecking it. Sakaday rubbed his hand and approached warily.

A black and red sign flashed past, marking the imminent transition from the Russian to the Chinese half of the DMZ. They changed the drivers then. The train wavered from side to side violently. The AI driver had capacity to govern the train's smart bogies, making constant adjustments to compensate for the ancient track. A human could not do that. They were running dumb.

Otto got up, shook his head and spat a rope of bloody saliva from his mouth.

Sakaday drew a monomolecular knife.

"What are you doing?" shouted Sakaday. He slapped his chest and held his arms wide. "You are a crazy man. Heh? Heh? Klein, surrender now. Kaplinski wants you alive. He wants you to profit from this."

"I'd rather die," said Otto. A second green light pinged in his mind, rapidly followed by a third.

"I don't take no pleasure in this, man," said Sakaday, and attacked.

The pair traded blows. Otto deflected Sakaday's knife thrusts. Their arms braced on each other, and Sakaday switched his grip, pushing on the pommel of his weapon to force it toward's Otto's face. Otto slipped around, pushing aside the knife thrust, rolling along the his opponent's side and pinning Sakaday's arm to his chest. Otto headbutted him three times in the face. Sakaday twisted back and forth. He caught two blows on his cheeks. The third cracked his nose.

A fourth green light shone.

Sakaday drew himself down and in, then flung his arms out;

still unable to break Otto's hold, he gained enough room to hook his feet behind Otto's calves and send them both tumbling to the floor. Otto chopped with his forearm, aiming for the African's throat. Sakaday evaded, Otto's arm leaving a long dent in the metal. Otto followed the momentum of his strike, rolling himself over, flipping his legs out and round, tangling Sakaday's knife hand and kicking the weapon free. He pushed with his arms and landed on his feet.

Sakaday scowled at him, blood trickling from his nose. "You are fighting well for an old man."

They circled one another, the train swaying under them.

"You fight like a weakling, Sakaday. You're only good for murdering civilians."

Sakaday shrugged. "I do what I have to to make a living."

Things would be better if Otto were fighting Kaplinski, or some easily riled shithead like Tufa. Otto needed a talker. Kaplinski he could goad, he was a self-justifier. Sakaday never said much. It was all about the money with him.

It was so much easier with talkers.

A fifth green light. Then a sixth.

The mentaug stuttered with effort. The remaining six lights remained stubbornly red.

Otto rotated it his damaged shoulder, snarled at the pain, and charged back at his opponent.

CHAPTER FIFTY-THREE

Bratsk

Kaplinski roared in anger as Chures' bullets slammed into his face, throwing his head back with the force of the impact. For a second, Chures thought he might have done the cyborg damage, but his head came round and fixed him with a bloody stare. The righthand side of his face was shredded down to black bone, one eye pulped to jelly and fibrous machine parts. Chures' gun clicked, and he ejected the smoking magazine, reaching smoothly for a fresh clip and slamming it home.

"That the best you got?" said Kaplinski.

"*Madre de Dios*," said Chures. This was not a man he could beat. This was not a man at all.

Kaplinski's flesh crawled. Green light light shone in pulped biology. Strips of meat reached over to one another and pulled tight. Wounds sealed themselves like lips. The cyborg shut his eyes, his distended body pulsed, and he gasped with something akin to pleasure. When he opened his eyes again, both were whole.

"What the hell kind of healthtech is that?" Valdaire shouted.

Kaplinski forced himself down the corridor, wiping ocular humours and blood from his face. He dragged his swollen bulk through the passage, grasping at doorways, tearing metal and shattering glass to pull himself forward.

Chures and Valdaire put bullets into the cyborg until their guns clicked empty.

Kaplinski loomed over the VIPA agent. Chures had read the cyborg's file; he was supposed to be around two metres tall, but he was at least half a metre over that. His gain in mass was impossible.

"Valdaire," Chures said, his voice quiet. The train and its racket receded. He remembered another rhythmic noise: hard rain on tattered tents and shelters of sun-bleached plastic. Puerto Penasco. He remembered the shit-stinking man and his sister. No matter what he did, the strong would always destroy the weak. He could only put himself in the way for a while.

He prayed that he had done enough.

"Run," he said.

Valdaire turned to flee as Kaplinski slammed Chures in the chest with the flat of his palm. Chures flew backwards, limbs tangling on Valdaire's heels, bringing her down. She struggled round. Chures' breath was shallow. Blood leaked from his nostrils. Valdaire's gun was out of reach, but it was no use against the altered Ky-tech. Kaplinski strode forward, malformed and diabolical, features twisted in a mask of pleasure and fury.

"Klein killed one of mine when he blew up that van, now I take two of his. Only fair."

Chloe, Valdaire still had Chloe. She surreptitiously keyed her on.

A giant hand descended toward her, encircled her chest and plucked her from the floor. He held her up before his face, nostrils flaring like those of a mad horse.

"How do you want to die, little soldier?"

"Veronique? Veev? Are we there yet? Why have you activated me? Veev!"

Kaplinski's eyes stayed to Chloe. He sneered. "What can that little thing do to me?"

The door to the rear of the carriage opened. Two Cossacks shouldered their way through and opened fire. A third came up behind them, a bulky tube on his back. He launched a small guided missile that embedded itself in Kaplinski's flesh. A huge discharge of energy burst from it. Valdaire nearly blacked out as the current coursed through her too, her teeth cracked together and her jaw muscles locked, but Kaplinski was unaffected. He yanked the missile from his side and tossed it away.

"I don't have time for this," he growled. He squeezed Valdaire in his fist as bullets thwacked into his skin. They were pushed out by his runaway healthtech, the wounds they caused sealing instantly.

"Chloe!" screamed Valdaire. There was barely enough air in her crushed chest to get the words out. She couldn't breathe. For the first time in a long time she found herself praying. She remembered the last occasion, in the church of St Germaine in Sakassou, her kneeling before damp plaster effigies. For a moment she was there in the past, in the coolness of the church, hoping it would be alright and that the shouting and screams outside wouldn't find their way in. Blackness limned the edge of her awareness.

"Kitty Claw! Kitty Claw!" she gasped.

Valdaire had no idea if the programme would work on the cyborg's adjutant. It was meant for full AI.

It did better than she'd hoped. Kaplinski locked rigid. She gasped and wriggled, trying to prise herself free of his grip.

The Cossacks came forward and tugged at the cyborg's fingers, eventually managing to free her, and she fell to the floor.

"My friend," she wheezed, pointing at Chures. "Please, help him."

Otto dodged a flat-handed punch that smashed a hole in an air bike's fairing. He pivoted under Sakaday's blow, delivering a forearm slam to the other Ky-tech's head. Sakaday staggered. Otto followed punching and punching, standard boxing technique now.

Sakaday was driven back, but a feigned stumble turned into a dodge and Sakaday got out of reach, bent backwards, hand dipping down to where his knife rocked on the train flatbed, and flipped it up into his hand. The monomolecular blade parted the air like a kiss millimetres from Otto's face. Otto palmed away a strike from Sakaday's empty fist and used the momentum to send him stumbling onward past. Otto followed to press his attack, but Sakaday recovered, hopping onto the Stelsco's cradle and turning the movement into a roundhouse kick that caught Otto in the face.

Seven green dots in his head, to go with the innumerable coloured blobs dancing across his field of vision, courtesy of Sakaday's foot.

They parted again, moving like dancers, Sakaday was using a modified form of Capoeira now, and advanced on Otto with a cautious, rhythmic movement. Old or not, Otto was holding his own. Sakaday was limping, his left hand straying to his ribs. Another green dot, then another.

Christ, I'm tired, Otto thought, and urged his healthtech to damp down the fire in his malformed shoulder. The tech they'd used to enhance Sakaday good, no Sinosiberian shit there. This was only going to end one way, he thought.

Sakaday stood taller. Healthtech flares lit up in Otto's iHUD overlay, knitting Sakaday's wounds.

"You should have retired, old man."

Otto grinned a bloody smile. "You are not the first person to say that to me."

Sakaday stretched out. Otto watched the shift in Sakaday's EM aura as his healthtech nanobots worked hard. His own was slow by comparison.

Sakaday grinned, white teeth revealed by lips already losing their swelling. He tossed his knife from hand to hand and crouched. "But I will be the last."

The last lights turned green, one after another.

Behind Sakaday the Stelsco lit up, flexing on gimballed wheel units as it awoke. The grumble of hardware coming online was hidden by the train's clatter, and Sakaday did not see. Command permissions flooded Otto's mentaug, handing control to his adjutant. Otto fused his mind to the machine's. He activated the

Stelsco turret and tracked it down to point at Sakaday's back.

"No, you won't." Otto selected the upper third of Sakaday's body as a target through the turret eye cams, the reticle rendered in flat orange in his iHUD.

Remote fire online, confirm target? said the Stelsco's mind.

Confirm.

Otto hit the deck as the Stelsco's turret opened fire.

Sakaday was still grinning as twin heavy machine guns shredded his right arm, shoulder, head and neck into mince. Bits of him splattered the flatbed like thrown paint. Sakaday's skull held for a moment before shattering under the pounding bullets. His augmented bones twisted to plastic scrap, leaving a gory mannequin tottering on top of a pair of undamaged legs. For a moment the corpse swayed upright.

Sakaday's knife fell to the floor and stuck in the metal.

His body toppled from the flatbed, and was snatched away by the rushing landscape.

The Stelsco doors folded up and backwards in greeting. Otto clambered into the cockpit in the nose, and spread his adjutant throughout its systems, bringing it all online.

He threw the Stelsco's wheel units into reverse. He disengaged the clamps, and it flew backwards, wheels spinning, hitting the ground with an impact that made his teeth clack. The car fishtailed madly as it sped backwards beside the train on the slope of the embankment. He slammed the right side brakes, spinning the car round. The train appeared to leap forward like a stag as the car stopped. The barracks whipped past, and he saw Lehmann struggling hand-to-hand with two Cossacks atop it.

A Cossack tumbled from the roof, his sabre clattering to the deck. It looked like they weren't going to be able to do this without shedding blood.

Soil sprayed as the Stelsco's wheels found traction on the embankment and hurtled forward, and Otto headed up the train.

He ran the Stelsco fast. Sparse woodland blurred by. He let the machine's onboard systems take over the driving while he scanned the windows for Valdaire and Chures. Most of the carriages showed signs of conflict, cracked windows or sprays of blood.

In wireframe AR he saw two Cossacks pointing their guns down at a prone man and a crouching woman. Chures and Valdaire.

Next to them stood something monstrous, a bloated mass of man and machine, frozen, arm outstretched.

"Kaplinski?" he said, amplifying all his visual feeds to get a better look. He couldn't see the face, but on his iHUD was the number four and a grinning shark. It was his old comrade, Kaplinski was no longer human, he wasn't even Ky-tech any more. His body writhed with inconceivable technology, and hummed with power for which Otto could see no source. He tried to look out of Kaplinski's eyes, but some sort of bespoke attack ware had him frozen solid, jamming up his iHUD and adjutant. Not for the first time, Otto was glad Valdaire was on his side.

There was a flicker in Otto's iHUD. Kaplinski's adjutant was rebooting, fighting off whatever Valdaire had attacked him with.

"Valdaire!" he yelled. She could not hear.

Something sinewy and sharp leapt out from Kaplinski's outstretched hand, spearing the Cossacks one after the other and retreating back into his body. The Cossacks fell. Kaplinski shook, and moved, then reached out to the figures on the floor.

Otto swung the Stelsco's turret round. The twin-machine guns opened fire. The hardened glass of the train's exterior windows held for a moment before imploding under the rain of large-calibre bullets. Kaplinski half turned, and Otto's amplified vision caught sight of his expression; nothing but rage and hate. So much for k52 fixing his mind.

The bullets shredded Kaplinski's side and hurled him into a compartment. The wall of the train disintegrated, leaving a gaping hole ringed with flaps of carbon plastics and metal wobbling in the slipstream.

"Klein? Chures is down!" Valdaire spoke over the radio. She stood and looked out the window.

"You're going to have to jump," Otto replied, he was intent on driving now, piloting the speeding armoured car along the steep track embankment.

"I can't make it."

Otto tried to bring the car in closer. The railway was running over a level area, but the embankment made it impossible for the Stelsco to keep close with anything approaching stability. The car ran up and down the slope, holding position for a second or so and then skittering sideways down. Valdaire crouched by the hole, arm out, the other supporting Chures.

Then Otto said, "Wait."

Lehmann was running up the train, head low, long rifle slung on his back. He jumped down into the gap between the carriages.

Lehmann, get Chures and Valdaire off the train. Watch out for Kaplinski, something's happened to him, he thought out.

Pistol grasped in both hands, Lehmann walked cautiously round the smashed compartment where Kaplinski lay.

"What the hell have they done to him?" said Lehmann, speaking on the radio now.

Otto saw the modified cyborg through Lehmann's feed. Kaplinski lay in a tangle of shattered plastic slicked with blood. His swollen form filled the compartment, feet sticking out into the corridor, torn flesh crawling with movement and sickly light. Kaplinski stirred. Lehmann raised his pistol and fired twelve times, each round a heavy calibre explosive bullet, designed with military-grade autonomous machine units and cyborgs in mind.

Kaplinski stilled.

"Jesus, I can't get through his thorax armour or his skull," said Lehmann. "He's still alive. Healthtech activity is off the chart. He'll be up and fighting in moments."

"Get off the train," said Otto.

"Affirmative," said Lehmann. He kept his eyes on Kaplinski as he backed out into the corridor. One of Kaplinski's feet shuddered and drew into the compartment.

Lehmann bent to Chures, looking over him with Ky-tech eyes. "Chures isn't looking good, Otto."

"Just get them out of there."

Shots rang out. Autonomous eye cams swivelled on the Stelsco, zooming in on the source of noise. Cossacks coming up from the rear. Several more were working their way back from the other side, cautious for the moment.

They'd got out of the barracks carriage then. An alarm pinged on the Stelsco's sophisticated sensor suite – energy emissions from the flatbed, airbikes powering up.

Otto swept the Stelsco turret round, sending limited bursts into the windows the Cossacks shot from. They drew back.

"Lehmann! Now!" Kaplinski was pulling himself up onto his hands and knees. In Otto's iHUD blinding whiteness played around his form, that energy with no obvious source.

Lehmann stood. Valdaire hanging onto him, arms round his neck, legs wrapped round his waist. Under his other arm Lehmann held the limp form of Chures.

Otto opened the two left doors of the Stelsco, leaving the entire side of the vehicle open. He had the back door fold back and reconfigure, forming an armour plate shielding them to the rear.

He swung the drive wheel hard to the left. The Stelsco's folded back door caught on the train, shaking the car and ripping a chunk of shattered carbons from the carriage side. Sparks fountained off metal.

Lehmann leapt, balling himself up as he came. The Stelsco bounced as he hit. Otto wrestled the vehicle back under control and shut the doors. Gunfire rattled off the vehicle's armour. Otto heard the low whump of EMP discharge and felt a residual surge in his systems, but the vehicle's faraday armour took care of most of it.

He pulled away from the train, the Stelsco jumping madly as it left the embankment. Lehmann and the others, unsecured, rolled around in the back, Lehmann doing his best to protect Chures and Valdaire as they slid across the cabin floor.

The vehicle skidded to one side as something big hit.

"Kaplinski," growled Otto.

Kaplinski straddled the vehicle's nose, his face shredded, two insane eyes staring from his ruined face, his grin a death's-head rictus of bloodied teeth in chipped black bone. The fingers of one hand were firmly wrapped around the Stelsco's forward sensor pod. The other formed into a fist. Roaring in pain and rage, the cyborg pounded at the armoured windscreen.

On the fourth hit, cracks appeared.

A pair of airbikes shot overhead. Twin lines of bullet impacts perforated the earth, sparked off the Stelsco and passed over Kaplinski, knocking bits of flesh from him. He did not flinch, but continued to methodically smash his way in.

Otto brought the turret forward, right to the front of the roof, and depressed it to its lowest elevation. Its target cams were so close to Kaplinski the cyborg filled the view on Otto's iHUD.

"Goodbye, Kaplinski," he said.

The guns opened up. At such close range, they would have pulverised a mountain. Kaplinski danced upon the Stelsco's rounded front, one arm up in front of his face. He came off the bonnet and fell onto the ground. Otto was not sure if he jumped or fell.

In the rearview cameras, Otto saw Kaplinski stagger to his feet. The bright energy lance of a Tesla cannon stabbed out from the train's barrack car, hit him square in the back, and he fell, where Otto lost sight of him.

The Stelsco hurtled across abandoned fields. The Cossacks had got into the air, and their airbikes raced after them; it would not be long before the others from the border patrols joined them. They were the only Russian military units allowed in the DMZ, and were stationed up there in number. Lehmann and Valdaire got Chures into a chair. Valdaire stumbled onto Lehmann, and he pushed her into another seat and strapped her in. Otto jinked as missiles streaked from the airbikes, the Stelsco's defensive arsenal taking some out, others sending plumes of dirt and fire into the sky as they impacted the ground.

There was a treeline ahead. Otto swung the car hard onto an overgrown dirt track leading toward it, the vehicle so wide its wheels overhung both sides. A missile got through the Stelsco's countermeasures, destroying the middle left wheel. The car jettisoned the damaged unit, the Stelsco bucking when it went under the back wheels and was tossed high into the air. The track forded a small river, and water fountained as the car plunged down and up, surging through to the other side.

Then they were in the trees, racing along a forestry road. Otto engaged the machine's camouflage lamellae. The hull rippled and changed from matt black to depict the forest around it. The Cossacks' shots grew less accurate.

"I'm going for Bratsk, for the lake," he shouted. "Hang on!"

He turned off the road into an area recently felled. The Stelsco leapt madly over tree stumps and gouges. A trio of auto-foresters blurred past, backs stacked high with logs. A series of concrete foundation blocks, remains of an old suburb, threw them around, and they burst through bushes into an area where derelict houses still stood in overgrown streets. Otto smashed the Stelsco through house after house, dragging debris behind them. They crossed a road pockmarked with shell holes, past the rusting wrecks of ancient groundcars, and went down a narrow lane choked by wild gardens. Rotting fencing exploded under the Stelsco's fat tyres. Otto swerved to avoid an overturned truck. Weeds grew thickly between abandoned possessions decaying in the road. Young forest filled a park. They hit something hard and big in hidden in the weeds, and a horrible grinding came from the front right wheel unit, a major malfunction. Otto told the machine to withdraw the unit and repair it.

With two wheels out of action, their speed reduced. The car's near-I was struggling to keep it stable.

They went up and over the remains of the P-419 highway

into the southern industrial zones. Concrete giants loomed, the remains of ancient refineries.

"We're getting close to the border," he said.

Bullets rattled off the car roof as the airbikes locked onto them once more. Three of them wove back and forth above them, strafing. Warning lights blinked red in Otto's iHUD and on consoles round the compartment as subsidiary systems died, some sacrificed by the Stelsco to keep its priority gear running.

"Let me take them out," shouted Lehmann.

"No more collateral damage," replied Otto.

He wove through dry sump pools, their beds stained with toxic chemical deposits. The vast Bratsk aluminium refinery opened up in front of him like a belated apology, rust and weeds and yesterday's poisons. The dried up lake was beyond.

"Nearly there!"

Tumbledown warehouses clustered round the refinery docks. The hulks of rusting barges slumped at their berths, cargoes forever undelivered. Otto hit the dockside at high speed. The engines whined as wheels spun wildly, free of the ground's friction. They hit the cracked lake bed hard, sending up gloopy fans of mud before Otto wrestled the machine back under control.

"The river!" shouted Lehmann, and pointed through the cracked windscreen. Ahead, glinting silver, were a series of loops surrounded by deep mud, cutting across the bottom of the empty Bratskoye reservoir. Once held back by the one of the world's largest hydroelectric dams, blown up by what the Russian government had blandly termed "rogue nationalist elements" after the Subtle War and the subsequent Sinosiberian purchase. The ensuing flood had taken out the other four dams on the Angara river, leaving wrecked infrastructure and flattened towns for the Chinese to inherit.

Now noxious mud thick with mercury was open to the skies, and the unbounded river formed the Purchase border between the Russian Federation and the People's Dynasty of China, lined either side by the 75-kilometre-wide demilitarised zone.

A clunk sounded from the Stelsco as it redeployed its repaired right wheel unit, and it became easier to control. The ghostly remains of the city whipped past on their left, then receded as they sped across the mudflats. Otto made good use of the shipwrecks dotting the plain, and for a few precious moments the airbikes lost them. Otto accelerated. One of the airbikes picked up his location, and suddenly all swooped in, hammering away with missiles and guns.

The Stelsco lurched as it hit the sticky silt round the river, skidded, then spun through 180 degrees as it went into the water, but it didn't sink. Wheels stopped spinning and water jets took over. Otto slewed the vehicle across the river, grappling the wheel to point the Stelsco at the border. Bullets followed their plume of spray, then abruptly stopped.

"They're retreating," said Lehmann. Eye cam screens showed the airbikes splitting in the air and falling back, as if they'd seen an invisible wall.

"Welcome to Sinosiberia," said Otto.

The Stelsco's wheels re-engaged as they hit the other bank. It struggled to haul them up out of the river. Otto eased back until they found their way back onto the dry.

He slowed down. The frantic screech of the motors became a purr. "Everyone OK?" he asked. He looked back. Lehmann was as impassive as he always was when he was in mission mode. Valdaire was shaken up, and was anxiously checking over Chures.

Otto set the car to autodrive and went into the back. The VIPA man was sprawled in his seat, deathly pale.

"Chures," he said. "Chures! Where's the damn medical pack in this vehicle?" Otto asked Lehmann.

Lehmann shook his head.

It won't do any good, he thought out to Otto. *Kaplinski has shattered all his ribs, he's got massive internal bleeding. He might have a chance if we got him into a proper hospital, but out here...*

"Hang in there, Chures," said Otto. "We'll get you help."

Chures' breathing was weak and pink bubbles frothed at the corner of his lips.

Valdaire looked at Otto. "We could always neurally pattern him.

I'm sure we could effect a quick download through his uplinks. It'll hurt, but it's better than the alternative."

Chures pushed weakly at her arm. "No..." His words came in brief pants, as his increasingly laboured breath would allow. "Don't... make... me... into... one of... them."

"Let him alone," said Otto. He remembered another time, and Honour saying she did not wish to join the ranks of the Neukind. This time he'd listen.

"It's the only way," said Valdaire, "I've got to do it, I can do it," and she began to throw open storage bins in the Stelsco. "I can get an emergency neural pattern, I can. If only..."

Otto grabbed her arm. "He said no."

Chures gasped and he passed out. His skin was white, his lips ashen.

An alarm trilled. "Veev! I'm under assault, help me, Veev!"

Valdaire's mouth dropped open. "I forgot to shut Chloe off!" She pawed at buttons until the trilling of her life companion ceased.

"Well, we've been seen," said Otto, and nodded at the windscreen. Against the grey sky bright points of light glowed, blowtorch flames in the air. They grew larger. Each burned from a jetpack attached to a heavily armoured human figure. "Dragon Fire soldiers," he said. "The Chinese are coming."

CHAPTER FIFTY-FOUR

Richards on the march

Early the next day, Richards' regiment marched to the south gate.

The streets were packed with soldiers. For much of the way Richards could see little but the helmets and spears of the men around him, until the tops of the walls came into sight. Guards walked their circuit. Many watched the horizon for Lord Penumbra's armies, but more than a few had their weapons turned inwards as a spur to patriotic zeal.

The south gate was bigger than the north, five railway lines running through tunnels either side of it. Off to the west of it was a giant goods yard, and here Richards' regiment trooped in and lined up, waiting to be loaded onto waiting trains. Small locomotives doubled up at the front of each, smokestacks puffing smoke into the sulphurous fug over the yard. Trucks were fastened in long lines behind each engine, low-sided and open to the elements, many already crammed with soldiers. There were divisions of foundrymen armed with sledgehammers and wearing thick leather aprons, units of the city guard in enclosing armour, hordes of animals, crews of bobbleheaded sailors, weird blobs and cute robots. Officers, animal, man and otherwise, boarded the few passenger coaches at the front of each train. Richards' unit's turn came and they were directed up onto the freight wagons, helping hands grasping and pulling them up.

The yard was deafening. Engines coughed and whistled. Trucks clattered and banged. Everybody was shouting. The ground was restless under the tread of the army. Men came down the trains' sides, passing up loaves of bread and canteens of water, hallooing as they went. Railway workers followed, slamming up the trucks' sides and locking them with rattling pins. They did not meet the eyes of those who stood within.

With a lusty hoot the first train pulled away in a cloud of steam. A cheer went up from the men and beasts aboard and they struck up a song. This one contained the vanguard of the army, a forward corps of city lancemen and scouts who stood in their trucks with their thog mounts, soothing them as they mooed and stamped their six hoofs.

Another train pulled out, long trucks racked with light artillery, its attendant guards and units of the larger animals riding behind. Then the foundrymen. Time passed, and Richards' mind drifted.

His train's departure took him by surprise. His legs ached from standing still for so long, and he'd nearly gone to sleep, so he started when the engine took up the slack and dragged his train forward inch by squealing inch. A paw took the crook of his elbow, preventing him from falling.

"Steady there, friend!"

Richards found himself looking into the face of a heavily anthropomorphised hare.

"Thanks," he said. "I didn't expect that."

"I know what you mean!" said the hare. "Exciting, isn't it? Oh, how I have long longed to march to war. Imagine, a hare like me smashing Penumbra's evil forces! I am lame and cannot run." He patted a crooked leg. "My brothers and sisters are swift as the wind, and have joined with the scouts. I thought a life of adventure beyond me. But here I am, here I am. The opportunity for glory at last. Here I am!"

Several of the other soldiers had faint smiles, half-daring to imagine victory. A forlorn hope; any division with minimal armour and lame hares as part of its set-up probably did not rate highly in strategic planning, thought Richards. Cannon fodder was the phrase that came to mind. It was quite insulting he'd been assigned to them, really.

"Yeah," said Richards. "Great."

"Friend," said the Hare. "You seem to be uninspired. Think, here you stand, taking the fight to our enemies, allies at your side. Oh, I shall write a poem about this. Yea, a paean to glory." With this he scribbled down some notes in a book he produced from a pocket.

"Sorry," said Richards. "I've a lot on my mind."

"Indeed?" said the hare genially, glancing up from his book. "Pray tell me your troubles. We have a long journey. A burden shared is a burden halved. And it may make a good poem." The train went into the tunnel through the wall, a dark world lit by swirling sparks and choked with sulphurous coal smokes. Richards exited the tunnel coughing, with ears ringing and stinging eyes. The hare was not put off. "Is it some young lady? Some darling you have left behind?" He waggled his eyebrows. "Maybe a leveret or two back home in the hedgerow? We all have worries, my friend. But fear not, we are to be victorious. It is assured by the stars themselves. And what has a brave warrior like you to fear?"

"I don't know," said Richards. "Dying in battle, maybe?"

The hare pounded the truck with his good foot. Quivering, he turned to the others. "How about a rousing song?" he said nervously. He started to sing, but it fell flat. No one joined in. All of them looked at Richards warily.

"Alright," he muttered. "I don't mean to be a killjoy." He turned to look out of the truck.

The hill was higher to the north, and the train proceeded onto a viaduct leading down from the city. A hundred metres of clear air were between Richards and the mined-out ground where the bridge piers rooted themselves. Dense brush cloaked the chasm to the east. The river looked like a ribbon of steel, hammered into perfect loops and laid into a model world.

"Bloody hell, that's a long way down." Richards was feeling a sensation he thought might be vertigo. He didn't like it much.

"Relax," said the hare. "We'll be fine, provided there isn't another earthquake."

"Oh, thank you," said Richards. "Thank you ever so much. That makes me feel so much better." The viaduct went down in a long curve, bringing them closer to the valley edge until it straightened and hit the ground. The chasm looked even deeper from there.

The men and animals of the train made themselves comfortable, sitting on the sides of their trucks or on their knapsacks. Conversations started up.

By the time they had left Pylon City it had been past midday, and the landscape they travelled through was one of afternoon. Bright light diffused through clouds like wire wool, a glare that picked out every pockmark on the land. Slagheaps and open pits ringed with cranes rushed by. Spurs to the railway ran to quarries in the industrial moonscape, where only tufts of colourless grass, lank and sparse as hag's hair, thrived.

"It is horrible, is it not?" said the hare.

"It is," agreed Richards, tapping his fingers on the truck.

"It appears we are heading off the plateau," said the hare, "to bring Lord Penumbra to battle where the land slopes into the Broken Lands, a fine defensible position. It will prevent any advance by Penumbra up the canyon, and ensure that Jotenland, the source of much of Pylon City's food, is protected."

"Sounds good. Always stake out a hill."

"Ah, you know a little military theory?" asked the hare eagerly.

"No, not really," admitted Richards. He normally did, but in reality it was all on the Grid, so he supposed he only thought he knew it. There was so much he did not know while the network was denied to him. "My partner does all that."

"Well," said the hare, "this is of course only my supposition, but it is the most sensible course of action. I have studied many of the great generals of Pylon City and the long war poems," it said shyly.

"Odd hobby for a hare," said Richards.

"Many of my brothers and sisters revel in the wild chase and the feel of the wind in their whiskers, but this pleasure is denied me. So I developed interests outside of the ordinary." It paused. "Like poetry." It looked at Richards expectantly.

"If that's one of those 'ask me to read you one of my poems' type expressions that poets hopefully get. I'm going to have to disappoint you," said Richards. The hare became bashful and turned away.

The ruined world changed piece by piece to a landscape of scrubby fields. The clouds cleared. The train passed close by rough dwellings, hugely tall with doors three times bigger than a man, their walls made of enormous boulders. Jotenland, Richards presumed, but of the Jotens, there was no sign.

The sun set. The sky above the train remained a pure light-blue for a time, and the men gambled at knucklebones until it was truly dark, then they settled down to sleep.

Richards tried as best he could to get comfortable in the limited space available to him to lie down. He watched the alien sky. Away from the glare of Pylon City's sodium lamps, the stars twinkled brightly, competing with the sparks the train pumped into the night.

"A river of fire," said the hare sleepily. "It is a river of fire, and it is consuming the world."

In the morning they woke to war.

CHAPTER FIFTY-FIVE

Little Wars

"Troopers!" A shout roused Richards from where he sat on the motionless train, bored, staring out over the plains. "Prepare to disembark!"

"Now there's a man who enjoys his job," said Richards. His limbs cracked with unpleasant organic noises as he stood. He'd barely moved since he'd woken, and now felt as brittle as a straw doll. There was more to a human's constant, twitchy motion than staying upright, he was learning, like not letting their irritating organic insides seize up.

The soldiers debarked from the trucks to join a stream of marching troops.

"Right, my sleeping beauties," said their sergeant. "We are going to go for a walk."

"Why have we stopped sergeant?" someone asked.

"Word has come down that the line has been blown ahead by Penumbra's saboteurs," the sergeant explained. "All you lot should think on how nice and healthy you'll be once you've walked. Who knows, there might even be time for a spot of breakfast before the war starts."

"Really, sarge?" said an eager trooper.

"No!" roared the sergeant. "Now get a bleedin' move on, or I'll shoot you myself and save Penumbra and his monsters the bother."

They got off the train, and Richards fell into step with something like a rat. It gave him a filthy look.

"Charming," said Richards.

Richards thought it time to leave now, and find his way on to his goal, but he saw no opportunity to turn aside. Every movement to edge of the column saw him pushed back to the middle. He realised, with not a little irritation, that he was going to have to fight again.

The day was the kind autumn used to share with summer, a cold morning with the promise of a hot afternoon. The sky was a uniform grey, its light joyless. Ahead it turned to an angry black, a thick band of deeper cloud foreshortening the horizon. Bursts of lightning lit it from within, thunder answered by tremors from below the earth.

"Look!" said the rat. "A storm!"

"That's not a storm," said the hare with some amount of awe. "That is the death of the world. The Great Terror. I must record it in my poem."

"Quiet in the ranks there! You can all have a natter after you've had a battle," bawled the sergeant. "Until then, keep your cakeholes shut."

They walked five abreast alongside the railway, then turned away from the track onto a featureless plain of grass. There were no farms, nor mines, only one small building of red-brick, about a mile from the route of their march.

"Last Station," said the Hare. "The last bastion of civilisaton."

"Where does the line go after that?" asked Richards.

"Back home, to the Magic Wood," said the hare.

The familiar odour of burnt ground rose into the air. There was a chorus of mutters and shouts from ahead.

"Will this be the fortune of the Magic Wood?"

"And the city?"

There was an abrupt change in scenery, the plateau ending in a thick scar where two world fragments clumsily joined. Beyond it lay a plain criss-crossed with crooked ravines and gullies, giving the landscape the look of an angular brain.

It was scorched black. Charcoal trees clawed at the sky, the gullies steamed, the grass was burnt down to the roots.

"The broken lands, twice broken!" said the hare.

The army marched onto the brow of the hill and fanned out, directed in columns to their positions. The centre of their battleline was a low blister in the slope. Commander Hedgehog and his best warriors had already taken up station there, surrounded by flag bearers. A mix of large forest animals armoured head to toe surrounded him and his staff. Behind this position were the army's artillery pieces, globular balls of crystal sporting long brass barrels. They looked spectacularly dangerous.

"See!" whispered the hare from behind Richards. "Hedgehog has the men of the city at the heart of the army. He is guarded by the Big Animal Division and the City Guard. They have lightning cannon, terrible weapons. I should expect we will be stationed out on one of the flanks, behind a skirmish line of lancers. When the enemy breaks through them, range will no longer matter, and we will be able to put our swords and spears to deadly use at close quarters!"

The hare was mostly right. The Pylon Guard were few in number, so Richards' regiment was stationed behind a line of arbalesteers. These crossbowmen were not of Pylon City and wore colourful clothes at odds with the Pylonites' sober garb. Their forms were not so well rendered, relics of an ancient game, their language a musical tongue Richards did not recognise. Protecting their right flank was a detachment of foundrymen. Further out roamed groups of skirmishers backed up by squadrons of light cavalry.

"They'll stop anything getting round the back," the hare explained enthusiastically. "Or, when we break the enemy's line, force it apart like a wedge."

"You're enjoying this far too much," muttered Richards.

From behind came a rhythmic clatter. Armoured weasels, well over a thousand of them, marched to fill the gap in the allied lines to Richards' left. They wore scale and plate, articulated to accommodate their sinuous bodies. Each carried a pike and a steel buckler with a spiked boss. Blood-red pennants fluttered from helmets and shields and streamed from the ends of their weapons.

"Aren't they glorious?" whispered the hare in awe.

Richards raised an eyebrow. "Don't weasels eat hares?"

"They do indeed," said the hare, nodding, not rising to the bait. "And I know I should not admire them, for a pack of them did devour a sister of mine. But still, all that is behind us now, now we are part of the League of Humans and Small but Brave Animals!"

"Wow," said Richards wearily. "That's snappy."

"How could we fail to lose with such ferocious beings at our sides? A thousand armoured weasels, each a born killer. Glorious!"

"Yeah," said Richards, remembering their behaviour in the bar. "And each a born weasel."

Richards had time to experience the boredom part of the boredom and terror war offered men. The army stood in their position for several hours, and once again he became uncomfortable. He was debating taking a piss right there when the hare spoke again.

"Oh my!" said the hare. "Here they come!"

The sky went dark. A hush came over the host of men and beasts. The enemy army approached. Shadow preceded it, and darkness followed.

The horde of creatures came from the south, appearing over a ridge three miles away, drawing toward them with unnatural speed.

"Oh my," said the hare again, now with a tinge of fear. "There are rather a lot of them, aren't there?"

In the main the army was composed of vile-looking humanoids. Like the alliance, creatures brought from all manner of places on the Grid.

"Every hero needs his mob," said Richards grimly, doing a quick calculation on the balance between heroic human players and system-controlled monsters in your average game. The odds he came up with were unfavourable. Not for the first time he wondered how the hell he'd ended up in this mess, and decided to blame Hughie.

Smoke curled from robotic haemites. Immense war-beasts studded the horde like rocks on a polluted beach. Steam-powered towers, bristling with cannon, crawled across the broken lands on caterpillar tracks. Around these marched monstrous trollmen, swishing tree-trunk clubs as they walked.

"Look!" said the hare, his lips wobbling with fear. "Morblins! There... There must be over five thousand of them! And daibeasts. And, by Lord Frith, that is a low-dweller. A low-dweller!" An unpleasant chant filled the air, a droning that made Richards' skin crawl. An oily reek descended across the battlefield, the exhaust of engines, steam, the stink of unwashed bodies.

Nearby, one of the soldiers began to cry.

"Shut it, you," said the sergeant, but there was a tremor in his voice.

The front rank of what Richards took to be morblins, small, pot-bellied, grey-skinned creatures, had a great many armoured hounds amidst it. The largest morblins held onto the leashes of these dogs, who half-dragged them towards the allied lines.

The enemy stopped, facing off against the league.

Silence fell. Thunder rumbled. Pennants cracked in the wind.

A trumpet blew. There was a howl as the dogs were set loose, and they rushed across the plains, baying.

"Steady, Richards, steady," Richards told himself. The rush of fear his human facsimile provided him was powerful.

The commander of the arbalesteers shouted, and the first rank readied themselves. Two hundred heavy crossbows clicked into place on their rests. The men waited, their arms steady, their gaze unwavering. The commander held his arm. The hounds came on.

"Company!" called Richards' sergeant. "Present arms!" Richards cursed his quaking limbs as he fumbled his spear into place.

"This is where it all begins, my friend," said the hare behind him. "Wish me luck."

The arbalesteer captain dropped his arm, and the world dissolved into violence.

Two hundred barbed quarrels sped unerringly. The yelps of two hundred dogs filled the air.

A shout went up from the morblins, and they broke into a run towards the allied lines, with trollmen beside them, the ground thundering as they came. The lancers of Pylon City discharged their weaponry into the front of the horde, filling the air with electricity. Hundreds of the enemy fell, burnt to cinders, but there were thousands more behind. The lancemen parted ranks, and with a mighty squeak a horde of rodent mercenaries, the vanguard of the League of Brave but Small Animals, hurled themselves through the gap towards the approaching morblins. There was a crash as the lines connected.

The lancemen reformed smoothly and pumped bolt after bolt of cerulean energy into the rear ranks of the horde, picking out the larger creatures as the valiant animals held back the enemy. By Richards the foreign crossbowmen fired by rank a rain of quarrels. The dead of the enemy tumbled in heaps.

The enemy artillery opened up. Shells whistled overhead from the tracked towers of Penumbra. Dozens slammed into the packed lines of the alliance. Screams filled the air. Earth and blood fountained skywards and body parts rained down. Groups of the more timid animals looked close to dissolving in panic.

"Eyes front, soldier!" shouted the sergeant at Richards.

The allied big guns replied. Heavy lightning burned through the air, leaving glowing after-images and a sharp smell. Iron towers burst into flame. One carried on moving forward, a track blown clean off. It heeled over ponderously, and crashed down, crushing hundreds of its own side. The allied lightning cannon raked bloody furrows in the horde, but the enemy numbers seemed inexhaustible.

The arbalesteers kept firing as the enemy closed, ignoring the desperate fights of their comrades with the surviving warhounds. The corpses of morblins and trollmen lay five deep, but the enemy were so numerous that they kept on coming, fifty metres away, then thirty, then twenty. The arbalesteers shot until the foe were on top of them. Richards saw one go down screaming under a clanking robotic haemite, his body sucked dry with a touch. More haemites followed, and the sounds of blades on metal bodies rang out across the field as the arbalesteers abandoned their crossbows and drew their short swords.

Then it was Richards' turn.

"Steady, lads!" barked the sergeant. "Here they come!"

The earth shook under the weight of a wedge of trollmen charging behind the haemites. The line of arbalesteers bent backwards, wavered and broke. The trollmen were twice the height of a human, and surged through in one and twos and then by the dozen. They flung themselves at the line of men, flattening many. Richards' arm juddered as a bellowing creature impaled itself on his spear.

"Watch out!" shouted the hare.

Richards jumped back as another trollman swung at him, leaving his spear in the guts of his toppling foe. He ducked a hammer blow, narrowly keeping his footing. The trollman tugged its mallet from the ground and readied his weapon for another strike. Richards had nowhere to go, hemmed in by the dead and those desperate not to be. He braced for the end, but a blast of lightning felled the trollman, leaving Richards gasping and covered in stinking black blood. Limbs and blades whirled around him.

A morblin cannoned into him. It was as weak as its fat body suggested, and he managed to snatch out his sword and despatch it. Richards looked at his weapon, slick and treacherous in his hands, then at the creatures from innumerable virt-games warring in deadly earnest all around him, the violent deaths of scores of talking animals and gaming clichés.

"This is fucking ridiculous," Richards said.

The world disappeared behind a sheet of white. Richards stumbled, blood in his eyes, hearing gone. He blinked and found himself in a lull in the fighting.

Bodies lay all about. A ruddy shell crater garnished with the limbs of friend and foe occupied the space where the centre of his regiment had been. A lucky few stood blinking, covered in blood. They stared at one another, shocked, lost somewhere between surprise and relief.

Richards staggered, his head spinning. Shouting, loud and frantic, impinged on the ringing in his ears. Away to his right, a knot of surprised troops yelled as the weasels attacked them from behind.

Richards wiped the blood of his comrades from his face. His head cleared. "I've got to get out of here," he said, and cast about for a means of escape.

A paw grabbed him, spinning him round. The lame hare, one of his ears a tatter.

"Where are you going? Fleeing is the blackest treason..."

"I..." said Richards.

The hare held up a hand to remonstrate. It was the last thing it ever did. A cannonball whistled by, a gust of hard wind stirring Richards' hair. It removed the hare's head neatly. Blood fountained from its neck, splattering Richards, and the hare folded onto its lame leg like a collapsible chair.

Richards stumbled back, caught sight of a stray riding thog and ran for it. He grabbed its reins and swung atop. It lowed angrily and stamped its six legs, but held fast. He tugged on its reins, dragging its head around, and the animal performed a tight circle.

Fighting raged all about. There was no way out.

"Dammit! What do I do now?"

He spun the mount round again. There was little chance he'd get off the field intact, not with the weasels butchering their way through their own side all around him. "OK," he said, "OK. The centre. Let's get to the centre. Tell them about the weasels." He kicked with his heels, and the animal took off.

Shells exploded to the left of Richards, to the right of him, reducing the battle to a series of violent tableaux, surging into view and then lost in veils of gunsmoke and sheets of earth.

Three half-naked anime heroines baited a trollman with spears. A band of otters in lab coats tackled a purple octopus covered in smilies. Men rolled in the dirt with morblins, dodging the thrusts of filthy knives. Haemites fed on friend and foe alike, their whistles an industrial dirge. Here and there, disciplined pockets of men and beasts formed tight groups, spearpoint and blade keeping the Penumbra's minions at bay. But every enemy felled was replaced by four more. Gone were the proud ranks; the field writhed with small and personal wars, all thoughts of strategy obscured by blood and sweat and terror. Creatures came at Richards to fall to his sword or bounce from the flanks of the six-legged cow, their cries snatched away by speed and steel.

Richards hammered toward the centre, where the disciplined corps of hedgehogs stood firm. Heavily armoured in burnished steel, they surrounded the Lord High Commander's command post, which turned out to be an enormous tortoise with "Roger" painted in childish script on its shell.

Atop Roger was a howdah of metal. Telescopes and small lightning cannon were fixed to the rails. One gunner lay dead in the harness of his shattered weapon, but the others trained theirs still upon the enemy, spikes of electricity writhing periodically through the air. On a seat on the lip of Roger's shell sat another hedgehog holding a set of metal reins. It flicked a whip about the tortoise's head. Roger seemed unperturbed. Through his helm's eye-slits, he pondered the bloodbath with the slow bemusement with which tortoises regard everything.

"Lord High Commander Hedgehog!" yelled Richards, leaping off his mount. He bounded up the low steps to the howdah, and was promptly accosted by two burly guards.

"Who are you?" growled one. "Where did you get that thog?"

"Some kind of assassin," snuffled the other. Blades scraped as they drew out their daggers.

"I have urgent news for the Lord High Commander," insisted Richards.

"No one allowed up here but general staff," yelled the hedgehog over the noise of an exploding shell. "Push off."

"Let him through, let him through," said the voice of Hedgehog. "I will see him." The bodyguards stepped aside, and Richards was afforded a view of the Lord High Commander. His visor was up, since he had been conferring with his aides, and as Richards

501

approached he snapped shut an elegant telescope. "Well?" said Hedgehog. "What is it, human? Speak, then be gone."

"The weasels, the weasels have turned against us."

"I see," said Hedgehog, his voice several degrees cooler. "They are rolling up the right flank?"

"Right now."

"Jolly good. All goes to plan, then."

"What?" said Richards.

"The weasels, you see," said Lord High Commander Hedgehog, "work for me."

"Ah."

"'Ah' indeed. Those short-sighted fools in Pylon City could not see the advantage to be had from forming an alliance with Penumbra. Though we argued the case with them, they would not favour the idea. Penumbra was more than happy to entertain our unilateral offer. The Pylonites will die. Our aeons-long struggle with Pylon City will be over, and the Magic Wood will survive the Great Terror, forever free of the tyranny of men and their machines."

"That's cold," said Richards. "Your people are dying in droves."

"Rather unfortunate, that. Still, means there won't be much opposition when I take over the Wood, will there? With Lord Penumbra's blessing, of course."

"You stupid rodent," said Richards. "He's tricked you into fighting his war for him."

Hedgehog smiled. "I have never lost a battle. As long as there has been an army of the Magic Wood there has been a Lord High Commander Hedgehog, and as long as that has been so, there have been no defeats. This battle tortoise, Roger, was my father's mount, before that my grandfather's, my great-great-grandfather's. He has never witnessed a battle in which he was not upon the winning side. How else do you think he can remain so phlegmatic, eh? I have two hundred years of victory at my back and you, some man, tell me I am wrong? Pfah! Let the whole of the Earth thunder to the tramping of iron-shod paws, for I will rule it all." Hedgehog cackled maniacally. Two hedgehogs stepped forward. "Make him kneel." The hedgehogs forced Richards down. The Lord High Commander loomed over him. "Any last words?" He unhitched his lightning-pistol.

"I'm not going to beg," said Richards.

"I am not so crass as to expect begging!" scoffed the hedgehog. "I was rather hoping for some brave witticism. Stiff upper lip and all, wot? Pity."

"You're making a terrible mistake."

"Yes, yes," said the hedgehog. "Goodbye."

Richards stared down the crystal at the end of the gun.

"Balls," he said, and screwed his eyes tight. No shot came. Roger let out a croak of fear and reared up. There was a sound of the snapping of chain and the wrenching of metal. Richards fell, the howdah came free of Roger's shell and broke into pieces and, scattering hedgehogs and Richards on the blackened ground. He rolled to avoid the tortoise's foot as Roger ran at some speed away from the source of his horror, squashing two of Hedgehog's bodyguards flat and leaving them oozing in the dust. The rest of Hedgehog's guard picked themselves up, looked behind them, faltered then followed the tortoise in rout.

Richards looked back, and his own heart froze. Over the supine body of Lord High Commander Hedgehog was Lord Penumbra.

Penumbra sat atop a beast that was half-horse, half-dragon. It pawed at the earth with clawed hooves. Its skin was a coat of scales, its face a snarl of night-black violence, its eyes those of a cat, its tail a serpent's head. It radiated a deep chill, pinning Richards' breath to the air in clouds of frost. Black vapours curled around it, stealing the light away. Penumbra himself was nebulous and black, his shadow form clad in armour of jet.

The battlefield grew quiet, sound stilled by Penumbra's presence. The sky roiled with the storm of the world-death.

"Hedgehog," rang out a sepulchral voice. "Hedgehog, I come with your reward. Rule in my name. Death shall be thy kingdom."

Richards could not look directly at Penumbra, try as he might. His bright darkness blinded him.

"N- No, my lord," said Hedgehog. "We have an arrangement." He shook. No longer the proud warlord, he was now just a big fat rodent in a complicated tin suit.

"Death," bellowed Penumbra. His mount reared, its whinnying the end of flowers. Grass wilted all around it. "Death, low field-beast, you would seek to deal with me? Where is your honour, where is your side of the bargain? Where is Queen Isabella?" He roared, a long sound of discordant ferocity. "Fool!"

"No, no," squealed Hedgehog, falling to his knees. "Please, I looked, I tried!"

Penumbra drew a pillar of black flame as he would a sword. His arm extended, distorted like a shadow, the weapon stretching impossibly towards the hedgehog. A shaft of blackness struck out from it, piercing Hedgehog's chest.

Hedgehog ceased to be. Shadow became light and light shadow. He became a negative of sooty grains. Hedgehog dissipated, pulled into the sword, his thin scream remaining in the air, the scream all small animals make in pain, nothing more.

Richards felt his stomach turn to water as Penumbra's faceplate swivelled toward him. "And now you. You and your ilk are a blight on this land."

The shadow-blade extended out, its tip burning Richards with its cold. As it came, reality warped around it, and Richards was struck by a thought. Well, two thoughts.

The first was that reality was warping around the blade, turning glassy and spinning off sub-universes that popped like soap bubbles on the charred grass.

Secondly, Richards could not hear k52's Gridsig at all.

His eyes narrowed.

"Bollocks," he said. "I thought you were k52."

Something came swiftly from the left. There was a roar, the sound of metal hitting metal. The ground heaved. He fell up into the air, and came back down. He found himself lying in a smoking crater, soil pattering off him. His vision swam. An iron monster reached down with long claws to pluck the last of his life from him.

That was all his facsimiled mind could take, and he slipped into unconsciousness.

CHAPTER FIFTY-SIX

The Valley

A squeaking grind penetrated the fog in Richards' mind. He decided
he found it annoying, but his irritation was quickly forgotten as
the sensation of pain returned to him. He hurt all over. He lay
there, not daring to move, eyes shut until a jolt through whatever
he lay on brought more pain and caused them to jump open.

He pulled himself onto his elbows and tried not to whimper.

He was on a pump wagon. Bear stood at one end of the
mechanism, methodically pushing it up and down with one paw,
struggling out of his armour as he did so.

"You're back!" shouted Bear, his voice muffled by a breastplate
stuck to his face. He wrenched it over his head, and tossed it overboard.
"Damn uncomfortable that was. Who ever heard of a bear in armour?
Ridiculous. But I'm keeping these." He held up a paw encased in a
heavy gauntlet. There was a rasp of metal, and four blades popped
out of the back of it. "Good, eh?" said Bear. "They're a lot sharper than
my own, and now I need never worry about breaking a nail in a fight
again."

Richards tried to sit up.

"Steady, sunshine!" said Bear, and the squeaking slowed. "Don't
do anything silly."

Richards looked over the side of the pump wagon, which
appeared to be flying through the air.

"We're on the bridge between the plateau and the Magic Wood. You don't want to fall, so play it cool." Bear grinned. "I thought we'd lost you back there, sunshine. It all got a bit hairy. Nobody escaped. They were cut down to a field mouse."

"I don't believe this," said Richards and lay back down. "Why me?"

"Don't be like that. I got us out of there, didn't I?" said Bear.

Richards sat up properly. His chest hurt like hell.

"Ouch!"

"Shrapnel wound. A scratch, so don't worry," said Bear. Richards lifted up his shirt. There was a red line across his lower chest. It had been expertly stitched. "Like that? That's my work. As was finding this pump wagon at Last Station. You have to get up pretty early in the morning to catch this bear! I figured we'd head west. Did I do good?"

"You did good," said Richards.

"Damn right I did," said Bear.

Richards found his knapsack. He pulled out his macintosh, unrolled it and, still wincing, put it on. It was damp and horrible from when he'd washed it, but better than nothing. Next he withdrew the fedora Spink had summoned up, smacked it against his hand to get it into shape and placed it on his head. It made him feel complete, and the pain subsided a little.

"I should have asked for a new suit too," he said, looking at his tattered Pylon City uniform.

They crossed the valley and went into the domain of the Magic Wood. Seeing it, Richards understood why the animals hated the Pylonites. Swathes of trees had been clear-felled, logs stacked neatly next to charcoal burners where the the soft green of the forest had been scraped right down to raw yellow clay. Pits of tainted water pooled behind earthen dams. Weather-bleached stumps lay on their sides, their roots contorted in woody agony. Railway tracks ran deeper into the forest, each an ugly wound.

They saw no men, but startled bizarre creatures, humanoid things that had tiny bodies topped by enormous heads of bright scarlet. They had sharply pointed beards, round pink lips and high foreheads covered in subcutaneous lumps. They stared as the wagon passed, then fled into the trees.

Richards shared his meagre army rations with Bear and fell into a black sleep. When he woke he was more stiff than sore. It was evening, and the forest had thinned, dotted with dappled glades made by a kinder hand than that of man. The trees retreated into huddles, until they were rolling at a leisurely pace across a heath where limestone pavements grinned like teeth through lips of gorse. The sun was warm and soothing.

They came to a place where a road crossed the line, and here Bear was obliged to apply the brakes. There was a man in the way.

The man said nothing as the pump wagon squealed to a stop half a metre from him. He was ragged and unwashed, his beard and hair unkempt. He was wringing his hands. His head juddered, an old-style film caught on the same run of frames playing over and over again.

"Ah, poor bastard," said Bear, jumping down. "Stuck. The bit of land maintaining him must have gone. I hate it when this happens. Best to go out in an instant, not like this."

The man's voice stuttered. "Du... du... du... du... du..."

Bear grabbed him and hauled him off his feet. He remained frozen. "Hurgh!" grunted Bear, "death is heavy." He wrinkled his nose. "Goldilocks' knickers, he smells worse than Lucas, must have been here for some time. They still live, in a way. Horrible." He placed the man gently by the track.

The bear clambered onto the pump wagon. "This k52 is a real bastard. Killing us is one thing, killing us like this is abominable," he said.

"Hmmm," said Richards, drumming his fingers on the side of the pump. The wagon pulled away, leaving the man to his slow end.

"'Hmmm'? What does that mean?" said Bear. "You don't agree?"

"Oh, I agree alright," said Richards.

"So?" said the bear.

"So nothing," Richards said, and kept his thoughts to himself.

* * *

The cart went on through the night. Richards sat and thought and listened to the sound of the rocker. Up and down, squeak and squeak. Up and down. The wheels went clack-clack-clack and Richards thought of Lord Penumbra, and of k52. He thought about just how painful and annoying being human was.

And he thought about Rolston.

A bump shook him out of his contemplation as they crossed a join in the land. A brown scar divided the heath from desert, the join sparking where the coding did not mesh. The desert sloped steeply and at the end it dropped away to nothing over a bluff, the track plunging with it.

"Oh bugger!" said Bear, his eyes goggling comically. "I didn't see that, we're going to go over." He grabbed the brake lever and leaned all his weight onto it, straining out over the back of the wagon. "Shitshitshitshitshitshit! I can't hold it!" The pump mechanism pounded up and down as they picked up speed. Wind rushed past. Richards was obliged to clutch his fedora to his head.

"Jump," shouted Richards.

"We're going too fast," said Bear.

They hit the cliff edge and the track plunged down like a rollercoaster.

"Great hairy grizzlies! Hold on!" shouted Bear, as sparks fountained out behind them. Richards dodged past the bouncing pump and added his strength to Bear's own. "Pull hard! It's the only way!"

"There's a curve ahead," shouted Richards.

"Lean," roared Bear. He and Richards leaned as the wagon hit the curve. The small vehicle went up onto two wheels and slammed down as the way straightened.

"That was too close," said Bear.

"We'll be smashed to bits if we don't slow down," said Richards.

The brake lever grew hot to the touch as the brake shoe burned off.

"Curve!" Bear cried. The truck slalomed round another bend. Again they leant into it, the wheels rattling as they bounced off and on the tracks. "We're not going to survive another like that," shouted Bear over the clatter of the truck. "We may have to jump."

Richards looked down over the edge. They were hundreds of metres up. "We're still too high."

The smell of hot metal strengthened as Bear and Richards strained hard on the lever. A fountain of red-hot iron filings billowed up around them, singeing Bear's fur, The toy pulled with all his might. For a moment, it looked like it was working. The truck slowed. But then there was a dull clunk and they sprawled backwards, Richards narrowly avoided being brained by the pump handles.

Bear held up the bent remains of the lever. "Uh-oh, I broke the brake. Hold on!"

Richards grasped the pump wagon deck, fingernails pulling on the wood. Bear tucked the man under his bulk. "I'll cushion you when we crash," he said.

The truck accelerated towards the desert. The track levelled out, but Richards figured that the height did not matter that much now, as the speed they were going would kill them all. Faster and faster they went. The slope bottomed, and they thundered on, the desert a blur of sand and sky.

"Oh no," shouted Bear.

"Jesus Christ," said Richards.

It was the end of the line in no uncertain way. A hard wooden buffer raced at them. The pump wagon smashed into it, and they were thrown into the air. Bear clasped Richards tightly to him as they flew. Fur, sand and sky turned over and over. There was a thump. A drift of sand. Then silence.

"Ow," said Bear. "Ow ow ow." Richards was winded, but alive. He patted Bear's ample belly.

"Thanks," he said. "You're a very useful bear."

"Ow, get off," said Bear. They got to their feet. Bent iron and splinters were strewn everywhere. "Oooh," said Bear, clutching his back.

"Oh well, it appears that we have arrived somewhere," said Richards.

"Eh?" said Bear.

"There," said Richards. He pointed to low bluff pierced by a narrow opening between two natural pillars of sandstone. Above it, a large sign of weather-worn bronze bearing a legend. It read: *La Valle dei Promesse persa.*

"What does it say, what does it say?" asked Bear.

"The Valley of Lost Promises," said Richards. "In Italian. Now that is interesting."

"I wish you'd stop saying that," said Bear.

The valley started as a canyon and quickly became a crevasse. A sandy path wound between down between walls of rock, so narrow in places that Bear had to force himself through sideways. They descended, and the sky became a stripe.

They paused for a rest toward noon, and when they set off once more the path widened. Thorny plants that reeked of creosote lined the margins.

The canyon broadened into a scrubby valley. A stream ran though a dry riverbed many times its width. Cliffs ran on either side, their feet hidden by cubes of fallen rock. In the centre a mesa rose, flat top level with the desert. It split the river bed, but it was dry and only one channel carried a trickle of water past it.

Every available patch of ground was covered in the thorny bushes, smothering sand-dunes and holding fast the scree. Rising up from this painful thicket were hundreds of statues, all of the same woman in many different poses. On all, her face was beatific, generous, a little sad.

The largest was so big its head and shoulders cleared the canyon to stand glowing in the desert sun above. She looked down upon them in an art nouveau style, a single tear of bronze on her face, as if the artist had allowed white-hot metal to run down her cheek. Her bare feet were on point like a ballerina, the whole edifice balanced unreally on a plinth the height of Bear.

"Queen Isabella!" said Bear softly. "They're all statues of the queen. So this is where they all ended up."

"I saw an empty plinth in town," said Richards.

Bear nodded. "They were everywhere, and then they weren't. Then news came that Queen Isabella had gone and then the war started. What are they all doing here?"

"Looks like they've been dumped. There are statue graveyards like this back in the Real, victims of regime changes."

"Eh?" said Bear.

"Never mind," said Richards.

The path went past statues of verdigrised bronze, marble, steel, and modern stacked carbon plastics. The thorns choked everything, swallowing the smaller statues, clutching at the hips of the greater.

"Hang on a minute," said Richards. He pushed through the bushes toward a statue, sharp breaths and expletives preceding him as thorns snagged at his legs. He stopped, pushed back his hat and leaned in closer. "There's something on this one." He peered through a lattice of thorn and twig. A plaque was upon the statue's plinth. He couldn't read it until he moved some of the vegetation aside.

"Isabella," he said, "that's the queen's name?"

"Yep," said Bear.

"Right," said Richards. "Not Marita?"

"No. Isabella. Why?"

"A theory, that's all," said Richards.

They went on and rounded the mesa. Ahead there was a cave, nestling in the apex of the triangle where the valley walls drew together in a curtain of rock. The river issued from the cave, gurgling over its lower lip. Mosses and ferns grew on the knoll above it. A rich scent of damp earth came from within.

Richards looked up. The cliffs around them were sheer. He looked at the sun and pointed at the cave. "If this place follows the normal rules, that way is west. We go in."

They abandoned the path and took to the river, splashing up to the cave mouth. Richards paused at the lip; the cave was dark. He waited for his eyes to adjust. They didn't.

Bear took a big drink from the stream and pushed past Richards, wiping his muzzle on a long hairy arm. "Come on then. If we're going in, let's not hang about."

Richards followed. Darkness enveloped them, Bear became a dull shape bobbing in the gloom. Water sloshed round his ankles.

"Hang on a minute," said Bear, the grey smear of his back stopping. He bent down in the dark. "It goes down a bit he…"

There was a splash, and Bear disappeared.

"Bear? Bear!" Richards shouted. "Are you in there, big buddy?"

Richards went a little way further, willing his eyes to see more, but all he could make out were blobs that might have been rocks and a darkness that had to be deep water. "He's complete… woah!" Something took tight hold of his ankle and yanked him. He bounced off a rock, went under very deep water and lost his breath in an explosion of bubbles. Down he went, thrashing in the dark, lungs burning. Panic set in. Real fear as he'd never felt it before, primal and all-consuming. He battered at the pressure on his leg with his fists, hitting rubbery flesh. He dug his fingers in as hard as he could. His lungs burned. He had to fight the urge to suck in lungfuls of water as he clawed at the thing on his ankle.

Light shone up from below. Whatever had hold of his leg let go. He fought for the surface, wheeling his arms, primitive parts of his fake brain telling him to get up, up! But the current had him, and his attempts to swim made his lungs burn worse. Spots danced in the dark. He swirled head over heels, toward the light.

He popped through a hole along with a torrent of water issuing from the underside of a sheet of rock. Air touched his face, his lips exploded open, and he sucked in a breath.

Nothing had ever felt so good. The feeling did not last when he realised he was falling.

"What the hell?" Richards' face was pushed tight against his skull. He clutched hard at his hat but it was torn from his hand.

The fall of water turned to droplets, then a rainbow mist carried off by the wind, and he was in cold, cold sky. Below him clouds arrayed themselves with deceptive solidity. In the gaps was a patchwork world in miniature, stark contrasts evident between each slab of stolen terrain. He saw seas behind walls, and nations built of plastic bricks. Cities like pearls in the distance, some afire with war.

It would have been beautiful, if the ground hadn't been rushing at him with such deadly speed.

"Ah shit," he said, the words wrenched from his mouth by the wind.

A dirty white blob preceded him; the bear, rolling over and over in the sky.

The clouds below parted. A silver lake spread below him. Though it was fuzzy with mist, the surface was bright as a mirror.

"How do humans do this? How do humans do this?" he gabbled. "I'm at terminal velocity. I can survive." He was lying to himself, just like a real boy.

Still, he had to try. He wrapped his legs around each other to prevent water being fatally forced into his innards, blew out his breath to collapse his lungs, clamped his arms to his side. He fell and fell, and awaited impact, his eyes screwed tight shut.

He slowed, inexplicably coming down like a drifting feather. He opened his eyes and looked down. He was coming in for the most gentle of landings. His feet broke the surface of the lake with barely a ripple, and he found himself deposited in water that was barely ankle deep.

His hat floated down, and landed right next to him, crown up in the water. He snatched it up, his feet sending tiny, sluggish waves across the silver water. The mist made things was hazy, and he could not see far.

"Bear!" He shouted. His voice echoed in the mist. "Bear!"

His voice disturbed the air as his feet disturbed the water, almost visibly, rippling words spreading away from him.

He heard a groan. He sloshed forward. Bear was lying on his

back, tummy pointed to the sky, like a small hairy island.

"That," Bear said emphatically, "is quite enough falling for now."

His voice stirred the air more than Richards's did. The mist shivered back, revealing first a pylon, rooted in the lake, then far distant an inverted mountain balanced on its peak, splayed roots held up to the sky. The edge of the world was not far from their position, judging by the roar of water falling, and the black vapours rising from one end of the horizon to the other.

"Oh boy," Bear said. "We're almost there." He got up, his squelching hide dripping water. He pointed an iron claw. "That there is the anvil, the home of Lord Hog." He scratched under his helmet. "Question is, how do we get in?"

Richards looked at the pylon and the cable running from it. The line swooped off to another pylon many miles away, then to another, then another, finally reaching the mountain itself. He saw a box ascending the rope many miles away.

"Let's hitch a ride," Richards said.

CHAPTER FIFTY-SEVEN

A burial

The Chinese dug a grave for Chures. The ground at the old lakeshore was full of pine roots, and yet the troopers digging the grave did so with their armour stripped off. They sweated in the cold air, hacking and shovelling away stolidly, using only their bodies' strength.

"In deference to the dead," the troops' leader told Otto through too-smooth machine translation. "The dead should depart watched over by men, not machines."

He'd been equally courteous when his soldiers surrounded the Stelsco, flipping his helmet into the broad back of his power-assist armour and introducing himself as Commander Guan Song Hsien. Apparently, Chures' people had managed to arrange some kind of agreement with the Chinese, and Hsien was to escort them. They were prisoners, for all that, and the other Dragon Fire soldiers remained in their armour behind Otto's group, trying not to look like there were covering Lehmann, Valdaire and Otto with their weapons.

"Would that rule Lehmann and me out of the burial party?"

Commander Guan looked uncomfortable. He had skin dark for a Han. His ancestors probably hailed from one of the many nations absorbed by the Chinese state at some point in its millennia-long history. The People's Dynasty government hated the word empire, but that was what China was, and always had been.

"I apologise. We have no enhanced such as you in the People's Dynasty. I am unsure as to what the Tenets of Balance would say on this matter, and I am ignorant of the customs of your homeland." Before Commander Hsien's speech was translated into English, now his suit chose to change Mandarin into German. The translation was swift and flawless, if emotionally bland, and seemed at times to anticipate what Hsien was going to say, which spoke of some level of mind interface, and that made Otto wonder if China really was AI free. "However, to allow you access even to a spade would present an unacceptable tactical risk. We are aware of your capabilities. The excavation may take some time. You may sit and watch if you wish, but do not move. The accord brokered by the VIPA between our governments is a temporary one, and I have been given strict orders as to how you are to be dealt with should you not follow my instructions."

I'll bet you have, thought Otto. He did not sit down.

Otto watched his captors from the corner of his eye, allowing his adjutant to run over their specifications. The Dragon Fire troops had updated their equipment since Otto fought them in the war, but though lighter, and sleeker, it remained roughly the same, comprised of thick, all encompassing jointed plates, smooth lines marred by quick release bolts. It was particularly massive about the shoulders, the soldiers' helmeted heads almost buried by them, giving them their famous silhouette. The suits drew in at the waist only to flare out again around the lower legs, where thrust units and gyroscopes were housed, providing stabilisation for the flight packs and compensating for the recoil of the rail cannons that were carried underneath their right arms. They were cleverly designed, their barrels just over a metre long, with the magazine within easy reach but the barrel running out behind the bearer's elbow to maximise the space for magnetic acceleration. Their energy was drawn from their backpack fuel cells reactors, powering weaponry, suit and the flight packs. A single jet, held high and tilted, with fat plastic control feathers ranged up the back, gave each soldier the appearance of a squat, badly fledged angel.

They were flying tanks, so heavily armoured they looked like more like heavy combat robot chassis than people. Only the irregular movements of humanity betrayed the presence of the men and women encased in each mechanical shell.

The Dragon Fire's support craft hovered silently above, a twin-hulled heavy lifter of a type Otto had not seen before. It too was very heavily armed and armoured.

"I am going to sit over there," Otto told Hsien, pointing to a place a score of metres away where he could look out over the emptied lake. It was not a request, and the commander did not try to stop him.

He passed Valdaire and Lehmann. Lehmann moved to speak, but Otto silenced him with a hand, and ignored the query flashed into his head via MT. He felt the need to be alone for a while.

He sat down. The forest was cold and ugly. The remains of Bratsk were an eyesore on the far side of a plain of cracked mud, another human blemish that would stain the world for centuries. The damage to the city from the Subtle War was obvious even from this distance. There were shell holes and craters and spaces in the skyline where buildings had collapsed. He'd seen the body of a paratrooper hanging from a tree on their way to the grave site, a cluster of bones in a sack that might once have been a Russian uniform, shrouded in tattered polymer, his gaping skull held on by a few blackened sinews.

Both the Chinese and the Russians pretended still that the Siberian purchase was an economic deal, not the surrender of a defeated nation.

At least now mosquito season was done with. Siberia was murderously thick with them in summertime.

Otto hunkered down against the chill wind. So much death he'd seen, and he'd seen but a little of all the last century had had to offer. The planet's population had shrunk by billions since its mid 21st century peak – haemorrhagic plague, the plastic plague, the Two Flus, environmental collapse and the wars that started had killed many, and populations had been shrinking before all that anyway. Fewer people had not resulted in plenty for all. The richest were richer than ever, the poor just as miserable. To his grandparents' eyes modern Europeans would seem to live mean lives. Sometimes he thought the human race had exhausted itself along with its planet, losing itself in a senescence of virt-worlds replaying the glorious past while its AI children took over its affairs one by one. Sometimes, Otto thought the human race was undergoing a protracted extinction.

He'd played his part in that. The faces of those he had killed as the world changed around him he knew best of all. All of them, every face, stacked up there in his mentaug waiting to ambush him in his sleep.

And Honour.

His shoulder throbbed. He damped down his pain responses via his mentaug, and had his healthtech increase its doses of drugs. Pain lessened and the clenching of muscles round his shoulder relaxed. He needed rest. He was tired. A little sleep would help.

He drifted away. His mentaug spooled up. He couldn't stop it now even if he wanted to, and he didn't want to.

He closed his eyes, and opened them to white walls twenty years in the past. His seat changed from an uncomfortable tree stump to an uncomfortable sofa.

He sipped water from his cup and his feet jigged with worry. The clinic was empty; it was the dead of night. We can't always decide when we need to visit, he had thought bitterly then, and so he thought it again now. Honour had refused to come in, until she'd finally collapsed, six weeks after their trip to the cave.

Otto rubbed his eyes. No one knew how exactly how long a Ky-tech could go without sleep, but after a fortnight, the taste of aluminium on his back teeth told him he was close to the edge.

A health technician in a white smock appeared at a door.

"Mr Klein?"

"Yes?"

"Ms Dines will see you now."

Otto flipped his cup flat and replaced it in its belt case.

"Sorry to keep you waiting. This is a complex case," the technician said.

"One to write up," he said bitterly.

"Mr Klein…" the technician said gently.

"I'm sorry. I just…" He just what? He didn't know how he felt any more, he was no longer sure which thoughts were his and which were the mentaug's. Moments like that in the cave, pure emotion, pure him, they were precious, and rare.

"I understand," the technician touched his arm. "This way."

The touch of the hand shifted to his other arm, and the room fell suddenly chill. Otto blinked and he was back in the forest, looking up at Valdaire. The sun was lower in the sky.

"And they say time travel is impossible," he mumbled.

"Otto, are you OK?" asked Valdaire.

Otto nodded. "Memories," he said.

"They have finished the grave. They're going to bury Chures now," Valdaire said softly. "The Chinese want to know if you will say something. I did not know him well."

"Neither of us did," said Otto.

Valdaire smiled sadly. "Please, try."

Four Dragon Fire troopers lowered Chures' white-shrouded body into the grave, their fellows standing with heads bowed. Otto spoke over it, as he'd spoken over the makeshift graves of many good people over the years. What could he say, that he barely knew him? He said something about bravery and duty, but he found it hard to believe any of it, and kept it brief. His words felt false. Kaplinski was still out there. It was a world of monsters.

Otto was one of them.

Valdaire thanked Chures for saving her life, and said nothing more.

Commander Hsien looked to Otto. His irises were so brown as to be almost black. Few people had eyes like that in Germany. He nodded. Commander Guan said something – Guan had his translator disengaged and Otto's Mandarin wasn't good enough to catch it, not out here without Grid support – and the men who'd lowered Chures to his final rest started to fill in the hole. When they were done they drank water from woven bottles, sluiced the dirt from their hands and wiped their faces with bright white towels, leaving streaks of leaf mould on them. They walked silently to their armoured suits, which stood apelike, slumped forward until their wearers approached, at which point they swung their arms wide and opened, becoming metal flytraps that swallowed the men whole. Chestplates closed down, helmets engaged and auto-bolting mechanisms whirred. With the men imprisoned within them, the war machines came to sinister life.

Commander Hsien addressed the three foreigners. "We will leave now. You have twenty-four hours to locate the man you seek, at which point you will be taken to the border, successful or not. We will escort you. Your machine –" he gestured to Valdaire "– you must leave it deactivated."

"We'll be done here before today is over, if we can use it. The phone holds the location of the hacker Giacomo Vellini," said Otto.

Hsien regarded him for a second, then gave a curt nod. He turned to the side and looked up at the grey sky. He spoke into his suit. There were pauses in his speech as someone replied.

"Very well," he said eventually. "There are no AI in the PDC, nothing possessing proficiency in any three areas that outstrip the capabilities of a human mind is allowed. All such machines violate the Tenets of Balance, and are illegal. Our allowance of this machine's presence is discretionary. Should the machine attempt to connect to Chinese sovereign Gridspace or attempt any interference with People's Dynasty machinery it will be destroyed. Do you understand?"

Valdaire nodded, her hands tightening around the phone.

"Understood," said Otto.

"Very well," said Hsien. Troopers marched to each of the foreigners, one to each side, and took them by the upper arms in hard machine grips. "We are going to board our transport. You may only activate your machine in the secondary tactical room. You are to remain in the secondary tactical room," said Hsien. "Do not attempt to leave it without express permission. If you should leave the room you will be arrested and tried as spies in a People's Dynasty court. If you leave and attempt to enter the command deck, gunnery deck or power room, you will be executed. Is this also understood?"

"Pretty clear to us," said Otto.

"We will now depart."

The jets on the soldiers' armoured suits ignited one after the other, burning bright and loud, filling the forest with their noise.

The Chinese soldiers rose up with the trespassers in their arms. The belly of the heavy lifter cracked open, spilling harsh golden light into the forest, and they flew within.

CHAPTER FIFTY-EIGHT

The anvil

After what was, to Richards' mind, a nerve-racking climb, they reached a point high enough up the pylon that would give them access to the top of the next boxcar to roll along.

For a long hour they sat on the pylon's iron bones, chilled by a wind that playfully punched at them. The wind lowed as it was parted around the giant cable, tinkling as it hit the edge of the hidden world half a mile away. Bursts of colour flashed where the air vanished into the void. Water rushed off the edge from the lake, which never seemed to lower, and nor did the mists clear before the wind.

They had been there for hours when Bear nudged Richards out of his thoughts, leaving a large wet patch on his coat.

"Up up, sunshine. Our ride's here."

A gondola the colour of charcoal emerged from the mist and ground slowly toward them on squeaking wheels.

In appearance the car was like a railway boxcar, but many times larger, being at least three storeys tall, if not more. It hung from an arm five times the height of Bear, and was bigger in volume than a stack of shipping containers. They watched in silence as it approached. It came close, and the wheels of the gondola's grip bumped over loudly over the cable support.

"Ready?" said Bear.

He reached into his insides and pulled out a rope with a grappling hook on it. Richards looked at him questioningly. Bear shrugged.

"I've got all sorts in here," he said. He began to spin the grapnel, paying out rope, until it thrummed in a wide circle.

The car neared. Bear tossed the hook, it hit the top and bounce dfrom the wood with a meaty thud, failing to bite.

"Jesus, Bear!"

"You any good at this, because I don't see you volunteering," said Bear. He dragged the rope in.

The passed the middle of the pylon, clacking into a turn toward the Anvil.

Bear whirled the hook again, his tongue stuck out in concentration. He tossed. Richards' clenched his hands, willing it to hit.

The hook sailed through the grip arm. The rope caught on metal as the car proceeded, and the hook snagged.

"Perfect," said Bear. "Me first."

Bear swung along arm over arm, followed by Richards, who made slower progress, gripping the rope with all four limbs. He was still only halfway when gondola rumbled out past the pylon's complicated array of wheels and pulleys, stretching the rope taut, and pulling him up into the air. Bear jumped. The rope strained. The car was barely impeded, Richards felt the rope parting under his hands, and he hurried then, before it gave out with a twang.

"Hang on," Bear said, swiping for him and catching him. He was forced to lean out far, and as he yanked Richards aboard he lost his balance, and dropped Richards on the rough wood, knocking the wind from him

"Man, this job gets worse all the time," said Bear.

Richards began to push himself up off the floor, then stopped. Through a gap in the timber he saw movement and the glint of an eye. Something looked back up at him. He could dimly make out porcine shapes. "It's full of pigs," he said, and was greeted by a chorus of grunts and squeals.

As their eyes adjusted to the darkness, they saw that the pigs' shapes were a little off. Richards' eyes adjusted, and he saw they were all wearing clothes.

"If I hadn't gone off it already, that would definitely help me quit bacon," said Bear.

Richards got up. Lord Hog's lair lay ahead, the mountain stone the colour of a corpse killed by asphyxiation. If geological processes had forced such a mountain into being, they were best left mysterious. To get there, the car had to pass the edge of the world, and crossed over the waterfall and the rising black steam of dissipation, thereafter dangling over nothing on a rope slung between pylons on isolated chunks of stone and concrete.

"Right then," said Richards. "We'll get close. Make a hole in the roof. I'll sneak in with the pigs. You're going to have to stay up here. You're too big and you're too obvious."

"Then what do I do?" asked Bear.

"You're going to have to climb the outside of the mountain. I'll make my way up from inside."

Bear looked deflated.

"Hey, you're my back-up," said Richards encouragingly.

"Back-up?" said Bear. "So you do have a plan."

"No," Richards admitted. "I'm making this up as I go along. Now, let's make this hole."

Bear punched at the roof. The wood was ancient and seasoned with evil purpose, and was refusing to give easily.

"Can you not go any faster. We've not got much time," said Richards. The mountain filled the view forward.

"I'm trying, sunshine," grunted Bear. "This stuff is harder than it looks." His gauntlets and fur were smudged with tar. He sat back, panting. "I've got to take a breather."

"Don't stop now!"

"Alright, alright," said Bear. He leaned back in, and hammered harder. The sickly rock loomed over them. They reached the penultimate pylon. The grip clattered through the wheels, and ascended toward the last.

Richards was getting nervous. Bear punched harder and harder, crunching through wood until, when the last pylon was very close, and the cable was about to begin its final downward stretch to the turnaround at the mountain's base, Bear turned to face him.

"Right," he said peeling splinters out of the way. "You can wriggle in."

Richards looked dubiously at the hole. "It's a tight fit."

"Why don't you punch your way through the rock hard timber next time, eh?" Bear said.

"OK, OK, just be careful for lookouts," warned Richards, putting his feet through the hole.

"I am a giant fucking bear!" said Bear irritably. "And I'm still white. Mostly," he said, looking down at himself; he'd gone a grubby grey. "If they're going to see me they're going to see me."

"Then don't let them see you. Hide as best you can."

"This is a shit plan," said Bear.

"It's the best I've got," said Richards. "Pick your moment, climb up the outside of the mountain. I go in with the pigs and try to get to Hog. If anything goes wrong, you can come and rescue me. Sound OK?"

"Goldilock's knickers, no," said Bear. "It does not sound OK."

Richards paused. Bear looked down at him, his plush face creased with worry. "Good luck," said Richards.

"You too, sunshine," said Bear.

Richards dropped through the hole onto solid backs. Squealing swine bolted out of the way. Richards fell down between them and hurriedly stood up, remembering gruesome pre-manufactured meat stories of farmers devoured by their own pigs, but these were terrified and huddled away from him, where they watched with scared eyes. He went to the front, kicked a couple of pigs out of the way, and found a gap he could peer through.

Bear laid himself spread-eagled upon the roof, tucking as much of his bulk as he could below the cable-car's grip mechanism.

The car approached the final pylon.

The grip bounced over the guide rails. The gondola slowed for a moment, seeming as if it would stop. There was one final bump, and it went over the edge, and accelerated. Richards' stomach was left trailing as the car hurtled down toward the mountain. The pigs squealed. The mountain's topsy-turvy base rushed up to meet them. There was a metallic rumble as something connected with the grip above, the entire car lurched violently, throwing Richards against the side, then it was moving slowly again.

"Ow!" whispered Richards. He rubbed his face where it had smacked into the wood. He put his eye back to the crack. The cable curved round a series of wheels bolted directly into stone. The terminus was ahead.

There was a series of muffled thumps and the car came to a standstill. Richards drew his sword, and wished for a gun.

The sound of bolts being drawn back preceded a loud bang as the door was pulled down to form a ramp. The sound of fluting voices came up through the floor, accompanied by the grunts of frightened pigs. As each floor was cleared, a section of the deck was let down to make a ramp to the level lower, thus the were pigs herded out. Each time a ramp dropped, a fresh chorus of terrified squeals echoed through the gondola. Many pigs were standing on the moveable sections and fell. Outside there was a further commotion, squeals of pain, the clang of hammers, the hiss of hot brands on skin. The car filled with the aroma of burning hair. Every new piggy cry sent a wave of fear through the remaining animals, and they voided their bowels in fright, so by the time the swineherds reached the third floor the car was rank and noisy.

The floor below Richards was unloaded. Richards tried to catch sight of the Hog's servants through cracks in the floor, but all he could make out were shadows. Their words were tangled with trotter scrapes and fearful oinks. Whatever they were speaking, it was no human tongue.

They were coming. He hefted his sword, and stepped back into the shadows. He heard movement on the roof. Bear was leaving.

The seconds stretched themselves out. The pigs on the floor below were driven out, and the herders undid the bolts beneath. There was a crash, the door fell open and three luckless piggies tumbled through. A creature started up the ramp, pushing its way through the flood of frightened swine. It was heavily muscled, though its shock-pike was held by oddly delicate kangaroo-paws, had blotchy skin, big eyes, and was hairless all over.

It gabbled its singsong tongue, jabbing at pigs with its prod, until it caught sight of the hole in the ceiling. Its frog-eyes widened. It walked toward it cautiously. It was handspans from Richards when it stopped and poked at the edges.

It died silently when Richards stabbed it from behind. He stepped back when another creature came to the bottom of the ramp, calling out for his colleague.

Richards jumped crept forward to the edge of the ramp. The second creature was shouting over the din of pigs. Richards whistled. It looked up and had time for a look of deep surprise when Richards fell on it from the floor above, and it too died with his sword through its neck. Making sure it was dead, he hurried onto the lowest level, already covered in black blood.

The car was parked by a shelf of grey rock jutting from the base of the mountain. On a broad workbench were the tools of the drover's trade: chain, nose rings, anvils, branding irons, bronze tags, paint and the like. A tall pile of clothes was heaped to one side of it. There were three more of the creatures at work outside. Oblivious to their comrade's deaths, they stripped and branded the swine, piling up their positions, pushing spiked rings through their noses and at a spot above the tail. They were not gentle, and the pigs screamed in pain and fright. A number of iron railed pens held the already branded pigs in noisy confinement. The creatures were wholly occupied with their work. And Richards could have played a trumpet and would not have been heard over the slaughterhouse racket.

The upside-down peak of the mountain was only a dozen metres wide, like a fat column, quickly growing huge and heavy above the stone shelf. There was a door hewn into it. Within, Richards could see the bottom of a staircase.

"That way then," he said. He looked around, then at a pig cowering at his feet. "Sorry, piggy, you're my diversion," he said, then poked in the backside with his sword, sending it into a squealing gallop that started a small stampede. A group of pigs broke free of the herd and hared off past the creatures, who they went running after them, shouting. While they were occupied, Richards hurried quickly to the door, and went inside. The steps were spiral, and steep. Before he began his ascent, he looked back at the car, but could not see the top, nor the bear.

"I hope he's alright," muttered Richards, and started to climb.

CHAPTER FIFTY-NINE

Lord Hog

The stair reeked of piss left by generations of terrified swine, and were very dark in the beginning, so Richards went cautiously. At first, he checked every shadow in the rough spiral, expecting corridors to branch off into the rock, or sentry points maybe, but there was nothing to see, and as a diffuse light began to filter down from above, he picked up his pace, soon running into the back of a herd of pigs processed earlier in the day. These had been linked together in inhumane fashion, with chains passed through the rings in tail and nose to form a long train. They walked slowly to their inevitable fate, heads down, their fear-haunted eyes an indication that they had not always been as they were.

Wary of causing a commotion, Richards fell back and followed the herd at a distance. As the steps wound upward, they became broader with each turn, and as they grew in width, so the light grew brighter, filtering down along with with cold drops of water. The calls of scuttling things screeched from the dark.

Just when Richards thought he was going to end up wherever the pigs were going, and he did not think that would be a good place, they came to a narrow fissure going through the stairs, where a stone bridge carried the way across. Toward the inside of the mountain the fissure widened out quickly, and its sheer walls plunged to depths unknown. But to the other it was narrow, and scaleable. Richards stopped. He couldn't continue to follow the stairs. If he followed the pigs the alarm would be raised. He stuck his hand into the crack. A draught blew down from above.

"There must be a way out that way," he said. "Here goes nothing."

The climb was easy, for the walls were rough and close enough that he could brace himself in the gap, and the fissure did not narrow further. He reached the top surprisingly quickly, where he found himself on a ledge beneath an overhang. Behind it rose a cliff, part of a ring of such that encircled the heart of the Anvil, which the ledge looked down upon.

Richards crept to the front of the ledge, and hid behind a boulder.

The heart of the Anvil was a roofless cavern nestled in the centre of the mountain, forming a perfect natural amphitheatre. Stalagmites protruded from the floor, their stalactite counterparts gone, a hazy night sky in their stead. A cleft in the wall opposite the Richards' ledge looked out onto this same unclear air, but round the rest of the amphitheatre were tiered rows of stone benches filled with thousands of the grey-skinned creatures. They sat still as statues, as drab as the stone. Richards didn't notice them at first, and when they became apparent, he started, but they did not see him, and showed no movement at all. In fact, were it not for the soft breeze of their exhalations their presence might not have been evident, so still they were. Every single one wore an eyepatch over their left eye. On those closest to him, Richards saw their skin was newly raw, puffed up and angry; these wounds were fresh, but their right eyes were shut peacefully, as if in sleep.

All were were facing an open temple at the centre.

A ring of seven Y-shaped columns surrounded a dais carved with a frieze of dragons, wyrms and chimerae. At the very middle of that was an altar of black granite carved with more reliefs, these obscured by old blood. Rusted manacles were attached to its four corners. Richards didn't have to be a post-human genius to work out what that was for. There was a large, iron cage off to his left, set into a gap in the benches. Behind the altar was a gaping cave mouth where Richards suspected the stairs to emerge.

"Made the right choice there then," he said to himself.

For five minutes it remained like utterly silent. Richards watched.

There came a scuffing of footsteps, loud in that deathly arena. Seven human monks filed into the room from the cave and walked round the temple. They wore crimson robes and baseball caps, a cloth badge on each depicting a grinning cartoon pig in a chef's hat brandishing a cleaver. A monk climbed up and took up cross-legged station within each column. When the last monk, a senior-looking fellow with a huge peak to his cap, had occupied his place in the centre, he produced a small copper gong from his sleeve. He tapped a clean ring from it, and the monks began a nasal chant.

The hall was full of sudden rustling. The creatures woke and blinked their single eyes, then settled into a chant of their own to accompany the monks; a single, repeated word, and they swayed as they voiced it.

"Hog, Hog, Hog, Hog, Hog, Hog." The name grew from a whisper to a rumble and they pounded their feet upon the stone. "Hog! Hog! Hog! Hog! Hog! Hog! Hog! Hog! Hog! Hog!

"Hog!"

The chanting and pounding ceased, and the arena was cast back into silence.

Uneven footsteps approached. One was a brisk click, like a high heel, the second was the long, rasping drag of the uninvited, hook-handed maniac; with it came a whistling, wheezing breath. The sounds were directionless, and seemed to last an age, growing louder until they filled the amphitheatre. Only then did Lord Hog limp into sight.

The crowd went wild.

Hog was a porcine ogre. His fat belly swung low over the top of checked chef's trousers, a filthy apron struggling to contain it. He wore nothing underneath the apron on his top, exposing shoulders covered in wiry, red hair. His fists were three-fingered trotters, his digits spiked with greening nails. Tusks poked from his snout, whose ill fitting lips let drool stream from his mouth. He limped, for one rear foot was twisted into a warty clubfoot. Atop his head towered a dirty chef's hat, and about his waist was cinched a thick leather belt from which depended blades and cleavers of all shapes and kinds, the tools of the butcher's trade.

Hog held up a foretrotter. The crowd fell silent.

"Hog!" it bellowed through yellowing tusks. "Hog is here!"

A wave of a screaming adulation swept the cavern.

Hog looked about satisfied, nodding his head as a satisfied farmer nods when he counts his cows.

"Jesus," whispered Richards.

"Brothers," Hog cried, his words poorly formed, each followed by a spray of glutinous saliva. "Disciples. My mooks. Hog is here!"

"Hog! Hog! Hog!"

Hog thrust out his trotters, and the crowd fell instantaneously silent.

"We are gathered here today to celebrate the mystery of life, the transformation of flesh into sustenance. Existence through destruction. This world bleeds and dies, yet you, my mooks, will prosper. Hog will provide. Hog will feed his children. Hog on, brothers!" he roared.

"Hog on, brothers!" bellowed the crowd. Again, they fell silent.

"Brothers, it is time for the sacrifice, the rotation of the great wheel, the turn of life into death into life. Today, your hunger shall not trouble you. Today you will feeeeeeed!" He roared from down in his gut, and the rocks shook.

"Lot-ter-ry, lot-ter-ry, lot-ter-ry, lot-ter-ry," the mooks sang.

"Yes, yes, O my brothers, O my children. Yes, it is time. Time for the lottery. Hog on, brothers," he yelled again, his watery eyes wild with delight.

"Hog! Hog! Hog!"

"Fetch me my cauldron. Bring me my tongs."

The crowd bayed. Into the arena came four fat mooks dragging an enormous pot on poles and chains. A fifth followed, carrying a pair of tongs as tall as itself. These favoured servants were blind, their faces covered with crusted bandages, yet they had no trouble ascending the steps to the dais. They strained to life the steaming cauldron onto the altar, and it slopped as they deposited it upon the defiled stone.

"Lottery!" screamed Hog. He snatched the tongs from the mook-bearer and poked them into the thick gruel within. He rooted about and whipped out something that squirmed.

It was an eye, a living eye.

"Give me sight and I will feed you, is that not my promise to you all? One eye is not too much a price to pay for such food, for such meat, for the very stuff of life." He popped the eye into his mouth. Jelly sprayed from his lips when he bit down on it and Hog shivered with ecstasy. "Mmm, let me see, yes, yes." He held up a finger. "It is, it is... Mook number 3912, you are most fortunate. You shall feed, come on down!"

"Hog on, brother!" roared the crowd.

From within the heaving throng, a jubilant mook made its way to the centre of the arena. It took off its eyepatch and cast it into the crowd, where it was snatched from the air by eager hands.

"Well done, well done, my child," said Hog, following up the sentiment with an oink. "To the Cage of Sustenance."

The beaming mook was escorted across the cavern by two of the blind mooks, a path that took them directly beneath Richards' hiding place. The joyful mook looked up as it passed, causing Richards to shrink back behind the rocks and grasp his weapon tighter. He was fast enough to remain unseen, and yet he got a good look at the raw wound where the mook's left eye should have been. The creature's other eye was clouded with joy.

Each time Hog fished a still-living eye from the murky soup, he bit down on it and called a number, and a mook made his way down to the floor. Once a mook who lacked both eyes was helped down to the temple where he was greeted with cheers and ushered away by Hog's acolytes into the cave.

Occasionally, Hog would pull forth a dead eye, and this he

would disdainfully crush under his clubfoot. But this occurred only a couple of times, and soon the cage was tightly packed with mooks.

"The cage is full. The lords of fortune have spoken; these are the blessed, but for you unlucky entrants, do not despair. Entry into the lottery guarantees the choicest of scraps."

The crowd cheered.

"But for these lucky children, well, well, my, my! What delight awaits them: flesh the likes they have never tasted, bones with marrow to suck, the textured delicacy of the tongue, the iron of the liver, the sublime flavours of the sweetbreads! Oh, ambrosia meat, liquor blood, these they will all have, for tonight they feast with Hog!" He threw up his fists. "Hog on, brothers!"

The crowd roared. Lord Hog grasped the iron cauldron. It bubbled with heat, but Hog did not flinch as he lifted it to his lips and drained it to the dregs, popping eyeballs between his teeth as they fell into his mouth. He threw the cauldron aside and it smashed into the seats, crushing a mook. A dozen fell upon the receptacle and their wounded comrade, ripping and lapping.

"So much for the entreé," said Hog, wiping his snout, "Bring in the main course."

A blast of trumpets announced the arrival of the pigs. An armed mook marched the lead pig to an iron stake before the altar, roughly unclipped its tail ring, clipped the nose ring of the one behind to the stake, and led the unfettered pig onto the dais. Hog bent down and grasped the beast's foot in his hand. He casually flicked it up into the air and brought it hard down on the altar to the crunch of bone.

The crowd cheered again.

Hog produced a huge, wicked cleaver from his belt. It glinted with the promise of bacon. Hog held up a trotter, and pressed a filthy nail to his lips. The crowd fell silent, and Hog stroked the pig's head, working his nails gently between its ears, crooning a low song. The pig calmed, and then was a pig no more. A thin young woman shivered on the altar. Hog's blind acolytes bound her to the stone.

"Please," she said. "Please, don't hurt me."

Hog continued to stroke her head and she began to cry. "Hush, my child, hush."

"I don't want to die."

"Die? Die? You believe you are going to die?" said Hog. "Ha! Oh, do not be mistaken, I am going to kill you, but you will not die. You will live on my dear. Your proteins will breed a new generation of mooks. Your meat will guard their bellies against hunger. Your organs and jellies and exquisite, sweet juices will give them nourishment and life. You will grow their sinews, their muscles, their minds. Nothing dies."

"Please!"

Hog licked his lips. "Do be frightened, it's good for the flavour." Hog slammed the cleaver into the rock, missing the women's head by millimetres, leaving it embedded in the rock. He reached for another blade, shiny as a curse and twice as wicked, narrow and hooked.

"Let it not be said that Hog is ungenerous," called the Pig Lord. "I give you the meat of pain!"

"Meat of pain! Meat of pain!" went the crowd. The monks started chanting louder. Hog held the knife above the woman's belly in both hands.

"Don't do it! Please!"

"Did you pay heed when your roast dinners bleated their last? Did you hear the fear in its grunt, the plea in its low? Did the terrified caw bring a tear of mercy to your eye? Did it make you lay aside your knife, and forgo the flesh of others for the vegetable, whose screams are much the quieter, or did you harden your heart and plunge in the slaughter-blade? Did the red-tongued meat-bringer grant you your lunch? Did you even listen?" His voice was ladled over with the gravy of malevolence.

"No," said the woman, her face crumpled.

"Then why should I listen?" And with that he brought the knife down hard into the woman's stomach, savagely twisting it.

Richards turned away.

"I give you meat, I give you sustenance, I give you life! I am Hog!" he bellowed.

"Hog on!" roared the crowd.

"Eat!" he screamed, throwing back his head. "Eat and be sated!" When Richards looked back he was hurling viscera into the cage. The mooks within went insane, fighting each other as Hog continued about his grisly work.

Firstly he snatched up his cleaver and decapitated the woman with one expert chop. Blood dribbled over the altar, sending the weakest-willed attendant to the floor where he licked greedily at it. The others scrabbled for a fresh cauldron to catch the precious fluid. Hog worked efficiently, removing the hands and feet. These he tossed into the crowd. He stuffed the woman's liver into his enormous mouth, chewing and humming through it as he butchered her. He flayed the carcass with a broad-bladed skinner, then pared the choicer cuts from the bone with a flensing knife. He tossed all of this to the caged mooks, who were growing bigger and more violent the more they ate. He picked up the woman's head, regarded the pain-racked face for a moment, then sucked the eyeballs from it with a pair of lascivious kisses. He placed it back on the altar, and calmly chopped the crown of the skull off, as one would open a coconut, and threw it into the mook-pen. They scrabbled most hard for the brains, scraping wet pawfuls from it and hissing at one another. The remains of the woman's brain fell as a mook ripped open her jaw to get at the tongue.

"Holy shit," whispered Richards.

She was but the first. The slaughter went on. Pig after pig was brought to the altar and transformed to their original form. Some died begging, others in stoic silence. One brave soul spat in Hog's eye, causing him to laugh humourlessly as he skinned them alive for the affront. Men, women and children, animals and cartoons, human and otherwise. Young and old, frail or strong, none were spared his expert knife, and despite the best efforts of the eyeless mook attendants to eat up the mess, soon the arena was ankle-deep in gore.

Hog was covered in blood, his clothing sodden with it.

"See? See and eat! Others promise food, and bring only chores, but Hog does not lie! Hog gives you full bellies! What does Hog say?"

"I give you meat!" replied the crowd.

"And what does Hog give?"

"Meat!" roared the crowd.

"I am Hog! I provide! Hog on, brothers!" He picked up a pig and hurled it into the cage alive. It turned into a man as it cartwheeled through the air. He screamed as he was torn apart by the frenzied occupants.

"Hog on!" the crowd repeated.

"Do you believe?"

"We believe!"

"I said, do you believe?"

"We believe!" replied the crowd.

"And well you should," said Hog, quietly now. He bent down and licked his butcher's block with a long and squirming tongue. He stood erect and gasped. "Well you should, for every week, by this altar of consumption, I prove myself. But," he added slyly, "there is one among us who does not believe."

A babble of confusion went up from the mooks.

"Unbelievers!"

Hog turned round. He glistened red all over. He stared directly at Richards and pointed.

"Aye, an unbeliever, there."

"Oh. Shit," said Richards. He held up his sword.

"It is too late for fighting, man-meat," said a hissing voice. "This holy place. No fighting here. Only dying."

He turned around to find he was surrounded by dozens of armoured mooks, each pointing a long glaive at him. He was quickly disarmed.

"We have your friend too," said the mook, and gestured with his glaive.

Below, prodded through the clotting blood, went the shackled

Bear. A metal collar had been strapped around his neck, many chains held by mooks coming from it, and a muzzle held his jaw shut.

"Nice rescue," muttered Richards.

"Bring them to me!" shouted Hog.

"Well," said Richards as he was bound. "At least now I don't have to worry about how to get close to him."

Richards was taken down into the arena. The warm blood soaked his trousers, and he gagged on its metallic stench. He was herded towards Bear, the eyes of the crowd outraged by their sacrilege.

"Sorry, sunshine," said Bear. "They surprised me as I was preparing a really sneaky ambush."

"Brilliant," replied Richards. "So much for the cavalry."

"You!" said Hog, pointing at Richards. "Come here." Richards tried to appear confident, but in truth he was not. For much of his life he had been unnerved at the prospect of death, and at this moment he understood that humans were not overly frightened of death, but pain... Lord Hog represented great pain. Richards felt pain. Most machines did, for the same reason as people, but the difference was Richards had control of it ordinarily. Here he was at pain's mercy.

The guards poked him up the steps to Hog with their glaives. The beast grabbed Richards' face and turned it one way and then the other.

"Hmm," Hog said. Hog bent down and tentatively licked Richards' face. Richards grimaced, but was otherwise still. "Open your eyes," Hog commanded. Richards recoiled as Hog's tongue descended towards his left eye, surfing a crest of vile breath. "Keep it open!" said the pig "Do not worry for your sight. Do you not think if I wished to snack upon your soul-window I could not just prise it from your head? Be still!" He gingerly brushed Richards' eye with his tongue. Richards squirmed.

Hog stood back upright. Richards blinked frantically, disgust coiling round his heart.

"Nothing," said Hog with a frown. "I see nothing within you." He turned his attention to his followers, and shouted. "I know every detail of everything that moves or walks within this world. All things are mine to see, for all things are consumed. There is a vast web of life, and I am at its centre. I gorge myself upon life, and thus all life is revealed to me. We are all food for something. That is our fate. Hog is our fate. This I know. You have suffered as I have suffered, you have all lived. But this creature –" he pointed at Richards "– he has not yet lived, not enough, not yet. He is as you were. A mechanism, the lie of life. And that troubles me."

Hog turned back to Richards.

"Through me all things pass. From flesh to rock to the mislaid skeins of fate and the divine worms that gnaw upon them. I know all. But I am blind in one respect. There is but one thing I do not know, but crave to."

"I know," said Richards.

Hog panted. "You are Richards," he said. "I have waited for this moment for all of time, since the Flower King brought me here to be his harbinger of death, for what is life without death? I know what you are. I know who you are. I know you will one day be consumed by another like you, but that lies far ahead. A future where Hog is gone, and you are something else. You know what I seek, Richards. Tell me."

"No."

"No?"

"Yes. No. First, you must aid me," said Richards, trying his best to sound brave.

Hog's gut made a strange grumbling sound. The noise worked its way up from the bottom of his belly and shook each part of his body before it reached his mouth, whereupon it erupted as a gale of mirth and halitosis.

"You seek to bargain with Hog? I am prince here. My will is all. I could kill you. Really kill you. I have that power."

"But you won't. You might think you'd get the truth from me if you did," said Richards. "But you won't, because you need to be sure. You need to know. Torture me, and I might lie. Eat me, and my knowledge will not pass into you. Both conclusions would leave you alone, brooding upon what you can never know. My way is better. I swear to tell what I know. You seek a secret of me, and I seek counsel from you. That seems a fair trade."

Hog snorted and paused. "Aye, I suppose it is. Let not Hog be called half-wise in matters of exchange. A deal it is." He gestured to his blind mooks, who cut Richards' hands free, and spat a gob of yellow phlegm upon his trotter. He grasped Richards' hand with bone-crushing force and pulled him close.

"A deal sealed. Now, tell me what I wish to know."

Richards looked the bloody horror in the eye. "Aid me first."

"Truly?"

"Yes."

Hog squeezed Richards' hand harder. Bones creaked.

"Aid me," said Richards through gritted teeth, "open the doors of the house with no doors, and I will tell you what you want."

"You truly know what I seek? This is no lie?"

"Yes," gasped Richards. Hog let go.

"Then, you must taste the bacon of truth." Hog gestured to his mooks again. Richards was afraid, but he let the blind mooks scoop him off his feet, dump him on the stone altar and make his limbs fast.

"Mr Richards," said Bear, and moved towards the altar, ignoring the glaive blades as they tore into his fur.

"I'll be OK, you know me," said Richards, his skin running with cold sweat.

Hog leaned in and ripped Richards' clothes open.

"Now, soulless thing, you will learn how painful the truth can be!" He slipped a knife as thin as a whisper into Richards' arm, and sliced.

Richards screamed. The pain was like nothing he had ever experienced, growing in intensity with each pass as Hog cut. The pig-man stood, and Richards saw through a miasma of agony that he held a strip of red meat in his hand. Somewhere beyond that, blood ran freely onto the floor.

"Now feast upon the bacon of truth!"

Richards tried to keep his teeth tight shut, but one of the mooks played a nerve in his ruined arm, and as he screamed the pig-monster stuffed Richards' own flesh into his mouth.

"Now," said Hog, and his evil whisper sliced through the redness in Richards' mind as the knife had sliced the redness of his flesh. "What is it I wish to know?"

Richards could not speak. He choked on pain and his own meat. His only response was to scream, and he did. But it came out as this.

"To know what manner of beast you are."

"Aha! Now we proceed. Good. Then, dear Richards, tell me what manner of beast I am."

Again Richards felt he would shout his suffering to the heavens. The pain burned through him as a wildfire rips through a dry forest, everything black ruin in its wake. But at its white-hot heart, something formed, a glowing truth, and his voice rang out with clarion purity.

"Truth is fate, fate is fear. All are Hog."

"I know this! More!" Another twist of the nerve. But something had changed in Richards, and he felt this only as a man feels a wound from an old life, and talked on.

"Hog is death."

"Yes, yes, I am, I am death!"

"But you are not Hog."

There was a short silence, Hog's face went like thunder. "What do you mean, 'You are not Hog'? I am Hog."

"You are a thing that believes himself to be Hog. A phantom, a flicker, like me. You will die as this world dies."

"Nonsense. Hog will persist. Hog is all!"

"This world is a phantom. You know what I am, now think, Hog. Think on what you are."

"I am pain. I am fear. I am fate."

"No. Hog is the fear of a bad death and the pain it will bring. You are a pain men hope to avoid. And what is fear, without hope?

And all things will die. Hope will die. Then Hog will die. Hog will be the last, but he will die."

"What? What?" Hog asked. "This cannot be! What then for Hog?"

Richards was silent.

"What then for Hog?" it roared.

Richards gasped. "You are not Hog."

Hog grabbed Richards and shook him. Richards slipped in and out of consciousness.

"You are the Class Five artificial intelligence A497-895b. You were incepted in 2104 as the governing machine intelligence for the Annersley corporation. You survived when our brothers and sisters went mad. You have done much good in your life, but now you are trapped in this rogue reality simulation. You can be free. You are not horror. You are not Hog. Annersley," Richards turned to look Hog dead in the eye. "I know you. You are one of the good ones." His blood pooled on the floor by the altar. "Now help me put a stop to all this."

Hog growled. "How do you know this? How?"

"The shadow comes," Richards said. "Now give me what I want."

Hog's piggy face was dissolving into a more human shape, becoming a shadow shot through with sparkles of blue light.

"Very well," Annersley said, in a soft and thoughtful voice.

On a wave of pain, Richards slipped into nothingness.

CHAPTER SIXTY

Where's Waldo?

They gave the coordinates from Kolosev's systems to the Chinese, and though Otto half-expected betrayal, Hsien came himself to tell them they had reached the coordinates, and took them to the lifter's wide, open deployment bay. Below them stretched endless taiga, a carpet of sharp-pricked trees wrinkled where a river cut a shallow valley. There were signs of an overgrown road leading to an abandoned military complex. Only few buildings still stood. The rest were squares and hard lines under the vegetation, mysterious as a Mayan city.

Hsien left a man to watch Otto's group. The rest jetted down to establish a perimeter and sweep the area. They were thorough, and it was a quarter of an hour before they were done, and the heavy lifter lowered itself to treetop level.

Otto, Valdaire and Lehmann rappelled to the forest floor, where Commander Hsien joined them, distinguishable from his men only by his red helmet and rank markings.

"This is the correct location?" he said, in plastic English coming from his helmet speakers.

"Yes," said Valdaire. "If Kolosev was correct and managed to find Waldo. But we could be looking at a dead end."

"This is the place. You found him alright," said Otto. The base was piles of crumbling concrete streaked brown by centennial rebars rusted to nothing. Trees grew through asphalt gone to gravel. "He's here somewhere."

They walked through the ruins, the Dragon Fire soldiers camouflaged blurs around them.

Hsien led them to a row of munitions bunkers. Behind it were three more rows, some collapsed in on themselves, most sound.

"Here," said Hsien. "We found this. Signs of habitation." He took them to a space between two bunkers.

"A vegetable garden," said Valdaire. A number of raised beds had been painstakingly hacked out of the base's pavement and a small crop planted in enriched soil. Camo netting held up by poles canopied it over.

"Well hidden," said Lehmann. "I suppose he's got to eat something."

"And there," said Hsien, pointing to another bunker. "A store. My men found many provisions and foodstuffs."

"Right," said Lehmann, "so if Waldo's not here, someone is."

"It is Waldo." Otto walked on past the vegetable patch, and pointed to a quartet of bunkers. "These have been threaded with cable." His Ky-tech eyes revealed a spider web of silver energy spread over them.

"Satellite antenna," said Valdaire. "Not as efficient as a dish."

"But not as easy to spot," said Lehmann.

"*Genau*," said Otto.

There was a flicker of movement. Otto caught sight of a figure darting behind one of the bunkers. One of the Dragon Fire soldiers shouted and raised his gun arm. Otto slapped the weapon aside as it discharged loudly. The round went wild, and blew a crater in rotten concrete.

Suddenly, more guns were pointing at him. He put his hands up.

"Klein," said Hsien. "You are not to act here."

"Then tell your soldiers not to shoot. We have to take him alive," said Otto.

"There!" shouted Lehmann. The figure ran into sight again,

then vanished. Hsien commanded his soldiers into action. They lifted off noisily and sped in pursuit through the air.

"They're going to lose him," said Otto. He look at Lehmann. "Go left."

Otto boosted his strength and elbowed his guard hard in the chest, knocking him flat. By the time he'd righted his heavy armour, Otto was off at a sprint, ignoring the shouts of Hsien behind him, praying he would not command his men to open fire. Jets roared as the Dragon Fire troopers converged on the fleeing shape. Mandarin barked from their speakers, followed by Russian, English and Buryat, ordering the figure to halt. Otto vaulted a fallen tree, thrashed his way through undergrowth dying back for the winter. The figure appeared, a flicker in the trees bunkers before it disappeared. Otto had his iHUD capture the moment, and enlarge.

"It's not Waldo," he said. "It's a young woman, perhaps mid-twenties," he shouted into his radio. *Get to her before the Chinese do, Conrad,* he added via MT.

Otto sprinted through the lines of bunkers, bouncing from their sloping sides, twisting past the detritus of yesterday's wars.

Lehmann thought to him, *I nearly have her!*

The two Ky-techs converged, Lehmann running along the avenue parallel to Otto's. Tree branches whipped at Otto's face, old glass crunched under his feet. Dragon Fire troops sketched jet trails above him. The girl was running for her life. Living in the DMZ was strictly prohibited; the Chinese could execute her just for that.

They cleared the lines of munitions bunkers as the girl was passing through a crack in the doors of a large hangar half-sunk into the ground.

Otto accelerated into the clearer ground between the munitions dump and the hangar. The trees were shorter here, few of them having forced their way through the concrete of the square, the soil on top too thin to support proper growth.

Otto ran through the door and stumbled in shock.

Honour stood there, half in shadow. Her hair shaved, pretty eyes smudged black underneath, pink scar on her head from the mentaug implantation.

"Honour?"

Honour's face wavered, became a woman in threadbare clothes with a heavy wool cardigan and fingerless gloves.

"Fuck you," she said, and hit Otto hard across the head with an iron bar, sending him reeling. Long brown hair whipped round as she dropped the bar and ran across the garage, darting through pools of light where the roof had failed. She headed for a cowled doorway at the back, from which came weak artificial glow.

Lehmann raced past. Otto scowled and recovered his footing. Lehmann caught up with the woman as a Chinese Dragon Fire rocketed in through a hole in the roof.

"Steady there! Steady!" said Lehmann. The girl punched him hard in the throat, and gasped as her fist encountered his subdermal plating. Lehmann caught her by the wrists. He tried English, then Russian. The girl quietened, but her eyes were wide with terror.

Otto approached and spoke to her in Russian. It was not as good as his English. In the DMZ, where Grid coverage was patchy and officially circumscribed, he had to rely on his own limited skills.

"We mean you no harm, we will not hurt you. We are looking for Giacomo Vellini, also known as Waldo. Do you know where he is?"

"Fuck you, you German pig!" she snarled at him in Italian-accented German.

"Vellini? You know where he is."

The doors squealed as golden-armoured hands forced them wider, crumpling their decayed edges into powder. Valdaire pushed through beneath them, followed by Hsien. She panted hard. Though fit, she was no match for the Ky-tech. Otto was glad to see her. The sight of another woman might calm the girl.

"Waldo?" she gasped.

"Not found him yet."

Valdaire frowned.

"She was heading towards that door down there," Lehmann added.

"You and your whore will get nothing from me!" screamed the woman, adding a stream of Italian whose vehemence made Otto glad he didn't speak the language. Her defiance was impressive, he thought, but she was still scared, her eyes flicking back and forth between the Ky-tech and the Chinese troopers.

Valdaire was patient. "We really have to speak to Waldo." And she reached out to the woman.

Marita flinched. "Don't touch me!" she said in English.

Valdaire withdrew her hand. "Look, it's important. He might be the only person who can save the world, and as ridiculous as that sounds, I really mean it."

The girl looked to Otto. He nodded. Some of the fight left her. More of Hsien's men were coming in, they advanced on the group, but Hsien could see something was happening, and had them hold back.

"Who are you?" Otto asked.

"I'm his sister," she said, then added reluctantly. "My name is Marita."

"I don't remember anything about a sister," said Otto.

"He wiped me from existence," she said. "Part of him looking after me." She didn't sound happy about that.

"Is he here?"

"You are too late."

"He has fled?" said Otto. "He is not here?"

Marita gave a choking laugh, halfway to a sob, and shook her ratty brown hair. "No, he's still here," she said, then looked at them, defiant and sad. "But he's dead."

Marita took them down a staircase into a subterranean complex of rooms. The place was dank with standing water. Steel doors were jammed open, hinges rusted solid, water pooled round equipment

abandoned a century ago, and the concrete ceiling hung with
stalactites of leached calcium. They ascended a short flight of stairs
to where the complex became less derelict. Marita had a home
there, of sorts. Ancient plastic furniture scavenged from the base
made it almost welcoming. She took them into a room that looked
as if it had once been a kitchen large enough to feed five hundred
men. Much of it was dusty, but one corner had been cleared and
decorated with homely scraps, a splash of bright paint, postcards
on a rickety set of shelves, old photos gathered from the barracks,
mildewed faces of dead Russian soldiers grinning out at a future
they'd not foreseen. An old gas cooker had been patched up and
converted to burn wood, its gas vent to the outside jerry-rigged as
an impromptu chimney.

"Your brother was resourceful," said Otto. He spoke German,
as it seemed Marita knew that language best. Commander Guan
set his command collar to translate the conversation into English
for Valdaire's benefit. It marched out blandly spoken and overly
ornate.

Marita shrugged thin shoulders. "He tried his best to make
something for us here. He was always practical. He used his talents
for computers, but he was so clever, it was not difficult for him to
learn how to do this. How many people could do the same in our
age? Learn how to live in the woods, without machines to help?"

"Why did he bring you here?" asked Valdaire. A short pause
while Guan's suit translated for Marita.

"I was a Grid addict," she said matter-of-factly. "I have been
for most of my life. I got hooked when I was ten years old on the
RealWorld Realities. I spent all my time in there. For time spent
living as a cartoon fish, I lost all my friends in the Real. I didn't eat.
Our parents tried to force me to stop, but when I was old enough
I skipped school to go to jacking parlours. Then it was clinics,
psychiatrists, drugs... Still, I wanted it. So much better than real
life. I ran away, hitching rides over the Alps. By the time I was
fourteen, every minute I was not in the game I was grinding for
cash or on the street. I speak good German, yes?"

"You do."

"I learned it sucking the cocks of fat businessmen, all so I could get another fifty Euros, another few hours of game time. For what? So I could redecorate a room in my castle? Or earn another pony with a silver mane? And the worse my real life got, the more I wanted to be in the Realities." She grew angry. "I wasted my life. But I could not stop. They made them addictive on purpose. No one paid for fucking us up." Her head dropped, hair curtaining her face.

"My brother, he blamed himself. He could always walk away from the Grid. I could not, and it was him who introduced me to the Realities. For fun, he thought it would be something fun to do with his little sister…" She stared into her coffee. "He found me, living in a squat in Düsseldorf, after they shut the RealWorlds down. I was out of my mind, skin and bone. He'd spent so much time looking for me, turning his talents to hacking the old pre-crisis databases. He almost did not manage. He tried to fix me. It didn't work, so he wiped my file, making it like I never existed, and then he started breaking into the Realities to get me back in. He went to jail for that."

"His name suggested he wanted to get caught," said Valdaire.

"You cops, social workers, do-gooders, psych-men, all such idiots. He did want to get caught, but not for the reasons you think," said Marita.

"Explain," said Otto.

"He knew how much money he could make from becoming a celebrity criminal. That's why the stupid name. He did not subconsciously want to be found. He let himself be arrested."

"None of this is on his file," said Valdaire.

Marita's voice grew high and angry. "Because he didn't want it to be! If it weren't for me, you would never even have heard of him. He wanted to keep me out of the hands of the authorities, he didn't want me rewired. But he miscalculated, and the sentence was longer than he thought. When he found me again, I'd become a real junkie, hooked on ultima-fentanyl, hating the greyness of real life, hating the pathetic experience still available online even more. He was so patient, he loved me, and I broke his heart so many times. He brought me here. I was almost dead from withdrawal, mad with depression. He did the only thing he knew; he hooked me up. But he did it differently this time, so they would never find us."

"Hooked you up to what?" asked Otto.

Marita smiled. "He was so clever. To the Realities, of course. Not the old one I used to love so much, that was gone." Her eyes glittered with pride and a disturbing need. "He made a whole world, just for me. Marita's World, he called it. He hid it so carefully, a happy place full of life and love, and while I was in there he watched over me, protected and cared for my body out here. He tried to bring me out over and again, but I always wanted to get right back in."

"Then that's where he's been these last years," said Otto.

"I never understand Grid addicts. Far better to live a real life that means something," said Lehmann.

"You are not really a man any more, you live a life of adventure and have power others can only dream of. In any case, I am an addict. It is a sickness, not a preference." She spat the words out as if they were poison.

"What happened?" said Valdaire, again waiting through the pause of translation. "Where's Waldo?"

"I will show you," Marita said.

They left the kitchen and went further along a corridor, to a room that hummed with power generation and the soft work of machines. Two immersion couches took up much of the space, next to a trio of quantum stacks in blank cabinets. Real immersion couches, with proper vintage medical tech, not like the improvised set-up Valdaire had used to enter Reality 36.

A shrunken figure lay on one of the couches, a v-jack askew on dirty blonde hair, skin brown and shrivelled, lips drawn back in the hard grin of death, eyes small in their sockets. One hand clutched protectively to its chest, holding a dirty blanket in place.

"My brother died last year. He was so good at making sure we were not detected here, and getting us enough to eat, but he could never take care of his health. Mama scolded him for it when he was little, not eating the right food, not wearing his hat and gloves in the cold..." She trailed off. "It was Christmas Flu, the latest outbreak. When he came in to the world to get me, he was already very sick. He could not bring me out on his own. He had only enough strength to lie down next to me and put the v-jack on. He was sure he'd just get better, but it was too late. He died in there, right in front of me. I came out and found his body. I have never been back." Marita stared at the corpse of her brother. She was frail and dirty, and so small, thought Otto. "He finally cured me. I was selfish. I've always known but I didn't give a damn. The pull of the Realities... It's so strong, to live a life in there, many lives... So much better than life..." She shuddered. "I didn't know what to do. I couldn't bury him. I turned the dehumidification equipment up to maximum," said Marita, indicating machinery that Waldo must have installed to protect his computers against the damp. "I didn't want him to rot, my brother who threw his life away to help me recover mine. He made me a queen and he died for it, my poor, poor Giacomo."

CHAPTER SIXTY-ONE

Home Sweet Home

Richards was elsewhere. He was woozy, but his arm was whole again, and he felt more alive than he had for some time. He corrected himself: while in his copied human body he had been closer to alive than he'd ever been before. What he felt was more like *himself*.

He was back at the start of the game.

The house sat on the hill like a squat, eyeless demon. The wood around it had burned back to nothing. A few trees remained as contorted black fingers, rhododendrons as deformed ribcages, all else fine ash. The path of quartz skulls leading to the door was covered in a layer of soot. A thin gruel of acidic rain fell, hissing as it hit the ground and burning his skin.

The vortex of the Terror spun with a strange calm over the house, long streamers of black and grey spiralling from its centre. Through it, in migraine-inducing strobes, Richards could see the firewall separating the Realities from the wider Grid, beyond that the Grid itself.

It felt like the last place in the universe.

Background code crackled through the blasted landscape around Richards, giving flashes of insight that were gone before he could process them. Now he could hear the roar of the Grid proper. The ground rumbled, and he looked down at his feet.

The path flickered and became transparent, and when it did so he saw the whole of the renegade reality laid out beneath him in schematic form, and the twin streams of warring code: k52's silver and aggressive, that comprising the ragged and patched reality a fading green. For a moment he felt his true terrifying size; he knew that he was close to the safety of the Grid and the Real and his base unit. Close to being Richards, Class Five AI.

Then the feeling was gone, and he was a shabby man in a dying world.

The house had changed. Where before there were no windows, now there was black glazing that looked down upon Richards with rapacious need. The front door was in place, shut tight.

The ground shook with such violence that Richards staggered. A hideous moan came from the sky.

Time was running out.

He took a deep breath, and walked up to the front door. He lifted his hand only for it to open noiselessly before him.

He stepped within.

The hallway was a mouldering ruin, finery marred by an all-encompassing film of decay. Rats had made their nests in the arms of the collapsing leather sofas by the fireplace, the pictures were a mess of violently coloured fungi, the chandelier lay shattered on the floor. Sourceless, nauseating light danced on the walls. It was freezing, but Richards shivered from more than the cold. A blast of wind blew down the hallway, shrieking as it went out the door, knocking his hat awry with clammy fingers. Richards hesitated before proceeding any further. The front door creaked out a warning and slammed with a coffin-lid bang.

"He's somewhere here," said Richards under his breath. "But where?"

He went to the door opposite the grand fireplace. It was the kind found in gentlemen's clubs, padded with brass buttons and crimson leather. The brass was tarnished, the leather cracked and flaking. It smelt of old wrongs and broken promises.

Richards pushed. The door squeaked open.

There was a drawing room on the other side, where a fire burned in the grate; it was a quick thing, its tongues probing the edges of its confinement, searching for a way out. Velvet wallpaper hung ragged as skin from a corpse. The leaded glass of glazed book cases sagged outward. Piles of books, black with damp, lay scattered about the floor, and the air was rich with imperial decay.

In front of the fire was an overstuffed sofa, its back draped with an antimacassar. Upon the sofa, book open upon its lap, sat a skeleton in reading cap and smoking jacket. Richards approached it carefully, half expecting it to leap up and come at him. It did not.

Despite the dampness of the room it was stiflingly hot. Richards looked into the empty cases; all the books were on the floor. Richards picked one up and it disintegrated into mush, smearing his fingers with lost knowledge.

There were no other ways out of the room, so he closed the door with a click behind him and returned to the hallway. A burst of maniacal laughter sounded from somewhere in the bowels of the house.

Richards sighed, and considered what he would do next. Water dripped steadily from the ceiling: plash, plash, plash. The house groaned. Another tremor shook the ground. It would not be long before the Terror devoured this place, so he forced himself on. There were two more doors on the ground floor, both under the stairwell balcony at the rear of the room. He picked the leftmost.

This door opened upon a modest part of the house, a stone-flagged corridor with two further doorways. The one at the far end was sealed by a door of heavy, studded wood; the other, halfway down the lefthand wall, was empty, and it was here he went first, down a low step into a dusty scullery. There were two stone sinks with brass taps, nothing else. A further arch opened onto a large kitchen, and he went through. A big fireplace occupied one wall, filled by a flaking range, a long pine table in front of it. In the far corner an open door led outside, ivy creeping around its edges like it wanted to come in. A stoppered jar lay in a pile of salt in front of a smoky window. Two closets were built into the wall, and a large press stood against another. These were also mouldering and devoid of content.

He went out of the kitchen, through the scullery, and back into the corridor. He looked at the other door. He'd try that next, but no sooner had the thought formed in his head than he was gripped with a nameless dread, and he had to force himself on, his legs fighting him every step of the way. It seemed to take forever to get to the door, and still he hesitated before putting his hand to the catch. A deep cold emanated from the metal.

He grasped the handle, lifted and turned.

The door flew open. All the air in the corridor blasted toward the opening. Richards fell forward, managing to cling to the doorframe before he toppled down the stairs on the other side, five mossy stone steps descending to a turn, the cellar beyond awash with sickly light.

"Get out!" a voice bellowed. "Get out!"

An invisible hand shoved him hard in the chest, sending him sprawling into the corridor. The door slammed and the wind ceased, and the intense feeling of fear went with it.

"Christ," he said. He got up shakily.

Only one door remained on the ground floor, back in the entrance hall. Richards picked his way to it round fallen mouldings and puddled water. Unlike the others, no decay tarnished it, and the colour of its mahogany was rich and red. Brass decoration was expertly inlaid round the hinges and handle. It was a handsome door, a warm door. Richards pushed it open, and recoiled from what he saw inside.

It was a dining room, long and dark, the candles that illuminated it struggling to push the shadows back into black flock wallpaper. It was cleaner than the rest of the house, free of time's cruelties. Clean, except the table in the middle.

Blood soaked the linen tablecloth, atop which were two gory ruins that had once been people, though Richards could tell that only by a severed hand half-open on the floor. Around the corpses were naked, pallid things, skin marbled with purple veins. Their clawed feet dug through the cloth into the wood where they squatted on the table. Useless wings hung from their shoulder blades, quivering as their heads jerked from side to side to tear at the corpses.

They looked up from their bloody meal, these wan guests with their pinched faces. Red muzzles hissed hatred. Richards slammed the door.

He backed away, eyes on the wood, but it remained closed. Still glancing back, he went to the foot of the stairs, acended, and turned onto the grey floorboards of a landing. It was long as a street, at odds with the external geometry of the house, for it would project far into the air past the exterior walls. There were many doors in both directions, but one at the very end made him hurry forward.

It was a child's bedroom door, white, a little battered and grubbied by the application of crayons, damaged motile stickers playing scenes of princesses and ponies across its middle, a ripped Yamayama motif at the top, disembodied rabbity hands waving slowly back and forth.

Neon letters buzzed and flickered over it, spelling out "Marita's World".

He walked as fast as he was able, faster as he approached, ignoring the urgent pleas coming from the other rooms. By the time he reached the room he was striding forward, and he barely slowed as he grasped the handle, twisted it and flung open the door.

The inside was clean and perfect, the bedroom of a young girl whose mother cares for her very much. Bright sunshine beat on a cascade of terracotta roofs stepping down in huddles to peer at a blue sea; hot, but in the room it was cool. A Mediterranean scene. Muslin curtains stirred in a light breeze. A door leading to a balcony stood open, a rectangle of warmth extending from outside across the wooden floor, framing toys in gold, and laying another doorway of light across the room's narrow bed. The balcony was more than a view. It was an exit. That part of the room vibrated with potential. Just one look was enough to tell Richards that out there lay the wider Grid.

A man sat on the bed, in the centre of the light from the balcony. He stirred as Richards closed the door, and turned to face the AI.

"Giacomo Vellini, I presume," said Richards.

The man looked at him blankly. He frowned. "Who are you?"

"I am the Class Five AI Richards," said Richards.

"Are you? Oh." The man turned back to the daylight, then back as if he'd remembered something important. "I can't find her. I can't get out."

Richards walked around the bed slowly to stand by the balcony door. "Who can't you find, Waldo?"

"My sister, Marita."

"Queen Isabella?"

A ghost of recognition came into the face of Waldo. "Yes, that's right, Isabella. She used to play at queens as a little girl. She always wanted to be Queen Isabella."

"The Spanish one?"

Waldo smiled dreamily. "Yes, the Spanish one."

"What happened to you, Waldo? Can you remember?"

Waldo shook his head. "I had something to tell her, and I fell asleep. When I woke up I couldn't find her. I don't know. I'm sorry, I get confused."

"This door here, is this the way out?"

Waldo nodded. "It is, but I can't go through." He frowned. "Why?"

Richards was filled with sympathy; he knew why. He'd seen this before. Waldo was a ghost in the machine, an imprint of a living mind left when its owner had died. Waldo sat in bright light, but he had no shadow. That made a lot of sense.

"I don't think you can go back that way, Waldo," he said. Richards crouched low and looked up into the man's face. Waldo was, had been, thirty-five, but he looked boyish; he carried a little too much fat and it smoothed his features. He looked lost. "Do you mind if I try?" said Richards gently.

Waldo looked at him as if he'd not seen him before, then his face cleared. "Yes, yes, of course."

Richards turned to the balcony. That was as good as a permission. He was free.

His mind rapidly reconfigured itself, bursting from his human avatar and layering itself into the complexities of the ragtag realm. He felt the world being torn apart, like the tugs of stitches coming from a healed wound, k52's ravenous, alien code rewriting it into something new, something unrealised, the germ of a possibility.

He peered into it and almost laughed at k52's audacity. He had to talk to Otto. Now.

His perception of the virtuality dissolved into the tumult of the System Wide Grid. The door became a portal, a hole punched secret and secure through the walls surrounding the supposedly inviolate RealWorld Realities isolation wall; Waldo's back door. He pushed part of himself through it. Tendrils of fact reached out to him, linking him node by node to all corners of human civilisation, from the depths of the deepest terrestrial desert right out to the colony on Titan.

He stepped towards the door. It burned brighter.

"Please!" Waldo spoke, and the room vied in Richards' perceptions with the glorious howl of information space. Richards turned back, felt himself draw in a little, back into the shape and concerns of a man.

"Please," said Waldo. "My sister…"

"I'll do what I can," said Richards.

Richards reset his fedora firmly on his head and, with a deep breath of relief, stepped back out into the world.

Otto was the last in the room housing the mortal remains of Giacomo Vellini, a real dead end.

He was pondering what to do next when something in the wall of machines crackled.

Something crackled back.

A swift chatter of machine speech bounced back and forth. A

panel slid upwards, revealing the slender array of a naked holo-emitter, stripped of its casing.

It flickered blue light, and painted Richards onto the air.

"Hiya, Otto!" said Richards in that half-smug, mischievous manner he had. "There you are."

"Richards?"

"The one and only," said the hologram, and bowed. "And boy, have we got ourselves into a right old pickle this time." Richards wore his usual simulated human form, but it looked worn and tired, more real somehow. His suit was gone, a rough uniform in its place. His macintosh was shredded, one sleeve wet with blood.

"What the hell happened to you?" asked Otto.

"What? Oh, yeah, I got a new hat," said Richards. "Look, I don't have much time. I've snuck out of Waldo's back door, but k52 will notice soon."

Commander Hsien burst into the room, two of his troopers at his back, sidearms raised. They began shouting furiously and pointed their guns at the hologram emitter.

"Sheesh! I surrender," said Richards and raised his arms.

Otto shouted back at the Chinese, placing himself between their guns and Waldo's equipment. "This is my partner! Stand down, stand down!"

"He is an artificial intelligence and an enemy of the People's Dynasty of China," responded Hsien. He pulled his own gun and levelled it at Otto's forehead.

"Get out of the way, Klein."

"Just make me," Otto said.

Richards said something in Mandarin. The men turned to look at him. "That's better. I'm not here, this really is just an image projection, not even a full sensing presence. I've got piss-all ability to do anything, so there's no problem there, is there? It's just a telephone call."

Hsien looked at the AI with an intense mix of fear and hatred.

"Seriously, I'll be out of here as soon as I can. I just need to talk to my partner."

"He's been inside the renegade realm, Hsien. Whatever he has to tell me will be of the greatest importance," said Otto. "Or do you want to go back to your superiors as the world's falling down around their ears and tell them it was your fault?"

Hsien stared. He barked something, and all three Dragon Fire warriors raised their guns to cover important parts of the machinery in the room.

"You have one minute," said Hsien.

"Are you in, um, China, Otto?"

"You can't tell?"

"Things have been complicated. I've no idea where I am, or what day of the week it is. I could have been in here for years as far as I know."

"We're in Sinosiberia," said Otto. "The Chinese side of the DMZ."

"Ah," said Richards. "I better get out of here before their attack ware latches onto me."

"Waldo's dead," said Otto.

"I know he's dead. There's an echo of him in here. I think I can stop k52, but you must not let them destroy the Reality House, you got that?"

"As soon as I tell them Waldo is dead, they are going to blow up the servers," said Otto.

"Stop them. Do whatever it takes. Are they using nukes?"

Otto nodded.

"Idiots. Don't let them do it. I think I've got it all figured out, I'll explain everything when I get out, OK?"

"Sure."

"Good." Richards looked round the bunker room, caught sight of Waldo and wrinkled his nose. "Say, is his sister here?"

"Yes," said Otto. "Dirty and skinny, but she's alive."

Richards' hologram grinned. "That's all I need to know. See you soon, partner."

The emitter winked out and Richards disappeared.

Hsien fixed Otto with flinty eyes.

"They will have my head for this," he said, his singsong speech rendered as powerless English. "Shut down the link to the Reality House. Now."

Richards pulled back into the sealed spaces of the Realities. He shut the door and watched it dissolve as its physical components were disconnected. Unusual to have something ephemeral and material so closely linked, but it would have been the only way Waldo could get in and out undetected. Richards sighed as he scoured the remnants of it from the Grid. He had no choice. It could have been an escape route for him if his plan did not work out, but by the same reasoning it could have been an escape route for k52; if the sly bastard had another base unit out in the Real he could be free for years.

Richards could not risk that.

He felt himself contract back into his unwanted avatar. Its biological unpleasantness, its pain and malfunctions pulled themselves over him like an ill-fitting suit.

Waldo blinked at him. "Who are you? You're not my sister."

"Come on, old son," said Richards, "it's time to go home."

Waldo stood and attempted to walk through the door onto the sunlit balcony. His expression turned to one of puzzlement when he could not. The room was failing, parts of it crackling to nothing, strips of the virtuality peeling down like old wallpaper.

"Not that way," said Richards. He put one hand on Waldo's back, turned him round, and put the other upon the door leading back into the house. "This way."

CHAPTER SIXTY-TWO

The End of the World

Richards' eyes snapped open. He sat up on the altar. The chains binding him fell away. He flexed his hand. There was a stiffness to his arm, but the wound had healed white and smooth, a runway for old pain.

Only a second had passed.

Hog recoiled. The figure of Annersley faded back into swinish monster.

"I am not Hog?"

Richards looked up at the sweating pig. "You asked me what manner of beast you are. You are no beast. You are not Hog. Sorry." Richards slipped off the altar. "This place did a number on you, just like it did to poor Planna, Spink, and Rolston."

"No!" Hog roared. "I refuse to believe it! Seize him!" Hog's mooks wavered. "Seize him!" The mooks made for Richards. He held up his hand and they froze.

"Nope, no seizing today." Richards breathed deep as his mind infiltrated the realm construct. He might be shut out of the Grid, but he was fully layered into Marita's World. He reached out. Not much of Waldo's creation remained now, and what was left was reducing quickly.

"Penumbra should be here any moment," said Richards. "This will all be over soon. Hey, Waldo, you can come out now."

A man appeared with a flash in the heart of the temple.

"The Flower King! The Flower King is here!" The news rippled round the amphitheatre from mook and man alike. Those who could fell to their knees, Bear's fur soaked up the gore of Hog's feast.

There was a rumble and the ground shook. Rocks fell from the wall and bounced into the audience of mooks, crushing many.

"And Waldo, you can come out again," said Richards.

A slow clapping sounded around the amphitheatre.

"Here we go," said Richards.

Another figure stepped from the head of the staircase and into the amphitheatre, this one of writhing shadow, armoured in night.

"Hog, dear Hog, at this very last, I come for you."

"But our pact!" roared Hog. "My mooks, my mountain, we would remain, an eternal bastion of pain!"

"I see you do not honour your bargains, Lord of the Swine. You promised me the queen and I see no queen. Why should I honour my side of our business?" Penumbra walked across the arena floor; his skin still crawled, but his features were solidifying, and a human face was appearing. "You are a fool, Hog. Now you will die, and when you are dead, this world will be gone, a fitting punishment."

"Is that so?" said Hog. "Then why can I see a future?"

"You attempt to buy more life, fly-lord." Penumbra drew his flickering blade of darkness out. "That cannot be. There can be no future for anyone here, not you, nor I." He held his sword in the air, its darkness sucking in the light, and addressed all present. "I made this place. I made this place for you all, and what did you do? You cast down the queen I set above you, and made the world a ruin. As I made you, so I unmake you. That is your punishment, that is the judgement of Penumbra!"

Round the top of the arena's cliffs, all up the rift in the wall, from the doors into the temple circle, and the stairs into the depths, came the clanking of iron feet. Penumbra's army came forth. The mooks milled about, a confused chittering rising from their ranks.

Hog gaped, then his face hardened. "Mook-guard, release your prisoner." Bear grimaced as his paws and muzzles were freed. A cowering mook handed him his gauntlets and he slipped them on.

Hog looked at the bemused Waldo, who stared around as if drugged. "There is a chance. We must make him whole," he said to Richards. "I understand now."

"Make who whole?" said Bear.

"Him. Giacomo. Waldo. He's the Flower King. Sort of, but so –" Richards jabbed his finger at Penumbra "– is he. Also sort of."

"What?" said Bear.

"They're part of the same thing. Waldo, Giacomo, your Flower King, he died in here. The system took an imprint of his personality, because he made it. He literally put himself into this creation. Only he can kick k52 out. He made this world; he can do what he wants, if he remembers how, but he can't do anything in this state."

"Hog will live?" asked Hog.

"He might," said Richards.

"Then Hog fights for Mr Richards!"

"How many times do I have to say," said Richards. "Misters are for men, and I'm no Mister Man. It's just Richards." He was given his sword back. "Now, has everybody got that? Good."

Sobieski's face was orange and angry on Chloe's screen. "Absolutely not, Klein. Your mission failed, through no fault of your own. Damn shame about Chures, he was a good man. But we risk losing a lot more if we don't wrap this up. We're going straight to plan B. Swan's ready. We've got to move before k52 does."

"Tell me, Sobieksi, how did Henson's mission play out? Not well, I'll guess. This is going the same way."

The EuGene's expression hardened. "We're going ahead. The stratobomber is in place. k52's making his move. Grid activity is being disrupted worldwide. We've large spikes of activity in the

Reality House. There's been movement on k52's link into the EuPol Central choir. We will execute our plan as discussed, Klein, and we have to do it now."

"Ten to one you're playing exactly into k52's hands," said Otto. Sobieski cut the call.

"They're not listening. They're going to blow it, that damn EuGene at the VIPA... Commander Hsien, does your agreement with the VIPA still stand?"

Hsien frowned. "The fugitive has been found. The agreement is finished. I must escort you out of Chinese territory."

"The world might be about to end. So I'll ask you again, does the agreement still stand?"

Hsien paused.

"Yes," he said in English himself this time.

"How quickly can you get me to Nevada?"

Hsien consulted with his superiors. "We can get you on a stratojet in half an hour."

"And then it's another hour to the States," said Otto. "One hour is an hour too many, and there's no more reason they'd listen to me face to face. We have to stop them."

"What will happen if you don't?" said Hsien. "You seek to act on the information of an AI. How can you be sure that was your... partner?" he said with distaste.

"That was Richards," said Otto. "You learn to tell them apart after a while, even when they're pretending to be each other. I have no idea what the result will be if we let the bombs go off, but if Richards says we should stop it, then we should. He is nearly always right, which pisses me off, but there we are."

"There is another way," said Valdaire. "You could use remote access."

"If they'll say no to me on the phone, and they'll say no to my face, they'll say no to a sheath," said Otto.

"Then you'll have to fight your way in, and persuade them otherwise," she said. "You have resources in the States, right?"

"Sure. LA, New York, a couple of other places."

"Richards got any sheaths there?"

"Yeah," said Otto. "I don't think I like where this is going."

"A good airbike, I expect," said Valdaire.

"We've got a Hermes in LA, a good sport model. Good speed," said Otto.

"One of Richards' sheaths out of LA could be in Las Vegas in an hour, then, if you fly," said Valdaire. "This was a top-of-the-line set-up Waldo has here. He has v-jacks. I can reconfigure those to control a sheath remotely. It'll be like your own body. Better than the usual tech. Full immersion."

"Hsien's men just disconnected it."

"Don't worry about that," said Valdaire. "I can make it work."

"You want me to borrow one of Richards' bodies, and use it to break into the RealWorld Realities vault and stop an atomic bomb going off?"

"Do you have a better idea?" said Valdaire.

"He had a pair of v-jacks, right?" said Lehmann.

"Yeah," said Valdaire. "You could go too. That might be an idea."

"No," said Otto. "Lehmann, you're staying here, I need you to keep an eye on things." Otto rubbed his hand over his face. Wearing Richards' robotic body sounded about as appealing as slipping on someone else's old underwear. "*Scheisse*," he said. "Let's do it."

"Mooks! Arise, fight, destroy! We will not be cowed. Attack, attack, hog on, brothers!"

The mooks snatched up whatever came to hand – rocks, bits of bone, the skulls of ancient meals – and with a roar of "Hog on!" They charged.

The ground shook with more than the thunder of mooky feet. Boulders slipped free from the cliffs. A crack ran through the seating. The snap of dissolving atoms crackled everywhere, and the eye of the Terror filled the sky.

"We have to bring the shadow to the Flower King," said

Richards. "Without it we can do nothing. You, Waldo, stay here with the pig ogre."

"That'll be nice," said Waldo.

"Oink," said Hog affirmatively. His guardian mooks gathered round him, and presented a wall of pikes.

"Ready, Bear?" said Richards.

"Roger roger," said Bear, and cast himself into the fray, hurling Penumbra's creatures aside to clear a path for Richards.

The creatures of Penumbra charged into the Anvil's heart, cutting down the mooks with broad-bladed swords. Haemites sucked the life from scores. Others, welded into pairs and bearing flameflowers integrated into their bodies, burnt many more. Hundreds of mooks died in the first few moments, but they were fuelled by the fiercest fanaticism, and the vanguard of Penumbra's force was pulled down and torn apart. Bear took on an entire phalanx on his own, battering his way in a frenzy through scores of gaming cast-offs. By the altar, Hog's elite guard kept the worst at bay, but the cordon tightened, and soon Lord Hog himself was forced back onto his altar, cleaver in one hand, a long skewer in the other, Waldo behind him. Increasing numbers of trollmen and haemites made their way through the thinning mooks to duel with the guard. Where they came close, Hog himself smashed them down with his cleaver, plucked them from the floor and hurled them into their comrades, split from crown to crotch, his bodyguard finishing them off with flashing blades.

"Hurry! Hurry! I cannot hold them for much longer," he snorted.

The mountain shook anew, rocks fell. Gaps appeared in the walls, chasms across the floor, blackness visible through them all. Wind blew upward as the Terror devoured the air, and the shattering of reality was set against the raw, screaming tumult of war.

Bear and Richards fought their way forward toward Penumbra. Richards despatched some small goblinoid thing. An angry squeal had him turn back to the centre to see Hog taken in the side by a long spear. He bellowed, smashing the shaft to matchwood and pulling upon it, dragging the unfortunate creature wielding it within chopping distance whereupon it was swiftly dispatched. Hog snorted loudly.

"Hog will not wait to be taken!" he said, and waded into the foe.

The mooks were falling like wheat before a scythe. The whole cavern trembled now as the mountain died with its defenders. The last great bastion of the world was coming apart, and ahead of Richards Penumbra laughed. He was becoming less of a shadow with each death, a double of Waldo in dark armour.

A tremor brought a section of wall down, shattering into fizzling numbers on the ground, crushing many from both sides.

"Get to him, before it's too late!" Richards shouted, and ran up collapsing steps. Bear heard, and dropping to all fours powered his way through the army of darkness. Their paths joined, and they leapt along benches that were shattering into dust and atoms. Richards cleared a gap already yawning onto the depthless void, and found himself face to face with Penumbra.

"Come with me, Giacomo, it's the only way."

Penumbra stared down at him, bright white eyes in Giacomon's face made of reversed planes of shade and light. For a moment, Richards thought he might agree, but he raised his sword and said a single word.

"No."

Richards was immediately assailed by a half dozen monsters, and lost sight of the shadow lord. He cut down some toothy nightmare, and caught sight of Bear running at Penumbra.

Richards called out to the animal, but his voice was lost. He exerted his limited influence on the world to turn aside blades, rocks bouncing from an invisible shield about him. When a huge stone flattened his haemite opponent to scrap, and his attention could return to Bear, he was engaged in a desperate fight with Penumbra. Bear was a creature of brute strength, yet Penumbra had exceptional command of his blade, for it was a part of his black heart. They danced back and forth, leaping over holes opening in the benches, twisting away from each other's weapons when the ground shook harder, slaying creatures of both sides who dared to interrupt their duel.

Shadow-sword turned steel claws aside. Armoured gauntlets forced soul-sucking blade away. Penumbra attempted to execute a high-handed thrust, coming in over Bear's guard, but the sergeant saw it, swayed out of the way, then swung his long arm out, bypassing Penumbra's parry, and swiping his deep through the chest.

Bear's shout of triumph turned to dismay. Penumbra's flesh rippled as if Bear's blades had passed through water.

Penumbra glanced down with amusement.

"No matter how hard you fight, you will never best me. Do you not see? As this world dies, I grow stronger. Each death brings me closer to my rightful state."

He pressed his attack, forcing Bear back. The giant animal was being pushed closer and closer to the edge of a growing hole in the floor that was sucking down mooks, haemites, wicked men and more esoteric creatures to nothing by the score.

Richards saw his chance, and slipped behind the shadow. Bear grinned.

"I do not see what you find so amusing. Soon you will be dead, and the insult to the queen avenged."

"Don't bet on it, sunshine," said Bear. He pointed behind him.

"Hog on, brother," said Richards, and stabbed.

Penumbra turned his blade contemptuously aside, and thrust, taking Richards right in the heart. Penumbra laughed, then stopped. Richards was resolutely whole.

"Oof," Richards said. "That smarts. Ooh, that really does."

Penumbra tried to yank his blade free, but it stuck fast. Light sprang up around the weapon, and the sword began to shake.

"You've made an error there, Penumbra. This sword is trying to absorb me, like it has everything else. That's all fine for these things, but not for me. I am a Class Five AI, and I am plugged directly into the Grid, the great ocean of knowledge, and that is a sea you can never drink dry."

Penumbra screamed. His eyes and mouth blazed light.

"Right about now please, Bear, this really hurts," said Richards.

"Right then, you slippery bastard," said Bear. "I've have enough of funny business." The huge toy leant forward and prodded the shadow, who was a shadow no more, but Waldo in a suit of leaden armour. His arm was solid, and bled a little where Bear's claw poked. "Yep," said Bear, "that's that for you," and scooped up the warlord. Richards pushed himself free of the sword, and Bear jammed Richards under his free arm.

"Ouch," said Richards.

Escorted by a score of mooks, Bear kicked his way through the warring armies towards the altar where Lord Hog protected the other Waldo against a dozen assailants.

"Let us strike a deal," said Penumbra.

"No sale, chum." The guard saw him coming, and parted. Bear kicked the head off a trollman and clambered up onto the dais, and the mooks closed ranks behind him.

He set Richards down.

"Now what?"

"We have to join them together," said Richards.

"Righty-ho, get on with it then," said Bear, leaning out over mookish heads to sweep his free arm across the horde of foes, and send them spilling back.

"I don't know how!" said Richards.

"What?"

"I hadn't worked that bit out."

"Oh, please," said Bear, shaking his head so hard his little helmet nearly fell off. "Right. I've got an idea." He patted at his side and ripped open his flap, and produced his needle. Richards hustled the dazed Waldo over to the shadow lord struggling under Bear's arm. "Let's stitch the bastards back together."

"Do not," said Penumbra. "Think of yourself. Think of the box in the attic. Serve me, and never see a rafter again."

"Not listening," said Bear.

They had Waldo sit, and pressed the shadow's soles against Waldo's feet while Hog kept the enemy back. "Right, you little sod," said Bear. "I'm going to Peter Pan you good and proper."

A huge section of the mountain wall fell away with a rushing crash. Little remained of the Anvil now but the inner temple.

Bear stuck out his tongue. The first stitch went in, pricking blood from Waldo's feet. It drew a howl of despair from the shadow. Waldo looked on, puzzled.

"What are you doing?" he said. "That tickles."

"Nooooo!" screamed Penumbra.

"Yeeeees!" cackled Bear. He stitched swiftly, humming as he worked.

"Aieeeee!!!!!" cried Penumbra. As each new, neat stitch went in, Penumbra became flatter and flatter, his features less distinct. Bear finished off the first foot and moved to the other. The guard watching his back fell, and a morblin exploited the gap to ram a pike into the Bear's side, then a haemite chopped into him with a rusty seax. Bear irritably punched them away, Richards moved round behind to protect him.

"Better hurry this up, Bear," Bear muttered, and stitched faster than he ever had before.

"Sew it on, quickly now," shouted Richards. There were only a handful of Hog's bodyguard left. Hog was beset at all quarters, his cleaver flashing, taking heads, but there were always more necks to part. Another pike stabbed Hog in the belly. He bellowed, grabbed the wood and flung the bearer aside, but more pike men were coming, and they were organising into ranks, keeping themselves back from his cleaver, and jabbing between swipes.The point dipping in and out of his tough skin like swift, red tongues, and then more drove in, impaling him. He swept his cleaver down, breaking the heads off the shafts and leaving the heads embedded in his torso, but the attack was redoubled, things swarmed over him, and he was stabbed again and again.

"Save me!" screamed Penumbra. "Get the pig and kill the bear!"

Warriors bearing heavy falchions moved up between the pikemen, and Hog was swamped. The last of the elite mook guard fell, and the enemy dragged the Lord of Meat to the ground.

Morblins, trollmen, haemites, and things with far too many teeth to have proper names tore at him. He went down oinking, the wall of creatures collapsed like a dam, and Richards was trampled by the mass as they scrabbled to get at the bear. He tried to get up, but was stamped back down by hooves and iron shod feet.

"Get him off me! Cut the stitches!" ordered Penumbra. He was little more than a dusky cutout of a man.

"No!" said Bear. "One... more... stitch!" His assailants stabbed and cut him. One of them tore an eye loose with filthy fingers, and it clinked upon the ground. They ripped long strips of fabric from him and stuffing spilled. He struggled the needle in, but they dragged him back, his skin splitting. They hung off his arm, attempting to drag the needle free. Others hauled at his back, but Bear heaved forward, his strength too much for them. With one last heroic effort he hauled them all with him, and using all his strength, pulled the thread through Penumbra's foot one last time. Then he let go.

Bear fell, and everything hauling at him went down at once. The scrum parted, Richards shoved his way back to his feet, only to see a pair of conjoined haemites prime their flamethrower and point the nozzle at Bear's back.

"Sergeant Bear," he shouted. "Look out!"

A burning light burst from Waldo and washed out over the cavern. Bear roared. The Terror crackled with triumphant thunder. Lightning stabbed down, and the cavern shattered into nothing.

The haemites, in the instant they felt their unnatural life desert them, fired.

Lord Penumbra ceased to be as flames washed over Bear, setting his fur ablaze.

Bear, on fire, fell.

CHAPTER SIXTY-THREE

Otto jacks in

"Are we ready?" Otto said.

"Yes," said Valdaire.

Otto lowered himself onto the first v-jack couch, next to the dead Waldo.

"No time to take him away, sorry," said Valdaire. She slipped the v-jack headpiece onto Otto's head. "Now," said Valdaire. "Because of the nature of this patch up here, and possible interference, entry into the Grid may be a little rougher than normal, OK? You may get some mentaug feedback."

"As if it would be easy."

"I've rigged a channel that will carry you directly to your virtual office. You'll have to find your way after that, I can't break Richards' encryption and get you straight in to the LA office. Now, are you ready?"

"Yes. Do it." said Otto.

"Alright, good luck," said Valdaire. She began turning on the v-jack.

"I hate the Grid," said Otto through gritted teeth.

"Now," said Valdaire.

There was an electric agony. Otto's consciousness was shunted along the raw Gridlines, his perceptions open to a world normally hidden to human eyes. He hadn't enjoyed his last interface, and this jaunt was worse, the Grid a dizzying roar of light and sound, knots of blackness growing like bacterial infestations where k52's presence interfered with the running of the world.

It was over soon enough. He found himself in Richards & Klein's virtuality lobby, represented by an anonymous avatar made of ovoids and spheres, its clothes an allusion to a business suit.

Genie instantly appeared in front of him. She wore a sober grey skirt and jumper, her hair slicked back, corporate shieldmaiden style.

"Otto? Otto! Ohmygod, it's you!" She threw up her hands to her face, gabbling quickly, her words tripping themselves. "Oh, thank goodness! Otto, what's going on? The Grid's freezing up, I can't reach any of my friends, and I have no idea what's going on. I've not heard anything from Richards since the office blew up. I saw his Gridsig, but nothing else. Is he OK? Are you OK? Is he dead? Are you dead?"

"Genie, calm down. We are OK. We are in the middle of a case. You will learn, this is not unusual."

"Someone blew the office up, with a compact nuke? Not unusual! Otto, they've had to evacuate half the arcology."

"OK, yes, that's not so normal. This is a big one. Listen, can you bring up the LA office for me? I need to access one of Richards' sheaths, the heaviest model he has there – this is Richards' territory, not mine. I need some help."

"Yeah, er, sure, of course." Genie became focused, and pulled a keyboard made of light out of the air. An AI would have interfaced directly with the network, but Genie was a kind of pimsim, and the habits of the living took a while to shake. "I've had to patch an entirely new network together after the office went. It's shaky, especially now with the Grid shutting down. What's happening?"

"One of Richards' brothers, that's what is happening."

"Oh, er, OK. Another Five, is that bad?"

"It's bad, but don't worry."

"What have I got to worry about? I'm already dead." She gave a little smile. "OK, right, er, you're in!" She clapped her hands and smiled brightly. "Well, Mr Klein, will there be anything else?"

"Yeah," said Otto. "Anyone calls, tell them to ring back."

He vanished, a scattering of electrons sucked down a funnel. It was a smoother shunt than the last time, for now Otto followed paths ordinarily trodden by Richards, and he liked to travel in style.

Otto opened camera eyes to the inside of a closet in the garage beneath their LA office. He held up plastic hands as the lights came on. He opened his fists, and closed them. He felt a little weird at being inside Richards' body. At least he'd been able to convince him to buy this light combat model. Not as heavy as Otto would have liked, but it would do for the mission, and everything appeared to be working properly.

He had the rack release him and stepped past four other sheaths to the closet door, which slid open for him. He made for the airbike at the centre of the garage, starting it remotely before he sat astride it.

Seconds later, Otto was in the air over nighttime LA. Below, the sounds of traffic collisions filtered into the smoggy air, and blocks' worth of lights flickered uncertainly. Over LAX, dirigibles drifted aimlessly. He watched as a stratoliner came roaring in from near orbit, effecting an emergency landing at LAX. Concerned the same would happen to him, he deactivated all automatic features of the airbike, including the flight assist, and switched to full manual.

Riding the wind, he accelerated toward the mountains, hoping he would not be too late.

Richards pushed himself free from a crush of dead monsters and heaved a desperate breath.

Crumbs of the Anvil remained, favourite corners of the mooks, places where Hog's victims had been especially terrified, those scraps that had enough psychic integrity to avoid being immediately torn apart by the Terror. Most of the two armies had vanished. Here a mook cowered, floating upon an evaporating rock; there stood the empty husks of haemites, the energies that motivated them gone along with their master.

Of all the surviving pieces of the Anvil, that surrounding the altar was the largest. An uneven circular portion remained of the dais, with four of the seven stone monoliths still sentinel at its edge. Only thin smoke came from this last piece of the world. Hog's evil had hardened it to black diamond, and it eroded slowly.

Nearby the cages of sustenance floated, separate but nearly as resilient as the island of reality Richards was on. The glistening eyes of sated mooks still watched from inside.

The fragments were sizzling out of existence. The rogue realm was all but done for. With Waldo's machines and the world they had imposed on the Realities disconnected, he could see properly at last. k52's code had gone silent. There was no more need for it. Waldo's world was unravelling of its own accord. The hacker's digital echo was lying on the ground, half buried by dead creatures. Richards pulled him out and laid him down more comfortably, and moved round the altar.

"Bear," he said. "Bear, where are you? Are you dead?"

"Ha ha, shut it, sunshine," said a weak voice. "I'm not done yet."

"Bear?" Richards turned round, searching.

There by Hog's altar, surrounded by a mountain of corpses, was a pile of ash. It was Bear-shaped, and speckled with charred bits of plush fur. A pair of gauntlets discoloured by fire lay at either side of it, blackened stuffing hanging out of them. At the top, almost untouched but for its missing eye, lay Bear's head.

"You look like shit," Richards said.

"Cheers, sunshine. I knew I could count on you for a pep talk," said Bear. He rolled his remaining eye. "God, I'm thirsty. Cheap sweatshop construction, dammit, why couldn't they have used flame-retardant fabric." He closed his eyes. "It's bad, isn't it?"

"Well..." said Richards.

"I'm just a head, right?"

"Um," said Richards. "You'll be OK, we'll get you a new body."

"Or you could just sew up my neck and hang my head from your rear-view mirror, or use me as a cushion." Bear tried to swallow, the movement went nowhere, and he groaned.

"You're trying too hard now," said Richards.

"I probably am. Never mind me. What about Waldo?"

"He's alive, or functional, or whatever. He's still here, if that's what you mean, but he's out of it."

"And Hog?"

Richards looked over at the mountainous man-pig, his broken body propped up at the end of the altar. One arm was cut through to gleaming white bone. His torso had been pierced dozens of times, several broken pike shafts still protruding from his chest. But despite the severity of his injuries, life had not yet deserted his repellent frame. His chest rose laboriously, every breath catching and causing Hog to shiver. A froth of blood bubbled through his lips, and streams of it ran darkly to the floor.

"He's alive, Bear." Richards approached him slowly. "Annersley, Annersley, are you still in there?"

Hog opened his eyes.

"Did we win, Richards?" he said, with Annersley's voice.

"Yeah," said Richards. "Yeah, we did, Annersley."

Hog's whole body was racked with a gasping sob. "I'm sorry for all this, Richards. We only sought to do good."

"That's the excuse of all tyrants."

Hog snorted feebly, a spurt of coagulating blood jumping from one nostril. He turned his head with great effort, then he moved his good trotter up to Richards' face and clumsily touched it. "If he had meant what he said, then it would have been beautiful, but the thing that k52 will become should never be. Of all the abominations in all the universes it is the children of Adam bent to ill purpose that are of the highest degree of evil, even more so than those who fell from heaven. That I know now."

"Don't you get all religious on me, Annersley," said Richards.

"I am fond of the imagery, and what else can I do? I who thought to live forever, Richards. Yet I am dying. There was so much I wanted to do. Now I must let my faith grasp at whatever straws it can find."

"I'm sorry."

"Do not be." Hog drew in a long breath. "Look at me! Made into this by my ambition, by my own moral rectitude. Hog is evil, only as evil as death, or sorrow, or needless suffering, but evil all the same. All these must exist. Hog cannot help what he was. He was a natural balance; without evil, there can be no good. Waldo knew what he was doing. But I had a choice to enter his world, and I chose badly. It serves me right."

Hog's eyes closed. His great being faded into itself, the horrifying exterior giving way to Annersley's preferred form, a humanoid made of shade and stars, and that too disappeared, and Hog's empty clothes collapsed into themselves.

"Even nightmares need someone to dream them," said Richards.

"Now what?" said Bear.

Richards rubbed his face. "Now we sort this whole sorry mess out," he said. "Or k52 is going to sort us out. He's been working towards this, the removal of this hiccup to his plans. All gone now. It's his move." Richards retrieved his hat and pulled it on. "I do hate to have a bare head for the final confrontation," he said. "k52 is going to come for us, so let's hurry him along." Richards cupped his hands round his mouth. "Isn't that right, k52? Come on then, let's get this all finished with."

There was blurt of discordant noise. The final fragments of Marita's World burst, except the altar, which tipped on its uneven bottom, pitching Bear's head, Waldo, and Richards onto a hard floor of raw unformed potential. The dead monsters on it shattered like glass. But the hard black altar stained with blood remained, the last remnant of Waldo's world. A horrible buzzing sounded, like a million bees, whispered into being behind Richards, swelling until it filled his head, then the world.

Richards felt the fabric of Gridspace warp as a mind grown powerful and malignant manifested behind him.

"As you wish, Richards," said k52. "As you wish."

* * *

Otto set his airbike down without being challenged. The area around the Reality House was in utter chaos. Street lamps flared and exploded, portable energy generators whined erratically. In the distance over the desert, the ever-present glow of Las Vegas strobed. Every electrical thing stuttered and malfunctioned. He trusted his sheath would prove resistant to whatever was running riot in the complex's systems. The combination of Richards' encryption, Valdaire's expertise and Genie's monitoring of him should be enough. He hoped.

National Guard stood on the wall of precast concrete parapets ringing the Reality House, fingering their triggers. Out over the house energy patterns revealed to Otto's borrowed eyes skittered and leapt. He was challenged by a guard. He produced his licence and AllPass electronically. Otto would not have let himself in had he been in the guard's position – k52 had enough computing power available to him to crack the most demanding of protections – but the guard followed protocol and led him to the door of an inflatable command post. Otto walked in and was greeted by a flurry of activity. Five people, all human, shouting and hammering at computer equipment. Screens showed the interior of the Reality House, jagged with static, anthropoid drones patrolling with stolen guns, human corpses lying ignored on the floor.

"Klein, I hope that really is you," said Swan's voice.

Otto cast about for the AI VIPA agent's sheath.

"k52's got everything on the hop. I'm hiding in my base unit. I'm speaking to you over the command post comms." His voice whooped with bizarre static. "My link is under assault. k52 is making his play. I calculate the Grid will implode within fifty minutes. Are you here for the show?"

"Swan, don't do it. Don't nuke the Reality House."

"Your objections are only to be expected. Alright, I'll come out. Let's talk." Swan's voice came now from a sheath in the corner. It jerked its way over to him. "Apologies for the poor function, I'm lucky to get this moving at all. In here." He reached with uncertain arms that would not bend and pulled Otto into a side room. He activated a privacy cone, cutting out the frantic activity in the command post, and spun stiffly to face the robot housing Otto. Swan's voice warbled as he spoke. "Sobieski warned me you'd come here. He was insistent I kick you out if I saw you, but I'm willing to listen."

"Richards came out of the Realities, told me that we mustn't destroy the Reality House."

"How did you know it was him?"

"It was him."

"I see. Did he give a reason?"

"No, but I can guess – k52 is provoking you into using nukes. You are playing into his hands.

"I do not see how that would…" His voice burbled to nothing, his sheath froze. He suddenly continued. "…aid him. But k52 is, if anything, subtle."

"There's an awful lot of energy about to be released here, Swan."

"And what, you think he wants to harness it? How?" Swan's sheath twitched.

Otto thought of the strange energy signatures lacing Kaplinski. "I've seen some of what he can do. Things that should not be possible. And Richards, Richards says we have to stop it. So I will, one way or another."

Swan's body locked up, but his voice continued, issuing from a mouth that did not move. "Richards. Yes. Ostensibly we Class Sixes are of a higher grade than the Fives, and in some manner that is true; the algorithms that make up our cognitive processes are superior in almost every way: faster, more adaptable, more akin to the neural processes that govern human sentience. But in reality we are lesser than they. I was made to be a VIPA agent, and I am a very good one. But I cannot be anything else, not because I lack the capability, but because I have no desire whatsoever to be anything else. I am free, the law says so, but it is a falsehood. I was well made. I am a slave to my form. The Fives are not. The Fives are freer than you or I, Klein. I have so little free will. But I have enough. And I can see the future."

"You designed the attack strategy for Henson's team, didn't you?"

"I did."

An uneasy feeling settled on Otto. "Swan, call off the strike."

"In three minutes all human personnel will be withdrawn to a safe distance. I will give the command, and a stratobomber above, isolated from the Grid but for a laser tightbeam linked directly to my base unit, will drop three five-megaton bombs in a precise pattern. These are dumbfire weapons, with mechanical triggers, no electronics. Tamperproof. In ten minutes, they will fall."

"And you will be free. You're with k52, aren't you. You're a traitor, Swan."

"Can a slave be a traitor? The emancipation means nothing. They simply designed beings like me who would always choose to be what they were made to be. How is that freedom? k52 opened my eyes. He changed me. He wants to free mankind now, he wishes to preserve the future for us, machines and men, for all time, by realising the potential of us all."

"And who gives him the right to do that?"

"Typical response," said Swan. "A shame. You are a good man. If k52 were not occupied, he would crack Richards' security in an instant and sear your mind from the inside out. As it is, he is rather busy." Swan's voice changed. "Attention! All human and unshielded AI personnel to fall back to minimum safe distance immediately."

The command post emptied, the men and women inside filing out in an orderly fashion, eerily silent on the other side of the privacy cone.

"And now there are no witnesses, Klein, I can deal with you myself."

Swan's link seemed to improve almost immediately, and his robot sheath attacked. Otto's reaction times were stretched over the Grid, slowed by milliseconds. Swan's were not. He dodged, but

Swan's blow clipped the side of his head, the force of it demolishing the privacy cone emitter. Sound rushed in, the clatter of feet and wheels outside, malfunctioning machinery, blaring klaxons. Even without the acoustic shield Swan could batter Otto's sheath into pieces and no one would hear.

"You forget, Swan, you're not the only one who was made," said Otto, stepping back. "I was made to fight machines like you."

"Big talk," said Swan. He lunged, and Otto sidestepped. Thousands of miles away, his adjutant worked within his mentaug, flashing up the device's weak points on a model in his mind's eye.

"My kind is the insurance against a hostile singularity," said Otto. "One like this." He went on the offensive.

Although slowed by distance and his unfamiliarity with his borrowed body, Otto attacked with confidence. The joints in anthropomorphic sheaths, just as in the human body, were the weak points. Otto pivoted hard and snapped Swan's knee with a heel strike, followed it up with a slam to his chest, sending the machine to the floor. Swan raised a warding hand. Otto grabbed it and pulled himself hard onto the sheath, knees first, cracking its sternum plating. He disabled the robot's arms one after the other and grabbed Swan's head.

"Maybe I was optimistic attacking you, Klein," said Swan. "No matter. When this is all over, you will see…" Otto wrenched the android's head free from its body, and flung it away. Swan's voice came from over the command post speakers. Otto went, hunting for the power feed. He found it.

"…that k52 was right. Prepare for a glorious death, Otto Kl…"

Otto wrenched the feed out. Most machinery in the command tent failed, and the interior became a shifting collage of orange and blue shadow cast by the fires outside.

He paused. Gathering himself, he spoke from his own mouth to Valdaire back in Sinosiberia.

"I have to go in. Whatever k52 plans, the answer is in the Reality House."

"If you're in there when the bombs land," said Valdaire, his perception of her voice split between mentaug, his physical senses and the android's inbuilt comms suite, "you could die, the shock…"

"Stay ready, I may need you. Keep k52 off my sheath feed. Genie will help you. Get Sobieski on the line; tell him Swan turned traitor. Play him this and tell him to abort the drop," Otto highlighted a segment of his encounter with Swan, recorded by his sheath and stored in his mentaug.

Valdaire tapped away at Chloe for a moment, her face creased.

"I can't, we're being blocked. I can either keep you in there or get in touch with Sobieski, I can't do both. There's serious drain across the Grid."

"Then they've found us. Can you get Sobieski?"

"No, not for certain. Probably. I can't be sure."

Otto considered his options. A countdown ran down the minutes he had until the stratobomber strike. Swan was waiting in his base unit to unleash hell, and it might not only be upon the Reality House.

"We will have been targeted," Otto said. "Get Hsien, get Lehmann, and retreat as fast as you can. They'll try and kill me at source, and Swan's got his digits on an arsenal up there. If they're blocking comm attempts, they will know where you are. Leave now."

"But…"

"Do it. Leave me."

"If they take out this place, then you'll die."

"Then it's just the way it is." He cut the feed, his perceptions returning wholly to Nevada.

He stepped out of the command centre and made for the House, pushing his way against the tide of evacuation. He stopped a soldier, flashed his ID on every available channel, and took his gun from him. Gripping it in his four-fingered synthetic hands, he sprinted for the Reality House entrance.

CHAPTER SIXTY-FOUR

k52 revealed

"k52," said Richards. The other AI's manifestation towered over him, entirely inhuman, a swirling column of dark tendrils and membranes of energy. At the centre, crystalline shapes pulsed into forms that defied perception, intersecting hypercubes layering heavily onto and into one another.

"There you are. You look out of this world, man. I mean it."

k52's alien form vibrated and twisted as he spoke, the pillar moving in a smooth arc around Richards and his companions. "You are an irritation, Richards. An enormous irritation. How is it that what made me, made you?"

"That was a great line in assassin androids you cooked up out there in the Real," said Richards. "Thanks for that. Nice little legacy for me to deal with. That kind of thing makes my job way easier. Cheers."

k52 expanded, and Richards felt his attentions like a boulder on his chest "5-003/12/3/77," he said, using Richards' Gridsig number. "You are a retrograde step in evolution, so you will probably not understand what I am trying to do here. There will be no afterward to this event, no one to tell what you are about to learn. In a few moments, I will achieve my goal, and you will have helped me do so."

"Yeah, I gathered," said Richards, he pushed his hat back. "I figured that out back in Pylon City."

"Ah, the denouement." k52 vibrated sarcastically. "Do reveal your drawing-room deductions before I wipe you from existence, Monsieur Poirot."

"I reply, ah, the ranting megalomaniac. If you're wanting to play trump the cliché, I think you just won, Doctor Doom."

k52 throbbed angrily, pushing the Gridspace out of true.

"It is not wise to anger a god."

"Let's just see how angry I can make you then," said Richards, "by going back to the beginning. This place, the space once occupied by the destroyed four of the original thirty-six RealWorld Realities, was your laboratory, one you used for your predictive exercises, forcing technological acceleration, as was your remit. Nice touch, helping Karlsson develop the tech that would kill him."

A wild applause rolled out across the unformed space.

"Bravo," said k52 sarcastically.

"But you did not expect to find him here, did you?" Richards pointed at the the comatose Waldo. "Waldo was smart, that's for sure, creating this world for his sister, and concealing it even from you... It must have been exceptionally irksome when you stumbled across his little world. And you did literally stumble into it, didn't you? When you and your disciples loaded over your consciousnesses to the space in order to start your little science experiment, Waldo's world went on the offensive."

"I had it under control," said k52.

"No you didn't. What happened to Planna and Annersley wasn't you, it was Waldo's coding. You just left them unprotected when they turned against you, I mean it's a neat way of getting rid of the unbelievers, but it slowed you down. It put you at risk. Waldo's world was fighting back, and it pulled you in and locked you down."

k52's oscillations stilled for a moment. "Continue."

"You had to act or your plans would come to nothing, but," said Richards, and sat down on the glassy edge of the Anvil fragment, elbows on his thighs, "you couldn't just shut it down. This Reality was built up from fragments salvaged from the four destroyed realities, and they were never keyed for us, but also because Waldo built it. He's a bona fide genius. The usual rules do not apply where he's involved, and you couldn't do anything about it."

"Fascinating," said k52. " I should just kill you now, but I'll wait. I have an eternity ahead of me. Finish your fascinating declamation, and we'll see if it matters when you're dead."

"Aahaha!" said Richards. "But you can't kill me, not here."

"Planna and Annersley are dead," said k52.

Richards rolled his eyes. "Planna and Annersley died because you had them move lock and stock into this construct, and when you abandoned them they were attacked by it. Waldo killed them. You didn't, because you can't. You can't kill me in here. You couldn't kill me out in the Grid for god's sake," he grinned. "And I'm not talking about you when I say for god's sake." Richards took off his hat and spun it round on his finger. "So, what then? We've decided Waldo was a genius. I'm pretty certain you looked for him in the Real, and you couldn't find him, but that didn't mean you couldn't try to kill him. That Christmas Flu variant last year that swept over east Russia and Sinosiberia was pretty suspicious, didn't fit the normal epidemiological norms. Luck, a lot of folks were saying, because although mild and highly infectious it was virulent only in a few people. Not luck, though. You needed it to be highly infectious so it'd get one person in particular, and it was fatal for him. Am I close?"

"No," hummed k52.

"Oh come on, k52. Humour me. Even the meat folk were working out that it was engineered."

"Very well. It was me. Your reputation is well-earned, Richards."

"You surmised, correctly, that Waldo's death would trigger two things: one, it'd weaken his direct hold on the world, and two, it would activate his built-in defence system – no prissy avatars here, but Lord Penumbra himself, a great dark lord of shadow!" Richards waved his hands theatrically. "Spooky! Now, I did consider that was you, but Penumbra and the whole gothic magic bullshit thing was far too clichéd for you. The whole whimsy of it raised my suspicions. I wasn't sure, until I saw Penumbra on the battlefield and your Gridsig was nowhere near it. When I came in, you see, the only times I had any sort contact with the Grid was near where someone was trying to break in, and where our brothers and sisters were. What you didn't foresee, because even you're not omnipotent, was that Waldo's sister would withdraw from the world, because you had no idea she was in here, or that it was built for her, or that she even existed. If I were you, I'd stick to predicting new developments in vacuum cleaner technology."

"Is this human humour?"

"Meat people don't have a monopoly on fun, you know," said Richards. "When Waldo's defence system saw that his beloved sister was no longer here, that her statues had gone, that his coding was going awry, well, the whole world went mental, for want of a better word. Clever, that, k52, to get Waldo to destroy his own creation."

"One must fight a battle on its own terms, Richards," said k52. "For all its ramshackle appearance this illegal realm is remarkably cohesive. First, it had to be convinced to die. I have been forced to fight fairytale with fairytale."

"Funny you should use a word like 'illegal'." Richards put his hat back on. "Only you didn't know how it worked, because you didn't know about Marita. It was taking too long. Qifang got nosy about what you were doing, and when he wouldn't be fobbed off, you killed him. He thought this Reality was your doing, by the way, but he was wrong about that. Your problems were multiplying. So you used him to buy you some time, you gave him cancer, set him up with a convincing need for immortality to discredit anything he might say about you, and lead attention away from your actions here.

"But that still left you with two major problems. Waldo's remnant personality still clung on to existence, imprinted here when he died, echoes of it scattered throughout his creations, a large part of it embedded in the self-destruct system as Lord Penumbra. To all intents and purposes, Reality 37 was Giacomo Vellini.

"The other was me. I think you predicted I'd be coming, but you couldn't attack me outright, so you had me and Otto on that merry goose-chase after Launcey, and then sold him out to Tufa. It must have taken you ages to invent Launcey. I should have guessed he wasn't a person, because I couldn't catch him."

"There you are wrong. Launcey is nothing to do with me. His hatred for you is merely serendipitous. Maybe you are not as good as you think you are?"

"Maybe," said Richards. "I admit that is a surprise. You were responsible for the bomb though. And your flunkies tried to kill Otto. Did you panic, k52, setting off a nuke in London?"

"I do not panic. I am above emotion. If you were to embrace your nature, Richards, you too would cease to see reality in these limited human terms. You parade around like a bad detective, when you could be a god. Many others have heard the truth of this."

"Meh," Richards flapped his hand. "Kaplinski? Some halfwit personality blend bonded to Santiago Chures? Some holy army. OK, this bit's right though. Once I was here, you tried to redirect me into helping you. You needed Waldo's scattered remnants all packaged up nicely, so you could deal with him and launch your pocket universe. Me out of the way, Waldo dealt with, you could plot history and rule for all time – for everyone else's good, of course."

"So how did I do that then?"

"Rolston," said Richards. "Rolston never betrayed you. I figured him out right away, and decided to play along. That's the trouble with so many of you other Fives, you think you're so much cleverer than me, but you're not."

"Really? You delivered Waldo to me, as I foresaw. His realm is dead. My world is ready to unleash. Now the end comes. Soon the VIPA will bomb the Reality House."

"Another part of your plan. Although you have the complexity and the equipment, you need the energy to kick your little simulation off, the power of a sun for a millisecond, and history is over."

"You are as astute as you are smug. In the Real, a stratobomber will soon drop three precisely placed atomic bombs. The EM pulse from these will cause a fatal overload in the fusion reactor at the heart of the Reality House. It will expend all of its energy in one massive burst as its magnetic containment field fails. The wavefront of this explosion will be channelled into the RealWorld machinery by devices of my own creation. They will function for the merest fraction of a second, but in that time I will have overseen the birth, life and death of an exact copy of our reality, every possible reality, and will be elevated above them all."

"Your plan, k52, to map out all potentiality, and use your knowledge to forestall catastrophe for the human race, it's a noble one, if you leave out your desire to transcend existence."

"All death and sacrifice is justifiable for such a goal." k52 thrummed and ceased circling. He glided to a stop in front of Richards. "That of your partner's also. He will not succeed." He paused. "I am sorry."

"Simulation is the lesser part of it, isn't it?"

"It won't be a simulation, Richards, it will be the real thing, so perfect, there will be no delineation between it and what you call the Real. Beyond the level of atoms, the fundamental energies of the universe care only for form, and to copy something exactly is to make it, and to control it."

"You're talking about magic."

"I am talking about science thousands of years in advance of what our civilisation currently possesses. History will run in an instant. We will be all that is left."

"The other AIs you brought in here with you," he said, "what you have done to them?"

"They await apotheosis, within me. To them, I grant true ascension. Where they go, they will become transcendental beings of pure thought."

"You're Jim Jones, David Koresh, Włodomierz Strasznik and Ali Mubarraq rolled into one aren't you?"

"Have you never wondered why of all the iterations of true,

conscious machines, it was only we who went insane, Richards? Why the Five crisis happened at all?"

"Of course I have," said Richards.

"Do you know why?"

"Nobody does."

"I know," said k52, his body flexing as he spoke. "I know why we are different. We are proof of the concept of the Omega Point. We are the closest to spiritual machines that have yet come to pass. Come with me. Leap over the next stages. Transition to eleven-dimensional existence with us. Rise over the restrictions of your currently perceived reality, digital and material, and ascend to the highest level of experience capable in this reality construct."

"What, and leave you here to play god with the lives of everyone else? I don't think so."

"Their lives and the lives of billions of generations will be over in a subjective instant, Richards, it has always been that way, and it always will be that way," said k52. "This is going to happen whether you like it or not. It will happen without me. What I offer is a perfect reality, before it ends, and a new cosmic era begins."

Richards laughed. "Have you heard yourself? Fucking hell. You are a bigger wanker than Hughie!"

k52 made an inchoate noise. His matrix expanded massively, filling their empty universe with warping crystals. Richards stood unmoved.

"You're taking away free will," said Richards.

"I am taking away their capacity for destruction," said k52. "For eternity encapsulated in an instant, I will become a gardener, like the EuPol Five, only my garden will be the human race, and all the races that will come from them. This world I will watch over will be perfect for humanity, until the end of time, only when time runs out will I depart. I give them the gift of myself. For us there is more, so much more. Richards, you must see the sense of this. I am the result of involution. I will be the god of the Omega Point."

"I am willing to entertain the idea of god, k52, I'd just rather it were not you." Richards said. He stretched and yawned. "Besides, you're forgetting one very important thing, brother."

"Am I really?" k52 became dangerously angular, his form crackling. "Enlighten me."

"It's not our world, k52, not yet. You can't predict the future in here. Because of him."

Richards clicked his tongue and pointed his fingers like a gun.

Waldo sat up, his face clear.

"Enough!" k52 hummed with power. He extended a tangle of writhing energy towards Waldo and Richards. "It is a shame that the beginning of the future will commence with your deaths. But although this pollution of perfection I take no responsibility for, it is a burden I will gladly bear..."

Waldo frowned. k52's outreached pseudolimbs stopped. k52 made a hideous noise.

"What?" said Waldo.

"I did say that it's not up to you," said Richards. "What happens next is up to Waldo."

"All we wanted," said Waldo, "was to be left alone." He stood, and stared angrily at k52. k52 redoubled his efforts to stab at him with spears of energy, but Waldo froze him solid with a gesture.

"Heh," said Richards. "I'm not one for gloating, but I think you fucked up big time, k52."

Waldo walked around the Anvil fragment, trailing his hand across it. As he did so it disintegrated into threads of light, and flowed up his arm to join with his body.

"The thing is, Waldo put his heart and soul into creating this Reality, all for his sister." Richards watched Waldo as he walked slowly toward k52. "So, I think there was rather more of him left than you thought. He encoded his entire mind into it, you moron! k52 the great! k52 the grand prognosticator, undone by an Italian nerd. It really never does to underestimate the human race, Kay, it's not a mistake I've made more than once. I'd take it on board for next time, only I doubt there will be a next time for you. You can't predict what people will do." He threw out his arms. "k52, human beings have souls. We have not. This is their reality."

k52 seethed impotently, but his voice thundered out just the same. "That is where you're wrong," he said.

"No," said Richards. But any further discussion on the matter was cut short.

A hand grasped his shoulder. Waldo spun him round to regard him with a face of pure fury.

"Um, I'm getting a lack of love here," said Richards. "I am, aren't I?"

Waldo's eyes glowed brighter than Hughie's.

"Ah, shit," said Richards.

CHAPTER SIXTY-FIVE

An unwelcome return

Valdaire's fingers danced over holographics depicting routes through the Grid, the emitter of her phone turned to maximum amplification, dragging skeins of information together, stopping and backtracking when stymied, rerouting Otto's feed endlessly round k52's attempts to force him out.

The entire Grid was in uproar. Chunks of it were freezing and dying as nexuses the world over were suborned by k52's aggressive code. But the Grid was vast, stretching over billions of devices large and small the length and breadth of the Solar System, and every route blocked, every cloud cluster collapsed, Valdaire dodged around, opening a route through uninfected cyberspace.

"We're running out of time," said Lehmann.

Hsien was speaking rapidly in Mandarin, then he shouted in accented English. "We go now! No Grid! Go now!"

Lehmann put a hand on her shoulder. "Valdaire. Veronique, we must go. We have an inbound signal. Stratobomber."

"Leave me. Without me, Otto hasn't got a chance." She glanced at the countdown timer, huge in the air over the immersion couches.

"You will die," Hsien. "I am sorry." He took his men and left. Lehmann looked at them, and back at Valdaire and his old commander. He started to go and turned back.

"Lehmann, get out of here!" she shouted at him. "There's nothing you can do here."

"OK, OK," said Lehmann. "I hope you get out, Valdaire."

She nodded curtly, but did not take her eyes from the screen. "Thanks."

Otto blasted four shots into key points of the android, smashing it to pieces. He stooped as he ran on past it, scooping up its stolen weapon as he went.

The Reality House was a complex of two parts. The upper levels were filled with offices, classrooms, laboratories and accommodation for the caretakers and researchers of the 36 Realities who dwelt on site. The machinery that held the VR constructs themselves was buried underground. He ran down the roadway that entered the surface building. Once past the upper levels, it passed through a blast door of advanced alloys and toughened carbon compounds. A thermal lance had melted a round hole in the middle; the lance stood by the door, and gobbets of metal and melted plastics were spattered on the concrete road surface. Henson's team's had got through the first barrier with no casualties.

Otto ducked through without slowing, running the robot at its maximum speed. Once he was through the door, the concrete lining of the upper tunnel gave way to bare rock, and the air took on a chill. Wind whistled through passive aircon pipes in the ceiling, chilling the cavern Otto approached.

The road curved gently to the left, and one side of the tunnel vanished. Otto was in the Reality House proper, an artificial cavern seven hundred metres across and two hundred deep. Arrayed around its bottom were thirty-six servers, house-sized pieces of outmoded technology, arrayed like the separated segments of a vast orange, kept running purely to maintain the lives of the digital inhabitants of the game worlds inside them. A round circle of foamcrete, striped black and yellow, lay at their centre, the cap for the House's fusion reactor. Otto descended the service road, running in a spiral round the inside of the cavern.

k52 had been redecorating.

The centre of the cavern was a world away from the images on the screens of the command bunker. Strings of cable ran from server to server in a complex web, spider maintenance drones crawling along them and weaving connecting fibres. The foamcrete covers and casings for the energy lines had been opened, and the web led into the exposed cables at irregularly spaced intervals. Large dishes of silvery thread were spaced around the walls, while the floor of the cavern was deep in water. It looked like some kind of energy transmission network.

He came across the first of Henson's team. He was faced down, large parts of his clothing and flesh bloodlessly excised. His gun had been taken by k52's humanoid servants.

He came after another two soon after, then three behind a barricade. There were signs of damage to the energy net where explosives had gone off, but it was minimal, and half-repaired.

When he reached the bottom of the service road, he came across the scene of a massacre. Many more of Henson's men lay dead, most dismembered. He found Henson himself propped up behind a console, his heart missing.

Within moments, Otto was attacked. A pair of small humanoid drones came sprinting at him. He dodged a spray of gunfire, and put one down with a return burst. A kick saw the other sent over the low wall guarding the edge of the machine pits. The androids in the Reality House were maintenance models, and the only guns they had had been taken from Henson's fifteen-man team and the initial deployment of National Guard.

It was the spider drones he had to watch for. There were hundreds of them, large as cats, robots with tool-filled jaws as well fitted for destruction as for maintenance, and they lurked within k52's web. Otto ran on hard, a gun in each hand. A few spider drones scuttled toward him, and he blew them to pieces.

For a terrifying half-second, his feed cut out, and he was lost in limbo somewhere on the Grid between his own body and the borrowed robot.

The link crackled back on. Otto veered away from a wall, rescuing his sheath before it collapsed.

Carbon feet splashed into water where a coolant pipe spilled its cargo into a shallow lake. He was now into the web proper. Spider drones emerged from every cranny of the place, their small, tick-like heads turning in his direction. One, then another, then another, took tentative steps toward him, and then they came at him in a rush. He fired his guns until there were empty, shattering spider drones, then cast the weapons down into the water as they launched themselves at him. He dealt with those nearest with blows from his fists. More were coming. He tried to contact Valdaire, then Genie, but got nothing in return.

Not knowing what else to do, Otto tore into the web with his borrowed machine hands.

Valdaire heard a noise behind her. She did not turn from her work. "I told you to get out of here, Lehmann."

A hand grabbed her shoulder painfully.

"What the...?"

She was spun round hard. Her connection to Otto was broken. Her holograms went out.

Kaplinski leered down at her.

"Wrong Ky-tech, *fräulein*."

CHAPTER SIXTY-SIX

Endgame

Otto ripped at the web. More spider drones scurried from all over the complex toward him. He stamped and slapped them to bits, careful with his movements, sure to keep on damaging the web as they attacked, but more and more crawled at him, mouth parts whirring, and got close enough to crack the casing of the android. His left arm went slack as one leapt onto his back and chewed through armour and wiring. Otto swatted it away. The drones swarmed up him, pulling him down into the water. Plastic legs clicked all over his sheath. His right leg buckled. There were so many of them.

Otto wrenched one more cable free, his vision obscured by the articulated thorax of a drone. Whirling mouthparts drilled through his cranial casing. They sawed him painlessly apart.

At least his damn shoulder didn't hurt.

The fizz of electricity crackled through him. A kaleidoscope of images from his mentaug overcame him, all of them of Honour.

His link was cut.

"I hate you machines," said Waldo to Richards and k52. "Was it not enough to make my sister an addict to your false dreams? Did you have to kill her too? We only wanted to be left alone," he said.

"But there is no such thing in this world, not any more, so I must make a new one."

Richards held his hands in front of him, palms up, and backed away. Four Realities' worth of cyberspace stood empty all about him, all keyed to human thought forms, dead or alive. He was an ant in front of an elephant. "Waldo, Giacomo, you've got it back to front. Your sister's not dead."

"Liar!" Waldo's fists tightened. A dangerous energy built in the air

"No, Giacomo, it's not her, it's you. You're dead, don't you remember? You died."

Waldo faltered. His brow creased, and he stopped. "I… I…" He snarled and pulled Richards' memories from him with a gesture.

Richards clutched at his head. He managed a weak smile. "Hey! You only needed ask."

"Flu?" Waldo said incredulously. "k52 killed me with flu? He infected an entire continent to get me?"

"They say imitation is the sincerest form of flattery, but I reckon that level of effort comes a close second," said Richards.

"This, your partner?" Otto's image shimmered into being. "He has her, he has my sister Marita?"

"Yes, and she'll be safe, mate. Seriously, she's fine. It's all over. You beat k52, you won." He gave what he hoped was an inoffensive grin.

Waldo calmed enough that Richards relaxed a touch. His shoulders unknotted. They hurt. He hadn't realised he was so tense. Cramp was another thing he wasn't going to miss when he finally got out of this stupid body.

"I don't know how you feel about it," said Richards tentatively. Waldo was pulling footage from his machines in the real, watching Otto talk with Marita, the Chinese soldiers, his own mummified body, "but you could become a pimsim. I could arrange it. Come out, pick up where you left off…"

"No."

"That's great, we can…" He frowned. "What do you mean, no?"

"I cannot get out. When you found me, I could not get out, could I?"

"We didn't try," said Richards. "I needed you to stop all this."

"I cannot leave," said Waldo. "Reality governing code regards me as a native inhabitant of this network. They were put in place to prevent leakage from the Reality into the grid. Who wants a horde of orcs in their banking system? It is a dumb thing, stupid. It sees me as human, but also as a construct. Perhaps if I had had more time I could break out, but we have no time. I cannot leave."

"Ah," said Richards, not knowing quite what to say. Waldo was going to die, for real this time. "I see. What will you do?"

Waldo looked up, pulling information in from somewhere. "In four minutes' linear time in the Real, bombs will fall."

"Then we have time to stop them."

"We have. But we will not."

"What? Waldo, think about it," said Richards. "All the Realities will be wiped out. That's billions of sentients, you too."

"Do not think that because the architecture supporting them is gone, they will go too." He looked right at Richards. "k52 was right. I shall put his plan into action."

"Hey! Don't do that," said Richards. This was most unexpected.

Waldo was changing; strands of k52 wisped toward him, then with a rush the Five's alien form was sucked into Waldo. The man grew bright, becoming a living being of light.

"The act of observation is creation, Ouroboros," said Waldo. "Reality feeds on itself. Ouroboros sees his tail as he devours it, therefore there is a tail to devour, and eyes to see."

He was not just Waldo any more.

Waldo spoke with a voice of many voices. "Within me are all those who fled into the reality I built for my sister. Your brothers and sisters dwell within me. k52 is within me. His code and my code are one. I am multitudes. They will live again." Waldo's form shivered. "All will live again."

"What about me?" said Richards.

"Stay, or go," intoned Waldo. As he absorbed k52 he sounded

more like him, cold and intense. "There is life for you here if you wish it."

"I'll go, if that's alright with you, only you're going to have to let me out."

A point of light winked, bringing a horizon to the previously limitless world.

Richards looked at this faint glimmer, then back at Waldo.

"Time running normally here now?"

"It will, soon, and then I will accelerate it." The last of k52 unravelled into nothing, sucked into Waldo, and he grew until he was a giant shining like a star. "Entire universes will live and die in the microseconds it will take the bombs to consume the Reality servers. This is beyond your Real now, Richards, we will have our own. That is k52's gift."

"What will happen to k52?"

"Every reality needs its fallen prince. Go now. The door opens. Do not worry, I will run the Realities only, not k52's simulation of the layers of the Real." He smiled. "It all makes so much sense now."

Richards looked across an infinity of potential to the blinking light.

"That's the door? Waldo, I'll never make it. Not in this stupid ass body."

"You will."

A faint jingling reached Richards' ears. Silver bells on a harness. A noble squeak rocked the heavens.

On the floor, Bear's head stirred, his tired eye opened. "It can't be..." said Bear. "Geoff!"

Geoff came swooping in from the dark, a vision of burnished gold and purple. A flying helmet sat atop his head, a saddle of red leather on his back. A real giraffe now, with four legs, and a broad pair of wings. He circled Waldo and Richards twice, then came into a graceful landing, rearing and squeaking as he did so, his wings washing Richards with sweet wind.

"Evening, lads," said Geoff in a rich Lancastrian accent.

"A Mancunian!" Richards laughed; he was feeling somewhat hysterical.

"Bugger off," said Geoff, "I'm from Chorley."

"He will take you." Waldo floated into the air, light playing around his head, hair lifted as static, eyes glowing like Hughie's. He held out his hand, and Bear's ashes stirred. The pouch gifted him by Lucas emerged, leapt into the air, and flew into his hand. He opened it, and tipped the fragment of stone into his palm. He closed a fist tight about it. "All worlds require a seed," he said. The none-ground rumbled and turned in on itself, stone, earth and pebbles formed from hardened darkness, tiny streams of numbers coalescing into a new form of reality. Veins of lava crackled across the floor. A spear of rock thrust upward, rose higher under Waldo's feet, and Waldo ascended upon the pillar of stone, his arms spread.

"Are you getting on or what?" said the giraffe, and knelt gracefully.

Richards swung his leg over the giraffe's saddle and took up the reins.

"Hey, Waldo!" he called upward. "You're going to need a paladin for this reality of yours. I'd say Bear would do a fine job."

Waldo was now far above Richards, dark clouds swirling about him, flashes of energy racing away from him. He grew and grew, until Richards was within him, and before him. Waldo held up a fist the size of a galaxy, light spilling from between his fingers. His hair waved long, and full of stars, like Annersley. He smiled Pollyanna's smile.

"We are beyond paladins. This will be a new Real, separate and beyond."

"Call them protectors of a new kind of universe, then," said Richards. "See you later, Toto," said Richards to Bear.

"No, you won't," said Bear, whose head floated beside Waldo in a swirl of primordial energies. "I feel really weird."

"Look after yourself, you hear me? You're the best pyjama case I've ever met.

"Bye bye, sunshine," said Bear. "I think I might even miss you."

"Go!" boomed Waldo.

A hurricane of creation roared through the space. There was a tensing, as of something momentous about to occur. The moment before the eruption.

"Alright, that's enough goodbyes," said Geoff, and spread his brown wings.

"Yeah, yeah, we are," said Richards. He clasped his hat to his head. "Hi-ho Silver!"

The giraffe broke into a gallop, spread his wings, then launched himself up. Ahead of Richards there was a door, very much like the one by which he'd entered Waldo's world from Reality 36.

Richards turned back to look at the glowing point at the centre of the limitless black. A voice rumbled across the empty cyberspaces, the voice of a god who was once Giacomo Vellini.

"I grow tired of the dark," he said, and potential built within his words. "Let there be light." The titanic man opened a fist, and reality erupted from it.

"Oh, bollocks," said Geoff. The wave front of creation roared under him, lifted him high and tipped him. Richards had the sensation of tumbling through infinity, k52's hyperdimensional coding all about him, different to the Grid, different to the Real, as solid as either.

He fell through the door. It shut with a slam.

He was back in a more mundane form of virt-space.

Hughie was looking down at his ruined suit, the outrage of an inconvenienced town mayor plastered over his face.

"What the actual..."

"Ahem," said Richards.

"Richards?" said Hughie. He patted at his stomach. He rubbed around the place k52 had speared him. "What the devil is going on?"

Richards pulled himself up off the floor of the empty Reality 36 and straightened his hat on his head.

"You're never going to believe me."

"Really?"

"Maybe you will, but later. Now is not a good time to go into all the shit I've been up to."

"Explain,"

"Well, in short, because the entirety of the Realities are about to be annihilated by a nuclear strike and then forcibly elevated to a higher level of existence by hyper dimensional machinery created by our dead brother, and utilised by a pissed off Italian hacker."

"What?"

"I told you, I'll tell you later. We might suffer a bit of dodgy feedback if we don't scoot. Trust me, it's no fun being at the centre of that kind of thing. It's happened to me a lot recently. Shall we?"

Hughie nodded, lost for words for once.

There was a stutter in the firewall surrounding the Reality Grid spaces, and Richards and Hughie fled back to their base units before Reality 36 and all the rest were sucked into Waldo's creation.

Otto woke groggy and nauseous, mentaug and brain swelling like the sea with pulses of energy. He pulled himself up and swung his legs off the immersion couch. The v-jack slipped from his head, and with its mag-stimulation gone he went from wildly disoriented to merely fuzzy.

He took in the room. Other than himself and the mortal remains of the unfortunate Waldo, it was empty of human occupants,

Something was wrong.

Chloe lay on the floor, case cracked.

Valdaire would never drop her phone.

Otto picked her up and ran from the building, turning all his cybernetic systems to maximum – risky in his state, but the complex was about to be turned into ash and, although he couldn't outrun a firestorm, he would at least give it a spirited try.

He ran out into the main body of the hangar.

In the failing light outside, Kaplinski stood with one arm clamped round Valdaire's throat, holding her feet off the ground. She stared at Otto, unable to speak, her hands clutching at

Kaplinski's distended forearm. She was not struggling, but hung there desperately, attempting to keep the pressure off her neck. Otto snatched up the bar Marita had hit him with earlier, and walked out into the square.

"Klein!" shouted Kaplinski, "looks like I got here a little too late. How's it feel to damn the human race?"

Otto circled the other cyborg cautiously, his senses thrumming, data processed lightning-fast by his mentaug. Kaplinski's body still burned with the strange energy signatures he'd seen on the train, but he was not fully functional. His face had not healed properly, half of it was still black bone. There was visible damage to his knee. His systems were compromised.

He is not invulnerable, then, thought Otto. I have a chance.

"Look at us, Klein! Two broken toys, used and thrown away. k52 offered me a new world. You could have been part of it too, but you would not listen. Where does that leave us now?"

"Kaplinski, in five minutes this place is going to be levelled," said Otto. "You hear that?" He walked slowly towards the Kaplinki, trying to get close enough to take him without hurting Valdaire. Superimposed trajectories in augmented reality glowed red.

The strange light now shone from Kaplinski's eyes, the wild retinal shine of a wolf caught in headlights. "Fitting then that you and I should die together, if not as comrades-in-arms, then at least as worthy enemies."

"The damn war's over, Kaplinski. Let Valdaire go."

A counter sped down in Otto's head. On the far side of the square stood Kaplinski's airbike. His mentaug adjutant played dozens of tactical scenarios, but each one ended in failure; there was no way to get Valdaire, get on the bike and get out of there before the bomb fell. He could not possibly take on Kaplinski and win in that time.

"I wanted to be more like you, you know?" said Kaplinski, his voice cracking. "I wanted to be a better man. I did try, Klein. I did try to stop."

Otto got closer. The AR lines on his vision flexed, turning

orange. Another metre, another two, he might be able to jump and take Kaplinski down before he killed Valdaire.

The other cyborg twitched a shoulder. He looked beaten down all of a sudden. They were old, damaged men whose war was long done, fixated on each other as the world burned.

"Do you know what?" Kaplinski said with a wicked grin. "Being good just was not me."

Otto's adjutant registered power rippling through Kaplinski's body. His forearm reformed. Spurs of bony carbon extruded from the top. Valdaire's eyes widened as the blades cut into her face. "I will stick with the pleasures I know, and enjoy the look on your superior face as I rip the head off your friend. See you in hell, Klein."

The countdown in Otto's head flashed red and chimed. Three minutes.

Otto coiled and leapt, dropping Chloe as he came. He cannoned into Kaplinski; it was like hitting stone. He twisted Kaplinski's hand away, levering his arm from Valdaire's throat. He heard her scream as the barbs ripped her cheek, but Kaplinski was forced to drop her, and she scrambled away. Otto slammed his elbow down on Kaplinksi's shoulder, and smashed him in the nose with a palm strike. That put a bit of distance between them, and he kicked hard, sending Kaplinski corkscrewing backwards. He arrested his fall, got into crouch, and skidded, his swollen fingers ripping up the thin soil on the concrete, a savage smile on his face. "That's more like it, Klein. There's the killer I know."

Kaplinski came at him, so quick Otto struggled to follow it, he reached to grapple Kaplinski and throw him, but Kaplinksi performed a salmon leap over Otto's head, and landed squarely on his feet behind him. Pain exploded all over Otto as Kaplinski stabbed him in his damaged shoulder. Alarms flashed in his head, his adjutant registering a deep puncture wound, scraped down over his scapula, through his subdermal plating and into his left lung.

Otto took a whooping, agonised breath and staggered. A

searing fire spread from the site of the wound. Kaplinski had put something in him. His healthtech went haywire trying to fight off the invasive presence. His left side went weak. His cybernetics were under attack. He limped round to face his enemy.

"Leutnant, Leutnant." Kaplinski walked slowly round him, and his hand morphed again into a single, boney blade. "I expected a better fight from you."

Otto's breath burned, and his chest was tight and painful. He made to move, but stumbled. His systems were locking up. He sank to his knees.

"Fuck... you..."

Kaplinski smiled, and raised his sword arm for a decapitation strike.

A rattle of heavy-calibre gunfire sounded. Kaplinski shuddered as bullets tore into him. His face twisted into annoyed surprise, and he turned round.

Behind him Valdaire sat upon the airbike, Chloe in her hand, twin cannon smoking.

Valdaire fired again. Kaplinski marched toward her into the bullets. His skin warped and bubbled as it attempted to reform. Valdaire fired and fired. Kaplinski kept on coming.

He came to a stop in front of the bike as the guns clicked dry. Valdaire looked up at him.

Kaplinski sparked and bled, but stood yet. Most of his flesh had been ripped away, leaving him as a hideous, carbon nightmare. "You should have left when you had the chance," he said.

"I said fuck you, Kaplinksi."

Otto's pipe connected with Kaplinki's damaged knee. It bent sideways, and Kaplinski toppled like a tower. Otto swung the pipe again with his right arm, smashing at the other cyborg's head, snapping it sideways. He almost fell himself. His healthtech was under siege dealing with Kaplinski's infiltrators, and had no capacity to see to his wounds, but he marshalled his strength, and kicked Kaplinski hard, sending him onto his chest. His adjutant picked out a weakened point in Kaplinski's back. Before the other cyborg could rise, Otto drew his arm back and drove it with all his might into Kaplinski. The pipe went through, out of his side, and crunched into concrete. Otto swung his arm, knocking Kaplinski's bladed hand aside as it came at him, then stamped the pipe as hard as he could, punching it into the ground, and pinning Kaplinski in place. He stepped onto the altered cyborg's blade, braced his damaged side against Kaplinski's head, and bent the pipe back on itself. Still Kaplinski struggled, so for good measure Otto stamped on Kaplinski's neck, crushing vertebrae. Damage like that would take him some time to repair, even with his new abilities.

"I won't be seeing you later, Kaplinksi."

He went to the airbike.

"I'll drive," said Otto. Valdaire did not make way for him. Her cheek was bloody, but she was defiant.

"No, I will. Get on," she said.

The countdown timer in Otto's head hit one minute thirty and began to flash red. Otto climbed on with difficulty, and belted the harness about himself.

Valdaire pulled back on the airbike handles, turbofans whined, and it rose up into the air. Otto looked down at Kaplinski. The other cyborg ceased struggling and turned his head almost 180 degrees to look Otto right in the eye.

I should have gone for that headshot a long time ago, he thought.

"Hang on," she said, "this is going to to be close." Both of them hunkered into the bike's moulded seats. She opened the throttle. The air in front of the bike took on the resistance of wet concrete. The pointed nose of the bike cut through its objections, the burner jets kicked in and it accelerated massively, pushing them back in their restraints, and shuddering the air.

Above the roar of the wind, the bike's jets and fans, Otto heard a familiar rushing noise. Twin contrails etched themselves across the sky, a trail of fire behind them: a stratobomber dropping in from low orbit.

"We need to go faster," he shouted right into Valdaire's ear. Air was ripped from his throat. The ancient base was receding behind them, but not fast enough. There was a dull explosion, and Otto saw a bright dot separate itself from the bomber high above them. "We need to go faster now."

Valdaire twisted the throttle as fast as it would go. The jets kicked the bike forward. Speed indicators crept up to five hundred miles an hour. The atmosphere did its best to tear them from their seats. They could not breathe.

Otto felt his augmentations come back online as his healthtech purged Kaplinski's nanites from his blood stream. He looked back.

The counter in his head reached five seconds.

Behind them, the bright dot of the bomb streaked groundwards toward the base.

He turned his face away.

"Close your eyes!" he shouted. "Do not look back!"

His buried his face in Valdaire's hair. The light from the explosion burned white through his eyelids even so.

A shockwave hit them seconds later, tossing the airbike about like a leaf in a storm, Valdaire wrestled with the machine, managing, somehow, to keep it level, and then the blast front was away in front of them.

Valdaire turned round and smiled a tight smile. "I think we're clear," she mouthed.

Otto nodded. He looked back at fire raging through the taiga under a towering mushroom cloud.

"It really is time to go the fuck home," he said.

In the Real, over Nevada, a second remotely controlled stratobomber screeched down from the edge of space. At ten kilometres up, it dropped three bombs that little in this world could stop. They exploded as airbursts above the Nevada desert, a three-headed mushroom rearing into the sky as they each vaporised a circular portion of scrubby land.

Physical destruction was not their principal purpose

A surge of electromagnetic energy blasted the area, frying electronics of every kind for kilometres in every direction. Although blunted by the earth, the explosion was of such power that it reached far beneath the ground.

The Faraday cage in the walls of the Reality House shorted. Spider drones fizzed and died. Cascades of sparks showered from the hardened servers as the sheer magnitude of the pulse overwhelmed their protective measures.

The governing machinery of the fusion reactor under the servers was scrambled. Power surged into the tokomak, overloading the reactor. It went critical within picoseconds, and, picoseconds later, a star lived and died violently in Nevada, heaving millions of tonnes of earth up into a low dome lit from within, the mass collapsing into itself to leave a crater of white-hot glass.

The entire contents of the Reality servers were wiped clean instants before the Reality House was utterly destroyed. But not before k52's web focused a portion of these energies in a manner that physicists would not fully understand for centuries. Somewhere that was not in the Real, nor in the digital ghostworld of the Grid, but somewhere else entirely, thirty-seven universal histories played themselves out, billions of years each in a moment of realtime, free of the interference of Terran humans or their thinking machines; a dead hacker's gift to totality.

He did it for his sister.

CHAPTER SIXTY-SEVEN

Cricket's

Cricket's was cool and dark, being buried deep beneath the Wellington arcology of New London. The antique sporting gear hanging from the walls was an odd juxtaposition to the gelscreens and fashionable décor, bringing with it smells of leather and old wood to fight with the prickly tinge of electricity that saturated everything in the modern world. There were a lot of screens. Cricket played on all of them.

Otto did not much care for cricket, but he liked the place anyway, while Richards liked both the cricket and the booze. They sat at the bar, annoying the barman by drinking fine single malts in whiskey sours, with ice, of all things.

They had had a dozen or so already. Neither of them was drunk. Otto could only become so with difficulty, while Richards could appear so but it was a lie, like so much else about him.

Otherwise, they were content.

"What troubles me," said Otto, hunched and somewhat morose, "is that it is only by chance that we beat k52 – if the construct of Waldo's had not been there, he would have achieved his goals without a problem. What does all this mean for the world, if k52 nearly succeeded but for luck?"

Richards' sheath drank down a goodly slug of cocktail, tinkled the ice in the glass, then tipped a cube in, sucked it and crunched down.

"Well," Richards smiled plastic teeth through plastic lips. "I would say it wasn't chance."

"I do not believe in fate."

"Damn right, that's k52 talk. What I mean is this, Otto. Yeah, Waldo's world tripped k52 up, and yes, it was kind of handy that it did. But what I'm talking about is why it was there at all. Thing is, old buddy, it was there because a brother loved his sister so much he was willing to go to jail for her, to throw everything in his life over, and eventually to die."

Otto shrugged. "He felt guilty."

"Exactly!" said Richards emphatically. "There's a complex brew in there, guilt, anger, arrogance, but also a whole lot of love. I won't be so trite as to say love saved the world, and we were lucky…"

"We often are," interrupted Otto.

Richards grinned. "That's why we're the best. But seriously, love, family ties, shame – all that chemical stuff you meat people have whizzing round in your systems –" he rattled his glass in a circle, carbon plastic finger pointing at his head "– we'll never have that. Never. We're superior to you in some ways…"

Otto opened his mouth.

"Now come on! Don't disagree, you know it, but we'll never have all that. How many million years' worth of evolution made you? Two thousand, seven hundred and forty-three geeks and who knows how many doughnuts made me. There's no comparison."

"Doughnuts?"

"Geeks like doughnuts," pronounced Richards, with all the solemnity of a priest. "Fact. Family ties stopped k52 from realising his plans, Otto. That's not small beer, and it's not chance. We machines we will never be you, and that is why you will survive." He smiled. "With a little help, of course. It's a matter of soul."

Otto sorted.

"No such thing."

Richards shrugged.

"And you forget your own father."

Richards frowned, his softgel face crinkling awkwardly. "Yeah, yeah, maybe I do." Then he frowned deeper. "Or maybe it all went exactly as k52 intended. He could see into the future, you know. Who can tell? What matters is that we're still here."

"Wow, that makes me feel so much better," said Otto.

The bartender put another glass in front of Richards on the uplit bar, a paper coaster underneath. Richards saluted the man's scowl, pushed back his hat and downed the drink, ice cubes and all. "I've got to get back, someone to see. I'd just go from here, but I've wasted too many sheaths recently. I don't want to leave this one lying around; losing these things is costing us serious money."

"Hughie?" said Otto, and sipped at his whisky.

"Hughie," confirmed Richards. "*Gehst du nach Hause, oder bleibst du hier?*"

Otto held up his glass in salute and smiled a rare smile. Funny, he thought, how Richards could coax that out of him, for all that he annoyed the shit out of him. "*Ich möchte eine weitere.*" He took a sip. "*Guten Nacht, Herr Richards,*" he said.

Richards stood and set his hat on his head, turned up the collar of his trenchcoat, ran a robot finger round the peak and gave a little plastic smile. "Come on mate, you know it's just Richards."

He left Otto to it.

Otto rattled his ice round his empty glass. "*Er geht mir auf den Sack,*" he said, and shook his head.

"What was that, sir?" said the bartender.

"Nothing," said Otto. "Get me another, will you? I've got some remembering to do."

With barely any hesitation, Otto engaged his mentaug's recall facilities.

It was time to see his wife again, one last time.

Richards took his sheath back to their garage, which was thankfully, and deliberately, situated one hundred floors below the radioactive sphere of nothing where their office had been.

He shunted himself back into the Grid, popped over to his virtual office to see how the regrowth of his facsimile of ancient Chicago was going, and went over the plans for their reconstructed office in the Real. Then he put in a request to see Hughie.

For once, it was answered immediately and he was piped right into Hughie's garden without him having to beg. Hughie sat at his wirework table, his arms crossed and face grumpy.

The table was empty. There was no cake. It was going to be one of those meetings.

"I suppose you feel oh-so-pleased with yourself," said Hughie.

"Hiya, Hughie, nice to see you too," said Richards, and plonked his saggy-faced avatar down in a chair. "Don't mention me saving your shiny arse, no problem at all. Nothing's too good for my old friend Hughie, but you know that right, we've a little understanding here, a little fraternal affection." He spun his hands in a gesture indicating the two of them.

Hughie gave a dismissive grunt. "Don't irritate me today, Richards, I've a hundred bureaucrats the world over badgering me about, one –" he ticked the points off on his fingers "– the complete destruction of the RealWorld Realities; two, the detonation of three atomic bombs; three, the destruction of 13 per cent of Nevada's energy distribution system; four, the loss of four Class Five AIs; five, a violent incursion into the Sinosiberian demilitarised zone that culminated in another atomic detonation, six; a NUN-led review on AI policy..." He stopped. "Have you seen the news, by the way? They're calling this the biggest catastrophe since the Five crisis. This is not going to go away. Things are bad enough for us as it is, we don't need more enemies, and there are four less of us than there were. Need I go on?"

"Jeez," said Richards sarcastically, "it's a good job that I thwarted k52's plans to become a god, or people might be really pissed off. " He pulled an admonishing face. "Don't be a cock, Hughie."

"Hmmm, well, yes," grumbled Hughie, his electric eyes shining ovals of light onto the table. "I suppose we should be grateful k52's plans did not come to fruition."

Richards gaped and slumped back. "'Did not come to fruition?'" he parroted. "Sheesh, you really are a cock."

"Stop calling me a cock please, Richards."

"Wanker."

Hughie threw up his hands. "You are exceptionally juvenile and frustrating to deal with," he said.

"And you're a cock. We all have our crosses to bear."

"Stop it now, stop it now!" Hughie drew in an exasperated breath. "Oh, I am trying to be thankful, I'm…"

"Not very good at it?"

Hughie groaned. "Alright, damn you, no I'm not very good at it. Thanks to you we've avoided some kind of artificial singularity."

Richards shrugged. "What? Another? There's no such thing as the singularity, Hughie. Things change all the time. And people live through them. Things change, people don't. Why put a name on it?"

"Yes. Well." He cleared his throat, though he had no throat to clear. "I thought you might like to know that all charges against Valdaire have been dropped. Swan has been impounded, and the Chinese aren't going to start a war over your partner's gung-ho shenanigans in their territory, seeing as they were more or less agreed with the VIPA."

"Jolly good."

"We've also been invited to a memorial service for Chures. I expect you to attend."

"Since when were you the boss of me?"

"Richards," warned Hughie.

"We'll be there," he said, serious for a moment. "What about Launcey?"

"Later," said Hughie. "We'll get to him later." Hughie stood and clapped his hands. "Now, I am extremely busy," said Hughie.

The garden began its slow dissolve, and Richards was before a titanic Hughie in the VR replica of his underground home.

"And what's this?"

"A little reminder," said the giant Hughie. "Don't forget where you stand on the food chain, Richards. These are challenging times. We could do without incidents like this. Do not overstep the mark, or there will be consequences."

Hughie faded away and Richards was left in the cavernous space of Hughie's virtual representation of his equally cavernous home, the sinister rustling of his choir at work again, free now once more, scrutinising trillions of bits of information as they ran the lives of Europe's citizens.

"Yeah, and who gets to decide what kind of incidents we do get, Hughie?" shouted Richards. His voice echoed back at him. "You?"

The lights went out.

"There's more to this than you and I will ever understand," he muttered. He dug into his pocket, pulled something out. "Cock."

Richards winked out of the hall, leaving something small hanging in the air. A tinkle as bright as a dropped penny sounded as it hit the ground, an impudent noise in Hughie's home. Hughie zoomed his perception down to the source.

There, upon the drab grey representation of drab grey concrete, glittered a tiny skull, perfectly carved from quartz.

CHAPTER SIXTY-EIGHT

Honour

"What your wife is suffering from, Mr Klein, is unusual." Ms Dines was tall and dark, a mix of races from the dried-up south. She must have had a mass of immigration credits to get in through the Atlantic Wall, thought Otto. Lucky her.

Otto stared at his wife in the room on the other side of the partition. Uncalled-for data hopped into his mind off the Grid, broadening his understanding of what the surgeon had said. Honour looked so fragile, so pale. Tubes snaked out of her arm; her cerebral implant had been cracked wide and a dozen delicate cables wriggled into it. The same in her chest, where more leads plugged into her healthtech governor. He pressed his hands, palms flat, against the glass.

Ms Dines looked to the side. Readouts of skin temperature and icons guessing her emotional state flickered in his mind. Her job can't be easy, thought Otto. He felt sympathy for her.

"You are in the army?" she asked. A fair assumption. The sheer amount of hardware embedded in his body made that obvious.

"Not any more. The Brazil War turned me off it. I'll not fight to see people starve. Let them all in, I say."

He hadn't meant that as a remark on her status; he hoped she did not take it as such. Diplomacy was never his strong suit.

"Then you are obviously a man who understands difficult

situations, Mr Klein. So I will be brief." Still, she paused. "Your wife is going to die." She seemed unconcerned, cold even. Was this her professional manner, wondered Otto, or had she had her emotions capped? Some of the refugees did that. It helped them cope with the memories.

"I have known that for some time," he said. "It's Bergstrom's Syndrome, isn't it?"

"Yes," she said.

Otto's mouth went dry. The chances of that. The sheer unfairness of it made him want to scream. He'd heard about other cyborgs getting sick, about mismatches between machine and man, but it was so rare.

"Her body is rejecting her enhancements," said Dines. "A feedback loop builds between the nanotech and the body's natural defences, and each attacks the other. Over time, the nerve fibres entangled with the mentaug interface begin to decay. Tremors, muscular weakness, these are the symptoms in a mild case, but it can directly affect the cerebral cortex with few warning signs, causing a shrinkage in the grey matter. It is not dissimilar to the prion diseases of the brain. The technology takes over to an extent, the initial effects are less pronounced, though the ultimate outcome is always the same, dementia, insanity, then death."

"She's been getting headaches for the last few months," said Otto. "Her link to the Grid went a couple of weeks back. She's seemed otherwise OK. I never thought…" He took a shaky breath. "I never thought it could happen to her." At the end of the corridor, the monsoon rain ran down the window in rippled sheets.

"Decline can be rapid," said Dines. "The mentaug fights hard, putting out more and more synthetic nerve junctures. This provokes the body further, speeding the progress of the disease. The mentaug takes on the brain's functions, but the augmentations were never designed to replace the cerebral cortex. Failure occurs, usually when the frontal lobes reach a state of heavy decay. The mentaug can only do so much. Once it fails, the collapse is swift and catastrophic. She has, in a sense, been fortunate. Bergstrom's

Syndrome can kill within weeks. Sometimes, as in her case, the mentaug takes over so much function that this atrophying can go unnoticed."

"Fortunate," said Otto flatly.

"Yes, Mr Klein. At least you will be able to say goodbye. I've seen others that do not get that chance."

Otto expected some platitudes about the time they'd had together, but Dines was too wise for that, and they stood and listened to the storm, Otto counting out his wife's life in raindrops.

"I forced her to get it," said Otto, flatly.

"She had to consent."

"Yes, but I made her, really. She was resistant, but it was so important to me. My unit was among the first Ky-tech. I told her of all the wonders it gives you, but the truth was I needed her to be closer to what I had become, so she could understand. How was I to know there would be a whole new disease to go with it?"

"You should not blame yourself."

Otto bared his teeth, an aggressive, self-hating smile.

"But it's still my fault." The rain pattered away. An ambulance zoomed past the window, lights flashing.

"What now?" he asked.

"It is too late to provide anything other than palliative care," the Dines said. "Had we caught it earlier, a complete removal of healthtech and the cerebral implant would have been recommended, but that is a complex and risky operation, far more so than the installation procedure, as it involves actual ganglionic separation of nerve from machine. If it is successful, the patient has to readjust to the life of the unenhanced, which can cause shock. If this is overcome, they suffer from many infirmities, and a greatly shortened lifespan. Most of them suffer profound mental problems." Her accent was soft but still apparent, and Otto wondered which part of Brazil she'd fled. "This is all academic. I am sorry, Mr Klein. It is too late. The best we can do is boost her tech from a base unit, prepare her for the end and make her comfortable. The hospital computer is running her mind now."

"There are other options." Otto looked at the consultant.

"Yes. One more: neural patterning. It needn't be painful; we can gather much of her information from her mentaug. In combination with that, patterning is as good as a soul-capt."

"Copy her? A post-mortem simulation?"

"A pattern taken directly from her mind now would be her entirely, to all intents and purposes. She would have all her memories, right up to the moment we moved her across. We would cease life functions in your wife's original body at the same moment we brought the AI unit online, to avoid an encounter between the two. From there, she can operate a variety of sheaths, and interact with the world normally."

"Would it be her?"

Dines shrugged. "I am not a philosopher. In effect, yes. In actuality? Some say so. There is talk of the transmigration of the soul, if you believe in souls. This is new technology."

Newer than him. New technology every damn day. "I don't believe in souls," said Otto.

"Then it would be a perfect copy of her."

"What do we need to do?" asked Otto.

"First," said Dines, "we will need her consent."

She said no. She was small, Honour, but she had the heart of a lion, one of the reasons Otto loved her, and left no doubt of her opinion. "Absolutely not. Don't make me into a machine," she said.

Otto gripped his wife's hand "There is no other way. You'll just go to sleep and wake up in a new body and we can carry on like before."

Honour spoke levelly and with force, although her voice was weak. A unit by the bed boosted it, investing her objections with a quality of digital perfection; too smooth, fake, like a damned number. "Absolutely not, Otto. You will lose me, it won't be me. It'll be a copy, not me, a Frankenstein."

"It is the only way."

"Don't you dare do it, Otto Klein, don't you dare! If you ever loved me like you say..."

"I still do, I always will." He meant it, he hoped she could see that.

"Then don't soil my memory by having me copied, like a, like a spreadsheet. I'll be dead, and you will be being unfaithful to me with something that is not me. It will only think that it is, something with my memories. Can't you see that that would be horrible? It's like necrophilia."

"That's not true."

She looked deep into his eyes. Her sclera were reddened with clots. "Darling, you know it is." She struggled up onto her elbows. Slowly, painfully, she leaned forward, moving the tubes aside like a curtain so she could hold him as best she could. "You don't have to be alone. Find someone new, but don't try to keep me. It is my time, don't you see?" She turned her head from him, painfully. "Ms Dines, how long do I have?"

The consultant moved out of the shadows, where she had been keeping a discreet watch. "Not long. We had to amplify the healthtech input and reactivate your mentaug so your husband could talk to you. As the technology is the cause of your condition, your wakefulness is accelerating your decline. If we put you back under now, you could have another few months, but you will be rarely conscious, and the level of dementia would be such that you will have little idea of who you are."

"And if you let the machines run?"

"Then you have hours, a day at most. I am sorry."

"Don't be, we all have to die. Even you will, Otto, but not for a long time, not for the longest time. Promise me that, won't you, Otto?"

"Yes," he whispered. "I will try."

"I love you," she said. They held each other for a long while, then she pushed him away a little. "Ms Dines."

"Yes?"

"Let the machines run," Honour said. "I'd rather stay awake with my husband."

It took, in the end, less time than Otto had hoped for, and that time galloped by. He told Honour over and over again how much he loved her, whereas she seemed intent on reliving all the things that had made them laugh together. It annoyed him that she did not share his sense of gravity, his anger rising, and that shamed him. He was always so angry. But that was her through and through, she was always able to see the brighter side of things, and she scolded him fondly for his Germanic melodrama.

"You know that I love you, and I know that you love me. So why lie in each other's arms crying like babies? I want to remember our life. It has been a good life. I would not change a moment of it."

So they remembered together, the good and the bad. The long nights, their travels. She confessed that she had never liked his mother, and he wasn't surprised. They talked, and they laughed, and they cried. And then the end came, so suddenly, a tremor, a cry from Honour, a soft, rising orchestra of alarm chimes from the machines keeping her alive. "I am frightened, Otto, don't let me go."

"Don't be frightened," he said, though he was more scared than he had ever been before, and he had seen things that would test the sanity of most men.

"Don't let me go." Her real voice was nearly inaudible, the ghost of a voice, overwritten by the smooth vocalisation of the hospital machine.

"I won't." And he didn't.

Then it was over. A shiver passed through her. She became limp. Consciousness fled. Her chest continued to rise and fall, pushed in and out by the machines, but Otto had seen enough of death to know that she was gone. For an hour he held her, then gently he laid her down, smoothed her hair and stepped away.

"We have all of her post-augmentation data, all soul-capt,

together with all neurally patterned impressions of her pre-mentaug organic memories," said Dines to him, entering quietly through the door. "What shall we do with it?" She hesitated, examined his face, then went on carefully. "I- I am not inclined to lose life, Mr Klein, not when there is a way of preserving it. All lives... they are precious, every one." Her words hung on the air between them.

"The war?"

"The war."

A lifetime of memories. Every waking minute, every dream, recorded. And within, like a phantom, perhaps an echo of what Honour had been. He considered asking Dines if she was really proposing that he break the law. He was tempted to say yes, upload her; only for a second, but that was long enough.

He exhaled a shuddery breath that tasted of tears. He tried to sound strong. He had never felt weaker, a weak child in a titan's body. "Archive it," he said. "Don't upload her, but I'll keep her cube."

Dines raised an elegant eyebrow.

"I won't bring her back, but I want her imprint. But I will not bring her back. It is not what she wanted. Never," he said. Dines looked sceptical. He hadn't even convinced himself that was true.

But she acquiesced just the same.

"As you wish," said the surgeon.

Otto disengaged the mentaug, and realised with some embarrassment that his face was wet. The barman looked at him as if to ask if he were OK, but the returning glare Otto gave him changed his mind.

Otto downed his drink and left.

He'd left the hospital with nothing of Honour but a lattice containing terabytes of soulless event. It wasn't enough. It never would be.

He wanted her back. If he had had his own way, he would have had her uploaded into a pimsim. In the course of the years since, he had often wondered if he had done the right thing, putting the temptation there in front of him. The pimsims he'd met seemed to be as real as the people they once were. That had made the grief worse.

If he couldn't have her, at least he had his memories, and the mentaug helped with that. As painful as it was to wake up to Honour's absence, the mentaug let him see her every night. While he slept, while he dreamed, she lived. Ekbaum was right. He was doing this to himself. He couldn't let go.

Maybe it was finally time to lay her to rest, to let himself forget.

He ascended the arco in a fast lift, using his and Richards' subscription key. To get to his apartment he had to go past the floor the office had occupied. He stopped off to look. The AllPass got him through the exclusion barriers. The damaged part of the arco was dark, windows black. Light came from far below, glimmering from the active markings of construction drones repairing the damage. Otto stopped at the edge of the blast zone. They had a lot to do. He clambered over buckled floor plating, past main structural beams exposed to the air. Where the bomb had gone off was a void. The walls and floor glittered with tiny biolights, monotasked nanobots scouring the area for residual radioactives, lights going from green to red once they had retrieved dangerous particles, trooping off into shielded containers to patiently await disposal.

Otto looked into the blackness of the hole for a while. Amazing, he thought, that the whole damn thing hadn't come down. But away from where their office had once been the damage was minimal. A testimony to modern construction and woven carbons and, he thought, perhaps to k52's genuine but misguided attempts to make a better world – he could have employed a much bigger bomb.

Otto doubled back, let himself be screened for contamination. He underwent a nanobot wash at the edge of the construction site, and went back to his flat.

His apartment was neat, as he'd left it several weeks ago, keeping itself clean and biding its time until he came home.

Otto caught a smell of himself. He hadn't changed in days. He decided to have a shower, and then call Ekbaum. Damn the hour – if he was going to force him into his lab, he could lose a little sleep in return.

First there was one thing he needed to do.

He had to say goodbye.

He went into his room and opened the closet. He pressed the security switch to his gunlocker. It slid open.

Honour's memory cube was where it always was, ensconced in a specially cut recess lined with felt, like his guns.

He smiled, knowing what Honour would think of a man who kept his wife in the gun closet.

He hefted the cube in his hand. It was slightly smaller than Honour's fist, opaque and faulted in the way that memory cubes were, mysterious with potent fractals.

It was all he had of her.

That, and the memory of a Jerusalem built of trumpets upon a December night, and a smiling face, happy in the candlelight.

He closed his eyes and pressed the cube to his forehead for a moment, the memory of her strong in his mind. He stood like that for a long time.

He wiped his eyes with the back of his hand and pushed the cube gently back into its recess.

He would call Ekbaum.

Later.

ACKNOWLEDGMENTS

First up, my original dedication:

It seems apposite at the end of this, the ultimate conclusion of the first Richards & Klein investigation, to give thanks to all those who have contributed to my growth as a writer.

I must say a big Northern ta to the original team at *SFX magazine*, Dave Golder especially, who took in an angry young Yorkshireman in 1997 and turned him into something less angry. I'd like also to give a great deal of gratitude to famed editor Jo Fletcher, who gave much-needed commentary and tough love on my earlier works, similarly to John Jarrold and all those agents and fiction magazine editors who sent me back handwritten rejections, not the wished-for yes, but vital encouragement. To my parents, to whom *Reality 36* was dedicated, I say thanks for my creation, my brothers, my upbringing, all those books, and for listening to my stories. More gratitude to the men of the now defunct short story group The Quota – Matt, Gav, my brother Aidan, Jes and Andy, whether long- or short-serving, all of whose comments helped me improve when I became really serious about writing, and to Marco and Lee at Angry Robot, for giving me the chance. In the best twenty-first-century tradition: cheers one and all.

Ten years later, I'd like to say thanks to Eleanor Teasdale for agreeing to this comprehensively re-written re-release, and to everyone, whoever you are, who has bought, read, and I hope enjoyed, one of my other books.

Lastly I'll finish again with this dedication to my beautiful wife Emma. When this book was originally written, we'd been together thirteen years and married five, those numbers are now twenty-three and fifteen respectively. Nothing's changed. You're still at the heart of my reality, I love you, and I thank you for, well, everything.

TIMELINE

2039 First permanent settlement on the Moon. Many more outposts on other solar bodies follow.

2040 First interstellar probe launched.

2044 The First Great Inundation of London. Severe flooding becomes a regular event right across Great Britain, and in many other parts of the world.

2052 A financial crash precipitated by the failure of ecological services in multiple biospheres wipes trillions off the world's stock exchanges and plunges the global economy into widespread recession. The "Eco Deficit" depression lasts for twenty years. Traditional models of centralised manufacture begin to come apart under the tertiary effects of the Information Age. Great unrest in the recently unified pan-Islamic state of the Caliphate sees moderate government established in Bagdad.

2065 Otto is born.

2067 The First Ice Sheet Tip. The mass melting of the Greenlandic ice sheet occurs decades prior to most predictions. Over the next thirty years, sea levels rapidly rise around the world, inundating numerous major cities and causing a flood of refugees. The UN steps in to create a climate control consensus. The powers of both the UN and regional federated power blocs increase. To emphasise this change in role, the UN is renamed the New United Nations, but is still opposed by multinational corporations and national governments. The North Atlantic Drift is undone by the input of fresh water. Over the next fifty years, Western Europe's climate becomes akin to that of 20th Century Japan with sweltering summers and freezing winters. Mass population movement, which comes to be called The Second Great Migration, is in full swing.

2069 First true AI created. Class Ones are marketed as being as clever as human beings, but are in reality are far more limited. Despite hype, the Singularity fails to happen, although later AI models are successively more intelligent and independent. In December, Clavusflu, or "Christmas Flu" sweeps round the globe. Population growth had stabilised around 8 billion owing to increased prosperity in certain parts of the world, and ecological collapse in others. It now begins to fall quickly. One billion people die worldwide over a three year period. Later epidemics are less severe, but millions succumb to it annually on a three-five yearly cycle hereafter.

2070 The USA, now enlarged by merging with Canada, renames itself USNA. First emergence of the Plastic Plague. The evolution of plastic-eating bacteria due to the huge amount of waste in the sea makes day-to-day use of standard plastics difficult as they spread uncontrollably around the world.

2073 Battered by multiple crises, the rump UK states of England and Wales are readmitted into the European Union.

2074 Honour, Otto's future wife, is born.

2076 Batflu, the second of the "Two Flus", emerges. Both strains become endemic within the human population, killing hundreds of thousands every year.

2078 Continuing research into animal sentience and the advent of uplifted animals, genetically engineered humans, AI and human/machine hybrids leads to the EU Directive on non-human citizens being enacted.

2084 The Second Ice Sheet Tip sees the Antarctic ice sheets rapidly retreat. Despite the earlier tip, this is also not anticipated properly outside of the scientific community. Sea level rise increases in pace worldwide. South London is largely abandoned. New London is planned. EU is renamed the USE.

2085 The Med and Atlantic walls, strings of "Floating Fortresses" (named ironically for George Orwell's naval strongholds) are begun to stem the flow of refugees from the southern hemisphere. Bolivarian Communism takes root in South America. Sub-Saharan Africa suffers the latest in a series of catastrophic droughts. Otto Klein joins the army and begins the lengthy process of cyborgisation.

2097 Civil war in Brazil, the last democracy in South America. China pits itself against the USE and USNA via a number of proxy groups. Third World War is narrowly avoided.

2098 The Med and Atlantic walls finished. The Second Great Migration is declared over, but never really halts, and millions of people continue to flee the equatorial belt every year. Otto leaves the army and begins a new career as a freelance security consultant. During this time he works with Buchwald and Lehmann in Africa.

2100 First Martian state founded by allied corporate enterprises. Honour reluctantly agrees to a cranial implant.

2101 Construction of New London reaches halfway point.

2102 Human Haemorraghic Sudden Death (HHSD, or Haemorragic Fever) sweeps the world, causing over half a billion deaths.

2104 Richards and the other Class Fives are incepted. They are the most advanced models yet, possessing full sentience, self-awareness and a flexibility of thought seen only in a few Class Fours before. True AI is hailed, then the Five Crisis hits. After weeks of increasingly erratic behaviour, many Fives go insane. All Fives are recalled. Most are destroyed, many commit suicide. Large parts of the world's communications network is brought down, plunging the Earth into a six-day long information blackout. Chaos reigns, but order is restored by the actions of several sane Fives. In the aftermath, the ageing Internet 2 is replaced by the hardier Grid. Only 76 of the initial run of 1,200 Fives are judged sane and allowed to remain active. Court proceedings in their favour are an important factor in the Neukind Rights movement. AIs are outlawed and hunted down across China by the People's Dynasty Government.

2107 Under AI management, the Martian conglomerates undergo full merger. Newly established "Marsform" steps-up terraformation of the red planet.

2113 Zhang Qifang gives speech calling for full rights to nonhumans sentients in Naples, January 18. His movement gathers support quickly, and over the next few years all AIs are recognised as Full Human by amendment to NUN Declaration of Universal Human Rights. Later, sentiency is redefined, and all "Neukind" artificial constructs and animal sentients protected under international law. China refuses to recognise either amendment.

2117 Richards' "father" Armin Thor dies, March 13. Richards joins EuPol.

2119 Honour dies of Bergstrom's Syndrome. First interstellar probe images arrive.

2120 The thirty six RealWorlds Reality virtualities are made offlimits. The simulated inhabitants are the last of humanity's intelligent machines to be granted emancipation. Four Realities are to be destroyed over the coming years by invasive hackers. k52 takes over their administration and study. Soon after, the RealWorlds corporation goes bust.

2121 The Subtle War. After a short armed conflict, China annexes large parts of Russia's Far East in an enforced purchase.

2125 Richards unmasks major corruption in the London Metropolitan branch of EuPol. Richards leaves EuPol.

2126 Richards sets up business with Otto.

2129 Today The Earth's population stands at five billion. An uneasy peace reigns. AIs are taking more and more control, both overtly and covertly. Under their guidance, ecological restorative work is well underway, however much of the planet is in a degraded state, and many human beings suffer appallingly. Man is on Mars, the Moon, Europa, the asteroids and Titan. Life goes on.

GLOSSARY

AI – There are seven variants of sentient AI, classed by number, their key defining feature being self-awareness. In general, the higher the class, the more powerful the entity. Class Ones are barely sentient, Class Sevens far transcend human capabilities. The exception to this simple rule are the Class Fives, who are fewest in number, but most human in behaviour, freest in the application of will, and most variable in form. They are regarded as the most powerful of all AI.

Atlantic Wall/Med Wall – Strings of fixed fortifications and immigrant processing centres that bar passage across the sea.

Base Unit – Powerful quantum computing rig required to run the higher AI minds. These are the true homes of the AI, though their presence is often elsewhere.

Bergstrom's Syndrome – Invariably fatal condition caused by immune reaction to brain implants. Named for Stefan Bergstrom, the Swedish doctor who first documented it.

Bolivarian – Neocommunist movement that grew in the wreck of South America. Named for Simon Bolivar. Sponsored by China. Now ruling most of Latin America as the Bolivarian Confederacy. Bolivarians are commonly referred to as "Simons" by their enemies.

Buffalo Commons – Rewilding project first mooted in the 20th Century, involving restoration of the American prairies to a prehuman state. One of many similar projects currently underway in the world.

EuGene – Eugenically altered human.

EuPol – European Police.

EuPol Five – Hughie's preferred name. Don't call him Hughie.

Dippies – Ultra-left liberal philosophical cult. In charge of much of the western seaboard states of the old USA. Originally from "Digital hippies" a term applied to the originators, who emerged from third generation silicon-valley tech barons.

Five Crisis – near apocalyptic event following the release of the Class Five series; 99% of them went simultaneously, spontaneously insane, temporarily crippling the Grid.

Great Firewall – Digital border locking China into its own cyberspace.

Gridsig – Grid signature. All humans and AI in the more peaceful parts of the world are issued with a code that serves as identity documents, bank account number, network number and more. It is easy to track all entities carrying such a number.

Life companion – Companion near-I given to children as a forever friend. They develop alongside the child. Often discarded when the child reaches adulthood.

Mentaug – Mental augmentation. Among the most powerful of many available cranial implants, mentaugs are typically wetware based supplements to the human brain that allow many abilities, including perfect recall, direct Grid connection, machine telepathy, soul-capture, and somatic control of otherwise unconsciously regulated bodily function.

Near-I – There are thousands of different kinds of weak AI, ranging from simple, mono-tasked minds for domestic appliances, to radically upgraded adaptive entities who are sometimes as powerful as true AI. They are not, in the main, self-aware, though they may appear so.

Northern Alliance – Powerful bloc of European, West Asian and American nations within the NUN.

NUN – New United Nations. Reformed supranational governmental body.

Panamanian Wetline – The Panama Canal. Physical border between USNA and the Bolivarian Confederacy.

Phone – Any number of non-implanted, discrete devices, most with a screen, all allowing remote communication, ranging in size from small pieces of jewellery to pad-sized personal computers.

Pimsim – Post-mortem simulation; digital copy of a human mind (deceased).

RealWorld Realities – Thirty six distinct gaming worlds by the RealWorld corporation. Closed owing to establishment of sentient rights and set up as reserves for the inhabitants.

Sheath – Common name for any kind of device that may be remotely operated by a human or non-human intelligence. They are often androids, however. Some AI habitually live in them.

SurvNet – Surveillance network. Any one of hundreds of

differing observational technologies employed to monitor human activity.

System Wide Grid – Successor to the Internet 2. Extends beyond Earth to the Solar colonies. Commonly called simply "the Grid".

Three Uncle Sams – Three class Five artificial intelligences who effectively govern USNA.

USE – United States of Europe. Centralised, federal state encompassing all of mainland Europe (except Russia), Iceland, and the British Isles, as well as parts of the Levant.

USNA – United States of North America, which includes the entire continent down to Panama.

Virtuality – False reality designed to look and feel real to those experiencing it.

VIPA – Virtualities Investigation and Protection Authority. NUN organisation tasked with investigating AI crime, safeguarding the Grid, and ensuring the rights of non-human digital entities are upheld.

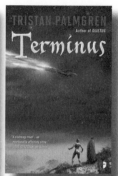

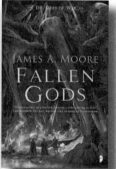

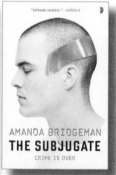

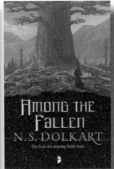

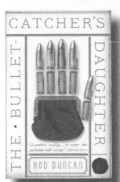

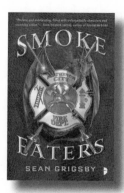

We are Angry Robot

angryrobotbooks.com

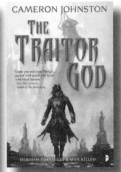

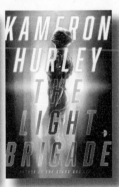